HALF A SIXPENCE

East Kent, 1830. Catherine Rook takes her peaceful life for granted. Her days are spent at the village school and lending a hand on her family's farm. Life is run by the seasons, and there's little time for worry. But rural unrest begins sweeping through Kent, and when Pa Rook buys a threshing machine it brings turbulence and tragedy to Wanstall Farm. With the Rooks' fortunes forever changed, Catherine must struggle to hold her family together. She turns to her childhood companion, Matty Carter, for comfort, and finds more than friendship in his loving arms. But Matty has his own family to protect, and almost as quickly as their love blossomed their future begins to unravel.
With the threat of destitution nipping at her heels, Catherine must forge a way out of ruin...

HALF A SIXPENCE

HALF A SIXPENCE

by

Evie Grace

Magna Large Print Books
Long Preston, North Yorkshire,
BD23 4ND, England.

British Library Cataloguing in Publication Data.

A catalogue record of this book is
available from the British Library

ISBN   978-0-7505-4629-4

First published in Great Britain by Arrow Books in 2017

Copyright © Cathy Woodman 2017

Cover illustration © Ildiko Neer/Arcangel by arrangement with
Arcangel Images Ltd.

Published in Large Print 2018 by arrangement with
Random House Group Ltd.

LP

Magna Large Print is an imprint of Library Magna Books Ltd.

Printed and bound in Great Britain by
T.J. (International) Ltd., Cornwall, PL28 8RW

In memory of my grandparents
who taught me resilience.

Acknowledgements

I should like to thank Laura at MBA Literary Agents, and Viola and the team at Penguin Random House UK for their enthusiasm and support. I'm also very grateful to my mum for her help with researching Victorian Kent and sharing her memories of hop picking.

1830

Chapter One

The Bonnet

Overshill, East Kent

Catherine looked at the sea of golden corn in the field next to the stony road, and her heart soared. She gazed at the gently rolling countryside, a patchwork of hop gardens, orchards and meadows filled with wild flowers, then glanced at her companion.

'There'll be no school on Monday,' she said.

'Or the Monday after,' Emily Millichip, the miller's daughter, replied. She was heavily built with plump arms and ruddy cheeks, whereas Catherine was what other people described as delicate in appearance.

'There'll be no writing, reading or 'rithmetic.'

'Or sewing, or taking a turn looking after the little ones.' Emily was twelve years old, a year younger than Catherine, who was envious of the way Emily's straw bonnet struggled to confine her blonde ringlets, while Catherine's own dark hair hung long and wavy from under her bonnet, down to the small of her back.

'Shall we go the long way through the woods?' Catherine asked as they passed the end of the drive leading to Churt House, an imposing building with many windows and tall chimneys that stood on a rise looking down on the village of Overshill. She imagined taking off her boots and cooling her feet in the chalk stream that babbled through the vale below the village, but Emily wasn't in the mood for dawdling.

'I must go straight home,' she said, looking towards the top of the hill ahead at the windmill with its four white sails and beehive cap set against tarred weatherboards. 'Ma will give me a good hiding if I'm late.'

'We'll say Old Faggy kept us back to sweep the schoolroom floor.' Mrs Fagg ran the dame school at Primrose Cottage for the village children whose parents were willing and able to pay for them to attend.

'She's bound to check with her when she comes to buy bread. Come on, let's hurry.' Emily took Catherine's hand and they continued past the vicarage and the Church of Our Lady where they went every Sunday with their families. The church was built from grey ragstone with a red-tiled roof and stained-glass windows. It had a chapel to the side and a central tower which, according to Pa, the villagers had used as a lookout in the past. The main door was made from oak and was partly hidden from the road by the dark, forbidding yews that watched over the dead.

Catherine and Emily turned along the path where the flint wall bordering the churchyard came to an end and the ground opened up into rough scrubland with a leafy hedgerow of blackthorn and brambles to one side.

The smell of bad eggs assaulted Catherine's nostrils as a grey-green stagnant pond overgrown

14

with weeds and bulrushes came into view. She shivered. She'd never liked Ghost Hole Pond, even before Old Faggy had taught them about the reign of the Jutish kings when people and horses were sacrificed in its murky waters to secure a good harvest for the village. Sometimes as she grew near it, she fancied that she could hear the screams of the victims and the splashing as the horses plunged in their fight against the spirits who dragged them without mercy to their grave.

'There's Matty Carter,' Emily said, pointing towards a boy of about fourteen who was striding towards them with a bag slung over his shoulder.

Catherine disapproved of his coarse manners and his raggedy clothes that reeked of hops and smoke, and she hadn't liked the way he used to tease her at school.

'He's trouble. We must keep out of his way,' she said, but it was too late. He stopped in front of them. His brown hair stood up on end like a stook of corn, the bridge of his nose was spattered with freckles and his cheek was smeared with dirt.

'How's Old Faggy?' he asked with a glint of humour in his green eyes. 'Does she miss me?'

'She's never said so.' Catherine unhooked a stray bramble from her skirt.

Matty had left school the previous year, his income from work being more useful to his family than the education provided by an elderly spinster. Not that Old Faggy was a bad teacher. Pa set great store by her methods – she had taught him to read and write when he was a young man.

'She probably didn't notice me and Jervis were

gone,' Matty said, referring to one of his older brothers. There were seemingly endless Carter children, some still at home and others long grown up and moved away, but Matty had two older brothers who still lived in Overshill: Jervis, the eldest, who laboured on the farm when he wasn't lurking on the Canterbury to London road, waylaying any unfortunates whose carriages had become stuck in the mud; and Stephen, the middle one, who was apprenticed to Overshill's blacksmith. 'She's as deaf as an adder and blind as a bat.'

Catherine couldn't help wondering if Old Faggy's afflictions were more contrived than real, her way of coping with the challenge of maintaining discipline in the classroom. What the eye didn't see, the heart didn't grieve over. If she did notice the older boys getting up to no good, flicking pieces of chalk at the girls, she would send them outside to chop wood.

'Get out!' she'd shout after them. 'I don't want none of you besoms in here.'

'I never thought I'd say this, but now that I'm having to earn my living, I wish I was back at school,' Matty said.

'We don't feel the same, I'm afraid. It's a lot more peaceful without you,' Catherine said. 'What have you got in your bag?'

'Nothing.' Matty's fingers tightened around the hessian sack.

'You must have something. Show us.' She reached out to take it, but he hugged it tight to his chest.

'It's none of your business.' His eyes flashed

16

with annoyance tinged with fear.

If, as a small boy, he hadn't relished scaring the life out of her with slugs and slow-worms, or laughing at her when she filled her shoes as well as her bucket with water at the pump in the farmyard, Catherine might have backed down. But remembering the sensation of the mouse's teeth nibbling at the back of her neck and the sheer panic as it slid between her skin and the fabric of her blouse while they sat in class at Old Faggy's, she made up her mind.

She grabbed at the sack.

'No, miss. Please don't.' Matty tore it from her fingers and threw it back over his shoulder, but it was too late. She knew what he'd been up to from the scent the hessian had left on her skin.

'Leave him alone,' Emily sighed. 'He isn't worth our notice.'

'Where did you get them onions from?' Catherine said.

'I haven't got no onions. I've bin collecting herbs for me ma.'

'I can smell them.' Catherine watched his face turn dark red like boiled beetroot. 'Where did you get them from?' she repeated.

'I found them by the wayside.' Unable to meet her gaze, he traced circles in the earth with his boot, showing off the scuffed leather patches across the toe.

'You stole them,' she said, shocked. 'You took them from my pa, you thieving scoundrel.' Her blood surged with fury at his betrayal of her father's trust. Pa had a soft spot for the Carters, although she didn't know why when none of them looked as if they'd ever had a wash in their lives. The Carter family rented the cottage at Toad's Bottom, not far from Wanstall Farm where Catherine lived with her parents and brother John. Matty and Jervis worked for Catherine's pa, who had also employed their father, George Carter, for as long as she could remember.

'If I'd have picked up things I'd found just lying around, and they did belong to your pa, he wouldn't notice as much.'

'Of course he would.' Pa counted each and every onion – that's how he had made a success of the farm, and why Squire Temple showed his gratitude by keeping the rent the same year after year. He looked after the land, ploughed the straw and muck back into the ground, walked the fields to check on the crops, and sent the labourers out to pick the caterpillars and mildewed leaves off the hops. He knew every stone, every tree, every bird's nest, every flower. 'I'm going to make sure he hears about this.'

Matty lashed out and grabbed Emily's bonnet from her head, as she was the closest to him. Catherine tried to snatch it back, but it was too late.

'No,' Emily cried. 'Ma will have my guts for garters.'

Matty ran off and scrambled along one of the sloping branches that leaned across the surface of the pond. He stopped and balanced on his heels, holding the bonnet over the water.

'Promise me you won't tell,' he called fiercely.

'I shan't promise anything,' Catherine shouted back. In spite of her fears, she scooped up her skirts, petticoat and all, and started to climb along the branch. Emily's ma had a temper on her and she didn't see why Matty should involve her closest friend in their disagreement.

'Please don't.' Emily grabbed at her arm. 'He wouldn't dare.'

Catherine freed herself from Emily's grasp and pulled herself along the branch.

'They call your pa "skinflinty Rook" at the beerhouse because of the niggardly wages he pays,' Matty jibed.

'He gave your pa a flitch of bacon and a sack of flour after the haymaking,' Catherine countered. 'You and your family don't have to work for him. There are other masters.' She glanced down at her sleeve which was covered with a dusting of lichen, and at the water below where the arms of the ghosts were outstretched to catch her and pull her into the depths. The branch trembled, making her perch seem even more precarious.

'Listen.' Matty's eyes were wide with desperation. 'I swear them onions were lying scattered across the ground, all round and swelled up. I seen them and I thought of my brothers and sisters and how they haven't eaten anything but bread since Sunday night, and before I knew it, they were in the bag.' A tear ran down his cheek. 'I'm truly sorry, Miss Rook. Please don't tell. If I'm dragged up in front of the magistrate, I'll be locked up or hanged. My family will starve.'

Catherine didn't like to think of the little Carters with their runny noses and dirty clothes dying from hunger, but surely Matty was exaggerating about the punishment. When his brother

19

Jervis had been caught with apples in his pockets, he'd been whipped and sent on his way, laughing in the magistrate's face.

'I won't keep secrets.' She had been brought up to be open and honest. 'Now, give me that bonnet, or else.'

'Or else, what?' Matty growled. 'You're going to tell on me whatever I say. I'm doomed.'

She watched his fingers slacken and the bonnet fall and spread across the surface of the water with the ribbons drifting behind it.

Emily screamed. Catherine snapped off a hazel twig and caught the bonnet, lifting it out of the water before she clambered carefully back to safety, leaving Matty sitting astride the branch with his head in his hands.

'Ta.' Emily took the bonnet by her fingertips as though it was stained with blood. 'Oh no, it's ruined.' She started to cry.

'Wring it out carefully and lay it across the bushes around the corner so it will dry in the sun,' Catherine ordered. 'You can have my bonnet and I'll come back for yours later. That way your ma will never know.' She didn't look back. She placed her own bonnet on Emily's head and fastened the ribbons, and, having done her best to dry her friend's tears, they continued on their way along the path, turning left onto Overshill's main street.

They passed a pair of black-and-white timber-framed houses before reaching the forge and its attached cottage where a pair of carthorses stood in the shade of the spreading chestnut tree, waiting to be shod.

Stephen Carter, dressed in a shirt, trousers and

brown leather apron, was untying one of the horses from the iron ring that was buried in the tree trunk.

'Hello, Miss Rook and Miss Millichip,' he said shyly, touching his forelock of wavy brown hair. At seventeen, he was taller than Matty and his arms were all sinew and muscle. He rubbed at his side whiskers as if he had some kind of rash. 'How are you today?'

'We'd be much better if your brother hadn't made off with Emily's bonnet, thank you for asking,' Catherine said.

'I'm sorry. I'll box his ears for you.' He clenched his fist around the horse's rope. 'That'll learn Jervis not to terrorise innocent young ladies on their way home from school.'

'Oh, it wasn't Jervis,' Catherine said. 'It was Matty. And please don't trouble yourself on our account. We can stand up for ourselves, can't we, Emily?'

Emily nodded, but Catherine wasn't convinced. Emily's ma had taught her to act helpless, not fight back when she was wronged.

'Stop your cotchering and get that nag over here now, lad,' yelled a voice from within the dark depths of the forge where the coals were burning brightly. 'Have you finished sharpening those scythes? George will be here for them on his way back through. There'll be hell to pay if they aren't ready.'

'I'd better go, or the master will be after me,' Stephen said cheerfully. 'I don't know why he scolds me for gossiping when it's he who can talk the hind leg off a donkey. Good afternoon.'

21

'Len's always shouting,' Catherine said as she and Emily watched Stephen lead the horse away. Len was married to Catherine's sister Ivy. He could be a bit grumpy, and she didn't want to hang around. 'Let's go.' She saw him emerging from the forge. 'Hurry!'

'Don't you want to say hello to Ivy?' Emily said. 'You haven't seen her for ages.'

Catherine shook her head. Ivy was much older than her and they didn't have much in common. She never felt entirely welcome at Forge Cottage. When she did visit, Ivy would offer her a drink and something to eat, before returning to her needlework. She was a good seamstress and her services were much in demand in Overshill.

Catherine and Emily walked on past a terrace of brick cottages where the gardens were filled with pale pink and deep blue geraniums, bright sunflowers and the mauve spikes of buddleias clothed with butterflies and buzzing with bees. On the opposite side of the road was the butcher's shop, then the greengrocer's and the Woodsman's Arms where a pair of elderly men in their smocks were sitting outside on a bench. They raised their tankards in greeting. Catherine nodded in return.

'Stephen is very polite, don't you think?' Emily observed.

'He isn't at all like his brother. They're like chalk and cheese.'

'I thought you should have been at least a mite grateful to him, considering that he made so bold as to offer to box Matty's ears. Do you remember how he hardly spoke to us when he was at school?'

'I didn't take much notice of him,' Catherine said.

'I wouldn't say no to Stephen Carter if he should ask me to marry him one day,' Emily went on. 'He's very handsome.'

'Ma would absolutely forbid me to walk out with any of the Carter brothers. She's devoting her spare time to making sure that I marry up.' Catherine pursed her lips and twirled an imaginary parasol as if she was a lady. Laughing, Emily joined in and they danced the rest of the way up the hill past the oast house, an old barn with a round kiln tacked on to the end for drying the hops in September. The wheelwright was perched on a ladder that was leaning between the barn roof and the kell so that he could repair the white-painted cowl on the top.

Catherine parted from Emily at the mill where one of Emily's brothers was leaving the bakehouse next door with a basket of bread on his shoulders. He waved at Catherine and held the door open for his sister, like a gentleman, she thought, not like certain other ruffians who lived in the vicinity.

Instead of continuing north towards the turnpike road that ran between Canterbury and Faversham, Catherine followed the left fork at the crossroads, passing Toad's Bottom Cottage where the Carters lived. The porch was propped up with a chestnut pole that appeared to have been appropriated from the Rooks' hop garden, and patches of damp had crept up the walls. Ten people shared the one-up, one-down tumbledown hovel. She'd often wondered how they fitted in, if they topped and tailed in the bedroom under the eaves of rotten thatch, or took it in turns to sleep.

She began to run, not stopping until she reached her wonderful home: Wanstall Farm. She passed the front gate to the red-brick and tile farmhouse, where a shingle path ran across the lawn to a green door with a wrought-iron handle. The path continued on, disappearing behind a tall hedge into the garden behind it where the Rooks grew fruit, herbs and vegetables for the kitchen.

Catherine turned into the farmyard, entering through a wooden gate in the wall that made up one side of the yard. To her left was a henhouse, pigsty and woodpile, along with a long timber barn where Pa stored feed and tools. In front of her, twenty brown chickens were cawing and scratching through the chaff outside the granary and stables. Between them was another gate that led out into the orchard and fields beyond while the rear of the house completed the fourth side of the yard.

Looking up, Catherine noticed that the sash windows were still open from earlier that morning when Ma had sent their live-out maid round to air the rooms.

She walked past the pump and stepped inside the back door where the cooler air made her skin like gooseflesh.

'Catherine, is that you?' her mother called.

'Yes, Ma.' Catherine found her in the kitchen along the corridor from the pantry.

'Where have you been, young lady?' Margaret Rook looked up from the oak table where she was pitting plums for a pie. She was a handsome woman with clear blue eyes and round cheeks. Silver and blonde strands of hair had escaped from her braids, and it seemed that her figure would burst from her dress if it wasn't for the ties on her apron.

'I walked straight back home from school with Emily.' Catherine glanced towards the fireplace where the housemaid was stirring fruit and skimming the stones from the surface of a pan that was suspended above the flames. Drusilla was a country girl who'd been in the Rooks' employ since she was fourteen years old. Now seventeen, she was a young woman whose hands and knees were calloused from scrubbing floors. Her greasy hair was tied back from a face scarred by pockmarks from an illness she'd had as a child. There were many who wouldn't have taken her on because of it, but Ma hadn't been able to afford to be fussy.

'There's bin no gallivantin'?' Ma went on.

'No, Ma.'

Her mother stared and Drusilla gave her a sly glance, but Catherine didn't waver.

'How many times have I told you not to linger when I'm working my fingers to the bone? Where's your bonnet?'

'I must have left it behind,' Catherine said defensively. She couldn't help feeling that Ma blamed her for coming along so many years after her three siblings. There was Young Thomas Rook who was thirty-two and married with five children. He farmed land to the south of Selling, a moderate acreage that Pa had received in lieu of a debt when he'd rented out horses, waggons and labourers, and provided stock to the previous landowner. Then there was Ivy, who'd married Len the blacksmith. Catherine's other brother John was twelve years older than her at twenty-five, and destined to be the future tenant of Wanstall Farm, so it was imperative that he find a suitable wife. He'd been courting Mary, a farmer's daughter, for ages, but she seemed keener on him than he was on her.

'How can you have forgotten it? Don't you have any idea how much it costs to feed and clothe you? I despair. The sooner you're wed and off my hands, the better.'

She was far too young for marriage, Catherine knew, but Ma's words still stung. At least they were just words, though, not the sting that Emily would have received from her mother's hand if she'd been the one to arrive home without a bonnet.

'Go and feed the pigs and chickens, and make sure you collect the eggs before you come back in here and take over from Drusilla.' Ma mopped her brow with a muslin cloth. 'I've been on my feet since the crack of dawn, and I've yet to call on Mrs Browning.'

Catherine went outside with a bowl of scraps and meal. She tossed out handfuls of chicken feed and the hens came running. She watched them scrabble for the tastiest morsels, the bossiest hen harrying at the rest of the flock to keep them in their place. Poor Mrs Browning, she thought. The wife of the new vicar was being subjected to a barrage of visits by the other wives of the parish as, like the hens, they established their positions in the pecking order.

Catherine hunted out the eggs, finding them in the henhouse that her brother John had made, and in the straw in the barn, and even one on top of the threshing machine that Pa had had repaired by the wheelwright and stored safely away in the granary ready for the harvest. She filled the bowl with eggs and returned it to the kitchen where she fetched a bucket of slops to feed to the pigs. Her favourite sow was in pig and it wouldn't be long before she gave birth to her piglets. As she leaned over into the sty to scratch the sow's back, she smiled at the thought of their tiny pink snouts and curly tails.

'It won't be long now, Margaret,' she said aloud.

'Margaret?' Pa's voice cut across the sow's noisy slurping.

'Pa?' Catherine jumped and turned to find her father moving up beside her to look into the sty. She noticed how his grizzled hair was thinning on the top of his head.

'I didn't know you'd given her a name,' he said, smiling affably.

'I-I-I...' Catherine stammered, her face hot. She hoped that Pa wouldn't be cross that she had called the pig her mother's name.

'She's rather keen on her rations,' Pa went on, his brown eyes twinkling with humour. 'She's getting a good bellyful there.'

Catherine had often wondered how Pa had turned Ma's head. Married for thirty-four years, they were ill-matched in appearance and disposition. Pa was quick-witted, short and wiry-bodied with a tanned complexion. Ma was well spoken but sometimes slow of thought. They were in their early fifties, which Catherine considered to be very old, much older than Emily's parents anyway.

'Your ma is a good woman, you know,' Pa said, more seriously. 'She was born and bred to be a farmer's wife in spite of all her airs and graces. I always tell her that she churns the best butter in the parish.' At the sound of the horse and cart rolling into the yard, he turned and raised his hand. 'Afternoon, George.'

George pulled the horse up and clambered down to the ground. He looked older than Pa, Catherine thought, even though they were apparently the same age. He could have passed for five years short of a hundred with his stoop and magnificent grey beard. He wore a smock and a hat with a single brown feather.

'The scythes are all ready for the cutters, Tom.' George started to unload the tools that he'd taken to Len for sharpening. 'The Irish are at Boughton, itching to start work on the harvest tomorrow.'

Pa cast an eye towards the sky. He was always on edge in August, looking out for rain that might spoil the grain and worrying that there wouldn't be enough people to bring in the crop. He would be relieved to hear that the travellers had arrived for the harvest, Catherine thought. She'd watched him out in the fields, breaking open an ear of corn to check it was ripe before leaning on his stick to listen for the snapping sound of the barley as it dried in the summer sun.

'We're all set for Monday,' Pa said, confirming

her expectation that there would be no more school for a while. All hands would be needed to bring in the harvest, then when all the barley was gathered and carted away to the granary, Pa would provide supper and flagons of beer for the labourers, and they would dance the night away with George and the Carter boys playing the accordion and fiddle. Everyone, even Ma, would be happy.

George unhitched the horse while Pa closed the gate across the entrance to the yard. Catherine waited to speak privately with her father.

'Thank you, George,' Pa said.

George smiled and walked away.

Pa turned to Catherine.

'He's a good man. He doesn't ask for much.'

'That's because his family steal whatever they want from you,' Catherine said matter-of-factly.

Pa's expression darkened. 'What did you say, my girl?'

She sensed the weight of her father's disappointment, whether it was in the Carters or in her for telling him something he didn't wish to hear, she wasn't sure.

'Is this hearsay, or do you have evidence?'

'I seen it with my own eyes and heard it through my own ears. Matty confessed to filching onions.'

Pa rubbed the ridge of his hooked nose with his fore-finger.

'You shouldn't go around telling tales.'

'It's the truth. I thought you should know, Pa. The onions are your property and there are some who would make an example of him.'

'Every family has their struggles, some more

29

than others. The Carters have more children than they can look after, and the pure strain of having all them children has taken a toll on Ma Carter. The eldest is only a few years younger than our Young Thomas, and the littlest littl'un is barely out of swaddling clothes. Ma Carter might be younger than your ma, but all that child bearing has made her an unwell, weakened woman. She can't do much, except for a little basket-making. The poor family can't afford for Matty to be charged with larceny for the sake of a few onions.'

Catherine shrank a little under Pa's disapproving frown. She wished she'd held her tongue.

'A long time ago,' Pa began, reminding her of when she was a little girl and he used to sit her on his knee to tell her a story, 'when George and I were littl'uns, we were larking about at the pond. There were a couple of branches leaning across the water and I reckoned I could balance on the top with my arms outstretched and walk the furthest. I got to the end and turned to come back, waving victorious, when there was a loud crack.' He clapped his hands together to demonstrate. 'The branch fell away and I went with it. I felt this sharp blow to my head and the chill of the water, and when I tried to swim up to the surface, the ghosts kept dragging me back.'

Catherine shuddered as he continued, 'I thought my lungs were going to burst. Then I heard George's voice telling me to calm down and lie still. He fought off the spirits and saved my life. If it wasn't for him, I would have drowned there and then in Ghost Hole Pond. I've never forgot. I swore I'd treat him as a brother from then on. Always.'

It made sense now. Pa had persuaded the parish to pay the apprenticeship fee for Stephen to be bound by indenture to the blacksmith. He had employed Jervis, in spite of his reputation for unlawful behaviour, and ensured that Matty had attended school for long enough to have learned the basics of reading and writing. No doubt he would support the younger Carter children in similar ways.

'I've had a bit of luck – the squire has always favoured me for the way I can coax more bushels of barley than anyone else from an acre of ground. I've risen in the world while others have stayed the same or been lowered, but I will never forget my roots. In my opinion, everyone, even those like Matty from the most humble background, should have the oppor*too*nity to better themselves and make a good living for their families. The Carters have very little, Catherine. The littl'uns often go to bed with empty bellies. How would you feel if you were in their situation?'

Catherine felt ashamed. She'd only wanted to protect Pa's interests, but she wouldn't have said anything if she'd known all the facts beforehand.

'True friends are few and far between – make the most of the ones you have. And keep your own counsel in future. It's a principle that's served me well. No harm's been done so that's all I have to say on the matter. You'd better run along. Ma has a great deal to do' – Pa grinned, revealing his crooked teeth – 'as she takes much pleasure in telling me.'

Catherine returned indoors. While Ma went to call on Mrs Browning, she boiled some eggs and helped Drusilla prepare a cold supper for the evening, along with potatoes and carrots for the Sunday roast which they would eat after church the following day. The shelves in the pantry were groaning with food for the workers' lunches on Monday, which only added to Catherine's guilt. Everyone knew that the Carters were poor, but she hadn't understood how bad things were for them. It occurred to her that she could apologise to Matty in a practical way. No one would notice if some pie and cheese and a jar of preserves went missing, and who would condemn her when it was for a good cause?

While Drusilla was distracted, standing on the slatted wood mat in front of the sink in the scullery, washing the dishes, Catherine slipped out with a wicker basket of provisions on her arm.

Swapping it from one arm to the other, she made her way back up the hill to Toad's Bottom. She couldn't open the cottage gate which was firmly stuck on its hinges, so she climbed through a gap in the wall where the flints had fallen away, and walked up the path to the door. She stepped over several pairs of boots that were filled with grass, and raised her hand to knock. The door opened and Matty appeared in front of her.

'Od rabbit it!' he exclaimed roughly. 'What are you doing here?'

A small boy of about four, naked from the waist down, clung to his leg, staring at her. His cheeks were hollow and his eyes glittered with hunger.

'I've brought some food for you,' she said, sensing she had made some kind of mistake. She held out the basket.

Matty pushed it aside as a woman's voice called weakly from somewhere inside the dark depths of the cottage.

'Who is it?'

'Nobody, Ma,' Matty called back. He glared at Catherine. 'We don't need the Rooks' charity.' The timbre of his voice was more like a man's than a boy's.

'I wanted to say sorry for accusing you of stealing. Well you did take the onions without asking, but I understand it wasn't thieving. Why won't you accept these things? You're more than happy to receive money and food from my father.'

'That's in return for a favour done in the past. This is charity,' Matty said emphatically. 'You know it doesn't suit you, going around with your nose stuck in the air like you're better than everyone else.'

'I don't,' she stammered. 'That isn't fair.'

'You think you're so special. Even your parents treat you different–'

'How?' she cut in.

'Your ma wishes you'd never bin born while your pa puts you on a pedestal.'

It was close to the truth, but she didn't like to hear it. She often thought that Ma didn't like her, and Pa did spoil her a little, but she assumed that was because she was the youngest and the last child in the line.

'There are some around here who say you're a changeling with your pale skin and long black hair,' Matty went on, taunting her, 'but you're flesh and blood, the same as the rest of us.'

'All I'm doing is trying to help. I can't bear the thought of the littl'uns having empty bellies.'

The child began to wail. Matty scooped him up and held him on his hip. He kissed his forehead and stroked his face, calming him down.

'Be on your way.' He closed the door in Catherine's face, leaving her standing on the step, wondering how she could have misjudged the situation so badly. She was upset that Matty had rejected her offering, but what really hurt was the way he had expressed his opinion of her.

She left the basket on the wall, hoping that he might give in and take it before she returned from fetching Emily's bonnet, which she found torn by the brambles where they had left it to dry. On her way back to the farm, she collected the basket, disappointed to find that its contents had been left untouched.

'Catherine, wait for me,' she heard Ma call. She turned. She was in the mire now, she thought with a jolt of panic. Her mother was almost upon her, giving her no time to hide the basket in the hedge, but Ma was too distracted to notice, her head filled with the lingering excitement of her visit to the vicarage.

'Oh, you have no idea what a lovely time I've had,' she sighed as they walked back towards the farm. 'Mrs Browning is truly a lady of quality and merit. Her son, Hector, is a handsome fellow – he returns to school in Faversham in September. Her daughter Jane is a beauty to behold, a little pale maybe, but that's because they've been living in London for the past several years. Mrs Browning allowed me to recommend the salt marsh lamb to her cook. That will soon put some colour back into her daughter's cheeks.'

'What about the vicar?' Catherine said, keen to encourage her mother along this train of thought to divert her from the basket and its contents. 'What is he like?'

'He was out preparing for a meeting of the vestry, so I can't say. We'll find out soon enough. Mrs Browning says that he is determined to encourage the congregation to return whole-heartedly to the fold.'

Catherine smiled to herself. The previous in-cumbent had been an unassuming man whose dreary sermons had sent his flock scattering across the countryside on a Sunday as he grew fat on his annual stipend paid from the tithes contributed by all the residents of the parish, rich and poor. He'd retired and the Church had given the Reverend Browning the living at Overshill. The church would no doubt be filled with people eager to view the new vicar. Ma began to stride ahead as they approached the farmhouse. Catherine hung back so she could deposit the basket's contents back on the shelves in the pantry.

'What was in your basket?' Ma asked a little later when the family – apart from John, who was still working out in the fields, making the most of the fine evening – were eating supper at the kitchen table.

'My bonnet, of course,' Catherine said. 'I col-lected it from school.'

'How strange when you could have carried it

home on your head,' Pa observed, chewing noisily on a crust.

'She's always bin a peculiar child.' Ma passed him a second slice of ham to add to the bread and butter on his plate.

Ma's remark reminded Catherine of what Matty had said about her being a changeling and later, as she repaired the tears in Emily's bonnet by the flicker of candlelight so that they wouldn't show, she began to wonder what he meant by it.

She wondered too if the harvest would be a good one.

She laid down the bonnet and snuffed out the candle before retiring to bed. All was silent apart from the occasional creak of a rafter in the old house and the regular ticking of the longcase clock in the hall. It didn't seem possible that anything would ever disturb the peace and tranquillity of Overshill.

Chapter Two

The Harvest

On the Sunday morning, Catherine walked into the village with Pa, Ma and her brother, a tall, handsome man of twenty-five with hair the colour of ripened barley, bright blue eyes and good teeth. He was wearing his corduroy jacket, matching trousers and recently blacked boots.

'John has put an unusual amount of effort into

his appearance,' she remarked.

'He looks quite the dandy,' Ma agreed.

'You're making me blush, Ma.' John turned and grinned before walking on with a spring in his step.

Catherine doubted it. Her brother was used to compliments. He'd always had his pick of the village girls because of his light-hearted attitude to life, his charm and his prospects, but now it seemed that he'd settled for Mary Nobbs.

'It's a pity that you had to let us down by wearing that grubby bonnet on the Sabbath, Catherine,' Ma went on. 'It's in a terrible state. It looks like the cat's put her claws through it. I'll have to have a word with Pa about buying you some more clothes.'

Catherine smiled to herself as they reached the mill where the aroma of meat cooking in the bread ovens, ready for some of the other villagers to collect after the service, rose into the air. She knew exactly what Pa would say about the prospect of a new bonnet. Not until after hop-picking when the money came in.

The Millichips joined them on the street. The miller was wearing a suit that seemed to bear a light dusting of flour, and his sour-faced wife wore a grey dress and cape bound with red braid. They greeted Pa and Ma Rook, the men shaking hands, and the women nodding politely. Emily linked arms with Catherine and the pair of them dropped back behind the rest of the party.

'Did your ma say anything about your bonnet?' Catherine said.

Emily raised her finger to her lips and shook

her head.

'Did you snitch on Matty?' she asked quietly.

'I spoke to Pa, but nothing will come of it. And then I tried to make up for what I'd done, and now Matty hates me. His family is so very poor. I didn't realise what a struggle they have to make ends meet.'

'I'm sure you meant well,' Emily said, turning towards the carriage that had stopped outside the church. Mr Hadington, the lawyer who owned Churt House, held the door open for his wife and grown daughter, who stepped out in their finery and feathers. With his smart coat, curly whiskers and brown teeth, he reminded Catherine of a rat, sniffing out opportunities to enhance his fortune. He stared at the girls, his eyes settling on Emily. She glanced away, but he continued to stare.

'Don't you think that Mr Hadington is rather odd?' Emily whispered. 'He's always looking at me. Last week when we came out of the church, I could feel his eyes burning into my back.'

'Don't take any notice. We'll never need to have anything to do with him.'

'Do you remember how we used to stand at the bottom of the drive and crane our necks to catch a glimpse of Churt House?' Emily said. 'You told me how you wished you were a rich man's daughter.'

'Imagine how different life would be if you had too much money rather than just enough,' Catherine said wistfully. 'I'd help all the poor families in the village.'

'If they'd let you,' Emily pointed out. 'The people around here might be poor, but they're also very proud.'

They walked up the steps into the churchyard and joined the throng entering the church, curious to see the new vicar and his family. Catherine glanced around at the familiar sight of the elegant stone pillars that separated the nave from the aisles on either side, and at the soaring arches that formed the roof. There were stone bosses where the ribs met: one in the form of a nun's face, another of a rose, and her favourite of a man with a beard of leaves. She turned to look over her shoulder at the west gallery above the entrance to the church where the choir were shuffling around, taking their seats behind the carved wooden screen.

'Catherine, stop your daydreaming and come and sit down.' Ma's voice broke into her consciousness.

'Wake up, little sister. You can't possibly miss out on this great occasion.' John winked at her as he escorted her along the nave, then whispered, 'It's only fair that we all suffer in equal measure.'

Catherine suppressed a chuckle.

'That's her. That's Mrs Browning,' Ma said loudly as they settled in their pew, the Rooks alongside the Millichips and three rows back from the squire, the lawyer and other dignitaries of the parish. 'That's her daughter, Jane.'

Catherine gazed towards a girl of about her age who was dressed demurely in a bonnet and dark blue dress with long sleeves and lace gloves. She kept glancing behind her with a smile playing on her lips. Her upturned nose gave her an air of superiority.

'And that is her son, Hector, who has a most handsome countenance, don't you think?'

Several heads had turned at the sound of Ma's voice. Catherine wished she would keep quiet.

The boy was a year or two older than her, pale and uninteresting, she thought, with his chestnut hair neatly combed and his shoulders rounded as he slumped in the pew with his head in his hands. His mother gave him a nudge as the new vicar, dressed in cassock, surplice and stole, stepped up to the lectern. His hair was brushed forwards onto his fat cheeks and he wore silver spectacles with pebble lenses. He raised a tin vamping horn to his lips – the villagers used to use it to call the cattle home in the days before the lands were enclosed, but the last time Catherine could remember hearing it was when the parish clerk called for help after a candle fell over in the vestry and set the vestments alight.

'Pray, silence,' the vicar lisped through the vamping horn. His voice echoed around the vaulted ceiling, sending a ripple of amusement through the crowd. 'Ladies and gentlemen of Overshill! Silence! I cannot hear myself speak.'

A loud thud from the west gallery caught the congregation's attention instead. George Carter, who was with the other members of the choir, had dropped the trombone. There was a chuckle, followed by deep, booming laughter.

'You oughta be more careful, Pa.' It was Matty's voice from behind the wooden screen. 'You've broken it.'

'I 'aven't.'

'Yes, you 'ave. Look at it there. No, there.'

'Well, maybe I 'ave just a little bit, but equally you could say that it broke itself on the way down. No matter. The churchwardens will pay for the repairs, for what use is a choir without its instruments?'

'We will see what use this choir is by the end of the service,' said the vicar. 'Sit down, sirs. Open your ears and hearts to God's Word, and pray forgiveness for your sins of drunkenness and lack of respect for the hallowed Church of Our Lady.'

The choir began to settle as the vicar preached and prayed about salvation and wickedness, and each time Catherine thought he was about to say, 'Here endeth...' he continued. His lisping delivery became louder as he became more fired up with wrath against a congregation that had only returned to the church for one purpose: to observe their new vicar.

Eventually, he stopped and the singing of the psalm began. The Reverend Browning was not happy with it. He raised both his hand and the vamping horn, and sprang up on the balls of his feet to call for the choir to pause.

'I cannot hear the singing,' he complained, and Catherine wondered if it had more to do with the state of his ears than the efforts of the choir. He handed the horn to one of the village boys who carried it up the stone staircase to the gallery and gave it to Jervis Carter.

Jervis, who was taller and rangier than his brothers with knotted brown hair and a poor impression of a beard, put it to his mouth. George beat the rhythm with his hand, the trombone being out of action. Stephen played the clarinet and Matty drew his bow across the strings of his fiddle.

Jervis's voice sang out, high-pitched like an angel's, while George joined in with a lusty bass. The music began very slowly, too slowly for the congregation, making the sound most mournful, but as the psalm progressed, George gradually beat a faster rhythm until it was more like a sing-song at a beerhouse.

Catherine and Emily began to sway. Mr Millichip began to tap with his foot. The vicar's forehead became lined with discomfiture and Catherine could almost feel his relief when the singing came to a drawn-out end complete with one final toot of the clarinet.

Reverend Browning continued with his sermon while the farm servants yawned in the pews – most of them had been up at dawn, putting in three or four hours' work before church. John was fidgeting and sighing. Ma was fiddling with a piece of lace. Pa was writing with a stub of pencil on a piece of paper inserted into his psalm book. Every so often, he would put the stub behind his ear and sit, frowning. When Catherine peered across, she could see that he was making notes and drawings on improvements for the farm: cropping; planting; a fantastical machine with pulleys and belts and smoke belching from a chimney on the top.

The light glinted through the stained-glass window of Our Lady onto a brass of some old knight in armour on the floor. Above that, set in the wall, was a white marble plaque that marked the lives of Squire Temple's ancestors, the men all of courage, the women entirely virtuous, and their children pure and innocent.

Squire Temple himself was asleep – she could tell from the slope of his shoulders and the way his head jerked forwards now and then. Jane kept her eyes down and head bowed in supplication as though praying for her father to stop and let them out into the bright sunshine to enjoy their day of rest.

Catherine thought of the meal they would have later: roast beef and taters. And her stomach rumbled. When would it ever end?

'I were praying for him to stop,' Pa said on the way back to the farm after the service. 'Doesn't he realise the harvest is almost upon us? It's no wonder that people don't go to church any more when the parson don't even offer a prayer for good weather. It's all very well preaching the virtues of temperance to the choir, but it won't make no difference. That was time wasted when I should have been setting up for the morning. What do you think, Ma?'

'I think I shall reserve judgement, you being a churchwarden and that,' she said. 'You'll feel better when you have some food in your belly.'

'I'll feel better when everything – the grain, the hops and the rest of the apples – are safely gathered in.' A smile crossed Pa's face. 'And then it'll be time for ploughing and planting, and threshing with the new machine. That will be the making of us, you'll see. By next year, every farmer who's seen it in action will want to hire it and I'll have made enow money to buy another, and maybe more. Our future is golden like the barley in the meadows.'

The next day at dawn in the two-acre field behind the farmhouse, the reapers were already at work under Pa's watchful eye when Catherine turned up with John, who was carrying his scythe on his shoulder in readiness for mowing. She was to act as one of the gatherers until it was time for her to help Ma bring the midday meal out for the workers.

'Matty will fetch and carry too,' Pa said, and Catherine frowned at the thought of having to face him again, knowing that she would feel awkward and embarrassed.

The shadows shrank as the sun rose in the clear sky. John took his place alongside the other men and began to cut the corn. He swung his scythe close to the ground with ease and rhythm, moving from his hips and waist. The cradle on his scythe caught the barley which fell onto the ground in a neat swathe.

Catherine walked after him, taking handfuls of stems and laying them on the ground so she could place some of the barley that John had cut on top. One of the bandsters followed behind her, binding the swathe with knots of straw to make a sheaf. Mary Nobbs, the farmer's daughter from nearby Sinderberry Farm, and Drusilla had also been drafted in to help with the harvest.

It was Mary who took her place behind Catherine so she could impress John with the speed of her knotting, and keep her eyes on him as he scythed his way through the barley. Her dark hair was braided and her lips were full and pink, and she was exposing far more of her bosom than Catherine thought necessary. As she bent down to tie the band around each sheaf, her bodice could barely contain her flesh.

'John, keep straight,' Catherine called to her brother as the windrow began to waver across the meadow.

'I am going straight,' he shouted back.

'You aren't – you're all over the place like you've bin drinking Pa's cider.'

'I've bin doing nothing of the sort.'

'Then something's distracting you. Or someone.' She placed her finger on her lips, pretending to think. 'I wonder who that can be.' She smiled as she watched his complexion flush the colour of a ripe apple. It was her sisterly duty to embarrass him.

'Eyes forward.' Pa laughed as he took up a scythe and began to cut the corn alongside his son. 'I'll race you to the end.'

Matty and two of the other labourers stacked the sheaves, leaning them against each other to form a stook. Jervis added an additional sheaf across the top to act as a hood to keep the rain off while the stook dried.

The sun rose higher and the day grew hotter. Their shirts stuck to their backs and the sweat dripped from their foreheads. John and George stripped down to the waist as they continued to mow the field. George's scythe needed frequent sharpening, slowing the reaping down. The Irish complained about the lack of beer, and Pa grew impatient about the lack of progress.

45

'At this rate, we won't be done before winter,' he grumbled. 'I don't know what's got into everyone.'

Catherine felt the perspiration trickling from beneath her bonnet. Her back and arms ached, but when the burning sun reached its midday zenith, Pa gave her some respite, sending her and Matty to fetch food and beer for the labourers. Matty mopped his brow with his shirt as they walked side by side to the farmhouse in awkward silence.

'I'm sorry,' they both said at the same time.

'I shouldn't have done what I did,' she said, keeping her face averted. 'I didn't think about how it would look to you.'

'And I didn't think of how you'd feel about me turning you away with a flea in your ear when you'd come to us out of kindness. I shouldn't have said those things about you either. I was angry.'

'Ta. Let's say no more of it. How is your ma?'

'She can't work in the fields no more, but Pa and I can, and my brothers and sisters as soon as they're old enough.'

'How do you manage?' Catherine dared to ask.

'Stephen gives us money when he's able to, and after the harvest, we'll have earned enough to pay the rent and settle our debts, and I'll have leather for a new pair of boots.' He grinned from ear to ear. 'As long as your pa keeps us on for the threshing, we won't need no charity.'

They entered the house, and fetched and carried according to Ma's instructions.

'Don't you dare get your grubby fingers on

those loaves,' she called as they struggled to carry a basket of bread together across the farmyard and out past the granary to the field. As they turned the corner, Catherine lost her grip on the wickerwork handle, and the basket fell, tipping a loaf onto the ground.

'Oh no. Ma's going to yell at me.'

'She'll never know.' Matty picked up the loaf and gave the crust a quick rub to remove some of the dust.

'You've made it worse.' Catherine giggled as Matty buried it beneath the others in the basket

'Keep it to yourself,' he whispered.

'Oh, I shall.' She had learned her lesson about telling tales.

There was cheese and beer, and caraway cake as well as bread for the reapers who sought the shade beneath the hedges and farm buildings, where they ate, drank and swore aloud. The more they drank, the more they cursed, and the more anxious Pa became. He rounded them up and set them back to work as the heat shimmered from the stubble.

The harvest continued over the next fortnight. Catherine was out in the fields from dawn until dusk, day after day, but at last, the final cart laden with barley was brought to the barn by a horse decorated with ribbons and a garland of flowers around its neck. The corn dollies that the women had plaited from the last standing sheaf to keep the spirit of the corn goddess alive until sowing the following spring sat on top of the waggon. The ensemble was accompanied by a motley marching band comprising members of the church choir and a pair of the Irish playing a pipe and fiddle. George Carter played the accordion while the three older Carter brothers and the rest sang their hearts out.

Catherine danced with Emily all the way to the farmyard where the men unloaded the cart onto the rick. As soon as the hops had been picked, they would thresh the grain ready for milling.

Ma, Catherine and Drusilla prepared food in the farmhouse kitchen. Emily and Matty carried it to the long tables that Pa had had set out in the meadow behind the house. There were barrels of strong beer from which everyone helped themselves, and quite quickly, the conversation became loud and the mood merry.

Before the band struck up once more, Pa stood on the table and raised his tankard.

'A toast,' he shouted.

'Speech, speech,' chanted the workers.

'Let's have none of your speechifying this year, Thomas,' Ma sighed, but Catherine could see the pride in her eyes. Whatever Pa had done he had done right, because the yields of grain were higher than the year before, and the one before that.

'A toast to the King. Long may he reign over us,' he said.

'To the "Sailor King".' The crowd applauded.

'And a toast to you all. Don't spend your wages all at once!'

'To us.'

'May you pay us what we're owed,' a high-pitched voice called out.

'Don't I always do that, Jervis?' Pa said with good humour.

'Hear, hear,' someone else shouted out, one of the Irish.

'Thomas Rook is a generous man with his shillings and beer. That's why we come back to Overshill every summer.'

'And I'm very grateful for that.' Pa glanced along the table to where John was standing up. 'Wait.' John sat back down again, rocking the bench. 'There's plenty of time for singing and dancing. I haven't finished yet.' There was a barely suppressed groan from the members of the band who were fidgeting to pick up their instruments and start playing.

Pa straightened his back and raised his tankard for a third time.

'Lastly, let us raise a toast to the new machine. May she thresh fast and furious.'

Silence fell. Catherine shivered at the slight chill in the air as the sun's rays crept away from the table. She'd heard her father talking animatedly about this new miracle machine that would halve the manpower required to thresh the harvest. But she'd also heard other men mumbling these past two weeks about how it would be the end of their livelihoods, and she wondered why her father had even brought it up.

Matty stood up with the setting sun like a halo around his head. Jervis moved close behind him.

'Go on, speak,' he muttered.

Matty, emboldened by the drink, and the support of some of the other young men, wiped his palms on his trousers.

'Sir, I will not toast the machine,' he said.

'Sit down and shut your mouth,' George said

sharply. 'I'm sorry, Tom. He's had a mite too much beer.'

Catherine wondered why Matty had been put up for the argument. Perhaps it was because the other labourers perceived that Pa would listen if it came from one of his favourites. Or perhaps this was how he really felt, although she found it hard to imagine him going against her pa so openly. This was another side of Matty altogether.

'Never mind. I was a young man once,' Pa said. 'Let him have his say.'

'It's flailing and winnowing that keeps us in work for the winter, sir.' Matty's eyes flashed with a boldness that Catherine hadn't seen in him before, not even when they had been at school. He'd cheeked Old Faggy often enough, but when she'd turned on him, he'd run away, or blushed and lowered his eyes, knowing he'd been in the wrong. Now, he was speaking against her father in front of everyone, convinced that he was in the right. 'How will we provide for our families then?'

'There'll still be plenty of work for all,' Pa said. 'The machine needs men to keep it going, not just farm workers, but wheelwrights and blacksmiths too. I'm not blind. I can see how people struggle, living hand to mouth, and that's why I want to do my bit to embrace new methods of farming. By using machines, I can bring more bread to the table. No one need starve ever again.'

'What's the use of more bread if no one can afford to buy it?' Matty said sullenly.

'There'll be other work. You'll soon see that there's nothing to fear.'

'What about the danger in it?' Jervis joined in. 'I've heard of a farmer upcountry who got his hand caught in the drum. They tried to stop the horse, but it panicked and tried to get away. It smashed his hand to atoms it did, and he died the next day from the shock of it.'

'It's just a rumour spread by those who are afraid of change. The machine is complete safe. I'll prove it to you. We'll have it running tomorrow morning. Everyone is welcome. In the meantime, let's eat, drink and be merry.'

Amid the cheering, Catherine thought she heard someone, Jervis maybe, say, 'While we can.'

As more beer flowed, the mood lightened. The band picked up their instruments and began to play. Jervis and Stephen sang at the tops of their voices with Drusilla looking on.

'Drusilla has taken a fancy to Jervis,' Emily observed as she and Catherine were dancing on the stubble with some of the other village girls. 'And Stephen has his eyes on you.'

Matty and Stephen paused the music for a moment while they propped their father up against the back wall of the barn so he could continue playing his accordion. Stephen caught Catherine's eye and smiled. She smiled back out of politeness, hardly thinking of Stephen at all. Matty and her father wanted the same thing, prosperity for everyone, but they had different ideas of how to go about it.

The dancers began to tire. The lyrics to the songs became coarser. As they started to sing about a modest maid of Kent who didn't know what kissing meant, Catherine and Emily took themselves off to see if Margaret had produced her piglets.

'I can't see any,' Emily said as the sow snuffled around in the straw.

'Maybe tomorrow,' said Catherine as another noise caught her attention: a giggle and the deep tones of her brother's voice.

'Who's that?' Emily whispered.

'It's John and another.' Catherine caught her friend's hand. 'This way.' They crept past the open door to the barn where she caught sight of the silhouette of a couple against the moonlight, wrapped in each other's arms. 'It's Mary.'

'One of the sisters from Sinderberry Farm? What are they doing in there?'

'What comes naturally.'

'What's that? What do you mean?'

Catherine smiled. She had seen the boar and the sows together so she knew all about it, more than poor Emily who'd led a sheltered life at the mill.

'Hush. They've been courting for ages.' If she'd feared that they would disturb the lovers, she needn't have worried. She felt a sudden flood of emotion in her breast, a sadness and yearning, and a hope that she would one day fall in love, but with whom? She knew that Ma had plans for her, which didn't seem fair when John appeared to be free to choose whomever he pleased – as long as she was a farmer's daughter from a line of fertile stock, and she was modest, clean and respectable.

The morning after the harvest supper, Catherine fed the chickens and plucked the young cockerel that Pa had despatched earlier. The tabby cat watched as she put the feathers in a bag and took the bird indoors to the pantry where it would sit until Drusilla was ready to add it to the stew-pot for supper. The maid was upstairs emptying the slops and airing the beds. Ma was in the kitchen rubbing cold cream made from lard, wax and oil of lavender into her hands.

'Look how my skin suffers,' she moaned. 'I don't suppose that Squire Temple's wife has to endure the effects of bodily labour like I do.'

'Where is John?' Catherine asked, ignoring her mother's complaint.

'He's on his way. Can't you hear the sound of his big feet on the stairs?'

Catherine looked towards the doorway where John appeared.

'You look well for someone who was completely pickled last night. Where did you get to?' she said with a wicked smile as he took a whole loaf of bread from the pantry.

'I'm not telling you,' he said with a grin.

'I seen you in the barn with Mary.'

'Your mind must ha' been playing tricks on you.' John's cheeks grew pink as he tried to deny it. 'Or it was Jervis having his way with Drusilla.'

'I hope he wasn't interfering with our maid,' Ma said. 'I'll be having a word with her.'

'I seen you clear as anything,' Catherine repeated.

'I'll shut you in with the hens tonight if you aren't careful,' John said lightly.

'You wouldn't dare. Pa wouldn't let you.' Catherine giggled, but she was a little fearful that her brother might carry out his threat. When she was younger he had tipped her up and dangled her over the horses' trough, dunking her head in the ice-cold water when she had refused to tell him where she'd hidden his shoes.

'Stop your teasing and leave the poor lad alone. Don't put him off,' Ma interrupted gleefully. 'It's taken him an age to get this far, but now I have high expectations that there will soon be an announcement.'

'It won't be for a while,' John said. 'There's too much to be doing on the farm.'

'If you leave it too long, she'll walk out with somebody else,' Ma said.

'Pa says there's no hurry while he's fit and well.' John began to demolish the loaf, slicing it into hunks and spreading them with butter and jam. 'I don't want to put a noose around my neck before I have to.'

'Is that how Pa describes his marriage?' Ma said sharply.

'No, not exactly. I reckon he was talking of getting hitched in general, not in particular.'

'Well, Mary's a good match and you'd be a fool to let her go.'

John started to eat a piece of bread and took the rest outside with him, just as someone rapped at the front door.

'Aren't you going?' Ma said pointedly.

'Of course.' Catherine hurried out to the hall-way and opened the door to find the Reverend Browning, dressed in a gentleman's attire and a shirt with a collar, on the doorstep. He poked the end of his silver-topped cane just inside the door as if he feared she might close it on him.

'Good morning. I should like to speak to Mr Rook,' he lisped.

'Let me take you to him,' Catherine said.

'Allow me,' Ma said from behind her. 'Good morning, vicar. It's a pleasure to welcome you into our home.'

'Good day, Mrs Rook. I must speak with Mr Rook immediately,' he insisted.

Ma showed him through to the yard where Pa was shouting at John, Matty and George as they set up the threshing machine so there was enough room to manoeuvre the horses. Catherine followed, eager to listen to what the vicar had to say.

'Can't this wait until the next vestry?' Pa grumbled. 'That's the place to discuss parish matters.'

'It is a matter of urgency.' The Reverend Browning nodded towards the machine. 'Naturally, I should hate to interrupt the course of progress, but I have to express my disgust at the orgy of drunkenness and lechery that went on last night. The people of Overshill are debauched and depraved. They have been allowed to stray for far too long.'

'The harvest supper's always a riotous occasion. People like to keep their spirits up with a good song and dance,' Pa said, one eyebrow raised.

'I would like to think that, as a churchwarden and respectable member of society, you would know better than to encourage them. Last night there were goings-on in the churchyard, and this morning there is graffiti chalked on the door of the church.'

'I'll send someone over to scrub it clean. Don't worry, vicar. It's high jinks, that's all,' Pa said impatiently. 'George, fetch the horses.'

'I intend to bring the harvest celebration into the church next year to promote the virtues of sobriety and high moral standards.'

'I don't like the sound of it.' Pa rubbed his chin.

'I trust I can count on your support.'

The sound of hooves clattering at speed along the road towards the farm broke into their conversation. Squire Temple and his bailiff swung into the yard on their horses, much finer creatures than the pair of carthorses that George was bringing out of the stables to power the threshing machine.

'We will take a vote on it at the next meeting,' the vicar said before the squire greeted him and Pa, and introduced him to the bailiff who oversaw the home farm on the squire's estate and collected rent from the tenants.

Squire Temple was wearing a hat, coat, breeches and long leather boots. He sat on his sway-backed horse, leaning back in the saddle, with his toes sticking forwards and downwards and his hands held high. In his forties, he had a reputation for hunting, drinking and getting involved in local politics. He and Pa had a mutual respect for each other because of their interest in farming and custodianship of the land.

Pa called John to his side. John doffed an imaginary hat.

'Good morning, Master Rook.' The squire smiled. 'I've come to see what this machine can do. According to your father, every farmer will have one by the end of the year.'

'Indeed, sir. That's what he believes,' John said, nodding.

'And do you believe it too?'

'Of course, sir.'

'Do you agree with everything your father says?' the squire asked with a hint of challenge in his tone.

'Yes, sir. Almost. Except for his decision to plant barley instead of peas on the long acre next year.' John was referring to one of the strips of land to the south of the farmhouse. 'I've told him he shouldn't put all his eggs in one basket.'

'The squire doesn't want to hear about our bickering,' Pa said quickly. 'I haven't settled on barley yet, but there's a growing market for it. The brewers at Faversham can't get enow.'

'When's the threshing going to start?' Squire Temple said, changing the subject. 'I don't have all day.'

'It won't be long, sir,' Pa said, glancing past him, to where Mr Nobbs, Mary's father and tenant of Sinderberry Farm, was rapidly approaching. Behind him, the young Carters were making slow progress, helping their mother along the lane. 'John, go and help Ma Carter.'

John, perhaps fearing a confrontation, didn't wait to be bidden twice.

'Good morning, Ed,' Pa said, shaking his hand. 'I knew your curiosity would get the better of you. How is your wife?'

'She is well, thank you, but don't try to soft-soap me.' Mr Nobbs was an ebullient character with red cheeks and roughened hands to match.

57

His head was bald and shone in the sunshine, yet wiry curls sprang from the back of his neck and chin. He was taller and broader than Pa.

'You've heard that Mary is walking out with my son,' Pa said.

'Who hasn't? It's all over the village and has bin for some considerable time. I'd appreciate it if you'd make it clear where his duties lie. I expect him to do right by her very soon. I don't like the idea of a long drawn-out courtship, not for one of my daughters. It's best that these things are settled so there can be no wrongtakes.'

'They're young yet.'

'Mary is twenty-two. There's nothing I'd like more than to see her walk down the aisle with the son of one of East Kent's finest farmers, but by Christmas, or not at all. Send the lad over to me this week,' Mr Nobbs went on.

'I'll speak to him on the matter,' Pa said.

Other people were arriving, some of the labourers turning up with their flails as though they were expecting the machine to fail. Ma Carter was among them, having struggled the short distance from the cottage to watch, two of her little ones bringing a chair for her. She sat down, her hair straggling from beneath her bonnet, her face pale and pillow-like, and her eyes bulging rather like a toad's, Catherine thought, feeling sorry for her.

The vicar, who had remained to see the machine, went to speak to her to see if there was anything his wife could bring her to make life a little easier.

'If Mrs Browning was able to bring me good

58

health, that would be all I would ask of her,' she said, 'but failing that, a loaf of bread and a fat hen for the pot would help put some food in the little ones' bellies.'

'I shall see what I can do. Let me remind you, Mrs Carter, that a prayer to God and attendance at the church will bring you much comfort. It seems that as you can get yourself to Wanstall Farm, it wouldn't be much of an effort for you to walk to church on a Sunday morning, especially if you gave yourself plenty of time to get there. It's my belief that many of these ailments among the poor could be prevented if they only took some fresh air, and opened their minds to the Lord. An hour listening to one of my sermons can do wonders for a person's health.'

'He thinks himself a doctor as well as a clergy-man,' Catherine said. 'Listening to one of his sermons for an hour feels like a leety death.'

'Shh,' said Ma Rook. 'You mustn't talk lightly of dying like that. It comes to us all too soon.'

'But he is so dull.'

'It is a vicar's calling to be dull,' Ma asserted. 'That way nobody can be accused of going to church for entertainment.'

Mr White the wheelwright was a guest of hon-our, and present, Catherine suspected, in case the machine should require emergency repairs. Emily joined her, and the crowd swelled to about fifty people. Some stood on upturned buckets and ladders that they'd brought with them for a better view.

'Let's see this miracle of engineering,' said Mr Nobbs.

59

'It doesn't look much,' someone else observed as they gazed at the wood and metal monster with its belts and pulleys.

A pair of horses were harnessed, standing patiently for work to begin. George Carter was at the lead horse's head. When Pa nodded, George made a clicking sound in his throat and the horses stepped forwards, their movement powering the drive shaft that sent the spinning drum and straw rollers into motion with a great shaking and shuddering. For a moment, the machine stopped abruptly with a jerk and the crowd held their breath. George urged the horses on and gradually the machine squealed and grated into action. Pa clambered onto the top to untie the first sheaf and feed it into the drum, which gobbled it up in an instant.

Matty forked up more sheaves from the barn and George kept the horses moving while the spinning drum broke the grain from the straw and fed it across the rollers, where the grain fell through the sieve beneath and into a sack.

'Three or four men can thresh as much corn as twelve can the old way,' Pa shouted as he clambered down to let John take his place, untying the sheaves and feeding them into the machine.

'So what will the rest of us do over winter?' Jervis shouted out. 'I tell you, we will all be starvin' by Christmas.'

'Have faith,' Pa called back. 'We will be able to plough more land, sow more seed and reap more corn. This beauty heralds the start of a new age of prosperity and enow food for all. Step forward, Jervis, and help me take the first sack of grain.'

Someone pushed Jervis forwards and, to applause, he and Pa loaded the first sack of grain onto the waggon.

'The sails will soon be turning at the mill,' Emily said, smiling broadly. 'Ma will be happy.'

Which meant she wouldn't be chasing her down with a rolling pin or leather strap, Catherine thought.

'My brother is going to ask for Mary's hand in marriage this week,' she told Emily.

'How do you know? Has he said so?'

'I overheard Pa speaking to Mr Nobbs. It seems quite decided. Oh, I don't know,' Catherine sighed. 'Mary has taken a fancy to John, but I don't think he feels the same way about her.'

The question troubled her as all around the sounds of late summer filled her ears: the regular dunk of the machine and the rhythmic sawing of timber from the woods. She noticed Drusilla waving at Jervis from an upstairs window in the farmhouse. Jervis smiled briefly before the scowl returned to his face. Catherine wondered if Pa had managed to allay Jervis's fears over the machine and the potential threat to his livelihood. Pa was right, of course, about this machine. He always was right about everything. She trusted him implicitly, and she was proud to be a daughter that loved her father with all her heart.

Chapter Three

Laudanum and Smelling Salts

Catherine was feeding the hens early on a cold October morning as the mists were rising from the vale. The grass was wet with silver dew and the middlings left on the apple trees were rotten to the core. She blew on her fingers in an attempt to warm them up. The blood started to flow, making her chilblains red and itchy. She checked on Margaret's piglets – they were growing fast, snorting and snuffling through the fresh straw in the sty. One stopped and looked up at her, then scampered away squealing, making her laugh.

She headed back towards the house, passing the granary where John, Matty and George were working the threshing machine. George was having trouble keeping the horses in order. They seemed a bit fresh, tossing their heads and swishing their tails. Matty was feeding the sheaves into the machine, which rumbled and shook as it sent the straw flying and the grain tumbling into a sack. John tied the top, dragged it aside and replaced it with a fresh one as soon as it was full.

Noticing Catherine, John smiled. She smiled back. He had proposed to Mary and been accepted, and plans were afoot for their wedding. She was pleased for them, and confident that John had overcome any doubts he might have had over the match. With their impending marriage, the Rooks appeared to have secured the tenancy of Wanstall Farm for another generation at least. Catherine was looking forward to the wedding celebrations that Ma was planning.

The sound of an altercation on the track outside the yard cut through the rumbling of the machine.

'Jervis Carter!' Pa was yelling, his words ringing out like iron through the mist. 'I've told you before. I don't need you today, tomorrow or the next. Get off my land!'

'Look at you,' retorted a familiar, high-pitched voice. 'You have everythin': a son engaged to a farmer's daughter; a winter coat; a decent pair of boots. Your wife grows fat like a pig from the fruits of our labours.'

'I beg your pardon?' Pa growled.

Catherine realised that the machine had stopped, and George, John and Matty had appeared from the mist to face Jervis and her father as they entered the yard.

'Jervis, think before you speak,' George cut in. 'Tom, he don't mean anything by it, do you, son? Where have you bin anyway? I haven't seen you for a week and a day.'

'And why do you think that is?' Jervis stood in front of them in a torn jacket and muddy boots. 'Why do you always assoome that I'm up to no good? I've bin trampin' the countryside lookin' for work, and it's the same everywhere. All you can hear is the sound of the threshin' machines and grown men cryin' as their women and children starve.' His eyes glittered with anger and tears. Catherine could smell strong beer on his breath. 'It's men like you who take advantage of the poor,' he said, turning to Pa with his fists clenched.

'Don't you raise your fists to me!'

'That's enow.' George stepped between his friend and his son.

'I don't know why you bother with him, George,' Pa said. 'He's like a mad dog. He's always bitten at the hand that feeds him. His attitude doesn't do him any good.'

'How can I be to blame for my attit*oo*de? You've brought me to this, favouring my younger brothers over me. Look at them. Stephen hardly speaks to me now, he's so swelled up with his self-importance.'

'I've done all I can for you boys out of my eternal gratitude to your father. You would have been apprenticed by virtue of being the eldest if you hadn't upset Len so bad that he refused to consider you, and Matty can always be relied upon, whereas you...' Pa's words appeared to fail him for a moment.

'Tom has only ever been kind and generous to the Carters. He would ha' gi'n you work if you'd turned up with the rest of us the other morning. You could have joined the watch with Matty on Saturday night, if you hadn't been out and about.' George forced a chuckle. 'You was walking out with your sweetheart, i'n't that right?'

Jervis set his mouth in a grim straight line, refusing to answer.

Catherine glanced towards Matty, whose face was a mask. She could sense the tension between

64

Pa and the Carters, and between George and his sons.

'I reckon that if you apologised in a proper, genuine manner, Tom would find something for you to do,' George said.

'I have enow hired hands for the present,' Pa said stiffly.

'Please,' George begged. 'I'll vouch for his good behaviour in *foo*ture if you'll give him work.' He slapped his son on the back. 'Come on, my lad. Say you're sorry.'

'I'm sorry, sir,' Jervis said. 'I spoke out of turn. I didn't mean to offend.'

'That's better,' Pa said. 'I was afraid you were coming round to Captain Swing's way of thinking.'

'No, sir. Of course not, sir.'

Catherine had heard Pa talk of the mythical Captain Swing, named after the action of the hand flail. Pa had attended a meeting with the squire at the Rose Inn in Canterbury to discuss how they could protect their farms from the rioters who set ricks and granaries alight, and broke threshing machines in protest against the wealthy farmers and landowners, and the law of the land which had changed to disadvantage the poor. There were troops patrolling the country roads on the way, and when he'd walked to the top of the Dane John, he'd seen ricks and farms ablaze in the distance. That had made him realise the seriousness of the situation, so he and the local farmers around Overshill had set up a regular night watch from the church tower.

'Will you hire me, sir? I can dig out the rotten

poles in the hop garden, pull onions or lift turnips. I'll do anythin'.'

'The vegetable patch needs digging over. You can start with that.' Pa turned to Catherine. 'Go and fetch Jervis some bread and cheese. A man can't work on an empty stomach.'

'Pa, I'll be late leaving for school,' she protested.

'Do as I ask. It won't take long.'

She went indoors. The cheese dish was empty so she returned with the bread and some butter.

'Here you are,' she said.

Jervis snatched it from her and started tearing pieces from the loaf and stuffing them into his mouth. He paused for a moment.

'Thank you, Miss Rook,' he said grudgingly, his lips covered with crumbs and spittle, before he turned abruptly and walked away into the mist while the machine groaned back into action.

Catherine carried on with her before-school chores, fetching water for the pigs in the heavy wooden bucket. As she struggled to tip it into the trough, there was a screech and a terrible grating sound, as the machine slowed down. She stopped what she was doing to watch her brother trying to get the rollers moving smoothly again.

'These are blocked,' John called. 'You must have put too much in at once.'

'I didn't mean to,' Matty shouted back from the top of the machine. 'The straw is longer than usual. It keeps getting stuck.'

'Pull it out then, son,' George called. 'I'll hold the horses.'

'I'll do it,' John said impatiently. He scrambled

up to join Matty and reached in to clear the straw, but George hadn't yet managed to bring the horses to a halt. The spindle caught John's smock and started to wind him in.

'Stop, Pa,' Matty yelled.

As George pulled the horses up, John's smock tore apart, releasing him from the mechanism.

Catherine uttered a gasp of relief, but as the machine jerked to a stop, John lost his balance. He reached out to save himself, but there was nothing for him to hold onto. He toppled and fell to the ground, landing head first. For a moment Catherine stood paralysed in shock, then she screamed and ran over to him, dropping to her knees at his side. George left the horses to join her where John was lying out cold.

'Matty, fetch Tom,' he said. 'Quick as you can.' Matty ran off, shouting for Pa.

Catherine patted her brother's face and begged him to wake up. His eyes rolled to the back of his head. He began to twitch and foam at the mouth.

Pa appeared from the barn, grim-faced and shaking.

'Oh Lord, what have I done?' he exclaimed. 'What happened?'

'His smock caught in the spindles as he was trying to clear the machine,' Catherine explained. 'He fell and broke his head, and now he won't wake up.'

Pa ordered Matty to take one of the horses and fetch the doctor from Boughton-under-Blean.

'What shall I say to Ma?' Catherine asked, getting up.

'I wish we didn't have to tell her. This will break

her heart,' Pa said, running his hands through his hair. 'What are we to do?'

'I think we should move him into the house,' she said, trying to be practical. 'He can't stay out here.' She bolted indoors to find Ma who was negotiating the purchase of a brace of pheasant from a higgler who had turned up on the doorstep.

'Why aren't you at school?' Ma said. 'You'll be in trouble with Mrs Fagg.'

'Come and sit down,' Catherine said.

'Can't you see how busy I am?' Ma said, annoyed. 'I'm right in the middle of something.'

'I'm sorry. It's urgent.'

Ma looked at her properly for the first time, catching something in her tone. 'Something terrible has happened, hasn't it?'

Catherine nodded.

'Is it Pa?'

'Come and sit down.' She sent the higgler away and led her mother to the kitchen, where she sat her on a chair near the fire. 'There's been an accident. It's John. He's in a bad way.'

Ma got up, her face as white as lard.

'Please, don't move.'

'I have to see him.' She pushed her aside. 'You can't keep a mother from her son.'

Catherine ran out after her. Pa, George and Jervis – who had appeared from the garden – were moving John onto an old door. Ma wailed and beat her chest. Catherine restrained her to allow the men to carry the patient upstairs un-hindered and put him to bed.

'Try not to worry. Pa's sent for the doctor,' she said.

'It's too late. He's dead,' Ma exclaimed, wringing a sodden handkerchief.

'He's breathing.' Catherine helped her to John's room. 'Let's pray that he wakes soon.' She called for Drusilla to bring boiled water, clean cloths and the smelling salts. When they arrived, she opened the vinaigrette and held the sponge to John's nostrils. He uttered a long, low groan.

'Oh, my poor, darling boy.' Ma sat on the bed at his feet, snatched the vinaigrette and took a deep breath of hartshorn. 'This is your fault.' She looked accusingly at Pa. 'If only you hadn't insisted on buying that infernal machine. I knew it wasn't safe.'

'I should have had a guard made for the spindle,' he said quietly. 'Mr White advised me to, but I didn't get around to it. It was expensive.'

'Oh, how I wish to hear the sound of the flail again,' Ma went on, rocking back and forth.

Catherine loosened John's necktie and mopped the spittle from his lips and the blood from his scalp.

'What did you think you were doing, being so careless around that machine?' she murmured under her breath. 'I'd give anything to see you open your eyes.'

'Where's the doctor?' Pa said with a curse. 'What's keeping him?'

Catherine offered silent prayers, Ma cried, and Pa paced up and down the landing until the doctor arrived on his horse a few minutes after the clock in the hall struck twelve.

'Dr Whebley, thank goodness you've come,' Ma said when Drusilla showed him up to the sickroom. He strolled in, dressed in a great coat and boots, and carrying a leather case. He was about sixty years old, his face deeply lined and his moustache the colour of salt.

'The boy told me what happened,' he said gruffly. He examined John, looked inside his eyelids, pinched his fingers and toes, and listened to his chest with his ear to a paper cone. 'You were right to send for me in such a case of insensibility. Concussion of the brain as a result of a contusion cannot be regarded too seriously.'

'What can be done for him?' Pa asked, his voice raw.

'He's a young man and his body is strong. I prescribe regular doses of laudanum mixed with water to allow him to continue to sleep quietly and without pain while his head repairs. I advise you to cut his hair short and apply cold to the bruise. It wouldn't hurt to apply hot water bottles to his feet as well to try to bring him out of this suspended animation.'

'You've seen this before? He will get better?' Pa said.

'It's too early to give an opinion on the likelihood of his recovery, but I shall have a better idea upon my return on the morrow.' The doctor bade the family farewell and rode away down the lane at a smart trot on his chestnut mare.

Pa left the room and Ma sat with John until she seemed to be unable to bear her grief any longer. Catherine remained with him, willing him to live, not just for her sake, but for Mary's and the rest of the Rooks too.

News of the accident spread fast, resulting in a

constant stream of visitors during the afternoon. Mrs Browning called with her daughter, Jane, bringing an offering of junket.

'Oh my dear Mrs Rook, we heard of your terrible misfortune, and came as soon as the milk had set,' said Mrs Browning as Ma showed them into the sickroom to see the invalid for themselves.

'It is the end of the world. My lovely boy is brought to this! He's as good as d-d-dead,' Ma sobbed.

'Please, don't say that. What if he can hear you?' Catherine said.

'Catherine is right,' Mrs Browning said. 'Words like that are of no encouragement in bringing him round. We should remain optimistic and pray for his recovery. Jane and I will leave you in peace. If there's anything we can do, let us know.' The visitors left, taking the junket with them. Catherine assumed it was destined for another invalid – Ma Carter, perhaps – one able to appreciate it.

Young Thomas Rook rode over to see his brother as well. He looked in on the patient and talked briefly to Catherine, giving her news of her nephews and nieces before returning to his farm. George Carter called in at the end of the day to offer his regards and express the wish that it had been him, not John, who'd got caught up in the machine, which wasn't very helpful because it set Ma off into an attack of the vapours which necessitated her retiring immediately to bed.

Catherine was dripping water laced with laudanum into John's mouth when Drusilla brought her a supper of soup, bread and cheese.

'What is that, miss?' she asked, putting down the tray and picking up the chemist's bottle.

'It's medicine – Dr Whebley prescribed it.'

'Is it sleeping drops?'

'I believe it is similar.'

'Is there any change?' Drusilla put the bottle down.

Catherine shook her head. Even Ma's frenzied sobbing hadn't made John stir.

'I will cast a spell to make him better.'

'Thank you.' Anything was worth a try, Catherine thought, although she was a little dubious about the practice of witchcraft. The Reverend Browning wouldn't approve.

'Is there anything else you need, miss? Only it's time I was goin' home.'

'No, I'll see you in the morning.' Catherine wished her goodnight.

She nibbled at the bread, but the soup went cold on the dressing table. The candle at the bedside flickered and the smell of burning tallow filled the sickroom. A barn owl, a harbinger of doom, started to shriek into the dark night. She leaned across and looked closely at the patient's face. His eyes were half-closed. He seemed sleepier than ever after the laudanum. Now and again his breathing stuttered, as if it were about to stop altogether. She reached out and held his hand.

'Don't leave us,' she begged. 'You have everything to live for. Please, John, squeeze my fingers, do anything to show you can hear me. I love you, my brother.' She waited, but there was no response, just the clatter of a small shower of stones against the window.

Frowning, she got up from the chair and looked out into the darkness. A figure moved into the light cast by the moon.

'Matty?' She opened the window. 'What do you want?' She pulled her shawl around her shoulders to protect herself from the icy draught.

'To come up and see you, but your ma won't let me in cos of me dirty boots.'

'Can't you take them off?' Catherine called back.

'She says my feet have the fago of a pigsty. I've got something for you.' He pulled this something from his jacket pocket and held it out. 'I didn't steal it,' he added quickly. 'Here. Catch!' He tossed it upwards. Catherine reached out through the window and caught it.

'Thank you,' she said, examining his gift of a ripe apple. 'That's very kind.'

'I thought it would help you feel better. I'm sorry about your brother. It's a terrible thing that's 'appened. I shouldn't have put so much of that long straw through the machine in one go, but you know what your pa is like. He always wants things done by the day before yesterday.'

'It wasn't your fault. No one is blaming you.'

'Is that you, lurking about in the bushes, Matty Carter?'

He shrank back into the shadow at the sound of Ma's voice, then turned and scarpered as fast as his legs could carry him.

Catherine closed the window. She would have appreciated the comfort of another's presence in the sickroom. The responsibility of caring for John was weighing her down and she could hear her parents arguing downstairs.

'We should go and fetch Mary,' Ma was saying. 'Maybe she can wake him.'

'I don't want no more people coming round to take joy from the Rooks' calamity,' Pa said. 'Mary would come of her own accord if she wanted to.'

'She must come. She and John are engaged.'

'She won't want to marry him now. He kept her waiting, so why should she come here and be dragged in to looking after an invalid? Or be a widow by the time a year has passed?'

'You are an insufferable husband. Why do you never take your loving wife's side?'

'Because you talk such nonsense.' Pa raged against Ma, who raged against Pa and the machine.

Catherine curled up on the mattress that she and Drusilla had dragged in from her bedroom, and placed her hands over her ears to block out the noise. Eventually she fell into a fitful sleep, waking twice to check on her brother and a third time to find Ma prodding at her with her foot.

'Get up, lazybones. You're supposed to be watching over John, not lying around doing nothing. You've let the fire go out,' she snapped. 'I shall blame your negligence if he should pass away. Go and fetch a comb for his hair. He must look respectable for the doctor.'

Even if he's dying, Catherine thought resentfully as she stood up. Not for the first time in her life, she wondered why Ma cared so much more for John than she did for her. She couldn't understand how a mother could treat her own daughter so cruelly.

'I'm sure Dr Whebley is used to seeing people at a disadvantage,' she called after her mother who disappeared at the sound of a horse's hooves, only to return shortly afterwards with the doctor. He'd had time to remove his coat on this occasion, revealing a red waistcoat and gold chain for a pocket watch.

'What is your opinion?' Ma asked in hushed tones while he gave the patient a cursory examination.

'There is no change. He remains in a state of insensibility. Continue with the laudanum and I will come back tomorrow. Your young nurse here is doing a grand job.' He smiled at Catherine. 'Good day, Mrs and Miss Rook.'

Catherine showed Doctor Whebley out and made her way back to the sickroom. Pa joined them, still wearing his boots which appeared to have half the farmyard stuck to them.

'Well?' he said, moving up to the bed. 'Catherine, you speak more sense than anyone else around here. Did the doctor show any sign of optimism? Did he examine my son, or prescribe a different medicine, perhaps? Did he express a wish to bleed him or call the surgeon?'

'No, Pa. He stood at the bedside and saw what I could see.'

'Is that all?'

She nodded. 'He proclaimed that his condition is about the same.'

'In a few days' time, he'll hand me his bill and expect me to pay for his opinion, which is no different from yours,' Pa said scathingly. 'I reckon he's no more than a quack. In fact, I might just as well turn him away tomorrow.'

'Dr Whebley is a polite and learned gentleman,' Ma interrupted. 'He's been the only medical man in Boughton for many years.'

'All he does is ride about the countryside making house calls and giving airy opinions.'

'He's renowned for his cures and bedside manner. Don't you go sending him away for the sake of a few shillings.'

'Guineas, more like.'

'The money doesn't matter. Our son must be well again.' Ma's face crumpled.

'Don't I know it. After all the work we've done to get this far. We've nearly broken our backs for it.' To Catherine's astonishment, Pa stepped towards his wife and took her in his arms. 'I'm sorry, my dear,' he said in a husky voice. 'I wish I'd never clapped eyes on that damned machine. It's cursed.'

'Where are you going?' Ma exclaimed as he turned and pushed roughly past her.

'To make sure that nothing like this can happen again,' he yelled, his feet thundering down the stairs.

Ma, Catherine and Drusilla followed him out into the farmyard.

'The Lord have mercy on us,' Ma cried as he picked up an axe from the woodshed and carried it across to the threshing machine, the hens scattering feathers in front of him. 'He has lost his mind.'

He raised the axe and took a swing.

'No, Pa,' Catherine screamed.

'Stop!' Ma rushed towards him, but the axe

came down onto the machine, splintering the timber with a terrible cracking sound that brought Matty running out of the granary with George limping along behind him, flail in hand. Jervis and another farmhand emerged after them.

'No, Tom!' George bellowed.

'Stop him,' Ma shouted. 'Please! He'll do himself an injury.'

George threw down his flail and flung himself at Pa's back, catching him by the arms, but Pa shook him off.

'Leave me alone. This has to be done.' He took another swing with the axe, smashing it down and raising sparks from the ironwork.

'The madness has taken him,' Jervis gasped as Pa took another swing, again and again, until all that was left of the machine was a heap of firewood and metal. He threw down the axe and sank to his knees on the wet ground, sobbing uncontrollably.

As Catherine moved to comfort him, Ma stayed her with a hand on her arm.

'Leave him be,' she said quietly. 'Go back to work, everyone. The grain won't flail itself. Drusilla, stop gawping and get back indoors. Catherine, you're neglecting your duties.'

Feeling guilty for having abandoned her patient, Catherine returned to John's bedside. Her heart missed a beat, for something had changed. His eyes were wide open, and his expression reminded her of a fox she'd once seen cornered by the squire's pack of baying hounds.

'Oh, my dearest brother,' she reached for his hand, 'you are returned to us. Ma, Pa,' she shouted from the window. 'John has woken! Come quickly.'

Ma was in the sickroom in an instant, thanking God for a miracle. Pa arrived a few moments later, supported by George on one side and Matty on the other.

'The breakin' of the machine has brought him back to us,' George marvelled. 'The sound has roused him from his stupor. Well, I never. Well, I never did.'

Pa stood at the end of the bed, unable to speak.

'Who are you?' John muttered, addressing Catherine.

'I'm your loving sister. Don't you recognise me?'

He frowned and her joy quickly turned to sorrow. His eyes turned to Ma.

'Mama?' he said.

'My darling boy. You used to call me that when you were a baby,' she said softly. 'You gave us quite a scare. We thought we'd lost you.'

'But I am here,' John said.

'I know.' Ma turned to Pa. 'Thomas, we must send for Mary straight away.'

'It is too soon,' Catherine interrupted. 'If Doctor Whebley was here, he'd recommend peace and quiet for a while longer.' There was more than one reason for keeping Mary away. She wasn't sure what effect the sight of John's future wife might have on him, and if he didn't remember her, what effect this might have on Mary.

Ma seemed to accept her opinion, clothed as Doctor Whebley's. She kissed John's forehead and ordered Pa, Matty and George to leave the room.

'My head hurts,' John groaned, touching the bruise on his temple with his fingertips. His lips were dry and cracked.

'Don't move,' Catherine said gently as he tried to sit up.

'I'm hungry,' he said.

'I'll arrange for Drusilla to bring something,' Ma said, 'and then I'm going out to let everyone know that the Rooks are back stronger than ever and the tenancy of Wanstall Farm is secure.'

'No, Ma. Don't say anything, not just yet,' said Catherine.

'Why not? This will put an end to all the gossip I've had to endure.'

'Wait a few days until he is up and about again. Without proof, people are bound to speculate about his condition. I would have thought that the last thing you'd want is for Mary to find out that he isn't as well as you're making out, and break off the engagement for that reason.'

'Perhaps it is better to delay in case he has a relapse,' said her mother begrudgingly.

'Thank you,' Catherine said, feeling much older than her years.

Ma left the sickroom and Drusilla turned up with a bowl of light gruel some time later.

'I want bread and jam,' John said.

'Sup this first,' Catherine said, smiling. He hadn't lost his appetite.

He tried to reach out for the bowl with both hands, but his right arm flopped uselessly from his shoulder.

79

'Let me help you.' Catherine tucked a cloth beneath his chin, spoon-fed him then wiped his mouth while Drusilla stared. She took her aside on the landing.

'I shouldn't need to remind you where your loyalties lie,' she began.

'With the Rooks, a'course,' the maid said.

'That's right,' Catherine confirmed. 'If you value your position here, you'll choose your words wisely when it comes to talking about my brother.' Catherine didn't want idle gossip spreading through Overshill, ruining her brother's reputation before he was back on his feet. If people thought that John wasn't fully recovered, it would damage him, their whole family and their position as trusted tenant farmers. Would Squire Temple be so keen to continue having the Rooks run his land if John was no longer capable?

'Are you threatenin' me, miss?'

Catherine stiffened at the tone of her voice. She glanced from her small pale blue eyes to her roughened red hands, and wondered what she was capable of.

'I'm doing what anyone would do, protecting my family.'

'You'll soon learn that it isn't that easy. Don't worry, I won't say anythin' out of turn. Is there anythin' else?'

'No, that will be all for now.'

Over the next two days, the colour began to return to John's face. The swelling on his head diminished and the bruise at his temple started to retreat. Doctor Whebley expressed the opinion that the accident had caused congestion of the head with consequent softening of the brain which could result in a variety of symptoms, including slow thought, poor speech and a privation of voluntary movement with paralysis and a lack of sensation in the limbs. He couldn't confirm that John would regain all his faculties. On the contrary, he doubted that he would make a full recovery. Once he saw the patient on his feet, however, unsteady but able to move around, he did say that John was much improved, and Pa dispensed with his services.

Catherine dispensed with the laudanum as well, locking it in the top drawer of the bureau in the hall for safety. She didn't see the point in it. It sent John to sleep when her instinct was to keep him awake so he had time to learn how to move again and recall lost memories. She didn't believe Pa's theory that the doctor was a quack. She thought it more likely that he had made a mistake. She decided not to mention withholding John's medication.

All she wanted was for John to go back to his old self so she could have her brother back, then his marriage to Mary could go ahead, she could go back to school and Pa could return to normal. A week later, though, Pa was hardly speaking still, except to berate himself over the machine, and John couldn't recall a single detail of the accident. He could scarcely remember his own name.

Chapter Four

The Watch

Catherine didn't go back to school after John's accident. She continued to nurse him through the ever-shortening days of October and into November, when the easterly wind blew across the vale with a nasty bite, nipping at her fingers and toes and tearing deep into her bones. No matter how many clothes she wore, and how close she got to the fire in the parlour where John spent most of his waking hours, she couldn't get warm.

Pa grew impatient at his son's failure to recover fully. He was determined that John would return to normal despite Doctor Whebley's gloomy prognosis, and decided it was time that he carried on his usual business just as he had before the accident. Getting him back to work on the farm and out into the community, he reasoned, would hasten his convalescence. To that end, Pa asked Catherine to help John dress in his outdoor clothes. He took him by the arm and led him out to the farmyard where he placed a stick in John's right hand. It fell to the ground.

'Wake up, lad,' Pa exclaimed.

'You have to remind him to use his left hand. His right side is weak,' Catherine said protectively.

'Thank you, sister,' John said as Catherine picked it up and handed it back to him. Did he recognise her now? She wasn't sure if he remembered her from before the accident, or he'd created fresh memories since. Doctor Whebley seemed to have been correct in surmising that the accident had softened John's brain.

He pointed at the hens and the cat, and grinned with delight.

'I told you you'd feel better for a bit of fresh air,' Pa said. 'Let's go to Faversham and have a look round the market.'

George brought the horse over and helped John into the cart. There was a time when John would have taken up the reins, but it was Pa who had to do the honours because John didn't seem to know what to do.

Catherine fetched a blanket to put around his shoulders, afraid that he would catch a chill.

'Stop pampering him,' Pa complained. 'He needs to do things for himself.'

'He can't. He's like a baby.'

'He's a grown man,' Pa said sharply.

She watched them pass through the gate onto the track at a plod. The piebald mare didn't like leaving home without one of her companions, and Pa had to crack the whip across her rump to keep her moving. Pa was burying his head in the sand, Catherine thought, because she hadn't seen any change in John's condition in the past two or three weeks. John was a half-wit, or maybe not even as much as that. Awash with sadness, she went to feed Margaret and the piglets they were keeping to fatten over the winter.

When Pa and John returned after their long day's expedition, they sat down to supper with Catherine and Ma.

'John and I have been thinking about how to move forward and we reckon it would be a good idea to rent a cottage and a few acres on the marshes where he can run a flock of sheep. There were some Kent sheep, long-wools, at the market – I fancy they could make a fair profit,' Pa said.

'John can't live alone,' Ma said. 'I won't have it.'

'Mary's a good woman. She won't let him down.'

'What's she got to do with it? She hasn't paid us a single visit since John's accident, and Mr Nobbs has been avoiding us. He almost ran out of church the other Sunday so he didn't have to speak to you.'

'I'm sure Mary will hold fast, but anyway, it doesn't matter. Our boy will be perfectly capable of looking after himself and a wife by then,' Pa insisted. 'That's right, isn't it, John?'

'I'd like some more,' he said, looking down at his empty bowl. Ma nodded towards Catherine who fetched him a second ladleful of stew.

'What do you say of our plan, son? We talked about it this afternoon.'

John continued to eat, scraping the bowl with his spoon.

'Stop!' Pa seemed to snap. He grabbed at his hand and held it still. 'Look at me and listen. What did you think of the sheep?'

John nodded and smiled. Slowly, he formed the words, 'I can look after myself.'

'There you go,' Pa said. 'Case proven.'

84

Catherine frowned, silently questioning her father's sanity. John's accident had turned his hair completely white and there was no telling what effect it had had on the inside of his head.

'What about the farm?' Ma asked. 'Who will do John's work here? Thomas, this will tear our family apart.'

Catherine knew why Pa didn't want him here any longer. John's bumbling presence was a constant reminder that he had a simpleton for a son and it was his own fault.

'I won't discuss this further. The decision is made.'

Ma scowled and tutted, and cleared the plates. Catherine served up plum pie and custard. Pa didn't touch his portion. John took it from under his nose and finished it off.

Catherine hoped that the trip to Faversham would be the last attempt that Pa made to return John to his former self, but it wasn't to be. On the following Sunday, he decided to take him to church.

'I reckon he will shine when he's in the presence of people he's known all his life,' he said.

Reluctantly, Catherine tied her bonnet and pulled on her cloak to accompany them. She feared that John would be mocked for his slow, mumbling speech and the way that he walked.

'The love of a good woman will make him well again. When Mary sees him, her breast will flood with compassion and affection. They will be married within the month. Trust me.' Pa placed a walking stick into John's left hand and picked a second one from the stand in the hall for himself.

'Let's go.'

The bells rang out as the Rooks strolled towards the church.

'We should have brought the wheelbarrow for him,' Catherine remarked. 'He is too slow, walking along and dragging his foot like that.'

'He's got to do it himself,' Pa said. 'It won't be long before he can move faster and be more graceful than a hare.'

They walked along the path between the gravestones and into the church, where they took their places alongside the Millichips. Catherine noticed how Pa settled John at the end of the oak bench beside the aisle, sitting him upright with a hassock tucked under his right arm.

'How are you?' Emily asked quietly. 'I haven't seen you for ages.'

'I haven't had a moment to myself.' Catherine returned Emily's smile, but she could hear the whispers echoing around the nave: *He's an idiot, thanks to that machine. I said no good would come of it.*

A draught whisked along the aisle as Mr and Mrs Nobbs rushed with their daughter to their seats.

'I told you we'd be late, Mr Nobbs,' his wife grumbled.

'We're here to a dot,' he said, taking off his coat.

'Oh my.' Mrs Nobbs touched the brooch at her throat.

'Look who's here.'

Mary uttered a small cry.

'John, it's you.'

Ignoring her mother's entreaties to stay at her

side, she crossed the aisle to where he was sitting, his body slowly slumping to one side. She leaned across and touched his cheek.

'John, it's me, Mary.'

He gazed at her, his mouth half-open and one eyebrow raised.

'If this is one of your jokes, please stop.' Mary turned to Pa. 'Mr Rook, what's the matter with him?'

'There's nothing amiss.' Pa gave John a hefty dig in the ribs, making him grunt. 'Son, stop pretending like you've never seen your wife-to-be before.'

Deep furrows formed across the left side of John's forehead.

'I never seen this lady before,' he mumbled.

'Come on. How many times have we talked about Mary? Only yesterday, when we took the cart to market, you were telling me what joys marriage to such a beautiful and accomplished, and I have to add, suitable, young woman will bring you.' Pa looked straight at Mr Nobbs who was at his daughter's side, staring at John as if he was trying to associate this John with the engaging young man that he remembered. 'He was fair aflame with passion,' Pa said aside to Mary's father to emphasise his point.

Catherine sensed that Mr Nobbs didn't believe a word that Pa was saying, which was unfair, she thought, when Pa was never anything but scrupulously honest. She had never heard him tell a lie. He just wouldn't, but the whole congregation was silent, anticipating a scandal. His words simply didn't ring true.

'We must arrange for the banns to be read forthwith, so we can unite our families in celebrating the union of your daughter and my son,' he went on. 'Isn't that right, Margaret?'

'It is indeed, Thomas.' Ma played along. 'There's nothing that will give me more pleasure than seeing the matter settled.'

'I shan't marry a simpleton,' Mary cut in, her eyes filled with tears. 'It's impossible.'

'Don't be too hasty,' Mrs Nobbs said. 'John is still a fine young man. Look at him, sat there in his Sunday best.'

'It would be cruel to let him down now, after what he's been through,' Ma said.

'I shan't be made to feel obliged. When we were walking out together, it was John who delayed and made excuses about why we shouldn't be married. He doesn't remember me, so it won't be any loss to him. That's the only consolation I have, for I was fond of him – as he was.'

'You're right, Mary. There are other, more eligible bachelors around here,' Mr Nobbs said. 'I don't see why my daughter should be hitched to but half a man.'

'Eventually, John will inherit the tenancy,' his wife said in a shrill voice. 'They will have security and a good living.' But not a happy life, Catherine thought.

'The succession of the tenancy isn't a foregone conclusion,' Mr Nobbs said. 'The squire is at liberty to change his mind at any time. There's no reason why Wanstall Farm should remain in the hands of the Rooks.'

Catherine could sense Ma bristling with fury.

'Why, I'd like to get my hands on it, if I could, but not like this,' he went on.

'What is John's opinion?' Mrs Nobbs said.

There was a pause as they waited to see if he would express a desire for marriage to someone who was apparently a complete stranger to him, but he seemed overwhelmed.

'I'm hungry,' he said eventually.

'I'm sorry.' Mary unfastened the delicate chain that hung around her neck and let the locket from it slide into her palm. She pressed it into John's useless hand. It dropped to the floor and bounced under the pew. No one moved to find it. 'Take that as confirmation that we are no longer engaged.' With a cry, she ran out of the church with her mother following close behind.

'Good day, Mr and Mrs Rook, Miss Rook, John,' Mr Nobbs said. 'I'm glad we've had that out, Mary has been fretting so. I'm sorry for your troubles.' He put his coat back on. 'We won't stay for the service. We've bin through more than enough suffering for one day.'

He walked away as the Reverend Browning ascended the pulpit and struggled to attract the congregation's attention.

'Why didn't you stand up for our son?' Ma hissed. 'Why didn't you insist that Mary married him?'

'Because anyone could see she didn't want him. She would have made his life a misery.' Pa scowled at his wife. 'There's more than enow misery around here without that.'

The Reverend Browning thumped the pulpit with his fist.

89

'I told you not to bring him and you wouldn't listen to me. You've shamed our family in front of the whole village,' Ma went on, and she would have continued to harangue her husband if Matty hadn't appeared with the vamping horn and passed it to the vicar, who put it to his lips.

'I will have quiet!' His voice, magnified by the horn, silenced her. 'That's better. Perhaps members of the watch would like to return church property to its correct place in future.'

'Perhaps they would,' Matty said brightly as he headed back to his place in the gallery.

Catherine couldn't help smiling at the inconvenience inflicted on the vicar. Pa and the local farmers had continued to employ some of the men to look out for rioters during the weeks after John's accident. The men had borrowed the vamping horn in case they needed it to warn the villagers of impending trouble.

The choir struck up at the required time. The fiddle broke in first, followed by the slow boom of the bassoon, and the whining tones of Jervis Carter, who sounded as though he was still in his cups from the night before. Stephen joined in three beats later, and the whole ensemble sounded like an elegy at a funeral.

'Stop, stop, stop!' the vicar lisped.

Jervis stopped singing and peered out over the gallery. The fiddle paused and the bassoon continued.

'Please, sirs, you cannot proceed,' the vicar shouted, but the bassoon didn't stop until the verger went up the steps to the gallery to relay the message.

'What's the problem?' George asked. 'Do you want us to play something else? A more cheerful toon?'

'Something to counteract the mournful tone of this service would be most acceptable,' the squire said.

'Hear, hear,' came a murmur from the congregation.

'How about "Who Would True Valour See"?' George suggested. 'Or "Salvation! O the joyful sound!"?'

Matty plucked idly at his fiddle strings and Jervis waved at someone seated near the back of the church.

'May I remind you that you are performing in a holy place as part of our worship, so the utmost care should be taken to avoid this indecent levity? I implore you to avoid strong beer before Sunday service in future.'

'You can't make us,' Jervis muttered.

'I can lobby the churchwardens to cut your pay if you persist in turning up in an unfit state and unable to enter thoroughly into the sentiments of each chosen psalm.'

'You can't tell me how to play. I come from a moosical family,' George said.

'So you know that the sound that you make should die away gradually and in harmony. Everyone should follow the same beat so the congregation can sing along with you. At the moment, they are totally lost. I shall have to press ahead with my plan to bring in a singing master,' the vicar said sternly.

'We've never had any complaints before,'

George said, his tone one of sadness and confusion.

'We sing as we feel at the time,' Jervis said.

'Can't you discuss this at the next parish meeting?' the squire said impatiently. 'It's irrelevant to the rest of us.'

'Irrelevant? It's in everyone's interest to have a competent and clean-living choir to assist us in our worship.'

'I'd be more interested in finishing in time for an early luncheon so I can ride out before dusk than quibbling over the rules of music-making,' the squire said.

'I'm very hungry,' John said loudly, causing a ripple of laughter. 'Mama, what's for dinner? I should like bread and jam.'

'May these disruptions stop!' the vicar exclaimed. 'Mr Rook, please remove your son from the church.'

'There is nothing wrong with my John,' Pa said, his eyes gleaming with fervour.

'And some tripe and onions, and a slice of brawn,' John added.

'He can return when his head is mended and he no longer behaves like a child. He is driving me to distraction.'

'There is nothing wrong with him,' Pa repeated.

'I shall keep him in my prayers, hoping that it pleaseth the Lord for him to make a complete recovery; but he can't stay here.'

'Look at him. He's walking and talking like he was in the months before the accident. Stand up, lad.' Pa held out both hands to help John up. He struggled to rise from the pew, knocking his arm against it as he extricated himself from his seat.

'Are we going home for dinner now?' he said.

'Hush, John,' Pa said.

'Oh, he is sadly changed,' Mrs Millichip observed. 'He has but half a smile on his handsome face.'

'He is like a baby,' said her husband.

'Don't listen to them,' Emily whispered so only Catherine could hear.

'It's the Rooks' punishment for their greed,' Jervis called down from the gallery.

'Tom Rook is a good man,' George interjected. 'I won't hear of anyone speaking badly of him.'

'Come on, John. And you, Ma, and Catherine,' Pa said, his back stiffening. 'We aren't stopping here to be made fools of by those who are more foolish and feeble-minded than us.'

The Rooks' silent trip back down the aisle was the longest walk Catherine had taken in her life. It was shameful and embarrassing, and she doubted that Pa would ever bring John to church again.

During the ensuing week, she continued to care for her brother and do more than her share of the chores. She cooked mutton with rosemary, churned butter and scalded milk. She packed apples in crates of straw and made spills from waste paper, putting them in a box in the hall for lighting candles and fires for the winter while Ma bewailed her situation: having a mad man for a husband and a son who could no longer work on the farm or hope for marriage now that everyone in Overshill knew exactly what damage his fall from the threshing machine had done to him.

Pa hardly spoke. He spent many of his waking hours wandering through the woods and vales while George assumed responsibility for the farm in his absence and Matty stepped up to help his father, working every day except for Sunday.

On the Saturday night, Matty joined the watch that Pa had organised with Squire Temple and some of the farmers, including Mr Nobbs, to look out for the gangs that were roaming the countryside as part of Captain Swing's campaign for fairer conditions for the labourers who worked on the land. The previous week had been quiet, but there had been rumours of a group of about twenty men armed with bludgeons and matches going around the villages of Chartham and Chilham to the south the night before.

Normally, Pa would go and speak to the men and boys who were on the lookout at the top of the church tower to raise their spirits and find out if they'd seen any signs of trouble, but tonight, he complained of an attack of gout that kept him off his feet.

He couldn't be that worried about the possibility of the rioters targeting Overshill, Catherine thought, as she took it upon herself to deliver beer and food to the church. She picked up a lantern and basket, and hurried past Ghost Hole Pond in the dark, praying that she would avoid a confrontation with the spirits. She reached the church tower safely, and climbed the steep spiral staircase to the top where she stooped to pass through the tiny doorway onto the roof.

'Is there anyone there?' she called.

'Me,' Matty said. 'I'm over here.'

She found him sitting under a blanket with the hood of his cloak over his head. He was looking out between the stone balustrades.

'Where is everyone?'

'It's just me for now.'

'I've brought your supper. Pa is unwell.'

'He hasn't been himself since John had his accident.'

'It's been a terrible ordeal for him. He had his heart set on him taking over the farm one day.'

'He says there's still a chance that he'll mend.'

'Yes, he is hopeful,' Catherine affirmed.

'But you aren't?'

She shook her head.

'Poor John,' Matty said softly.

'Pa blames himself for making the situation worse by taking him to church last Sunday,' she said, relieved to have found someone with whom she could talk about John. It was impossible to talk to Pa because he was refusing to face up to the truth about John's recovery, and whenever she asked Ma for help looking after him, her mother would dash back her tears and tell Catherine it was her duty to care for him as a loving sister.

'Squire Temple won't sign the tenancy over to my brother, having seen that performance played out,' Catherine went on. 'Once Pa is gone, the Rooks will lose Wanstall Farm.' An icy gust of wind made her shiver.

'I'm sorry. That will affect the Carters, an' all. Come and share my blanket.' Matty patted the floor, inviting her to sit beside him. 'What are you waiting for?' he added when she hesitated.

95

'I'm not sure. I don't know that Ma would approve.'

'She isn't here.' Matty's teeth flashed white from the darkness.

'This might be one of your tricks.'

'I promise you it isn't. I'm not at Old Faggy's now. Please, Miss Rook. You'll catch your death.'

His chivalry took her by surprise.

'I shouldn't stay,' she said, marvelling at the changes she'd seen in him. It seemed that they were becoming friends, having put the Ghost Hole Pond incident behind them.

'I could do with some company to keep me awake.' He yawned. 'Jervis was supposed to take over from me, but he hasn't turned up.'

'I'll sit with you for a while,' she said, relenting. The idea of spending time away from the farm appealed to her. John would be safe with Ma. She placed her basket and the lantern on the floor, catching sight of a book in its soft yellow light. 'What's that?'

'Your pa lent it to me. I asked him.'

'It's all right. I believe you, although it does seem odd that you would want to read about' – she picked it up and flicked through the pages – 'sheep farming.' A chuckle threatened to erupt from her throat.

'Why do you laugh at me when I'm trying to better myself?' Matty sounded hurt.

'I'm not mocking you,' she said, feeling guilty. 'But can you read it? L'arning wasn't one of your strengths.'

'I can get the sense of some of it. Would you teach me some of the long words that I'm not

96

familiar with?'

'I suppose so,' she said, wanting to be helpful.

He smiled. 'Don't tell anyone, though.'

'There's nothing wrong in being bookish.'

'Promise you won't breathe a word?' he said fiercely.

'I promise.' Catherine sat down beside him. He laid his blanket across her shoulders.

'If you would be so kind as to read from the first page.' He started to eat one of the slices of pie from the basket.

'You haven't got far. You didn't tell me why you were so interested in sheep all of a sudden.'

'You'll laugh at me again.'

'I won't.'

'It isn't long ago that I turned fourteen, and I'm already feeling like an old man. I have a lifetime of labouring ahead of me. I work in the fields, rain or shine from dawn till dusk. I dig and hoe, pull onions and pick hops for a few shillings a week, just enough to buy bread and meat. I strive until my arms and legs ache, and my clothes are dirty and my boots are falling off my feet. When I get home, I help my little sister make meals and do the laundry because Ma can't do it. I put out buckets to catch the water that leaks through the roof when it rains. I have to beg and steal wood for the fire. By night-time, I'm asleep as soon as I rest my head on the pillow. All that I have to look forward to is more of the same.'

Catherine didn't know what to say as he continued, 'I wish I'd been born Squire Temple or even Hector Browning.'

'The vicar's son?'

'His hands are always clean and white – haven't you noticed them? He wears clothes that are neither too big nor too small.'

'He's been sent away to boarding school,' Catherine said.

'Where he feeds on beef and suet every day, and l'arns from books and rubs shoulders with the sons of the wealthy who rake in the money from breweries and brick-fields.'

'You wouldn't wish to be like Hector, though? He has no friends here in Overshill.'

'He's a prig,' Matty pronounced, 'and you're right. I'd hate to be sent away from my family. I mean, I'd like to travel the world too, but always come home at the end of it. When I get down on my knees in church to pray, I wish for Ma's good health, and food for my brothers and sisters. All I dream of for myself is having a cosy cottage, clean clothes and a vegetable patch, and maybe a pig to fatten. I'd like to have my own bed and one day, I'd like to run a few sheep on the marshes, or rent a few acres where I can plant an orchard.' He turned and looked her in the eyes. 'It isn't much to ask, is it?'

She didn't answer, afraid that his idea of contentment was too much for a farmhand to expect.

'There's one more thing,' he added. 'I'd like us to be friends.'

'We are friends, silly,' she laughed, although his sentiment warmed her heart.

'I mean good friends for ever. For the rest of our lives.'

'Well, yes, of course.'

'Even if I leave Overshill?'

'I don't see why not, but why are you planning to leave? It's home. It's where we belong.'

'No one can tell the future,' Matty said with a shrug. 'If it's meant to be, it's meant to be.'

Catherine gazed at him. He was being serious. 'You're a strange one, Matty Carter,' she said gently.

She picked up the book, opened it at the first page, and in the light of the lantern began to read about the role of a shepherd from a text that resembled one of the vicar's sermons.

'This is as dull as dishwater,' she said after a while. She paused to blow on her fingers in a feeble attempt to warm them up. She admired Matty's determination to improve himself by acquiring knowledge, but she couldn't help feeling it was going to take a very long time until his efforts bore any fruit. She thought of the damp environs of Toad's Bottom Cottage and Ma Carter's swollen body and limbs, and the younger members of the family, half-starved and unwashed. George had spent most of his life working on the land. What had he achieved? What had he got to show for his labours?

'Keep going,' Matty urged. 'I don't want to end up poor like my father. Your pa has done well out of him.'

'What are you saying?' Catherine said, hurt at the implication that her father had somehow taken advantage. She hoped that Matty didn't hold these sorts of resentments against her dear father, like his ungrateful brother Jervis seemed to do. Catherine always thought of Matty as a quiet and hard worker rather like Stephen, if a bit more mischievous, but now he sounded disgruntled.

'I don't mean to give offence.'

'He's been good to you. He's given you both work in the winter months when there was little or nothing to do.'

'Don't I know it,' Matty exclaimed bitterly. 'And he's paid for Stephen's apprenticeship and kept Jervis on when others wouldn't. I'm sorry, Catherine. I'm grateful, but it's hard to accept that we're completely dependent on Thomas's goodwill.' He leaned back and dosed his eyes. 'Please read.'

'Aren't you supposed to be on the lookout?'

'There's nothing to see. Nothing will happen until the beerhouses close.'

Reassured, she obliged, returning to the rather woolly subject of the husbandry of sheep, until the sound of shouting disturbed her.

'Did you hear that?' She tugged at Matty's cloak and was answered by a light snore. She extinguished the candle in the lantern so she could see better into the distance towards Wanstall Farm. The glint of Ghost Hole Pond and the silhouette of the mill were visible, highlighted by the bluish touch of the moonlight. She caught sight of people out in the field near the rick which was bright with a halo of flames. She could see and smell smoke. Her heart began to pound.

'Wake up! The hayrick's alight.' She shook Matty by the shoulders.

'Fire?' he muttered.

'Yes, at Wanstall Farm.'

With a yawn, he reached out and picked up the vamping horn, then he jumped up and put it to his lips. He blew hard, the sound piercing through the

100

darkness over and over again.

'Fire!' he yelled. 'Fire!' The horn clattered against the floor as he dropped it and took Catherine's hand. 'Let's go.'

They ran down the spiral staircase, one behind the other, out past the vicarage where the Reverend Browning had stepped outside to tie the knot on his robe. They joined a throng of people sweeping along the road to the farm: the Millichips; the butcher and his wife; Ivy Len and Stephen from the forge; Mr Nobbs and Mary; and George Carter. They rushed through the farmyard to the field behind where the rick was well ablaze, sending glowing cinders of hay high into the air.

The fiery fragments drifted over the tops of the barns towards the house and granary, and fell to the ground. Those that fell on stone or muddy ground blacked out, while those that landed on the thatched roof of the stables and the straw in the pigsty began to burn more strongly, sending out licking tongues of flame.

Margaret squealed and the horses in the stables started to panic, kicking out at the barriers between their stalls.

'Pa,' Catherine called, but she couldn't find him. George was at the pump, passing buckets and bowls of water along a human chain through the gate to the rick.

'The pigs.' She snatched a bucket from Ma, who had joined the line, and poured the water onto the burning straw. 'Matty, help me.'

'Take one.' He was back at her side, having picked up a couple of short poles from the woodpile. 'We can drive the pigs to safety.'

'What about the horses?'

'All in good time. Hurry.'

Catherine opened the gate into the sty.

'Come on, Margaret,' she urged, but she had to step inside and push the sow out. Her piglets followed, trotting across the yard towards the back of the house, which was all very well, but where were they going to put them so they didn't escape into the woods and disappear as fodder for the charcoal burners and travellers?

Matty threw a bucket of water onto one of the piglets which had stopped to snuffle at George's feet. It oinked and scampered towards the farmhouse, where Catherine opened the door and sent the pigs inside.

'Your ma will go mad,' Matty observed as he watched her shut them in the scullery.

'She might be grateful for once. Come on. We need to free the horses.'

Matty reached up and grabbed a coat from the hook in the passageway and they ran outside again. The horses were whinnying and kicking so hard that the buildings quaked. The rick and the pigsty continued to burn. More people had arrived, along with Squire Temple, his bailiff, kennel-man and groom, who were already in the stables, trying to cajole the horses outside. Matty handed the coat to the squire. He threw it over the lead horse's head. Calmed by the blindfold, the horse walked quietly out into the yard.

'Pa,' Catherine called again. Where was he? Was he injured? Where was John?

She ran round to the rick where the fire was

under control. The hay that was left was damp, blackened and smoking, and completely useless for feeding to the livestock during the long, cold winter. The pigsty was ruined and the thatch on the stable roof had gone, leaving the timber beams exposed. The men, women and children of Overshill put down their buckets and looked on as a gaggle of men appeared from the fields.

Pa was at the head of the procession with John stumbling along behind him. Next came three youths, flanked by five others, farmhands from Home Farm over the hill. They drove the three youths into the farmyard.

'Tie them up,' Pa ordered. He looked around, his gaze settling on Matty. 'Fetch the ropes from the barn.'

The three youths were swiftly roped together and surrounded. Who were they? Catherine wondered.

'Jervis, what are you doing here?' she heard Matty say.

'For the love of–' George's voice broke off.

'I didn't do nothin', Pa,' Jervis stammered. 'Honest.'

'We chased them down to the chalk pit,' one of the farmhands said. 'We found matches on this one.' He showed Pa his haul.

'I saw them drinking at the Woodsman's Arms earlier,' said another. 'They left at closing time and joined some other troublemakers in the woods. They've bin trying to rally others to their cause.'

'They have no cause,' Pa said. 'They're vandals who don't spare a thought for the ordinary working man when they're ruining people's property. Jervis, I've given you work out of the goodness of my heart and for the sake of your father, who is an honourable man, a gentleman in manners if not by wealth. I don't understand why you run amok.' He turned to the other two youths. 'What do you have to say for yourselves?'

Unlike Jervis, they had a lot to say, including the fact that they had met Jervis at the beerhouse and he had persuaded them to accompany him in setting the rick on fire as retribution for the miserly wage that Pa paid him, and for the resentments he felt at being passed over for the opportunities that his brothers had received.

'I can't turn a blind eye this time,' Pa said angrily. 'I'm not made of money and I'm tired of trying to do the right thing by people like you. You've damaged my livelihood and put lives at risk with your thoughtless actions. If Matty hadn't spotted the rick on fire and sounded the alarm, it could have taken hold on the barns and the house. You were supposed to be on watch yourself. I can't forgive you.'

Jervis swore.

'One day, Mr Rook,' he said, finding his tongue, 'if I have my way, people like you will find out what it's like to be destit*oo*te and without hope.'

The back of Catherine's neck pricked with unease as Pa responded.

'You aren't welcome within a mile of this farm or my family ever again. Go, before I change my mind. Other men have hanged for less.'

'Thank you for your compassion,' George said. 'He is a foolish, weak-minded lad and I'm ashamed of him.'

Jervis spat and cursed again as he struggled against the rope that bound his wrists.

'I did that for you and you alone, George. If I ever see him here on my property again, I will have him arrested and let the full force of the law come down upon him.' Pa nodded towards Matty. 'Untie them. You'd better run before the special constable arrives from Faversham. Go on. Get out of my sight.'

The three youths hastened from the farm and up the lane.

'Why did you let them go?' Squire Temple asked. 'We should make an example of them.'

'We can still set the hounds after them,' the bailiff said darkly. 'They'll bring them down. Failing that, I would have them shot ere they show their faces back in Overshill. It would be no loss to anyone.'

Catherine shuddered. Matty put his cloak around her shoulders, but she wasn't cold. She was even more fearful for the future now with the bailiff's violent threats and the thought of Pa being forced to choose between buying in hay and selling the animals that she loved. With the talk of shooting and arson, she didn't feel safe any more.

'Keep hold of my cloak until tomorrow. I'm off,' Matty said. 'I don't want to be here when your ma finds out the pigs are in her scullery. Goodnight, Catherine.'

'Thank you, Matty.' She smiled ruefully as she watched him hasten away. A few pigs in the scullery were the least of the Rooks' worries.

She thought back to the harvest and how she had wondered if the tranquillity of Wanstall Farm and Overshill could ever be broken. Within less than three months, everything had changed. John's accident with the threshing machine had set his life and the fate of the Rooks on a very different course. Tension had grown between farmers like Pa and the farm labourers whom the introduction of threshing machines had put out of work, and now there was the fire and the fallout from that to cope with.

It wasn't all bad, though, she mused as she wrapped the cloak tightly around her. She had made a friend in Matty Carter.

1833

Chapter Five

A Silver Sixpence

Overshill, East Kent

It was three years after the rick fire and a kind of peace had settled over the Kent countryside. The incendiarists had been apprehended thanks to the reward of one hundred pounds offered by the Kent Insurance Company for their detection. Some had been hanged to put fear into other would-be rioters. Farmers like Thomas Rook had raised wages and lowered the rents to help their farmhands, and the poor seemed to have settled for their lot. Wanstall Farm had recovered from the rick fire, but Catherine wasn't sure that her father would ever be quite the same again, his spirit diminished further by Jervis Carter's betrayal and his concerns for the future.

One morning in June, a day after Catherine's sixteenth birthday, she was in the kitchen with her mother. Pa had gone to market in Faversham with Matty and John while George remained at the farm, supervising the workers. Drusilla, having turned up late as had become her habit, was trying to catch up with her chores. Catherine could hear her stamping along the passageway with buckets of water for the copper.

'I was talking to Mrs Nobbs at church the other

day. It turns out that Mary has made a good match,' Ma said as he rolled pastry out on the table. 'Not as good as if she'd married our John, if things had been different, of course,' she added sadly. 'Her husband has inherited a farm near Maidstone, and she has one child and another on the way.' Ma lifted the round of pastry on the rolling pin. 'Don't you think that Hector is rather handsome?'

'He doesn't look well,' Catherine said. He'd grown into a pale, sickly-looking creature that might have crawled out from the depths of the pond.

'When he follows his father into the Church, he'll need a capable woman at his side.' Ma laid the pastry across a dish of plums. 'You'd do very well for him – you're pretty enough. And you can cook.'

'I couldn't be a vicar's wife, making much of her good works, and looking down her nose at people.' Catherine was smarting at Ma's comment about her appearance. Even though she said it herself, she had grown into a good-looking young woman. She was taller and had curves where she hadn't had them before, and her hair was as dark and glossy as a raven's plumage.

'You mustn't talk of Mrs Browning in that way. I'm fondly acquainted with her.'

Catherine frowned.

'Don't you think it's odd that she takes a gift of calf's foot jelly around to Ma Carter's on a Friday, and by Sunday, her husband is sermonifying against the idle sluggards of the parish who lie abed day and night, avoiding their duty to their families and the church?'

'I'm sure she doesn't influence her husband in any way.'

Catherine had always fancied that it was the voice of Mrs Browning that echoed through the church at every service.

'I fear that the vicar is more an instrument of his wife than one of God.'

'I wish you wouldn't speak so. One of these days, you'll be struck down by lightning.'

Catherine raked the fire out of the bread oven in the alcove and placed the pie inside.

'If you won't consider Hector, there's poor Mr Johncock, recently made a widower by the death of his wife in childbirth.' Ma tipped her head to one side as if considering. 'Of course, he has four little ones who need a ma.' She smiled at Catherine's confusion. 'He's a farmer with ten acres of his own and another twelve rented from the squire. You could do worse.'

'He has no teeth,' Catherine said, repulsed at the thought of marrying an old man who had taken to drowning his sorrows at the beerhouse.

'Better a husband with no teeth than to spend the rest of your life in the sorry state of spinsterhood. I was married by your age. It's time you were off my hands.' Ma handed Catherine a bowl. 'Go and fetch the buttermilk.'

In the pantry, she found lines of emmets marching into and out of the honeypot. She picked out as many of the ants as she could and placed a board on top with a jar of pickled eggs on top of that to keep them out, before she returned to the kitchen.

Ma yawned and patted her mouth.

'I'm going to retire for an hour. I can feel one of my heads coming on and if I don't rest, I won't be fit to accompany Mrs Browning on her visit to see the Norths this afternoon. You'll be coming with us.'

'I'd prefer not to,' Catherine sighed.

'It won't hurt you. Now, finish off here before you help Drusilla with the laundry.' Ma took herself off to bed.

Catherine added potatoes and carrots to the stew-pot, gave the peelings to the pigs and returned indoors. She slipped into the scullery to find the water boiling in the copper, a piece of lye soap ready on the side and the mangle set up, but no sign of Drusilla. Wondering if Ma had stirred and called her away, Catherine went into the hall-way where she noticed that the top drawer of the bureau had been opened and the key left in the lock.

The sound of light snoring from the parlour caught her attention. She pushed the door open to find Drusilla sprawled out on the chaise with her eyes closed and her mouth ajar, and the bottle of sleeping drops at her side.

'What do you think you're doing?' Catherine hissed. 'The laundry doesn't do itself.'

'More's the pity,' Drusilla murmured as she came to her senses. 'I thought to take some medicine for my womanly pains.'

'You stole it,' Catherine accused her. How she regretted not pouring the laudanum away after she'd decided that John had no more need of it. That way, Ma would never have acquired a taste

112

for it. Their voices must have roused her from her sleeping-drop induced slumber, because she arrived in the parlour, her expression dark with anger.

'What's going on here? Catherine? Drusilla? How dare you take advantage of the fact that I'm indisposed?'

'I was feelin' unwell.' Drusilla laid the back of her hand against her forehead in the manner of an actress at the New Theatre in Canterbury.

'You've been unwell a considerable amount recently. Is there something you aren't telling me? You can't deny that you've been walking out with that rogue Jervis Carter. It's all round the village. You've been seen in the Woodsman's Arms of a Saturday night, drinking and carousing.' Ma spotted the bottle. 'What's that?'

'Nothing, ma'am.' Drusilla picked it up from the floor and staggered to her feet. 'I swear 'tis mine. Jervis got it for me.'

'Let me see.' Ma held out her hand. 'For goodness' sake, give it to me.' Drusilla laid the bottle in her palm. 'What is the meaning of this?'

'I found the bureau unlocked and the bottle gone,' Catherine said.

'So you stole it, Drusilla,' Ma said.

'I had to take it to get me through the day. Washin' all those sheets and garments is backbreakin' work.'

'It's no wonder you haven't been yourself lately. When you are here, you're usually asleep on your feet. Now I find out that you're nothing but a common thief.' Ma stamped her foot. 'You are dismissed.'

'No, not that.' The maid's eyes were dark pools of fear. 'I'll do anythin'. I'll come in an hour early and finish an hour late every day to make up for it. I can't afford to lose my position here.'

'And I can't afford to lose sleep worrying about what my lazy maid is going to steal next. Go! You can't be trusted.'

'What about my wages, ma'am?' Drusilla held out her hands. 'I need somethin' to tide me over until I find another position.'

'You won't find one around here,' Ma said sharply. 'I'll make sure of that. I shan't be providing you with a reference.'

'But where shall I go? What shall I do?'

'I don't know and I don't care. Go and take your shame with you. Don't darken our door again.'

Drusilla looked towards Catherine.

'Please, miss,' she begged. 'Can't you put in a good word for me?'

In spite of their differences, Catherine's heart went out to her. They'd worked alongside each other for years and suffered together from her mother's scolding tongue. Didn't she deserve a second chance?

'Ma,' she began.

'Don't go feeling sorry for her when she's brought this upon herself,' Ma interrupted.

'It was the drops,' Drusilla said. 'Once I started, I couldn't stop takin' 'em.'

'I won't listen to anymore of your excuses.' Ma wagged her finger at her. 'I won't have you setting a bad example to my daughter.'

'That's the pot callin' the kettle black,' Drusilla

muttered, at which Ma escorted her from the house.

'What will she do for money?' Catherine asked as she and her mother returned to the kitchen. 'How will she live?'

'I don't know. She should have thought about that before she took a wrong turn. Now, you must go and do the laundry in her place.'

'When will we have a new maid?' Catherine looked at the mound of dirty linen on the floor in the scullery 'Have you got someone in mind?'

'Oh no, not yet. I'm too weary to think about it now.' Ma touched her brow. 'Besides, I'm not sure that we need another. You're sixteen years old and perfectly capable. And you don't cost me a maid's wages.'

'What will people think when they find the Rooks no longer have an indoor servant?' Catherine tried to play on the importance that Ma placed on her status in Overshill to make sure she got more help round the house.

'I'll tell them that we're looking out for a suitable girl. In the meantime, we will manage.

'I wish you wouldn't take those sleeping drops,' Catherine said, wondering if the laudanum had affected her mother's mind. 'You take them day and night. I've seen you.'

'They're a great comfort to me. You shouldn't deny me my small pleasures – I should suffer much worse without them.'

They all would. Catherine smiled wryly. When Ma suffered, everyone was compelled to suffer with her.

Catherine scrubbed Pa's collars, put the wet

115

sheets through the mangle and hung the washing out on the line. Later, she accompanied her mother to the vicarage with a basket of flummery and apple pie on her arm. When they met Mrs Browning, Ma suggested that Catherine carry her basket as well.

'Thank you,' the vicar's wife said, handing it over.

'It's no trouble at all. My daughter is healthy and strong.'

It was all very well Ma demonstrating her ability, if not her willingness, to carry two weighty baskets, Catherine thought.

As they trudged up the hill to the wooded ridge, she began to feel the heat.

'Look how her complexion glows,' Ma said proudly.

'Indeed,' said Mrs Browning. 'She is turning into a fine young woman, like my Jane.'

'There is no one more beautiful than your Jane. She takes after her mother in appearance, and her father in bookishness.'

'She is extraordinarily well read.'

'She will make the perfect wife,' Ma went on. Catherine shrank beneath her bonnet.

'She is far too young yet. I didn't marry until I was twenty-one.'

'I was betrothed at sixteen,' Ma said. 'I should like Catherine to attain such happiness as I did at a young age. I can't see the point in waiting.'

'Surely, it's better to give a young person's character time to settle before making a lifelong match.'

'I'm of the opinion that it's better for a couple

116

if their characters form while they are together so as to create the conditions for a life of marital harmony.'

'My husband and I are perfectly content in our marriage. I really wouldn't recommend betrothal at sixteen, unless the girl was in the family way.' Catherine became aware that Mrs Browning's eyes were on her.

'Oh no, not that,' Ma said quickly. 'My daughter has been brought up to know right from wrong.'

'It is a pity she hasn't had the benefit of some formal education.'

'She attended the dame school. She can read and write and is far better at 'rithmetic than me. She can add numbers in her head, while I have to count on Mr Rook's and my fingers if it is a big sum.'

Catherine smiled. It was her father who did the books and paid the bills.

'We had a tutor to school the children. Jane has an ear for music, while Hector is a scholar of the classics, which will serve him well when he follows his father into the Church. We have a match in mind, although it will be many years before he is free of his studies and able to take a wife.'

'Who would that be?' Ma said as they continued through the woods. 'Do tell.'

'You wouldn't know them. A friend of my husband, whom we met while we were living in London, has a daughter who is fair of face and virtuous of spirit, and has been brought up to understand the particular duties of a vicar's wife.'

'You never know what might happen during the

years that they are apart,' Ma ventured. The trees above them bowed and creaked in the breeze.

'I have my heart set on it,' Mrs Browning said rather curtly, as a small cottage came into view in the valley below.

When they grew closer, a dog like a rack of ribs on stilts came rushing out, barking and baring its yellow teeth.

'Get away, cur,' Ma shouted, taking a stick to fend it off. To Catherine's relief, it slunk away and lay down on a mound of leaf litter to watch from a distance.

Mrs Browning knocked on the door and a woman emerged, blinking in the sunlight. She had a child at her breast and two more hiding their faces in her skirts.

'Good afternoon, Mrs North.'

'I hardly think so. Who are you that risks her life to call here?'

'It's Mrs Browning, the vicar's wife, and her friend, Mrs Rook and her daughter, Miss Rook.'

'Forgive me. I haven't been to church for ever so long.'

'The Reverend Browning hopes that we will see you there again soon. We've brought food for your children. My commiserations for your recent sad loss.'

The woman's eyes gazed hungrily at the baskets as if she would pounce on them and devour, them whole, wicker and all.

Catherine felt sorry for her. What had brought her so low and desperate?

'Catherine, take hold of the baby for Mrs North,' Mrs Browning said.

She looked around for somewhere that wasn't filthy and alive with flies to put the baskets down, eventually settling for a bench made from a plank and two logs underneath the window. When Mrs North handed her the baby, the infant took one look at her and screamed. The other children joined in and Mrs North began to sob.

There was little comfort the women could give her. She had lost her husband in an accident with an axe that had severed his arm at the elbow. He had died within an hour, leaving her penniless with three small children.

'I promise to keep you in my prayers,' Mrs Browning said as they left. 'Have faith that God will provide.'

Ma and Catherine expressed their hopes for an improvement in the Norths' fortune, and returned through the woods with Mrs Browning. They visited Ma Carter and left bread, scraps of cold meat and some pickles for her hungry family.

'I wish you had stood a little straighter and walked more ladylike,' Ma said after they had parted with Mrs Browning at the vicarage.

'How could I? Them baskets felt like they were filled with stones.'

'You could have made more effort when Mrs Browning was looking in your direction. How am I going to find you a husband?'

Catherine walked on. She reckoned she could find one herself.

'You see what will happen to you if you don't marry well. Marry a poor man and you'll always be wretched. Take a wealthy husband and you'll have all the happiness that his money can buy.'

'Money can't buy happiness.' She thought of the things that made her happy: a basket filled with eggs; the piglets playing in the muck; the feeling of exhaustion and elation at the end of the harvest; John's slow smile; and most of all, Emily and Matty's friendship. As far as she was concerned, her life was complete. She didn't need a husband or his money, although she had no doubt that in the way of things, she would end up with the former, if not the latter.

When they reached the farmyard, they found the gate shut and their way blocked by a flock of sheep.

'Oh my, what's going on here?' Ma said.

'What do you think of my purchase?' Pa said, pushing the ewes aside to let Ma and Catherine through.

'You've bought them?' Ma said.

'That's what I said.' Pa smiled.

'This is turning out to be one of the worst days of my life,' Ma went on dramatically. 'I've had to send our maid packing and now I find you've wasted good money on these scabby creatures?'

'Drusilla has gone?'

'Forgive me for enquirin', but why has she left?' George said, joining them. Matty and John moved up to his side. 'I thought you were pleased with her on the whole.'

'She's bin a good maid, but I've been leery about her for a while. I thought it had something to do with her stopping out late, but I caught her taking sleeping drops and neglecting the laundry. I have an inkling that she's walking out with Jervis and she's under his influence.'

'The rest of us Carters don't have anything to do with him now that he's living out Dunkirk way. He hasn't been to visit his poorly ma for months. She's very upset about it.'

'Perhaps Drusilla will go to him,' Ma said, fishing for gossip.

'Oh, I don't know about that,' George said.

Ma returned to berating her husband.

'Where is your sympathy for your poor wife's aches and pains? Where is your compassion? You keep telling me there's no money for new clothes, yet you go and spend out on a flock of sheep. Look at me, Thomas. These rags make me look like something the cat's dragged in.'

'There's no use in going around the farm dressed in finery and feathers. You complain about the mud as it is.'

'I'm obliged to keep up appearances when I'm doing my charitable works around Overshill.'

'Mrs Browning doesn't wear the latest fashions. She's a modest sort of woman,' Pa said. 'You wouldn't wish to outshine her, would you? You must hope to be renowned for your piety and generosity of spirit, not the richness of the laces and silks that you wear.'

'You know what it's like. I can't possibly go around the village dressed like a poor person.'

Catherine glanced at Matty's face. His expression was frozen. He looked torn between embarrassment and anger, and for a moment Catherine wasn't sure which side would win. But Matty wasn't Jervis, he had a sensible and respectful head on his shoulders and he let Ma's comment slide off him.

'The sheep will give John a purpose,' Pa said. 'Matty, show him what to do – drive them out of the yard.'

'Yes, sir,' he said cheerfully. 'Come with me, John.'

Pa, George, Ma and Catherine followed Matty and John into the field behind the stables where the sheep promptly scattered in a panic, unnerved by their new surroundings. Three escaped through the hedge into the orchard.

'You'll have to run faster than that,' Pa hollered after Matty. He turned back to Ma. 'There'll be a nice bit of mutton for the pot, and fleece to card and spin for wool.'

'You'll be the death of me. How can you do this to me? I have more than enough to do without attending to a flock of toothless ewes.'

'Margaret, light of my life, this is one venture that can't possibly go wrong. Trust me. Catherine, go and help Matty round them up.'

Catherine ran down through the field and opened the gate into the orchard where Matty was scratching his head as he stared at the three sheep. She pulled a stick from the hedge and shouted instructions. The sheep bunched up and headed up the hill away from him towards the gate, but when they spotted Catherine, one turned and fled and the others followed.

'They're a skittish lot.' Matty laughed.

It took three more attempts to persuade the sheep through the gate. When they hesitated, Catherine tapped the ground behind them with the end of her stick, which was enough to convince them to move on. They trotted into the field and made their way back to the rest of the flock.

Catherine closed the gate and Matty slipped the rope over the gatepost to hold it shut. He was seventeen now. He was taller and his shoulders were broader, but it would be some time before he filled out. His legs were like bean-poles.

'You're pretty skilful for a girl.' He smiled.

'I read the chapter about sheep farming when we were sitting up on watch that time, remember.' She smiled back. 'That seems like ages ago.'

'It was.' Pa said that sometimes it felt like the fire happened only yesterday, but Catherine didn't feel that way. She counted the beginning of her friendship with Matty from that night, though it felt as if they had been friends for ever. They had grown closer, now and then sharing the responsibility for John's care. In fact, Catherine depended more on Matty than Emily these days. Caring for John took up so much of her time that she hadn't been able to see Emily so often. She missed her and the carefree times they had spent walking to and from school, but now when Catherine was looking for company from some-one close to her in age, Matty was always close by at Wanstall Farm.

'I'm looking forward to learning about shep-herding,' Matty said as they walked slowly up the field back to where Pa and George were standing talking, Ma and John having gone indoors. 'Your pa says that if I do well, I can have one of the ewes as my own and keep her lambs. Just imagine, one day I could have a flock of Kent sheep.'

Catherine admired his enthusiasm and ambition. It was odd, because there'd been a time when she had thought herself superior to Matty, but today, she felt that they were equals.

On the Sunday, Catherine and Pa went to church. Ma asked her to remember Mrs North in her prayers while she stayed at the farm to look after John. Catherine took her place beside Emily. There was so much she wanted to tell her, but the sermon went on for what felt like hours, and the choir became restless, attracting everyone's – apart from the vicar's – attention.

'I could do with a pint of a good strong beer,' George sighed.

'The hair of the dog,' Matty chuckled.

'I didn't touch a drop last night.'

'That's because you poured it straight down. It barely wet your whistle.'

'Hush,' Stephen said. 'We're drawing attention to ourselves. The Reverend will have the music master back onto us.'

George swore. The very act of uttering an epithet under the roof of the church caught Reverend Browning's ear. He picked up his prayer book and aimed it at the west gallery. It flew through the air, caught the balustrade and bounced into the choir. There was a gasp and a handclap from the congregation.

'Well done, my man,' said Squire Temple. 'Good shot.'

'Out!' shouted the vicar. 'Get out of my church.'

'Now?' said George, leaning over the parapet.

'All of you. You have tried my patience one too many times.'

'What about our wages?' Matty joined in.

'The wages of sin is death,' the vicar lisped fiercely. 'This choir is disbanded with immediate effect.'

'Who will sing the psalms?' George said, crestfallen.

'The congregation will find their voice.'

'Where will they take their timing from? What will their singing be without the uplifting tones of the clarinet and fiddle?'

'They will do very well,' the vicar insisted. 'Do as I say and walk out along the aisle to show yourselves as the unruly rag-tag rabble that you are. I should have done this long ago.' He held up his hands. 'Thanks be to God for giving me the strength.'

'What if we refuse?' Stephen asked.

'I'll send for the special constable.'

'On a Sunday?'

'I believe that he upholds the law every day of the week.'

There was a murmuring, a confabulation from the gallery, and a scraping of chairs as the choir stood up and headed down the steps to the body of the church with those instruments that belonged to them. They walked along the aisle, dejected and defeated, with all eyes upon them.

'Don't you feel sorry for them?' Catherine whispered to Emily. 'They always put so much effort into their playing.'

'Sunday mornings won't be the same without the choir's tomfoolery,' she whispered back. 'There won't be any entertainment.'

'We'll be bored to tears,' Catherine agreed. 'We should go for a walk sometime like we used to. I have so much to tell you.'

'Whereas I have very little to say that's new,' Emily sighed.

The vicar picked up the vamping horn and began to recite the Lord's Prayer, bringing the congregation back together again with the familiar chant and final 'Amen'.

Outside the church after the service, Matty and Stephen were standing talking at the gate.

'You keep your eyes and your hands off our daughters,' Pa joked as they passed them. 'What do you say to that, Mr Millichip?'

'I think that it will be easier to prevent the latter than the former,' he responded. 'Eyes are always prone to wander when there are pretty girls in the vicinity.'

'We aren't doing any harm,' Matty said.

'I'm glad to hear it,' Pa said. 'I'm sorry about the choir. I know you depend on the perks that it brings. I'll do my best to persuade the vicar to reinstate you, but he seemed quite definite about his decision.'

'My decision is final and unassailable,' the Reverend Browning interrupted. 'We've been trying to find ways to reduce the church's budget and this is an excellent way forward. The choir was the biggest expense in the accounts last month, what with the addition of the cost of new reeds for the clarinet and a barrel of beer to lubricate the voices when they seem perfectly well moistened from the night before. The tower needs urgent repairs and some of the ladies have expressed a desire to replace the hassocks. The money would be far better spent on thread and sherry for the vestry.'

Aware that Matty and Stephen's eyes were upon them, Catherine linked arms with Emily and stepped out onto the road. They began walking in the direction of the mill.

'I think that Stephen has a fancy for you,' Emily said. 'He keeps looking at you.'

'You have a vivid imagination.'

'No, I've been observing him and what I say is true.'

The sound of horses' hooves and the clattering of carriage wheels broke into Catherine's consciousness. She turned her head to find Mr Hadington's carriage moving up behind them at speed as the driver whipped the horses up to a gallop. They were a matching pair, two black creatures in harness with glittering bits and buckles. She could see the scarlet lining of their nostrils and the whites of their eyes as they bore down on her and Emily.

Catherine tugged at her friend's arm, trying to pull her away from the oncoming vehicle before it reached them, but she was too late. The driver hauled at the horses' mouths and used his whip to redirect them. They moved aside, but not quite enough, because one of the carriage wheels glanced against Emily's side and knocked her to the ground.

'Emily!' Catherine screamed. 'Someone stop him.' She flung herself to her knees in the dust, her heart beating fast as the accident replayed itself in her head.

'I'm all right,' Emily said, attempting to sit up.

'Let me be the judge of that.' Catherine sup-

127

ported her. 'Any bones broken?'

'I don't think so,' she gasped. 'I'm just winded.'

'No harm done then,' Mrs Millichip said over Catherine's shoulder. 'My daughter has a strong constitution. Don't go using this as an excuse to avoid the bakehouse, my girl, because it won't wash with me.'

Matty and Stephen stepped in to help Emily to her feet. Catherine looked up the road to where the carriage had stopped. She noticed now that the driver was in fact Mr Hadington himself, in a hurry to get his family home for dinner. When he saw that Emily was upright, he sent the horses off again.

Catherine was indignant.

'Isn't someone going to stop him?' she said in front of the crowd who had assembled. 'Pa, he can't be allowed to tear around the country like that without a thought for anyone else. You must speak to the magistrate at least.'

'What good would that do? Mr Hadington is a lawyer so he knows about justice, how to deliver it and how to evade the consequences. He defends people in court and gets them off the charges, more often than not. If challenged, he'll merely state that Emily was walking in the middle of the street, chattering with you, so she didn't hear the carriage. He'll lay the blame for the accident on her inattention.'

'He was in the wrong. He was driving too fast,' Catherine countered. 'He'd whipped the horses up to a frenzy. He didn't give Emily a chance to step aside.' She felt weak thinking about how it could have been so much worse. 'We could have been killed. We should at least talk to him.'

'It's never wise to get on the wrong side of people,' Pa told her. 'If they make the hairs on the back of your neck stand on end, then best to conceal it. You never know when you might need their assistance in future.'

'I'll never have any need of a lawyer. They're for the rich.'

'I've used him before to transfer the deeds to the land I acquired for Young Thomas.'

'Then you must never use him again.'

'There is a saying, beggars can't be choosers.' Pa stared down at the ground. 'He is a man with a reputation, and by that I mean not a good one.'

'I can see why.'

'No, you can't.' Pa shook his head. 'You're too young to understand and it was a long time ago. It's best not to plough poisoned earth – I implore you to let this subject lie fallow. You, my precious daughter, are worth twenty of him.'

They returned home to the farm, and later the same afternoon, Emily called. Catherine invited her into the kitchen where John was on the prowl for food.

'Are you well?' Catherine gave her brother a barley sugar twist from the jar on the windowsill. She offered one to Emily and took one for herself.

'I'm a little battered and bruised.' Emily had a bandage wrapped around her wrist.

'Is that new?'

'Ma was cross with me. She said I should get my head out of the clouds and watch where I'm going.' Emily smiled ruefully.

'Good day, Emily. What brings you here?' Ma came sailing in and stood waiting for any crumbs of gossip that Emily might have brought with her I from the bakehouse.

'Let's go outside,' Catherine said, and the two of them walked out to the yard. 'Ma doesn't have to know everything. What are you here for?'

'I've brought you this for saving my life.' She put her hand in her pocket and withdrew her fist.

'I don't need a present,' Catherine said shyly. 'And I didn't really save your life. I pushed you out of the way. Anyone would have done the same.'

'I know how close I came. I felt the hot breath of those horses and the wheel of that carriage. Without your intervention, I should have been killed, so' – she took a deep breath – 'please accept this humble offering from your best friend without further ado.'

Catherine opened her hand and watched a silver sixpence fall from Emily's clutch into her palm.

'It's all that I have.' She folded Catherine's fingers around the coin and clasped them together. 'I want you to keep it as a token of good fortune and friendship.'

'We will always be friends, whatever happens.'

'Of course.' Emily smiled.

The cat was sunning herself on top of the pigsty, perfectly content with her situation, whereas Catherine felt a sense of restlessness as she gazed around the farmyard. She envied Matty's dreams of travel and a life beyond Overshill, but she loved the animals and the woods, and the idea of staying in the village to bring up her children alongside

Emily's. But what of the future of Pa's beloved farm? Upon his demise, or before if Squire Temple so chose, it would pass to someone else, and not one of the Rooks. It wasn't fair. It wasn't right that she would be overlooked for the tenancy by virtue of her sex. If she'd been born a boy, she would have saved Wanstall Farm for the family. As it was, she was doomed to marry the likes of Hector Browning or poor Mr Johncock – she gazed at the coin that Emily had given her – and the few possessions she had would become rightfully theirs.

She wondered what the future held for the Rooks and Wanstall Farm, and how long she would be able to avoid making an unsuitable marriage. At the moment with Pa running the farm and Ma needing her to look after John and do the chores, there was no rush, but she knew from the experience of John's accident that life was prone to taking unexpected twists and turns.

1837

Chapter Six

Smoking out the Bees

Overshill, East Kent

In the twelvemonth that Catherine turned twenty, it seemed that the corn dollies from the previous year had failed to impress the goddess of the fields because the barley went mouldy on the stems and the harvest was poor.

Catherine was in the garden at Wanstall Farm, picking the last of the gooseberries, and topping and tailing them as she moved along the row.

'Catherine?'

She sighed at the sound of her mother's voice. 'Yes, Ma.'

'I need you to take the pot that's on the table along to the forge – the handle's come off.'

'I'm in the middle of something. Can't you go?'

'I'm asking you. When you've done that, you'll come with me to call on the Brownings. I believe that Hector is at home.' Ma gave her a stern stare. 'I still have hopes that you will win him over. There's no sign of this other young lady of whom Mrs Browning once spoke. What are you waiting for?'

For an excuse not to have to visit the vicarage, she thought. She wondered how long she could loiter at the forge.

'Don't be long,' Ma said as she left with the broken pot. She passed Matty in the yard where he was repairing the henhouse. John was holding the pieces of wood while he knocked the nails in.

'Morning, miss,' Matty said.

'Good morning,' she said, heat flooding up her neck. Why when they were just great friends did his address have such an effect on her? Why did she sometimes find herself kissing him in her dreams?

She walked to the forge where a mare with a colt foal at foot was tied to the chestnut tree outside. Len glanced up from where he was trimming the mare's feet. Catherine quelled a shudder at the sight of the dent in his forehead and the crescent scar that filled most of the socket of his left eye where he had been kicked by a horse when he was an apprentice.

'What do you want?'

'Ma sent me to have this pot repaired,' she said awkwardly. Len was one of the few people who made the hairs on the back of her neck stand on end. 'Would you mind? She wants it back in rather a hurry'

'That's typical of your mother. Can't you see I'm busy?' he grumbled. 'Go and see my apprentice. He'll do it for you.'

She thanked him and went to find Stephen, who was stoking the fire inside the forge. He greeted her with a smile and an elaborate bow, then stood back with his hands in his pockets, hardly able to meet her eyes.

'Len said you'd be able to repair Ma's pot.'

'Of course,' he said, moving round to take it

from her by the handle. It fell apart and clattered across the ground. 'I'm sorry.' He picked it up. 'Oh dear, I've put a dent in it.'

'Never mind,' Catherine said.

'I'll fix it. You can take a seat on the bench over there. Take the weight off your feet, not that you're a hefty sort of a lady.' His face was bright red. 'I always say the wrong thing. I get fanteeg.'

'You don't seem flustered.' Catherine dusted down the bench before she took a seat to watch him at work. His limbs were long and gangly like the colt's, and the sinews in his arms looked as hard as iron. 'You can take as long as you like over it,' she went on. 'I don't want to go home – Ma has plans for me later.'

'I shouldn't like to upset your mother.'

'But you'll take a while – for my sake?'

'Of course, miss.' He placed a strip of metal in the fire and waited until it glowed white-hot when he picked it up in a set of tongs, applied it to the pot and reattached the handle. Once he was happy with the joint, he dropped the pot into a bucket of water that bubbled and hissed as it cooled. He pulled it out again, and hammered at the dent before wiping the pot with a cloth and handing it back.

'There you are, miss. Happy to oblige.'

'Thank you,' she said. She made her way back to the farm where Ma criticised her tardiness and the quality of the repair before sending her upstairs to change.

'You must wear the green dress,' she said. 'It sets off the colour of your eyes.'

She didn't have a choice, Catherine thought.

137

She had one smart dress that still fitted her. She had outgrown the rest and there was no sign that there'd ever be enough money for new ones. When she arrived downstairs, Ma insisted on brushing her hair and putting it up.

'You'll do,' she said eventually. 'Come along now. We haven't got all day.'

She and Ma walked to the vicarage to find that the Reverend, perhaps wisely, had locked himself in his study. Mrs Browning showed them into the parlour, where Jane was working on some embroidery and Hector was standing at the window.

Ma dropped a curtsey.

'You are back from university for the summer?' she said.

Hector, pale and ethereal as if he never stepped out into the summer sun, nodded.

'I'm looking forward to returning to my studies. I'm finding Overshill rather dull.' He spoke with a lisp like his father.

'Oh, Hector, it isn't that bad.'

'Mother, you've said yourself that you will die of boredom unless you can find a way to return to town. You're always telling me how East Kent is filled with dullards; farmers and labourers, and their tedious families.'

'Hector! You have completely misunderstood me.' Mrs Browning flushed the colour of the velvet curtains. 'Mrs Rook's husband is a tenant farmer. He has many interests.'

'He is an educated man?' Hector enquired.

'He reads books,' Ma said.

'Ovid, the *Metamorphoses*? The *Conquest of Gaul*?'

138

Ma frowned.

'He studies farming texts on the breeding of sheep, for example,' Catherine said, trying to help her out. In spite of the way Ma treated her sometimes, she didn't like seeing her being put in a bad light.

'Not the classics, then.'

Catherine met Hector's eye.

'I don't know what they are,' she said.

Ma gave her a dig in the ribs, making her bite down hard on her lip. How was a young woman supposed to act when her mother wished her both to make herself noticed and maintain a modest silence at the same time?

'The classics would be of no use to Miss Rook,' Jane said.

'Except to provide her with an intelligent and engaging topic of conversation,' Hector said rudely.

They didn't stay long after that. As she and Ma trudged back to the farm without speaking, Catherine felt her lack of education sorely, but she knew that Jane was right. What use was it to a farmer's daughter? Ma remained silent on the subject until Pa and John returned from the fields that evening for supper. When they were sitting down around the table, she opened her mouth.

'I have had the most dreadful day,' she began. 'I have never been so offended.'

'Who has crossed you this time, my dear Margaret?' Pa asked as John shovelled food into his mouth.

'Mrs Browning and her son. Who would have thought that a well-educated young man like

Hector would have been so contemptuous of our family?'

'What do you mean?' Pa put down his spoon and sat up straight.

'When I heard that he was at home, I took it upon myself to call upon the Brownings – seeing that you have little or no interest in pursuing a suitable match for our daughter.

'It isn't something that needs to be pursued, as you put it. It will happen. A young man will come along and ask for her hand soon enow.'

'That isn't how it works and you know it,' Ma snapped. 'There are very few bachelors in the area, and even fewer that are eligible.'

'Hector couldn't make any woman, let alone Catherine, happy.'

'But he will follow his father into the Church and make a good living,' Ma argued.

'And for the sake of being able to tell the world that your daughter is married to a vicar, you would have her be miserable for the rest of her life.' Pa rested his elbows on the table. Ma glared at him, but he ignored her. 'We've brought our children up on the land and that's where they belong. Our youngest should marry whom she pleases, preferably a man who is content to get his hands dirty, not some lisping, lily-livered laggard who's only interested in books. And that's the last thing I shall say on the matter.'

Inwardly, Catherine thanked her father for having her best interests at heart. It was a relief to know that Hector Browning was no longer a consideration.

August turned into September. On a sunny day when the swallows were gathering on the roof-tops to fly to warmer climes, Catherine was out-doors collecting eggs when she heard the familiar sound of Matty's whistle.

'Where are you?' She picked a feather from one of the freckled brown shells.

'Over here.'

'Show yourself. I can't see you.'

'I don't want your ma catching sight of me, or she'll have me back in the fields.'

'Is John with you?'

'My pa is looking after him until I get back.'

'Where are you going?' She moved around and found another egg in the straw in the empty stable. She shooed a couple of the hens out. 'I wish you'd do all your laying in the coop.'

'That's just it. I want to show you something.'

'No, ta. This is bound to be one of your childish tricks. I don't care if you are now twenty-one years old.' She closed the stable door behind her.

'It isn't, I promise.'

'How can I trust you?' Catherine laughed.

'You'll have to take a chance.'

She caught on to the suppressed excitement in his voice. It had been a dull day so far. She had been waiting for something to happen. Maybe this was it.

'Please come, Cath – I mean, Miss Rook.

'Call me Catherine. None of this "Miss Rook" nonsense.'

'We haven't much time. Please, hurry.'

She took the eggs indoors and fetched her bonnet before hastening across the farmyard to where Matty was waiting for her. He'd washed his face and it looked as if he might have spat on his boots and given them a rub from the state of his cuffs. He carried a basket on his arm.

They walked swiftly side by side along the track and past Toad's Bottom Cottage to the crossroads where they slipped into the wood. The chestnut underwood was in full leaf and the sound of sawing filled the air.

'I should really go back,' Catherine said, hesitating. 'I don't want Ma to notice I'm gone.'

'There's something I want to show you. It isn't much further.'

She followed him along a deer track that wound between the trees until it reached a small clearing. He balanced his basket on a tree stump and moved close to her.

'Look up there,' he whispered. He pointed towards one of the trees, one bare of leaves and almost bereft of branches with a hole in its mossy trunk. A bee flew into the hole. 'Where there are bees, there's honey. What do you think?'

Catherine's mouth watered at the thought of sweet, sticky honeycomb as Matty knelt down and began to scrape dry leaves and pine needles into a small mound.

'You will be careful,' she said.

'It's all right. I've done this a hundred times.' With a flint and stone, he lit a flame in the leaf litter and blew it out to leave it smoking.

'Look at you.' Catherine laughed as she gave him her shawl to protect his face.

'Keep your voice down,' he chuckled. 'We don't want to have to share.'

142

He collected up the smoking heap and held it at arm's length, stepping slowly and quietly up to the hole in the tree. He dropped it inside and ducked back quickly. A dark, buzzing cloud of fury emerged from the hole, followed by a stream of the smoke that was supposed to have quietened them.

Catherine gasped.

'Stay back,' Matty warned. He squatted on his heels, watching the bees' flight and waiting for the right time to extract the honey. When the buzzing subsided, he pulled a knife from his bag and approached the nest. Another bee flew out and hit his face. He slapped his cheek and pulled the shawl down further over his eyes. He reached into the hollow trunk and started cutting. He pulled out a dripping section of honeycomb and walked across to Catherine. He broke a piece off and handed it to her.

It was chewy and sweet, the most delicious honey she had ever tasted.

Matty wrapped the rest of the comb in a rag and they started to stroll back towards the village.

'Are you looking at me?' she asked, aware that he was staring at her.

'I hope you don't mind me saying, but you're a beautiful woman,' he said, blushing. 'Very fine.'

'Too fine for you,' she said, trying to make light of his compliment.

A shadow crossed his eyes as if he'd taken her dismissal to heart, but he pressed on.

'Would you do me the honour of walking out with me?'

A dragonfly hovered nearby as though waiting

like Matty for Catherine's answer. He was twenty-one to her twenty, tall, good-looking and strong. He had filled out, his limbs now clothed with muscle, and his jaw had grown squarer and more manly. She felt a surge of attraction for him as they stood face to face in the dappled shade, which was all very well and slightly disturbing, as she had looked upon him as a friend and almost as a brother since she had lost John in the accident. She scolded herself for her self-deception. There had been occasions when she had thought of him otherwise, but walking out with him? He had taken her by surprise.

'Before you say anything, the honey wasn't a trick to get you alone. I saw the nest and thought of you.'

She wiped her hands on her skirt.

'You know you have no right to think of me in that way.' She wondered immediately why she had said that.

'Why not? Are you taken? Is my brother courting you?'

'Stephen? Whatever gave you that idea?'

'I don't know. He likes you, that's all.'

Her laughter rang hollow in her ears.

'Ma wouldn't approve of me being courted by one of the Carter brothers.'

'So you are spoken for?'

'Not yet.' She didn't yet know what she wanted and it wasn't fair to take it out on him. She opened her mouth to apologise for her contrariness, but it was too late. He was angry.

'You are a spoiled brat. Where do you think you sprung from? Royalty? The way you talk, anyone

144

would think you were Queen Victoria 'erself. Yet your grandfather' – he paused – 'that's Thomas. He was just a farm worker in the beginning.

'Thomas?' Matty was deliberately trying to confuse her. 'Thomas is my father, and Thomas was my grandfather before him.'

'The man you call Pa is your grandfather, didn't you know? Your ma is your grandmother.'

Catherine felt her heart fluttering like a bird in a cage.

'You must be mistaken,' she stammered. Her dearest Pa was her father. She'd never had any reason to doubt it, except... A memory flowed back into her head, like the water passing under the bridge, catching a stick briefly then carrying it on downstream, a thought she had long ago dismissed.

'Ivy's your ma.'

'It isn't true.' She stared at Matty. 'How dare you suggest such a thing? Ivy isn't my ma. She can't be. She and Len haven't been blessed with a child.'

'She had you. My ma says it's a punishment for what Ivy let that man do to her.'

'What man?' Tears sprang to Catherine's eyes. How could he be so cruel?

'Ivy was in service,' Matty said.

She'd known that, Catherine thought. Ivy had been a maid at Churt House, but her time there had been cut short for some reason.

'Even though he were a married man, she seduced him with her fancy looks' – Matty seemed to moderate this opinion – 'by some accounts. She was sent home in disgrace. After you was born, she

145

was married off quick as lightning to the black-smith.' He tipped his head to one side. 'You're a bastard.'

'And you're a tale-telling, lying weasel. I shan't speak to you again.' Catherine stamped her foot and turned away from him before briefly glancing back over her shoulder to spit out the words, 'I hate you, Matty Carter.'

She ran along the deer path, haring along as fast as she could to get away from him, but he was quicker. He jumped over a tree stump to overtake her and stopped in front of her, blocking her path.

'Get out of my way,' she ordered.

'I didn't mean anything by it,' he said, moving close to her, his voice hoarse. 'I didn't want to hurt your feelings. It was supposed to be a secret – my pa let it slip one day. I'm sorry I spoke of it.'

'Why did you then?'

'Because I wanted to get back at you for turning me down. I'm fond of you, Catherine. Your past doesn't matter to me.' He cleared his throat. 'I thought you might be sweet on me.'

She denied it, even though she could recall more than one occasion when she had been tempted to hold his hand, or lean in for a kiss.

'I hope I've never given you that impression. I'm not and never will be. We were friends, that's all.' She looked him up and down. 'Look at you in your threadbare clothes, with your hands and face dirty from working on the farm. Why would anyone want to walk out with you? Get out of my way,' she repeated, 'or else.'

'Or else what?' he said scornfully. His chin

146

jutted out in defiance, but his lip wobbled as if he was about to cry.

'I'll scream.' She pushed him aside and ran home to the farm, where she almost bumped into Ma who was carrying a trug of beans towards the house.

What happened to you?' she sighed. 'I hope you haven't been laying yourself open to accusations. You know how people round here talk.'

'They should mind their noses,' Catherine said sharply. She couldn't bring herself to ask Ma outright just yet about what Matty had told her.

'I need you to fetch bread and beer. Here.' Ma dropped a couple of coins into her palm. 'Ivy has darned some stockings and let out a dress for me. You can collect those and take the pie I've made for her as well.'

Catherine compared her mother's pudsy hands with her own slender fingers. She was a little different from the rest of the Rooks, physically and in spirit, so was there some truth in Matty's tale that she wasn't one of them? There was only one way to find out, and Ma had given her the perfect opportunity.

There was a pair of big bay dray horses with silken feathers and soft brown eyes standing outside the forge. Len, dressed in his leather apron and heavy boots, was bent over, hammering nails into a grey cob's hoof. The horse shifted its weight as the blacksmith twisted off the clenches. He uttered a growl of annoyance. The horse raised its head and flicked its ears nervously back and forth. Len's presence had a similar effect on Catherine, but today she was feeling brave, spurred on

147

by the mixture of anger and disbelief that she felt at Matty's revelation. At one moment, she thought he must be right, the next that he had to be wrong.

Len looked up, and spoke with nails in his mouth. 'What brings you here?'

'I've come to call on Ivy.'

He limped across to look inside her basket. She lifted the muslin from the top to show him the pie's golden crust.

'She's indoors.' He nodded towards the door into the cottage, a thatched building with a timber frame, then looked back towards the forge where Stephen was standing with a glowing horseshoe on the end of a pritchel. 'Lad, get back to your work. What are you gawping at?'

Flushing, Stephen hooked the shoe over the end of the anvil.

'Good morning, miss,' he said, acknowledging Catherine with a shy smile.

'Good day to you,' she said, looking down her nose. He was one of the Carter boys after all, and he didn't even know what time of day it was. She walked away and knocked on the door to the cottage. There was no reply, but she entered anyway. Ivy wasn't one for keeping the home spick and span. Catherine was never sure what she did do, apart from mending and sewing.

'Ivy, are you there?' she called as the musty odour of damp and rats bit her throat.

She moved into the kitchen, where she found her sister sitting sewing at the table with the drapes letting in just a chink of light which fell across a rent in the garment that she was working

148

on. She turned her face away and began rummaging in her sewing box.

'Why is it I can never find the scithers?' she said sharply.

'I've brought you a pie,' Catherine said, sensing that something was wrong. She removed it from the basket and placed it on the table.

'Tell Ma, thank you.' Ivy squinted to rethread her needle. 'Off you go now.'

'I thought you'd be outside. It's a lovely day.'

'I'm indisposed.'

For a moment, Catherine wondered if the family's prayers had been answered and she was with child at last, but Ivy turned and gazed at her. Her eyelids were swollen and her eye half-closed.

Catherine gasped.

'Don't say anything to Ma and Pa. I walked into a door. I am a dolt and a clodpole.'

'No, you aren't. Len did that to you.' Ire welled up in Catherine's breast. She had never seen Pa raise his hand to Ma, even when she'd goaded him to anger. 'You must leave him.'

'How can I when I'm bound to him for life?' Ivy said bitterly. 'Oh, he's a good husband in many ways. He doesn't look at other women, only their menfolk to check that they aren't looking at me. You must promise me you won't breathe a word of this.'

'Don't ask me to keep a secret,' Catherine said curtly. 'That's why I'm here. To find out about what you've been hiding from me all these years.'

She noticed how Ivy's hand shook, her needle hovering above her handiwork.

149

'Don't deny it,' she said, biting back tears. 'All I want is the truth.'

'We'll talk outside. Bring your basket.' Ivy put down her sewing and Catherine followed her into the garden and down the cinder path that ran between the vegetable and flower beds to the privy.

Ivy was tall, like Ma, and blonde, but she wore her hair down and her clothes were dirty, and her shoulders stooped. She turned to face Catherine in the shadow of one of the pear trees that grew at the end of the garden. For a moment, Catherine thought that she was going to tell her that it was idle gossip and send her on her way, but it wasn't to be.

'I knew you'd find out one day,' she began. 'It was only a matter of time.'

'So you aren't my sister?' The ground seemed to fall away from beneath Catherine's feet. She reached out for the tree trunk to steady herself as her head swam. Her identity had been torn apart. She had been betrayed by those closest to her, the people she loved most. 'How could you?'

'Ma made me promise to hold my tongue.'

'I mean, how could you give me up? A poor defenceless baby? Your own flesh and blood?'

'I did it out of desperation. I was scared and ashamed. I had no choice. Ma wanted me out on the street. If it hadn't been for Pa's intervention, I would have ended up dead.' She took a breath before continuing, 'Your father disowned you before you were born.'

'Who is he?' Catherine prayed that Matty had got that part wrong at least.

'The year before I turned fifteen, Ma helped me pack a basket with my belongings and walked me to Churt House where I went into service as a housemaid. They wanted me when I was younger, but Pa forbade it.' Ivy glanced nervously towards the cottage.

'Does Len know about this?' Catherine asked, as the sound of hammering rang out from the forge.

'He knew of the rumours, then on our wedding day and against Ma's advice, I confessed because I didn't want to start married life keeping secrets from my husband.' Ivy began to cry bloodstained tears. 'I wish I'd never told him. He's held it against me ever since.'

'Oh, Ivy,' Catherine exclaimed. 'I'm sorry.'

'None of this is your fault.' Ivy touched her throat.

'Tell me more about my father.'

'I can't think of the man who sired you as a father – he isn't like dear Pa. He's hard and ruthless, and deeply unkind.'

'Who is he?'

'It was Mr Hadington, the master,' she whispered.

'But he's so old. He must be at least fifty,' Catherine exclaimed, thinking of the lawyer with his fine coat and cane who strolled up the aisle in church to take his pew every Sunday and who'd almost run Emily down with his horses and carriage. 'And he's married,' she added, thinking of his wife. She felt sick.

'You are sadly innocent in the ways of the world, as I was back then. I didn't know that such men existed.'

'What do you mean?' It was common knowledge that Mr White, the wheelwright, had had a connection behind the oast with Mrs Clackworthy, the landlady of the beer-house, so Catherine thought that she knew a little about men.

'Mr Hadington has a preference for girls on the verge of womanhood. He pursued me for over a year, often inviting me into the library alone, and trying to entice me to sit on his knee or climb the library steps to reach a book for him, so he could grasp me around the thighs and bury his face in my skirts to keep me "safe" from falling.' Catherine noticed how Ivy shuddered at the memory. 'One afternoon, we were alone in the house. He contrived it. It was the lady's afternoon for calling on the neighbours, and the kitchenmaid was in bed with the fever, so he dismissed Cook for the rest of the day. When he called for tea in the library, I found him sitting behind his desk. He was in his cups, which was, a relief to me.'

'Why?' Catherine frowned.

A smile briefly crossed Ivy's lips. 'Have you not heard of the term "brewer's droop"?'

Catherine had heard the term being shouted about at harvest time when the men had taken too much strong beer. She blushed as she recalled how Matty had once offered a crude explanation to her and Emily behind the hayrick.

'I thought that if I could persuade him to take a little more whisky, he'd fall into a slumber, but the more he drank, the more insistent he became and then...' Ivy's voice trailed off '...he ruined me, and when my belly started to swell, he said I must lay my child to someone else or take something and kill it. I wasn't the first, or the last. My lady paid me what I was owed, I packed my basket and walked home to Wanstall Farm. I had nowhere else to go. I couldn't work anywhere else because the lady refused to give me a reference.

'The one piece of advice I give to you is to keep yourself pure and your reputation beyond reproach until such time as you are legally married. Never listen to a man's promises, no matter how much you love him. They will say anything in the heat of the moment. Mr Hadington told me that he cared for me and would make sure I was looked after. He lied. Fancy that from a man of the law,' Ivy said sarcastically. 'Never mind, eh? That's the way it is and nothing can be done about it.'

'It isn't fair. Why should a man get away with sins such as these while the woman has to suffer? Why should you be punished?' It wasn't enough that Ivy had been censured by her mother. Her husband was still wreaking revenge on her for her past. Catherine gazed at the yellowing bruise on her sister's – her mother's – cheek and the fresh one around her eye.

'I'm grateful to Len,' Ivy said as though she'd read Catherine's mind. 'He took me on when other men wouldn't–'

'He beats you.'

'He isn't a bad man.'

'Don't you wish you had married for love?'

'I do love him,' Ivy insisted. 'He's given me a home and security. He doesn't mean to lose his temper. When he has the gripes, he suffers so.'

'That's no reason for him to make you suffer as well.'

'It could be worse. We want for nothing, except a child, but that is God's will.' At the sound of a low shout from the cottage door, Ivy straightened. 'We will not speak of this again. Go and pick some peas. I'll cut some flowers.'

Catherine placed handfuls of fat pea pods in the basket and Ivy laid stems of mallow and orange blossom across the top. They were beautiful, she thought, running her fingers across the soft, smooth petals. They were like bright truths in an otherwise grey day of dishonesty. If she hadn't been desperate to protect Ivy from further trouble with Len, she would have broken down, but she had to appear strong so that he wouldn't suspect there was anything wrong.

'I'm labouring over a fire, killing myself, while you're here cotchering,' he grumbled as she and Ivy returned to the cottage.

He could hardly criticise them for gossiping, Catherine thought, when if anyone wanted to know their neighbour's business, they came to ask him.

'I wanted to send some peas and flowers to Ma in return for the pie.'

'Doesn't she have her own peas and flowers?' Len said scathingly. He stepped up close to Ivy and held her by the chin. 'You should be more careful where you walk in future, my lubberly woman.'

'I fear that calling someone clumsy only makes them more so,' Catherine dared to say.

Ivy uttered a small gasp and bit her lip.

154

'You should learn not to come between husband and wife,' Len said, scowling.

'Go, sister,' Ivy said. 'Thank Ma for the pie. I'll bring her dress to the farm as soon as I've finished the alterations.'

'I'll tell her,' Catherine said, torn between getting away as fast as she could, and her concern for Ivy's safety. She didn't feel anything for Ivy as a mother. She felt sorry for her as she would for any human being who was under threat of abuse. She would rather have been brought by the stork than be Ivy's daughter. Ivy had always been cold to her and now she knew the reason why.

She turned and fled. As she hurried past the forge, Stephen stepped out into the sunlight as if he had been waiting for her. He was wearing a shirt with the sleeves rolled up, trousers and a leather apron. His arms were long and lean and his shoulders were bulky with muscle.

'Hello, Miss Rook. How are you–' He stopped abruptly. 'Not well, I see. Can I see you home?'

'I'm all right. Really. Thank you for asking.' She could barely speak.

'Oh, come here,' he said. 'Let me take your basket for you.'

She was too upset to argue. She handed it over and walked alongside him.

'Are you sure you can spare the time?'

'For you, Miss Rook, of course. Has something happened? Has Matty upset you? Because if he has I'll give him a good hiding. Has he said something? Has he done something to hurt you?' He hesitated. 'I thought there might be something between you, that you had a fancy for him.'

155

She stopped and turned to face him. 'No, Stephen. Absolutely not. I hate him. He's a horrid creature. In fact, I can't believe that you two are brothers.'

'I'm the quiet one, while Matty...' He shrugged.

Matty had more of a spark, she thought. He was more like Jervis in some ways, whereas Stephen was dutiful and steady. But whatever the differences between the three Carter brothers, Catherine wished she had never allowed herself to become friends with Matty.

At the crossroads, she held out her arm for the basket.

'You must get back to the forge. Thank you, Stephen.' She told him that she was going to the mill to see Emily, but it was a ruse to walk back through the woods to avoid passing Toad's Bottom Cottage and the Carters. She needed to be alone for a while to think.

To avoid running into the Irish who had set up camp ready for hop picking, she crossed the chalk pit, the stones sliding underneath her feet. She had learned some important lessons today. She was special, but not in the way she had imagined. She was a bastard, born out of wedlock and sired by a drunken lecher who'd taken advantage of an innocent girl. She shuddered at the thought. How many times had she seen Mr Hadington at church on a Sunday? She'd had no clue that he had any idea who she was. She recalled how he never once looked in her direction, whereas – she remembered now – Emily had once said that he'd stared at *her* in a strange way. Catherine understood now. He was a truly wicked man.

She thought of Ma, her grandmother, resentful at being put in the position of having another mouth to feed, and jealous of the way Pa favoured her. Her grandfather had treated her kindly, but why? Was it because he'd felt sorry for her? And who else knew of her situation? Ivy, Ma and Pa, George and Matty. What about John and Young Thomas? Why had no one thought fit to enlighten her before?

She felt sick at heart. She had been flammed, deceived. How could she ever trust anyone again?

Chapter Seven

Hop Picking

Catherine was crying when she went past the pump to the house. Ma opened the back door and pushed the cat who was waiting outside with her kittens away with the toe of her boot.

'That cat should be drownded,' she said. 'I've asked your pa but he's too soft. He'd rather that she steals the food from our mouths.'

Catherine felt as her erstwhile father did. The cat was a friendly creature who kept the granary and barns free of vermin. She spent a lot of time in the stables with one of the horses, rubbing against his face and sitting on his back. Each litter that she had disappeared once the kittens reached a certain age, and the cat would howl as she searched for them in every nook and cranny.

157

'Is that how you felt about Ivy?' A bitter taste rose in the back of Catherine's throat. 'Did you wish her child drownded too?'

'What are you talking about?' Ma said sharply. 'Is Ivy all right? Did she send you my clothes? Have you forgotten, you dunty girl?'

'I did not forget. And don't call me stupid. You have no right.'

'I have every right. You're my daughter.'

'You've bin lying to me. I am not your daughter.'

'I don't know where you've got that from.' Ma rested her hands on her hips. 'That's enough of your insolence.'

'Why did you do it? Why did you wrench me from my mother's arms?'

Ma's mouth fell open. There was a fly buzzing around – Catherine wished it would find its way inside and choke her.

'Who said so?' Ma said eventually. 'Ivy?'

Catherine shook her head.

'It doesn't matter who said what. You and Pa are my grandparents.'

'Well, maybe we are, but that's neither here nor there. We think of you as our daughter.' Ma continued, 'Let me help you understand the situation we found ourselves in. There are many who are envious of what your pa has achieved and believe that they are more deserving than him of the squire's favour.'

Catherine thought of Jervis and how he resented the Rooks.

Ma turned away to scoop a boiled ox tongue from a pan of boiling water. She placed it on a

158

plate and stood brass weights on top of the meat to squash it down into a good shape for slicing once it had cooled.

'Life was rosy and we didn't want anything – unmarried mothers and illegitimate children – to damage John's prospects of taking over the tenancy in the future. Pa was all for taking a shotgun to the man in question, but I persuaded him to keep his head. What good would it have done? He would have hanged and we'd have lost everything we'd worked for. We hatched a plan. Ivy would go away to have the baby. I would make out that I was with child, and then when you was born, I would take you on and pass you off as mine.'

'There are some with a child born out of wedlock who have gone on to marry respectably,' Catherine ventured, 'Drusilla's sister, for example.'

'She made a disadvantageous union with a drunkard. As for Ivy, Len would never have considered Pa's proposal of marriage if she'd had a child in her arms.'

'Pa proposed to Len?'

'He had a word with him. He pointed out the merits of such a match, considering his age and unfortunate appearance. Anyway, that's by the by. There was gossip, but no proof that you were anyone but my daughter. You were one of those babies that sometimes comes along unexpectedly in one's middle years.'

Ma fell silent as Pa entered the kitchen with John following along behind him.

'Something smells good,' he said.

'I'm hungry,' John kicked off one boot and left

159

it in the middle of the floor.

'Catherine, help him with the other one, and take them outside,' Ma said.

She did as she was told, hardly able to bring herself to look at the man she'd thought was her father. Her chest ached. His betrayal had broken her heart.

'Is everything all right?' Pa asked. 'I can see steam coming out of your ears, Margaret.'

'No, it isn't all right. After all we've done to keep our secret from her, Catherine knows everything.'

'How did she come to find out?'

'Does it really matter?'

'I thought we had everything battened down and watertight.'

'It wasn't Ivy, so it must have been one of the Carters who said something to Matty, because I'm sure it will have been him who told her. He'll have blabbed to everyone by now. Catherine is ruined.'

'Oh please, don't exaggerate,' Pa sighed.

'No one will have her after this. She will be passed over by every eligible bachelor this side of Canterbury.' Ma was crying with frustration and disappointment.

Catherine walked outside. Pa followed.

'I'm sorry, ducky,' he said gently. 'We did what we thought was best at the time.'

'I thought I was special,' she said, thinking back to when Pa used to carry her out to the orchard to pick the ripest cherries, or pluck the sweetest apples, depending on the time of year.

'You are. Haven't I always treated you like a princess?'

'I'm different. Why didn't you tell me?'

'We weren't sure you could keep a secret being so young, so we thought we'd leave it until you were older, but the longer we waited, the more difficult it became to speak of it. May God forgive us if we made the wrong decision!'

Catherine turned furiously on the man who'd been her beloved father.

'How can I believe anything you say again?'

'Haven't I always treated you as a daughter?'

Catherine steeled herself against the raw emotion in his voice. He was hurting too, but as far as she was concerned, he had brought it upon himself. How had he and Ma ever imagined they could keep their secret from the gossips of Overshill?

'Don't you ever call me "daughter" again,' she snapped. She walked away, scattering the hens as she hastened through the yard and out of the gate into the fields. She didn't stop until she reached the orchard, where she sat down beneath one of the apple trees and watched the sun set on her innocence. Knowing about the likes of Mr Hadington made the world seem a dirtier place.

She took her supper on her own, sitting in the back of the cart that George had made ready to carry the hops the next day. She threw crumbs for the hens that clucked and cawed at her.

'A penny for them?'

She looked up to find Pa approaching her. Not Pa. How should she address him? As Thomas or Mr Rook? Grandfather? Her throat tightened as he took a seat alongside her.

'Leave me alone,' she said. 'I have no wish to

speak with you.'

'John is distressed that you didn't eat with us. Catherine, you are acting like a child.'

'Which is how you have treated me.'

'I don't want there to be bad feeling between us. I've apologised. That's all I can do. Maybe we did make a mistake in keeping you in the dark, but we could see no other way. Ivy had been wronged and Mr Hadington was – and still is – a man with influence. All we could do was protect the family's interests as far as we could from the scandal that would have broken out if it had become common knowledge.

'What I'm trying to say in a roundabout way is that life goes on. The seasons come and go the same, year after year. The great turnwrest plough turns the soil, we sow the seed and the corn goddess bestows rain and sunshine for the grain to grow and ripen. We reap and thresh, and we plough again, and the cycle is repeated. Your life will go on the same as before.'

'How can I trust you?'

'Nothing like this will ever happen again, I promise. All will be well. You will marry and have children, and then you'll find out that you will do anything that's necessary – lie, cheat and steal – to protect them.' His voice tremored.

'Oh, Pa,' she whispered.

He opened one hand to reveal a few crushed hops. The tips were brown and beginning to break apart from their golden centres.

'What do you think?' he asked.

She took one and rolled it between her fingers, making it rustle and release a sweet aroma.

162

'They're ready,' she said.

'That's my girl. Come indoors back where you belong with your family. I don't expect everything to be right between us straight away, but time will mend.'

Catherine wasn't convinced. She felt as though their relationship was beyond repair after Matty's revelation, but she returned indoors and she gave John a hug. He smiled gormlessly.

'Oh, my darling brother.' She smiled back. She would always love him as her sibling, no matter what.

'I'm hungry,' he said. 'I could eat a sheep.'

'I don't think your pa would approve.' The flock had grown significantly since the ewes had arrived at the farm, but this year's lambs were not yet fat enough for the table. 'I'll cut you a slice of pie. How about that?'

She sat with him until it was time to retire to bed. Ma had already gone upstairs having taken some sleeping drops for one of her 'heads', and Pa soon made himself scarce. Catherine remained awake for a long time that night. Tomorrow she would see Matty again. How could she face him, though? She was still seething with anger. Not only had he disturbed her peace of mind with his unwanted revelation, he had turned out to be insufferably, unbearably right, which was what rankled her the most.

She wondered about pretending to be sick so she could stay in her room for the duration of the hop picking, but her sense of duty and loyalty to the farm meant that she was up at dawn the following day when the mist began to rise from

163

the vale.

'Hurry, Margaret, and you, Catherine,' Pa said as she was lacing her boots. 'The hops won't pick themselves.'

They walked to the hop garden where thirty or forty people, including the Irish families with their horses and carts, Young Thomas Rook and his family, the Carters, and a handful of strangers, were already gathered. Two of the strangers, a man and a woman, were wearing cloaks with hoods. One of the Irish – Catherine recognised him as being the head of the group, a man of about forty years old, dressed in dark clothes and carrying a cudgel – stepped forwards.

'Mr Rook, sir,' he said.

'Mr O'Brien?' Pa said.

'Just to say that none of us is prepared to work until you pay us the balance of what you owe from before.' Catherine stiffened – his voice was as bitter as gall. What was going on? Pa had grumbled about the yield of barley this summer, but had not mentioned being unable to pay the harvesters in full. She didn't think he'd told Ma either – she was being supported on either side by two of the village women.

'I said I'd settle up after hop picking. I'm a man of my word.'

'Words won't feed our wives and children.'

A young woman stepped up, holding a baby in her arms. It started to cry.

'My child is sick, Mr Rook. I've tried the old ways, but she needs medicine.'

'I don't see why I should break my back picking hops for you when you might or might not pay

164

us, Mr Rook,' one of the regular labourers called out 'I seen Mr Nobbs last night and he says there's work for some at Sinderberry Farm.'

'Why did you come here, then?' Pa asked.

'To tell you, sir.' He touched the brim of his hat. 'You've always been good to us, so we felt it was only right to speak to you in person.'

'Well, I thank you for that at least, Mr Moon, but can't I persuade you to stay? I'll pay you half of what I owe when the hops are picked and the rest when the brewery have paid me for them.'

'I'm sorry, sir, but our minds are made up.' Mr Moon turned and walked away with three of the local men and their families.

'What do you think of that?' Pa said, standing his ground. 'Aren't you going with them?'

'We've heard that Mr Nobbs is stingy with his beer,' Mr O'Brien said.

'We should go.' The woman with the baby grasped the Irishman's arm. 'We've come all this way to work the whole summer to take money home with us. It's too much of a risk when all he's offering is his word.'

Catherine stared at her father. He wouldn't let them all go, would he? If the hops weren't picked, there'd be no income for anyone.

'I have a reputation for being an honest man,' Pa said, his voice loud and clear. 'I have made a promise and I shall keep it. The beer is excellent and in a plentiful quantity. What's more, I'll give you money for the child's medicine, whether you stay on to pick the hops or not.'

There was a low gasp and a few moments of chatter as the families made their choice.

Mr O'Brien turned back to Pa.

'We will take you at your word, Mr Rook.' He spat on his palm and held out his hand. Pa took it and shook it firmly. The deal was done.

Pa lined the workers up, including the handful of strangers, to collect their baskets. The presence of the hooded ones made Catherine feel a little uneasy, but she knew her father couldn't afford to send them away when he was short of pickers, thanks to Mr Moon.

She took a basket and began to pick the hops from the bines, scratching them from the plant as quickly as she could. On the good ones, the hops were the size of small pears while on the bad ones, they were more like peas and took longer to strip. Gradually, her fingers turned brown and her nose filled with the scent of hops, a mixture of apple, yeast and wild garlic.

When she had filled her basket, she took it over to the row of bins standing at the entrance of the hop garden. She tipped the contents into the Rooks' bin in front of Pa, who was acting as the tallyman.

'You're one of the quickest,' he said cheerfully.

'You are your father's daughter,' George said, overhearing him.

Catherine frowned, wondering if Matty had spoken to his father about the revelation he'd made the day before, but George appeared to have commented out of innocence. He must know, though, she thought, gazing around at the hop pickers. She wondered how many people knew her shameful secret.

George emptied the Rooks' bin, scooping the

hops into a bushel basket. Catherine watched to see that he was fair. It was all too easy for the measurer to crush twenty bushels into a dozen.

Pa carried two sticks, one long one and a shorter one. He put the two pieces of stick together and scored a notch across both pieces with a knife for each five bushels picked. He entered the amount into his book, scratching the number onto the page with the stub of his pencil. He gave Catherine the shorter piece of stick to look after so there could be no dispute later over the amounts she'd picked because when the two sticks were put together, the notches would tally.

The next person to take a basket to the tally-man was one of the strangers, who held his cloak across his face. Pa looked into his basket, ran his hands through the hops and pulled out several leaves. He held them up level with the man's eyes.

'What is the meaning of this?' he thundered.

'I don't understand, sir,' came a high-pitched voice. 'You always get a few leaves in it.'

'That there is more leaves than hops. I won't have it.' Pa reached into the basket and pulled out a folded blanket. His voice rang out across the countryside. 'How dare you cheat me!'

'I-I-I don't know how that got in there,' the man stammered. 'It's nothing to do with me. Someone must have put it there.'

Pa yanked at his hood and pulled it from his head.

'Jervis Carter!' he exclaimed. 'I guessed it was you. You know you aren't welcome here. Leave your basket and get off my land. I never want to have the misfortune of seeing you around here again.'

'What about my money?' Jervis swore.

'I won't pay you a single penny.'

'You took me on. You gave me work. I insist on being paid what I'm owed.'

'You tricked me,' Pa insisted. 'George, what's the meaning of this?'

'I don't know. I didn't know anything about it and that's the truth. Son, what are you doing, risking everything in coming back here? Don't you remember the last time when Tom threatened to set the constable on you? All you think about is yourself. You haven't a thought for your father or brother who work here, bringing them shame by association.'

'Pa, why are you talkin' like that? You're supposed to take my part.'

'Because you are no longer my son. I turn my back on you and your so-called wife who even now at this moment is sitting in the shade sipping at her sleeping drops. I've seen her. The woman in the cloak is Drusilla.'

'She is my wife,' Jervis said. 'There's nothin' so-called about it.'

'It was a marriage made over a broomstick,' George said.

'Take that back,' Jervis growled. 'I won't have you speakin' of my missus like that.'

'She i'n't your wife in the eyes of the law. Go, and take her with you.'

'I came to see Ma and make some money, at the same time. I was goin' to give it to her to help her out.'

168

'If you cared that much, you would have come back a long time ago.'

Jervis turned back to face Pa, squaring up to him as if he was about to hit him.

'I want my money, or else.' He swore and cursed, uttering epithets that Catherine had never heard before.

'Or else what?' Pa said, standing his ground. 'Are you threatening me?'

'Jervis, that's enow,' George snapped, pushing his way between them. 'What would your poor ma think of the way you're behaving?'

'Oh, I made a big mistake comin' back here,' Jervis said. 'Nothing has changed. Pa, why do you still creep around on your belly to please the Rooks? Why do you make yourself beholden to the likes of Thomas Rook, who would make himself rich at the expense of others? I'd watch your backs, all of you.'

Neither Pa nor George deigned to respond, and Catherine watched them escort Jervis and Drusilla out of the hop garden.

'Close your mouth or a beetle will get in.'

She turned to find Matty alongside her.

'Go away,' she said and she returned to the picking. The sun grew hotter and the beer began to flow. Whenever she thought she'd escaped Matty's presence, he would be back, picking from the bine next to her. She scowled at him, picked up her basket and moved on. He followed.

'Don't blame the messenger,' he said. 'I wish I hadn't said anything.'

'Leave me alone.'

He seemed to take notice of her this time, leaving her to continue picking until the sun began to sink into the horizon.

George drove the cart laden with hops to the nearby oast for drying before they were packed into pockets and taken to the brewery owned by the Berry-Clays in Faversham. The locals made their way home, some via the Woodsman's Arms which was stocked by the same brewery, while the travellers settled down for the night.

As the children's laughter echoed around the woods and fields, Stephen dropped by at the farm to confirm the rumour he'd heard about Jervis being in Overshill that day.

'We heard at the forge that he turned up with Drusilla,' he said, meeting Catherine and Matty in the yard. Matty was on his way home while Catherine had decided to call on Emily. 'My brother has the cheek of Old Nick.'

'He's either mad or desperate. He's gone, anyway,' Matty said. 'Catherine, let me walk with you. I'm going in the same direction.'

'I can find my own way, thank you.' She turned away and walked out of the yard, aware that Matty was at her heels with Stephen not far behind.

'Please don't ignore me,' Matty said as they headed into the village.

She glanced back at his face. She didn't understand why he should be the one looking hurt when it was he who'd injured her with his words. She walked on apace.

'What do I have to say to make you understand?' she said as he caught up with her.

'Excuse me, Miss Rook. I see that my brother is pestering you. Matty, push off.' Stephen strode

170

alongside them.

'No, I shan't. Push off yourself.' Matty gave him a shove. Stephen grabbed him by the collar, and twisted it until he was choking.

'Miss Rook doesn't want you bothering her.'

'What's it to you? And why all the "Miss Rook"? She's called Catherine.'

'I'm being polite, addressing a young lady in the proper way,' Stephen argued, 'something you should learn to do.'

'You?' Matty exploded.

'She i'n't interested in you. She's said as much.'

'You mean you think she has a fancy for you?' Matty began to laugh, inflaming his brother's, wrath. 'You're clung, duller than ditchwater. You'd bore her witless.'

Stephen hit out hard. There was a crunch as his fist made contact with Matty's nose.

'Ouch!' Matty reeled and staggered against the wall, steadied himself, took a breath, and with blood streaming from his nostrils, put his head down and charged like a bull. He brought Stephen to the ground, threw himself on top of him and started pummeling his chest.

Stephen grabbed Matty's arms and wrenched them apart so that he couldn't rain any further blows upon him, but Matty twisted his body and dug his knee into Stephen's stomach, making him grunt with pain and release his grip.

Matty leapt up and offered his hand. Gazing warily at his brother, Stephen allowed him to help him to his feet. He backed off a couple of steps then squared up to Matty for a second time.

'Fight!' someone yelled. 'Hey, come quickly.

171

There's a proper scrap going on.'

A crowd appeared from nowhere.

'Fight! Fight!' they chanted. There was Mrs Clackworthy and a handful of regulars from the beerhouse, Mr and Mrs White, and Mr Millichip and Emily who came running down from the mill. Some of the Irish, including Mr O'Brien, also stopped on their way from the farm to buy beer.

'What's this about?' Emily was at Catherine's side. 'They are killing each other.'

Catherine watched with a mixture of awe and fear that one or both of them would be badly hurt.

'This is stupid. There's been a misunderstanding.' She stepped forwards. 'Matty, Stephen, stop. Please, someone stop them.'

'Catherine, don't get involved.' Emily restrained her. 'It will do you no good to make a scene. Everyone will talk.'

'I don't care. How can we stand by?'

'They are both strong fellows,' one of the Irish said. 'Don't worry, lass. You're Tom Rook's daughter, aren't you?'

She nodded.

Mr O'Brien stepped in. He grabbed at Stephen's shoulders, but Stephen ducked away, turned and punched Mr O'Brien on the nose. Mr O'Brien thumped him back.

One of the other Irishmen joined in, helping Mr O'Brien to pin Stephen against the church-yard wall.

'Watch his right hook.' Mr White grasped Matty by the waist and pulled him back, but

172

Matty fought him off. Another of the Irish joined in and soon there was a fist fight raging along the street.

Emily pulled Catherine back into the shelter of the church gate as the vicar came running out of the vicarage.

'What in God's name is going on?' he lisped, but no one heard him without the vamping horn.

Len and Ivy appeared from the forge. Len strode into the fray. He took one of the Irish by the wrist, pulled him off his opponent and threw him sideways so that he staggered back across the street, landing in the hedge of one of the cottages opposite. His opponent took one look at Len's scarred visage, turned and ran, sparking confusion and panic in some of the other men who were scrapping in the street. Len took on another one, rendering him incapable of further violence, before he caught sight of the brothers rolling around on the ground.

'Stephen!' he hollered 'What do you think you're doing?' He stood over the brawling pair as everyone else stopped to watch. He leaned down and dragged Stephen up. Matty struggled to his feet.

'What's this? Two Carter boys fighting like cat and dog,' Len bellowed.

Stephen had a bruise across his cheek and his eye was half-closed. He dusted himself down while Matty leaned against the wall, keeping his head back and pinching his nose. Blood trickled through his fingers and down his arm.

'What the hell is this about?' Len went on.

'It's over a girl,' said Mr O'Brien to laughter.

'It's always about a woman.'

'I've a mind to send you packing for scrapping on the street. You're on the verge of finishing your apprenticeship and you show yourself up by doing this.'

'I'm sorry,' Stephen mumbled. 'Matty, I haven't finished with you yet.'

'That's enow. Forget it,' Len insisted. 'Come on, lad. You're a mess.'

'Go home, sister,' Ivy said, turning away to follow Len and Stephen back along the road, but Catherine couldn't leave Matty in the state he was in.

'You should make sure he gets home safely. We can meet up another time to talk.' Emily hesitated. 'Is it important? You don't seem yourself.'

'Matty told me something terrible,' Catherine said, unable to keep her secret from her friend. She lowered her voice. 'I thought it was a dirty lie, but it's true. Promise me you won't say anything.'

'You know me – I'm no telltale,' Emily said quietly.

'Ma and Pa are not my true mother and father.'

'Oh, I see.'

'You don't seem surprised.'

'There's always bin rumours, but nobody takes any notice of them. Don't fret. It will all come out in the wash.' Emily smiled. 'Whatever that means.'

'Thank you.' Reassured that Matty hadn't told anyone else and thereby made her the talk of the village, Catherine caught his eye. He nodded, an unspoken understanding passing between them. She walked back in the direction of the farm and he followed, keeping a few paces behind until they reached the crossroads when he caught up with her.

'I'm sorry you had to see that. I don't know what's got into my brother. He's usually the calmest, most gentle person in the world.'

'He thought you were bothering me. He was only trying to do the right thing.'

'I suppose so.' Matty tried to smile.

'You look terrible.'

He pinched the bridge of his nose and looked down at the front of his shirt. When he spoke his voice was thick with blood.

'I look like I've killed a pig.'

'Come back to the farm – you can wash your face and borrow one of John's shirts. If your ma sees you like this it will make her ill. You can wait in the granary so no one sees you.'

'Are you sure?' He hesitated. 'I thought you hated me.'

'I did at first after what you said.' She softened. She had wronged Matty with her scorn. She had made him cry. 'I'm truly sorry for how I treated you. I hope you can forgive me.'

'It was my fault. I upset you. There's nothing to forgive,' he said. 'I should have kept my mouth shut.'

'In a way it's a relief to find out because it explains so many things that I've wondered about. Now I know why I'm the odd one out, why I have dark hair not blonde, like Young Thomas, John and Ivy.'

'It doesn't matter. You are beautiful,' he said quietly as they entered the farmyard.

She couldn't bring herself to look at him. What did he mean? What was he trying to say?

'Go and hide yourself. I'll fetch a shirt.'

It was dark inside the house, since everyone had retired to bed ready for another early start in the hop garden the next morning. She slipped in through the back and filled a dish with lukewarm water from the copper kettle. She sneaked out through the hall and up the stairs, avoiding the fifth step which would creak and give her away if she placed her foot on it. In the spare room, she opened the linen cupboard where she found a piece of soft muslin. She listened on the landing to check that she hadn't been discovered, but all she could hear was Ma snoring.

On her way out, she took one of John's crumpled but clean shirts from the scullery.

Matty was waiting for her in the granary, sitting in the heap of straw that had been left from when the men had laid down their flails to harvest the hops.

Catherine sat down beside him with the shirt and muslin over her arm and the bowl in her lap. She dabbed the end of the cloth in the water.

'This might hurt,' she said softly, turning to face him, her heart aflutter.

'It's all right. You make me brave.'

She touched the damp cloth to his lips. Slowly, she dabbed at the blood and wiped it away. She rinsed the cloth, squeezed it out and started again, cleaning the smears from his cheeks. She could hear his breathing quicken as she took his hands and dipped his fingers into the bowl, entangling them with hers as she washed the blood away. She wrung out the cloth again and dried his hands as best she could.

'There,' she said. 'Now you must change your shirt. You can leave yours here and I'll have a go at getting those stains out.'

'I don't want to get you into any kind of trouble.'

He was smiling. She could tell just from the tone of his voice.

She watched him unfasten the two buttons that held his shirt together.

'I'll mend that at the same time,' she said, pointing towards a rip in the sleeve.

Her breath caught in her throat as his hand rose and trapped hers. She could feel his roughened skin against her fingers and smell his musky scent.

'I haven't anything, any way of thanking you, apart from this,' he whispered. He leaned in close and planted the briefest of kisses on her lips. Trembling, she gazed into his eyes.

'Is that all?' she whispered. 'I reckon you owe me one more at least.'

'Really?' He pressed his mouth to hers. The contact sent her head spinning with joy and desire. She giggled. She'd never felt such happiness.

Eventually, he pulled away.

'Would you do me the honour of walking out with me?' He blundered on. 'If you aren't already spoken for. And Mr and Mrs Rook don't object.'

She held her fingers up to her lips.

'Hush, Matty. I'm not spoken for. Stephen has no claim on me. I'm sure Ma will have her say, but Pa favours your father so I don't think he'll have any objection.'

'You mustn't feel obliged. I don't want to ruin

your life.'

'Why on earth would you do that?'

'I don't know. Sometimes when things are bad, I get this feeling of dread. I get this sense that I'm doomed.'

'Don't be silly. There's no reason why anything terrible should happen.'

'I know,' he sighed. 'So you will walk out with me?'

'Yes. Yes, of course.' She'd been caught off guard when Matty had asked her the day before, but with all the drama and conflicting emotions since, she had realised how she needed him, and how the strength of her feelings wasn't only friendship. She kissed him again. 'I have to go indoors now before anyone misses me. John sometimes wanders and it's my duty to send him back to bed. The last thing I need is for Ma to discover that I'm not in my room.'

'I could sit up all night with you.'

'I'll see you in the morning,' she said firmly, standing up and straightening her skirts. She picked up the dish, cloth and shirt.

'Thank you for everything. Remember that I would do anything for you in return.'

'You can show that by leaving when I ask,' she teased. She waved him away as he began to put on John's shirt, shooing him like she did with the hens, but he looked so sorrowful that she walked up to him, threw her arms around his neck and kissed him again.

'Be careful,' he said, 'more of that and I won't be able to tear myself away. When shall we meet again?'

'Tomorrow, but we must keep it from Ma and Pa for now.'

'I think that's very wise.' He grinned. 'Goodnight, Catherine.'

She wondered how long they would be able to keep their courtship secret and, when it did come out, whether Ma and Pa would approve. Did it matter? she thought as she retired to bed. Why was she worried about their opinion? They didn't have any right to say whom she could or couldn't walk out with when she wasn't their daughter, but she was still dependent on them and she had a conscience. It riled her that they'd kept the truth from her, but they had brought her up when they could have given her away. She had that, and more, to thank them for.

Chapter Eight

Carrying the Anvil

'There'll be a few sore heads tomorrow,' George opined as he leaned against the trunk of the chestnut tree where Catherine, Emily and Matty had taken shelter from a sharp late September shower. 'The vicar will be lucky if just half the pews are filled. Hardly anyone attends the Sunday service any more, not since he sent the choir packing.'

'It serves him right for bringing his newfangled ideas to Overshill,' Matty said.

'I wish I'd brought my accordion,' George went on. 'We could do with a cheerful toon to add to the occasion. I've never bin so proud. To think that everyone here is drinkin' beer and breakin' bread in honour of one of my sons.'

'Stephen has done well for himself,' Matty commented.

'He deserves it. He's worked hard to get through his apprenticeship,' George said.

Catherine gave the crowd who had come to join in the celebrations a cursory glance. The Irish had left the area after hop picking – Pa had stumped up the money to pay them. Catherine wasn't sure if he'd taken out a loan on top of the payment from the brewery to do it.

She turned back to gaze at Matty, who seemed more beautiful than ever. His wounds had healed after his fight with Stephen, and the scruffy boy had gone, replaced by a young man with his hair trimmed and combed, and wearing a clean shirt with a collar. She felt his fingers tangle briefly with hers, sending a shiver of longing running through her body. He winked at her and she blushed, wondering if he knew what she was thinking.

The rain stopped and a few cold drops of water dripped from the tree down the back of her neck, as Len and Stephen emerged from the forge.

'Do you remember the first time you tried to carry the anvil?' Len said. 'You were worse than useless. You came here a weedy boy who wouldn't say boo to a goose, and now you've become a strong young man and able smith who's made me proud.'

'Thank you,' Stephen said, reddening. 'I'll

180

always be most grateful to you, and Mrs Gray.'

'You used to struggle to get in the forge at six in the morning,' Len teased. 'And I can't remember how long it took you to learn the sizes of all the nuts and bolts and the names of the different tools.'

'I found it better when I got to work with the horses, taking the shoes off and finishing the hoof.'

'You soon got pretty handy with the fire, if I remember rightly. And you can make a well-tempered hoe. We'll send you off to Faversham where you'll do your two years of improving, and then you'll always be welcome back here as a master blacksmith, and maybe take over when my back's given in and I can't do no more.' Len handed Stephen a copy of his indenture, releasing him from his apprenticeship. The crowd applauded as Stephen tucked it into his pocket.

'Now show us how you handle that anvil,' Len said.

Stephen stepped forwards, cracking his knuckles. He bent down and put both forearms under the anvil. He took a deep breath and tensed the muscles and sinews in his neck before he straightened, slowly lifting the heavy weight off the ground. A roar of cheers went up as he held it steady.

'His arms are very strong, very strong indeed. He's handsome, don't you think?' Emily said as Stephen gently lowered it down again.

'He's very fair,' Catherine said in a low voice, 'but he isn't like my Matty.'

'You're making me blush now,' he said, smiling.

181

'It's true,' she said archly.

'I'll leave you to talk with Emily in peace.' He moved out from the shelter of the tree and joined some of the labourers in the street.

'You're a dark horse,' Emily said. 'I had my suspicions. Why didn't you come running to tell me?'

'I didn't want it to be common knowledge straight away. It was our secret, but now it's out.'

'What's it like? Do you think you'll marry him?' She reached out and clasped her hands. 'Oh, Catherine, what is your ma's opinion?'

'Emily, that's far too many questions for me to answer all at once.'

'Answer one at a time then,' she giggled. 'Have you kissed?'

'What do you think? It isn't something that a young lady talks about.'

'So you have. I can tell. What about your ma?'

'She doesn't know yet. We want to keep it that way for as long as possible.'

'I won't say anything.' Emily gazed towards Stephen. 'I wish I had someone special. I can't wait to have an excuse to get away from the bakehouse.'

'I shouldn't harbour hopes in that direction,' Catherine said. 'It's true that he's a good-looking young man who's done very well for himself, but I've heard that his affections are engaged elsewhere.'

'Of whom do you speak?'

'I'm not sure. It's just a rumour that I heard.'

'From Matty, I suppose.'

Catherine didn't confirm or deny it.

'I'd better go. Ma will be expecting me,' Emily said. 'I want to be the first to hear the news of your engagement.'

'It is a little early for that, I think. Matty hasn't talked of marriage, not yet.'

'Oh, Catherine, you're very serious today. I'm teasing, although I'm sure that Matty will seek your father's permission very soon.' Emily touched her arm. 'I'll see you in church tomorrow?'

'Ma's expecting me to stay at home with John. Another time.' Catherine wished her good evening and was about to look for Matty when Stephen sidled up to her.

'Miss Rook, please allow me to speak with you for a moment,' he whispered. 'It's important.'

Assuming he was about to give her an overdue apology for the fight with Matty, she stepped aside and walked a little way along the street away from the crowd. He turned to face her and she noticed the petals trembling on the posy of flowers in his band.

'I've built myself up for this and I don't think I'll be able to do it again when the moment is more convenient.' The words came spilling out of his mouth, hot and passionate and heartfelt. 'I know you probably haven't even thought of me, but I dream of you all the time, while I'm working at the forge with the heat and the smoke, while I'm lying in bed at night. Miss Rook, you are always in my thoughts.'

'Please don't say any more,' she said, reading the anguish in his eyes. 'This is wrong.'

'I have to speak. I cannot restrain myself. You must understand how much I admire you. I

183

worship the ground that you walk on.'

'This is too much,' she exclaimed, but he blundered on.

'Will you say that you will walk out with me, if not now, then at some point in the future when you've overcome your shock and become used to the idea?'

For the briefest moment, she wished that she could love Stephen, for he expressed his affection for her more deeply, more strongly than Matty did, but that was only because he was cleverer than his brother with words. When she was with Matty, he didn't need to speak to reveal his feelings for her.

'I'm sorry, Stephen. My answer is no.'

'Why? At least give me a reason so I know how to change.'

'You don't have to change who you are. No, it isn't you. I thought you might have guessed.'

'Guessed what?'

'That I'm walking out with Matty.'

Stephen frowned. 'I don't understand. You didn't say you had no feelings for him – you said you hated him.'

'I know, but love and hate are similar passions. There is little difference between them, don't you think?'

'They are opposites in my book. And you are a most contrary girl.'

She hated to see him hurt. 'I didn't mean to mislead you. I mean, you've always been kind to me. I didn't realise that you paid me attention because you had taken a fancy to me. I would never have encouraged you if I had.'

'How dare you suggest that I was kind to you merely because I wanted you to fall in love with me! You led me on with your fine figure and beguiling eyes,' he said fiercely. 'That was a wicked thing to do.' He was almost in tears. 'I was prepared to give you everything: the security of a blacksmith's life above the unpredictable nature of farming; my love; every part of me. I still would if you would only say yes. At least give me a chance.'

'There is no point. I can never love you, Stephen. I'm taken. I'm with Matty.' She watched the rise and fall of his chest as he fought with his emotions.

'Then I accept your answer,' he said eventually. He dropped the posy and ground the flowers into the earth with his heel. 'I wish you and my brother all the luck in the world.'

'And I wish the same for you,' she said sadly. 'There's someone out there for you, but it isn't me.' She watched him turn and walk away, his hands in his pockets and his shoulders slumped. She felt wretched for turning him down. Any other young woman would be proud to be seen on Stephen's arm, but she only had eyes for Matty.

She turned to look for him, finding him talking to Old Faggy, who had made an appearance to wish one of her pupils well on completing his apprenticeship.

'How are you, Catherine?' the elderly teacher asked. She had powdered her hair and repaired her gloves with dark thread for the occasion.

'I'm well, thank you. How are you, Mrs Fagg?'

She spoke politely even though she was still in shock at Stephen's declaration.

'My memory is as sharp as ever, although the body is failing day by day,' she said with a twinkle in her eye. 'I always knew you two would end up courting.' She pointed towards them with the end of her walking stick.

'We most certainly aren't,' Catherine said quickly.

'Don't worry, my dears. I'll keep it to myself,' Mrs Fagg said. 'It's lovely to see you. Good day.' She moved on towards the church, disturbing a small flock of sparrows that came flying out of the hedge on the way.

'Matty, will you walk me home?' Catherine asked.

'We'll go the long way.' He smiled, and they walked arm in arm through the woods, stopping to find their secret place, a bowl-like depression in the ground hidden within a clump of hazel saplings and brambles.

'I have something to tell you. You mustn't be cross,' she said as she crawled after him into the shelter of the undergrowth.

'What is it?'

'This afternoon, Stephen asked me to walk out with him – he didn't know about us.'

'I told him not to pester you.' Matty pulled off his jacket and spread it across the ground.

'Please, don't get into another fight over it.' Catherine sat down beside him. 'I made my feelings clear.'

'Let's not waste time talking about my brother.' Matty slipped his arm around her shoulders, and turned his face to hers. 'Kiss me.'

'Where have you bin?' Ma demanded later. She was waiting for Catherine at the front door in the dark when Matty gave her one last goodnight kiss and left her outside the house.

'It can't be nine o'clock yet,' Catherine said.

'It's gone ten. It's way past my bedtime, you thoughtless girl.'

'You didn't have to wait up for me.'

'I thought something had happened.'

As Catherine walked up to the door, her mother grabbed her by the ear and pulled her indoors.

'Ouch!' she exclaimed 'Let go of me.'

'This way,' Ma said, releasing her. 'Pa is in his office.'

'What is this about?' Catherine protested as Ma directed her towards the room where her father carried out farm business and, on occasion, hid away for peace and quiet.

'You know very well. I've bin watching you since you started going around, smiling like a cat that's got the cream. You're walking out with Matty Carter. Don't deny it. I've just seen you with your tongues down each other's throats. Ugh.' She flung the door open. 'Thomas, I told you so.'

Pa looked up from his desk where he sat with a pencil and a blank piece of paper. The candle flickered as Ma and Catherine entered the room, Ma prodding her in the back as if she was one of the sows being sent for despatch.

'You must thrust them apart.'

'You mean Catherine and Matty?' Pa said

187

calmly as if he'd known all along.

'She must be forced to work in the house at all times. She must not on any account enter the fields without a chaperone.'

'I believe that their proximity should be encouraged. Matty is fond of her. He'll treat her right.'

'He's nothing but a poor labourer with coarse manners.'

'That isn't fair. He's a clever lad. And he knows where she's come from so he won't have any nasty surprises in the future. He's patient with John, which I would have thought would be worth more than anything to you.'

'Thomas, you will be the death of me.'

'How many times have you accused me of that? Look at you,' he goaded. 'You're still alive and kicking.'

'You can't blame me for not liking the boy,' Ma argued. 'His tongue is too loose in his head. Look at the way he let the Rooks' secrets slip out like water through a sieve. He isn't to be trusted. We will find someone else to care for our son.'

'Whom do you suggest?'

'George will do it.'

'He is old and weary,' Pa said. 'John would run him ragged within a day. Listen to me, Margaret.' He stood up, moved round the desk and took his wife's hands. 'John is very fond of Matty. It would break his heart if Matty should decide to leave because we banned him from seeing our daughter.'

'Catherine?' Ma said.

'Who else? Oh, Margaret, you can be very wearisome. I shall always think of Catherine as

188

our daughter – that will never change.' Pa paused for a moment before going on, 'Think of John.'

'I wish Matty to stay for John's sake, but I can't bear the thought of him courting Catherine. What will everyone think? What about our reputation in Overshill?'

'That doesn't matter. All things considered, we should give our blessing for them to walk out together and see how it works out between them.'

'I'm not happy with this. If she marries a Carter, her life – and ours – will be steeped in misery. Can't you see that?'

'We aren't talking of marriage. We're talking about courtship, time for two young people to get to know each other and decide whether or not they're suited.' Pa turned to Catherine. 'Run along now.'

She left the room, smiling to herself. Pa had betrayed her over her birth, but he had proved that he was on her side. He wanted her happiness, admittedly with some consideration for John, even if Ma didn't. Her pulse began to race as she thought of Matty's arms around her and his kisses sweet on her lips.

A week after the celebration at the forge, she was walking through the village with her basket and money to buy beef and cheese. The leaves on the chestnut tree were fading to yellow as late summer turned to autumn. She could hear the sound of a threshing machine in the distance, a steam-powered beast that Mr Nobbs had invested in. Everyone had been invited to see it, but Pa had declined. The word was, though, that Squire

189

Temple had been impressed by its speed and efficiency and now he was sending grain from the home farm to Sinderberry Farm for threshing.

Stephen was trotting a horse up and down the street near the forge. He pulled it up and greeted Catherine.

'I hope you are well, Miss Rook,' he said awkwardly.

'I'm well, thank you. I thought you'd moved to Faversham,' she said, a little embarrassed to have run into him after what had happened at their last meeting.

'Not yet. I have some business to complete here in Overshill first. Did you know that I'm walking out with Emily?'

'I have to admit that's news to me. Do you wish me to congratulate you?'

'I believe that would be appropriate in the circumstances.'

'Congratulations, then.' She hesitated before going on, 'I don't think you can love her, not so soon after declaring your affection for me.'

'You might disapprove of my change of heart, but it was only to be expected. Rejection is painful. It's like the wind and rain turning iron to rust. It fair takes the shine off. I'll always be fond of you, but your preference for my brother has altered my feelings.' The horse nuzzled at his arm.

'Emily and I are to be married within three weeks.'

'I beg your pardon?'

'She hasn't told you?'

Catherine shook her head.

'We'll be moving to Faversham together as

190

husband and wife.'

'I wish you every happiness, Stephen.' Was it really love that he could turn it round so quickly and court Emily? That wasn't the kind of affection she sought and not what she wanted for her close friend. Her instinct was to protect her as she'd always done since the moment Emily had first slipped her hand into hers at dame school when she'd been overwhelmed by the presence of the older children. 'It seems rather sudden.'

He shrugged. 'I can't live like a monk for all my life. I need a wife at my side, someone to help me at the forge, to work in the house and keep the bed warm at night. Emily is a pretty, sweet and capable village girl. She is fond of me. And she will do very well. She will have rule of her own domain and be free from her bullying mother. I will give her everything she could ever want or need. We are going to be happy together. I'm determined.' He paused. 'Some of us can't afford to have such scruples as you. We make the most of what we can have. Emily is a good match for me.'

'Well, I am glad,' she said. 'Truly.'

'Good afternoon, Catherine,' he said. 'I may call you Catherine, as I have every expectation that before very long we will be brother and sister by marriage.'

She bade him goodbye and went straight to the mill, where she knocked on the door of the cottage which adjoined the bakehouse.

'Come in,' Emily called.

Catherine stepped inside, relieved to find that Mrs Millichip appeared to be out.

'I'm in here,' Emily added and Catherine followed the sound of her voice into the kitchen. She coughed as the scent of burning caught her by the throat.

'What's going on?' she asked.

'I'm cooking supper.' Emily, who was wearing an apron over her clothes, pointed her ladle towards a pan that stood on a brand-new metal rack on the table with its contents bubbling over the rim. 'I'm hoping that I can retrieve it.'

'I'm afraid that it's too late for that.' Catherine took the ladle and gave the stew a stir, bringing blackened carrots and mutton to the top. 'That's hardly fit for the pigs.'

'When we are married, my husband and I will be forced to live on bread and cheese.'

'You mean Stephen?'

'Oh! How do you know?'

'He told me.'

Emily frowned. 'I wanted to tell you myself. Never mind. I wanted to call on you, but Ma insisted that I finished the chores first.' She wiped her hands on her apron. 'It's the most wonderful thing that's ever happened to me. Stephen came to see my father this morning, and he said yes, without hesitation. Stephen is the most suitable man. I couldn't have imagined making a better match.'

'I'm delighted for you both,' Catherine said, unsure how to proceed. Looking at dear Emily's face, brimming with joy, she didn't know if she could bring herself to mention Stephen's pursuit of another.

Suddenly, Emily burst into laughter.

'Oh dear, I'm going to be a useless wife, aren't I? He will have so much cheese, he will end up squeaking like a mouse.' She became serious, once more. 'Ma's going to beat me for this when she gets back.'

'Let's see if we can fix it before she returns,' Catherine said. 'I can show you how to make a pie from one of Ma's recipes.'

'Would you? I can bake bread blindfold, but anything else is beyond me.'

'Have you any flour? And meat and onions?'

Emily went to the larder, took a bowl of flour from the bag and two onions.

'There is meat.' She brought out a pair of rabbits. 'I'm not sure how to skin them.'

'It's simple. I'll show you.' Catherine had skinned them before under Pa's watchful eye. She butchered them and chopped up the meat while Emily sliced the onions.

'You don't seem all that happy for me,' she said, wiping one eye.

'Of course I am. Now, tip those onions in with the meat and get on with the pastry.' Catherine told her what proportions of lard and flour to use.

'Has Matty spoken of marriage yet?' Emily went on.

'Not yet.'

'How can you be so patient?'

'All in good time.'

'Do your parents know that you're walking out with him?'

'Pa approves, but Ma will never give us her blessing. She's a mean-spirited bigot.'

193

'Isn't it a mother's duty to disapprove of her daughter's choice of match? My ma wasn't enamoured of Stephen until he offered to repair her locket and chain.' Emily peered into the bowl where she was rubbing the fat into the flour to make a crumb. 'What's next?'

'Add water. Not too much,' Catherine warned. 'You can use a knife to pull the crumbs and water together to make a dough, but don't overwork it, or you'll end up breaking your teeth on it.'

Emily rolled out the dough and placed it in a dish. Catherine blind-baked it before showing her how to fill the pastry case with the meat and onion mixture and arrange a lid of pastry on top.

'You have to flute the edges to stop the juices bubbling out. Wait a minute,' Catherine said as Emily put the pie in the oven. 'You haven't made any holes in the top to let out the steam.'

Emily put the pie back on the table, and under Catherine's guidance, she pierced the lid and turned the pastry trimmings into leaf shapes to put on the top.

'Waste not, want not,' Catherine said, watching her finish the pastry with a wash of egg and milk. 'That looks perfect.'

Emily returned the pie to the oven and Catherine helped her clear up the pots and pans as the kitchen filled with the mouth-watering aroma of meat pie.

'I can't believe I made that. Stephen will be delighted when I bake it for him in the future. When we have a home of our own, I'll keep house and he'll make new things for it. Look at the rack on the table – he made that.' She paused, a beatific smile on her face, before going on, 'With his own hands. He is a craftsman of the highest order.'

She hardly stopped praising her betrothed while Catherine tormented herself with the question of what to do. The guilt of keeping her secret from her friend was threatening to burst from her lips like the steam that rushed out of the slits in the pastry lid when she took the pie from the oven a little later.

She could hear Matty whispering in one ear, 'Keep quiet: least said, soonest mended,' but the voice of her conscience was strident. She knew only too well that a secret was like a stash of gunpowder, quiescent and harmless until something, a stray comment or a spark of suspicion, ignited it. If it should unexpectedly explode in the future when Emily was already married, it could cause untold injury and hurt, whereas now, she would have the option of breaking her engagement, no matter how painful it would turn out to be.

'Emily, are you sure that Stephen loves you?' she began.

'Of course. Only yesterday he brought me a horseshoe that he'd decorated with flowers.' She smiled. 'What on earth makes you say that?'

It was now or never, Catherine thought.

'Not so long ago, he professed his love to me.' Emily stared at her.

'I don't believe you.'

'I'm sorry, but it's true.'

'Why are you trying to spoil this for me?'

'I'm not. I want you to be sure about what you're getting in to.'

'I don't understand. Oh, it's because you're jealous because Matty will never make all that much of himself compared with Stephen.' Emily's eyes flashed with anger.

'He asked me to walk out with him,' Catherine went on stubbornly.

'When?'

'It was when we were hop picking. That's why Stephen and Matty got into that fight.'

'They were scrapping over you?'

Catherine nodded. 'Stephen asked me again when he was celebrating the end of his apprenticeship at the forge.'

'If that's really so, why didn't you tell me before?'

'You and Stephen getting together – it's all been such a rush, and I was scared of hurting your feelings–'

'So you thought you'd enlighten me after I've gone and agreed to marry him,' Emily cut in.

'It isn't too late. You can break an engagement, but it's almost impossible to unpick a marriage.'

'How can you suggest that I give up the one thing that is precious to me? How can you ruin it like this?' Emily started to cry. 'I thought you were my friend. Why would you do this to me?'

Catherine's blood ran cold. Stupidly, she hadn't anticipated the intensity of Emily's response. How would she feel if the boot was on the other foot?

'No matter how much you try to poison me against him, I will not change my mind. Whether Stephen loves me or not, I can't afford to have principles. Neither can you, for that matter.'

'I'll do anything to hold true to my beliefs,' Catherine insisted.

'I can see that. You've shown yourself quite prepared to break up a friendship with your thoughtless, cruel words. What would it have cost you to keep quiet?'

Catherine felt herself wilting under Emily's gaze. She hardly recognised her. Where was the down-trodden Miss Millichip? Her confidence seemed to have soared since she'd accepted Stephen's proposal. She knew exactly what she wanted and where she was going.

Catherine's chest was tight. She could hardly breathe as Emily continued, 'I have no wish to see you or speak with you again.'

'Please, don't say that,' Catherine begged. 'I'm sorry.'

'I'm sorry too, sorrier than you'll ever know, but I can no longer be friends with you. You have planted the seed of suspicion in my heart and I will always see you as a danger to my betrothed's constancy. I insist that you leave immediately.'

'But, Emily–'

'Go!' She pushed her towards the door. Catherine tripped over the step and into the cold. She looked back through a skein of tears, but Emily had gone, slamming the door firmly on their friendship.

She had done the right thing, or so she thought, but had it been worth it?

Catherine tried to see Emily again on several occasions, but she made excuses not to see her, and turned her back on her in the street.

The Rooks were invited to the wedding, which was held a month later. Catherine offered to stay at home with John so that she could avoid any awkwardness, but Ma insisted that one of the labourers and his wife would sit with her brother while they attended the church and the celebration at the mill afterwards.

'I have no wish to go,' she told Matty when he arrived at the farm to walk with her to the church on the morning of the wedding. He looked well in his clean shirt, patched trousers and polished boots.

He held out his arm and kissed her cheek.

'You must be there for Stephen's sake, if not for Emily's. Besides, I want you nearby. I'm my brother's best man as Jervis isn't here.'

'Where is your ma? I thought she might be with you.'

'She can't leave the house any longer – people stare at her when she's out. She was crying when I left – her spirit is willing, but her flesh is weak.'

'I'm sorry. Perhaps I should call on her.'

'She'd like that very much,' Matty said. 'She can't wait to hear about the wedding, what the bride was wearing and who was there.'

As they walked along the road, he reached across into the garden outside Mill Cottage and plucked some sprigs of laurel and holly, making a nosegay of them. He handed it to her.

'For you, my love.'

'You shouldn't have,' she said with a rueful sigh. 'These don't belong to you. They aren't yours to give.'

'They belong to you now,' he said. 'The Millichips won't even notice they're gone.'

Catherine forgave him. The sun was shining,

the church bells were pealing and she was with the man she hoped to spend the rest of her life with. All he had to do was ask.

When they reached the church, she went inside, leaving him to wait on the step for the groom.

'Have you been dilly-dallying?' Ma said as she took her place in the pew.

'Leave her alone,' Pa said.

'Look at all these leaves and ribbons,' Ma went on, pointing out the decorations along the aisle. 'Anyone would think that the Millichips were made of money.'

'It's their special day. Don't spoil it, Margaret,' Pa said.

'Hush,' Mr Nobbs said from behind them. 'Here's the groom.'

They turned to watch Stephen walking towards them, his face pale against his new frock coat. Catherine had to smile because it was far too big for him, as though he'd bought it to grow in to. Matty stood alongside him and fidgeted as they waited for the bride.

'The wait would be made more enjoyable with some moosic,' George Carter said as he joined his sons.

'Please, let us not forget that this is a day of celebration, and no time to visit past disagreements,' the vicar said. 'We're considering the purchase of an organ. The outlay will be considerable, but the cost of maintenance far less than keeping the old choir.' He looked past George. 'Here comes the bride.'

Catherine turned to see Emily, who was dressed

in a veil and a yellow dress with lace trimmings, walk past her without a glance. Her heart sank – she was still angry with her.

Reverend Browning officiated and the ceremony went smoothly until Matty fumbled for the ring. There was a collective sigh of relief as he found it deep in one of his pockets along with a coin and a piece of string. He handed it to Stephen, who slipped it onto Emily's finger. The couple signed the register and they walked out of the church as husband and wife, looking neither to the left, nor the right for good luck.

The congregation followed. Catherine waited for Matty to pay the vicar for his services before they called at Mill Cottage for refreshments. They approached Emily who was seated with Stephen in the corner of the main room, receiving the guests.'

Catherine held out her hand, but Emily didn't take it.

'Congratulations to you both,' she said, her eyes flicking from her old friend to Stephen and back. He dropped his gaze. 'I wish you all the happiness in the world.'

'Thank you, Miss Rook,' Stephen said. 'My wife and I are most grateful that you could join us. Aren't we, Emily, my love?'

'Not particularly. I would rather not be reminded of–' She stopped abruptly.

'I shouldn't have come.' Catherine took a step back and turned away, her face burning as Matty slipped his arm around her shoulder and led her outside.

'She will never forgive me,' she said.

'She will, given time. It's too fresh in her mind.'

'Look, you go back and celebrate with your brother. I'll go and see your ma on my way home.'

'If you're sure,' he said.

She nodded.

'I'll call upon you later. Perhaps your parents will retire early so we can sit up.'

'We can always hope.' She smiled at the thought as she headed back to the farm, making a detour to Toad's Bottom Cottage. The gate was open, half-dropped from its hinges, the path was slippery with fallen leaves and someone had boarded up one of the windows. One of the younger Carter boys walked around the corner of the house with a brown rabbit tucked under his arm. His sister accompanied him, her skirts wet with mud.

'What do you want?' the girl said.

'I've come to call on your mother.'

'Go on indoors. She's in the kitchen.'

'Thank you.' Catherine pushed the door open, scraping it across the doorstep. She stepped into the dark, damp, cold interior and found her way to where Ma Carter was lying on a mattress on the floor in front of the fireplace where the frail skeleton of a log sat in the ashes. 'Good afternoon,' she said. 'How are you?'

'You find me about the same as yesterday and a little worse than the day before.' Ma Carter tried to sit herself up. Catherine helped slide a bolster behind her back. 'Oh dear, I'm sorry to put you to this trouble. Have you bin to the wedding?'

'That's why I'm here, to tell you how it went.' Catherine took a seat on the wooden settle which bore the shiny imprints of years of use. 'Stephen looked very handsome and Emily, well–'

'What was she wearing? There's no point in asking my menfolk. One will say that the dress was red, another will say blue, and then they'll argue about it and agree on green, and I'll be none the wiser.'

'Her dress was yellow and covered with lace.'

'And her shoes?'

'I believe she was wearing new ones of pale leather.'

'How I wish I could have been there, but I have the dropsy, and there's nothing that can be done. Would you mind putting the kettle on for tea?'

They drank weak tea from chipped cups and without saucers to catch the drips.

'I can't tell you how happy I am to hear that you're walking out with our Matty. He's always talking about you, Catherine. I know he has his faults, but he's turning out to be a steady young man. It's such a shame that people can't see the same in my Jervis. I don't know what it is about him, but he's always been misunderstood.'

'He started the fire at Wanstall Farm. Don't you remember?' Catherine said.

'That what everyone says, but he'd never do such a thing. I know, because I'm his mother.' Ma Carter gazed at her visitor through tears. 'I wish your pa had taken him on again. I miss my son. I wonder if I'll ever see him again before I pass.'

'I'm sorry. I'm afraid I've upset you. I should go home.' Catherine stood up and smoothed her skirt.

202

'You will come back soon,' Ma Carter said. 'I like to hear of the goings-on in the village. Mrs Browning calls on occasion with bread and cheese, and junket, but she doesn't enjoy a good gossip.'

'I'll call another time,' Catherine promised. She wished her goodbye and returned to the farm, glad to be away from the oppressive confines of the cottage.

One afternoon soon after Stephen and Emily were married, Catherine was in the village with Matty when they saw the cart taking them and their few possessions to Faversham.

'I'm surprised they didn't have a big send-off,' she said.

'We said our goodbyes last night. Ma was very upset,' Matty said, waving after them. 'You're very quiet today. A penny for your thoughts, my love.'

'I'm sad about what happened between me and Emily. She'll never forgive me.'

'I told you to give it time. We'll hear news of her, at least because Stephen has promised to visit Ma as often as he can.' He stopped and took both her hands in his. 'I've been thinking about us.'

Her heart began to beat faster as he continued, 'Would it make you happy if I spoke with your father?'

'Oh, Matty, is that a proposal?'

He nodded. 'Yes, of sorts. To be honest, I've been holding back.'

'Why?'

'I suppose I've bin scared that the strength of

your feelings for me might not match mine for you.'

'You should have no worries on that account,' she said softly.

A smile spread across his face.

'So you'll do me the honour of becoming my wife?'

'Of course. As long as Pa approves, which he will because I won't let him say otherwise.' She squeezed his hand, her heart bursting with joy. It wasn't the great romantic gesture she had dreamed of, but it didn't matter because it was real. When they walked on through the woods with the autumn leaves scrunching underfoot, they talked of their plans: where they would live; how many children they would have.

In the days that followed, she was on tenter-hooks, waiting for him to speak to Pa, the person who held their future happiness in his hands.

On a cold November morning, she was bring-ing some turnips in from the clamp. Her nose was frozen and her chilblains were itchy and sore. She paused on her way back to the house to watch George and one of the other farmhands who were repairing the roof of the barn to make it watertight. John stood counting the new tiles in the pile on the ground. 'One, two, three, five,' over and over again. George asked him to hand one up. John chose one, but the morning dew had made it glincey and it slipped from his grasp and shattered across the stones.

'Never mind,' George said.

'Never mind,' John echoed.

'What's John doing out here? He'll catch a

chill,' Ma exclaimed as she emerged from the house dressed in her best clothes and carrying a basket. 'Catherine, bring him indoors.'

'All right,' she called back, reluctant to leave the men's company. It had been quiet in the house since Drusilla had gone and there was no sign that Ma was ever going to find a replacement she could trust. In four years, they'd had three girls start. One had left under mysterious circumstances – Ma said that she'd had her eye on John. The other two hadn't lived up to Ma's high standards – one had burned a side of bacon rendering it inedible while the other had damaged her favourite porcelain figurine while dusting.

With all the other work that had to be done, the farmhouse had begun to appear neglected. The window frames had started to peel and crack, and a pane of glass had fallen from the upper floor and been left to gradually disappear into a mound of stinging nettles.

Catherine blew on her fingers as she struggled to open the door while holding on to an apronful of turnips at the same time. The sound of horses' hooves caught her attention, making her hesitate. She looked back past the pump to see Squire Temple and his bailiff tying their horses outside the stables which had been rebuilt a few months after the fire at a cost that Pa could ill afford.

She took a couple of steps closer so she could hear what they wanted.

The squire greeted Pa with a handshake and expressed his wish that the meeting would go smoothly.

'I don't know if you've heard, but Mr Francis

over at Boughton has taken up a most peculiar charitable cause. He has only been persuaded to take in Sir William Courtenay to his home at Fairbrook.'

'I've heard of that fellow,' Pa said.

'It is said that Francis – or rather his wife and daughter – are under his spell,' the bailiff joined in. 'He is reputed to be a Knight of Malta, whatever that is, and a great leader of men.'

'I don't believe that he's any such thing,' Pa said. 'I saw him a few years back when he was staying at the Rose Inn in Canterbury.'

'Are you sure we're talking about the same gentleman?' the squire asked.

'The personage I'm thinking of is quite bizarre,' Pa said. 'He is tall and imposing, and has a long black beard. He has a habit of stroking his bushy locks and ample mustachios, and placing them between his teeth, and as for his clothes, well, when he was put up for election to Parliament, he wore a tunic embroidered with gold and carried a sword that he called Excalibur.'

'He didn't get elected,' the squire said, 'and he gained but three votes when he tried again in East Kent. There is some secret about what happened to him after that because no one saw hide nor hair of him for a while. Some say he went to his family seat in Devon, others that he got into trouble with the law and was committed to the lunatic asylum at Barming after being found guilty of perjury. I believe the case involved the smuggling of liquor, which makes it all the more surprising that Mr Francis would take him in. Who would willingly welcome a lawbreaker into their home?'

'I don't think that Sir William is a bad man at heart. When he was at the inn, I saw him give out pints to the people, and peppermints to the children,' Pa said.

'But he is against the natural order in that he would make the poor wealthy and the rich poor,' the bailiff said, frowning. 'I worry that, whoever he is, he'll stir up trouble around here, just as the rioters did in the time of Captain Swing. We don't want that again.'

'It won't happen. People remember the last time. Their antics did them no good.' The squire turned to Pa. 'Now, Mr Rook. Where can we talk in private?'

Catherine saw her father's face turn grey. He wiped his palms on his coat and invited the squire and the bailiff into the house to his office. She watched them go inside, then returned to her chores, pumping water from the well to take into the kitchen. As she stepped back to avoid the water pouring into her boots, she heard Matty's whistle.

She looked up to find he was almost upon her, striding along with his hands in his pockets, and dressed in his Sunday best. His neck was rubbed almost raw by the starched collar and his hair was so clean that it stood on end from his head. Her heart leapt because she knew why he was here.

'You look smart.' She reached out to straighten his cravat.

'I have a meeting with your father.' His face was pink and shining.

'You'll have to wait for a while. He's with the

squire at present.'

'How long do you think they'll be?'

'I don't know.' She hoped Pa hadn't forgotten about his arrangement with Matty, but it wasn't long before the squire and his bailiff emerged to collect their horses.

Matty helped Catherine with the bucket, carrying it indoors to the scullery, where they exchanged kisses before heading through the house to find Ma in the hall, waiting for Pa to come out of his room.

He appeared in the doorway, his head down and shoulders stooped as if he was carrying all the cares of the world.

'Well?' Ma demanded. 'What did they want?'

'The squire came to give us notice,' Pa said quietly.

'How can that be? Haven't we always paid our rent on time?'

Pa didn't answer. He didn't need to. His silence was more telling than words.

'Oh, Thomas.' Ma reached out to the clock for support. It swayed, the weights inside bashing against the case. 'You've given me a fair old shock.'

Catherine fetched her a chair from the parlour. She glanced towards Matty, who frowned. How could Pa contemplate the question of their marriage when the Rooks were on the verge of losing the farm, and everyone who worked for them was at risk of losing their homes and livelihoods? How would they all survive?

'I've been paying what I can since we fell on hard times,' Pa confessed. 'It all started with that machine – it's brought us seven years of bad luck.

We've been one man down since John had his accident – more than that because someone has to look after him. The harvest has been the worst in living memory. This situation is entirely of my own making.'

'You mustn't blame yourself,' Catherine said tearfully.

Her heart went out to him. He had tried so hard to make a success of the farm, for the family, for the farmhands and for the benefit of mankind, yet somehow he had failed. 'We can't stand here with the minnies crying over spilt milk. We have to do something.'

'I told him – I begged him – to give me time, and he agreed on one calendar year. I have a twelvemonth to turn our fortunes around.'

Catherine handed the smelling salts to her mother who was having an attack of the vapours, panting and rolling her eyes in her head.

'Calm down, Ma.'

'We are ruined,' she moaned. 'What did I ever see in you, Thomas Rook?'

'All is not lost, not yet. I recall that I have an appointment with young Matty this morning.' Pa turned to him.

'Oh no.' Ma pressed her handkerchief to her mouth. 'How can you entertain such an idea at a time like this? You'll send him away with a flea in his ear.'

Pa turned to Matty and Catherine.

'I assume that you've come here dressed up for one purpose,' he said.

'Yes, sir, to ask for your daughter's hand,' Matty said. 'I know I haven't always bin–'

Pa cut him short. 'There's no need for any flattery or flannel. I give you my blessing.'

'Thank you, Mr Rook,' Matty said. 'I promise I'll–'

'I know you will.' Pa gave him a brief handshake and raised his eyes towards the ceiling as though giving thanks to God.

'Thank you,' Catherine echoed, her heart filled with joy at her father's decision.

'You would have our daughter ruined, Thomas,' Ma interrupted.

'This marriage could be our salvation. Not only will husband and wife take care of John long after we've gone, but who better to take on the farm than Catherine whom we've brought up to be a farmer's wife, and Matty who's grown up on the land with her? Trust me,' he said. 'This is the answer to all our prayers.'

Catherine felt sick. Pa sounded far more concerned about the fate of the tenancy than for her and Matty's happiness. And as for John, as much as she loved her brother, she hadn't anticipated him being part of the deal. Her engagement felt like a business arrangement, not the romantic gesture and celebration she'd imagined it would be.

'Think about it, Margaret,' Pa went on.

'If you think this match should be encouraged and will find favour with the squire, I suppose I'll have to go along with it,' she said eventually.

Pa stepped to one side and showed Matty into his room.

'Come this way,' he said. 'We'll talk.'

Catherine watched the door closing behind them.

'That's that then,' Ma said.

'It's what I want,' Catherine said. 'I love him and I intend to spend the rest of my life with him.'

Ma stared at her, her eyes narrowed.

'Even though you aren't my daughter, I wanted better for you, but you've made your choice: now you have to live with it.'

Chapter Nine

Shooting at the Stars

Matty called at the farm on a Sunday afternoon three weeks after he'd spoken to Mr Rook.

Catherine was waiting for him, dressed in her woollen coat, stockings and boots.

'I've bin ready for ages,' she said, smiling as he held out his arm. She took it and stepped outside the house. 'Hurry up, John. We're going out.'

'John? Is he coming with us?' Matty whispered.

'I'm afraid so. Ma has retired to bed and Pa has shut himself away in his room, so there's no one to keep an eye on him.'

'One's too few, three's too many.'

John emerged from the house, his eyes lighting up when he saw Matty

'Come on, John,' he said with a sigh.

'Are we going to mend the gate today?' John asked.

'We finished that little job yesterday,' Matty said.

'What about the sheep?'

'They're fine. We checked on them this morning,' Catherine said. 'We're going for a walk in the woods.'

John smiled his lopsided smile and they set off along the track. Catherine walked with Matty's arm around her back, aware of her brother a few steps behind, dragging his useless foot through the fallen leaves.

'You're quiet today,' Matty observed. 'Is it John?'

'No. I'm used to having him around. I was just wondering when we shall be married.'

They reached the fallen tree in the clearing in the wood and sat down side by side.

'John,' Matty called. 'Come and sit here for a while. You can practise counting. How many trees can you see?'

John raised his good hand and pointed at each tree in turn.

'One, two, three, five,' he said. 'Seven, seven. One, two, three...' he repeated.

'That will keep him occupied while we talk about our wedding.' Catherine breathed in the aroma of damp and toadstools which mingled with Matty's musky scent as she waited for his answer. 'How about next week? Or next month? It's a quiet time of year on the farm.'

'Your pa suggested after the lambing.'

'He's being cautious, surely? I don't want to wait that long.' She was disappointed. She would be more than happy to set the date for tomorrow, although that would be impossible because there were preparations to be made.

'I would marry you today if I could, but I have

to be guided by your father's wishes.'

'I'm surprised he's thinking of a long engagement, considering he's depending on our marriage to secure the tenancy.'

'The squire has given him a year, so there's plenty of time,' Matty said, embracing her as the chill of the late November afternoon seeped through her clothes. 'Don't worry, my love. It will happen.'

'I have something for you,' she said, reassured. She put her hand in her pocket, pulled out the sixpence and placed it in his palm. 'Emily gave it to me as a token of friendship, but as she's no longer part of my life, I'd like you to take this as a symbol of my love for you.'

'Thank you,' he said, his voice husky with emotion. 'No one has given me anything like this before. I don't know what I can give you in return. Ah, I know…' He pulled a knife from his bag, twisted some of his hair around his fingers and hacked it off. 'May I?' he said, gesturing towards her head.

Catherine nodded, her skin tingling in response to the touch of his fingers against the nape of her neck as he selected a lock of her hair and sliced it through. He placed both sets of hair on his knee – the one dark, the other a lighter brown. He divided each set and plaited a section of each together to make two rings.

He picked one up and slipped it onto her finger.

'I promise to look after you until the end of time, my darling,' he whispered.

She picked up the second ring and pushed it

213

over the knuckles of the third finger of his left hand.

'And I swear that I will be at your side for ever,' she said, overflowing with happiness. She leaned up to kiss him. He responded passionately, sliding his hands inside her cloak.

'No, Matty,' she said quietly.

'I'm sorry. It's just that you're so beautiful,' he breathed. 'I can hardly resist. If John wasn't here...'

'We must wait until we're married.' She remembered Ivy's words of warning. She had experienced the consequences of bringing a child into the world out of wedlock and she wasn't prepared for it to happen to another poor innocent soul.

A shadow of regret crossed his eyes.

'We won't have to wait for long,' she said quickly. 'I shall speak with Pa. I'll persuade him to change his mind.'

But when she talked to him later, his mind was made up. There was a cottage on the farm that was rented out until the spring, when Matty and Catherine could take it over and do it up. He thought it was important that they didn't have to spend the first few months of married life sharing the farmhouse. Ma wouldn't like it, so after lambing it had to be.

Life on the farm went on much the same until the following year. When the cottage became available, Matty repaired the roof and Catherine whitewashed the walls. Matty blacked the stove and fireplace, and Pa had a bed made for them.

The seedlings began to come up in the field as the earth warmed, and the hop bines began to furl their stems around the poles. George and the other labourers spent many hours nidgeting on the land to get rid of the weeds. One of the mares gave birth to a healthy colt foal and two of the hens went broody and hatched chicks. Ma continued her mission to feather her nest in heaven while John and Matty prepared for lambing, driving the ewes to the orchard near the house in anticipation of the new arrivals.

There was room for optimism over the future of Wanstall Farm. The squire had even intimated that he would consider the renewal of the tenancy in a favourable light.

Catherine was in the yard beating the life out of a couple of rugs one morning, wondering why Matty hadn't dropped by to steal a kiss as he'd done before work every day since their engagement. Perhaps he'd gone straight to the orchard to help one of the ewes, but it was mid-March and the lambs weren't due for a couple of weeks. It wasn't like him to be late, and he was never ill. She paused on hearing voices. Pa rounded the corner of the granary with George and John.

'I don't know where he is,' George said, shaking his head. 'He went out last night – I assoomed he was on his way to sit up with Catherine. He didn't come home, but I reckoned he was...' He stuttered. 'Well, you know what young sweethearts get up to.'

'Not our young lady,' Pa said sternly.

'No, of course not. My mistake, Tom. I didn't mean to–'

'It's all right. No offence taken. Now, Matty isn't a shirker, so what has happened to him? Could he

215

have gone to the cottage? Has he met with some kind of an accident?'

Catherine winced at the thought.

'I've bin to the cottage to look and there's no sign of him there,' George said. 'Have you seen him, John?'

John shrugged.

'When did you last see him, son?' Pa asked.

'I can't rightly recall.' John swore. 'I wish I could remember.' Anguished, he started to beat his forehead with his fist as though he might be able to force a memory to appear.

'Steady there.' Pa took John's arm. 'Don't hurt yourself. Who is watching the sheep now?'

'I don't know,' John said.

'It would have been better if you'd stayed with the flock and sent one of the boys who's bird-scaring to deliver a message. George, you go and watch the sheep. John, come indoors and have something to eat. I expect Ma has a cold meat pie.'

'And boiled eggs? And cake, I hope,' John said cheerfully. Pa guided him towards the house and Catherine accompanied them.

'Do you know where Matty is?' Pa asked.

'No,' Catherine said, feeling somehow inadequate for not knowing. 'Why should I? I'm not his keeper.'

'Not yet,' Pa said. 'When you're a married woman, you'll keep him close.'

'I'm sure there's a good explanation.'

'Is he in some kind of trouble? Is he having second thoughts about the wedding? He wouldn't be the first. Oh, don't fret. I was a young man once, although it's hard to believe. But that's no excuse for leaving the sheep unattended. John relies on him.' Pa's eyes flashed with irritation. 'Soon, he'll be family, but I'm telling you, if he neglects his duties again' – his voice faltered – 'well, I don't know what I'll do. It's in your interest to make sure he doesn't disappear again.'

'I really don't know where he is.' Catherine's forehead tightened. 'Why do you keep asking me like this?'

'There are rumours going about. Some of the men around here have been getting themselves caught up with that Courtenay fellow over at Fairbrook.' Pa gazed at her, his eyes narrowed in question. 'My opinion of him has altered recently.'

'Matty would have told me if–'

'That's all right then,' Pa cut in. 'I believe you.' He turned back to John. 'Let's go inside.'

Catherine tried to slip out once she had finished cleaning the floors, but Ma caught her and forbade her to go anywhere until after supper. It felt like an age before she was free to leave the house. The past few evenings, she'd been patchworking to make a quilt for the bed in the cottage, but tonight it would have to wait. She threw on her cloak to hide her face and walked briskly towards the beerhouse.

She looked inside the door into a small room. It was dark apart from a pair of flickering candles that were spewing pungent black swirls of smoke into the atmosphere. Mrs Clackworthy was sitting on her seat at the serving area, beneath a row of pots hanging from hooks. She was talking to her customers; three fellows dressed in smocks and drinking beer at a table.

Catherine hesitated at the open door, catching snippets of their conversation.

'Squire Temple is in cahoots with the vicar. He won't provide beer no more for his men that do an honest day's labour on the farm. What do you think to that?'

'I reckon we'll have to move on come Michaelmas, for to work without beer is certain death.'

'Come in and sup with us, young lady,' one of the men said with a leer.

'No, thank you,' she said. 'Have you seen any sign of Matty? He's one of the Carter lads.'

'He's your sweetheart, isn't he?' said another, with white hair, side-beards and a bulbous red nose.

'Gone missing, eh?'

'Stop with us, dearie. We'll take care of you.'

'Don't listen to these wastrels,' Mrs Clackworthy cut in. 'I haven't seen hide nor hair of Matty Carter. I thought he was doing the shepherding for your brother?'

'Oh, he is. They work together on the farm.'

'So it isn't a case of the shepherd losing his sheep. It's more like the sheep losing their shepherd.' One of the men slammed his pot down and roared with laughter. The others joined in.

'Don't let them distress you, ducks. I'm sure there's a good explanation for your betrothed going missing. You're about to be married, aren't you?'

'Yes, very soon.'

'He'll be sowing his wild oats afore coming back to settle down,' one of the men said.

'That's enow, Samuel, or I'll turf you out on the street.' Mrs Clackworthy turned to Catherine. 'Have you tried the White Horse in Boughton? It isn't far away.'

'No, but thank you.'

'He might be at the Red Lion,' Mrs Clackworthy added. 'You've heard of Sir William, haven't you? Everyone's talking about him. There's many, men and women alike, who've gone to hear him speak as he travels around this parish and others.'

'I've seen him when he was staying with Mr Francis at Fairbrook,' said Samuel. 'He makes out that he's a gentleman but he's a fraud.'

'I'd heard he's the genuine article,' said one of the other men. 'He's heir to the Earl of Devon, would you believe?'

'He speaks a load of nonsense, but if that keeps the poor wretches happy, who am I to argue? He's harmless enow.'

'I should welcome him here with open arms and a cask of strong beer,' said Mrs Clackworthy. 'I'd rather he spent his shillings here than anywhere else.'

Catherine turned and fled. It was too late to be tramping around the countryside alone. Matty could be anywhere. She returned to the farm, but she couldn't concentrate on her sewing so she retired to bed.

Much later, the chinking of stones flying up against the window disturbed her. She slid out of bed, pulled her shawl over her shoulders and looked outside to see a familiar shadow moving across the grass towards the house. She slid the sash open.

'Psst,' Matty hissed. 'Is the coast clear?'

'No, don't come up.' Usually, he would come indoors and they would sit up together after Ma and Pa had retired discreetly to bed, but today was different. If Pa found out he was here, he would confront him over abandoning John and the flock. 'Meet me in the orchard.' She heard a floorboard creak somewhere in the house. She waved him away and closed the window, lowering it carefully so that it didn't make a sound. She put her clothes over her gown and tiptoed down the stairs, across the hall to the back door beyond the kitchen, where she put on her boots and slid the bolt open.

She held her breath, listening, but no one stirred so she slipped outside into the fresh air and walked briskly to the orchard where she kept to the lee of the hedge.

Matty stepped out from beneath one of the apple trees.

'Where have you been?' Catherine's heart leapt at the sight of his smile. She threw her arms around his neck. He pulled her close and spun her around, and it felt like they were dancing again in the meadows after the harvest.

'I've missed you,' he said gruffly, kissing her and burying his face against her neck.

'I've been worried sick.'

'I'm sorry.' He grasped her hands and took a small step back.

'And so you should be. You were supposed to be watching the sheep with John. Pa is furious.'

'Don't go on, Catherine. I'm not your hen-pecked husband yet.'

'I shan't be a nagging wife,' she said, feeling sore at his comment.

'I'm sorry. I didn't mean to say the wrong thing.' He smiled again. 'We will always be kind to each other.'

'It wasn't very kind of you not to let me know where you were.'

'I got distracted.' His eyes flashed in the moonlight. She could hear the excitement in his voice, 'I went to hear Sir William speak.'

'Why? What has he got to do with you?'

'I wanted to hear what he had to say. He's a wonderful man, good and true. It's a marvel to me that someone like him, born into riches beyond belief, is concerned with the plight of the wretched labourers.'

'What about our future, though?' Catherine said stubbornly. She didn't like seeing Matty's revolutionary side come out. It made her uncomfortable. 'What about looking after your own? We have rent to pay now.'

'Don't fret, my love. Whatever happens, we'll be all right. Sir William toasts good health to the poor and promises to fill everybody's bellies with victuals. He is Christ come down from the cross.'

'How can that be?' Catherine said, her tone scathing. She didn't want Matty to get carried away as she could imagine Jervis would over a man like Sir William. But here he was talking about Christ.

Matty grasped her by the shoulders, looked her in the eyes and said earnestly, 'He has shown me the nail marks on his hands. You see, there's nothing you can say against that. He styles his beard and hair in the image of Christ. What's more, he can hear everything anyone says from a mile around.' He delivered his final proof of Sir William's immortality. 'Last night, I saw him take out his pistol and shoot at the stars. They broke up and sparkled in the sky. I wish you could have seen it.'

Catherine wished she could have seen it too, to banish the doubt she felt at Matty's words. She wanted to believe him.

'Sir William is calling for people to follow him, to gather an army to rise up against the rich.'

'You aren't planning to join him?'

'I would see the wealth of the county shared equally.'

'But not all men are equal.'

'I don't see why they shouldn't be, though. Why should the squire have two hundred acres of land while my father struggles to survive on his wages?'

'At least your pa has money.' It was thanks to her father, who continued to employ George Carter even though he was too old and decrepit to do much more than gather wood and feed the pigs. There had always been this idealistic side to Matty, but Catherine had never seen it so alive before. She feared what it would mean for her and the future of her family. 'Matty, I'm scared.'

'Scared? Why?'

'I'm afraid that you're going against my father.'

'I look up to your father like my own. He's been good to the Carters, but I want to help the cause for all my brothers, not just those of my blood. Don't worry, my love.'

'You can't tell me not to fret and expect that to

be the end of it. I don't want you getting hurt.'

'I won't get involved in any fighting – Sir William is a peaceable man who will achieve his aims through words, not blows.'

'Don't risk everything for some madman's promises.'

'You must come and hear him speak. That way you can make up your own mind.'

'I will do, if I can get away from the farm.' She stared at him.

'Oh, don't look at me like that. I won't let your pa down again. I promise I'll turn up on time in future.' He touched her cheek. 'There's no reason for me to skip a day's work again.'

She softened a little. 'We shouldn't argue.'

'We'll be married soon, then we'll argue every day and enjoy making up afterwards.' Catherine smiled and Matty continued, 'I'll never let you down. I promise I'll be the best husband anyone could have.'

She kissed him full on the lips.

'Let's go to the cottage for a while,' he suggested. 'We can be alone there.'

Catherine bit her lip. She was sorely tempted. 'There'd be no harm in it,' Matty said.

She couldn't see the harm either, even though they hadn't set the date quite yet.

'I'll walk you back – no one will know you've been away.' His voice caught in his throat.

Catherine glanced down at the ring on her finger, their locks of hair intertwined. She wanted him. She needed to be close to him. They were meant for each other. Why should they wait any longer?

'No, you're right,' he began again. 'We shouldn't–'

'Let's go,' she interrupted, casting any remaining doubt aside. If she should by any mischance end up with child before their wedding day, it would be too early for it to show.

'Are you sure?'

'I'm sure. Our home is ready. There's nothing stopping us getting married.'

'We will walk down the aisle after the last of the lambs has been born,' he said. 'I promise.'

He took her hand and they made their way to the cottage.

The March winds turned to April showers and then May rolled in, bringing longer days and bright sunshine. As the lambs gambolled in the meadow, Catherine found herself afflicted by sickness that began from the moment she woke up until she fell into bed exhausted at night. At first, she dismissed it as nothing, but eventually she had to face facts. She was in a dreadful pickle.

Matty called at the farm one evening when day began to turn to dusk. She let him in to the kitchen.

'I thought we'd go out for a walk,' he said, placing a daisy chain around her neck. 'I made this for you.'

She caught the soft stems between her fingers and leaned forward to receive his kiss.

'Where do you think you're off to?' Ma said, entering the room.

'Out,' Catherine said.

'You'll get yourself into trouble – if you haven't

already. Matty, make sure you have her home by midnight.'

'Yes, Mrs Rook,' he said. 'She's a tyrant,' he added as they left the house. 'It's no wonder you can't wait to move out.'

'How about you?' Catherine asked.

'It will be hard leaving the littl'uns, even though the youngest is eight years old and well able to look after herself with a little help. I feel as though I've done my fair share of caring for everyone at Toad's Bottom.' He slipped his arm around her waist as they strolled out into the orchard. 'It's time that I looked after you.'

She glanced up at the sky where pinpricks of starlight began to pierce the navy sky.

'And our child,' she went on gently. She stopped and placed his hand on her belly.

'That's...' he paused. 'Are you sure?'

She nodded.

'That's a wonder,' he said, his eyes soft and dark with awe.

'It takes only one time,' she ventured.

He grinned. 'I know, but well, I didn't expect it to happen so soon. Does anyone else know?'

'You're the first, but I reckon Ma has her suspicions. I've been terribly sick of a morning.'

'Is there anything I can do? How can I help?'

'Just hold me in your arms and never let me go.' She smiled ruefully. 'No, we must set the date for the wedding so we can be married before I start to show.'

'Of course. How about around Oak Apple Day?'

That was less than a month away, she thought.

'I'll speak to the vicar.'

'I'll get Pa to have a word. You aren't the Reverend Browning's favourite person. You've hardly been to church since he got rid of the choir.'

'Why should I go? I can pray to God just as easily when I'm out digging Ma's garden, or–'

'Tickling trout and picking up firewood where you shouldn't be.'

'You're making me out to be a scoundrel,' he chuckled. 'I admit I can be enterprising. I have to be. I miss the wages in kind that I had from the vestry.'

'So I will speak to Pa?'

'Yes.' He smiled again. 'I can't wait to be a family – you, me and the littl'un.'

Within a week, her father arranged for the vicar to read the banns.

When he was reading them for the third time, Catherine stood side by side with Matty in the pew. George Carter was absent and the younger Carters were at the back of the church with Jane Browning, having attended her Sunday school. The gallery remained empty, the choir's music a distant memory.

At the end of the service, Jane came over to congratulate Catherine on her good fortune.

'It's lamentable that we'll never be able to call each other sister, but you wouldn't have found happiness with Hector, as your mother wished. He is a cold fish.'

'It is a pity,' Catherine murmured, unsure what to say. Jane was exaggerating – she wouldn't find it ernful not to be able to call her sister.

226

'He's to be married to Squire Temple's youngest daughter. It will be a long engagement, so she'll have the chance to experience some joy before they settle down together in the miserable state of matrimony.'

'Jane, how can you say such a thing?' Catherine exclaimed.

'Because it's true. When I see the sorrow that marriage has wrought on my sisters in the parish, I despair. You are the chattel of your husband, all your worldly possessions will belong to him and he can dispose of them as he wishes.'

'I have very little in the first place, and it doesn't matter because I'm marrying for love.'

Jane smiled. There was a bitterness behind her eyes, Catherine thought.

'Good day, Miss Browning.' She hastened along the street to catch up with Matt who was loitering outside one of the cottages, waiting for her. She slipped her arm through his.

'Shall we spend the rest of the afternoon together?'

'I'll call for you a little later,' he said.

He met her at the farm at about three, and they strolled through the fields and orchards and into the valley where the stream had dried out to a mere trickle. She took off her shoes and paddled in a shallow pool that had collected in a dip in the ground, letting the water cool her toes before Matty helped her up the slope of a grassy bank where they sat side by side. Catherine leaned against him and rested her head against his chest, listening to the steady beat of his heart.

'My ma is dying,' he said suddenly.

227

'I'm sorry.' Catherine sat up straight. 'Why didn't you say? Is she much worse than she was?'

He nodded, his eyes forlorn.

'You know the saying a creaking door hangs longest. I reckon she's about to fall off her hinges. Seriously, she has taken to her bed and is lying there moaning.'

'Is she in pain?'

'Some of the time she's in agony. Other times, she sleeps.'

'Does she have any medicine?'

'Your pa has paid for sleeping drops – they help a little. Anyway, what I wanted to say is that I wish to go and find Jervis. I need to bring him back to see his dying ma, not for his sake, but for hers. He doesn't deserve it for the grief he's given us over the years, but he's family, and blood is thicker than water.'

'We shouldn't be sitting here,' Catherine said, recalling how Ma Carter had expressed a wish to see Jervis when she had called on her on Stephen and Emily's wedding day. 'We should be looking for him. Have you any idea where he is?'

'I've heard that he's found work and a place to live. I believe that Sir William stayed at the very same cottage for a while after he left Mr Francis at Boughton and before he moved to Bossenden.' He pronounced it 'Bozenden'. 'Apparently, Mr Francis ordered him out of Fairbrook when he brandished a pair of pistols at him during a spat.'

'I don't blame him. I shouldn't wish to think that a guest of mine kept a pistol beneath his pillow.'

'He wouldn't have used them. I've told you

228

before – he's a peaceable man. People like him. He's well received by the Culvers at Bossenden.'

'What has Sir William got to do with finding your brother? You seem transfixed by this man.'

'I agree with his message, but I'm hardly a fanatic. I wouldn't take off to join his gang of followers even though I have sympathy for their plight. As you've rightly said before, I have work, and I have you, my love – I have too much to lose. No, as far as I know, Jervis is one of his followers. I figure that when I find Sir William, I'll find my brother.'

'I'll come with you. You were going to take me to listen to him speak,' Catherine pointed out.

'Not tonight.' He reached across and stroked her hand. 'I need you to cover for me if I'm not back by morning.'

'Oh, Matty,' she groaned. 'How will I do that when Pa watches everyone like a hawk?'

'You'll think of something.'

'I don't want to. You know how I feel about dishonesty.'

'Your parents lied to you. I'm sorry – I shouldn't have brought that up again, but that's how it is. This would be a white lie.'

'What about John?'

'You can keep an eye on him – it'll only be for a few hours, I promise. Please, Catherine. This means everything to my ma.'

'All right. I'll do it this once, but don't ask me to do it again.'

'I won't.' He squeezed her hand. 'I promise.'

She stood up and slipped her shoes back on.

'Let's go back,' she said. 'The sooner you find

Jervis, the better.'

'Thank you, my love,' he said, and he walked her back to the farm.

The next morning, there was no sign of Matty, but no one apart from Catherine appeared to have noticed his absence. George was hoeing the barley fields where the grass and weeds were threatening to overtake the crop. Pa had ridden over to see Young Thomas to talk farming and arrange delivery of a boar to service his new gilts. Ma was talking to a caller who was trying to sell her some goats' milk.

John was in the yard, unattended and staring at the ground.

'What's wrong?' Catherine said, noticing his perturbation.

He pointed at a heap of brown and cream feathers.

'The hens? Where are they?' Catherine called for them, but none came running. She followed a trail of feathers to the orchard, but the hens were missing and the culprit responsible for their disappearance was long gone.

Wiping back tears, she told John to wait and ran inside to speak to Ma.

'I've seen a wily-looking dog fox hanging around recently,' Ma said, bewailing their misfortune. 'I told your pa not to let them out too early, not until people were around to keep an eye on them. Oh, we are cursed. Has the cockerel gone too?'

'I can't see him anywhere.'

'I'll send Matty with the cart to tell Pa to fetch a few of Young Thomas's flock with him when he comes home.'

'Oh no, that won't be possible.' Catherine's heart sank. 'Matty isn't here.'

'Where is he then?'

'I believe he has gone to Faversham to borrow a suit from Stephen.'

'George didn't say anything about that,' Ma said, eyeing her with suspicion. 'I didn't think he could afford to take a day off when it is a holiday tomorrow, especially when he will soon have another mouth to feed.' She looked towards Catherine's belly. 'It's all right, my girl. I'm not stupid.'

'I am with child,' she confirmed. There was no point in trying to deny it.

'What were you thinking of?'

Nothing at the time, she thought, nothing but the heat of Matty's skin and the passion of his lips.

'No one need ever find out. You'll be married by Friday, thank the Lord. You'd better go and watch the sheep with John until he gets back. I'll tell Pa about the suit. It won't be a problem – we all know how important this wedding is, even more so now.'

Catherine was amazed. Ma wasn't as angry as she had expected, and in fact she was treating Catherine rather tenderly. She hoped that her marriage to Matty and all it promised for her family would be the making of her relationship with Ma.

Chapter Ten

Behold a White Horse

Where was Matty? Catherine was in the kitchen, feeling sick as she stirred the last of the eggs from the hens that the fox had brutally murdered into the mix of flour and fat for a honey cake. It was Oak Apple Day, the 29th of May, when they'd arranged to spend some of the holiday together, but he hadn't turned up. It was the second day running that she hadn't seen or heard from him.

When she heard shouting from outside the front of the house, she rushed to the door and threw it open.

'What's happening?' Ma bustled down the stairs to join her. 'Is it Matty?'

'No, Ma, it's Little Ed.'

A small boy with dirty knees stood on the doorstep, his cheeks flushed and eyes sparkling with excitement and self-importance. He clutched a coin in his hand.

'What news is there?' Catherine asked urgently.

'Master Carter asked me to let you know, miss. Sir William Courtenay himself is riding through the village. He and his men have stopped for refreshment at the Woodsman's Arms.'

Catherine didn't wait for any further explanation. She fetched her shoes and a shawl, and headed out of the house.

'Where do you think you're going?' Ma said, following her. 'At least, put on your bonnet.'

'I'd like to see this man everyone is talking about with my own eyes. Please, Ma. They say he is Jesus. Matty says he's seen him shoot at the stars and break them into pieces. This could be our chance to witness a miracle, if it's true.'

Ma didn't take much persuasion.

They hurried straight to the beerhouse. A gang of men and women, some wearing sprigs of oak, were standing outside Mrs Clackworthy's establishment, drinking ale from all kinds of containers: pewter tankards, glasses and china cups. There was a bugler standing with a white horse, an elderly man holding a white flag with a red lion painted in the centre, and Matty leaning against a pole which had a loaf of bread speared through its end.

Catherine was relieved and angry at the same time. Leaving Ma behind, she ran towards him.

'Where have you been?' she cried.

'Oh, listen to you, my love. You're already a nag and we aren't yet married.' He smiled, trying to make light of it, but he sounded different, tense and distracted. There was something wrong.

'Is everything all right? Are you well? Did you find Jervis?'

'Don't fret. You have no need to worry about me, and Jervis is fine.' He paused for breath. 'Please, take care of yourself and the baby.' He glanced towards the tiny swell of her stomach and lowered his voice to a whisper. 'Don't go into the woods alone.'

'Why do you say that? Aren't you coming home

233

with me now that you've seen your brother?'

'Not yet. Just promise me you won't put yourself in danger. There are many strangers travelling through the parish. It makes me feel uneasy.'

'I've walked through those woods all my life and I've always felt safe, even when the trees came down in the storms.'

'I'm afraid that a storm of another kind is brewing.'

'I wish you wouldn't talk in riddles. What is it you aren't telling me?'

'I can't say. People are listening.'

She wanted to ask why he cared, but the way he glanced nervously towards the bugler made her bite her tongue. A fresh thought occurred to her.

'You will be at the church the day after tomorrow as arranged?'

'Of course. Nothing will stop me. I love you, Catherine. All will be well. Trust me. I must go now, but I'll be back as soon as I can.' He took a step back. 'At least now you will see the man himself and form an opinion of him. Make sure you take his words with a pinch of salt.'

Catherine frowned. What did he mean? Had he changed his mind about Sir William?

She watched him turn towards the beerhouse where a roar of cheers went up as a figure emerged from the doorway. From his appearance, his long white hair, black beard and proud bearing, Catherine guessed that it was the notorious man himself.

'That can't be him,' Ma said over her shoulder. 'Where are his fancy clothes?'

Catherine was disappointed that his outfit

234

didn't match up to the rumours. He was dressed like the other men and about as flamboyant as a cockroach, not the kingfisher she'd had described to her. He was carrying a sword, but where was his Spanish sombrero and his tunic embroidered in gold with the Maltese Cross?

'He is a handsome man, though, in spite of his attire,' Ma went on. 'He is large and most pleasing to the eye.'

The bugler helped Sir William onto the white horse. Once aloft, he raised one arm, gathering his followers around him, and addressed the crowd.

'Let us go forth with the bread as a symbol of the future when all Men and Women of Kent will flourish and prosper. I promise that if you trust me and follow me, we can take the lands from the lords of the realm, of England, and divide them so that everyone has the means to support their family.'

The crowd cheered. Ma clapped. Matty stood with the staff and the loaf on top, his expression impassive.

'I am the reincarnation of Jesus Christ. For those who have doubts, hear this.' He paused for effect. 'The Book of Revelation reads, "...behold a white horse; and he that sat on him had a bow; and a crown was given unto him; and he went forth conquering, and to conquer". This is proof of my claim, and I will not let you down, my disciples.'

The bugler fell to his knees and raised his hands in prayer.

'Drink up your beer, and we will move on.

There is a farm near Boughton where we have been promised victuals.'

The bugler shouted out, 'Every man according to his works, our rights and liberties we will have.'

The crowd cheered and sang as they followed their leader along the road out of Overshill. Matty walked alongside the throng, holding the pole with the bread in front of him. Catherine was confused. She'd sensed that he was uncomfortable in the company of the gang, so why had he gone off with them and not come home with her? Had they threatened him in some way? She tried to dismiss her concerns. Matty was more than able to stand up for himself.

'What do you make of Sir William?' Ma said.

'I feel sorry for those who are gullible and desperate enough to believe him.'

'Like Matty, you mean. I would have thought that a loving fiancé would have arranged to spend this day with his wife-to-be, not traipse the countryside with the likes of Sir William and Jervis Carter.'

'Jervis?' When Matty had said that Jervis was fine, she had assumed that he had persuaded his older brother to return to Overshill straight away to see their dying mother.

'Didn't you see him? He was with the rest of them. And I thought I noticed Drusilla, that good-for-nothing, among them as well. She was wearing a cloak with a hood as if she was ashamed to be seen, as she should be.'

'Ma, do you really believe that Sir William is the Messiah?' Catherine asked.

'I have no reason to think otherwise. He makes an excellent speech – he uses clever words, although I don't understand entirely what he's saying. And he looks like those pictures of Jesus that are hung in some people's houses with his long hair and beard. What do you think?'

'I think he's an old fraud. How can he be Jesus and heir to the Earl of Devon at the same time?'

'God moves in mysterious ways, his wonders to perform. Anything's possible. But I do worry a little that he's going to rob the rich to help the poor. Where does that leave the Rooks, when we're somewhere in the middle, with assets but no land of our own?'

Catherine turned to head back towards Wanstall Farm, but Ma caught her arm.

'Where are you going, my girl? Let's call on Ivy to make sure she's finished altering the dress. You know what she's like. Come along,' she went on. 'Hold your head high – people are looking at us.'

There was no sign of Len when they reached the forge, but Ivy invited them into the cottage with barely a smile.

'We've come to try the dress on,' Ma said. 'It is ready?'

'I'll fetch it. You can change in there.' Ivy pointed towards the kitchen.

Catherine went behind the screen and moved the tin bath to one side. She wondered if Matty would wish to bathe in the kitchen when they moved into the cottage after the wedding. She stood waiting clothed in her bodice and petticoat for Ivy to bring the dress that Ma had given her from her wardrobe, one she had worn when she was a young woman.

'There's a little bit of moth, but I've added some lace to cover it,' Ivy said.

'I hope you didn't bring the seams in too much,' Ma said. 'Catherine is in the family way.'

Ivy rounded on her.

'I can't believe you got yourself into trouble after what I said to you.'

'She'll be married within two days. It's completely different from your situ–'

'Hush,' Ivy said. 'You promised you'd never mention it again.'

'Len isn't here, is he?' Ma said.

'He has gone out.' Ivy helped Catherine put the dress on over her head, a chemise made from pale blue muslin and trimmed with lace. Catherine smoothed it down over her stomach while Ivy fastened the back. She felt better, like a bride should feel, she thought, enjoying the swish of the skirt as she swayed her hips.

'Marry in blue – love will be true,' Ivy said. 'Marry in May and rue the day.'

'Thank you, Ivy.' Ma said sarcastically.

'I married Len in May,' she went on.

'At least you can be thankful that you didn't end up an old maid, or even worse, in the workhouse. Well, we can't stop here all day. Catherine hasn't started on the supper yet.'

The thought of preparing food made her feel sick again, but on their return to the farm, she managed to cut up onions, fry some pork and add stock, carrots and potatoes to the pan, leaving it to simmer for a while.

Later, the Rooks settled down to eat.

'Thomas, Catherine and I had the good fortune of seeing Sir William today,' Ma said.

'Oh, not that lunatic.' Pa sat down at the table. 'He's making a right nuisance of himself.'

'He was riding a white horse,' Ma said.

'That belongs to Mr Francis – he's stolen it from him. He's a thief as well as a fraud.'

'I thought you said he was a generous man, Pa.'

'He gave me that impression, but I know now that it was false. I don't think he will come to anything.' Pa's spoon hovered above his bowl. 'According to the reports I've heard from the vicar and at the forge, he's a powerful preacher who twists his knowledge of the scriptures to his advantage. His apocalyptic visions terrify the poor and weak-minded, but they say that the "Lion of Canterbury" – yet another name that he once gave himself – struggles to recruit.'

'He had many followers with him – twenty or so?' Ma looked to Catherine for confirmation.

'I think there were more like thirty.' she said.

'They'll leave when they realise how deluded he is.'

'He can shoot the stars, remember,' Ma added. 'There must be something in it.'

'He discharges his pistols into the night sky to impress, but it's mere trickery, involving gunpowder and tow.' Pa turned to Catherine. 'I thought Matty would have taken you out, seeing it's a holiday.'

'That's what I thought too. Didn't I say so, Catherine?' Ma said.

Catherine nodded.

'Did you see him today?' Pa went on.

239

'Yes, Pa.'

'Is he well?' he enquired.

'He is indeed well, and looking forward to our wedding.' She glanced towards Ma, grateful to her for keeping quiet about Matty's exact whereabouts. Ma wouldn't want to worry her husband with the fact that they had seen Matty with Sir William.

'That's reassuring anyway.' Pa continued to eat, a troubled expression on his face.

'They won't disturb us here, will they?' Catherine asked. 'Those men and Sir William?' She shivered as she recalled the rick fire and the heat of the flames as the stable roof fell in. She had no wish to go through an experience like that again.

'It's true that they're very close to home. Sir William and his men slept in the barn at Bossenden Farm on Monday night, and they visited Selling after that, just down the road from here. When I saw Len this evening, he told me that Sir William had stopped at Dargate Common, where he took off his shoes and proclaimed, "I stand on my own bottom," another marker of his insanity. You mustn't worry, Catherine.'

'But some of those people are desperate. Who knows what they might do?'

'They're totally disorganised. If they so much as threaten to break the law, the squire will send to Canterbury for the army.'

She sat back and pulled at a loose thread on her sleeve. It began to unravel along with her joyful anticipation of her forthcoming wedding. Pa had said everything would be well, but she wasn't convinced. She uttered a silent prayer: *Matty,*

240

please come home.

When she had done the dishes, she went out, hoping to find him. She called on the Carters at Toad's Bottom.

'I'm sorry for intruding,' she said when George opened the door to her.

'You're looking for Matty? Well, I believe he's gone to find a ring to present to you at the church.'

'Who is that?' Ma Carter's voice drifted on a cool draught of air from the kitchen beyond.

'It's Catherine,' George called back.

'Show her to me.'

'Yes, ducks. Come this way.' He showed her through. 'I'm afraid you'll find her much altered.'

'Mrs Carter?' Catherine said. She was lying on the mattress with blankets covering her up to her chin.

'I wish to give you my blessing, my dear,' she whispered. 'I fear that I'm not long for this world.'

'Please don't say that.'

'One day you'll be well again,' George cut in.

'I give you my best wishes for the future and I trust that you and Matty will care for each other kindly, as George and I have done.' She coughed.

'Don't tire yourself. I was telling Catherine how Matty's gone to look for a ring. Ma offered to give him hers, but he turned it down. It was my mother's, God rest her soul. I offered him a big brass curtain ring, but he wouldn't take it.' George changed the subject abruptly. 'Here, Catherine, let me give you some eggs to take back to the farm.'

'Oh no, there's no need for that.' She thought of the Carters' hungry children and their flock of

241

scraggy hens.

'We have more than enough for now, and your new poults aren't yet ready to lay. Wait here and I'll fetch them.'

She said farewell to Ma Carter then stood on the doorstep until he returned with three brown eggs which she placed carefully in her pocket.

'Ta,' she said. 'Did you mean what you said about Matty and the ring?'

'I'm sorry,' he said, shaking his head. 'I had to say something. I didn't want to raise Ma's hopes about Matty bringing Jervis home.'

'They are both with Sir William,' Catherine said. 'I spoke with Matty this afternoon.'

'At least they are together, and we have some idea where they are,' George said, stroking his chin. 'You are goin' straight back to the farm now?'

She nodded. Straight after she'd found Matty, she thought.

Having wished George goodnight, she walked to the cottage to see if Matty had gone there and then on to the Woodsman's Arms. There was no sign of him, so she decided to carry on towards Faversham, but it soon became clear that she was on a hiding to nothing. As the sky grew dimpsy, she gave up looking and turned back on herself, but it seemed an awful long way back to the farm by road when there was a short cut through the woods. She tried to forget Matty's earlier warning about walking alone. What harm could there be in taking it?

She ducked onto the footpath and made her way past a thicket of elder and blackthorn where a bramble snagged at her skirts. When she stopped to disentangle the thorns from the cloth, she heard the crack of a twig underfoot and the rustle of an animal – a deer or a badger – passing through the underwood, making the glossy chestnut leaves tremble. There was another crack.

She picked up a heavy stick.

'Who goes there?' she said. There was no answer, but she was sure someone was there. She could smell them. 'Show yourself!'

'I shan't,' a voice came back.

'You must make yourself known to me.'

'I'm not that stupid,' the voice answered, and she knew for certain then as a hooded figure stepped out from behind the nearest tree that it was Jervis. She caught the glint of a knife in his hand and shuddered.

'What is it that you want?' she asked, trying to control the quaver in her throat.

'I seek revenge.'

'I have no quarrel with you.'

'Except that you are a Rook–'

'She i'n't no Rook,' another voice cut in. It was Drusilla. 'She's Hadington's bastard and no better than us, even though she goes around pretendin' that she is. What shall we do with her now that we've found her here? It's a lonely place. No one would know until they found her body in the mornin'.'

'Would you harm a young woman and her unborn child?' Catherine said quickly. She held the stick out in front of her.

'You're with child? And not yet married,' Drusilla mocked. 'Well, well, well. Shall we take her hostage and deliver her to Sir William? It would mark the beginnin'.'

'The beginnin' of what?' Jervis said.

Catherine took a silent step back, and another.

'The fight, you dolt, the battle of all battles that will bring us riches and power.'

Catherine turned and ran.

'Quickly,' Drusilla exclaimed. 'Get after her, Jervis.'

Catherine heard footsteps behind her. She threw down her stick. There was a shout as someone tripped over it.

'Don't speak of this if you want your lover back in one piece,' Drusilla screamed after her.

'We'll never catch her. Who is the dolt now?' Jervis shouted, his voice fading into the distance as Catherine sprinted towards the village. She dodged the trees and branches and took random turns until she reached the road where she happened upon one of the young Carters who had a bag slung over his shoulder, just like Matty used to when he was a boy.

'Are you all right, miss?' he asked as she stood with her hands on her hips, trying to catch her breath. 'You look like you've seen a ghost.'

'Perhaps I have,' she said.

His eyes widened like saucers.

'Promise me you won't go into the woods. There is danger lurking there.'

'I promise, miss,' he said warily.

'Tell your friends.' She put her hand in her pocket and felt for the eggs, finding a slimy well of yolk and white mixed with broken shell. 'Now, run along home.'

She hastened back to the farm, touching her

belly and thanking the Lord that she'd been spared, but what about Matty? He wanted to get away from Sir William, but would his followers let him go? It was on the tip of her tongue to warn Pa and the others, but she didn't dare open her mouth for fear that Jervis and Drusilla would carry out their threat.

She went to bed, but she couldn't sleep. She'd made the wrong decision in keeping the incident in the woods to herself. First thing in the morning, she got up and spoke to her father before he left the house.

'I should have said last night, but I thought I was protecting Matty by keeping my own counsel. Now I've had time to think, I've realised that I was wrong. Sir William's followers are out to do mischief. Jervis and Drusilla accosted me and they would have carried me off if I hadn't run for my life.'

Pa frowned as she went on, 'I'm afraid for Matty and everyone else.'

'I'll spread the word in the village,' he said. 'Don't leave the farm today, and keep John with you. Have you seen Matty?'

'Not since he was at the Woodsman's Arms. George says he's gone to look for a ring – for the wedding tomorrow.' Catherine felt uncomfortable, using George's untruth to cover for the real reason for Matty's absence: that he was with Sir William.

'Well, that's good news,' Pa said more cheerfully.

But Matty didn't turn up at the farm for the third morning running and Catherine was forced into confessing the truth about his errand to find a ring. Pa was more intent on finding Matty than scolding her, and it was decided that George should go to Faversham to enlist Stephen in the search. Ma released Catherine from her duties in the house so that she could take care of John and the sheep. Pa went off to make his own enquiries as to the whereabouts of his future son-in-law.

When he returned to the farm that evening, Catherine was waiting for him.

'Did you find him?' she asked.

'No, but he will return,' Pa said. 'You have to believe it, Catherine. We all do. We're all depending on this marriage going ahead.'

'You don't think something's happened to him?'

'You know what he's like – he can look after himself. Stay strong – he has too much at stake not to turn up at the altar tomorrow morning.'

'There are extra slops for you this morning.' Catherine emptied the bucket into the trough. 'I'm getting married' – she glanced down at the slight swell of her stomach – 'and not a moment too soon.'

An elderly Margaret snuffled and slurped at her breakfast, seemingly unimpressed.

Having let the hens out into the sunshine, Catherine ran inside to wash and dress. She braided her hair, put on the dress that Ivy had altered, and picked up the small posy of blue cornflowers that she'd made up the night before and kept in a vase on the dressing table. Before she left her room, she glanced out across the orchards where the last of the pale pink and white blossom was drifting from the trees. The bines were spiralling up the chestnut poles in the hop garden and the woods beyond were swathed with green. She touched the third finger of her left hand, and prayed that Matty would come.

Downstairs, she bumped into John who was fumbling one-handed with the button on his collar.

'Let me help you.' She reached up to fasten the button before planting a kiss on his cheek. 'Dear John, how I wish I could have seen you married.' She wondered if he ever thought of Mary – she doubted it. 'Are you ready to go out?'

'I'm hungry,' he said.

'I know. Let's go and see what Ma says.' She hesitated. 'Have you seen Matty?'

John nodded.

'He's with the sheep?'

'I've seen him.'

'Are you sure?'

'I've seen him,' he repeated and a wave of relief washed through her. She shouldn't have worried. Matty had promised her that he'd be here and he'd kept his word. He would get on with his chores until it was time for him to prepare for the wedding and then they would have the rest of the day together.

Their cottage was ready. She had fresh bread and a sheep's head in the pot in the kitchen at the farm that would be cooked to take with them. The bedsheets were clean and scattered with handfuls of dried rose petals.

There was a knock at the door. John went to answer it.

'Good morning, John. Is your pa around? I

need to speak with him.'

Catherine took over. It was Mr Nobbs, looking grim-faced.

'He's somewhere outside,' she said.

'I'll make my own way.' He touched his cap.

She closed the door.

'What did that man want?' Ma said, rushing down the stairs. 'How dare he come here, trying to snatch the tenancy out from under our feet!'

'I don't know. He asked to speak to Pa.'

'You are an insufferable child. Why didn't you question him?' Ma hurried outside without giving her time to respond.

'Ma has a nose for gossip,' Catherine said wryly as she sat John down at the kitchen table and served him a slice of bread and butter, but when she heard her mother's voice shouting from the farmyard, she pulled a shawl over her shoulders and took John out with her. She trod carefully, avoiding the patch of mud around the water pump.

'Murder, you say,' Ma said. 'That's too close to home.'

'It's all right, Margaret,' Pa said, but it wasn't all right, Catherine thought as he went on, 'there's no reason to worry unnecessarily. The magistrate has sent to Canterbury for the army to come and restore order.'

'The squire and some of his men have taken shots at the rioters,' Mr Nobbs said. 'It's a most terrible thing that's happened.'

'Who's involved?' Pa asked. 'I assume that Sir William has had a hand in it.'

'I'm afraid so. He seduced four of Mr Curling's

labourers into joining his march–'

'Is that Mr Curling from Hernhill?' Pa cut in.

'That's right. Then Mr Curling spoke to Doctor Poore, who made out a warrant for the arrest of Sir William. He sent John Mears, the constable at Boughton, to execute the warrant, so he, his assistant and his brother set out for Bossenden Farm in the early hours.'

'Oh my,' Ma gasped.

'That's where it's said that Sir William shot the brother, Nicholas, dead.'

Catherine shuddered. She could hear the sharp crack of the gun and smell the acrid scent of gunpowder. She knew of Mears, but not his brother, and she could barely imagine how the family must be feeling, their lives torn apart by some madman's impulse.

'Catherine, close your ears. You shouldn't have to bear this kind of news on the morning of your wedding,' Ma said.

'No one should have to bear this on any day,' Pa commented. 'It's a tragedy.'

'I've come to warn you that there may be trouble later,' Mr Nobbs added. 'We must protect ourselves and our property from these marauders.'

'Thank you,' Pa said.

'I must go. Let's hope that everything is back to normal by the end of the day. I have every confidence that Sir William will be arrested very soon.'

'Where is he?' Pa asked.

'He's on the move with his men. He could be anywhere. Keep your men on guard and your family close. That's my advice. Oh, and send a boy with word of any intelligence that you might hear, and I will do the same. Let us pray for peace.'

'Indeed,' Pa said, then wished him good day.

'What are we to do?' Ma said once Mr Nobbs had gone. 'George and the men will keep watch on the house and yard for today. I don't think I should leave the farm.'

'You must. You're giving Catherine away.'

'The wedding can still go ahead – John can do the honours. My place is here. It wouldn't be right to delay the marriage, considering the circumstances. I'm sorry,' he added, turning to Catherine. 'I'll be with you in spirit.'

'I understand,' she said with a heavy heart. 'I must go and give Matty the news.'

'Don't,' said Ma. 'You'll see him soon enough at the altar.'

Catherine ignored her.

'I don't know where you'll find him,' Pa said.

'John says he's with the sheep.' She hitched up her skirts and ran down through the gateway into the fields. 'Matty.' she called. 'Matty!' She stopped halfway down the meadow. The sheep were grazing in the far corner, but there was no sign of him. Her heart plummeted like a bird of prey falling onto a rabbit. She should have thought. For John, one day rolled into the next, and one meal into another. He had remembered seeing Matty, but when?

She raced back to the farmyard where Ma and Pa were in conversation with George.

'Where is he? Tell me you've seen him,' she begged.

'Don't worry,' George said awkwardly. 'He'll be at home puttin' on his Sunday best.'

'But have you seen him with your own eyes?' Her mouth ran dry. She felt choked with fear. They knew now that Sir William was capable of murder. There was no saying what he might do next.

'To be truthful, no, I haven't, but it isn't right to assume the worst. There's nothing he wants more than to be married to you. It's all he's talked about for ages.'

'I know Matty. He'll be at the church,' Pa said.

'He'd better be, or there'll be a murder here at Wanstall Farm,' Ma said.

'Margaret, hush. It isn't right to make light of the fact an innocent man has been killed.'

'Don't tell me to be quiet. I've struggled to accept Matty into the family, but now that I have, it's all going wrong. He's with Sir William and his men when he should be here with us.'

'He'd be here if he could,' Catherine interrupted. 'I'm scared that he fears for his life and mine – if he walks away.'

'He wouldn't put up with that,' Ma said.

'He'd do anything to find his brother.'

'Hold your tongues.' Pa pressed his fingers to his temples. 'I need to think.'

'I'll check at the cottage. If he isn't there, I'll send Stephen out again to look for him,' George ventured.

'Stephen is here?' Catherine exclaimed.

'I fetched him from Faversham to help us find Matty. He's stayin' on at the cottage to spend time with his mother and see his brother married.'

Of course, she thought.

'George,' Pa cut in, 'go quickly and get Matty

251

to the church by hook or by crook. Ma, you take John and Catherine there while I call the men in from the fields to arm themselves with whatever comes to hand. That way, we'll be prepared to defend the farm should Sir William and his gang head this way.'

'You will be careful,' Ma said.

'Of course,' he said. 'Hurry along now.'

Catherine walked to the church with John and Ma. There were more people on the street than usual, as if they had been driven to find safety in numbers. The dame school was closed – Old Faggy had stopped outside one of the cottages near the forge to talk to one of her many acquaintances.

'Good morning, Mrs Rook, Miss Rook and Master Rook,' she said. 'It's a beautiful day for a wedding, but have you heard the news?'

'Mr Nobbs came to the farm earlier, Mrs Fagg,' Ma said. 'A constable's brother has been murdered.'

'That's right, he's been shot and stabbed through the heart, and now the troops are on their way from Canterbury, and Mr Knatchbull, a magistrate from Faversham, is riding hard to Boughton with a posse of seven constables.'

'How do you know of this?' Catherine asked quickly.

'Farmer Curling's son rode through Overshill a short while ago. He stopped briefly at the forge – his horse had twisted a shoe.'

'It never used to be like this around here,' Ma complained.

'Times change,' said Old Faggy. 'I shall walk

252

with you to the church. I love a good wedding.'

They walked on, collecting a gaggle of villagers who were eager to see the bride and groom on their way. When they reached the church, Emily was waiting at the gate.

'Catherine, how are you?' she said, stepping towards her.

'I didn't think you'd come. You've taken me by surprise.'

'Stephen persuaded me to put in an appearance. Don't think I've forgiven you yet.' She smiled. 'But I am here, and I do wish you all the best for the future.'

Catherine glanced down at Emily's figure. 'You are with child?'

She nodded shyly. 'We will be welcoming our son or daughter within the next three months.'

'How wonderful,' Catherine marvelled.

'We can talk about it later. In the meantime there is the more pressing matter of your absent groom. Stephen has gone to find him.' Emily lowered her voice and added, 'You see how he'll still do anything for you.'

Her words stung a little, reminding Catherine of why they had fallen out.

'Catherine, come here,' Ma called. 'The vicar is waiting.'

The Reverend Browning was at the church door, dressed in his robes.

'Ah, the bride is here, but alas, where is the groom?' he said brightly. 'It seems that he may have jilted you at the altar.'

'Please don't say that,' Ma said. 'I am in turmoil.'

'Matty will come,' Catherine said. 'He won't let me down.'

'He's here,' someone called from the gate.

Her heart lifted and she raised her eyes towards the skies, but her relief didn't last, because it was Stephen, not Matty, who appeared, almost doubled up as he tried to catch his breath.

'What news?' she asked. 'Where is your brother?'

'I'm sorry,' he panted. 'I've run almost all the way from the top of the vale. There's been some kind of skirmish, and now Sir William is at Fairbrook. You might have heard already that Nicholas, the brother of Constable Mears, has been shot. Sir William asked him if he were the constable and he said yes, which wasn't true. Since then, he has tried to recruit more men and is heading for the osier beds to make a stand against whomsoever takes a stand against him.' Stephen's statement seemed deliberately garbled, as if by creating confusion, he'd be able to keep the worst from her.

'What else? Please don't leave me in the dark out of respect for my feelings. I need to know.'

'I ran into Drusilla. She's with them. And Jervis.' He lowered his gaze, unable to meet Catherine's eye. 'Matty is with them too. I'm sorry.'

'Why haven't you fetched him here?' Ma said.

'Because I don't know exactly where he is,' Stephen said. 'Drusilla gave me false information as to his whereabouts.'

'Matty will marry her today. He has to,' Ma said.

'I can't wait for more than another half-hour,' the vicar said. 'I have a meeting and sermons to prepare. They don't write themselves, more's the pity.'

'Let's meet back here this afternoon,' Ma said. 'That way, it is of little inconvenience to you.'

'This is most irregular. No, I cannot do it. The law states that the wedding must be performed between the morning hours of eight and twelve. However, on seeing your distress, my dear ladies, I will agree to stay in the vestry where I can work in peace until midday. If you can deliver the groom by then...'

'Oh, thank you, vicar. I'm most grateful,' Ma said.

'Let me know when Mr Carter arrives.' Reverend Browning walked up the aisle and disappeared through the door into the vestry.

'I'll go and search again,' Stephen said. 'Perhaps I can persuade Mr Rook to lend me one of the horses.'

'Yes, I'm sure he'll lend you one gladly,' Catherine said, almost faint with panic, not about whether or not the wedding would go ahead, but for the safety of her beloved. 'Please, hurry.'

'I'll do my best,' Stephen said. 'I'll see you all later.'

Catherine went inside the church with Ma, John, Emily and Mrs Fagg. She turned her eyes to the cross on the altar and prayed as hard as she could, but Matty didn't come and neither did Stephen.

'You should go home,' Emily said quietly. 'You cannot be married today.'

'Come on, daughter, and you, John,' Ma said. 'We will not stay any longer to be made objects of ridicule. What was Matty thinking of going off with that man?'

'He must be in a terrible predicament,' Catherine insisted. 'He would have been here if he could.' Ma took her hand and almost dragged her from the church and down the path between the graves.

'I always said he'd let you down, but when did you ever listen to me? Now you can see why I tried so hard to get Hector for you. He would have turned up. His father would have made him.'

'It wouldn't have done any good for the farm,' Catherine argued. 'What does Hector know about growing hops and barley?'

'He could apply his understanding of managing a congregation to looking after the sheep,' Ma said seriously. 'Where are you going?' she added.

'To find Matty, of course.'

'Oh no, you're coming home with me and John. It's far too dangerous to be wandering about the countryside, and besides, how will he find you if you're out searching for him and he comes home?'

That made sense, Catherine thought, even though little else did at the moment.

'As soon as he turns up, I will personally drag him to the church and make him marry you. I hope he's all right.'

'I didn't think you cared. You've always hated him.'

'Oh, I don't like him at all. This is a completely unsuitable match, but I don't give a sixpence that you will marry and live in abject misery for the rest of your lives. What matters is that he makes

256

an honest woman of you when you're carrying his child, and more importantly, save Wanstall Farm for the Rooks.'

'I beg your pardon?' Catherine said, her cheeks burning with anger and resentment.

'You heard me.'

'I will be a Carter, and proud of it.'

'But there will be Rooks at the farm as long as Pa and I are alive. That's all that matters to me.'

Catherine stared at her. Now that her marriage to Matty might not be the saving grace the Rooks had hoped for, Ma was showing her true colours. She was a mean and selfish woman, and Catherine despised her from that moment. Ma didn't care that Matty was in danger. She didn't care for him at all. Her professed dislike of her betrothed wounded Catherine deeply. She had nothing more to say to her.

They returned to the house where Pa greeted them, his brow etched with worry. If he noticed the tension between the two women, he didn't mention it.

'Stephen's borrowed one of the horses. George is beside himself. I've tried to reassure him, but it's no use. When the miller delivered a sack of flour, he told George that he'd seen a detachment of the 45th Infantry marching along the London Road, and now he's convinced there's going to be a fight.'

'Do you think so?' Catherine asked. What hope did a motley crowd of labourers with Sir William in charge have against a group of highly trained soldiers?

'The sight of the army will send them scattering

across the countryside. They'll run for it. You mark my words.'

'Sir William has a pistol. He used it to shoot the constable's brother,' Ma said.

'I don't think one pistol will be a match for the infantry and their guns, do you?

'I'm hungry,' John said suddenly, reminding them of his presence.

'Come on, son, let's eat and then we'll patrol the farm.' Pa patted him on the shoulder. 'I'm sure Ma will have a cold pie and pickles in the pantry'

'How do you know that?' Ma said.

'Because I looked.'

'There's a sheep's head in the pot,' Catherine said, feeling sick at the thought of the soft meat falling from the bone. She turned and headed inside.

'Aren't you joining us?' Pa said.

'Let her be,' she heard Ma say. 'If she wants to starve herself to death, it's up to her.'

Upstairs, Catherine sat on the edge of the bed, resting her hands on her belly as she waited for news. Two hours passed before she heard the sound of a horse's hooves. She ran down to the yard to find Stephen dismounting from the cob that Pa used for pulling the cart. The mare was puffing and blowing, and foaming with sweat.

'Where is he?' she cried. 'Have you found him?'

'I have.' He was grim-faced as he turned and took both her hands.

'Tell me. Is he well? Why isn't he with you?'

'I'm sorry, Catherine,' he said.

Chapter Eleven

The Battle of Bossenden

Pa, George and Ma, having heard the commotion, came quickly to hear what Stephen had to say.

'There's been a battle over in Bossenden Wood. Matty has been taken prisoner at the Red Lion.'

'We must go to him,' Catherine said, trying to take the cob by the reins.

'Let's hear the details first,' Pa said. 'Forewarned is forearmed. Fetch the lad a drink, Ma. Not small beer. Something stronger. He looks as if he's had quite a shock. George, turn the horse out, let it roll and have some grass. Catherine, restrain yourself.'

Stephen sat on the bench by the woodpile. Catherine knelt in the grass alongside him. Pa stood with his fingers through his braces, tugging on them as if to hold himself upright. Ma returned swiftly from the house with a bottle of spirits. She pulled out the cork and handed the bottle to Stephen, who glugged back the contents. He rested his hands on his thighs and leaned forwards, coughing like a dying man.

'That sounds like it has bones in it.' Pa retrieved the bottle from his grasp. 'Now, tell us everything you know.'

'Go on, my son.' George offered Ma the re-

259

maining space on the bench, but she turned it down with a shake of her head.

'I hope I say this right,' Stephen began. 'It goes like this. Knatchbull – he's the magistrate – and a party of men followed Sir William to the osier beds.'

Catherine knew where the osiers were – they were clumps of coppiced willow grown for making withies, for thatching and basket-making.

Stephen continued, 'They didn't stay there all that long. Sir William gave a blast on his bugle to call his followers together and they returned to Bossenden. Knatchbull left some of his men to keep a watch on them from a distance while he met Doctor Poore at the inn at Dunkirk. By this time, the soldiers were there – a hundred of them, can you believe? Anyway, Doctor Poore read the Riot Act to the crowd outside the inn and the soldiers separated into two groups. One party entered the wood through Old Barn Lane. The other, led by a captain by the name of Reid, made their way into the wood further east.'

'And?' Pa said, when he paused for a moment.

'Something went wrong. A lieutenant who was with Captain Reid's party moved too quickly and was shot as he advanced to arrest Sir William.'

'Shot? Oh no.' Catherine pressed her fingers to her lips.

'Sir William fell in a hail of bullets. His men, armed only with staves of flayed oak, fought fiercely, so it is said. Eight are dead. Seven are injured. The rest have been rounded up and taken prisoner.'

'Matty?' she whispered hoarsely.

He nodded. 'And Jervis.'

'What were they doing there?' Pa exclaimed. 'Why did Matty risk everything, and on his wedding day?'

'How many times have I told him to mind his own business? All I wanted was for him to find Jervis so he could see his poorly ma, not get involved with Sir William's cause.' Tears rolled down George's wizened cheeks. 'Our family is ruined.'

'I can understand why Jervis would join him,' Catherine said, remembering how he had pushed his younger brother forwards at the harvest supper to denounce the arrival of the threshing machine. Jervis had always been on the edge of society. 'But Matty wasn't involved. He already knew that there was something not right about Sir William's claim that he was immortal.'

'I'm sure that Matty's capture is a mistake on some young constable's part,' Stephen said. 'Your father will have a word with the magistrate and he'll be freed by the end of the day.'

'We'll have to see about that,' Pa said. 'Where did you say he was being held?'

'The Red Lion at Boughton,' Stephen confirmed. 'The prisoners and the slain have been taken there.'

'Then we must go right now,' Pa said. 'We'll take the cart and one of the other horses. Sunny will do.'

'I'll come with you,' Catherine said.

'I don't think that's wise.'

'I'll drive,' George said. 'I need to see my sons.'

'John will have to come with us as well,' Ma said. 'I'm not going to miss out on the chance to see Sir William close up. Who knows? If Matty's wrong about him, we might be there in time to see him rise from the dead. I've seen him, and if he turns out to have been a liar, he'd be the most accomplished liar I've ever known.'

'That's a load of cock and bull,' Pa said as George walked away to fetch the harness and the fresh horse, a steady character who would be content to wait outside an inn for a while, as long as he had a nosebag.

They climbed onto the cart – George, Stephen, Pa, Ma, John and Catherine and three of the labourers, including one called Mr Lake whom Pa had recently taken on – and travelled through Overshill and on to Boughton, where it seemed as if the whole of England had descended. There were crowds of traders setting up their stalls of sherbets, pickled whelks, jellied eels, and penny pies; visitors laughing as if they were at a fair; mourners crying and comforting each other.

'What brings all these people here?' Catherine was sitting between Ma and Stephen in the middle of the cart on some old hessian sacking, but it did nothing to deaden the jolts as the wheels rolled through the ruts and potholes.

'They're coming to see for themselves that the great Sir William Courtenay is dead,' Stephen said. 'It's a momentous occasion.'

Catherine grimaced as he went on, 'You might judge that they are rather ghoulish in wanting to be part of history, but it's natural to be curious.'

'Of course it is,' Ma said. 'I'm here out of nat'ral curiosity, not ghoulishness as you put it, young man. Just imagine telling your grandchildren that you were there at the resurrection of the new Messiah.'

Catherine could hardly bear to look at her. How could she act so light of heart when men had been killed?

George dropped his passengers outside the Red Lion. Catherine pushed through the small crowd of people drinking beer to address the constable who was on guard at the door.

'Where are the prisoners?' she said urgently.

'They're in a room upstairs at the back, but you can't go up there, young lady,' he said, holding her by the arm as she made to head inside. 'We're waiting for the coroner to arrive, and to interview witnesses.'

She was so frantic to see Matty that she hardly heard what he was saying.

'I must get him out of there and take him home with me today.'

'There's no way that's going to happen,' the constable said harshly. 'Some of those men have committed a dreadful series of crimes. They have to remain locked up until the offenders have been identified so that justice can be served.'

Her eyes filled with tears.

'You might be able to see them from the yard through there, though.' The constable's voice softened. 'Is it your sweetheart who's up there?'

She nodded. 'I'm sure he's innocent. He wouldn't hurt anyone.'

'If I had a penny for everyone who's said that today, I'd be a wealthy man. I'm sorry. It's been a horrible day – I've lost two of my closest friends.' He cleared his throat. 'I hope for your sake that

263

he's freed without a stain on his character.'

'I beg you to let me see him. There must be a way–'

'Calm down, miss. You aren't the only one in a bind,' he interrupted. 'Every family in Boughton has been touched by this. If you want to catch a glimpse of your young man, go that way.'

She made her way to the yard at the rear of the inn and struggled through a wailing crowd of women and girls, the wives, sisters and children of the men who were being held upstairs. Shading her eyes, she looked up and caught sight of Matty's face pressed to the glass in a narrow window above.

'Don't worry, my love,' she shouted. 'You will soon be freed.'

'I'm sorry, ducky, but our menfolk aren't going anywhere soon,' an elderly woman said from beside her. 'That maniac who lies dead in the barn next door has had them snatched away from us. They'll all be hanged.'

'He's responsible for this,' another woman muttered. 'He's the one to blame.'

'My son is in that room. He has a wife and five children, and he helps me out whenever he can. I don't see how we'll survive without him,' the elderly woman said.

'You mustn't say that.'

'They're all doomed – I can feel it in my bones.'

'Well, I hope and pray that your bones are wrong,' Catherine said curtly.

The crowd shifted, allowing a constable through. He asked for one of them by name, and a woman of about thirty with long red hair pushed a pram

264

containing an infant towards him.

'What is it?' she said.

'I have to inform you that your husband has passed away as a consequence of the injuries he received earlier today. I'm sorry for your loss.' The constable, who was no older than Catherine, was crying.

The woman fell to her knees, wailing and beating her chest as the others crowded in to share her grief and offer their condolences, because the dead man was apparently well known and much liked. Biting back tears, Catherine turned away to find Ma at her shoulder.

'Oh, there you are,' she said. 'I couldn't find you. Have you found him?'

'He's up there with the other men.' She waved towards the window, but Matty had gone.

'Pa's trying to find one of the magistrates to speak to, and I've left John with Mr Lake. Will you come with me to view the body of Sir William?'

'I have no desire to do so—'

'You must come,' Ma caught her hand. 'I should be very afraid if he should rise from the dead and I was alone with him. Why, I wouldn't know what to say or do in that situation.'

'Who would?' Catherine said. 'It would be the rarest of miracles, and the unlikeliest.'

'But you can't deny the possibility.'

Catherine was unnerved by the gleam of anticipation in Ma's eyes. She knew why she was so desperate to see the body – if Sir William did prove to be immortal, she would be in possession of the greatest and juiciest piece of gossip that anyone from Overshill had ever had, and she would be able to feast on it for ever.

'I really don't want to go.' The less time she spent with Ma, the better, as far as she was concerned, but Ma was determined.

'We might come across someone who can help get your young man out of there.'

She'd do anything to that end, Catherine thought, and she reluctantly accompanied her mother to the barn that stood at the side of the inn.

A young man emerged, his pale face stained with tears.

'I shouldn't go in there if I was you. It's a shocking and pitiful sight to see our cousins' and brothers' broken bodies. Ladies, I beg you to reconsider.'

'Ignore him.' Ma pushed Catherine inside.

There were – she counted them – seven bodies lying on the ground, all with ghastly wounds. She retched at the stench of sweat, blood and other foul discharges that were soaking into the straw.

'This is a terrible sight, but one that must be endured, so we can report back,' Ma whispered. 'That one must be Sir William.' She pointed to the corpse that appeared like a giant compared with the rest. A woman was kneeling over the body, washing his face. 'He is of such fine countenance.'

'It can't be him,' Catherine said. 'He's shaven.'

'Look at the marks on his hands from the nails – it has to be him.' Ma gasped. 'Drusilla, is that you?'

The woman bathing Sir William's face looked

up, distraught. She was so overcome with grief that she showed no trace of recognition. She turned back and kissed the corpse.

'Give me a sign that you will soon return to us,' she begged. 'Give me a breath, anything, to show me that you are still living.'

Catherine gazed upon him. He was most definitely expired. There was a bullet wound in one shoulder and a bayonet wound starting from near his mouth and passing down his neck. His white smock was hanging behind him, steeped with blood and torn to shreds. Something flashed from the straw at his feet. She ducked down, picked it up and slipped it inside her dress.

'What's that?' Ma asked quickly.

'I thought I saw a coin, but it was nothing.' Catherine lied without effort. It was a man's gold ring with a jewel inset, and she didn't see why Ma, Drusilla or anyone else should try to claim it. She felt guilty stooping so low as to steal from a dead man, but Sir William owed her and Matty some kind of debt for his actions. If anybody offered to pay for a relic or souvenir of the man, she wasn't going to turn them down. The ring was insurance for their future.

'There you are,' she heard Pa say from the doorway. 'Ugh! What a picture of wretchedness!'

'What news do you have?' Catherine said, taking in a deep breath of fresh air as she stepped back outside with him.

'They won't let anybody go, but the magistrate, out of the goodness of his heart and knowing your situation, has agreed that you can see Matty. We must go straight there before they change their minds. Margaret, you'll have to wait down-stairs with John and Mr Lake.'

Catherine took Pa's arm and they pushed their way through the crowd of weeping women in the yard and up the steps to the landing, where another constable was guarding a door.

'That's where Lieutenant Bennett's body lies. You need to come this way.' He opened the door opposite.

'Prepare yourself.' Pa patted Catherine's hand, but there was nothing that could have prepared her for the number of prisoners, young men in the main, who were crammed together in the stuffy makeshift prison. Some were crying. Some were injured. One lay lifeless on the floor.

'I'll arrange for the body to be moved,' the constable said. 'Don't be long, ma'am. I don't want all and sundry thinking we've set a precedent, letting you up here.'

Someone swore.

'How do they do it? Why do the Rooks always end up getting special favours?'

'Jervis,' Catherine said, turning to find him sitting on the floor in the corner. 'Your father and Stephen are outside.'

'Why haven't they bin allowed in then?' he demanded.

'Hey, that's enow,' Pa said. 'If I can do anything to help you, I will – for your father's sake, not yours.'

'My dearest Catherine.' Matty came up to her and took her in his arms, wrapping her in his scent of woodsmoke and musk. 'I never meant to put you through this.'

She looked up and stroked the tears from his face.

'I should have carried you across the threshold by now.'

'Why didn't you come back to Overshill?' she said softly. 'That's all you had to do.'

'Sir William said if any of us wished to go home, we could, but if we deserted him, he'd follow us to the furthermost part of hell and invoke fire and brimstone from heaven upon us. He threatened me and then said he'd set out to harm you. I was scared witless.' Matty paused. 'You know that he killed a constable?'

Catherine said 'It was the constable's brother,' aware that Pa was listening intently to their conversation. She felt sick.

'He shot him, wounded him with a sword, kicked him and ordered us to throw him into the ditch, which we did because none of us dared to cross him after that. Then we went to buy bread and cheese, and returned to the wood. At about seven in the morning, he gave the last sacrament. He told us he had come down to earth on a cloud, and on a cloud one day he would be removed from us. Neither bullets nor weapons could injure him or us, and if ten thousand soldiers came, they'd fall dead at his command. I didn't believe anything he said any more, but I felt safer with him than away.

'We went to see Mr Francis, because Sir William wanted to make peace with his old friend, but all he did was give him gin and water, and send him on his way.'

'Oh, Matty, couldn't you have escaped from

him then?' Catherine asked.

He shook his head.

'After we left the osier bed and headed back to Bossenden Wood, I tried to give him the slip, but Jervis had his eye on me and told Sir William.'

'I never,' Jervis interrupted from the floor.

'He set one of the men on me, gave me a good hiding.' Matty raised the front of his shirt to reveal a livid bruise across his stomach. Catherine reached out and touched it with her fingertips.

'It's all right,' he said bravely. 'It doesn't hurt much.'

'You have blood on your hands,' she observed.

'I tried to help the soldier.' He turned his hands over to reveal his palms. 'This is his blood.'

'What happened in the woods exactly?' Pa asked.

'We ended up in the chestnut underwood, which Sir William thought would provide us with a little cover.' He gave a wry laugh. 'So much for that. It was barely up to our shoulders.'

'Go on,' Pa said when Matty hesitated.

'Sir William promised us glory and conquest,' he began again.

'I was up for the fight. We all were,' Jervis joined in.

'Speak for yourself, brother,' Matty said angrily.

'I'll do that. It's every man for himself,' Jervis said.

'A gentlemen rode up to us and told Sir William, "Desist, do not lead these poor men to destruction," but our leader called out, "Come on, my brave fellows, keep close." One of the soldiers moved forwards – Sir William shot him.

A private levelled his piece and shot Sir William by return.' Matty voice quavered. 'And then all hell broke loose. I tried to stop Jervis aiming his pistol at the man I now know as Catt, but it went off.'

'That's a lie,' Jervis growled.

'Well, I know which of you I'm more inclined to believe,' Pa said.

'There were guns firing in all directions.' Matty dipped his head as though he was trying to fend off flying shot. 'Sir William had told us that none of us would be harmed, but people were falling to the ground, wounded and screaming.' He frowned. 'We didn't understand it. It was such a shock that when the major ordered us to stop fighting, we didn't put up any resistance.'

'So you didn't hurt anyone?' Catherine said.

'No, I swear I didn't. I wouldn't. But I'm in a lot of trouble. I'm not sure I'm ever going to get back to Overshill.'

'Why, when you haven't done anything wrong?'

'I believe I shall be implicated in the murders of Lieutenant Bennett and the man called Catt – the one who came to assist the soldiers in catching Sir William – as will my brother.' Matty turned and looked towards Jervis. 'We'll both go down.'

'Not if I have my way,' Jervis hissed. 'If I should hang for this, I'll make damn sure that you do too.'

'Let's have no talk of hanging,' Pa cut in.

'There was a woodcutter in the clearing. I reckon he saw something. Maybe he could act as my witness,' Matty said.

'And mine as well,' Jervis added.

271

'I'll find him,' Catherine said.

'We'll see what we can do,' Pa said.

'You must go now,' the constable interrupted. 'I can't allow you to stay here any longer.'

Pa took Catherine's hand. 'You heard what the man said. We must leave.'

'Let me say goodbye.' She darted forwards and kissed Matty on the lips, her heart breaking at the thought of leaving him behind. 'I'll be back as soon as I can.'

'Goodnight, my love,' he said faintly.

She turned and followed Pa through the inn and back onto the street.

'I'm not coming home until I've found this woodcutter that Matty speaks of,' she said.

'Oh no, I'll send Stephen and one of the lads.'

'I have to go. How can I rest with him locked up here, wrongly accused?' She stared into Pa's eyes. 'He didn't do it, Pa.'

'I know that, and tomorrow the rest of the world will know it too. The witness will be able to give a statement in favour of his innocence and he will be released. Come home now. George is waiting over there with the cart.'

Pa helped her into the back where Ma was lying on the hessian sacks with the smelling salts pressed to her nose. Of the three labourers who'd gone to Boughton with them, only Mr Lake had reappeared, bringing John with him. John slumped down beside Ma while Mr Lake sat opposite Catherine and nodded off with his chin on his chest.

'Where's Stephen?' Catherine asked. 'Shouldn't we wait for him?'

'He's taken Sir William's horse to the farm,' George said. 'It's lame and useless as it is – he offered to take it off the innkeeper's hands to save him the expense of stablin' it. I hope you don't mind, Thomas.'

'No, that's fine with me.'

'Oh, I am quite overcome,' Ma cried. Whether or not it had anything to do with the thought of Sir William's horse taking advantage of the Rooks' hospitality, Catherine wasn't sure. 'I can't take any more.'

'We've spoken to Matty and Jervis,' Pa said, ignoring his wife's woe.

'Are they hurt?' George asked as he took up the reins.

'They have a few bruises, nothing serious.'

'Thank God for small mercies. I'll be able to give their ma the good news.'

'It isn't all good, I'm afraid. The coroner, Mr De La Saux, arrives tomorrow for the inquests. The prisoners will remain locked up while he decides which of them goes to trial. George, I'm obliged to warn you that Matty and Jervis may be implicated in the shooting of two men.'

'Both of them? How can that be? I can believe it of one, but not the other.' George flicked the whip across the horse's rump to hurry it along. It kicked up its heels in annoyance, jolting the cart. 'This will turn our lives upside down. How will I tell the missus?'

'I don't think there's any need to reveal more than the bare bones to her as yet,' Pa said. 'The coroner has still to discover the truth of what went on up at Bossenden today.'

'I shall never forgive Matty for this. He's put our daughter through hell,' Ma said, her words raising Catherine's hackles.

'I am not your daughter,' she cut in, but Pa ignored her, saying, 'That wasn't his intention.'

'He can't possibly marry into our family after this – we can't expect Squire Temple to favour a criminal for the tenancy of Wanstall Farm.'

'He i'n't a criminal, Margaret. We must be patient and not jump to conclusions.'

'Oh, you infuriate me. You're blinded by your loyalty to the Carters.'

'Mind your tongue,' Pa growled. 'George, I promise that I'll do everything in my power to make sure justice is done.'

'What can you do, little man?' Ma mocked. 'You have no influence with anyone of any standing in the parish.'

'Not wishin' to come between husband and wife, I'd like to say that I'm very grateful to you for your faith in my boy, Tom,' George shouted above the clippety clop of the horse's hooves.

The travellers fell silent for the rest of the journey back to Overshill. When they returned to the farm, they found Stephen had tied Sir William's horse up outside the stables. He held a knife in one hand and the horse's foot was caught between his knees.

'What news?' he asked, looking up at the sound of the cart.

Pa gave him a brief explanation of Matty's predicament.

'I thought you'd go and find this witness. You can take Mr Lake here.' He banged on the side of the cart and the labourer jerked awake.

'Please, let me unsee what I've seen today,' he groaned, rubbing at his eyes.

'I need you and Stephen to search the woods,' Pa said, helping him down. 'When you find him, you have to persuade him to give evidence on Matty's behalf. Arrange for him to meet me at the Red Lion in the morning.'

'How do we know that we can trust this fellow?' Stephen said.

'Tell him I'll pay him for his time.' Pa turned and went indoors with Ma and John. Mr Lake took a drink and washed his face at the pump, giving Catherine the chance to have a quiet word with Stephen, who was tearing up some hessian into strips.

'I need you to take me with you to find the woodcutter,' she said.

He gazed at her.

'Oh no, your pa wouldn't like that. It isn't safe for a woman–'

'It isn't safe for anyone out there, but Sir William is dead and most of the people involved in the riot have been rounded up. I'm not asking you. I'm telling you.'

'You'll have to cover yourself,' he said eventually.

'I'll fetch my cloak.'

'A beer and some bread would be good. I haven't eaten today.'

'Of course.'

'Are you sure about this? I don't want you getting into trouble with your pa.'

'I shall be in more of a pickle if I don't get Matty away from the Red Lion,' she said, glancing down at her belly.

'Oh, I see how it is now.' He forced a small smile. 'All the more reason to solve my brother's predicament.'

'What about Jervis?'

'What about him? I gave up on him a long time ago.' Stephen stirred something in a bucket, a steaming porridge of bran. 'Let me finish this and then we'll go. We should aim to be back before dark.'

Catherine fetched her cloak and some food, then waited impatiently for Stephen to apply the poultice and wrap the horse's foot.

'How will that help?' she asked.

'It'll draw out the poison. Within a few days, the horse will be sound. I'm hoping that Mr Francis will relinquish any claim he has on it when he knows that she's hopping lame, and as Sir William is expired, it will naturally fall to me to take her on.'

'That's very – um, enterprising of you.'

'The horse deserves a good home after today's events. She's been scared almost to death' He pulled a piece of string from his pocket and tied it around the hessian to hold it to the foot before leading her into the stable. 'All she needs now is time to mend,' he said, returning outside. 'How are you?'

'I don't know.' She handed him the bread and beer. 'I haven't had time to think.'

'That's probably for the best.' He drained the tankard and tore at the crust before stuffing it into his mouth. 'I'm sorry. Emily's always nagging me about my manners, but I'm starving. And I can

276

see that you're in a hurry to leave before your pa can stop you.'

As they walked through the woods, it began to rain. Catherine noticed the handle of a knife sticking out from under Stephen's waistcoat. He had come prepared.

'Now that we are alone,' she began, 'I need to ask you something. I can trust you not to utter a word about this to anyone else?'

'Apart from my wife. I reserve the right to consult with her.'

'Of course.' She thought she could rely on Emily to be discreet.

'What is it?'

'I've obtained a ring that belonged to Sir William.'

'You mean the imposter, Mr Thom. When I dropped in to the forge to see Len on my way back from Boughton today, he told me that he was just a plain maltster and innkeeper from Cornwall. He wasn't a member of the nobility at all.'

'Then I'm glad, because I don't feel guilty any more, knowing that the ring probably wasn't rightfully his.'

'I wouldn't be at all surprised if he stole it,' Stephen observed. 'How did you get hold of it?'

'I found it in the straw in the barn at the inn. I picked it up because I felt that he owed me something for sweeping us up into this terrible mess. I'd like you to sell it for me – you meet so many more people than I do. I thought I'd use the money that we raise to help Matty and the other prisoners, along with their wives and children.'

'Of course I'll help, but what about your pa? He has contacts in Canterbury. He might be able to get you a better price.'

'I'd rather he had no knowledge of this for the present.' She wasn't sure that he'd approve of her intention. 'He has more than enough on his mind with the threat of losing the tenancy.'

'Can't you use the money to help save Wanstall Farm for the Rooks?' Stephen asked.

'There are many others in more desperate need of support than my family. Promise that you'll keep this between the two of us.'

'And Emily.'

'And Emily,' she echoed. She slipped her hand inside her blouse, pulled out the ring and pressed it into Stephen's hand. He took a leather purse from his pocket and, having made sure that no one was watching, tucked the ring inside.

'Now, where will we find this woodcutter?' she said.

The light began to fail and her hopes to fade as they trudged through the woods and down into the valley. An owl swooped down, pale and ghost-like among the darting silhouettes of the flying bats. She shuddered.

'I can smell smoke.' Stephen reached for her hand and she took it, grateful of his reassuring presence.

She glanced through the undergrowth, catching sight of the glow of a fire, like the mouth of the Devil. Who were the people who tended it? Was it wise to confront them?

'You wait here,' Stephen said, as though reading her mind.

'Oh no, I'm coming with you.'

They moved towards the fire and stepped out into the open, where three children were playing in the shelter of an oilcloth spread between two saplings. A woman was sitting on a log with an infant in her arms, while a man moved towards them. Catherine caught sight of the gleam of a blade in his hand.

'Stephen, he has a knife,' she muttered, but he walked on without hesitation.

'It's all right, sir. We come in peace. We're looking for a woodcutter by the name of Testament.'

'That's you, husband. What you bin up to this time?' the woman said.

'Nothing. What do you want with me?'

'We're looking for anyone who witnessed the battle at Bossenden,' Stephen said

'I told the constable, I was nowhere near. I don't want anything to do with it.'

'Please, sir,' Catherine said. 'My betrothed has been taken prisoner and falsely accused of murder.'

'That's his problem, miss. I won't be dragged into this sorry affair. I have a family.'

'Then you are perhaps in need of financial recompense for your statement,' she said boldly, taking a purse from her pocket. She had saved a small amount of money over the years from selling eggs, thinking that she would use it for emergencies.

The man stepped up closer and made to snatch the purse, but she held on to it.

'I'll pay you after you've spoken to the powers that be. I wasn't born yesterday.'

'What should I say?' The man's eyes glinted in the firelight.

'All I ask is that you tell exactly what you saw with your own eyes.'

'Describe your young man to me so I can see if I recognise him.'

'He's a little shorter than the gentleman beside me. He has brown hair down to his shoulders, the most wonderful green eyes and even features. He is very handsome.'

'Oh, Catherine, you are exaggerating,' Stephen mocked lightly. 'Sir, he is my brother, and there is some family resemblance. My other brother was also present at the battle. The older one aimed a pistol at the lieutenant. The younger tried to take the gun from him.'

'Ah yes, I know them now,' Mr Testament said. 'He called out, "Put it down, Jervis."'

'That's right,' Catherine said, encouraged. 'The man who shouted is Matty Carter.'

'Why should I help you?' he said, suddenly backing down. 'Why should I trust you? What if I make my statement and you disappear?'

'I'll pay you half of the money now and half afterwards,' Catherine said.

'Take the money, Mr Testament,' his wife joined in. 'You would turn down a piece of good fortune?'

'What if someone should accuse me of being involved in the battle by virtue of being a witness? I reckon it's best to lie low.'

'We have three mouths to feed as well as our own. You cut wood day in and day out while I scratch around for berries and honey. We have almost nothing, yet when an opportunity like this comes along, you're too scared to act on it. You're a coward. I don't know what I ever seen in you.'

'We can go with you to find a constable,' Catherine said.

'We can't be seen to be influencing a witness,' Stephen pointed out. 'Mr Testament will go to the Red Lion tomorrow in return for half the money. When Matty is freed, he will receive the remainder. We'll meet when it's all settled.' He gave him his address at the forge in Faversham. Mr Testament repeated it while his wife stood up and walked across with the baby sucking at her breast to receive the money.

Catherine counted the coins and handed half of them over. Mrs Testament stared at them as though she couldn't believe their luck.

'Come now,' Stephen said, taking hold of her hand again for the walk back through the woods.

'Do you think we can rely on him?' she asked when they were out of earshot.

'We know what he saw, and it's clear that he needs the money. Let's pray for the safe release of the innocent men and justice for the guilty.'

It was dark when they reached the farm. The candles were out, but as Catherine sneaked stealthily up the stairs, she was waylaid by Pa, who was still dressed in his day clothes.

'You went against me,' he said, catching her by the arm.

'Yes, Pa, and if you were in my shoes, you would have done exactly the same.' She glanced down to where his fingers were digging into her flesh. 'You're hurting me.'

'I'm sorry.' He backed off. 'I've been worried sick.'

'I was with Stephen. You know he wouldn't let any harm come to me.'

'That's true. He's a good lad.' Pa began to calm down.

'So did you find the woodcutter?'

'Yes, and he'll be at the Red Lion in the morning to make his statement.'

'So there's room for optimism?'

She nodded.

'Good. Go and get some sleep. You're worn out.'

'I'm sorry for the trouble that Matty's caused.'

'It can't be changed now, Catherine. It's the way it is.'

'Goodnight,' she said, kissing him on the cheek.

She fell into bed, but she couldn't rest. She ached to be back in Matty's arms and to hear his voice whispering sweet endearments into her ear, but she knew she had to be patient, and trust that justice would prevail.

Chapter Twelve

The Red Lion

Boughton

Catherine returned to the Red Lion with her father every day after the affray in the expectation of bringing Matty home to Overshill.

The village of Boughton was overwhelmed with thousands of visitors from London who alighted daily from the Union night coach or travelled via Gravesend by steamboat. There were soldiers everywhere, guarding the bodies and keeping public order. The locals made hay while the sun shone – they sold pieces of bark stripped from the oak against which Sir William fell; bloodied earth scraped up from the ground; fragments of his smock and strands of his beard.

On Saturday, the second day of June, Lieutenant Bennett was buried at the cathedral in Canterbury with full military honours, and an inquest, held at the White Horse – the other inn in Boughton – returned a verdict of justifiable homicide on the deaths of Sir William and his followers.

Sunday turned into Monday, and they were still no closer to liberating Matty from the confines of the upstairs room at the Red Lion. Catherine sent food via one of the soldiers, but she wasn't allowed to see or speak to him.

On Tuesday, she and Pa were drinking tea in one of the cottages across the road from the inn where the occupant had opened their door to visitors who wanted to rest for a while in return for a few pennies. A young man in a suit, a fop from London, approached their table. He wore a high-collared cotton shirt and cravat, and a fashionable coat with narrow, pointed tails that fell just below the knee of his brown trousers.

'Miss Rook, I've been hoping to find you,' he said, doffing his hat. 'You are engaged to the prisoner who goes by the name of Matty Carter?'

'Ignore him, Catherine,' Pa said. 'He's a journalist. I can smell the print on his fat, grubby fingers.'

'My hands are clean, sir.' The man showed his palms.

'But your jottings are filthy lies.' Pa stood up. 'We must be going.'

'A moment of your time. I ask your daughter for her account so that I can write the truth. Everyone wants to know what really happened.'

'They should keep their noses out of other people's business,' Pa said.

'It's important that we spread the word about characters like Mr Thom, so that no one can be taken in again by the preaching of a lunatic and a liar. They unscrewed the coffin today to check that he wasn't shut in against his will. I saw him and he remains dead.'

Catherine had seen the coffin the day before, a plain box without even a nameplate, as if the authorities thought that the best way to punish

Sir William's desire for notoriety was by denying him any acknowledgement in death.

'I should point out that most of the men involved in the battle can't read their names, let alone a newspaper. All you're after is profiting from our misfortune. Now, leave us alone. You're upsetting my daughter.'

'Is that because she expects her betrothed to be committed to trial for murder later today?'

Murder? Catherine tried to suppress the shock that jolted through her body.

'Please, don't speak of this.' Pa clenched his fists and his face begin to turn a deep shade of plum. Fearing that he was about to lose his temper and his mind, as he had with the threshing machine many years before, Catherine pulled at his sleeve.

'We have to go,' she said forcefully, 'as you must too, sir, if you aren't to miss out on reporting the trial.' She flashed the journalist a warning glance. 'That is my last word.'

She and her father made their way across the road to the Red Lion, where the coroner was about to make his address. They squeezed into a corner of the room which was crammed with the prisoners' friends, wives, husbands and children, as well as some of the visitors who'd been attracted by the spectacle.

The jury were called and shown to their seats before the prisoners – men and a couple of women in bedraggled clothing – were led into the makeshift court. Catherine craned her neck to catch a glimpse of Matty who walked with his head held high. He glanced towards the crowd

285

and gave her a small smile. She smiled back to let him know that she believed in him, no matter what.

The coroner sat down at the table at the far end of the room, and began to talk about the conclusion of an earlier case that set a precedent for how the twenty individuals who were involved in the affray would be treated.

'If several persons meet for a lawful purpose and one commits murder, then he alone is answerable. If, however, those persons meet for an illegal activity, and one commits murder, then everyone who takes part in that meeting is equally guilty of the crime. Therefore, the living will be put on trial, according to that conclusion.'

There was a collective gasp as his words sank in. Catherine felt Pa's hand on her arm.

'Call the first witness.' The coroner read from his notes. 'Mr James Testament, woodcutter by profession.'

The sight of the man from the woods, the person who would confirm Matty's innocence, stepping up to address the jury lifted her spirits.

Firstly, though, the coroner raised the issue of Drusilla's presence at the battle with him.

'You have sworn that Mrs Carter was one of the rioters,' he said, but Mr Testament frowned and answered, 'I am now sure that I didn't see the lady in the woods.'

'Have you had a conversation with anyone since you gave your statement?' the coroner asked. 'Did anyone speak to you about it?

'No, sir,' Mr Testament said.

'Speak up.'

286

'No,' he said firmly.

'Let me read over again what you have sworn and now be cautious in what you say. Do you know Drusilla Carter?'

'I do. I've had the pleasure of meeting her on several occasions.'

'Was she in Bossenden Wood on the thirty-first of May?'

'I cannot say for certain.' Mr Testament twisted his cap in his hands and his face flushed. Catherine thought she could see beads of perspiration forming on his forehead and rolling from the end of his nose.

'What made you be so positive respecting her when you gave this statement?'

'I was trembling so, I didn't know what to do.'

'Are you sure that Drusilla Carter was not there?' the coroner asked.

'I know she was not.'

The coroner uttered a sigh of despair. He looked at his watch and put it back on the table in front of him, before turning back to the witness.

'Now tell us with whom you have had a conversation recently.'

'I had no conversation. Mrs Carter only said to me that I had sworn wrong.'

'And she requested you to say she had not been there?'

'Yes, when I saw her brought in, I knew I was wrong.'

The coroner turned to the jury. 'I recommend to you, members of the jury, that you give to the testimony of this witness such credit as you think it is entitled to.'

Catherine was devastated. The coroner had demolished Mr Testament's credibility as a witness. How could the jury believe him? What chance had Matty got now? Her belly cramped with nerves.

The coroner went on to read out Mr Testament's statement relating to the Carter brothers. He had seen Jervis raise his pistol and aim at the man known as Catt. The man he now knew as Matty Carter had tussled for the gun, which had gone off and killed Catt.

'Who fired the gun?' the coroner asked.

'It was Jervis Carter.'

'That's a lie,' Drusilla shouted as Jervis scowled from the dock. 'I told you what to say.'

'Silence!' thundered the coroner.

'I mean, it was the other one. Catt, no, Matty Carter,' Mr Testament stammered.

'You're telling us that you saw Matty Carter raise the gun and fire it at the victim?'

'Yes, that's right,' the witness said, but by this time the jury were glancing at each other and rolling their eyes.

'But it could have bin the other one, the brother.' He scratched at his temple. 'My head is like an addled egg.'

'This isn't looking good,' Pa whispered, and it got worse when one of the constables described how Matty had had blood on his hands when he arrested him. Catherine gazed towards where he stood, his expression impassive.

The jury retired. Pa and Catherine waited. Stephen joined them to hear the verdict three-quarters of an hour later when the foreman spoke on the jury's behalf.

'To the best of our judgement, we have discharged our duty to our country and to the satisfaction of our consciences. I'm happy to say that in all out decisions, we are unanimous. The names of those guilty of the wilful murder of Lieutenant Bennett are...' Catherine held her breath as he listed the names of eight men, including Sir William Courtenay, also known as Thom '... Jervis Carter and Matty Carter.'

'No, not that. Please, no. It isn't right.' Catherine felt the blood rush from her body and Stephen's arms around her waist as the foreman of the jury went on to announce that they had found Drusilla Carter not guilty.

The coroner held up his hand.

'No, I can't hear anything as to the latter point. My province doesn't extend further than to enquire as to which persons were concerned with the murder of Lieutenant Bennett. Now that this is concluded, I commit the prisoners to Maidstone gaol for trial at the Assizes in August.'

'You need some air,' Stephen said, trying to guide Catherine through the crowd, but she clutched at his shirt and held him back.

'I must see him,' she said, watching helplessly as Matty was led away.

'I'm sorry.' Stephen whispered. 'We have to go now.'

'He's innocent,' she cried. 'Why can't they see it?'

'Hush there.' He took a grubby handkerchief from his pocket and wiped a tear from her eye. 'All is not lost.'

'He's been found guilty of murder. My dear,

289

gentle Matty.'

'This is just a tinpot court. The coroner's decision doesn't signify anything. He'll have a proper trial at the Assizes in front of a judge. Listen to me,' he went on quietly. 'I haven't managed to sell the item that you gave me yet, but I've researched its value, and the money will be a great help to you. Catherine, he will come home. It's just going to take a little longer than we'd hoped.'

'Stephen's right,' Pa said, overhearing the tail end of the conversation. 'We must keep the faith.'

As they went outside, a messenger came pushing through with news of Sir William's burial.

'It is done,' he cried. 'Over one hundred people were there at Hernhill churchyard, but he was unwept and unhonoured.' A few desultory cheers went up as he continued, 'The coffin arrived at the church and was taken straight to the grave without a tolling bell to announce it. Then the Reverend Hanley read just the parts of the burial service that are necessary by law for a person buried in consecrated ground. The coffin was covered with earth and left unmarked. Sir William Courtenay is no more.'

'It's a good job for the country that he was buried without ceremony,' Pa observed. 'Now we can concentrate on how to get Matty off this charge of...' His voice faded then returned. 'He needs a good lawyer to represent him, someone with clout, but I don't know how to raise the money for that.'

'I have a little spare that I'd be willing to put towards the fee.' Stephen named a figure and Pa laughed out loud.

'That wouldn't go as far as hiring a lawyer's little finger, and what use would that be, except to direct Matty's way to the hangman's noose?'

Catherine sank to her knees.

'I'm sorry,' Pa said as he and Stephen helped her up. 'I should have kept my mouth shut.'

'Let's get her back to the cart. She should be at home in her condition,' Stephen said.

'So you've guessed?' Pa said with a shrug. 'Everyone will know soon enow.'

'I have to go to Maidstone,' Catherine said. 'I need to be close to him.'

'You're no use to anyone in this state,' Pa said. 'You need to rest.'

'Do as your father says for once,' Stephen said.

Exhausted and temporarily defeated, she half stumbled, half fell on her way to the cart. Stephen lifted her into the back, climbed in beside her and put his arm around her waist. She leaned her head against his shoulder as Pa took up the reins to drive back to Overshill.

What had Matty been thinking of? Catherine wondered. She loved him more than anything, but how could he have been so foolish? His recklessness had left her on the brink of becoming a fallen woman, unmarried and with child.

She wished she could have remained in ignorance of her condition – she'd heard that many women didn't know until they reached their fifth month, but she'd been certain of it within a few weeks. Now she would have no peace of mind until Matty was freed and they were wed. It had to happen. She couldn't bear to think of the alternative.

'I'm very, grateful for the ride back,' she heard Stephen say as the cart jolted along and she slipped in and out of sleep.

'It's no problem to me. We're all going the same way,' Pa said.

'I don't know how I'm going to tell Ma and Pa the news. It's preying on my mind.'

'It's terrible to think we have to wait another two months to learn of the prisoners' fate, but at least we have some idea of how long it will be.' Pa changed the subject. 'How is your wife?'

'She is well, thank you.'

'Make the most of the early days. They don't last.'

'That's what I've bin told,' Stephen said drily. 'Maybe absence will make her heart grow fonder. Since she's been with child, she's been like an angry cat.'

'I can't imagine that of Emily. She's always seemed so meek and mild.'

'There are times when I wonder if she's the same woman I married.'

'The female of the species is a changeable creature, while we men are simpler, more straightforward beings. You're a good man, Stephen. I know that you'll stand by your wife, whatever happens in the future.' Catherine heard the crack of the whip and felt the cart shoot forwards.

Before long they were back at the farm where George and Ma were waiting in the yard. George was leaning against the wall, chewing on a blade of grass, and Ma was sitting on a chair, shelling peas. They rushed towards the cart, tripping over the hens as Pa pulled the horse up.

'What news of my boys?' George asked.

'Where's Matty? Is he not with you?' Ma said, looking towards Catherine as she held up her skirts and descended from the cart.

'He and Jervis are to be tried in Maidstone. I'm sorry, George,' Pa said. 'The witness couldn't tell the truth if it hit him in the face. There was nothing we could do.'

George started to cry. Stephen moved round to comfort him.

Ma was furious. She turned on Pa.

'After all you've done for him: turned a blind eye to his thieving ways; sent him to school and l'arned him about shepherding.'

'A man should be presumed innocent until he's been proven guilty,' Pa said adamantly. 'Matty's never been violent – he wouldn't hurt a fly.'

'He's brought shame on us.' She glared at Catherine. 'You must send this sorry creature away, Thomas. I can't bear to look at her. I'm too old and worn out to take on another bastard.'

'I will hear no more talk like this, Margaret. You are a spiteful, vindictive woman,' Pa spat. 'This is how it's going to be. Matty is innocent, therefore, he will be freed by the judge. Then he will return to Overshill, marry our daughter and give her unborn child a respectable upbringing. He'll take on the tenancy of Wanstall Farm when the squire sees fit, John will be cared for and we'll live here comfortably for the years we have left.'

'I want her to go,' Ma muttered.

'Well, she's staying here, whether you like it or not. If you keep on like this, it'll be you who's packing her bags.'

'I don't think so. What would you do without me?'

Pa turned, unhitched the horse and walked away, leaving Ma standing in the middle of the yard, opening and closing her mouth like a trout out of water.

Stephen gave Catherine a questioning look as he took his father's hand to escort him home.

She nodded. She would be all right. It was Matty she was worried about. She had to find a way to help him get off the charge of murder. As she fed the hens and pigs, she began to make a plan.

Time passed. Stephen returned to Faversham, and the more mundane topics of repairs to the church tower and the sale of the Woodsman's Arms to a new proprietor gradually replaced talk of the riot. Catherine worked less in the house and more on the farm, looking after John and the sheep. The sickness wore off as her belly began to swell. She felt physically strong again, but her heart ached for Matty.

One day in the middle of July when the poppies were jostling for space in the cornfields, Stephen and Emily called at the farm.

'Do come and sit down.' Catherine smiled.

'Is your ma not at home?' Stephen enquired.

'She's taking a nap.' She'd pretty much taken to her bed since Matty's imprisonment. 'Would you like some tea?'

'We won't be stopping long – the forge doesn't look after itself,' Stephen said. 'I came to tell you that I've sold the ring to a Faversham merchant who desired a fragment of England's history. The gold, the stones and the association with Sir William made it a very valuable piece.' He pulled a wad of banknotes from his pocket. 'I hope that I drove a hard enough bargain for you.'

She took the money. It was more than she could have dreamed of.

'Thank you, Stephen.'

'I know you'll spend it wisely.'

'I'll use it to obtain legal representation for Matty at the trial. Any money that's left will go to the families of the prisoners and those that were killed. I have no wish to profit from this sad affair.'

'I pray that my brother will be swiftly and safely returned to us,' Stephen said. 'Is your father at home? 1 should like to speak with him.'

'He's walking the fields with John. He has high hopes of this harvest. I hope they aren't misplaced. There seem to be more weeds than ears of corn.' Catherine felt a stab of regret at memories of happier, more carefree times.

'I'll go and find him – if I have your permission, my dearest wife?'

'I'll wait here,' Emily said.

The two women moved to the kitchen, where Catherine made mint tea and cut slices of cherry cake.

'Married life suits you,' she said, observing the glow in her best friend's cheeks.

'It hasn't been plain sailing – I've been rather hard on my husband at times.' Emily smiled as she pulled up a chair. 'Stephen has no doubt that Matty is innocent.'

'I hope the judge can see that,' Catherine said,

sitting down. 'I miss him. It's like part of me has been torn away.' She listened out for his cheery whistle every morning, and looked for him when she stood at the orchard gate to watch the sheep nibbling at the grass. Sometimes, she heard his voice at her ear when she slipped into the woods to sit in the clearing in order to feel close to him. 'Let's talk about something else. When is your baby due?'

'Very soon.' Emily shifted in her seat. 'I'm scared, Catherine. I'm afraid I shall die.'

'Oh, don't be silly. You're the picture of health.'

'There we are, reassuring each other about uncertainties.'

'That's what friends are for. We are friends again, aren't we?'

'Let's let bygones be bygones,' Emily said. 'As it turns out, I couldn't have wished for a better man.'

The words stung. Catherine was still waiting to find out what kind of husband Matty was going to be.

'How are you finding Faversham?'

'I'm happy there. It's much livelier than Overshill, with the ships coming in and out of the creek. The house is very small and we have very little, so there isn't much for me to do. I cook and clean, and bake bread, and do the laundry.'

'Do you ever wonder if you're having a boy or a girl?' Catherine said, changing the subject back to babies.

'It's a girl. I did the test with the piece of cotton. It isn't definite, but I did it more than once, and it always gave the same answer.'

'Will you show me what to do?'

Emily removed her wedding ring, and tied it to a piece of thread that Catherine took from the sewing box. 'Now, you have to hold it over your belly.'

Catherine let the ring dangle over her stomach. At four months gone there was little she could do to hide her growing bump. The ring swung in a small circle.

'You're having a girl too. You know what that means.' Emily's voice was filled with excitement. 'One day our children will play together and be best friends like we were growing up.'

Catherine unfastened the thread and handed the ring back. She began to wonder if there was a chance that they would all live happily ever after as she and Emily had planned.

The next day, she put on her Sunday best and left the farm to call at Churt House. She walked up the long drive between the rows of willows and beeches through the sweeping parkland to where the house stood on a small rise with its many windows glinting in the sun. A pair of deer stalked across the drive in front of her, and a pony and trap passed at speed.

When she reached the buildings she wasn't sure which way to turn. Should she knock at the front door which stood at the top of a set of stone steps, or should she approach by the tradesman's entrance at the rear?

'Can I help you, miss?' came a voice. 'You appear to be lost.'

She turned to find the owner of the house riding astride a bay hunter. He wore a felt jacket with brass buttons and carried a silver-topped whip.

'I know very well where I am, sir,' she said rather sharply. 'I have come to call upon you, Mr Hadington.'

'What business can a person such as yourself possibly have with me?' He reined his horse in a half-circle. 'You have made a wasted journey.'

'Please, hear what I have to say,' she said. 'I need the services of a lawyer.'

He laughed. 'The likes of you could never afford my services.'

'I'm of limited means, that's true, but I've acquired a sum of money to pay your fee,' she said desperately. His curiosity apparently piqued, he jabbed his restless horse in the mouth at which the poor creature decided to stand still.

'Are you in some kind of trouble?'

'There is a man by the name of Matty Carter.'

'Do I know of him?'

'He's one of the Carter boys from Toad's Bottom. He grew up in Overshill and used to sing in the choir.'

'And he is now in one of the hulks waiting for the trial at Maidstone next month,' Mr Hadington finished for her. 'I read the papers. Tell me, why would I risk my reputation defending a common criminal?'

'Because he's innocent of the crimes of which he's been charged.' Tears sprang to her eyes. 'I'm sure, with your wit and learning, you can clear his name and enhance your professional reputation.'

'I can assure you that it needs no enhancement.

I am well known, even revered in legal circles. One day, I shall certainly become Lord Chief Justice.'

'I'm sorry for causing offence.' Inside, Catherine was burning with anger and resentment. So this was how her true father treated people! 'I wouldn't ask for your help if I wasn't desperate. I've told you – I have money.' She showed him the banknotes.

'I see. Well, let me tell you, I wouldn't defend this man for double that paltry sum, so if you don't mind, I'll be on my way.'

'So you will do nothing at all for the daughter you disowned, sir,' she challenged.

'Daughter?' He looked her up and down, scrutinising her features.

'We've been together in church almost every Sunday. Don't try to tell me you didn't know.'

'You can't be! You're the fruit of Thomas Rook's loins.'

'That's what he led you to believe. I am your daughter. You took advantage of my true mother when she was your maid and barely out of childhood.'

'That's a lie,' he said, his expression dark as he raised his whip. 'Take that back. Immediately.'

'I shan't, sir. I deal in truths, not falsehoods. I am your daughter, and I tell you this, Father' – she spat the word out in a fury of disappointment – 'if you don't agree to help me in this, the one and only request I will ever make of you, I shall contact the journalists who came to spin their yarns about the battle at Bossenden and make fun of those poor people who were caught up in

Sir William's web of lies. I'll let them know what kind of man you really are. I wonder how revered you'll be then.'

'Perhaps you are my daughter after all,' he said slowly. 'Your grandmother told me that you had died at birth. It was easier to believe her version of the story than any alternative. Ivy was a very pretty girl.' Catherine shuddered with revulsion at his lechery. 'Where did you obtain that money?' he continued.

'It was owed to me,' she said.

He thought for a moment.

'You seem rather sharp for a farmer's child, so maybe there's some truth in it. Let me see what I can do. Put the money away for now – you can settle my bill when we know what's what. I trust that this will be kept in confidence between us.' He cocked his head. 'No journalists. No revelations. I'll do what I can for the prisoner. You pay me in return. That's the deal.'

'I'm happy with those terms,' she said, marvelling at her courage in confronting the man who was both blood and a stranger to her, and wary of him at the same time. He was a sly old fox who would have the head off a chicken like her just like that if she crossed him.

'You must leave now,' he added. 'It isn't wise for us to be seen together. Goodbye, Miss Rook. I will send word.'

He kicked his horse in the ribs. It plunged forwards and headed down the drive at a gallop.

Catherine trudged back to the farm, sensing that she had won some kind of victory in standing her ground. Pa didn't feel the same, because when she ventured her news that evening as they swept the granary ready for the harvest, he was livid.

'How can you be so shameless as to beg a favour from that man?' he exploded.

She shrank back, startled by the ferocity of his opinion.

'Haven't I always supported you? Done everything for you as a father should?'

She saw that she had hurt his feelings, injuring him to the core, but Mr Hadington was the only lawyer she knew of, and who else would listen to her, considering the circumstances?

'I was going to speak with Mr Boyle when I next visited Canterbury. You should have told me what you intended to do.' Pa frowned suddenly. 'How can you possibly afford this?'

She explained about the ring.

'Mr Hadington's fees are extortionate. How did you persuade him to agree to represent Matty for that? I can't believe he would do it out of the kindness of his heart when it is made of stone.' A pulse began to throb at Pa's temple, bulging and swelling as though it might burst.

'I told him I was his daughter. I threatened to reveal it to the newspapers, the *Faversham Mercury* or even *The Times* of London.'

'You were going to blackmail him? What kind of person are you? Didn't I raise you to be honest and respectful? It's as if Matty has influenced you, leading you astray.' He looked around, his eyes wandering in blind confusion. 'Didn't I always encourage both of you to think before you speak and act, to do right by your fellow man and woman?'

'What's going on? I can hear you from inside the house.' Ma made an appearance at the doorway into the granary. 'Thomas, calm yourself. You'll have apoplexy. Here.' She forced the vinaigrette into his hand. He threw it down, sending it bouncing across the floor. 'Have some sleeping drops, then.' Ma gave him the bottle from her pocket, but he removed the lid and tipped out the contents. 'No! What did you do that for?'

'You shouldn't put that stuff inside you. How many times have I told you that it does you no good? It dulls the senses and deadens the mind. You are a shadow of the woman you used to be, as I am but half the man.' Pa walked out, crossed the yard and disappeared off along the track. He didn't return until the following morning, dishevelled and rambling on about the state of the barley.

'This is no way to impress the squire,' Catherine said as she put him to bed. She prayed that her father would make a quick recovery and continue his efforts to restore the farm to its former glory. How would he cope, though, if Mr Hadington failed to obtain Matty's release at the Assizes? Would he give up on the tenancy if he felt there was no future in it for the Rooks?

She gave herself a stern telling-off for weakening in her resolve to remain optimistic. Matty was innocent and one day soon he would come home.

Chapter Thirteen

The Assizes

Maidstone

Mr Hadington sent word that he was preparing to represent Matty at the trial, and in early August, the prisoners were set to face the Assize Grand Jury. Pa remained on the farm with John, watching and waiting for the weather to turn. The soft fruits, the raspberries and strawberries, had turned black and bitter on the plants in June and July. A dog had attacked and killed several of the season's lambs, and now the barley was beaten down and laid low by rain, while the weeds flourished.

George did what he could, but he was an old man with an invalid for a wife and two sons awaiting trial for the most serious of crimes. The only light in his life was news of the safe delivery of his first grandchild. Emily gave birth to a daughter, whom the couple named Jessie.

The day before the trial was due to start, Stephen and Catherine took the cart and the fittest of the horses to Maidstone.

'I hope Emily and the baby are well,' she said, as they travelled along the busy turnpike road.

'They're the picture of health.' Stephen smiled. 'I didn't want to leave them, but my master's wife

303

is at home to help, and I can't not attend the trial when my father has asked me to be there on his behalf. Besides, Emily insisted that I chaperone you.' He glanced towards her. 'Try not to worry too much about Matty. He has the best defence possible. It's Jervis who's deeper in the mire.'

'You're right, but I'm still afraid of what the outcome might be.'

'I know. So am I. I wish... Oh, what's the purpose of wishing things could have been different? It is as it is, and you can't do anything about it except pray, and I'm not sure that that does any good.'

'Stephen, you mustn't say that. It's the only thing we have left.'

After being on the road for almost six hours, they stopped at the Black Horse on the Pilgrims' Way in the hamlet of Thurnham. Catherine remained with the horse and cart while Stephen went inside to speak to the innkeeper. He returned shortly afterwards.

'I've taken rooms for the night,' he said. 'It turns out that we've been lucky to find somewhere to sleep. Apparently, hundreds have descended on Maidstone for the trials. I'll walk in to town to obtain tickets later.'

Catherine frowned.

'Without them, we won't be able to get in to the court-house,' he told her.

'Go quickly then,' she urged. 'I'll wait here with the cart and our belongings.'

In spite of her arguments to the contrary, Stephen carried their bags into the rooms and made sure the locks were secure before he left her.

'Promise me that you'll stay in your room until I return. I'll knock twice, like this.' He rapped his knuckles against the door.

'Just go,' she said, and he took the horse and cart into town for speed, returning with tickets a couple of hours later. They ate supper together before retiring to their beds, but she couldn't sleep for the heat and the people laughing and talking outside, and the drunkards stumbling up the stairs. She was lying on top of the sheets with her hand resting on her belly when she felt a fluttering movement like a butterfly beneath her fingers. Her heart leapt with joy. It was a good omen: the baby had quickened.

In the morning, she was ready when Stephen knocked on the door.

'Are you well? Only you look very pale,' he said. 'You must have some breakfast. You hardly ate anything last night.'

'Thank you for your concern, but I'm not hungry.'

'I'll send for some buttered eggs on toast and tea. At least try it. It's going to be a long day.'

She gave in and ate a little breakfast with him. They talked about Emily and the baby, and how Stephen, having cured Sir William's horse of its lameness, had kept it as his own. They reminisced about the dame school, and the time when Matty had hidden a frog in one of the desks.

'Old Faggy made him stand in the corner with a book balanced on the top of his head,' Stephen said, smiling. 'I wish I could have acted as bold and carefree as he did. I envy him that, not that

I'd want to be in his shoes now, though.'

She choked back a tear. She couldn't help it.

'I'm sorry, Catherine. I shouldn't have said anything. I've upset you. Let me hire a cab to take us into town. The landlord says there are horses and drivers available.'

'Oh no, I'd prefer to walk if it isn't too far.'

'It's about an hour and a half on foot.'

'That's nothing,' she said.

'Are you sure? Emily was afraid to walk more than a few yards when she was in your condition.'

'I'll be fine, I promise.'

Arriving in Maidstone some time later, they found the roads so thronged with people that it took a while to push their way through to reach the courthouse. When they got there, they found seats in the gallery among some ladies who seemed to be dressed far too gaily for the occasion. Lord Denman, Lord Chief Justice, took his place, and a pair of guards led the prisoners into the court.

Catherine leaned forwards to look for Matty, but he didn't appear at the bar.

'What's happened?' she whispered to Stephen. 'Where is he?'

'The judge is saying that today will be devoted to the murder of Mears, the constable's brother.'

Catherine sank back, her heart heavy with disappointment at the thought that Matty's ordeal wouldn't be over for at least another day. The hours ticked away painfully slowly as witnesses were called and cross-examined. Eventually Lord Denman did his summing up, impressing upon the jury that there was no justification for the prisoners to join in a criminal outrage, even if they feared for their own safety at the hands of Sir William Courtenay.

The jury retired at five, and the two prisoners present laid their heads on the bar. Half an hour later, the jury returned and declared them guilty of murder, but strongly recommended them to mercy.

'I sentence these men' – Lord Denman named them – 'to death.'

Stephen grasped Catherine's hand and held it tight. There were cries of shock and despair, and the gaily dressed ladies fanned themselves furiously, as if to waft the judge's verdict away.

'However,' the judge went on, 'their lives will be spared, thanks to the recommendation of this jury.'

Catherine didn't know what to think. They were to die, then they were to live. She looked at Stephen.

'What does that mean for Matty?'

'We'll find out tomorrow. As long as Mr Hadington does what you're paying him to do, he'll be cleared. As for Jervis' – he frowned – 'who knows what will happen to him?'

The next day when they took their seats in the courthouse, nine prisoners were led to the bar. Catherine caught sight of the two brothers. Matty was looking around the court when suddenly he saw her. His eyes lit up and he blew her a kiss. She smiled in return, but she felt only pain. He was haggard like an old crone, his cheeks sunken in and his ribs showing where his jerkin was torn to the waist. His hair was long and unkempt, and somehow, his scruffy appearance made him look ... well, guilty, she decided.

Eventually, Mr Hadington stepped up to address the court. He was counsel for Mr Matthew Carter who was charged along with the other men present with the murder of Lieutenant Bennett. Matty bowed his head as his lawyer spoke on his behalf.

'I am quite satisfied that this deluded man will find in your lordship a humane and merciful administrator of the law. There is no one who could agree that Sir William Courtenay's followers planned the act which that mad man committed.' He stroked his chin as though considering, giving time for his words to make an impression on the judge and jury.

'He should be on the stage,' Stephen whispered.

Catherine nodded as Mr Hadington continued.

'It is my duty not to struggle with the law as laid down by his lordship yesterday, and I have therefore advised Matthew Carter to plead guilty of the charge that is laid against him.'

'No,' Catherine said out loud. This wasn't what she'd asked for. What was he doing? 'This is wrong. He's innocent.' Matty's counsel flashed her a glance.

'Silence in the gallery,' Lord Denman ordered before he went on to examine the character of each of the prisoners.

'It will be soon,' Stephen whispered again. 'He'll address them shortly and give his decision.' He took Catherine's hand and held it tight. She waited with bated breath as the judge spoke.

'You, Jervis Carter, Matthew Carter' – he listed the nine men – 'have been severally convicted of the crime of murder and the law requires that I should pass a capital sentence upon you...'

Catherine's heart stopped. Her head began to swim. The verdicts from the day before hadn't set a precedent. Matty was going to hang.

'I think it right to state to you that your lives will be spared,' his lordship continued.

'Catherine' – Stephen's voice cut into her consciousness – 'my brothers are saved.'

'Your offence is of an enormous nature, with ignorance and folly thrown in. Matthew Carter, your counsel has advised me of your guilty plea which I take into account when considering your sentence. However, you and your brother Jervis Carter continued to follow your fanatic leader after the murder of Mears, encouraging him during the day in further violence.'

'It isn't true,' Catherine muttered as she watched the tears rolling down Matty's face. 'He was trying to prevent Sir William and his gang from causing any more injury. He wasn't part of it. Why can't anyone see that?'

'Hush,' Stephen said in a low voice. 'The decision is based on the evidence that's been presented in court. There's nothing we can do. Just listen.'

Lord Denman meted out Matty's punishment.

'With regard to you, it is perfectly clear that you cannot remain in this country. You must be made an example of in the severest way, short only of depriving you of your life.'

'He isn't to die,' Stephen said, but his face was white and his hands shaking. 'That's something, isn't it?'

She nodded weakly as the judge went on, 'You retire from this bar and from this country to be conveyed to distant parts where you will be removed from your dearest connections and relations for life.'

Catherine sank to her knees in despair. It was over. Matty was to be transported to the other side of the world, where he would remain for the rest of his days, and she would never see him again.

'Jervis Carter, you too retire from this bar and from this country.' Lord Denman sentenced him to transportation for life as well for his part in the affray. Another of the prisoners received a ten-year banishment while the other six faced a year's imprisonment, by which time every man at the bar was crying, as were their relatives and friends in the gallery. 'I have to finish by expressing my astonishment at the credulity that made these people of Canterbury and East Kent the dupe of a lunatic. I would anticipate that measures will be decided in Parliament to ensure that nothing like this can happen again.'

The audience started to surge towards the stairs and exits.

'How am I going to tell my ma and pa that two of their sons are to be sent across the sea to a place far away, never to be seen again? It will kill them,' Stephen said, helping Catherine up. 'Where are you going?' he added when she made to move away.

'To speak with him.'

'Mr Hadington?'

'No, Matty.'

'Miss Rook, a word.' Matty's counsel approached her and Stephen. 'I wanted to let you know that it was the best outcome in the circumstances.'

'I disagree,' she said. 'You advised him to plead guilty, which meant that he didn't have a chance to prove his innocence.'

'That wouldn't have happened anyway. You heard witnesses confirm that he had the pistol in his hand when the soldier was killed. Take cheer in the sentence if not the verdict. At least he will not swing from the gallows.' He paused. 'I will invoice you.'

She pulled the wad of banknotes from her breast.

'Take your money,' she said, thrusting it towards him.

'This is most irregular, and rather vulgar. Keep it for now. Let me know where you are staying and I will send a man to pick it up.'

'We are at the Black Horse in Thurnham for one more night,' Stephen said.

'He will be with you tonight. I trust I will hear no more from you after this.'

'I can assure you that I have no desire to impose on you again,' she said bitterly. Her true father had let her down for a second time, and she wanted nothing more to do with him. She turned her eyes towards the prisoners who were stopped in a line just beyond the bar.

A minute, she thought. If she could just have a minute to talk to her beloved Matty.

Leaving Stephen behind, she forced her way

through the crowd of weeping women who were trying to reach their menfolk. She recognised the elderly woman from the Red Lion, who stepped aside to let her pass.

'I'm sorry, ducky,' she said. 'My son is one of the lucky ones – he'll be back with us within a year. Go and say your goodbyes.'

It was too late. The prisoners were moved on and taken outside, and the door was shut in their relatives' faces. Catherine turned to look for Stephen.

'It's all right,' he said, forcing his way through the melee. 'You can see him. Mr Hadington's arranging it with one of the guards.'

'What did you say to him?'

'The sight of your distress triggered a touch of compassion in his soul. Perhaps something reminded him that you are made of the same flesh. It's all right. I know of the relationship between you, although in normal circumstances I prefer not to distress you by recognising it.' Stephen took her arm. 'Come outside quickly before the prisoners are taken away.'

They found Matty at the side of the court-house where a couple of reporters were taking notes and an artist was drawing caricatures of the convicted men. Catherine rushed towards them.

'Please, miss. Stand back,' said the guard, shoving the prisoners into line with a stick. 'These animals are a danger to the public.'

'This is my fiancé' – she pointed towards Matty, who was gazing at her, his eyes red from crying – 'and he's innocent.'

'Not in the eyes of the law,' the guard countered.

'Matty Carter's lawyer has arranged for this lady to speak with him,' Stephen interrupted.

'Ah yes, he did send word to that effect, but you'll have to talk here.'

'Can't we have a few minutes in private?' Catherine said. 'I beg you to show some kindness.'

'It isn't my job to be kind. You'll talk here, and if anyone so much as tries anything, I'll have them.'

Catherine shuddered. He was a short, well-muscled man with a scar across his cheek and a limp. He kept one hand on his stick and one on the knife that was sheathed at his waist. She could well believe his threat.

She turned to Matty.

'I'm so sorry,' she sobbed. 'I tried my best.'

'I know. And I'm sorrier than you can imagine for getting caught up in this terrible mess, but there's nothing we can do now.' His eyes filled with fresh tears.

'Will I see you again before you go?'

'I doubt it. I believe that I'm going to Rochester to await transportation.' He forced a smile. 'I've always wanted to travel the world and here I am heading for Tasmania, wherever that is.'

Catherine trembled. All she wanted to do was throw her arms around him and dissolve into him, to become one so they could travel together.

'You'll look after yourself and the child,' he said.

'It's a girl, our daughter. I checked with a ring and thread. It is certain.'

313

Matty bit his lip.

'It would make me very happy if you'd name her after my ma and yours: not Margaret, but Ivy. Agnes Ivy. What do you think?'

'They're beautiful names.'

'I've had an awful lot of time to think of them,' he said wryly.

Catherine blundered on, 'You'll see her upon your return. I'll burn a candle every night to light your way.' He shook his head.

'Don't wait for me. Mr Hadington says that I must have no expectation of ever coming back to these shores. Life means life.'

'No' – she clasped her hands together in anguish – 'I can't bear it.'

'I'll take comfort in the idea that you will think of me fondly now and again. I will think of you always, filled with regret for my mistakes and weaknesses.'

'Oh, Matty,' she cried.

'I have a request,' he went on hoarsely.

'Anything.' Her heart was beating painfully in her chest. 'You know I'll do anything for you.'

'This is the hardest thing I've ever done.' He took a deep breath before continuing, 'I'm asking you to break off our engagement.'

She could scarcely believe his words. 'How can you say that when we are promised to each other? How can you be so cruel?'

'I'm doing this for your sake, not mine.'

'I should rather remain betrothed to you, the father of my child. I will be ruined otherwise.'

'Catherine, how will you explain my absence?'

'I'll say that you are at sea, or away on business.

Please don't make me do this.'

'The very idea breaks my heart. You are the most beautiful, capable and loving woman, and it would be wrong to keep you bound to me for the rest of our lives when you have so much to give. I want you to be free to fall in love and marry, and have more children.'

'It's you whom I love. It's you I wish to marry. There'll never be anyone else.'

'That's easy to say, but it will be different when I'm half a world away. What if I don't make it to Tasmania? Many are lost while crossing the ocean. Conditions on the ships–' He stopped abruptly. He didn't have to go on. Catherine knew what he meant.

'Why don't we say we are married right here in the eyes of God?'

'I can't have that on my conscience.'

'I'll follow you. I'll earn my passage and bring our daughter with me.'

'Stay here, look after our child and love her for both of us. I'm giving you your freedom. Say that you'll accept it. I need to be sure before I go.'

'Catherine, what he's saying makes sense,' came Stephen's voice from her side. 'I think it fair to give him peace of mind by agreeing to his request, as painful as it is to both of you.'

She gazed at her soulmate, lover and father of her baby, reading the hurt in his eyes. He hadn't taken the decision lightly to ask her to end the engagement lightly.

'You have good reason to ask this of me, but you're wrong.'

'No, my dearest and only love, it's the right

thing to do. Please,' he whispered, inching closer under the watchful eyes of the guard. 'It will give me peace of mind. This is the one last thing I ask of you.'

'Your time is up,' the guard interrupted.

'Catherine?' Matty said.

'I'll do it,' she said softly. She removed the ring of plaited hair from her finger and dropped it on the ground.

'I have something for you and our child.' He kicked off his left boot. 'Look inside.'

Catherine picked it up and then handed it back, removing a small, hard object with a roughened edge from its malodorous depths as she did so.

'Hey,' the guard said. 'Show me your boot.'

Catherine palmed Matty's offering and slipped it into her pocket, while the guard searched his footwear for contraband before throwing it back at him.

'Move!' he snapped.

Matty looked behind him as he shuffled along in line with the other men.

'Always and for ever,' he mouthed, craning his neck for one last sight of her until the prisoners rounded the corner of the building and disappeared. She couldn't bear it. With a cry, she made to run after him, but Stephen caught her and held her back.

'It is no use,' he said, pulling her to him. 'He's gone.'

'Oh, my poor Matty,' she sobbed.

'Hush there,' Stephen murmured.

She was vaguely aware of his fingers tangling in

her hair as he held her close with her head against his shoulder. She felt his body shaking as she trembled with overwhelming grief. She had lost the love of her life, while Stephen had lost his brothers.

She and Matty would never walk through the woods at Overshill again. They would never kiss under the moonlight, or share cherries dripping with juice straight from the tree. He would never go out into the fields and show their daughter the hops curling up the chestnut poles, the deer walking among the trees and the ladybirds crawling around the runner beans, like Pa had with her. How must he be feeling now?

She wasn't sure how long they remained outside the courthouse, or what time they returned to the Black Horse.

Stephen ordered a light supper, and they ate half-heartedly. Mr Hadington's man came to collect his payment, and the next morning, they made their way back to Overshill with the horse and cart. Catherine sat in the back wrapped in blankets and exposed to the sun, but she still felt cold, as if she'd been turned to stone. The judge and jury had put an end to her hopes and dreams for the future. She had no husband and her child was without a father.

She slid her hand into her pocket and pulled out the object that Matty had given her the day before. It was a curious thing, half of a silver coin, the curve as smooth as the day it had been minted, and the cut edge across the centre rough and uneven, but she recognised it. It was half of the sixpence that she had given him. He must have spent hours while he was imprisoned filing it into two.

She gripped it tightly.

'You'll be all right, Catherine,' she heard Stephen say.

'How, when my heart is broken?' she exclaimed.

'I mean in a practical way. I'm sorry, I didn't mean to offend you. I know how I'd feel if anything should part me from Emily, but you will have Matty's child to bring you comfort.'

'Comfort? She will bring me only pain.'

'She will remind you of him.' He turned and looked over his shoulder. 'She will help us all to come to terms with what's happened.'

'Let's face it, Stephen. By the end of the year, I'll have given birth out of wedlock to a convicted criminal's daughter. Ma will never forgive me for that, and I'll be looked down upon by every respectable person in Overshill.' She gazed at him straight in the eye. 'Not everyone is fair and reasonable like you.'

The news had been carried to the village ahead of them by others who had attended the trials, and they found themselves the centre of attention as they turned off the main road. Some workers who were digging in the chalk pit downed their tools and touched their caps as a sign of respect, while the wheelwright and his wife emerged from their cottage to stare and make barbed comments about the unseemliness of associating with murderers, and of a married man consorting with his brother's betrothed. When they reached the forge, Len strode out, eager to hear the gossip first hand.

'It's bad news, in't it? Everyone's talking about it. I'm sorry, Stephen, and you, Catherine. We're all sore about Matty. He's always been a joker and a risk-taker, but his heart's always been in the right place. As for Jervis, well, something bad was always going to happen to him.'

'We're a little weary. Len, so we'll be on our way,' Stephen said. 'I have to call on my parents then get back to Faversham to see my wife and daughter tonight.'

'Don't mind me. One day soon, when you have a spare hour, come and find me,' Len went on. 'I have a business proposition for you, something for the future.'

He wished them both farewell and Stephen made clicking sounds in his throat to send the horse forward. It walked on more eagerly now that it was nearing home, and it turned into the farmyard at a smart trot.

'Thank you, Stephen,' Catherine said, as he helped her down from the cart.

'There's no need to thank me,' he said gruffly, turning away to unfasten the traces. 'I'm sure I've felt more grateful for your company these past few days than you've felt for mine. Would you like me to come with you into the house?'

'I'll be fine,' she said. 'You go and see George and your ma. And give Emily my kind regards when you get home.'

'Take care, Catherine. Look after yourself and the baby.'

She watched him lead the horse away before she walked indoors to face Ma. She found her standing at the top of the stairs.

319

'Ma, what are you doing?' she shouted as a hairbrush and a comb whistled past her ear.

'Clearing your room.'

'But this is my home.' She shrank back as a shoe bounced down the steps.

'You aren't welcome here any more.'

Catherine stepped back beside the grandfather clock that had chimed throughout the progress of John's recovery and her teenage years. It had stopped at two o'clock on the day of the riot at Bossenden Wood and no one had bothered to take the key and wind it up again. She saw the door to the parlour ajar and recalled the day when she had found Drusilla lying on the couch, under the influence of Ma's sleeping drops.

'You've been nothing but trouble since before you were born. You were the cause of your mother losing her position in service–'

'That's unfair.'

'The vicar has called to offer his condolences and prayers in a most disdainful way. Pa is no longer a churchwarden – it was suggested that he was no longer a fit person and should give up his post. I don't see how you can live with yourself. You have neglected your brother and half-killed your grandfather by breaking his heart. All this worry has made me ill. You have brought shame on our family. Now everyone knows that you are having a murderer's child.'

'Matty is innocent,' Catherine said.

'Not according to Judge Denman and every other right-thinking person. He was found guilty.'

'Let me speak with Pa.' He would listen to reason, she thought.

'He doesn't want to see you.'

'I don't believe you. Where is he? I shall go and find him.'

'Don't! He isn't himself. I fear he will kill you if he sets eyes on you.'

'You can't mean that.'

'In Pa's mind, everything hinged on Matty marrying you and now that it can't happen, he is lost. He blames himself for allowing Matty to deceive us and for not being able to keep Wanstall Farm in our hands. And he's livid at you for not keeping him on a tighter rein. He wishes that you'd never bin born.'

The words cut through her heart. Pa was the one person, apart from Matty, who had loved her unconditionally, or so she thought. How could he abandon her now?

'I'm sure I can bring him round.'

'There's no chance of that now.' Ma was spitting like a cat. 'We have lost the farm.'

Catherine was stunned into silence.

'Squire Temple was already unhappy about the state of the fields – the barley is hardly worth cutting, and the hops are riddled with the weevil, but Matty's conviction was the final straw. He sent his bailiff round as soon as the news came through. He didn't even come himself to give Pa notice. We have a month to get out. Where will we go? What will we do?' Ma took the smelling salts from her pocket. 'We have worked on this farm, worn our fingers to the bone, ploughed the money that we earned back into the land and buildings, and what have we to show for it? Nothing. Absolutely nothing. And it's all down to you!'

321

Grief surged through Catherine's body. She hadn't known it was possible to feel such pain. Poor Matty, and now poor Pa. The loss of the farm was the worst torment that he could possibly suffer.

'Can't we speak to the squire?' she asked. 'Just because I'm a woman doesn't mean I can't run the farm. I know the business as well as anyone else.'

'Only sad old widows run farms,' Ma said scathingly. 'Why should he listen to the Rooks when he already has a new tenant in mind?'

'So soon? Who is it?'

'Mr Nobbs. Can you believe it? Of all the people in the county, it has to be that sly, underhand snake of a man who's gone creeping around on his belly, ingratiating himself with the squire and stealing what's rightfully ours. He's been crowing about his good fortune as he struts around Overshill with his wife.'

'There must be something we can do.'

'By the end of this week, we will be homeless and destitute.'

'We can rent a cottage in the village. I can go out to work while you look after John.'

'We can't afford to rent anywhere, you numskull. The money has run out. Pa has spent what little we had left on running back and forth with you, and there's precious little coming in. We will starve.'

'What about Young Thomas? We can stay with him for a while, just until we are back on our feet.'

'When will you realise that there is no "we"?

You are no longer one of us.'

Catherine made to go up the stairs, but Ma barred her way.

'There's nothing left that belongs to you. Leave now. I can't bear to look at spoiled goods any longer.' She turned her back on her.

'Ma?' Catherine reached out her hand, her fingers quivering.

'Go! Get out and never show your face again,' Ma snapped.

'Where is John? I should like to see him before I go.'

'You can't. He's sleeping.'

Realising that she was defeated and nothing she could say would make any difference, Catherine picked up her basket from the hall, placed a few of her belongings inside, and threw her cloak over her shoulders before heading to the front door.

'Not that way!'

She turned and walked out to the kitchen. She took half a loaf and a block of butter and stuffed them into her basket before she left through the back of the house. As she made her way across the yard, the hens came running.

'I'm sorry, ladies.' She would miss them, and the pigs, and the cool darkness of the granary where she'd tended Matty's injuries after his fight with Stephen, and they'd shared their first kiss. Her chest grew tight and her eyes burned with tears. Where was he? What was he doing? Were the guards on the hulk treating him kindly? She doubted it.

She stood for a while at the gate into the

323

orchards and fields, gazing at the familiar view. She didn't know what to do or where to go, but eventually, she decided to make her way towards Rochester. If she couldn't be with him, she could be nearby.

She set out from Overshill and walked through the night making her way towards the coast. At dawn, she rested in the woods at the side of the road, drank water from a stream and ate half the bread and butter, before she carried on.

When a man rode towards her, she crossed the road to avoid him.

'Where are you going, ducky?' he called out to her.

She pulled her hood up to hide her face. It was no one's business, and she hardly knew where she was heading herself.

'If you're after some work, they're looking for fruit pickers at Whetstone Farm,' he said kindly. 'It's two miles from here. Turn left at the next crossroads and the farm is on the right past the oast house.'

'Thank you, sir.'

'I'll be on my way then.' He kicked his horse into a trot. 'Good day, ma'am.'

She headed to the farm that he'd mentioned. There was no work. The farmer already had enough labourers to bring in the harvest, but he took pity on her and sent her along to his neighbour, who was pleased to take on an extra pair of hands.

For five days she toiled in the fields alongside strangers, gathering in the wheat in the burning sun, and sleeping rough in the shelter of a hedge. Her feet grew hot and blistered, but she had food and a few coins to keep her going while she walked on towards the Medway, determined to find Matty.

The *Retribution* lay on her belly in the mud. The prison ship, a Spanish vessel, looked as though she'd been blackened by fire. Her timbers were dull and dirty, and some were broken. There were huts on her top deck for the guards and the only way to reach her was to cross the murky water by jolly boat.

There was a group of convicts in brown shirts, trousers, boots and double irons, loading a sailing barge on the quay. She moved closer, looking for Matty among the hundreds of men, but she didn't find him until the next day when she spotted him in a gang that was waiting for the jolly boat to return them to the hulk for the night. The overseer was yelling at one of the other prisoners who was limping and slowing the rest down. Matty shouted something and received a whack from the overseer's stick in return.

'Matty, my love,' she shouted, running towards them. 'Matty!'

By the time she reached the water's edge, he'd been dragged onto the jolly boat, and it had set out across the water. The overseer bellowed at the prisoners and the oars clunked in the rowlocks, the sound fading along with Catherine's hopes of attracting Matty's attention.

Her heart sank. She chastised herself for imagining that she could turn up, find him and steal him away on a ship to a place where they could make a new life together.

She stared at the boat which was slowly retreating into the desolate landscape. She hardly noticed the rat that ran across her foot and scuttled along a tarred rope to a nearby barge. What should she do next? Where should she go? Should she try her luck in London, or return to what she knew?

She walked along the turnpike road, stopping in Chatham to eat and drink at the Bear and Staff in the high street, choosing a table in the darkest corner she could find, afraid that she would be accosted by one of the men within the establishment. She'd picked on the inn because there appeared to be several young women present, but it wasn't until she was part-way through her fish and pea broth that she realised they were whores, drinking gin and plying their trade. She wasn't sure what to do once she'd finished her meal: take a room or move on? She peered through the grimy window where the lanterns outside barely pierced the darkness. Where would she sleep tonight?

She settled on taking a room for a shilling that she could hardly afford, but it was better than putting herself at the mercy of the naval men and pickpockets who were roaming the streets. In the morning, she rose early and spent the next few hours walking on through the villages of Rainham, Newington, Sittingbourne and Teynham. At about four o'clock in the afternoon, she was close to Ospringe when an elderly woman, a higgler with a basket filled with sprigs of heather, confronted her. Her eyes were glazed white like marble.

Catherine moved aside, not wishing to speak, but the woman caught her across the legs with her walking stick.

'What's a pretty young lady like you doing alone on this road? What beautiful hair and skin you have.' She touched the end of her stick to Catherine's belly. 'I see. You are with child.' A smile spread across her wizened face. 'You look as if you could do with a square meal, my lovely, and I think I can help you.'

'I don't want your help, thank you.'

'You could easily be a lady of breeding, fallen down in her luck.'

'I'm nothing of the kind,' Catherine said, feeling weak at the thought of food. She was torn. She was starving, yet she felt a strong sense of unease about the old woman's motive for offering to assist her. She bore an air of malevolence as though she was out to do harm.

'Come along with me and we'll do what we have to do to make ends meet. I think with new clothes we can pass you off as a damsel in distress. There'll be many a knight in armour who'll fall over themselves to help you.'

The woman's voice seemed to fade into the distance, and Catherine didn't recall anything else until she woke to find herself on a bed in dark, smoky room. She could smell beer and roast meats, the odour of stinking sheets and overflowing chamber pots and the faint scent of lavender.

She sat up abruptly. 'Where am I?'

'Keep your voice down, my lovely.'

Catherine recognised the old woman from the road. 'What are you doing?'

327

'Helping us both out,' she said. 'We're at the Ship Inn, where the landlord has offered us hospitality until you are well ... which might take a few days, give or take.'

'But I'm all right now. Who's paying for this? I have no money. I can't settle the bill.'

'Oh, don't you worry your pretty head. The young man from the stagecoach who saw you fall came to your aid. He's left money with me. It's safe in my pocket. Don't you worry, I can fix everything. When the baby comes, you'll give me money from what you earn while you're with me, and I'll place it with a couple who have no child.'

Catherine shivered. She'd heard rumours of the baby farmers who did away with the baby and took the money to the nearest tavern. The woman's breath reeked of gin. She had to escape from her clutches, but how?

When the woman left, she heard the turn of the key in the lock. She brought food later – bread and a little meat – and left again, keeping her confined. Catherine looked out of the window onto the street. It was too far to jump or climb down.

The woman returned again at midnight. She locked the door, shuffled around then sank down on the bed. Catherine shrank back, pretending to be asleep until dawn began to break, when she slid slowly to the edge of the bed, aware of every creak and groan of the bedstead. She sat up and lowered her feet to the floor, reached down and picked up her boots and basket. The woman's breathing stopped. Catherine hesitated, her heart in her mouth. The woman sighed and started to breathe again.

Catherine stepped across the floorboards, testing each one before she placed her full weight on it. On reaching the door, she slowly worked on the bolt then pushed it open. She looked out onto the landing and hastened towards the stairs. Down she ran and out through the front door of the inn onto the street. She kept running even though she was barefoot, passing the bakery and the village forge and heading away from Faversham. When she looked back and found no one following in pursuit, she slowed to a walk to catch her breath. She had pains in her belly and a raw sensation in her throat.

She checked her pockets – they were empty except for the half a sixpence. She checked her basket and found one single coin. She was alone, almost penniless and with child. She didn't see how it could get any worse.

Chapter Fourteen

Innocence and Temperance

Faversham

The rain began to fall. Catherine took shelter at the foot of a rick, crawling a little way inside where she curled up, shivering, like a half-drowned dormouse. The next morning, she emerged into bright sunshine to continue her search for work, but it was the same story at every farm. The great threshing machines were rumbling into action, some powered by horse, some by steam. They didn't need any more hands.

At the end of another day of walking, her boots began to fall off her feet. She tore some strips of material from her petticoat and wrapped them around her bleeding toes before moving on. She pulled an onion from a field and ate it raw. Its scent on her skin was a painful reminder of the time she had accused Matty of stealing onions from her pa. How she regretted that now. She hadn't known what poverty was.

She tried another farm.

A young woman opened the door and stared at her.

'What do you want?' She was wearing a crumpled apron and holding a wooden spoon.

'I'd like to speak with the mistress of the house, if I may.'

'You may not, I think.'

'Sarah, who is at the door?' A middle-aged woman appeared in the hallway behind the maid. 'How many times have I told you to leave spoons and the like in their rightful place before you greet a caller?'

'I'm sorry, ma'am.' The maid's attitude changed as soon as her employer spoke. 'This person is looking for work.'

'Tell her to go away. We have all the staff we need.'

'Miss, we have no work here.'

'I can clean and cook, and do laundry. I can sew,' Catherine said quickly.

330

The maid closed the door in her face.

She tried the farmyard where the farmer spoke with her as he supervised the labourers and the threshing machine.

'If I could afford to give you lodgings for a while, I would, but there's no work. Have you nowhere else you can go?' Tears sprang to Catherine's eyes when he carried on, 'The shelter of the workhouse would be better than being on the street.'

She shook her head. She would go anywhere but there.

She walked on through the woods, scavenging for sticks that she could sell or exchange for food, but the wood was wet and weighed her down. She sat down on a tree stump to rest for a while as the sun came out. Its rays crept across her body, drying her clothes, warming her skin, and bringing out the emmets that bit at her legs where her stockings had gone into holes.

Other than the raw onion, she hadn't eaten for three days, not since she'd baked half a potato in the embers of a fire that she'd made up from kindling and twigs. She gazed around at the trees and undergrowth looking for anything to break her fast, finding only a handful of fallen hazelnuts. She picked them up, broke them from their shells and nibbled at the shrunken kernels. She remembered how Matty had found the bees' nest, and the taste of the honeycomb: sweet dreams of long ago when she didn't have a care in the world. Now she couldn't find enough food to sustain a squirrel.

What should she do? Go back home to Overshill and throw herself into Ghost Hole Pond to the mercy of the spirits?

As she contemplated the idea of drowning, the baby kicked inside her.

'I'm sorry. I wouldn't hurt you for the world,' she whispered. Stroking her belly, she raised her eyes to the sky and offered a silent prayer for calm seas. 'Matty, my love.'

She stood up, turned and headed back to Faversham with her shawl wrapped tightly around her shoulders. Her stomach griped with hunger. She was starving.

She stopped at the next bakehouse that she came across. A woman stared from the door, guarding the loaves that were lined up in the window, and the faggots that were stacked up outside. A boy pushed past her with a bucket of frothing yeast as she searched in her basket for her last coin, and handed it over to the woman.

'That isn't enough for a loaf of bread,' she said, her eyes enquiring as they flicked from Catherine's belly to her face, 'but I can give you a few crammings. Put your money away,' she added quietly. 'Wait there.' She went inside the shop and returned with a paper bag.

Catherine snatched it. She tore the bag open and stuffed a lump of chicken feed into her mouth.

'Thank you,' she muttered, her mouth filled with rancid lard and bran, bound with water and baked in the oven.

'God bless you. Where are you heading?'

'Faversham.' The dry crumbs stuck in Catherine's throat. 'I have relatives there.'

'You'd better keep walking, so you can be safely indoors by nightfall,' the woman said.

Catherine lowered her eyes and went on her way along Lower Ospringe Road. She walked past the Union twice before stopping outside the entrance. It was a grand building, newly constructed from Faversham brick, and more imposing than any house Catherine had seen, apart from Mr Hadington's. The front gateway bore a sermon in stone carved above, reading 'Innocence and Temperance'.

She couldn't go any further. If she walked away now, she would be walking to certain death and she would have failed in her promise to Matty to look after their child. Taking a deep breath, she stepped up to the timber gates and knocked at the small door within them. The slot in the door opened and a pair of dark eyes peered out at her.

'Who goes there?' said a man's voice.

She didn't know what to say. Every fibre of her being burned with shame.

'I've fallen on hard times. Please, sir, I'm at my wits' end. I have no food, no money. I'm desperate.'

The door opened. She shrank back as a fetid odour wafted out from the courtyard beyond the gates. 'Uncover your head so I can see you.'

She pulled her hood back to reveal her face.

The gateman stared at her. He was about forty years old with a pale complexion and white-blond hair, as if he'd been laundered with onion juice.

'Where are your documents? Your written order from the parish?'

'I have none.'

'I'm obliged to peruse your paperwork. Rules is rules. Have you anything that will do?'

She shook her head. She had no energy left to walk back to Overshill to meet the overseer to authorise her admittance to the Union. She closed her eyes and began to sway. She didn't care what happened any more. She was exhausted, drained, prepared to lie down right there and let her life ebb away if no one would help her.

'I suppose that the first rule of rules is that rules are made to be broken,' the gateman said. 'You aren't the first and you won't be the last. Let's see what the Board decide tomorrow. Follow the corridor to the left.'

Catherine staggered through the door and into the courtyard.

'No, that way, cloth ears,' the man said, re-directing her. 'Keep going straight and you'll find yourself at the receiving ward.'

She entered the ward where the aroma of cheap lye soap and unwashed bodies assaulted her nostrils. She retched, partly from the smell and partly through hunger. A fire burned and belched smoke from the grate at the far side of the room, but it made no difference to the temperature. She stood shivering in silence for some time before a middle-aged woman entered the ward and approached her.

'There's no need to be scared, ducks,' she said as Catherine shrank back. 'I'm Mrs Coates, the matron here. What's your name?'

Catherine frowned. She wasn't expecting to be greeted by a friendly face. The woman had dusty brown hair pulled up into a bun with a cap on top, a round face with soft green eyes and a mouth prone to smiling.

'Your name? I thought that was a simple enough question.'

'Mrs Matthews,' she said. She had wanted to say Carter, to imagine that she was indeed Matty's beloved and loving wife, but she was afraid that because of his notoriety, her true identity would soon be guessed at.

The woman scribbled in a book, adding her name to a list.

'You'll be interviewed by the Board of Guardians tomorrow. If you answer their enquiries to their satisfaction, they'll approve your entry into the workhouse proper. Now, hold your arms up.'

'I have nothing but my clothes and what's in the basket,' Catherine said, her hands behind her back, fumbling for the half a sixpence that she'd tucked into her waistband. She placed it in her palm and turned aside to cough, covering her mouth so she could slip it beneath her tongue.

'You are unwell?' Mrs Coates said.

'It's just a summer chill.'

'Put your arms up then. Quickly. I have to search your person for valuables and contraband, and anything that can be used as a weapon. It's Union rules. Take it or leave it.'

Catherine struggled to keep her hands raised above her head as Mrs Coates patted her all over and checked her pockets.

'Now, take off your clothes then get into the tub over there. There's soap and a scrubbing brush.'

Catherine removed her clothes as the metallic taste of the half a sixpence stung her mouth.

335

Trembling and ashamed at exposing her nakedness, she stepped into the tin bath of greasy, grey, lukewarm water.

'Sit down.' Mrs Coates poured a basin of hot water over Catherine's head and checked her hair for lice with a comb, tugging roughly at the knots, before she made her scrub herself clean and raw all over.

'Out you get.' Mrs Coates handed her a cloth to dry herself. 'I don't want you catching your death when you haven't got anyone to give you a decent burial.' Her voice softened. 'Come over to the fire while I find you a uniform.'

'I'd like to keep my clothes, if you please.'

'I can't let you wear those rags in here. We'll have them fumigated and put away for the day when you leave us, if you don't end up in the parish coffin beforehand. You'll be given supper and sleep here until you see the medical officer and go in front of the Board tomorrow. When they admit you, you'll pick oakum until the time comes for your lying-in. The work is hard and the rations are moderate.' Mrs Coates bustled away and returned with a uniform.

Catherine dressed in front of the fire and hid the half a sixpence in the hem of the skirt.

Later, after a meal of potato, turnip and meat stew with dry bread, she settled down on a bench with a blanket for the night. The wool was scratchy against her skin, the mice scuttled across her feet and her heart ached for Matty and Overshill. She missed John too. How was he without her and Matty to look after him? She hoped Ma was struggling with John's care and keeping up with all the chores. It would serve her right for treating Catherine like she had. And as for Pa, she was angry at him for blaming her and Matty for the loss of the tenancy. Ultimately, Wanstall Farm had meant more to him than his own flesh and blood.

The next morning, the sound of a bell jolted her out of sleep.

'No lazing abed.' The sound of Mrs Coates's shrill voice reminded her where she was.

She dragged herself up and dressed in the uniform she'd been given the day before. As she pulled on her stockings, she became aware of another figure who was shrouded in shadow in the alcove beside the fireplace.

'Good morning,' she said, unsure whether she should speak or not.

'Well, I never did. It is indeed a good mornin', especially now that I have the chance to re-acquaint myself with Miss Rook.' The figure stepped into the light. The face was familiar, older and more careworn, but otherwise the same.

'Drusilla?' Memories came flooding back: the harvests at the farm, the night of the rick fire and the confrontation in the woods.

Catherine felt sick as the former maid went on, 'You've been brought down a peg or two. Who would have thought that you of all people would end up pickin' oakum like the rest of us?' She cackled like a witch. 'This is the answer to all my prayers, a little bird released from her gilded cage, all a-flutter and in need of a friend.'

'The name is Mrs Matthews,' Catherine said firmly.

Drusilla touched the side of her nose. 'I see how it is. It's all right. I'll help you keep your secrets.'

But it would be at a price, Catherine thought.

'I shan't be staying here long,' she said.

'We'll see. There's many a pauper who's said that. You owe me, and one day I'll take what I'm due.'

'Why do you blame me for your misfortune?'

'I blame you for lettin' on that those sleepin' drops were from the bureau at the farm, not ones Jervis had got for me, so I lost my position.'

'You'd have lost it anyway.'

'That's your opinion. And it's Matty's fault Jervis got done for murder. If he hadn't reached for the gun, it would never have gone off.'

'Matty was trying to stop him,' Catherine said. 'He went to fetch Jervis away from Sir William.'

'That's what he led you to believe.' Drusilla leaned close to her so she could see every scar and pockmark on her face. 'He was part of it. He was loyal to the cause.'

'That isn't true. He wanted to end the suffering of the poor, but not by unlawful or violent means.'

'You think what you like. My dear Jervis is a hero. He was one of the few brave enow to fight. You saw what it was like for people like Mrs North left impoverished by the death of her husband, and the labourers laid off in favour of them threshin' machines. You saw how they struggled, yet you were content to stand by and do nothin'.'

'We did what we could,' Catherine said, feeling a stab of guilt that she hadn't done more. 'The

Rooks were never wealthy. Pa paid rent to the squire and tithes to the parish. We never had much to spare, and now we have nothing. You might not know, but Squire Temple has evicted the family from the farm.' She broke off when she saw Mrs Coates approaching.

'Mrs Matthews, there you are. I see that you're back with us, Mrs Carter,' she said a little sharply.

'I found myself down on my luck after a couple of weeks outside, and thought it was time to renew our acquaintance.'

'I'll be watching out for you this time,' Mrs Coates said.

Drusilla smirked. 'You do that, dear. Just remember though that there's none so blind that cannot see.'

What did she mean? Catherine wondered as Mrs Coates retreated. She decided that it was better not to ask. She had no wish to invite trouble.

'To think that you've been brought down to this, and with a babe on the way,' her companion said. 'How does your ma face that snooty vicar's wife when she comes to call?' She mimicked Ma's voice. 'Mrs Browning, I expect you know that we have a daughter – who isn't really our daughter – in the Union over at Faversham. Oh, Mrs Browning, you've gone quite pale.'

'Drusilla, I don't want to hear any more of this.'

'What about your pa? What does he think of his little miss perfect now? Oh, just think of all the times I did your laundry at the farm. Perhaps you'll end up in the laundry here washin' my dirty linen.' She wiped a dab of porridge from her chin. 'I'd call that poetical justice.'

After breakfast, Mrs Coates announced that the Board was ready to see Mrs Matthews.

'That's you.' Drusilla gave Catherine a dig in the ribs. 'I'll go with her in case she should forget her name.'

'Oh no, you won't,' Mrs Coates said. 'You'll clear the dishes. You're a regular – they won't want to see you again.'

Drusilla smiled, revealing her blackened stumpy teeth as though delighted by the thought of her notoriety.

Mrs Coates went on, 'Mr James Berry-Clay from the brewery is a fair and reasonable man. He sits at the head of the table. His younger brother, Mr Rufus, is less amenable. Just answer their questions as honestly as you wish.'

Catherine found herself in an office with a high ceiling and a view of the gravel pits through the window. She wished she was outside flying with the gulls across the scudding clouds, not standing in front of the five stern gentlemen who were seated at a table veneered with the finest walnut.

She took a deep breath. She wasn't scared. There was nothing that people in authority could do any more to frighten her. She remembered standing in front of Mr Hadington – she couldn't bring herself to describe him as her father – and begging him to act for Matty at the Assizes. If she could deal with him, she could cope with these men who were only sitting in their places by virtue of their birth, sex and good fortune.

The gentleman at the head of the table, dressed in a red and black patterned waistcoat, a black tailcoat and dark cravat, was about forty years old. She assumed that this was James Berry-Clay. He had broad shoulders and an air of confidence that matched his flamboyant copper hair and beard. The man beside him had less presence but bore a distinct resemblance to his neighbour. He had red hair as well, but less of it, and he seemed in bad humour. He picked up a piece of paper and read it through a monocle, a deep frown etched on his forehead.

'This is a serious allegation. Mr and Mrs Coates were chosen for their compassion and efficiency of management,' Mr James said. 'Rufus, you were present at the vote.'

'What efficiencies have we seen? Name me one. The bill for bread has doubled in the past month since we changed supplier.'

Catherine waited. They didn't seem interested in her and she wondered if Mrs Coates had made a mistake and she wasn't expected.

'Which was the correct thing to do,' Mr James said. 'The old bread was mouldy and tainted.'

'Good enough for these people.'

'It was inadequate even for feeding the pigs.'

'Meat has gone missing from the kitchens.'

'Mrs Coates assures me that there's been an error in accounting. She's looking into it.'

'You are a fool to trust her.'

'She's an honest woman.' Mr James turned to Catherine. 'Name?'

'Mrs Matthews, sir.'

'So you are another who makes a pretence of being married?' Mr Rufus cut in. 'I see you have no shame.'

'I have nothing to be ashamed of.' Catherine

spoke out clearly.

'I beg your pardon.'

'I have nothing to be ashamed of,' she repeated.

'I heard perfectly well the first time.'

'In that case, why did you beg my pardon?' She would not be cowed.

'You are most impertinent. Where is the father of this child? Do you even know who he is?'

Catherine nodded.

'Speak up.'

'Yes, sir I am certain of it.' Her cheeks burned with humiliation. Hadn't she suffered enough?

'Why will he not support you? Why does he cast you onto the limited resources of the parish? Give us his name.'

'I will not.'

'Will not or cannot?'

'I am a widow.'

'There's no need for this, Rufus,' Mr James said. 'Gentlemen of the Board, let us be charitable towards this poor unfortunate woman who has fallen on hard times.'

'She has an attitude that may rouse the other inmates to dissatisfaction and rebellion,' Rufus persisted.

'We can't possibly send her away on out-relief when she has no fixed abode, and I will not have the death of a baby on my conscience.'

'If you have your way every time, we'll have the whole of the population of Swale requesting admission to the workhouse. We must make an example of every weak-minded woman to prevent others falling prey to their base urges.' Rufus's eyes flashed with passion and his cheeks grew high with colour as though he were growing excited at the thought of conquering any number of 'weak-minded' women himself. 'I see them on the wharves at night, larking about with the seamen with no reference to their virtue. I see them walking arm in arm along the street outside the brewery with their once maidenly attributes exposed for all to see.' There was a bubble of spit on his lips. 'The churchmen do nothing to stop this expression of debauchery.'

One of the other men grunted and shifted in his seat. Another tapped the end of his cane against the table.

'Gentlemen, I humbly request that we move matters along. I have a meeting at the Customs House in less than a half-hour.'

Mr James cleared his throat and turned to Catherine.

'Young woman, you will enter the main work-house where you will be entitled to three hearty meals a day in return for your labour until such a time as you will be required by the demands of confinement to move to the lying-in ward. There you will bring forth your child into the world under the protection of the Union.'

Under the protection of the Union? The words echoed around inside her head like thunderclaps.

'What will happen to my baby?' she asked, her voice tremulous.

'It will likely die or end up an orphan, like the rest of them,' Mr Rufus said harshly.

'I apologise for my brother's thoughtless words,' Mr James interrupted. 'He is wrong to condemn you without knowing your story. Go now. Mrs

Coates will set you to work.'

Immediately, she was set to work in the oakum room with eleven other women. She was given a spike, an empty basket and instructions to fetch some of the tarry old rope from the baskets in the corner by the door before she sat down at the end of one of the benches.

'Come and sit here, my dear.' Drusilla patted the place beside her and Catherine found that she had no choice other than to sit there where there was more room for her.

'Show Mrs Matthews what to do,' Mrs Coates said.

'Your hands will be cut to pieces by the end of today. You have to use the spike to untwist the old rope into strands then unroll them between your fingers.' She showed her how to spread them across her knees to turn the corkscrew spirals into a loose mesh. 'Then, when you're finished, you put 'em into your basket so Mrs Coates can keep an eye on how much you've done. No slackin'.'

'What is the purpose of this?' Catherine asked quietly.

Drusilla smiled. 'To keep us out of trouble. To make us suffer for being penniless, homeless and desperate. No, it's to make caulkin' for the boats at the shipyard.'

As they worked, the women talked, telling their stories of how they'd been forced to turn to the Union, how their families had been split up at the gatehouse and their husbands had been sent to work outside on the wharves and in the brick-fields.

344

'What about your children?' Catherine asked.

'I've lost two little ones,' said the woman sitting on the bench beyond Drusilla.

'I'm sorry.' She wished that she hadn't enquired, but the woman wanted to talk about them, a girl and a boy, twins who died soon after birth.

'It was God's will. At least He gave them breath that I might say goodbye to them.'

'You will have others,' another of the women said. 'Mine was with me until he was six months old.'

'My son was sold by the beadle to a shipbuilder,' said yet another. 'He guts fish, and cleans the decks of the ships that bring oranges and silk in to Faversham.'

Catherine continued picking at the rope on her lap, the strands cutting into her fingers, making them swell and burn. This was exactly what she feared; that someone would take her and Matty's child away from her. The thought of it brought her close to tears.

'How did you end up here, Mrs Matthews? Where is your husband?' Drusilla asked.

'I'm a widow,' Catherine said, sticking to her story.

'Such a terrible thing,' Drusilla sighed sarcastically.

Catherine didn't respond until later when they were in the women's ward, preparing for sleep.

'I wish you would hold your tongue,' she said. 'It's none of your business.'

'It's all right, miss. Your secret's safe with me, although there are one or two here whose husbands were sentenced with our men, who might recognise you from before. Look at you. You behave all meek and hard done by, but you aren't the only one to have suffered. My life will never be the same again without Jervis. Any heart that I had has been torn out.'

'I'm sorry,' Catherine said.

'We all have our burdens to carry, but life goes on. You have to make the best of it, and take advantage of every opport*oo*nity that comes your way. Jervis l'arned me to be ruthless, not shilly-shally about. I'll let you know when anything of interest comes my way.'

Catherine knew what she meant, but she wouldn't play any part in an unlawful act. No doubt Drusilla would set her up as revenge for what she reckoned Matty had done to Jervis.

She wished her goodnight before she lay down on the straw mattress and pulled the thin blanket over her shoulders. She prayed for Matty and their child before she fell into a deep sleep.

In the following weeks, she toiled hour upon hour in the workhouse until the oakum turned her skin brown and the stench of tar seeped into her body. She washed her hands before meals, but no matter how hard she scrubbed, nothing could make the stain and smell go away. Even more dispiriting was the fact that as soon as one pile of rope was done, Mrs Coates ordered the delivery of another.

One day in October, the Union came round to inspect the workhouse, staff and inmates. Mr James was among them, discussing a problem with the food in the corridor outside the oakum room. Catherine was inside, sitting on the bench alongside Drusilla. She was seven months gone and her belly ached with the weight of the baby. She could see the group through the open door and hear their conversation.

Mr Rufus was berating the beadle and Mrs Coates. 'You seem barely qualified to run a brothel, let alone an institution such as the workhouse.'

'I assure you we are the most honest people you could find in Faversham,' Mrs Coates said.

'We are the salt of the earth,' said the beadle.

'So why, whenever we inspect the place, do we find problems? The ledgers never match up with the numbers of occupants actually resident. Neither do the invoices and payments for the victuals. Today, there are three sacks of flour unaccounted for.'

'It is hard to keep track when we have so many in-and-outs,' said Mrs Coates. 'There are those who return to the outside to drink and sin, then come back to us when they can no longer cope.'

'Maybe, brother, you should take heed of Mrs Coates's words,' Rufus said. 'We are a laughing stock. The regime here is said to be less harsh than anywhere else in Kent. By providing kindness and food in abundance, we're encouraging those who are more than capable of supporting themselves to take advantage of the state.'

'For every one who takes advantage, there are ten or twenty who would die if left to fend for themselves,' Mr James said. 'Look at the number of lunatics and elderly, and the homeless. Why

347

shouldn't they have a life that is more than an existence? Why should they be denied shelter, food and drink? It's against my conscience to apply more deprivation than there already is to these miserable people.'

'If you struggle so much with your conscience, you should go to the Board for a vote so that I can take the burden from you.'

'You know that will never happen.'

'I do believe that you show more consideration to these people than you do to your wife.'

The group moved on, leaving the women who were picking oakum to gossip about what they had just heard. Catherine kept her views to herself. It was true that life inside was better than she'd thought possible. She'd lost her freedom, her life being ruled by the sound of the workhouse bell, but there were compensations. They had candles and coal fires so they could boil a kettle. They had enough food of adequate quality, access to a medical officer and plenty to occupy them.

Mr James reminded her a little of the way Pa had used to be before John had had his accident. She wondered how the Rooks were, if John missed her at all, and what had happened to Wanstall Farm. Had the Nobbs family actually got their hands on the tenancy? There was no news of their fate, and unless she exposed her identity, she had no way of finding out. It upset her, but it was having no news of Matty that hurt the most.

Chapter Fifteen

The Littlest Feet

It was the beginning of December and Catherine was beginning to wonder if the baby would ever come. One afternoon as she was unrolling a fresh section of rope in the oakum room, a pain caught her around her belly. She gasped and pressed her hand to her stomach.

Mrs Coates looked up from her table where she was writing notes into a ledger.

'Are you in some kind of trouble, Mrs Matthews?'

Catherine found that she couldn't speak.

'Put your work down and make your way to the lying-in ward.'

'I shall stay a little longer,' Catherine insisted after she'd managed to breathe through the pain. If the truth were told, she was frightened. She'd heard the moans and screams from the top floor of the Union as the women laboured to give birth to their babies. She'd heard the stories of how the nurse dragged them out, some dead and some alive, from their mothers.

'Go on, ducks,' Mrs Coates said. 'Babies don't wait.'

Drusilla snatched up the rope that Catherine had already picked through and took it for her own work, but she didn't care. She struggled upstairs to the ward where the nurse showed her to a bed. There were two new mothers there already. One held a weakly baby in her arms while the other was curled up on a mattress with her newborn swaddled in a grey sheet alongside her.

'That's Mrs Wilson,' the nurse said. She was older than Catherine, and had a squint and long bony fingers. 'I'm afraid she hasn't got long for this world.'

Catherine recoiled. She didn't want to be here. She didn't feel safe.

'You must lie down,' the nurse said as another wave of pain took Catherine's breath away and swept her into the realms of hell. She was barely aware of what was happening as she laboured for seven hours with the jangling of the workhouse bell marking the time. At midnight, her baby was born.

'It's a girl,' the nurse said.

Catherine waited for the cry. Would it come? Suddenly, there was a whimper and then a wail. The nurse placed the bawling creature against Catherine's breast and bustled away to attend to Mrs Wilson. Catherine held her daughter close, examining every detail of her face. At first she seemed like a stranger, but gradually, she made out Matty's features in her shock of brown hair and the breadth of her forehead. She counted her fingers and noted the rash of tiny milk spots across her nose. A fierce wave of love flooded her heart.

'You're beautiful,' she whispered as the infant continued to cry. 'Please, God, have mercy on you and let the world treat you kindly. How I wish your papa was here to greet you.' How she wished he was here at her side to support her and love her for the rest of their lives, as he'd once promised.

'She has an excellent pair of lungs,' the nurse said, returning to the bedside.

'Why won't she stop crying?' Catherine tried to latch her onto the breast, but she turned away.

'Your milk is too thin,' the nurse opined. 'I'll send for some bread and meat from the kitchen.'

'She's too young for that,' Catherine said, alarmed.

'Of course she is.' The nurse smiled. 'It's for you. You need to build up your strength. Don't worry – your milk will come in.'

A groan from the bed opposite distracted her. The nurse took a mirror from the pocket of her apron and held it to the mother's mouth.

'She's gone.' She closed the mother's eyes. 'God rest her soul. Annie, go and inform the beadle.'

Catherine said a silent prayer, hoping that she hadn't suffered.

Annie, the girl who was assisting on the ward, carried out her errand before reappearing later with a bowl of meaty stew and bread. Catherine forced herself to eat it by the light of a lantern while the nurse sat with the orphan baby, offering him milk from a bottle. Eventually, she fell asleep with her baby at her breast.

The first bell of the morning woke her. Two men came to collect the body of the lately departed mother. The orphaned baby started to cry most terribly. Foul miasmas emanated from the blankets, and the fire in the grate belched thick black smoke. Catherine couldn't bear it any longer. She rose and dressed.

'Where do you think you're going?' the nurse asked.

'Back downstairs. I'll be needed in the oakum room.'

'Not today. You must stay here until baby's feeding and your health is secure. Childbed fever can strike at any time for up to at least a week after confinement.'

'I'm just as likely to fall ill here as anywhere else,' Catherine said. More so, she thought.

'You need rest. I forbid you to return to work until I say so. It's the rules.'

'Aren't rules made to be broken?' she asked, recalling the gateman's words.

'Of course they aren't.' The nurse looked shocked. 'They're there for a purpose: in this case, to keep mother and child safe.'

'I can make my own decisions.'

'You can on the outside, but not inside while you're enjoying the hospitality of the Union. You will remain on the ward, unless you want me to call for the beadle to have you turned out onto the street.'

Catherine glanced towards the window where the rain was trickling down the panes of glass. As much as she craved the outdoors, her baby would never survive the winter weather.

'I'll stay,' she said reluctantly.

The workhouse bell rang again for breakfast. Annie brought porridge, bread and milk. The milk was sour, the porridge was blackened at the bottom of the bowl and the bread was stale, but Catherine forced herself to eat. She put the baby to her breast and, this time, she fed.

'What's her name?' the nurse asked.

'Agnes,' Catherine said, her heart breaking all over again as she thought of Matty and his request. 'Agnes Ivy.'

On the second day, Agnes started to screech, repeatedly pulling her legs up and forcing them straight. Catherine tried putting her to the breast, but she turned her head away. She paced up and down the ward, rocking Agnes in her arms to soothe her, but nothing worked.

'Please don't leave me,' she murmured, pressing her lips to her forehead.

'Why are you crying, Mrs Matthews?' the nurse asked.

'My baby's sick. Look at her. What can I do?'

'It's nothing serious. She has the symptoms of bellyache. The safest remedy is a few drops of peppermint in sweetened water.' She turned to the girl who was sweeping the floor. 'Annie, go and fetch a hot flannel. Each time the bell rings, you lay it across the infant's back to ease the pain.'

While Catherine tried this remedy, the medical officer called in to the ward to add his contribution: a little gin for the fractious child, and no onions or cabbage for the mother. The nurse wondered aloud if Mr James could be persuaded to provide a bottle of gin for the lying-in ward – for medicinal purposes.

Over the next few days, Agnes grew stronger and the bouts of colic less frequent without the aid of gin, and within a week, Catherine was back in the oakum room with her baby swaddled against her breast.

'Perhaps there is a chance that you'll meet your papa one day after all,' she whispered as she wielded the spike and separated the endless strands of tarry rope. Although her head told her that Matty would never return, her heart still harboured hopes that he would find his way back to her. In the meantime, she had to find some way of supporting herself and Agnes. She had no desire to remain at the Union any longer than she had to, but how could she possibly begin to build a life on the outside?

Over the next few weeks, the professional 'in-and-outers' like Drusilla came and went, and came back again, much to Mrs Coates's chagrin, and it appeared to Catherine that the only way to leave the Union for good was inside the parish coffin.

At Christmas, the inmates had a day off. There was a service with singing which reminded her of the choir at the Church of Our Lady at Overshill, followed by a feast of baked beef, plum pudding and strong beer. Mr James had provided snuff, tobacco and oranges out of his own pocket for the end of the meal, and he'd ordered all the fires to be lit and piled up with extra coal against the cold.

Catherine carried Agnes into the yard to escape the smoke and general merriment for a while. It was quiet outside and she took time to watch the few snowflakes that drifted down from the ochre sky.

Drusilla called to her from the doorway.

'I have somethin' that'll be of interest to you,'

she said as Catherine approached.

'I doubt it.' Catherine kissed Agnes gently on the forehead.

'You don't want to stay here for the rest of your days, do you?'

'Of course not, but I'll only profit by honest labour.'

'Oh, listen to you. You're such a prig. If you think like that, you'll never get out of here.' Drusilla tapped the side of her nose. 'Just between us, I've managed to get my hands on some snuff and a bag of oranges.'

'You stole them,' Catherine accused her.

'They were just lyin' around, going beggin'. Anyway, I need someone to carry them out for me, and I thought of you. You still owe me a few favours, after all.'

'I owe you nothing,' Catherine said firmly, but Drusilla continued.

'My plan is that I take care of Agnes while you carry the goods out wrapped in her shawl. I'll arrange the hand-over at the Bear. No one will suspect a thing. Oh, come on. This will give you a few spare shillin's to spend on the child.'

It was tempting. She would never be able to leave the workhouse without money, and a little put away would be a start. She was torn, but the prospect of what would happen if she was found out aiding and abetting a thief was unbearable to contemplate. She would lose Agnes for certain.

'I couldn't possibly. You know that Mrs Coates will lose her position here if the gentlemen of the Board find out that more supplies have gone missing.'

'Who cares? You have to help yourself in this life. No one else will.'

'I won't take advantage of the guardians' generosity of spirit, nor undermine Mrs Coates's security for anyone, least of all you.'

'I'll get you back for this, Miss Rook,' Drusilla hissed, her face so close to Catherine's that she could feel her spittle on her cheek. 'In the meantime, I'll find someone else to act for me.'

Catherine turned away and walked around the yard.

On the afternoon of New Year's Day, Mr James and Mr Rufus arrived at the Union, causing a flurry of excitement among the inmates who came rushing to the dining room. Even some of the lunatics were brought down from the ward for the occasion. Catherine joined them with Agnes in her arms.

'What's going on?' she asked Mrs Coates who was standing just inside the door.

'The brothers have made it their mission to give out money every year, sixpence for every adult and threepence for each child.'

'They give to make themselves feel better,' Drusilla cut in. 'Often, I wonder what would have happened if Sir William had been allowed to have his way. Jervis and I would have had our own lands and wealth beyond measure. We would have risen way above the brewers and merchants.'

'It was a terrible time. All that bloodshed for nothing. My nephew was one caught up in it and killed, God rest his soul. My poor sister followed him to the grave not long after.' Mrs Coates handed Catherine a heavy iron key. 'Will you fetch the rest of the snuff that was left over from Christmas? It's in the office. Mr James wishes to distribute the remainder to his workers.'

'I'll go,' Drusilla cut in, trying in vain to snatch the key. Catherine was immediately suspicious. Something wasn't right.

'I'd be grateful if you would come with me, Mrs Coates,' she said. 'I'm not sure I have the strength to turn the key in the lock.'

'Are you not feeling well, Mrs Matthews?'

'I have felt better,' she said.

'I'll come with you then,' Drusilla offered, showing off the strength in her wrists. 'I wouldn't let that one go alone, Matron. She knows all the tricks of the trade, how to lie and deceive.'

'What do you mean? I've found Mrs Matthews to be honest in our dealings so far, which is more than can be said for some.'

'Her name is Miss Rook. She was not so long ago betrothed to a criminal, one convicted of murder and transported across the sea: the man, in fact, who betrayed his own brother, my beloved husband, Jervis Carter.' Drusilla wiped an imaginary tear from her eye.

'Is this true?' Mrs Coates frowned. 'You have misled me?'

'I was engaged to marry Matty Carter, the prisoner who was sent to Tasmania with his brother. He was wrongly accused and convicted. It was Jervis who set Matty up, not the other way round,' Catherine said quietly. 'When we go to the office, I wouldn't be at all surprised to find that that snuff has gone. Drusilla asked me to smuggle it out on her behalf and I refused.'

357

'That's a lie.' Drusilla raised her voice, attracting the attention of the other inmates. 'I saw you take the snuff, and the box of oranges. I tell you, Matron, you'll find them underneath Miss Rook's mattress.' She was smirking as she and Catherine walked along the corridor and back to the ward where Mrs Coates joined them in front of the row of beds.

'It's that one,' Drusilla said gleefully, pointing at Catherine's.

Mrs Coates lifted the mattress and there was the snuff and the box of oranges. Catherine felt terrible about it, even though she wasn't responsible for putting them there.

'Oh, Mrs Matthews.' Mrs Coates's hand flew to her mouth. 'How could you?'

'I told you so. I saw her hidin' the goods this morning after breakfast.'

'You didn't,' a voice piped up from beneath a mound of sheets in the far corner of the room.

'Annie?' said Mrs Coates. 'What are you doing lying abed at this time of day?'

'I'm not well,' the girl said, slowly sitting up.

'You should be on the medical ward, not here.'

'I couldn't be bothered to move, which is why I can tell you that it was Drusilla who did what she's accusing Mrs Matthews of. One of the oranges came rolling out. I didn't say nothing. I lay here silent until she had gone, then picked it up and ate it. I hope I'm not in any trouble.'

'No,' Mrs Coates sighed. 'Drusilla, what do you have to say for yourself?'

'I'm not sayin' anythin'.' She was already at the side of her bed, scooping up a few possessions

358

from underneath it, and wrapping them in a sheet before rushing out through the door.

'Go,' Mrs Coates called after her. 'Return to the gutter where you belong.'

'Shouldn't we stop her?' Catherine said.

'What good would it do? She'll have a hard time surviving on the streets in this weather. She won't be allowed back here again. That's punishment enough, I think. As for you...' She looked Catherine in the eye. 'I reckon you have suffered more than enough too. Let's say no more about this, Mrs Matthews. Thank you, Annie. Please take yourself up to the ward later and see Nurse.'

Catherine went back down to the dining room where she overheard Mrs Coates speaking to Mr James.

'I can assure you that there won't be any more trouble in that direction, Mr Berry-Clay.'

'I'm happy to hear that,' he said.

The beadle thumped one of the tables with his fist.

'Line up. Line up!' he bellowed.

Catherine was last to receive the coins from Mr James. He smiled and gazed down at Agnes.

'She is a very bonny infant. She is healthy?'

'Yes, thank you, sir.' Catherine bobbed her head as he handed her the money, ninepence in total. Her heart beat faster. This was the beginning, a sign of better things to come. Drusilla had gone, she could continue living as Mrs Matthews without threat of being unmasked, and she reckoned that she'd found an ally in the girl, Annie.

Life in the Union continued quietly for several

359

months. When Agnes reached eight months of age, Catherine was obliged to leave her with the other children while she worked. She didn't like it, but she trusted Annie, who'd been moved from the lying-in ward to the children's ward, to look after her.

'You're needed to assist with the laundry,' Matron said, calling Catherine to her after breakfast one morning. 'I'm a couple of pairs of hands short.'

'I'd rather not,' she said.

'It isn't your place to say so.'

'Of course not. I'm sorry. I'll go.'

It was hot, hard work and her hands were soon red and raw. As she forced one sheet after another through the mangle, turning the handle until they spilled from the rollers into the basket on the other side, she began to recite a rhyme that she had learned at the farm.

'They that wash on Monday have all the week to dry. They that wash on Tuesday are not so much awry.' It reminded her of how Matty would drop by at the farmhouse to catch sight of her or snatch a kiss. Her chest hurt. She missed him more than she'd thought possible.

'Hey, stop your dreaming. I said, Mr James wishes to speak with you, Mrs Matthews,' Mrs Coates interrupted. 'He has asked for you in particular. He's most insistent.'

Catherine looked down at her apron – it was soaked through.

'I can't go like this. I'm not respectable.'

'I don't think you're in a position to have scruples. You'll do. Quickly, he's waiting for you in the meeting room.'

'What business can he have with me?' Was she in some kind of trouble? Was she about to be banished from the Union?

'That's up to you to find out.'

Catherine abandoned the mangle and made her way to the meeting room.

'That's no reason for all of the rest of you to stop and gawp,' she heard Mrs Coates shouting.

She wiped her hands on her apron and pushed a stray lock of hair back beneath her bonnet, before taking a deep breath and knocking on the door.

'Please, enter.'

She pushed the door open and found Mr James sitting at the head of the table with some papers in front of him. He smiled.

'Close the door,' he said.

She pulled it shut and stood in front of him with her hands behind her back and her head bowed.

'I prefer to do business with people who can look me in the eye.'

She looked up, uncertain.

'That's better. I like to be direct when conducting my affairs, but this is a somewhat delicate matter that I wish to broach with you. I have a proposition that could take you away from the Union.'

Catherine glared at him. What was he suggesting?

'Oh no, Mr Berry-Clay, I wouldn't even consider it.'

'You mean you like living here? You are content

361

to spend the rest of your life under this regime? It's strange, but I thought you would have wanted more, your independence, for example.'

'Not at the expense of my reputation and dignity,' she said, her cheeks burning.

Mr Berry-Clay frowned, then his red beard trembled as he chuckled, 'Oh, you misunderstand me. I wasn't suggesting ... I have a wife to whom I am devoted. I would never consider taking on a mistress.'

'I'm sorry, sir.' She wanted to run out of the room and as far away as possible. What on earth had made her think that he'd be the slightest bit interested in someone like her?

'How is your daughter?' he began again.

'She is well, thank you.'

'I know someone of substance and standing who is happily married. He has everything he can possibly wish for, a beautiful house, servants and wealth. There is but one thing missing, one joy absent from his life. Can you guess what that is?'

Catherine's heart missed a beat. She was suddenly afraid.

'No, not that,' she blurted out. 'Please don't ask me to give her up. She is the apple of my eye, my only happiness.'

'I appreciate your fondness for her ... little Agnes, but there are occasions when the greatest love of all means sacrificing what you hold dearest to you. Think for a moment. What can you give her?'

'A mother's love,' she said simply.

'Agnes would benefit from the love of both a mother and a father. She is bonny and blithe, and no one could fail to adore her. She would want for nothing.'

Catherine hesitated before asking, 'Would she learn to read and write? Would she receive a proper education?'

'Oh yes. She'll have a governess and be brought up as a lady.'

'Can you vouch for these people?'

'Indeed I can. I know them personally.'

'Can I meet them?'

'I understand your concerns, but that won't be possible. The couple wish to remain anonymous.'

'I'll be able to see her? Or receive letters at least?'

'That isn't possible either. It would be too unsettling for the child.'

'No, I couldn't agree to give her away on those terms,' Catherine said quickly. 'It would break my heart.'

'I understand the strength of your maternal feelings, but you must take your situation into account.' He stood up and looked out of the window, his hands clasped behind his back. 'This couple is offering to take your child and give her every advantage. In return, they will give you a sum of money to enable you to rent a small home.'

'Why my baby? Why not any of the other workhouse children?'

'Your daughter is a beauty with a bright smile. The others are ragamuffins and street urchins, the children of pickpockets and others of low birth. You strike me as a woman brought low by circumstance.' He turned back to face her. 'I realise that this is a decision that shouldn't be taken lightly, so why don't you think about it and we will meet again? Say the day after tomorrow, after evening service?'

'I will not consider it further, sir.'

A shadow crossed his eyes.

'It is the lady's dearest wish to care for a little daughter. She would cherish her as her own. Take a little time to reconsider.'

'I will not do that,' she said firmly.

'I don't think that someone in your position has a choice. I will await your final answer.' He showed her to the door. 'Good day, Mrs Matthews.'

'It is not a good day when a stranger offers to take your child.'

She returned to the laundry picked up a hot iron and applied it to one of the sheets that had been brought in from the yard, still slightly damp. She was aware of Mrs Coates's eyes upon her and the unspoken question hovering in the steam that rose from the cloth.

'What did Mr James want to see you for?' she asked eventually.

'I cannot say.'

'It is a most unusual situation. Have you come into money? Are you leaving us?'

'I told you – she's a spy for the Board,' one of the women muttered.

Another turned her back on her.

She caught her hand on the iron and winced, but the pain was nothing compared with the agonising thoughts that were running through her head. She'd told Mr James that she wouldn't consider his suggestion, but she knew she'd be a fool not to think about it.

When the bell rang for dinner, she rushed out to find Agnes. She was sitting in the dirt in the courtyard while some of the other, older children were pretending to roast a dead rat on some sticks.

Catherine recoiled.

'Agnes, I'm here.' She swept her up into her arms, spat on the corner of her apron and wiped her face and hands. 'What's that on your knee?'

Catherine tried to pick out the grit from the graze on her skin. Agnes grimaced but she didn't cry. It was as though she couldn't be bothered, her spirits weighed down by the black clouds and stormy sky.

'How did this happen?' she asked the other children. There were five – two girls and three boys, all under six – in Annie's charge. 'Annie, why haven't you been watching them?'

She looked thinner than Catherine remembered. Her elbows poked out from her blouse and her apron ties were wrapped twice around her waist.

'I've bin trying to keep my eyes on them, but they've worn me out.' Racked by a fit of coughing, she covered her mouth, but when the coughing stopped and she opened her palm, it was spattered with fresh blood.

'Oh my dear, you are sick. You shouldn't be looking after the children at all. Have you seen the doctor?' Catherine had more confidence in the junior medical officer who worked at the Union than she'd had in Doctor Whebley.

Annie shook her head.

'What good will it do? I know what it is. My mother and my sister had the same. They are both dead and buried.'

'You poor girl. Look, I'm sorry for shouting at you. I'll speak with Mrs Coates about what can be done.'

'Ta, miss. You're very kind.'

'Come along, the dinner bell has rung,' Catherine said, carrying Agnes inside.

She couldn't eat. What kind of life was it here for the children? She remembered her childhood: the farm, the hens, the fields and fresh food. Here, the sunshine crept into the courtyards and through the grimy windows for a limited time as though it feared being trapped like the inmates if it tarried for too long within the Union's walls. If Agnes stayed here for much longer, she could end up like Annie: skeletal and consumptive; or she might go mad like the lunatics who rocked back and forth and shouted out at night, and wandered half naked around the workhouse.

She bit her lip, recalling the bitter fragrance of the hops at hopping time, how her body ached at the end of a long day in the fields, the taste of a cool draught of beer and bread and cheese taken in the shade of the trees that rustled in the summer breeze. Agnes would never experience those joys, only the drudgery of the Union.

Was she being selfish, refusing to give up the most precious thing she had in the world?

Mr James had said that the couple who wanted her were prosperous. Catherine dreamed of wealth beyond measure: a house grander than Squire Temple's; clothes more fashionable than

Mr Hadington's; a golden carriage pulled by two pairs of white horses. But possessions didn't mean as much to her as the idea that Agnes would be educated and move in polite society, where she would meet potential suitors and marry for money as well as love, because, much as she'd refused to countenance Ma's suggestions that financial security was more important than affection when it came to marriage, she could see now that she'd had a point.

She had loved Matty and he had loved her, but it hadn't been enough. If they'd had money and education, and been born into a higher class, they would never have ended up in this situation.

Mr James was offering Agnes a free ticket to a new life, and Catherine the chance of independence. What should she do? What would Matty want her to do? What decision would he expect her to make?

Chapter Sixteen

This Little Piggy

The next morning, she sent word to Mr James, and within the hour, they were standing face to face in the meeting room.

'Do I take it that you've changed your mind?' he asked quietly.

She nodded.

'Thank you, Mrs Matthews. You've made the

right decision. She'll have the best of everything, I promise.'

'How can you be so sure?'

'I'm an honourable man who keeps his word. You have experience of my dealings with other people.'

'Indeed, sir.'

'Then you must trust me on this matter. Now, go and fetch the child.'

'At this minute?' she exclaimed. It hadn't occurred to her that it would be so soon. She'd thought she'd have plenty of time to prepare herself and say goodbye.

'It's the best way. I'll arrange for you to receive the money tomorrow morning.' He mentioned a sum that was beyond her wildest dreams. 'I know of a small property for rent in Faversham. You may live there rent-free for six months to give you time to find work of some description so that you are no longer dependent on the Union to pay the rent. You're making a wonderful gesture. You've made sure that she has a secure future, and restored delight and happiness to a marriage that's been devastated by a wife's grief over her barrenness. You will have other children. You are still a young woman.'

He was making out that a child was an object, something that could be easily replaced.

'Fetch her,' he went on.

'I insist on waiting until I have the money.' Catherine was careful, like her pa. You didn't give up the goods before you were paid.

Mr James thought for a moment, then smiled.

'You have an acumen for business which is

unusual in a woman. It's agreed then. I will bring the money tomorrow at nine o'clock sharp. You will bring the child to the boardroom.'

She nodded, turned and fled. One day and one night was all she had left, and she was going to make the most of it. She didn't go to work in the laundry. She took Agnes out through the wooden gate and carried her into the heart of Faversham.

She showed her the market stalls lined up beneath the timber-framed Guildhall where the traders sold eggs, fish, meat, butter, fruit and wool. She took her to the creek to see the boats moored at the quay, the barges and oyster bawleys. She told her about her father and how he had gone to the other side of the world in a sailing ship. Hiding her tears, she explained how much he'd loved her even before she was born, while Agnes smiled and cooed at the fresh sights and smells.

When her arms grew weary Catherine returned to the Union.

'Where have you been, ducks?' Mrs Coates said sternly. 'We thought you'd gone for good. You can't miss a day's work and expect to be fed.'

'I'm sorry. It won't happen again.'

'I should by all rights put you in front of the Board of Guardians in the morning.' Mrs Coates frowned as if she was grappling with her conscience. 'Oh, go on. The bell has been rung.'

Catherine didn't eat. Having made sure that Agnes was fed, she stayed on the children's ward with her. She filled a bucket with warm water and used the end of a cake of soap that she'd acquired from the kitchen to bathe her baby for the very

369

last time. She tore strips from a sheet to dry her, and combed her hair which was growing longer and darker, becoming less like Matty's and more like her own. She held her close and inhaled her soapy scent, trying to embed it in her memory for ever.

'Shall we say the little piggy rhyme?' she asked.

Agnes grinned. Catherine took hold of her big toe.

'This little piggy went to market. This little piggy stayed at home. This little piggy had roast beef. This little piggy had none. And this little piggy went, "Wee, wee, wee," all the way home.' She tickled Agnes's tummy. She was giggling and squirming to get away even before her mother's fingers touched her smooth, baby skin.

'Again?' Catherine asked when her giggles had subsided.

Agnes nodded and they played until she could hardly keep her eyes open. Catherine took her to bed with her and cuddled her, listening to her breathing and the tiny cries she made in her sleep.

'Sweet dreams, little one,' she whispered, pressing her lips to her cheek. 'I love you, my darling.' She felt like a monster. How could she be doing this cruel, wicked thing out of love?

The light of dawn came cold and quick, and all too soon she was back in the boardroom in front of Mr James, who was accompanied by a lady wearing a white bonnet and dark blue linen dress.

'This is Miss Treen,' he said. 'She'll be taking care of the child until she's placed with her new mother.'

Catherine felt sick as Miss Treen reached across to take Agnes.

'Where is the money?' she said, clinging on to her.

'It's here.' Mr James pointed to the leather purse on the table. 'There is a contract for you to sign. Hand over the child so that we can attend to it.'

'I insist on knowing what is in it first.'

'You are a shrew, Mrs Matthews,' Mr James sighed. He gave her the address, number eight, Davington Street. 'There is a neighbour at the property who is holding a key for you. Her name is Mrs Strange. The rent is paid in full for the next six months. After that, as I said before, it is up to you.' He pulled a document from his coat pocket and spread it across the table. She wondered how many times he'd rescued a child from the workhouse before.

'Can you read?' he asked.

'Yes,' she said, but although she tried, the copperplate hand was loopy and long on the parchment, and the words were too complicated. Frustrated, she pushed it back across the table.

'Read it to me, sir,' she said. 'I will not sign until I know what it says.'

He read it aloud. The terms were exactly those that he'd negotiated: that Catherine would hand him the child for him to deliver to the childless couple as their intermediary. She would never see Agnes again, or attempt to make contact with her.

She signed with his pen; blotting the ink with her tears.

'Take the child, Miss Treen,' Mr James said. 'We are done here.'

Agnes started to cry as Miss Treen took her in her arms and whisked her out through the door. Catherine pushed her fingers into her ears to block out the sound of her baby's screams. It was all she could do not to run after them and snatch her back.

'Goodbye, Mrs Matthews. We will not meet again.' Mr James left the boardroom. Catherine picked up the purse and walked out into the corridor where she ran straight into Mrs Coates.

'What's wrong, ducks?' she said. 'I saw the lady taking little Agnes.'

'She's gone.' Catherine's face was wet with tears. 'I'm leaving the Union today. I'd like my clothes back.'

'I don't know what to say.'

'Don't say anything. I wish to leave as soon as possible.'

Catherine followed her down to the receiving ward and Mrs Coates unlocked one of the linen cupboards with a key from the chain around her neck. She rummaged around on the shelves.

'Well, I never did. What a muddle. I don't hold out much hope of finding the outfit you were wearing when you arrived. Many have passed in and out since then, and they're not always honest in their remembrance of which clothing belonged to them.' She picked out a decent dress, coat and bonnet that smelled of bad eggs and dust where they had been folded and put away damp. Not that Catherine minded. She was beyond caring about what she looked like.

She put on the dress, a muddy-coloured muslin with a dark green ribbon sewn into the neckline, over her petticoat, remembering that Matty's half a sixpence was still safely secured within the hem. She slipped the purse into the pocket of the coat and placed the crumpled bonnet on her head.

'I'll miss you,' Matron said. 'Good luck, Mrs Matthews.'

'Thank you for your kindness, Mrs Coates. Farewell.'

Catherine stepped through the door in the gate and took a breath of fresh, untainted air before she set out on her new path.

She walked along the Lower Ospringe Road towards the centre of Faversham, and made a slight left onto Tanners Street, sensing the wind against her face and the drifting scents of the sea, fish and baking bread in her nostrils. She continued along South Road, and turned right into West Street. As she reached Market Place, her heart missed a beat when she recognised Pa Rook, his back bowed and his hair completely white, at the reins of a horse and cart. She turned her face away and ducked into the shadows beneath the stilted Guildhall until the cart had passed, then she scurried along East Street where the smell of malt and hops grew stronger as she approached one of the town's breweries. Before she reached it, she took another right turning and arrived at her destination.

Number eight was one of the houses in a row of ten, built from Faversham brick with tiled roofs. There was a pump outside and a sewer in the middle of the road. She walked up the path which was overgrown with weeds and peered through the window. Something scuttled away in the darkness, but she couldn't see anything else inside except for a broken pail lying on its side. She looked up at the window above. The drapes were drawn across and some ivy had started to poke its tendrils between the wooden frame and the bricks.

It would do, she thought. It just needed some love and attention. This was her one chance of independence and she wasn't going to waste it, especially after the sacrifice she'd made. There was no way she was going back to the Union. Ever.

She knocked at the neighbour's door as she'd been instructed.

'What do you think you're doing disturbing someone at this hour of the morning?' A middle-aged woman opened the door.

'I'm sorry.' It was gone midday. 'My name is Miss...' Catherine hesitated just long enough for the woman's eyebrows to quiver in question. 'Mrs Matthews. I've come to collect the key for number eight.'

'Welcome to the neighbourhood. I'm Mrs Strange – that's strange by name, but familiar by nature.'

'Good morning,' Catherine said, having no desire to befriend this woman with her over-powering scent of essence of roses, low-cut dress and rouged lips. Her skin was marked with pox scars, barely disguised with powder. She plucked out a key from her breast and handed it over. It was still warm from being in contact with her person, Catherine noticed, slightly repulsed.

'I don't know why anyone would choose to live here,' she said. 'There's bird's nests in the chimbley and mices in the privy.'

'That can all be changed,' Catherine said, undaunted.

'Have you any family? Will your husband be along to join you?'

'I am a widow,' she said.

'I'm sorry for your loss, dearie.'

'I'm planning to take in a lodger now and then to make ends meet.'

'If I hear of anyone looking for a room, I'll put him your way.'

'Thank you, Mrs Strange. It was nice to make your acquaintance.'

'I hope we shall see more of each other,' she said, closing the door.

Catherine let herself in to the house and took stock of her new home. The stairs to the next storey went up from the single room on the ground floor, where there was a fireplace and a three-legged chair. The floor was alive with vermin and beetles, and many spiders dangled from their silks as though they were inspecting the new occupant. The grate was filled with ashes and feathers, and a dead pigeon.

The back door led out to a narrow strip of overgrown garden and a lean-to privy. Agnes would love it – she corrected herself – would have loved it.

Overwhelmed with grief and regret, she returned indoors and headed up the narrow stairs into the bedroom, a single room with a window overlooking the street. The bedroom was small and the walls sloped in towards the ceiling, making it seem even smaller, but it would do. There was a brass bedstead suitable for a lodger, as long as he wasn't too tall.

There was much to do, and the sooner she made a start, the better.

She repaired the handle of the bucket and filled it from the well. She washed the dust from the windows, removed the cobwebs and scrubbed the floors. She cleaned the woodwork for bed-bugs and washed the drapes. She fashioned a table from logs and a board that she'd found abandoned in the back yard and paid some attention to the stinking privy.

She collected firewood on a couple of expeditions into the woods, hiding the sticks under her cloak as she walked home, and she purchased a small amount of coal to use in the grate in the kitchen. She obtained food – a bushel of potatoes, turnips and onions, and a ham hock from the butcher. She bought beer from the nearest alehouse. She cleaned the windows with cold tea to make them gleam, and stopped all the holes in the walls and ceilings with rags to stop the influx of any more vermin.

She chalked a sign on a piece of slate that she discovered on the ground in the yard, and placed it in the upstairs window to advertise her trade. Finally, she made a mattress for herself from straw tied together with twine, and hung a bine of hops above the fireplace for good fortune.

She was ready, but no one came and she began to worry that she would run out of money.

Every night, she put a candle in the window to light Matty's way back to her, and to remember Agnes. She prayed that God would guide him and that He would watch over their daughter, before she went to bed and struggled to fall asleep, listening to the drunken sailors shouting and cussing their way about town, and to Mrs Strange who entertained a different bedfellow each night, or so it seemed.

Every day, she walked the streets of Faversham, looking out for Agnes. Whenever she saw a woman with her baby, she was compelled to follow her until she caught a glimpse of the infant's face when she would be overwhelmed by a terrible, gut-wrenching sense of disappointment because it never was Agnes. It was as though she had disappeared from the face of the Earth.

Late one September afternoon, after she'd returned from yet another futile excursion, Mrs Strange called on her.

'I've found you a customer,' she said. 'I told him you're a respectable lady with a reputation as white as freshly laundered cotton sheets. He said in return that you'll never find such a clean-living, well-mannered gentleman.'

Catherine didn't know whether to believe her or not. How did you tell if a gentleman was truly respectable? Look at her own father, as in Mr Hadington. Appearances were deceptive and she certainly wouldn't take a man's self-professed opinion as the truth.

It turned out that Mr Wraith was just past the prime of life. He had a wizened complexion like an apple that had been hanging too long on a tree, and a twinkle in his eye.

'I'm a seafaring man, looking for a few days' lodgings until my ship sails,' he said, introducing himself when he arrived on the doorstep the same evening.

'Welcome.' Having agreed on a price, Catherine let him in and showed him to his room. 'I hope you will find everything to your satisfaction.'

'I'm sure I will,' he said, looking her up and down.

'I don't keep late hours and I won't have my lodgers rolling in at any time of night the worse for wear.'

'I expect you look forward to having a bit of male company, though. There must be times when you yearn for a warm body to join you in bed.' When he smiled, she realised he had no teeth.

'No, sir, I do not. I'm still in mourning for my lately departed husband,' she said sharply. 'An evening meal can be provided and laundry done at a cost per item if you so wish.' She didn't want to make him too comfortable. She didn't want him to stay. She needed the income, but she liked being alone in her little house.

He ordered a meal so she served him fish stew and brought bread to the table in the kitchen. Her skin crawled as she watched him devour his food and wipe his greasy chops with the back of his hand.

He stayed three nights. On the third night, Catherine was lying on the mattress in the room downstairs, listening for his heavy snores. Gradually, she drifted off, but later she felt a heavy weight shifting alongside her and a sudden chill as the blanket was pulled away. The stench of unwashed body and spirits assaulted her nostrils, and a pair of rough hands grabbed at her body. She fought to get up, but his fingers gripped her neck so she couldn't breathe. She had no option but to turn her head and bite hard into his flesh, at which he yelled out loud. Gasping for breath, she reached across him and grasped the poker. She scrambled away, holding it out as a weapon.

'Get out.' She threw his laundered clothes onto the street after him. 'Go and don't darken my door again.'

She bolted the door from the inside and took stock. Mr Wraith hadn't paid her, and she had to empty the slops the next morning and give the chamber pot an extra rinse with hot water and soda. She'd had a lucky escape, though. She checked for the half a sixpence in case her lodger had had light fingers as well as rude manners, but it was still in the hem of her skirt. She resolved to be far more careful in future.

When she returned from the market later the same morning, she ran into Mrs Strange.

'I heard you had a bit of trouble last night,' she said, tweaking the rather grubby lace on her scarlet dress. 'Come along to the inn with me and we'll drown our sorrows together.'

Catherine declined her offer.

'You know, there are easier ways to make money from men than offering lodgings. There's always some knave out there with money in his pocket looking for comfort in a woman's arms.'

Catherine's face burned.

'There's no need to be shy about it. If you change your mind at any time, just let me know. I have gentlemen friends who would pay generously for your looks and refinement, Miss...'

'Mrs Matthews,' Catherine reminded her.

'Mrs Matthews, that's right.' Mrs Strange held her gaze a moment longer than necessary, long enough to make her feel uncomfortable. 'A word of advice in the meantime. It would be to your advantage not to send your customers packing for the slightest misdemeanour. As I'm sure you know, men have needs that become all the more urgent when they've been away at sea for weeks and months on end. Added extras are always appreciated and the establishments that provide them are generally preferred, if you get my meaning. If I had to choose between respectability and making ends meet, I know what I'd decide.'

'I believe that you already have,' Catherine said sharply.

To her surprise, Mrs Strange smiled. 'I like someone who speaks their mind. Good day, Mrs Matthews.'

Catherine let herself into the cottage. She had only ever known Matty. She couldn't bear the thought of any other man touching her. That night she dreamed of him, recalling every detail of his touch, his face, his voice, his scent of musk and grass, and when she woke, she was distraught when she found that he wasn't there with his arms wrapped around her.

At the market the next day, she was bartering with a stallholder over the price of cheese when she heard someone call her name.

'Miss Rook? Catherine, it is you. I can't believe it.'

She turned to find Stephen right behind her.

'I thought you'd moved away,' he said, beaming. 'I'm so glad to have come across you like this.'

'Shh,' she said stiffly. 'My name is Mrs Matthews.'

'You are married?'

'Widowed. I'll explain. Let me pay for the cheese, then we'll find somewhere private where we can talk.' She decided not to invite him back to the cottage for fear that it would arouse Mrs Strange's curiosity.

'There's the Bear across the street,' he suggested.

She hesitated.

'Come on.' Stephen held out his arm to take her basket. 'Surely you can spare your old friend an hour of your time?'

She let him carry the basket across the road and into the inn. They sat in the snug, a private room screened with oak and frosted glass panels, where they shared a jug of ale.

'Have you heard anything from Matty?' she said. 'That's the one thing I've been afraid of, that he wouldn't know where I was to get in touch with me.'

'I'm sorry. He hasn't made contact with his family at all. We haven't received a single letter, but then he wasn't keen on writing.'

'He would have written or asked someone to scribe on his behalf if he could,' Catherine said sadly. 'I wish I knew he was all right, that he was at least content.'

'I feel the same. It would give me some sense of peace if I knew that my brothers were alive and well. It would certainly make a difference to my poor pa.'

'And your ma?' Catherine interjected softly.

'Ah, she has passed to the other side, God rest her soul. She is at peace.'

'I'm sorry for your loss.'

Stephen cleared his throat.

'You don't know how many times I've tried to find you. I have so much to tell you. Emily and I are planning to move back to Overshill to take over the forge. Len and Ivy are retiring to the coast for the sake of Len's health.' He grinned suddenly. 'Emily sent me to the market to buy barley sugar to satisfy her craving – she is with child for a second time.'

Catherine could taste salt tears on her lips.

'I've upset you.' Stephen passed her a hand-kerchief.

'It's my turn to be apologise. The last time I saw you, you were carrying–'

'I had to give her up,' she cut in. 'It was the worst thing I've ever done. When Ma and Pa sent me packing from the farm, I struggled to find work.'

'Why didn't you come to me and Emily? We would have found a way to help.'

'I couldn't, Stephen, you weren't yet established. You were working as an improver for your new master in Faversham, you had a wife and an infant on the way, and you were providing for your father and siblings. I couldn't possibly have imposed upon you.' She took a sip of beer. 'I admitted myself to the...' she could hardly bring herself to give it a name '...the place that some people call Gravel Pit House.'

'I know where you mean. When I found out that you'd left the farm, I went there and asked for you,' Stephen said, frowning. 'I came across Drusilla, who told me categorically that there was no person by the name of Miss Rook at the Union. She lied, didn't she? I shouldn't have listened to her. I'm an idiot sometimes.'

'She's pulled the wool over many people's eyes during her lifetime. She knew very well I was there, though. I went under the name of Mrs Matthews, a respectable widow who had fallen on hard times.'

'I could do her an injury. If I'd found you, I'd have dragged you back home to live with us.' Stephen leaned towards her. 'How are you living now?'

She explained.

'When Emily and I have settled back in Overshill, you can come and join us.'

'No, Stephen. I have no desire to return.'

'I'm sure you'd find paid occupation in the village.'

'I don't think so. I'd be Miss Rook who gave birth to a convicted murderer's child. Who would offer me a position? I'm grateful for the offer, but I'm making a life here.' She changed the subject. 'Have you any news of Wanstall Farm?'

'I'm afraid so. I don't wish to distress you–'

'It will distress me more if you don't tell me.'

'Your parents have gone with John to Selling to

live with your brother, Thomas. Pa said that they loaded up the cart with what they could, and took it away. The squire has since leased the farm to Mr Nobbs.'

It was as she'd expected, but it still pained her.

'I've heard through Len and Ivy that John's health is about the same, but your father is sadly aged, and your mother is unhappy at having to share a house with her grandchildren. As far as the farm goes, Mr Nobbs has made plenty of changes, and not all for the good.'

'How is Ivy?' Catherine asked.

'She's looking forward to enjoying the sea air at Whitstable. I believe that Len is treating her more kindly than he used to, now that he's about to give up the trials and tribulations of running the forge.'

'I'm glad to hear that.'

The bell chimed from the Guildhall tower.

'I'd better go,' Stephen said. 'I have an appointment to view a horse before I return to the forge. One day, I shall rent a few acres where I can buy and sell horses.'

'What about your smithing? How will you find the time?'

'I'm taking on an apprentice. He's a good lad.'

'I admire your ambition.'

'I want to be sure that I can clothe my children and put food on the table.' Catherine stood up and he did likewise. 'You must pay us a visit sometime in the near future. Emily would love to see you.' He gave her a small bow.

'Give Emily my regards And good luck with your new venture.' She accompanied him out

384

onto the street, where they parted. She didn't look back as she returned through the town with the sound of the rag and bone man and the street sellers ringing in her ears. She yearned for the peace and quiet of the countryside, but she couldn't bring herself to go back to Overshill. Her memories were too strong and her feelings too raw.

She didn't see Stephen again, or try to get in contact with Emily either. Seeing them together with their children would have been far too painful, a reminder of how she and Matty could have been a family with their darling Agnes.

For the next two years, Catherine concentrated on making enough money to pay the rent on the cottage. She saved money and firewood by pushing the bed up against the fireplace in the upstairs room, which put her lodgers off asking for the fire to be lit. In the evenings, she cut sheets in half and sewed the sides to the middle so the worn part was at the edges for reuse. She made soup with the fish heads that she bought at the market or straight off the wharf, and sold portions from the house. She planted marigolds and peas, onions, potatoes and raspberry canes.

She had some regulars – journeymen and sailors – whom she managed to keep at arm's length, and soon, by dint of hard work and frugality, she had a steady income, enough to live comfortably.

One of the men made her an offer of marriage. He was a journeyman bricklayer, rough and ready, but kind. He was about to be promoted to foreman and wanted a wife to accompany him to

London, where he would take advantage of the building going on around the London to Greenwich viaduct.

'I'm sorry,' she said when he made his proposal. 'It's a generous offer, but I can't accept. I will marry only for love.'

Her rejection disappointed him more than she'd imagined. He raised his voice in anger.

'You're a capable woman, and a most attractive one with a finely turned ankle and a blush on your cheek, but it's plain that you're burning a candle for another man. I shan't call or take up lodgings with you again.'

'I understand,' she said.

'When you're old and grey, and working your fingers to the bone, think of me and how I'd have looked after you while you made our house a home. Goodbye, Mrs Matthews.' He paid her what he owed and left.

'You are a madwoman,' Mrs Strange said when she asked after him and Catherine told her that he had gone, never to return. 'You turned down an offer of marriage to a man with prospects who would have built a life with his own hands for you in London. And he was decent-looking too.'

She hadn't been tempted. It had been hard at first, being a single woman living alone, but she was beginning to value her independence. She was no longer beholden to anyone. She didn't want to go to London – she'd heard about the slums, the rowdy crowds, and the dirt. Kent was home, where her heart was near Agnes whom she remembered in vivid detail: her toothless smile; her soft hair; her baby scent.

The area held her memories of Matty too. She had prayed that she would hold on to them for the rest of her life, but to her deep sorrow, they were beginning to retreat. She could recall neither the exact timbre of his voice when he whispered to her of love, nor the precise shade of his hair. Whereas once she knew exactly what he would have said in every situation, she was no longer sure. At first, that was more upsetting than anything, because it felt as if she had lost him twice, but as time passed, her grief started to fade.

1841

Chapter Seventeen

The Messenger

Faversham

On a wet and wild March night, Catherine was lying in bed when the sound of knocking began.

At first, she fancied that she was dreaming that Matty was at the door, having returned from the other side of the world to take her in his arms and tell her that he was free, then that the sound had something to do with Mrs Strange entertaining her menfolk next door.

Was it the knocker-upper come early to wake her neighbours and call them from their beds? Or was it someone out looking for lodgings? She couldn't afford to turn them away, unless they were three sheets to the wind.

She forced her eyes open, slid out of bed and crept past the embers of the fire to the door.

'Miss Rook, are you there?' came a man's voice.

'My name is Mrs Matthews.'

'In that case, forgive me. I'll leave you in peace.'

'No, wait.' Catherine pulled her shawl around her shoulders and picked up the stub of the candle from the windowsill before opening the door just a crack. There was a young man of no more than seventeen, shivering in a cloak, and holding the reins of a white horse much like

Stephen's on the doorstep. His hair was dark and slicked across his cheeks by the rain. 'Who is asking?'

A chill ran through her bones when he answered, 'I'm Daniel. I'm apprenticed to a smith who goes by the name of Mr Carter. I've ridden from Overshill with a message for a Miss Rook, but it appears that I've been given the wrong address.' He made to turn away.

'No, don't. I can convey your news to Miss Rook in person. She is well known to me. You'd better step inside.'

'Thank you, ma'am, but I can't stop. I'll get it in the neck if the master's horse catches a chill. He said to tell you – I mean, Miss Rook – that his wife is very sick. She's asking for you – I mean, Miss Rook.'

'Emily?' Catherine said.

'Mrs Emily Carter, that's right.'

'Shall I come in the morning or–?' she began, but Daniel shook his head.

'We need to leave now. You can ride the horse and I'll walk alongside,' he said, allowing for no further pretence about her identity.

'Let me pack a bag and leave a message with my neighbour.' It was an unseemly hour to call, but she needed someone to keep an eye on the cottage while she was away. Mrs Strange was up anyway, hanging out of her upstairs window, to see what the commotion was about.

Very soon, Catherine was riding through the driving rain back home to Overshill for the first time since she had walked away, half-starved and carrying Matty's child. She had been unloved, unwanted, an object of distrust and hatred, but she had no doubts about making her return. Emily was seriously ill. Her pulse beat with a sense of urgency as she wondered exactly how poorly she was. She was afraid that Daniel's gloomy silence was more telling than words. He seemed to be under the impression that her old friend wouldn't last the night.

The wind howled and the branches of the trees clattered together. The clouds raced across the moon, blocking out the meagre light. The horse stumbled its way through the muddy ruts in the road, its ears pressed back against its head. Daniel slipped and scrambled along at its side.

Catherine shivered as the rain seeped through her cloak. It seemed as though they would never get there, and if they did, it would be too late. She began to feel faint with cold. She clung on to the saddle, willing the journey to be over, but nearing Overshill, they had to make a detour around a fallen tree. Just as she was beginning to think that she couldn't hold on any longer, they reached the outskirts of the village and made their way to the forge.

There was a lantern hanging outside the cottage where Ivy and Len had used to live. It seemed familiar, but altered with an extra room added to the side and clad with painted clapboard.

'We are here, Miss Rook.' Daniel helped her down from the horse.

She rushed straight to the door and raised her hand to knock.

The door creaked open. The draught snuffed

out the candle that Stephen was carrying.

'You came.' He reached out for her hand and guided her inside. 'Thank God.' He glanced past her. 'Daniel, wisp the mare dry and give her some extra grub. Oh, and help yourself to tea and the cake the vicar's wife brought round today when you've finished.' He closed the door behind them. 'You'd better get out of those clothes – you're wet through.'

Catherine stood shivering in front of the fire in the kitchen as he held the candle in the flames until it flickered alight.

'How is she?' She removed her cloak and struggled to unlace her boots as Stephen choked back a sob.

Her heart missed a beat. 'I'm not too late?'

He shook his head.

'What's wrong? Have you had the doctor?'

'Dr Whebley has called, but he isn't hopeful. Catherine, I don't know what to do.'

'Lead me to her,' she said, and she followed him up the narrow stairs to the bedroom, where Emily was lying on the bed on her back with her arms tucked beneath the coverlet. Stephen placed the candle on the bedside table where the dancing flame illuminated his wife's face – she looked more beautiful than ever, her complexion pale and her cheeks a delicate pink. Her breathing was quick and shallow.

'She's asleep at last,' Stephen whispered as a baby let out a wail from the crib beneath the window.

'You have another child?' Catherine whispered in awe as the cry tore at her heartstrings, bringing back bittersweet memories of Agnes. She bit back tears. This was no time to be breaking down. Emily needed her.

'She took to her bed the day after she gave birth to our son.' Stephen reached out and touched his wife's hand. 'She has a fever.'

'What medicines has she had?'

'Laudanum and something to purge the impurities from her body.'

'Has she taken any food or water, a little light gruel?'

'Nothing. She refuses everything.'

'The baby? Has he fed?' Catherine moved over to the crib.

'Emily is too weak. I gave him a little cow's milk.' Catherine moved across to the patient and touched her cheek. Her skin was on fire.

'Emily, I'm here now,' she said softly.

Emily moaned in response.

The atmosphere in the sickroom reminded Catherine of nursing John after his accident, how the hot, stuffy air tainted with smoke and bodily odour seemed to worsen the patient's condition. She drew the curtains and opened the window just a fraction.

'Dr Whebley said to keep her warm,' Stephen said.

'Warm, but not roasting like a rabbit,' Catherine said lightly, looking at the fire raging in the grate. 'Have you got any help in at the moment?'

'One of the village girls helps out from time to time.'

'We'll require her services in the morning. In the meantime, I need hot water, bread and tea.'

She had an idea that cow's milk wasn't good for infants. 'Do you know anyone who has a goat so that we might have milk for the child?'

'I do. I reckon I know everyone's business around here.'

'Where is Mrs Millichip? Hasn't she called upon her daughter?'

'Emily's hardly spoken to her mother since our wedding day. They aren't on good terms. Catherine, I know what you're thinking – you're too kind and soft-hearted for your own good. There's no hope of a reconciliation between the two of them.' He left the room and fetched the items that she'd requested. He also brought cooled boiled water and cloths, and stood hovering over her as she encouraged the baby to drink a little liquid before returning him to the crib.

'Go and get some sleep while you can,' she said. 'I'm here now.'

'How can I sleep?' he said, beating his brow with his fist.

'Emily needs you to be well. Please ... I'll call you if there's any change.'

'You promise?'

She nodded.

Stephen moved to his wife's bedside and planted several kisses on her forehead.

'Remember that I love you,' he whispered. 'Always and for ever, my darling.'

Catherine thought that she saw the faintest smile on Emily's lips.

Always and for ever. That was what Matty had said to her when she had last seen him. Her love for him still burned brightly in her breast, but she couldn't help wondering if he still felt the same. Had the experience of living under duress in a strange land changed him as her trials of living in the Union and becoming a mother had altered her? If he did come back, would they have the same understanding, or would they hardly know each other from before?

She stripped the coverlet from the bed and loosened the ties of the gown at Emily's throat. She sponged her face and arms gently with water and ran her fingers through her tangled curls. This wasn't how life had been meant to be. They were supposed to have remained friends, married to two brothers, bringing up their children in Overshill, yet Catherine's desire for honesty and truth had driven them apart, and now it looked as if Emily would be snatched away before they had a chance to fully reconcile.

Emily continued to sleep peacefully overnight and through the morning, when there was a constant stream of visitors to the sickroom. Daniel arrived first with mud and chalk on his trousers, and a bottle of fresh milk.

'I had to catch the goat and milk it myself,' he said, smiling. 'There's plenty more where that came from. Mr Giles is bringing a daily supply until further notice.' He turned to show a young girl into the sickroom. She was about sixteen years old. She had braids of strawberry-blonde hair, blue eyes and freckles, and wore a clean but faded dress with worn cuffs and a cloak.

'This is Maud who's come to help with the children,' he said. 'Maud, this is Miss Rook. She'll give you instructions as to what to do.'

'Good morning, ma'am,' she said, giving a stiff curtsey.

'There's no need to be scared.' Catherine smiled gently. She wondered what was being said about her in the village. Was she still the infamous woman who had given birth to a convicted murderer's child out of wedlock, or had time begun to forget? 'You'll get the children up and dressed, and give them breakfast. You'll scrub the pots and pans, go to the bakery for bread and obtain some meat. You can cook?'

'A little,' she said.

'That will do. I'll supervise.' The girl continued to stare at her. 'You may go down to the kitchen now.'

Catherine picked the baby up from the crib. His grey-blue eyes were open and he was sucking on his fist. She sat in the chair beside the crib and fed him with spoonfuls of warm goats' milk, wiping away the few drops that spilled from his mouth with the corner of a muslin square.

'Poor darling, you were starving.' She rocked him gently against her shoulder and patted his back. If she closed her eyes, she could almost imagine that she was holding Agnes in her arms. Reluctantly, she put him down, swaddled him in a knitted blanket and placed him back in his crib.

At the same time, she heard footsteps stamping up the stairs.

Doctor Whebley entered the sickroom. He took off his hat and placed it on the bedside chest.

'Good morning, Mrs...?' he said, as if he half remembered her.

'Miss Rook,' she said.

398

'We've met before.' He frowned. 'At Wanstall Farm, when your brother broke his head.'

'Yes.' She bit her lip.

'Where is Mr Carter? I prefer to speak with him.'

'I believe he is at work in the forge. You have his permission to relay your opinion through me. You may go and check with him, if you wish.'

'I'll speak with him after I've spoken to the patient,' Doctor Whebley said. 'Please, close that window.'

Catherine refused, no longer afraid to confront anyone who was in a position of authority.

'Are you a doctor? Have you spent years studying the art of medicine?' His bloodshot eyes bulged, making him look as if he was in need of medical help himself. 'No, I thought not. It would behove you not to interfere with decisions that don't concern you. I remember now. You have some fanciful ideas which have no scientific basis whatsoever. Close the window immediately.'

Doctor Whebley might be above her in both social standing and intellect, yet her intuition told her that he was wrong.

'Your friend is suffering from childbed fever. It is not caused by foul air, but by the weight of the petticoats and skirts, and the infant growing in the womb in the early months of pregnancy. Instead of letting the poisons descend from the body in the normal way, they trap them so they enter the circulation where they cause putridity. You will obey my orders, madam, or I will have you banned from the sickroom and advise Mr Carter to take on a new nurse without delay.'

The patient stirred. A low moan escaped her lips, followed by the words, 'Catherine? Is that you?'

'It is I.' Catherine moved quickly to Emily's side. 'Oh, Emily, what a relief. You've given us all quite a scare.'

'I will be well for the sake of my husband and children.' She tried to sit up, but Catherine stayed her with a hand on her shoulder.

'Keep still. You need to rest.'

'At least we are agreed on that,' Doctor Whebley observed.

Catherine decided to close the window, not wanting any upset to disturb what she prayed would be the start of Emily's recovery.

'That's better,' the doctor crowed. 'Put a blanket across the doorway and a cloth into the keyhole. The body must be encouraged to sweat to remove the excrementitious matter, or the patient will die.' He gave Emily a perfunctory examination and glanced at the baby.

'I'd like to get up,' Emily said.

'There cannot be any reason why a woman should get up in less than a fortnight after their confinement,' the doctor said, and Catherine thought of how she had been on her feet within days. 'The period of after-repose is particularly required even at the second or third confinement. The mother's mind should be kept free from excitement and anxiety.

'I prescribe a glass of porter or ale once a day as a restorative, and forbid you to wear the patient out with excessive and unnecessary conversation,' he added. 'I'll let Mr Carter know the good news, and be back tomorrow morning.'

When he'd gone, Catherine turned back to Emily.

'I'm so glad you came.'

'I came as soon as I heard.' She gave her a few sips of water.

'Where is my baby?' Emily asked, looking around the room.

'He's sleeping. I'll bring him to you when he wakes. Don't worry – he's quite well.'

'Has he fed?'

'Daniel brought goats' milk for him. Maybe you'll be able to put him to the breast when you're up and about again.'

'I'd like to see Jessie and Matthew.'

'They are your other children?'

Emily nodded.

'They're with Maud. Stephen sent for her to attend to them and the house so you don't have to do anything except concentrate on getting better. Are you warm enough?'

'I'm too hot.' Emily pushed the bedsheet away. 'My head hurts. The light pains my eyes.'

Catherine moved to the window and opened it again. The view caught her eye: the Kentish landscape rising beyond the cottage garden. Some of the trees were laden with blossom and the hazels were dripping with catkins. She took a deep breath of the crisp scent of her childhood before closing the curtains and turning back to Emily.

'Let me wash your face and hands. You might find it soothing.'

'Ta,' she said weakly.

When she had finished, Catherine emptied the

401

bowl out of the window and hung the cloth over the fireguard.

'What's happening?' Stephen strode into the sickroom, bringing the scent of musk, horse and burned sulphur on his work clothes. 'I'm sorry I couldn't come straight here. The doctor's mare had cast a shoe. I had to fit a new one so he could ride home.' He sat on the edge of the bed and placed a clutch of windflowers in Emily's lap. Her eyes lit up.

Tendrils of envy wrapped themselves around Catherine's heart as she watched Stephen stroke his wife's face with his fingertips and plant a kiss on her lips. It was a painful reminder that she would never love again, nor marry, nor bear more children.

'I'll be back as soon as I can, my love,' Stephen said, reluctantly tearing himself away. 'I'll bring the children to see you later.'

'Don't be long,' Emily said.

Catherine pulled up the chair so she could sit with her.

'Often I dream that we are walking back home from Old Faggy's,' Emily began. 'Do you remember the day when Matty stole my bonnet and dropped it into the pond?'

'How could I forget?'

'I wish we had never been parted. We have wasted so much time.' She smiled. 'I was so glad when Stephen told me he had found you in Faversham. I wish you'd come back before, but maybe you have your reasons...' She reached her hand across the sheet. 'Stephen said... Oh dear, perhaps I shouldn't say anything.'

'You're asking about my daughter, Agnes. Yes, it's true. I had to give her up.'

'Have you seen her since?'

Catherine shook her head and gazed down at the coverlet.

'It was for the best,' she said quickly. She believed that fervently now that time had passed. If she had refused to give Agnes up for adoption, they would both have been stuck living in the workhouse among the sick and dying, and a couple more years down the line Agnes would have been sold into work outside the Union, and who knows where she would have ended up, or what suffering she would have had to endure. 'She'll be brought up as a lady. She'll have a jewellery casket filled with gold, and more bonnets than she can count. She'll drink chocolate every day if she wishes, but most importantly to me, she'll have respect and marry a suitable husband. I was assured that she would be loved and I have to believe it, or I should die.'

Catherine got up, stoked the ashes and put another log on the fire.

When she turned back, a pink spot had appeared in the centre of Emily's cheek. Her eyes seemed to grow larger in her face as she sank back into the pillows.

'Listen to me going on. You are exhausted.'

'I'm fine,' Emily insisted. 'I should like to hold the baby now. His presence will cheer me.'

Catherine fetched him and placed him in her arms.

'You're a darling boy,' Emily murmured, her voice thick with pride, as he gazed into his

403

mother's eyes. 'You look so much like your brother. You are like peas in a pod.' Emily looked across at Catherine. 'I really do feel much better. I can hear my children laughing and playing outside.'

Catherine frowned and called downstairs for Maud to fetch some stew from the pot. She couldn't hear the children, just the sound of the hammering of metal from the forge, and a blackbird's alarm call.

'I'm not hungry,' Emily said when she tried to persuade her to drink a little stock. She suggested some scrambled egg instead, but she ate no more than a mouthful. Her eyes glittered and her skin flared hot again, making Catherine uneasy. Was this the calm before the storm?

News of Emily's condition had reached the Millichips, for the sound of a disagreement floated up the stairs.

'We have to see our daughter. You cannot stop us.'

'This is my house,' Stephen said. 'It's up to me who comes and goes.'

There was the scuffle of feet and Mrs Millichip turned up in the room, closely followed by her husband and Stephen.

'Let me see her,' Emily's ma said, reaching the bedside. Emily flinched.

'I'd have come sooner if I'd known. I'm your mother, yet I've had to glean the news second-hand through the likes of George Carter.' She caught sight of Catherine with a flash of recognition. 'Miss Rook? What are you doing here? I'm surprised you dare show your face.' She looked at

404

Stephen. 'Why are you letting a woman of ill repute remain in the presence of your wife?'

'I invited her here. Her reputation is one that others have created for her. I believe her to be one of the sweetest, most generous and honourable people in the world, second only to my darling Emily.'

'She must leave forthwith,' Mrs Millichip said, the colour high in her cheeks.

'Stay,' Emily said as Catherine stepped towards the door. 'I will not have you insulted. Ma, you will apologise to my friend.'

'I will not,' she said.

'Then you must leave. In fact, I desire you to remove yourself from my home straight away.'

'You can't do that. I'm your mother.'

'You are no ma of mine.' Emily began to cry.

'Please go, Mrs Millichip,' Stephen cut in. 'You've done more than enough harm. Emily has told me everything: how you used to keep a strap hanging behind the door to beat her with; how you locked her in the bakehouse when she was only six years old. When I married her, I promised to keep her safe. I won't let her down now.'

'It's in the Bible. He that spareth his rod hates his son: but he that loveth him chastens him betimes,' Mrs Millichip maintained. 'I did nothing wrong. Emily, you will back your ma on this. You were a lazy, clumsy lump of a child. If I hadn't dragged you up, you would have come to nothing.'

'Get out,' Stephen snapped. 'It is Emily's wish that you leave forthwith.'

'I shall take my grandchildren with me. They'll

405

stay at the mill until my daughter is well again.'

'Absolutely not,' Stephen said. 'They don't know you. You're a stranger to them.'

Catherine noticed the muscle in his cheek tensing with anger at Emily's ma's effrontery.

'Come, Mrs Millichip,' her husband said. When she hesitated, he added, 'There's flour to be milled and bread to be baked. Your entreaties, unsurprisingly, are falling on deaf ears. I told you that I should have come alone.' He grasped his wife roughly by the hand and prised her from the sickroom. She opened her mouth as though she had more to say, but he gave her a look and she stayed silent. 'Promise me that you'll look after my daughter.'

'Of course, sir,' Stephen said.

'I should have done the same,' Mr Millichip said. 'For my failure to protect her, I am sorely ashamed. Good day.'

'I'm sorry, love,' Stephen said when they'd gone. 'I couldn't stop them.'

'I'm all right. Ma can't hurt me now. With you at my side, I have no fear.' Emily brightened a little. 'Would you bring the children to me? I'd like to see them now.'

Stephen came back with the children. The girl, Jessie, who was three and much like her mother in appearance with long, curly blonde hair and big blue eyes, scrambled up and bounced on the bed, throwing her arms around Emily's neck and smothering her with kisses. Matthew was eighteen months old and more like his father, quiet and reserved. He toddled along the side of the bed, holding on to the bedsheets.

'It's time for bed,' Stephen said eventually. 'You can see Mama again in the morning.'

Jessie looked close to tears, but she didn't argue and it wasn't long before she and Matthew were asleep in the room next door.

'I thought I'd sleep here with my wife,' Stephen said later.

'No, I'll sit with her,' Catherine said. 'I mean, spend as much time as you like, but don't stay up all night when I'm here to help out. She'll need you when I've gone back to Faversham.'

'You're right, Catherine. I don't know how to thank you.'

'There's no need. Thank you for standing up for me. I expect the whole of Overshill is agog at my return.'

'I'm afraid so. Although it happened some time ago, Bossenden is still fresh in many people's memories.' He gazed at her in the dusky light. The shape of his nose and the line of his jaw reminded her with a jolt of Matty. She turned away abruptly, dismissing the comparison.

She sat up all night with Emily, listening to Stephen tossing and turning in the room downstairs. She fed the baby three times and soothed Jessie when she had a nightmare. In the morning, she awoke with a start at the sound of flapping and the thud of a bird flying into the window which she had left ajar. The hairs on the back of her neck stood on end as she got up from her chair. The pigeon must have fallen down the chimney and onto the ashes of the fire. In its panic to escape, it had flown back and forth, scattering soot and feathers across the room, and now it was caught between the curtains and window-glass.

She crept towards it and slipped her hand between the curtains to push the window wide open, at which the bird flew out into the trees beyond. She took a cloth and cleaned up the evidence as best she could before Emily woke and Maud brought breakfast of bread soaked in weak tea.

'How are you, my darling wife?' Stephen asked as he entered the sickroom and went to Emily's bedside. 'You are looking quite well today.'

'I'm feeling a little better,' she said, her voice faint.

'But you haven't eaten anything,' Catherine pointed out.

'You must take some nourishment,' Stephen said, kissing Emily tenderly on the forehead. 'I love you.'

'And I love you,' she whispered.

Stephen turned to Catherine when she accompanied him downstairs to fetch milk for the baby.

'Do you think she's on the mend?' he asked.

'I believe it's too early to say,' Catherine said, thinking of the bird. It was a bad omen that only added to her sense of unease. 'I'll send for you if there's any change.'

'Thank you.' Stephen returned to his work in the forge with Daniel, while Maud minded the children. Catherine sat with Emily, awaiting Doctor Whebley's arrival.

'I'm so glad that you and Matty are happy together,' Emily said, suddenly grasping at Catherine's arm. Catherine took her hand and felt her pulse thin and thread-like at her wrist as Emily went on, 'Stephen says there are more lambs at

Wanstall Farm.'

Catherine's heart dipped.

'There are no sheep at Wanstall Farm. Not any more.'

'But I've seen them. Only last Michaelmas.' Emily's words slurred. 'Oh dear, and I've just remembered that I should be looking after them.' She tried to get out of bed, but her limbs were too weak. 'Don't let them take my children, will you, Catherine? Promise me.'

'No one will take them,' she reassured her.

'Not Ma and Pa.'

'You and Stephen will care for them when you are better.'

'I'm going to die,' Emily said. 'I told you – I had a premonition before Jessie was born...'

'I know, but that was a long time ago. Oh, Emily, if anything should happen to you, which it won't, then I promise you with all my heart that I will make sure that your children stay with their father.'

That seemed to satisfy her because she leaned back against the pillows.

'Can you hear the owls calling to each other?' she whispered.

'You're dreaming,' Catherine said quietly, noting how her skin had grown mottled and cool to the touch. 'Let me tuck you in, my dearest friend. I can hear the doctor on the stairs.'

Doctor Whebley was grave. The outlook was poor. He prescribed a laxative purgation and bled Emily by cup, and, bonded in their concern for their patient, Catherine didn't disagree even though the whole bloodletting episode seemed brutal. She'd do anything to make Emily better.

The doctor left, promising to return the following day, but from then on, Emily fidgeted and moaned in a delirium. They were heading into uncharted waters, Catherine thought, and who knew where they were going to end up.

Over the next two hours, Emily's body stilled and her breathing slowed to an occasional gasp. Catherine sent for the maid who sent for Stephen who called for Reverend Browning, and by midday, it was over.

Emily was dead, Stephen a widow and their children motherless.

Catherine covered the mirror on the dressing table and placed pennies on Emily's eyelids to keep them closed, so that nothing bad would befall her kin from looking into the glass or upon her eyes. The vicar came and said a few words over the body. The Reverend Browning raised one eyebrow when Catherine introduced herself, but he made no comment on the past. When he had gone, Stephen fell to his knees at his wife's bedside and held her hands to his face. Tears streamed down his cheeks as he kissed her fingers and gazed heavenwards.

'Why, oh why, did you take her in spite of all my prayers?'

'It isn't for us to reason why,' Catherine said softly, repeating the Reverend Browning's words, but she couldn't help wondering why anyway. What was the purpose of Emily's death? She was so young, only twenty-two. She was a wife and mother. She was needed here on Earth.

Stephen ranted and raved against everyone, blaming the vicar and the doctor, whether they were blameless or not, and everything that had sought to part him and his love. He blamed the baby. He blamed himself.

'What have I done to deserve this?'

'It isn't anyone's fault,' Catherine said, but he wouldn't listen.

'I promised you we'd grow old together, my angel, and I've let you down,' he cried.

Catherine stood back, biting her fist as he went on, 'I wasn't a good husband at first. I'll regret that for the rest of my life. But you forgave me, and in return, I've loved you more than anyone could have done, with all my heart and soul. You made me whole, and gave us the gift of children to light up our lives. Oh, Emily, my darling, I can't go on without you.'

'You have to, Stephen, for the children's sake,' Catherine said quietly.

'I wish I could have lain down and died in your stead.' He stood up, leaned down and kissed Emily's cheek before turning and walking out. Catherine heard his boots clacking against the stone floor downstairs, and the door slam behind him. A little while later, she heard the ringing of his hammer as he forged something from his love, anger and despair.

On hearing the children's cries, and Maud's futile attempts to console them, she forced herself to leave her friend's side and went down to the kitchen.

'I don't know what to do, miss,' the girl said tearfully. 'There's nothing I can do or say to make them feel better. It's a terrible thing to lose a mother at such a young age.'

''Rin,' Jessie said, taking her hand. 'Will Mama be back for teatime? Maud says she's in heaven which is in the sky.' She looked up through the kitchen window, her eyes wide with awe. 'How did she get there?'

Catherine knelt beside her.

'She was sick. Her body couldn't take any more, so our Father in His wisdom released her soul and carried her away to paradise.'

'I wanna go too,' Jessie said.

'You will do one day, but not for a very long time.'

'Will Mama be back for bedtime?' Jessie asked.

'No, she won't,' Catherine said, at which Jessie burst into tears.

'There, there,' she soothed as she took her in her arms.

'Your mama loves you very much. She'll be watching over you from above.' She thought of Agnes and how she had abandoned her, and wondered if she remembered her mother who had loved her, and still did. It wasn't fair. It should have been her who had died, not Emily who had three children who needed her. 'Now, Maud is going to look after you for a while. There's something I have to do.'

She glanced towards Maud, who nodded and said, 'Jessie, I need you to help me feed Matthew and baby Stanley.'

'Thank you,' Catherine said. She returned upstairs to wash and dress Emily's body in the best gown she could find, and sat up keeping watch over her. Her blonde ringlets tumbled across the pillow and her hands lay across her breast, linked together as though in silent prayer for her husband and children. As the clouds swept across the sky outside, casting a pall across the room, Catherine could almost imagine that she was sleeping.

She turned at the sound of a knock on the door. 'Come in.'

'It's me,' Daniel said. 'I've come to pay my respects to the late Mrs Carter.' He hovered in the doorway, holding his cap in his hands. 'She's been good to me. She welcomed me into her home and fed me, and she's treated my wounds on more than one occasion. I don't know how many times I hit my thumb with the hammer when I started here as a humble apprentice. Well, I wasn't humble at first, which was a problem – I thought I knew it all. And when the master threatened to send me away, it was Mrs Carter who stood up for me and convinced him to give me another chance. Why did she have to go and die, and so sudden? She was doing the laundry and fetching and carrying only the day before yesterday,' he added in a puzzled tone.

'The vicar says it is God's will, that she was too good for this world,' Catherine said. 'The doctor claims that she was taken by childbed fever. Daniel, I'd be very grateful if you would keep a close eye on Stephen. He is extremely distressed.'

Daniel nodded. 'Of course, ma'am. What about the little ones?'

'I'm going to stay for a few days after the funeral to make sure some arrangement is in place for the children before I return to Faversham.' She wasn't sure how Emily's babies would be cared for yet.

On the morning of the funeral, the bearers came to the house with the parish coffin from the church. They laid Emily, wrapped in a winding sheet, within the plain wood coffin, and put a sprig of rosemary on the top. The men bore her on their shoulders to the church with the family and other mourners, including George Carter and his daughter, following along behind. Catherine noticed Mr and Mrs Millichip standing well back near the ragstone and flint churchyard wall, watching from a distance. Remembering Emily's wishes, she suppressed an impulse to go and offer them her condolences. It was too late.

Stephen paid for the vicar to say a few words at the graveside, speeding her path to heaven, and Emily's body was laid in the ground in the winding sheet, and the coffin returned to the church. Her grave was set just inside the churchyard wall in the shade of a yew tree, covered with earth and marked only with a ridge of soil.

Chapter Eighteen

Least Said, Soonest Mended

Overshill

Stephen was inconsolable. He returned straight to the forge and threw himself into his work, leaving Catherine and the maid to care for the children.

'What will you do now?' Maud asked when she arrived at Forge Cottage for work the morning after the funeral.

Catherine was in the kitchen with Jessie and Matthew, eating eggs for breakfast, while the baby slept in his basket on the settle. She stood up and began to clear the table.

'I don't know,' Catherine said. 'Stay until the children and Stephen no longer need me, I suppose.' She couldn't abandon them at this time. People would talk, no doubt, but what did it matter? How could Stephen possibly cope with three small children? He could hardly afford Maud, let alone a live-in maid. 'We need more milk for the baby. Do you think you can send out for some?'

'Yes, ma'am,' she said.

'I'll mind the children for a while,' Catherine said, feeling a little uncomfortable about giving Maud orders. She didn't want anyone to think she was taking Emily's place, and she had no wish to hurt Stephen's feelings by making decisions on his behalf when he was the master of the house, but someone had to step into the breach and keep the household running.

There was a knock at the door. Maud went to answer it.

'It's Mrs Browning wanting to see you,' she called.

'Show her through,' Catherine said, quickly wiping her hands. 'Children, you go with Maud.'

'Where shall we go?' Maud said, showing Mrs Browning into the kitchen. She was carrying a basket, its contents covered with a white cloth.

'Please, take a seat, Mrs Browning,' Catherine said, pointing to the chair beside the fireplace. 'Maud, put their coats on and take them to ask Daniel about getting some more goats' milk.' The last thing Catherine wanted was for the vicar's wife to upset them again with talk of their dearly departed mother, which she assumed was the reason for her visit. She put Matthew's hat and coat over the top of his tunic dress while Maud helped Jessie with her outdoor clothes. Maud lifted Matthew up and carried him out on one hip with Jessie holding her hand.

To Catherine's relief, Stanley remained asleep.

'Good morning, Miss Rook,' Mrs Browning began as the front door clicked shut. 'We didn't have a chance to renew our acquaintance at the funeral. You'd rushed away before we could speak.'

Catherine sat down at the end of the settle.

'It is always sad when a family is devastated by the loss of a mother,' Mrs Browning went on. 'It's my Christian duty to see if there is anything I can

416

do to assist in their hour of need.' She reached inside her basket and pulled out a pie. 'This is for the poor, suffering widower and his children.'

Catherine thanked her, got up and took the pie and placed it on the table.

'How are your parents and John?' Mrs Browning asked.

'I haven't spoken to them for a long time,' Catherine said. 'I hear they have gone to live with my brother, Young Thomas, over near Selling.' She was sorry about John – she still missed him. But Ma and Pa were as good as dead to her. 'How are Miss Browning and Master Browning?'

'Hector remains engaged to Squire Temple's daughter and continues to pursue his studies. Jane is running the Sunday school as before, but I didn't call to talk about other people. I came to ask what you are doing back in Overshill.'

'Stephen sent for me – Emily wished to see me.' Catherine suppressed the sob that rose in her throat. 'She had a premonition and wanted to say goodbye. And I believe she decided that I should be here to take care of her children while Stephen grieves.'

'But you remain unmarried, Miss Rook,' Mrs Browning said. 'It is most improper for you to stay here at Forge Cottage, living under the same roof as Mr Carter.'

'There is nothing improper about it,' Catherine exclaimed. 'How can you suggest such a thing when my dearest friend was laid to rest only yesterday?' She picked up the pie and carried it back to Mrs Browning. 'We don't need your charity.' She dropped the pie back in the basket.

417

'I should like you to leave.'

'I haven't finished yet,' Mrs Browning said, standing up and straightening her skirts.

'I insist on you leaving,' Catherine said. 'Goodbye, Mrs Browning. Don't call again.'

'Good day, Miss Rook,' Mrs Browning said. 'You are making a mistake. People remember your history.'

'Let them,' she said. Trembling, she closed the front door behind the vicar's wife. Was this how it was to be? Was she to be punished for the rest of her life for falling in love with the wrong man? She took a deep breath before returning to the kitchen where the baby was starting to whimper. She picked him up and rocked him gently in her arms while she waited for the others to return with the milk.

Mrs Browning's censure was only to be expected, she thought, and she was going to ignore it. She was here for a purpose – to care for Emily's children until she was no longer needed, and that was what she was going to do. She wouldn't tell Stephen about the visit because she didn't want to upset him any further.

After two weeks of mourning when she avoided running into people in the village as far as she could, Catherine turned to improving the situation at the forge. She put on Emily's apron and set to work, cleaning the walls and floors, and removing the cobwebs from the corners of the rooms. She cooked pies and stews and churned butter. She fed and bathed the baby, and sang lullabies to him, just as she'd done with Agnes.

She taught Jessie to play spillikins, which wasn't a perfect success, because Matthew liked to join in, pulling not one, but several sticks at a time from the pile with his clumsy fingers, and moving Jessie to tears of frustration.

One day she took Jessie to visit Pa Carter, who was toiling in the garden at Toad's Bottom. He walked over to them and leaned on his hoe.

'How are you, Miss Rook?' he asked.

'I'm well, thank you. How are you?'

'I could be better,' he said, rubbing the small of his back. He glanced towards the cottage. 'My daughter looks after me well, though. She's a good girl. How is Stephen?'

'You will have to ask him. I cannot answer on his behalf.' She was finding it hard to speak to Stephen, he was so closed off. 'I think he'd appreciate a visit.'

'I don't like to intrude. I don't know what to say to him. I mean, I had plenty of time to prepare for the loss of my dear wife, but his loss came as a shock. Life is cruel. Emily was snatched away so young.'

'Your presence will be a comfort. You don't have to say anything.'

'I suppose not.' George turned to his grand-daughter. 'I believe there are tadpoles in the ditch over here.' He lifted Jessie over the tumbledown wall and showed her the puddle of water at his feet. Jessie squatted down to look. 'I expect you've heard the n*oo*ws,' George went on, turning back to Catherine.

'What news?' she said.

'Mr and Mrs Nobbs have moved out of Wanstall Farm.'

'How come? They've only just set up house there.'

'It's bin a while. They haven't managed to make a go of it. I think Mr Nobbs bit off more than he could chew, taking on a second place. He thought he was going to run it like your father did in the old times, but the changes he made didn't work out. He upset the squire, too, grubbin' out the orchards without a by your leave. I knew he was makin' a mistake, but who will listen to me?'

'I would, George,' Catherine said. 'You're very wise. Perhaps you know what will happen to the farm? What are the squire's intentions?'

'Rumour has it that he's lookin' for another tenant. I thought he might let the bailiff take it on, but he wouldn't be any good when all he's interested in is huntin'.'

She wondered about Stephen. Was he still thinking of buying and selling horses? Wanstall Farm had a yard with stables. She appreciated that he was still mourning Emily's passing, but maybe a new enterprise would help him to cope with his grief.

'I'm sorry for what happened between our families. I would have gone after Jervis myself if I'd known how it was goin' to turn out,' George said. 'Will you forgive me, Miss Rook?'

'There's nothing to forgive. Matty was a grown man, more than capable of making his own decisions. I'll always wish that life had turned out differently, but there's nothing we can do to change it. All we can do is make the best of what we have.' She gazed at the tumbledown cottage with its mossy roof and smoking chimney, and the garden which had been dug over and raked ready for planting the potatoes, marrows, herbs and carrots that George would harvest in the summer. He didn't have much, but he seemed content with what he'd got.

'I sound like an old man,' he said. 'I *am* an old man, but, Catherine, you've been through the mill, and now you must seize your chances of happiness when they come along. Don't hold back. Just take them.'

What did he mean? she wondered. Chances of happiness seemed very few and far between as far as she was concerned.

'Jessie,' she said. 'We must be on our way.'

'I wanna stay,' she said, looking up from the ditch. 'Look at all the wiggle-heads.' She put her hand in the water, stirred up the mud and wiped it down her dress.

'We have to go,' Catherine said sternly.

Jessie scowled and pouted.

'We'll come back another day,' Catherine said, wondering how to deal with her. She had to admit that she felt a little out of her depth, managing Emily's children. 'I promise.'

That seemed to satisfy Jessie, because she stood up to let George help her back over the wall.

'Say goodbye to your grandpa.'

'Goodbye, Gran'pa,' she said shyly.

'I'll see you again soon.' He smiled.

Catherine took Jessie past Wanstall Farm to show her where she used to live and play as a child. The house appeared unloved. The grimy windows were closed and the gutters were dripping water. They walked round to the yard, where a handful of abandoned hens cawed and strutted across the rotten woodpile.

'I'm surprised no one's had those for the pot,' Catherine said. 'Your Uncle Matty would have seen them as an opportunity.' She smiled at the thought. 'I used to collect the eggs and sell any extras that we didn't need. My father said that if I looked after the hens, I could have the profit.' She looked at Jessie and thought of Agnes.

She wondered how she was and what she was doing. She should have been walking here hand in hand with her daughter, not Emily's, telling her about the farm, how they'd picked hops every summer, and how they'd danced the night away to celebrate the grain being safely gathered in.

They walked back towards the forge, passing the churchyard where they stopped to lay flowers – daisies they had picked at the farm – on Emily's grave. There were flowers there already, fresh ones that must have been placed there that morning, along with a note on a scrappy piece of paper, which read, 'To my darling wife, how I miss you x'.

Tears welled up in her eyes. Life was short. Emily's passing had shown her that. She would always love Matty, but it was time to accept that he wasn't coming back and that this chapter of her existence was over. She should seize every opportunity that came her way, like George had said, and as Matty would do if he were in her place. She pulled up a handful of weeds that were threatening to encroach on the grave. In the meantime, she was thankful for small mercies.

She was back in Overshill for the foreseeable future, until she was happy that Stephen and the children were settled into a new routine, and then she would return to her cottage in Faversham.

'Sleep tight, Mama,' Jessie said. 'Shall we go home, 'Rin?'

'Yes, let's.' She uttered a silent farewell to Emily and returned to the forge with Jessie's hand in hers. Stephen was removing a shoe from one of Mr Hadington's carriage horses when she dropped by to let him know that they were back.

'We've been for a walk, Papa.' Catherine caught Jessie by the shoulder, keeping her back from the horse as it fidgeted and swished its tail.

'That's lovely,' Stephen said, his voice laced with the effort of putting on a front for his daughter.

'We saw Gran'pa and I tried to catch the wiggle-heads in the ditch.'

'I'd never have guessed,' Stephen said wryly. 'Your dress is muddy.'

'It isn't, Papa.'

'Oh yes it is. And look at your hands.'

She glanced down at her grubby fingers and chuckled. A smile crossed her father's face.

'George was gardening,' Catherine said. 'I'd like to sow some seeds in the vegetable beds sometime.'

'You have more than enough to do,' Stephen said. 'No, leave it. Emily loved the garden.'

'Did you know that Mr Nobbs has left Wanstall Farm?' Catherine went on. 'It's in a terrible mess. It's very sad to see.'

'I haven't been down that way for a while, but

there's been talk at the forge. Your pa would never have allowed the orchards to be grubbed out like that.'

'It would make good pasture for horses,' Catherine suggested.

'I know, but–' Stephen shrugged. 'I've rather lost heart in that project. It was supposed to be for us, for Emily and the children. What is the point in it without her?'

Catherine knew when to let the subject go. It was too soon.

Three weeks passed and the March winds were pushed out by April showers. The children became more light-hearted and Stephen, although still mourning his loss, was more like his old self.

'How are you, Catherine? What kind of day have you had?' he said as he walked into the kitchen after a long day's work at the forge. He carried a tankard of beer in his hand. He drained it, the amber liquid trickling down his neck and leaving a glistening trail across his skin. He put the tankard down and took off his boots, revealing the holes in his socks.

She wondered if she should offer to darn them for him, but he did his own mending to take some of the burden of running the household from her shoulders. He was kind and generous, and time had made him remarkably handsome. She recalled a distant memory of the tall, wiry boy who had declared his feelings for her one hot summer. What would her life have been like if she'd given him a chance? What if she had taken heed of Ma's opinion that she should settle for a man who could provide a home and comfortable living?

She dismissed that line of thought. Emily had been the sensible one, choosing to settle for Stephen, and it had worked out until fate intervened and cut her life short.

Catherine had been distracted by her attraction to the more elemental brother, the wilder, more rebellious one who had tried to do the right thing by going about it the wrong way, and realised too late that he had been sucked into a dangerous situation from which he couldn't escape.

'Something smells delicious,' Stephen said, bringing her back to the present.

'I have a pig's head in the oven,' she said with a smile. 'There's freshly baked bread too.'

'It's been a good day. Daniel's finally got the hang of making a decent shoe, and Squire Temple is sending his carriage horses to be shod. He's discovered the hard way that I'm more reliable than the blacksmith down the road in Boughton. One of his horses was nail-bound so I removed the nail and taught his groom to poultice the foot so the poison came out. The horse is sound now, so I'll put the shoe back on tomorrow.'

'I hope he's going to pay you handsomely for that.'

'He's paying a retainer to look after all his horses, the hunters as well.' He paused. 'Why are you looking at me like that?'

'I'm glad to see you're more cheerful than of late.'

Stephen frowned.

'I'm not being critical. It's good for you and the children.'

'I know. I haven't been very good company

lately. I'm sorry.'

'Don't be. It's natural to grieve. We all mourn in different ways.'

'Papa.' Jessie came inside from the garden with a basket with four freckled brown eggs lying in the straw at the bottom. She struggled determinedly to put it on the table.

'Jessie.' Stephen squatted on his heels and held out his arms. His daughter ran towards him, throwing her hands around his neck and planting kisses. He hugged her and looked up towards Catherine. 'You're right, of course. Life has to go on, for the children's sake if nothing else.'

She finished cutting slices from the loaf. Matthew toddled up, waving his hand.

'What do you say?' she said sternly.

'Please.'

She handed him a slice of bread and turned back to Stephen.

'Shall I fill your bath? I didn't realise you would be back quite so early.'

'I'll take my bath later. Daniel's clearing up in the forge. I thought I'd do some work in the garden as you suggested some time ago.' He smiled ruefully. 'I might have left it too late, but never mind.'

'Mrs White left some stocks and strawberry plants this morning. I was going to put them in the bed nearest the back door,' Catherine said.

'Oh no, that won't do. It's in the shade for much of the day. No, I'm going to dig over the beds at the end of the garden. They're full of weeds.'

Stephen ate his supper with relish, wiping the

plate clean with the last crust of bread. Catherine put Daniel's portion aside for when he came in later, then she fed the baby and put the children to bed, kissing each one in turn.

'Is Ma looking down on us from heaven?' Jessie asked.

'She smiles upon you all every day and night. You have been good children today. I'm very proud of you.' Catherine looked at how Jessie snuggled down with her brother. The baby cooed and gurgled from his cot. 'Sweet dreams.'

Her chest tightened at the thought that she would soon have to leave them. If she didn't return to her cottage in the next week or two, she would barely be able to scrape together the next month's rent. She was in danger of losing it altogether and then what would she do? She would be back on the street.

She stepped out through the back door into the garden, remembering a time long ago when she and Ivy had had the conversation about her parentage. At the time, she'd felt that her world had been turned upside down, but she'd learned since that it was nothing, that all love was precious, no matter how you were related or not. Ivy had loved her in her own way, letting her go to Wanstall Farm for a better life than she could have provided. In turn, she had done the same for Agnes. One day, she would visit Ivy to let her know that she had forgiven her.

She surveyed the scene. The fruit trees were in bud and the weeds, a carpet of forget-me-nots, had taken over the vegetable beds. Stephen was digging, stripped to the waist so she could see the rippling contours of his loins as he wielded the spade.

He thrust the blade into the soil, burying it in the chalky loam, digging deep as if he were burying some of his memories. He placed his foot on the lug of the blade and levered it through the soil, bringing up the loam from the depths and turning it into a heap on top of the bed. He then sliced through it several times to break it into a crumbly tilth. Every so often, he would stop to throw away a flint or stone. He continued along the row until it was complete, like a scar across the bed, the weeds torn up and tossed aside.

Catherine picked up the rake and followed along behind him, raking the tilth smooth as the sun sank low in the sky.

Stephen set up straight lines for the rows with sticks and string and Catherine sowed the seeds – ones that Emily had kept in the larder from the year before. There were peas, beans and carrots. Stephen raked the earth to cover the seeds and Catherine watered them to start them off.

Stephen began to sing, his voice filling the air as he planted the stocks and strawberries. He pressed the last plant into the earth, treading it down with his feet, then looked towards her.

'Let me have the bucket,' he said.

'It's all right. I'll water them in.'

'I'll do it. You have done more than enough for one day.' He took the bucket from her and poured the water over the new plants. He turned to her and smiled. 'You can tell you were brought up on a farm.'

'Are my manners that bad?' she said archly.

'I didn't mean that.' He blushed.

'I know you didn't.' She smiled. 'I'm sorry. I've enjoyed being out here this evening with the sun setting over the vale. It reminds me of the farm.'

'I assume that it reminds you of Matty as well.' He didn't wait for her response 'I miss my brother. Jervis deserved everything he got, but Matty, well, he had the best of intentions. I think of him often. If he'd stayed – and Emily had lived, we four and our children would have been as happy as larks.'

'We would,' Catherine sighed.

'I've made you sad again,' he said.

'A little. You know, you have made much of yourself. You should be very proud.'

'Who would have thought that Stephen Carter from Toad's Bottom would have come up to the top like the cream on the milk? Let's go indoors.'

'I'll fill your bath.'

'I'll do it,' he said. 'Put your feet up. Lord knows, you deserve it.'

She went inside and sat on the chair, watching the world go by out of the front window. Mr Hadington's carriage and four passed by at speed, black horses and a dark carriage disappearing into the night. A bat darted across the view of the cottages opposite where most of the windows were in darkness, the inhabitants having already retired to bed. A dog barked twice and a pair of shadowy figures stole past.

A shiver ran down her spine. They reminded her of the day she had been ambushed in the woods by Jervis and Drusilla. She took a breath, telling herself that it was over now. She would never be troubled by either of them again, except in her nightmares, the ones she still had, of the encounter in the clearing, of Jervis imprisoned in that room at the Red Lion with Matty, of the judge giving his verdict at the Assizes, of finding Drusilla of all people at the workhouse.

She wished she could put it all out of her head for good.

She closed her, eyes and listened to the sounds of the present. Stephen was splashing about in the tin bath behind the screen in the kitchen, just a few feet away from her. Another couple passed by, their conversation drifting in through the window. Catherine thought she recognised Mrs White and her errant husband, the wheelwright.

'I wouldn't mind betting she's giving him more than comfort,' Mrs White said. 'It's all over the village.'

'Hush, my good wife. Someone will hear.'

'I don't care if she does. It i'n't right, her being dead less than three months ago.'

'We have no evidence.'

'You know yourself the power of lust, Mr White,' his wife said haughtily. 'A woman should be able to control such base urges.'

'If she has any,' Mr White said.

Although hurt by Mrs White's insinuations about her moral standards, Catherine smiled at the irony in her husband's voice as they carried on along the street.

It was all very well, though. People were talking about her and Overshill's master blacksmith. It wasn't fair!

But, she thought, it was uncomfortably close to the truth.

She was falling for Stephen.

She checked herself. She couldn't let herself do that – Emily had been her childhood friend and Stephen didn't need any complications. It was far too soon.

She turned to find him standing alongside her in his trousers and a shirt unbuttoned to the waist. His hair was wet and tousled. His chest was glistening with droplets of water.

'I was thinking that I should go home soon,' she whispered.

'To Faversham?' he said huskily. 'I'm being selfish keeping you here for so long. I worry about how I'll manage with the house and the children without you, though. Jessie and Matthew are very fond of you. I know they'll be distraught when you leave us.' The regret in his voice tore her apart. 'I should take steps to find someone to take over from you, but it will take time...'

'I'll stay a little longer,' she decided.

'Thank you. I feel guilty now because the last thing I want to do is impose on you any further.'

He could impose as much as he liked, she thought, but it wouldn't do either of them any good. Her heart wanted to stay while her head told her to leave, to put some space between them before any awkwardness developed.

'Let me at least go and check on the cottage and bring some more of my belongings.' She had only the clothes she stood up in and a couple of Emily's dresses that she'd pulled in at the seams.

'Of course. I'll arrange for Daniel to drive the

horse and cart with you.'

'I can walk,' she said.

'I know you can, but I want you to travel in comfort, if not style.' He smiled. 'To be truthful, I'll miss you. I've got used to having you around. It's – well, never mind. If it is how you want it to be. Ma used to say, "Least said, soonest mended." Goodnight, Catherine,' he said, turning and walking abruptly away. She heard his tread on the stairs as he retired to his room.

She sat up for a while, pondering what had passed between them that evening, how his mood had changed from upbeat and cheerful while they were toiling in the garden, to a more sombre one that had come on when she had mentioned leaving Overshill.

She took pleasure in cooking and keeping house for him, and he seemed genuinely grateful for her efforts. If she'd thought that there was any chance that he could feel for her in the same way as she felt for him, then she would stay on, but there was no possibility of him treating her as anything other than a friend when she had rejected him for his brother all those years before.

He had loved Emily with all his heart and he had lost her. How could he ever love another?

Widowers did remarry, but she assumed that that was out of convenience. Stephen needed a mother for his children. What better solution than find another wife? And who would marry him when she was there in the way?

She promised herself that she would stay another month. That would be hard enough, because she knew that the longer she stayed at

Forge Cottage, the more painful it would be to leave.

A few days later, Daniel and Catherine set out on their expedition to Faversham. She would have liked Stephen to have been the one to accompany her, but it would only have added fuel to the fire of the village gossips.

'It is a lovely day, miss,' Daniel said as he drove the horse along the lanes. The sun was rising through a bright blue sky, its rays caressing the hop bines, encouraging them to unfurl their leaves. The spikes of barley were a lush green and the apple blossom was drifting in the air on a gentle breeze. 'Where are we heading for once we reach town?'

She gave him the name of the road.

'I should like to walk around the market as well,' she said. 'We should collect my belongings first, pick up some provisions and then you can drop me at the Guildhall. We can meet a couple of hours later.'

'The master expressed a wish that I stay with you at all times,' Daniel ventured.

'Knowing your master, I suspect that it was more of an order than a wish,' Catherine said lightly, 'but I can assure you I will be perfectly safe, and I won't tell if you don't.'

'I'll make sure I keep out of trouble.' Daniel chuckled.

They collected her belongings from the cottage, then went to the market together to buy provisions for the family: a sack of potatoes; a dress for Jessie; peppermints and cheese. Daniel loaded them onto the back of the cart.

'I'll see you soon,' Catherine said. 'Don't be late.'

'I won't be far from here,' he promised.

She inhaled a deep breath of fresh air, tinged with the scent of bad eggs and fish from the creek, before retracing the steps that she'd taken with Agnes on their very last day together. Her heart ached as she recalled the weight of her body in her arms, the way she had pinched her mama's cheek and giggled.

'Agnes,' she sighed. 'Where are you?'

She carried on towards where the Berry-Clay brewery stood, and as she walked through the crowd, she spotted a woman with a child. The child was a girl, the same age as Jessie, and dressed in a fine white lace dress, white socks and leather shoes. She wore a white bonnet that cast a shadow across her face, but she knew it was Agnes. She moved closer, her heart pounding. She recognised the woman – it was Miss Treen, dressed in a starched uniform with her hair up in a bun. Behind her walked Mr James with another woman – his wife, she guessed. And then she realised that she'd been duped.

Mr James had lied when he'd said that Agnes would be adopted by an acquaintance of his. He had taken her. It was his wife who had been unable to bear children. It was no wonder that he'd been prepared to set her up with the cottage and get her out of the Union. He knew that he would have been found out if she'd stayed. Some-one would have mentioned his child and she would have put two and two together.

434

She began to follow them, her mind in turmoil. All she wanted was to scoop Agnes into her arms and carry her away, but she had signed the agreement and if she revealed herself, she would be putting her daughter's future in jeopardy.

The child pulled away from her governess and ran back towards Mr James and his wife.

'Papa, Papa,' she cried, holding her arms up to him. He lifted her up, laughing with her.

'I wish you wouldn't spoil her so,' his wife said.

'She is young,' Mr James said. 'Of course we can spoil her. Agnes, Papa would like to buy you a toy and some barley sugar.'

'You will make her demanding and petulant.'

'It isn't in her nature. She is the sunniest, brightest and most loving child in the world.' Mr James gave Agnes a hug and put her back down on the cobbles. 'Agnes, run along to Miss Treen and take her hand. I can tell that your mama is worried about appearances. She wishes the people of Faversham to see that you are growing up to be a lady.'

'I wish you wouldn't talk so loudly,' his wife said, 'Someone might recognise her. I still think I was right to suggest we give her a new name, one of our own choosing.'

Mr James' face became uncharacteristically stern. 'Agnes' name is the one thing her real mother left her. I won't be the one to take that away from our daughter.' And with that he turned his back on his wife, and looked adoringly after the little girl.

The sun came out through the clouds. Miss Treen opened her parasol and held it above

Agnes' head.

Her daughter wanted for nothing, Catherine thought. She had an adoring father who would more than make up for the cold fish that was her adoptive mother. She had a governess and fine clothes and, what's more, she appeared carefree and happy, but it was no consolation. Not only had Mr James taken Agnes from her, he had changed her identity completely. He had discarded the name that she and Matty had chosen for their daughter. That hurt more than anything.

Catherine tasted the metallic sweetness of blood on her lip as she drew back and watched them go, Agnes growing smaller and smaller until she disappeared into the distance. She headed back to Market Place to meet with Daniel.

'Am I relieved to see you, miss.' He was slurring his words.

'I was thirsty so I sent a boy to fetch me a pint of ale.'

And the rest, she imagined.

'I was wondering where you'd got to. In fact, I was afraid that you'd come to harm – the master would have had a right go at me if I went home without you.'

'I'm well, thank you. Just a little tired.' She forced a smile. 'It's been a long day.' She spotted a boy trying to drag the sack of potatoes from the back of the cart. 'Hey, stop, thief!' she shouted. The boy ran. Daniel tried to run after him, but he could only stagger to the first corner where the boy disappeared.

'Little tyke,' he muttered. 'I wish I'd have got hold of him.'

'No harm done,' Catherine said, checking their purchases. 'We should be getting back.'

Daniel's face grew pale and sweaty. He clutched his stomach.

'I think I ate a bad oyster,' he groaned.

'Or drank one too many strong beers,' Catherine suggested.

'You will tell the master that it's the oysters that got to me?'

There was a time when she wouldn't have covered for him, but now a little white lie wouldn't hurt. Daniel was a good lad and Stephen would suffer if he sent him on his way for being in his cups.

'You get in the back. I'll drive,' she said.

'No, miss.'

'No arguing. Wrap yourself in one of the blankets. Go on. What are you waiting for?'

He clambered into the back of the cart and lay there groaning each time Catherine drove over a bump or a rut. The horse, a bay with a Roman nose and white feathers, plodded along as dusk began to fall – he knew his way home so Catherine didn't really have to do anything except make the occasional clicking noise in her throat to make him walk out a little faster.

Eventually, they arrived back at Overshill. She pulled the horse up outside the cottage and Stephen, who must have been waiting up for her, came straight outside.

'Where's Daniel?' he said.

'He ate an oyster or two. They've had an unfortunate effect on him.' She smiled and he smiled tenderly back. 'Would you put the horse away while I make sure he's all right?'

'Of course. I suppose I'll have to unload the cart as well,' Stephen said with a mock sigh.

'I've bought a new dress for Jessie.'

'I hope it wasn't too expensive.'

'It's a gift,' Catherine said firmly as he took the reins and unhitched the horse.

'I didn't intend to sound mean,' he said. 'I've been to see the squire about the tenancy of Wanstall Farm.'

'What did he say?'

'He didn't commit either way. He pointed out that I had very little experience of farming and that I'd be taking a considerable risk with my ideas for the land. It would be a stretch financially, if I were to go ahead.'

'I can picture you there with the children.'

'It could be possible if I let go of the forge. There's plenty of room for a workshop in the yard and the stables are still standing. I could employ someone to manage the farm side of things while I build up the horse business.'

'Is that what you want?' Catherine asked.

'For a while I didn't want anything, not without Emily at my side, but I have to provide for my children.' He smiled. 'I like being a blacksmith, but I'm happiest working with the horses. There's nothing more satisfying than getting a horse back to health after a bout of lameness.'

Catherine waited until he had led the horse around the corner to the stable before she woke Daniel, shaking him roughly by the shoulder to rouse him.

'Ugh, what's the hurry?' he moaned.

438

'Get up quickly,' she hissed. 'Go to bed and sleep this off.'

'I'm dying.'

'You aren't, I can assure you. Now, get up and take yourself off to bed before Stephen gets back.'

He rolled out of the cart, dropping onto his feet. With the blanket wrapped round him, he ambled inside, tripping over the doorstep and cursing out loud.

Catherine couldn't help smiling to herself. She doubted that he would drink too much again in a hurry.

'Where's Daniel? Did he look after you?' Stephen asked when she returned to the kitchen.

'I've sent him to bed. He has a touch of a fever, nothing serious.'

'That's strange. I've never known him to be ill. He has the constitution of an ox.' He eyed her inscrutably from his place on the bench against the wall near the fireplace. 'I suppose that even the ox has his weaknesses. It's all right. I won't punish him this time, but if it happens again...'

'He's a young man. He needs guidance, that's all.' She changed the subject. 'I saw my daughter Agnes today.'

Stephen sat up straight. 'Did she know you?'

'It was merely a glimpse, but I'm sure it was her. Oh, Stephen, I wanted to run up to her and take her in my arms.'

'She is well cared for?'

Catherine nodded.

'I'm sorry. That was an idiotic thing to say. Why should that be any consolation to a mother who

439

has given up her child out of necessity?' he went on.

'She looked happy. She was laughing with the man who is now her father. I know him. He's a good man at heart, and wealthy beyond measure.' Looking back, it reassured her that it was Mr James, not some complete stranger, although she was sad that he'd had to lie to her. At least she knew where Agnes was so she could see her again.

'I'm glad.' Stephen sighed. 'I've had a difficult day.'

Catherine sat down beside him and rested her hand on his shoulder. She didn't trust herself to move any closer.

'Grief is a wayward creature. It comes and goes. Sometimes you think you're free of it, that you've suffered enough, but then it comes back like a big black dog and takes you up in its jaws again. I miss Emily, but it isn't just that. When you are gone, Catherine, the house feels empty. When I walked back in for dinner in the middle of the day, I was expecting to find you here with the children. Without you, there is no laughter, no happiness, nor joy. Please, can you find it in your heart to stay a little longer? Another month or two, that's all I'm asking. What do you say?'

Chapter Nineteen

Catch him Crow, Carry him Kite

She stayed on for a month, then another, until a full four months had gone. She had to give up the cottage in Faversham, packing up her possessions and carrying them back to the forge on a second expedition with Daniel, who managed to avoid the drink on this occasion. The idea was that she would store them in the lean-to at the rear of Forge Cottage until such a time as she moved out and found another place from which to run her business.

In early August, there was a drought. The soil was etched with cracks and the stream stopped flowing, its course marked by a series of shallow pools. The beans were struggling to reach the tops of the canes and the marrows in the garden were failing to thrive.

Catherine's love for Stephen was stronger than ever. All it would take – as for the crops – was a drop of rain, a word or a touch from him, to bring it springing to life.

Then one afternoon, the rain came in long, stormy bursts, soaking the ground and pouring from the gutters into the valley. The stream swirled and gurgled, cutting a deeper channel for its progress. The beans flourished and the marrows swelled.

Catherine was standing in the kitchen, stirring custard to go with the cherry pie she'd made and watching the water running down the window, when Stephen appeared with an armful of bright flowers that glistened wet: larkspur, dahlias and delphiniums.

'Where are the children?' he asked as he kicked off his muddy boots at the back door.

She untied her apron strings and hung it on the hook.

'Maud has taken them for a walk in the woods. They were getting fractious.' She smiled. 'It wasn't raining when they left.'

'It won't hurt them to get caught in a shower or two,' Stephen smiled back. 'We can talk in peace.' He handed her the flowers. 'These are for you.'

'Thank you,' she said, turning to open the bottom of the dresser to find a vase.

'That can wait,' he said. 'Put them down.'

She straightened. 'They will wilt out of water.'

'There are plenty more where they came from.' He stepped up close, took them from her and placed them on the table. He reached for her hands. 'Why must you always be in such a rush? Come and sit down.'

He led her out to the bench where they sat down side by side.

'What's this about?' she asked. 'Is there news of the farm?'

'This has nothing to do with the squire's plans.' Stephen cleared his throat and it felt like they had gone back in time, and he was about to declare his fondness for her. He looked down and started to rub at a mark on the side of his forefinger.

'Let me have a look at that,' she said.

'No, it's all right.'

'I'll fetch a needle from the sewing box. It won't take two minutes. You'll see.'

'You are deliberately diverting me from what I need to say.'

'Wait there.' She returned with Emily's felt book of needles, picked one and asked him to hold out his hand. She glanced up into his eyes as she felt the warmth of his skin. 'This will hurt a little, but not for long.' She held his hand, feeling the strength in his fingers. 'Hold steady.'

'Haven't I always?' he said gruffly.

'You've been a wonderful friend to me, Stephen.'

'One of my biggest sorrows is that I lost touch with you after the trials, but what could I do? You disappeared without trace.' He looked down at his finger. 'Go ahead. I've braced myself for the pain,' he added wryly.

She pressed the end of the needle into the skin overlying the splinter.

'Ah,' he said, 'that's nothing.'

She dug a little deeper, removed the needle and squeezed his finger.

'Ouch.' He winced.

'I'm sorry.' She caught the end of the splinter between her fingernails and pulled it out. 'There. All done.' She flicked the metal filing away. Stephen sucked briefly on the wound then looked more closely at the damage.

'Shall I fetch you a bandage to stem the flow of blood?' Catherine teased. 'I swear that the baby is braver than you are.'

'Thank you, but no more teasing. I'm trying to

be serious.' He took her hand. 'I've been practising the words I was going to say, over and over again at the forge, but now they've completely flown out of my head, so I'll say it as it is. I want to marry you.'

She didn't know how to react.

'I've shocked you,' he said softly. 'I'm sorry.'

'You've taken me by surprise,' she admitted.

'I heard Jessie calling you Ma the other day.'

'She's asked me to be her mother, but I've explained that Emily must live on in her heart as she does in mine. I can't possibly replace her.'

'I understand.' He frowned.

'You want us to be married, so that I have a reason to stay on here in Overshill to be with the children.' It was a practical proposition and she would give a practical answer. 'I will consider it.'

'You will?' A shadow of regret and hurt crossed his eyes.

'There are many reasons why it would be a good match – for both of us. People are talking. They're saying that we've taken up with each other with indecent haste after.

'With Emily still warm in the ground,' Stephen finished for her. 'I've done my best to silence the gossip, but you know what Overshill's like. I don't like to hear anyone speaking badly of you. It isn't right when you are here out of the goodness of your heart.'

She gazed at him, wondering if he had any idea how she felt about him.

'I want to make a respectable woman of you, Catherine.'

'I imagine that it would improve your chances

of acquiring the tenancy of Wanstall Farm as well, if that's what you're planning.'

'I believe that the squire will look on my request more favourably if I present myself as a married man. Every would-be farmer needs a wife.'

'It doesn't seem possible that I should ever return to the farm.'

'But you'd like to?'

'In the right circumstances.' She was sorely tempted by Stephen's offer. She'd learned from Pa Rook how to coax the crops from the light, loamy soil and knew – she thought of Matty and the book she'd read to him at the top of the church tower on the night of the fire – how to round up sheep. She was fond of Stephen – fonder than she could say – and she'd learned that when you were ground down by poverty you didn't have choices. But there was something inside her, a mulish streak, that wouldn't let her accept. She hadn't compromised her principles when the journeyman bricklayer had proposed a comfortable marriage. She wouldn't give them up now.

'It's a lovely thought,' she began again, 'but I think it would be a mistake to marry out of convenience.'

'It wouldn't be on my side. That's what I've been trying to say, but it hasn't come out right because I'm a dolt,' Stephen said. 'Catherine, I've loved you since I saw you dancing at the harvest when you were about sixteen. I wanted you then, but by the time I asked you I was too late – you'd fallen for my brother. I knew I had no chance, which is why I turned to Emily. I grew to

445

love her more deeply than I imagined possible and I'm hoping against hope that you're willing to open your heart to me. I can offer you a home, friendship and a warm bed ... when you're ready.'

He loved her. He'd said in so many words what she'd been waiting to hear. She shivered, yearning to feel his arms around her and his lips upon hers.

'I don't think you realise how strongly I feel for you.' He slid to his knees at her feet. 'I couldn't bear to see you every day if you should decide that we cannot be together.' He took her hands, his touch like the fire that he conjured within the forge. 'I need you to put me out of my misery one way or another. My dearest, darling Catherine, will you marry me?'

She gazed into his eyes, her heart beating fast.

'Oh, Stephen, my dearest man. Yes, I'd be honoured to be your wife.'

His lips curved into a smile.

'Thank you,' he said, reaching his hands around her waist. 'I'll do everything in my power to make you happy.'

'I know you will, and I will do the same for you.'

Still on his knees, he leaned up and pressed his lips to hers, setting her whole being aflame. She was home, where she was meant to be, with Stephen, who had been and remained the one constant in her life. He had been at her side at the Red Lion on that fateful day of the riot and at the courthouse in Maidstone, and she had returned the favour, coming to his aid when Emily had sickened and died.

446

'We'll be a family and maybe one day we'll have children of our own,' she added, pulling away slightly.

'I'd like that. When we're married, everyone will have to acknowledge you or they'll have me to deal with. Mrs Browning will be compelled to speak with you when she comes with a kettle to solder, the same for Mrs White when she wants her ring mended. And Mr Nobbs when he comes with an order to beat out a ploughshare.' He grinned. 'I'm going to see the vicar before you can change your mind.'

'Do you think that's likely?' she said, tipping her head to one side.

He shook his head and kissed her again.

That evening, after Jessie and Matthew had returned from their walk, soaked through but exhilarated, and they had all eaten together, Stephen helped Catherine put the children to bed, then sat with her once again in the kitchen.

'We'll meet with the vicar as soon as possible. I don't want to miss out on a single day being married to you,' he said as the baby started to wail from his crib upstairs.

'I expect he's hungry again,' Catherine said, standing up and resting her hands on Stephen's shoulders. 'He's growing so quickly.'

'I'll fetch him,' Stephen said, getting up.

'I'll warm the milk through a little.' Catherine went into the larder to collect it. When Stephen returned with Stanley in his arms, they sat back down side by side on the oak settle. Stephen fed the baby and carried him back to his crib. When

447

he laid him down on his back, he started to fidget and cry.

'Please, don't wake the others,' Stephen groaned as he retreated to the doorway.

'Let me quieten him,' Catherine said, and she began to sing her favourite lullaby, one she used to sing to Agnes. She became aware that Stephen's voice had joined hers, melodic and deeply stirring, and by the time they'd uttered the very last notes, the baby's eyes were closed, and Jessie and Matthew were fast asleep.

'I shall retire to bed,' Catherine whispered. 'It's been a long day.'

'Goodnight,' Stephen said.

She dreamed about Matty that night. She told him that she was marrying his brother and he gave his blessing in return. She wasn't sure when she woke whether the dream meant anything or if it was merely wishful thinking on her part. She hoped that he would approve of the match. She thought that he would.

The next day, Stephen called on the vicar to arrange for the banns to be read, and in the second week of September, they walked to church together, just the two of them, hand in hand. Catherine wore a dress of Emily's made from light blue muslin with an overlay of lace across the bodice, and altered to fit. Stephen wore a suit that was too small for him, too short in the legs and arms, and too tight across the shoulders, but he looked no less handsome for it, she thought.

They made their vows in front of the Reverend Browning, signed the register in the presence of two witnesses, George and Daniel, and walked back out into the sunshine. They paused at Emily's graveside to pay their respects, the grave now marked with a small headstone.

'Let's go home,' she said to Stephen.

He smiled.

'The forge will be our home for another week, then we'll be moving into the farmhouse.'

She gazed into his eyes.

'You mean, Wanstall Farm?'

He nodded.

'Mr Hadington has drawn up the legal documents. I'm due to meet him and the squire to sign them later today, and then it's ours. We'll be the new tenants. I hope you don't mind. I wanted it to be a surprise, a wedding present.'

'It's certainly that, a surprise, I mean.' She smiled back.

'It will be a fresh start for all of us.'

'What about the cost?'

'We'll manage. Trust me. I have it all worked out.' He touched her face, the contact sending shivers of anticipation down her spine. 'I know we'll make a success of it – together.'

'Together,' she echoed as they headed out through the gate at the entrance to the churchyard. Stephen called for Daniel to accompany them, but he was nowhere to be seen.

'He's with one of the village girls, no doubt,' he observed with a grin. 'The wheelwright's daughter is much on his mind. She's always turning up at the forge with some or other excuse to talk to him.'

'I thought he was rather keen on Maud.'

'Oh, that's old news.' He held out his arm. Catherine took it and they walked quietly back to the cottage as husband and wife.

Mrs and Mrs Carter and the three children moved into Wanstall Farm, relocating the forge and taking on labourers to tend the hops and barley, while Stephen began to build a business in farriery and horse-doctoring

A year later, there was a knock at the door. Catherine, carrying the baby on her hip, opened the door to find the vicar on the doorstep. She ran her fingers through her hair, wishing she'd had time to make a little effort with her appearance for this unexpected caller, and wondering at herself for beginning to sound like Ma.

'Are you alone, Mrs Carter?' the Reverend Browning enquired.

'I am as far as it goes.' She frowned. 'Can I make you a cup of tea? I've made a cake – it's caraway.'

'Thank you, but there's no need for sustenance. Mrs Browning has directed the cook to make a beef and kidney pudding for tonight.'

She offered him a seat, Stephen's chair by the fireside in the former parlour which they now used as a family room. The vicar sat down and Catherine took a place on the settle opposite.

'I've received a letter from your husband's brother.'

'Matty?' Her heart stopped. Her vision blurred. What news and why now?

'It's a rather delicate situation, considering that you are only recently married. In fact, my daughter Jane, in her wisdom, suggested that I tore it up and burned it in the fire, but I couldn't have that deception on my conscience, so I am here to hand it over to you to do with it as you wish.' He lowered his voice as the sound of the children's laughter drifted in from the farmhouse garden which she and Stephen were bringing back to life after months of neglect. 'I shouldn't feel obliged to open it, if I were you. You are married now.'

She didn't need the vicar to remind her of that fact, she thought.

'Let no man tear such a union asunder,' he went on.

She gazed at the envelope, her heart pounding with apprehension. What if Matty was ill or asking for her help? She couldn't just throw the letter unread into the fire. She opened it.

His mark was at the bottom of the parchment, but another hand had written the body of the missive. She felt a little faint as she read through it. It was like hearing from a ghost.

'He says he is well,' she said. 'He has received a pardon. Well I never. He is a free man.'

'Is he returning to Overshill?'

She shook her head.

'He has raised the money to pay passage for me and our–' She broke off abruptly, not wishing to reveal more than was necessary. 'He plans that I should travel to Tasmania to meet him.' How many years had she waited to see or hear those words? She felt a rush of guilt that Matty had stayed true to her, while she had not done the same for him.

'That is rather inconvenient news at this time.' Catherine checked the date on the letter. It had been posted many months before.

'Would you like me to write back to him?' the vicar asked.

'No, thank you, I can do it myself.'

'I assume that you'll be letting your husband know about this.'

'Of course,' she said, 'we have no secrets between us. Stephen knows everything. I'm very grateful for your concern, but I mustn't keep you any longer. I'm sure you have sermons to write.'

'Indeed, I do.' He stood up. 'Good day, Mrs Carter. I'll see myself out.'

Once he'd gone, she checked for the half a sixpence which she'd hidden on top of the grandfather clock that Stephen had acquired as a debt from one of his customers. Matty's souvenir was safe, but she didn't need it any more. One day, when Agnes was old enough to understand, she would hand it over to her as a keepsake of her real father.

She called the children together and told them she was going to the forge to see their papa. She carried Stanley in her arms while Jessie and Matthew walked along, holding hands.

'Remember to mind the horses and the fire. And don't try to pick up the hammer again, Jessie.' She'd hauled it from the anvil on which it was resting on one occasion and it had fallen onto her foot.

'I won't, Mama 'Rin,' she sang out.

Daniel was at the fire, pulling a glowing metal bar from its heart.

'Hello,' Catherine called. 'Where's Stephen?'

'Over there by the granary,' he called back.

She turned and walked towards the building

452

where an elderly white horse was tied outside. Stephen was tapping nails into the horse's foot. She watched him with fondness as a dove cooed from the dovecote he'd recently installed. Eventually, he looked up and smiled. He lowered the horse's foot and straightened.

He moved towards them and took the baby from her. He held him up high, making him chuckle. Matthew stood, tugging at his father's shirt, wanting a turn too.

'And me, Papa,' Jessie joined in.

'Catch him, crow!' Stephen began. 'Carry him, kite.' The others joined in.

'Take him away till the apples are ripe. When they are ripe and ready to fall. Here comes baby, apples and all.' Stephen let go of the baby, catching him up quickly and swooping him above his shoulders.

'Please, Papa,' Matthew begged.

Stephen gave each of the children a turn before sending Jessie and Matthew off with a trug and strict instructions to keep hold of Stanley's hand while they hunted for eggs.

'What brings you here, my darling wife?'

'And children. I thought I would bring them out with me rather than let them get into mischief.' Her forehead tightened. 'I received a letter this morning.'

'The vicar delivered it. I saw him – he asked me about making a new gate for the vicarage. What was it about?'

'It's from Matty – he's alive and well. He has been pardoned.'

Stephen's face travelled through a range of

emotions from surprise to joy and then to sorrow.

'Is he coming back to England?'

'No. He asked if I would go to him–'

'Then so be it,' Stephen said abruptly. He stared at her. 'I'm glad my brother is well. I've prayed for him so many times. You have to do what sits right with your conscience. If you wish to find him, I won't stand in your way, although that will be the hardest thing I've ever done. I want you to be happy, Catherine.'

'Oh, Stephen, I'm not going to Tasmania. My place is here at your side. This is my home. I belong here in Overshill with you.'

'Do you mean that?' he said.

She nodded, hardly able to speak.

'My love.'

'You are my best friend and most wonderful husband, and what's more, I'm sure now that I'm with child. Our baby.'

He took her hands in his rough grasp and kissed her.

'You have just made me the happiest man in all of Kent.'

She smiled as the sun slanted across the farm-yard, its light banishing the shadows. She loved this man. He was the person who had been at her side, not Matty. They had been through good and bad times, the best and the worst. She would never leave him, just as she knew he would never dream of abandoning her. They were married, bound together, till death should part them.

This Large Print Book for the partially sighted, who cannot read normal print, is published under the auspices of

THE ULVERSCROFT FOUNDATION

About the authors

Nikesh Shukla is the author of the critically acclaimed novel *Meatspace*, the Costa shortlisted novel *Coconut Unlimited* and the award-winning novella *The Time Machine*. He wrote the short film *Two Dosas* and the Channel 4 sitcom *Kabadasses*. @nikeshshukla

Varaidzo is an undergraduate student and essayist working in film and the arts. She is currently an editor at gal-dem.com. @veedzo

Himesh Patel is an English actor best known for his role as Tamwar Masood in the BBC soap opera *EastEnders*. He also starred in the award-winning short film *Two Dosas*. @himeshjpatel

Chimene Suleyman is a writer. Her debut poetry collection, *Outside Looking On*, was in the *Guardian*'s Best Books of 2014. She has performed at the Royal Festival Hall, Book Slam, Literary Death Match, the Bush Theatre, Latitude and more. She has written on race and gender for the *Independent*, Media Diversified, and *The Quietus*. @chimenesuleyman

Vera Chok is an actress, writer and performance maker. She's also founder and director of theatre company saltpeter and The Brautigan Book Club. Her writing has been published by *Rising*, *Brautigan Free Press*, *Toast*, *Yauatcha Life* and *Ether* and performed at the inaugural BareLit Festival. In 2015, Vera acted for the National Theatre and The Kenneth Branagh Company as well as created the performance piece *These 12 Things Are True*. @vera_chok

Salena Godden is one of Britain's foremost spoken word artists. She is a regular performer at international and national literary festivals in a career that is now entering its third decade. Her short stories and poetry have been anthologised by Penguin, Canongate, Serpent's Tail, Influx Press, Polygon Books and many more. She has written for BBC Radio programmes including *The Verb, Saturday Live, Loose Ends* and *From Fact to Fiction* and has authored and presented several arts documentaries for BBC Radio and Channel 4. Burning Eye Books published her debut collection *Fishing in the Aftermath* in 2014 to mark twenty years of poetry and performance. Her literary childhood memoir *Springfield Road* was successfully crowdfunded and published with Unbound. @salenagodden

Bim Adewunmi is a writer. She writes about culture for BuzzFeed, and is a columnist at the *Guardian*. @bimadew

Daniel York Loh has worked as an actor at the RSC, National Theatre and Royal Court. As a writer he has written the stage play *The Fu Manchu Complex* and, along with composer Craig Adams, was the winner of the 2016 Perfect Pitch award to create an original musical, *Sinking Water*, based on events surrounding the 2004 Morecambe Bay Chinese cockle pickers disaster, which is now in development at Theatre Royal Stratford East. @danielfyork

Miss L is an actress and the creator of 'Casting Call Woe', a site where she highlights the very worst casting calls. She regularly writes about the trials of being an actress and her work has been featured on BuzzFeed and in the *Guardian* and *Grazia* magazine. @proresting

Nish Kumar is a British stand-up comedian, actor and radio presenter. He hosts *Newsjack* on BBC Radio 4 Extra. He has appeared on *Have I Got News for You*, Russell Howard's *Stand Up Central*, *Sweat the Small Stuff*, and *The Alternative Comedy Experience*. @mrnishkumar

Reni Eddo-Lodge is a journalist and writer. Her first book, *Why I'm No Longer Talking to White People About Race*, will be released in 2017. @renireni

Darren Chetty is currently completing his PhD at UCL Institute of Education, where he teaches on the BA Education Studies course. He taught in primary schools for almost 20 years. He is the author of the award-winning paper 'The Elephant in the Room: Picturebooks, Philosophy for Children and Racism'. @rapclassroom

Kieran Yates is a freelance writer on music and politics for *NME*, *Metro* and *Dazed & Confused*. She is the co-author of *Generation Vexed* and the creator of the magazine *British Values*. @kieranyates

Coco Khan is senior editor at Complex UK and editor of arts magazine, *Kensington and Chelsea Review*. She writes about class, culture and anything to do with hot boys. @cocobyname

Inua Ellams is an award-winning poet, playwright, and performer. Across his work, identity, displacement and destiny are recurring themes, in which he tries to mix the old with the new: traditional African storytelling with contemporary poetry. @inuaellams

Sabrina Mahfouz writes plays, poems, librettos and TV. She was recently a Sky Arts Academy Scholar for Poetry and an Associate Playwright at the Bush Theatre. Her play *Chef* won a 2014 Fringe First Award. @sabrinamahfouz

Riz Ahmed is a British actor and rapper. He has starred in *The Road to Guantanamo*, *Shifty*, *Britz*, *Four Lions*, *Ill Manors*, *The Reluctant Fundamentalist* and *Nightcrawler*. He records as Riz MC, with Heems as Swet Shop Boys, and with DJ Distance as Halflife. @rizmc

Sarah Sahim is a writer of Afghan and Indian descent from the West Midlands, UK. She co-hosts the intersectional feminist podcast *Not All Women*. She has edited for *Racked* and *Broadly* and written for *Rolling Stone*, *Paper*, *Playboy* and *Pitchfork* on race, feminism, pop culture and lifestyle. @sarahsahim

Wei Ming Kam is a writer and blogger. She works for Oberon Books and is the co-founder of BAME in Publishing, a network for black, Asian and minority ethnic people who work in publishing. She has written for Fantasy Faction and Media Diversified. @weimingkam

Vinay Patel is a writer for screen and stage. His work includes *True Brits*, which premiered at the 2014 Edinburgh Fringe before transferring to the Bush Theatre, where he is currently under commission. Most recently, he wrote BBC3's *Murdered by My Father*. @vinaypatel

Musa Okwonga is a poet, author, sportswriter, broadcaster, musician, public relations consultant and commentator on current affairs – including culture, politics, sport, race, gender and sexuality. He is the author of two books on football, and he has written for *Al Jazeera America*, *New Statesman*, the *Independent*, BBC Radio 4's *Today Programme*, Channel 4 News, Sky News, the *Guardian*, *New Humanist* and the *Financial Times*. @okwonga

THE GOOD IMMIGRANT

Ed. Nikesh Shukla

This edition first published in 2016

Unbound
6th Floor Mutual House, 70 Conduit Street, London W1S 2GF

www.unbound.co.uk

Text design by PDQ

Art direction by Mark Ecob
Cover design by James Jones

A CIP record for this book is available from the British Library

ISBN 978-1-78352-295-8 (trade hbk)
ISBN 978-1-78352-296-5 (ebook)
ISBN 978-1-78352-294-1 (limited edition)

Printed i

7 9 8

For Sunnie
and
Timothy Patrick York (1967–2000)

Dear Reader,

The book you are holding came about in a rather different way to most others. It was funded directly by readers through a new website: Unbound. Unbound is the creation of three writers. We started the company because we believed there had to be a better deal for both writers and readers. On the Unbound website, authors share the ideas for the books they want to write directly with readers. If enough of you support the book by pledging for it in advance, we produce a beautifully bound special subscribers' edition and distribute a regular edition and e-book wherever books are sold, in shops and online.

This new way of publishing is actually a very old idea (Samuel Johnson funded his dictionary this way). We're just using the internet to build each writer a network of patrons. Here, at the back of this book, you'll find the names of all the people who made it happen.

Publishing in this way means readers are no longer just passive consumers of the books they buy, and authors are free to write the books they really want. They get a much fairer return too – half the profits their books generate, rather than a tiny percentage of the cover price.

If you're not yet a subscriber, we hope that you'll want to join our publishing revolution and have your name listed in one of our books in the future. To get you started, here is a £5 discount on your first pledge. Just visit unbound.com, make your pledge and type **thegood** in the promo code box when you check out.

Thank you for your support,

Dan, Justin and John
Founders, Unbound

With special thanks to Joanne Rowling

CONTENTS

EDITOR'S NOTE

This book emerged out of a comment on a *Guardian* article. I know, I know, it's easy to say, don't read the comments. But I do. Because I want to know my enemy. The commenter took umbrage at an interview a journalist had done with five authors (including me) about their writing process. The journalist (Asian) had interviewed five or six people of colour. The commenter wondered why there wasn't a more prominent author interviewed for this piece. He supposed (for it is almost always a 'he') that perhaps we were all friends of the journalist, given we too were all mostly Asian. This constant anxiety we feel as people of colour to justify our space, to show that we have earned our place at the table, continues to hound us. For while I and the 20 other writers included in this book don't want to just write about race, nor do we *only* write about race, it felt imperative, in the light of that comment (and the many others like it), the backwards attitude to immigration and refugees, the systemic racism that runs through this country to this day, that we create this document: a document of what it means to be a person of colour now. Because we're done justifying our place at the table.

For people of colour, race is in everything we do. Because the universal experience is white. Another commenter (yes, yes, I know) on a short story I once wrote, was pleasantly surprised to see Indians going through the universal experience. Much as I was surprised that I was excluded from the universal experience, it hammered home the knowledge that the universal experience is white. This book collects 21 universal experiences: feelings of anger, displacement, defensiveness, curiosity, absurdity – we look at death, class, microaggression, popular culture, access, free movement, stake in society, lingual fracas, masculinity, and more.

Luckily, there are magazines and spaces emerging to give people of colour the space to write about their universal experiences, and not just write specifically on race. Check out sites like Media Diversified, gal-dem, Skin Deep, Burnt Roti, Rife Magazine.

I chose these writers for simple reasons: I know them, I rate them, I want to read more from them. I'm happy to admit that nepotism and networks played a part in my selection. And I'm happy to create a brand new old boys' network that circumvents the institutionalised ones we have to deal with on a daily basis. Because there is a secret cabal of people of colour, and contrary to the stereotypes we like to refute, we do all know each other. But that's because when we're the only ones in the room, we gravitate towards each other, and stick next to each other, because we intimately know the balance of race and universal experience particular to people of colour.

Before you enjoy these beautiful, powerful, unapologetic essays, a quick note on the title of the book: Musa Okwonga, the poet, journalist and essayist whose powerful 'The Ungrateful Country' closes the book, once said to me that the biggest burden facing people of colour in this country is that society deems us bad immigrants – job-stealers, benefit-scroungers, girlfriend-thieves, refugees – until we cross over in their consciousness, through popular culture, winning races, baking good cakes, being conscientious doctors, to become good immigrants.

And we are so tired of that burden.

NAMASTE

NIKESH SHUKLA

Namaste means hello.

Namaste means I'm bowing to you.

It's a customary greeting.

It's a respectful salutation.

It has become a bastardised metaphor for spiritualism. It's white people doing yoga, throwing up prayer hands chanting 'AUM' and saying 'namaste' like their third eyes are being opened and they can peer directly into the nucleus of spirituality.

You need to know this. Because of your skin tone, people will ask you where you're from. If you tell them Bristol, they'll ask where your parents are from. When they know you're half-Indian, one person will try to impress their knowledge of your culture on you.

I can't sleep.

It's 2am and a party is raging across the road. The flat is rented out to students on a regular basis. Your mother is, sensibly, sleeping with ear plugs in. I can hear you purring in the next room.

I know that in four hours time I have to drive you to London, to take you to see your dada and your fai and fuva. To spend time with the Indian part of your family. To say namaste to your Indian cousins, aunties and uncles.

I'm driving so I need the sleep.

It transpires that the reason the party is so loud is because someone on the top floor of the house is leaning out of his window, smoking and bellowing a conversation down to a person at street level, which, due to the peculiarities of the houses we live opposite, is about four storeys' worth of shouting. At 2am.

This is silly, I think. It's Friday night, sure, but it's a residential street. I may have been these kids once, but now I'm in my thirties. I'm a man of family now. I'm a man of red wine and Netflix. I'm a man of nights in and community cohesion. I get it. I get what life's about. It's about living like your actions affect the people you don't know, as well as the people you do.

I've done questionable shit, pissed in places I shouldn't have, left detritus for poor working souls to have to clean up the morning after, shout-screamed songs at the top of my voice running down streets where families lived, been oblivious to the rest of the world, carrying on like there's something out there in the rest of the world for me to interact with. Your mother reminds me of this the next morning when I tell her what happens next.

I tell her that I don't want to live with the thought that I'm intolerant of other people's intolerance.

I walk out of the house, just as the conversation, bellowed across four storeys, wraps up and the man on the street level leaves to the sound of his friend hoping he gets home safely. I approach the steps up to their stoop. I notice, in the shadows, a boy and a girl are sitting in the doorway of the main door, ajar, smoking.

'Excuse me,' I ask. 'Do you mind continuing your party inside?'

'Jah bless,' the girl in the doorway says. 'Namaste,' she repeats, over me.

I say it again. I change the words to become clearer. More forceful. 'Can you please continue your party inside?'

'Namaste,' she says again. I hear the boy stifle a laugh.

'Namaste,' they both say. 'Namaste, namaste, namaste, namaste, namaste,' until I'm drowned out.

I'm standing under a street lamp, wearing my white bedtime kurta and lengha pyjamas. My skin is bleached out by the fluorescence of the yellow lamp. There's probably no way they can tell I'm Indian from the lighting. It's dickery for dickery's sake.

The bellowing man leaning out of his window asks if the music's too loud. I look up to him, the voice of reason and I say again, can you please continue your party inside?

'Namaste, namaste, namaste,' the girl says.

I shout something wounded, along the lines of 'this is classy,' passive-aggressive, without a target.

I go back inside and I lie in bed staring at the ceiling, watching the arrows of passing car headlights pierce cracks in the curtains.

Eventually the party quietens. My mind doesn't. I'm rolling in a quagmire of ways to deal with this slight. Beyond writing 'Namaste, Dickheads' on a placard and placing it in my bedroom window, I don't know what to do.

The house residents go home for the summer, having moved in and warmed the house to celebrate. Any call for an apology I ask for come the autumn will be muted and months too late.

* * *

I walk past an arts space that's part bar/club, part sustainable restaurant, part hot-desking for freelance artists and part dance studio. They host morning raves and yoga classes there. Most mornings, the steps are daubed with hippies, wearing OM and Ganesha parachute pants, their hair in dreadlocks, bindis mark out the third eyes in the middle of their foreheads. They tie their dogs up to the bicycle racks using scratchy sari material and they enter the yoga studios to be natraja and ashtanga geniuses and salute the sun and greet and say goodbye to each other with a solid, heartfelt namaste.

'Namaste,' one of them says to me one morning as I walk down the road, listening to Jai Paul, swinging my two-tier tiffin up and down.

She offers me prayer hands as I pass and I see her mouthing something. I take my headphones off. Jai Paul's 'Str8 Outta Mumbai' is at its crescendo. *But you know I'll do anything for you. I'll do anything for you.*

'Namaste,' she says.

I grimace.

'Hi,' I reply.

'Namaste,' she replies and raises her prayer hands to touch to her bowing forehead.

She has faded henna on her fingers.

'It just means hello,' I say. She looks at me, confused. 'Namaste, it just means hello. That's it.'

'Namaste,' she says again, and I walk on.

I have three voices. I realise this when Nerm and his wife come to visit. You're inside your mother's stomach. Your involvement in this story comes just after your mother tells Nerm and his wife that she is pregnant, we are expecting. In his excitement, the typically expressive Nerm gestures wildly with his hands and knocks his pint of lager all over your mum's stomach. All over you.

It's funny, but it's not.

The way Nerm and I interact is an intersection of our Gujarati upbringing, our east London socialisation and acknowledgment that there's a white person in the room who needs to keep up.

Yes, bruv, we talk like goras be listening, innit. Fut-a-fut, we wipe away poi-nt spill, mite, while Katie gets fresss again. We call each other bevakoofs, cuss out each other's pronunciation, bruv. We greet with the kem cho, mite. We're cursive, glottal stopping, syllable-swapping rhythmic beasts of anarchic remixed English. Talking to him for the three hours he and his wife are in town, I feel like I'm with my peoples again. When I go home, it takes me a while to get my voice back.

It's an effort to type this way. In a way that's palatable to Westerners. In a way that's markedly different from my speaking voice, because my speaking voice holds rhythms that weren't made in the West.

My mum had three voices.

She had her white-people-phone voice, her Guj-lish talk-at-home voice and her relatives voice.

I have three voices too. I talk in Guj-lish, my normal voice and white literary party. I don't know whether my normal voice, where I feel most comfortable, most safe, even feels like me anymore. I've splintered into personas. This is the trick of living publicly online with increasing watch and scrutiny by others. When I first started out on Twitter, I had 10-odd followers, all people I knew in the real world, people I could be myself with. As my following increased, I had to become less of myself and more of the public perception of me as the writer. And it made me lose track of who I was and what voice I spoke in.

Nowadays, I ensure that whenever I tweet about literary things, I add the odd 'fam', 'bruv', 'cuz' or 'innit', just to ensure the execution of my thought or praise comes with the necessary rooting to where I'm from. I'm a hip-hop fan, and much as I agree that it's not where you're from, it's where you're at – actually, it's where you're from.

An agent who has rejected me twice tweets about an impending apocalypse because his intern referred to clothes as 'garms'. This sends me into a shame spiral. I've been using this word in two of my three voices since 1994. I reply to his tweet, saying 'slang's more important that "proper English", fam. No one talks in proper English, innit.' He doesn't reply. I delete my tweet. I know he's still smarting from when I pulled him up on a snarky tweet about diversity in publishing and his ennui towards it. His response was to say that there was a debate of merit worth having. I told him that it wasn't a debate for me, it was my life. I can't change my skin tone. White people debate it. We live it.

My conversation with Nerm makes me feel lonely.

I watch you in your mum's belly, squirming about, experimenting with spatial awareness, waking up as she and I settle down to bed after the pub. I wonder what voice you'll have? Who you'll be? What you'll sound like? And whether you'll have Gujarati reference points or if the extent of your lingual heritage will only be namaste?

I knock on my neighbour's door.

I know someone is home because a window at the top of the house is cracked open. I can just about make out the 'Keep Calm and Carry On' poster.

I wait, thinking about my opening line. I don't know whether to be angry or polite and firm, or treat it like it's a joke, like we're all friends here, like I know you guys were just dicking around and that's okay, but just know that words have impact.

Or whether to tell them how I feel.

One of the many online arguments I've had about the importance of language, how language can hurt, has been about tea. Chai means tea. Chai tea means tea tea. The number of times you see this on a menu makes you wonder why people can't be bothered to do their research. Like naan bread too. Bread bread.

A comedian, Kumail Nanjiani, an avid gamer, once expressed his delight that the *Call of Duty* series finally set a level in Karachi, the city of his childhood, now one of the top ten most dangerous cities in the world. He was appalled, on playing the game, to see that all the street signs were in Arabic. Not Urdu. He talks about the effort put into making each follicle on each soldier's head stand out, into making their boot laces bounce as they ran, the millions spent developing this game, and how at no point did anyone decide to Google the language of Pakistan.

In *Jurassic World*, they refer to some pachycephalosaurus dinosaurs as pachys, or pakis – 'the pakis are escaping' one of the techs exclaims. The budget for the movie was $150 million. If I had to place a value on how much people would have to pay me in order to call me a paki, it would be more than $150 million. Words matter. Words are important.

The casualness with which someone I'm working with refers to 'two coloured girls'. The casualness with which a person having her photo taken with a nice view, and me obscuring the corner of it asks her husband to ensure he gets

one 'without the Indian in it'. The casualness of being on the
last train home, from London to Bristol, in the same car as the
bar, listening to two drunk men in their early twenties shout
at each other, 'n****r, we made it', repeatedly, with excruciating
enthusiasm. They're just quoting rap, someone might think.
They're drunk, they're harmless, they're being exuberant.
Dickish, but exuberant.

Language is important.

Years before, I sat in an Indian restaurant round the corner.
It's called Oh! Calcutta![1]. I found the exclamation mark
alarming. The place was owned by a white guy. As I sat with
my best friend and his then girlfriend, starring at the disco
lights, I listened to Kula Shaker sing about 'Taatva', about
'Govinda jai jai, gopala jai jai'. I read the menu. One of the
dishes listed was Chicken Chuddi, described as an exotic blend
of authentic spices, tomato and peppers. It sounded so generic.
What was an exotic blend, what were authentic spices, also –
tomato and pepper? These were the biggest tastemakers aside
from chicken in the dish? What was Chicken Chuddi?

Also, as you know, chuddi means pants.

I told my friend and his then girlfriend. They laughed
at the whiteness of it all, ahahahaha, they said, cultural
misappropriation is hilarious, they said in so many words. I felt
mortified for the white guy owner, he had probably been duped
by some guy he'd asked for a word that sounded 'Eastern'.

---

1   *Oh! Calcutta!* was a long-running, avant-garde, sexy theatrical sketch revue put
together by Kenneth Tynan the theatre critic in the late sixties/early seventies,
mainly famous for the fact that the cast was naked a lot of the time. The title
of the show was taken from the title of a nude painting by the French surrealist
artist Clovis Trouille, *Oh! Calcutta, Calcutta!* which was a pun on the French,
'oh, quel cul t'as' roughly translating as 'oh, what an arse you have'. It has
nothing to do with India.

Maybe the chef was having a laugh with him. Maybe he was having a joke with his clients. I looked around. Everyone in the restaurant was white. It was a hipster student paradise. The mix of cod Eastern Britpop, minimal red lighting like a moody Ryan Gosling film and the prices, it felt like puppetry of food. The biggest crime. Not only was the Western balti curry now synonymous with my country's cuisine, but now we had white guys aping the food we made to fit in with the white guys.

I called the manager over.

'The Chicken Chuddi,' I said. 'You know chuddi means pants, don't you?'

He laughed. 'You having me on, right?' he replied. 'It's a specific blend of spices. Nice try.'

'It means pants,' I repeated.

He smiled, itching to get away.

I let him.

Language is important.

The door opens.

He stands in front of me. A boy, not yet 20, wearing a T-shirt that says GEEK on it in the all-caps of shouting pride. He holds a controller for a games console in one hand and a cider in the other.

'Hello,' he says politely. Nervously.

'Namaste,' I say, pressing my hands together in prayer. 'Hello.'

A car, a street away, pumps out a bhangra loop. The subwoofer bounces around my eardrum. I shake my head, turn around and head back across the street. Usually, when I leave for work, you're in the window, waving, propped up by your mum. Your smile is free. It doesn't know nuance yet. We should keep it that way.

A GUIDE TO BEING BLACK

VARAIDZO

With most people, their race is perhaps the only aspect of their identity guaranteed from the moment of conception. They'll be whatever race their parents are, and stay being that for life. For mixed-race children it's a little more confusing. We don't always come out looking like our parents, and often we'll be racialised differently to them. The process can take a little longer to figure out.

Because of this, I spent the first decade of my life unaware that I was black, and spent the decade that followed being not very good at it. They had a word for this in the playground, an 'Oreo': a kid that was black on the outside and white on the inside. I had 10 years of catching up to do, and it was showing, and I wished someone had written a guide to being black that I could have read and then just got on with it. Instead, I had to figure it out the hard way, through actually living.

Here are a few of the key lessons I learned, like what to do when you're the only black kid in a party when a Kanye song comes on, or how to decide which is the right hairstyle for you. It's the guide I needed when I was younger: this is the unofficial guide to being black.

1. Black is the New Orange: Explaining the 'One Drop' Rule

I first acknowledged that I was black in the back seat of my best friend Jenna's car. I was nine. Her mother was driving us, her older sister, and a couple of other kids that she carpooled, to their house for dinner. The older children had been having a debate over whether they were allowed to call someone Chinese if they *looked* Chinese but their country of origin was unknown. The word they were looking for, Jenna's mother informed the car, was Asian. Then she delved into a brief lesson on race.

'It's the same way our family is Scottish but yours are Irish, yet we're all still white, do you see?' she said, and Jenna, presenting further evidence to prove her mother's point, looked at me and declared, 'It's like you. You're English.... but you're also black.'

Nine is a young age to discover such a thing. My first four years of life had not really included race. A better description would be that race was so commonplace as to make it obsolete as an issue. I had a white mother and a black father, an Indian godmother and a Japanese lodger. I'd been moved from London to Zimbabwe and back again. When we finally settled in Bristol, my group of friends in nursery resembled a Benetton commercial, all races and genders playing together after lunchtime milk. We owned the Rodgers and Hammerstein *Cinderella* on video over Disney's pretty white animation, and I thought nothing of the Filipino Prince Charming having Whoopi Goldberg and Victor Garber as parents.

This post-racial utopia dissolved when I was sent to a primary school in Bath and I was the only brown-skinned child in my year. Around the same time I developed an obsession with the colours red and yellow. My bedroom had pairs of red and yellow walls, and I exclusively used those crayons to scribble. I understood how these colours interacted, that if combined they created a new colour: orange. I applied this logic to my own family. With one black parent and one white, I was the orange to my father's red and my mother's yellow, not quite either but rather something altogether new. Does an orange thing ever stop to think that it might actually be red?

I never had reason to consider I was anything other than mixed-race.

Until the car journey. Jenna sat back in her seat and grinned, triumphant that she knew more about the world than the other children in the car.

'I'm mixed-race, actually,' I mumbled, trying not to draw the entire car's attention to what I was or wasn't. And Jenna, relishing her new found state of knowing everything, rolled her eyes and crossed her arms.

'Well, obviously,' she said. 'But you're still black. That's just what we'd call you.'

She was right, of course. As a term, mixed-race could never fully illustrate my experiences. It described nothing; the act of being not one thing or another. To be a mix of races is to be raceless, it implied, and yet that had never been my reality. My race was distinct and visible, the thing that defined me as different to the rest of my classmates. Mixedness alone couldn't describe this difference.

Blackness was something more convincing, more tangible. It spread out across my features in big lips and long forehead and hair that grew out rather than down. It filtered through me like a beguiling beckon, drawing security guards towards me when I entered a store and tricking my teachers into thinking I could outrun anyone. The world saw blackness in me before it saw anything else and operated around me with blackness in mind.

There was a drama to blackness, a certain swagger and verve, an active way of experiencing and being experienced that mixedness could not accommodate, one that I was committed to embodying fully.

There was one thing I'd never considered about mixing red and yellow: a drop of yellow into red paint won't do much to change the colour, but one drop of red into yellow and the whole pot is tainted for ever.

2. Political Follicles: Black Hair

Growing up under the wing of my white mother and with no other black children around me, most of what I know about blackness I learned through an autodidactic education. Nowhere is this more true than with my hair.

For the most part, I perceived my hair the same way I did my elbow. It was just there. I had no teachers to show me what to do with it. No experts to learn from. The best I could do with it was attempt to copy what I saw on television.

Sitting on the bath, a mirror in one hand and cold blue gel in the other, I tried to work out how to slick my baby hairs down into swoops and spirals to frame my face (this is what the TV showed black girls were doing with their hair in '06). Instead, I'd ended up frustrated and crying, with my curls crispy and my forehead sticky with the attempts of my unsuccessful gelling. What was this black girl magic that I hadn't inherited? What was the secret to this process that they had all learned and I hadn't?[2]

2 A toothbrush, it turns out, used like a mini brush especially for baby hairs.

I assumed these bathroom breakdowns were unique to me, the result of being a black kid in a white town. When I migrated back to London, I realised most black women have some variation of this story in their memory banks. It's not uncommon for black women not to have learned how to care for their natural hair until well into adulthood. Instead, we learn that Afro hair is difficult and that it doesn't grow. We learn that it looks unprofessional and that it will prevent us from getting jobs. Hairstyles designed to keep Afro hair neat and healthy, like locs and braids, are often considered too wild and wacky for professional settings. On one occasion, I remember my Afro was described by a teacher as 'distracting' to others in my class. So what can we black women do? Well, we straighten it and cut it and cover it and we pretend that it is not our problem.

Certainly, I've never felt validation like I did when I got my first weave. I had to get a train all the way to Bristol and beg my mum to pay for the hair out of my allowance. The women at the hairdressers brushed out my small Afro with the vigour of a mother scrubbing stains out of school jumpers. Then they took it in turns to cane-row my hair so tightly that my whole scalp stung, cocking my neck at impossible angles, talking amongst themselves in languages I did not speak whilst fighting to be audible over the sounds of MTV Base on the wall-mounted TV screen. There is no need for customer care in black salons. Not when you're paying for miracles.

It never occurred to me to complain about pain because afterwards, with this coarse dead hair resting below my shoulders, I felt beautiful. I entered the hair salon with three packs of long black human hair and I left as Beyoncé. Nobody could tell me otherwise. Wearing a weave was like uncovering a version of myself that I could finally see reflected in mainstream media. I looked like the black movie heroines and music icons I looked up to. I walked taller and smiled at myself when I looked in the mirror for the first time in my life.

Nobody knows the transformative power of a new hairstyle like a black woman. All too often, aspects of our personality become attached to the way we wear our hair. Or rather, certain hairstyles become attached to rigid structures of personhood. Sometimes, it feels like changing your hairstyle is changing your entire identity. The Afro is the hairstyle for black radicals whilst locs are for Rastafarians and hippies. I enjoyed wearing weave because I enjoyed being accepted, for donning the modern black woman's *style du jour*. It made me feel like I belonged.

Although my hair was different, the real change wasn't the hairstyle, but in my attitude towards feeling accepted. By conforming, I felt like I had a place in the world, and the feeling felt good. The real lesson is learning to hold on to that feeling no matter what your hairstyle is.

For myself, and I don't doubt for many others like me, learning to look after our natural hair is also to learn the lesson that our hair does not define us, and it shouldn't determine our sense of belonging either. It's removing the comfort barriers of conformity; straighteners, extensions and perms, and confronting the insecurities that lie beneath. Nowadays, whether my hair is straight and conforming or unbrushed and everywhere, I don't rely on a change in hairstyle for a change in attitude. I've learned how to look after my hair, both when it's in its natural state and when it isn't. But more than that, my hair taught me how to look out for myself.

3. That Which Cannot Be Spoken: The N Word

At some point, the inevitable will happen. It will happen at a rave, or a club, or a party, where music is playing and people are dancing. A song will come on, usually a rap song, and amongst my generation it will nearly always be a song by Kanye West.

This is when an elephant will sneak into the room, walking straight out of Kanye's mouth, dressed as a word that can't be spoken. They will notice it at the same moment they notice me: the only black kid at the party.

It's Kanye, so everybody knows the lyrics, and everybody is looking at me. I've got 30 seconds to a minute before the chorus hits to decide what to do. If I chant the word it will be a public confirmation of my blackness, a deliberate display that says this word is mine and mine alone to say. That I am allowed. That this is damn near a birthright. And in that moment of vindication it seems obvious that I'm going to sing along, because if rapping along to Kanye is one of the few privileges afforded to me as a black person, then of course I'm going to take it.

Except, there are a few other things going on here. For a start, by being in the room, I am the only reason why the rest of the party can't say it. I'm a big red stop sign in the middle of the dance floor, a symbolic reminder of why they shouldn't use such a word and who they will offend. Without me there, the word is just another rhyme in a lyric. It's a tree falling in a forest conundrum: if a white kid raps all the lyrics to 'Gold Digger' and there isn't a black person around to hear it, is it still racist?

Secondly, I've never grown up with the circumstances where this word has been used. Never learned the difference between the -er and -a suffix, never picked up on the nuances of context. Where Kanye comes from, vocabulary has changed, history has been re-claimed in linguistics. That Which Cannot Be Spoken means so much more: means brother means friend means fool means black. I only ever learned the white rule for this word, of which there is only one: this is a word that should never be said. By anybody. Myself included.

Growing up with all-white classmates, there was no context in which this word could be used. I attempted it once, around the age of 12, the same age I was trying out other swear words in my vocabulary to see how they worked. And this was the only one that didn't. My friend responded, at first, with confusion, and then with a face full of pity. As if she thought me unaware that this word's purpose was to be derogatory towards me and only me, as if she was worried she might have to explain what it really meant. I felt embarrassed, and so did she.

Even when, at 14, I finally joined a school with other black people in my classes, it never came out comfortably when we used it.[3] We said it because we could, because it was cool, because it was delicious to be entitled to something that everyone else wasn't. Not because it came naturally.

Which is my third point. My white peers knew that we had only learned this word, not through any culture of it being used, but in the same way that they had, through hip-hop and American films. This was Somerset. Even those of us who adopted it smoothly into our lexicon would be lying if they said they hadn't done it consciously. Just because we could say it, didn't mean we could pull it off. And because it becomes so glaringly obvious that this word doesn't saunter so comfortably

---

3   There were still only eight of us, a particularly high number in comparison to other year groups, and every single one of us was also mixed-race.

off of my tongue either, there is always a worry that white people will take me using it, me who was brought up by their rules, as confirmation that they can as well.

This is when duality hits me in the face. Is the problem that I grew up as a black face in a white environment? Or is the problem that I possess whiteness within me, that I came from a white household, and was brought up with the white rule books? I can't provide the answers of what to do in this situation just yet. All I can suggest is to cross your fingers and hope for a radio edit.

4. The World is a Stage: The Performance

For as long as black people have been visible to the Western eye, our collective role has been that of the entertainer. From being ogled at in the human zoos of the nineteenth century, to now, where our television sets still mostly show us in limiting, stereotypical roles: the thug, the hooker, the fresh-off-the-boat minister, there is much fun to be had observing our queer, primitive ways.

The only way to control this gaze is to indulge in the role of the performer. To entertain is a passive process, it happens whether we wish it to or not. Whereas to perform implies the intent to entertain. And as anyone who has been to a black family gathering before will know, we are excellent performers.

We learn this, as with any art of performance, from the generations before us. We learn specific ways to dance, to sing, to tell stories, to laugh and make others laugh, to cook, to rap, to make a beat with anything at hand; with our fists, our mouths, our bodies. It is so deeply embedded within our culture that we appear to know these things innately, and of course, we don't. We learn these things just as anyone could.

I was only ever around my black family during school breaks, so all of these things I perceived them as knowing innately I sought to learn in other ways. I turned to the internet to teach me, because it was the only access I had to black culture as a pre-teen. There were the obvious (and with hindsight embarrassing) Google searches: 'how to dance like Beyoncé', 'how to gel my baby hair', and 'what are the full lyrics to Dizzee Rascal – "I Luv U"'.

Then there were the lessons I picked up more subtly. I spent hours in black haircare forums, dominated by African Americans, and without noticing I was mimicking their grammar, their way of speaking, to fit in: 'are's' became habitual 'be's'. 'She does' could end up being replaced by the rather more decisive, 'she do'.

But this was the wrong kind of blackness to be learning. I knew nothing of America, had never learned this new grammar, these new words by ear. Being black, partaking in this performance, was not as simple as just knowing I was black from birth. I was engaging in it as a conscious practice. And the more I recognised this, the more inauthentic I felt. I was not performing. I was acting. This deep sense of paranoia crept in, that invisible forces were going to catch me out for faking my own blacknicity.

I debated whether being in these online communities from such a young age meant that this was an authentic way for me to be now, the same way a child picks up an accent when they move to a new place. Of course, it doesn't really work like that. Anybody is capable of going online and selecting access to blackness. From fashion houses adopting black hairstyles on their runways to white pop starlets claiming they invented black dance moves, anybody is able to mimic the art of black performance and mistakenly assume that they are included within it. Just because I picked up on a dialect, albeit one used predominantly in black communities, doesn't mean it was authentically mine. Its creation is rooted in a certain space and a certain time, one I don't intend to misrepresent myself as existing in. Their lived experiences inform their online words which have accidentally trickled down to inform mine. And as long as that stays the case, there is no reason for me not to let my lived experiences do the same. Because, after all, I'm black too.

While being black can be a shared experience, not all black experiences are the same. With my family, we share the experience of being black through being Zimbabwean, through food, through music. With my friends, the context is being young and black in Britain in the new millennium. When it comes to the world online, sometimes the shared experience is as simple as being a confused black kid who hasn't yet worked out where they fit in. And that's enough.

My authentic self is my default performance, the person I am when I'm not thinking or when I think nobody is looking. And sometimes this is a person who tries to dance like Beyoncé in her bedroom with her eyes closed, or listens to 'I Luv U' by Dizzee Rascal because that song is a certified jam, or says all the lyrics to a Kanye West song because she knows all the lyrics to a Kanye West song and isn't concerned, in that moment, about what they might mean. Sometimes she is none of these people. My authentic self stays black. She stays black when people are present and she stays black when people are not.

My blackness is both a performance and a permanence, it will exist with me despite my actions. And another part stays with me too, the part that dictates how I experience blackness: with the awkwardness and the puzzlement and often with the privileges of being a light-skinned black child who is ethnically white too. My mixedness plays as much of a role in the way I'm experienced as a black person as my blackness does.

Because the truth is this: there is no singular way to be black, no universal set of experiences that we all share, no stereotype that can accommodate the vast array of personalities and histories and ethnic backgrounds that black people possess. And though a guide would have been a gift at times, especially as a confused, adolescent outsider, all of that confusion was just a small part of my experience. There is no one way to be black. Our worst performance is entertaining the idea that there is.

MY NAME IS MY NAME

CHIMENE SULEYMAN

One September I wrote my name as it would be seen in Turkish letters in fountain pen across my desk. The teacher, a thin woman with high cheekbones, wiped it clean despite my protests that she look at it first – Şimen. I don't know where the desire to do so came from. My parents had never spelled my name like this, nor wanted to. But I had seen the Indian and Nigerian kids in my classroom become Bobby's and Ziggy's as the heritage of their authentic monikers was redesigned. Standardisation is the backbone of the Empire, after all. But survival is forgiving. And these were kids who knew that the blow of being called 'paki' on the climbing-frames could be smoothed away faster with a whiter-sounding nickname.

Years later, I remember the surprising tastes of the Bangladeshi food from a workman's café buried behind a bus lane in Stepney. The collective flavours of what we grew to know as 'Indian' food were, of course, aspects of three or four nations' dishes and muted for a British palate. On TV and online, famous chefs even now attempt their 'own' versions of such resonant dishes as jollof rice, or rice and peas, one going so far as to ruin the dish, and enrage Jamaican viewers, by using green garden peas instead of kidney beans. Over the years, on mainstream radio stations where N.W.A., Souls of Mischief, or Kendrick Lamar should have played, Vanilla Ice, Eminem, and Macklemore did and still do. If cultures were to survive in England it would be on the shoulders of bastardisation. This was clear to people like my parents, who understood this to mean that simplicity and effortlessness were of themselves the root of Anglicisation.

They had the foresight to see that Chimene would sooner be pronounced 'chimney'. That schoolchildren would sing 'chim-chiminee, chim-chiminee, chim-chim-cheroo' in front of thoughtless teachers. Instead, my name was offered to the English in phonetics: Shimen. They had quite literally spelled my name out. At home my name would appear on birthday cakes and cards as Chimene. On my birth certificate, passports, and bank card it plainly read, Shimen.

The name itself is not a Turkish one. Pierre Corneille wrote the French play *Le Cid* some many centuries ago about the tortured love between a Spanish man and woman: Don Rodrigue and Chimène. The story is essentially that of Romeo and Juliet and my parents had enjoyed the sound of the name, perhaps even that it belonged to literature and love. It is scarcely recognised that my name is a French one. It is foreign, and I am foreign, and it is within this framework that I move. With family and friends I am Chimene – layered in cultures and afforded the romance of such a name. With the state I am Shimen – conciliatory and afraid that my difference is a thing of difficulty for the British.

One evening my father drove me to yoga. It was a practice then new to me, and in the freshly painted walls of an old Finsbury Park clothes factory a white woman with long hair would fold and bend until we repeated her motions.

It was as I stepped from the car that my father said, 'Your grandmother used to work here.'

Here, my mother's mother would stitch clothes behind a sewing machine with Turkish women who had only wanted from life the privilege of work. Some decades later I was rolling a mat out, as one rolls the carpet of gentrification over our ancestors' footprints, onto the floor of a room of exercising white bodies. I remember laughing when the instructor closed her eyes and placed her mouth in a way to make the 'Aum' sound. Others followed and I thought how easy saying things came to them without understanding their essential nature.

Words, names, and their noises are careless in England. They are not put to use in the way that obstructed communities have learned to pronounce every violence put upon us as though it is sacred. We carry our trauma in every word that we say. The three religions that this chant spread across did not exist in the instructor's mouth. Spirituality cannot be borrowed. Religion belongs to the cultures we are brought up in, and cannot be studied and replicated without family. There is no 'Aum' without Indian dharmas, as there is no 'Allah' without Islam, nor 'Pull-up!' without UK Garage, or two hands coming together to form a W without Wu Tang. That is to say: You cannot have meaning without knowledge of the environment from which it stems. This woman was not speaking of the infinite, the world, the truth. What she meant was, 'This is a calming noise for you, this helps you focus, this is the end of the session.' It did not mean 'Aum'.

There is a wretched scene in Brian Friel's play *Translations*, where Irish place names are transcribed at the behest of English soldiers. Poll na gCaorach – meaning 'hole of the sheep' in Irish – becomes Poolkerry in English. Druim Dubh – 'black shoulder' – turns into Dromduff. Words with significance become sounds without any. To repeat a word as it has been told to you is not to be invested in its force. As is calling me Shimen without knowing that my name is Chimene.

The Cyprus my parents were born to used characteristics and nicknames in place of surnames. A defining feature – a bushy beard, a long moustache, a hunchback, limp, or loud voice would attach itself to your first name – Ahmet the Beard, or Crazy Hakan. Last names became signifiers for your place in the family tree. Mustafa may have a son, Hassan, whose name would be Hassan Mustafa. Hassan would then have a child, Zalihe, who would take her father's name as her last, to become Zalihe Hassan.

As one might name their child after a beloved deceased relative, the rotation of names are as much the rotation of souls. Will a child named after her departed aunt bear further resemblance to her namesake, they will wonder. See how she speaks with her hands just as her aunt did, they will say. She loves swimming as the woman before once did. It is reincarnation for the spiritually shy. Just as the Juniors, and Junior Juniors, of African American communities know the importance of preserving identity. Such is the way for those communities who prepare for their fathers' murders. My father and his father continued the tradition. Suleyman Recep bore my father, Recep Suleyman. On a spring morning in 1964, Suleyman was tortured first and then killed.[4] Walked by

---

4   Unrest in Cyprus began with the annexing of the island by the British Empire from the Ottomans. Struggles against the British for self-determination shifted from a colonial dispute to an ethnic one between existing Greek and Turkish communities on the island. On December 21st, 1963, Greek authorities launched an offensive against Turkish Cypriots, which continued until a ceasefire was agreed in 1967.

Greek soldiers to a pig farmer's house, his body was probed, cut, then desecrated with a severance that belongs to those who have learned to take. I have seen this sense of property in the eyes of men who step to their girlfriends, who walk into children's bedrooms uninvited, in the policemen who slam a brown or black body against a wall for a half-smoked zoot – no, often less. It is there in the white men and women who do not understand, to the point of frustration, why we still walk with the noose of our ancestors around our necks, as we cannot comprehend how they do not carry the indignity of their ancestors tying it there.

But tradition is an inescapable trait of our communities – those who cannot rely on land or home for their identity. Our parents, and their parents, and theirs before, have little more to leave us beyond their names, beyond their language. We have inherited the knowledge that community means to remain. When we cannot return to our homes – or are waiting for them to be taken from us again – we must get the hang of how to recreate it elsewhere. It is in the particular smell of rice, or aubergines, the pastry that survived on the windowsills of our mothers' kitchens. It is present in the familial catchphrases of a sentence once uttered decades ago, resurrected every mealtime, 'The koftes are burnt!' We have been shown to grieve beneath beautiful scarves tied around our hair, and to eat and drink water in back rooms with shut windows so we may not be seen replenishing a life that another has lost. We are heirs to their favourite chairs, and wedding rings, and the noose around their neck.

Ten years after my grandfather's death, Cyprus would be divided through its middle – the South for the Greeks, the

North for the Turks.[5] My grandmother was assigned a home so recently abandoned in war that her children and their partners bore the task of burying the 15 or so bodies scattered throughout the house. One blisteringly hot afternoon in the '80s my cousins and I threw a football against a freshly painted wall that left a mark above the door. Inches below were bullet holes. There were more in the doorframe of the living room and around the windows of a room to the side. On her bedroom floor, beneath a worn red Turkish rug, the ageing stains of blood spread across marble. We were children who found leg bones of unmarked men beneath the lemon tree. We were children who listened to our parents crack jokes about being prisoners of war as one might recount a story of a badly gone date.

One evening we set about digging the mound in front of our grandmother's house where we knew there to be a body. We went at it with spoons. Perhaps someone had a stick. Our parents carried coffee over our heads and crescents of watermelon as we played in such a manner. This was not neglectful. Remember that in the capital, sandbags still lined the streets. In No-Man's Land[6] windows stayed open from where owners had never returned to close them. Such a 'business as usual' response to war is a poison. I know that now. But it is also an oath to our family and countrymen that is born of belonging to something so remarkable. It is a kinship I do not have with the English despite being born, educated, and brought up by the streets of London – north, east, and south.

---

5   In 1974 the ceasefire was disrupted by Greek Cypriot militia, prompting an
    intervention from Turkey. Since, the Turkish Republic of Northern Cyprus has
    become a sovereign entity with no international recognition beyond Turkey.
6   The United Nations buffer zone has been in existence since 1974.

When the border was put into place the official records on the island began. It was more practical to document the lives of Turks now that whole Turkish villages were no longer burnt and buried alive, or churned through mincers like those neighbourhoods of Sandallar and Murat Ağa. During this time my father was obliged to register a family name and from the ashes came a new one – Şehitoğlu. 'Şehit' to mean martyr, 'oğlu' meaning son. Recep Suleyman now carried his father's name twice.

I tell a lie. He carried it three times. High on his shoulder were the stains of a 13-year-old boy who had inked the Turkish flag into his own skin. Know that for many of us to be proud of our nationality is a death sentence. That my father was then a 13-year-old soldier and the only provider for his mother and her five children. Know that brown and black children are not allowed freedom from maturity. How can we call a child 'the man of the house' and not expect him to mark his body with a target so he too might be killed and taken from this responsibility and almighty grief? Some 10 years later he found himself a prisoner of war for a second time. With his brother they tattooed their father's initial 'S' into each other's arms. Stroking my own ancestral noose, my first tattoo mimicked theirs – a sweeping tail coming from the letter, jabbing towards my chest like a sword. It is not antiques and money we are waiting to inherit from our families, but their skin.

In the days that belonged to my school years, friends gathered in my bedroom to study album covers and eat family-pack bars of chocolate. These were white friends, British in a way I could never be, and outside my bedroom walls were the deeply woven rugs thrown atop each other, the colourful mosaics of Ottoman-styled lamps, paintings of my father regal in a keffiyeh, the beauty of my mother peeking between the folds of a niqab emblazoned in oil paints on a wall. My mother had drawn with some dedication the intricate designs of Ankara buildings. My father had painted in thick strokes the mosques of an Istanbul skyline. Someone mocked that this was a 'house of chintz'. They all laughed, but if this was a joke I needed the punchline to be explained. I should have asked. I should have made them spell it out, 'The horse is not sad, it simply has an elongated head. The chicken wanted to be on the opposite side. Your parents' heritage is strange and cheap-looking to us and doesn't belong here.'

This house, unforgiving in its Turkishness, became a place I would, over the years, ask my mother to change. I suggested that the flamboyant walls be painted eggshell or chantilly lace. I proposed that the elaborate light fixtures be replaced. I wanted an English home, whatever that meant. I wanted the decor to be Shimen, not Chimene. After all, my father had left the name Şehitoğlu in documents belonging to North Cyprus wars, where in London he was once again Recep Suleyman for the purpose of keeping civics away from the colony. As far as I saw it, we had adapted so much already, why not take it beyond all recall?

My parents and I have always known a different language to each other. We have always had different accents. Though love has never been lost in translation, our frustrations of this planet have been. When I was 10, a man who worked with my father called for him on the house phone.

When I answered he said, 'Oh, I must have the wrong number. How can a child that speaks like you have a dad that speaks with that ridiculous foreign mess?'

The mess was not that my father pronounces 'hatred' to sound like 'hatriot'. Rather, that there is a whiteness that exists to be so tone-deaf it cannot make out our words, nor our lamp-fixtures, gods, nor our names – where all are as good as the dog-whistle without the Labrador.

I think back to that afternoon of my school years with a kind of burning envy. What must it feel like to come into someone else's domain and believe in one's right to stand so tall within it. To have confidence that your jokes and your jibes won't land a fist against your face, a bottle against your neck, a grab of your sleeve or cuff and have you thrown from the building, or the land, or the world. My fear of being taken from this galaxy was in fact so strong that I rushed the pronunciation of my own surname. Where I should have elongated the middle to an 'eyy' I instead rounded vowels so that they may be lost to the wind and reappear on the other side as Soloman. After all, Suleyman was the name of a murdered man. Şehitoğlu was the title of our punishment.

We have learned that our ways make us homeless and fatherless, just as there is a whiteness that is fearless to the point of tenure – unmovable and permanent. We have become chameleons navigating the land, answering to white slave names put upon black nations, searching for directions not to Coaquannock – the 'grove of tall pines' – but Philadelphia.

'Change your surname to an English one,' my mother suggested before I moved to New York earlier in the year, 'I'm worried they'll wonder what kind of Muslim your name belongs to.'

Outside my grandmother's house between the mountains, the tarmac, and the sky is the street name — Şehit Suleyman Recep Sokak. Some evenings I watched my grandmother's dark sunken eyes stare into the road name, gaze into the olive groves behind, and the rocks behind that, and the coral skies, and the heavens beyond. This was not a man's life on a sign post, nor in our name, nor on our skin – rather, his death. How can I say this without sounding like I have not missed my grandmother's smell, her gravelly cackle, and the Pepsi-filled fridge of her modest home, every single day since she has died – but I was thankful for her passing. I am not a woman who has faith in an afterlife but, should there be one, I hope it is kinder to her than the life she knew. The slab of concrete that marked her grave was quickly replaced with its permanent stone. We took hold of the temporary one, discarded in the overgrowth, and washed the soil from it. There are images we never forget – my father standing in his mother's grave, my father carrying her tombstone, her name, beneath his arm as he walked with it through the graveyard. My grandfather's grave remained in the South of the island, which may as well have been another planet. Finally on her tombstone there became a place for us to grieve them both. It read, 'Emetullah Şehitoğlu, wife of Şehit Suleyman Recep'. How many times and in how many places can we say someone's name and hope they eventually answer?

Understand this – we do not carry our fathers' names without bearing with them their suffering. We do not grow in London, New York, or Berlin with the bravery we are forever told our parents and their parents had. Such courage is almost a fallacy. That they were lionhearted is part truth, part fable, told by the strugglers to soothe our pain, before being given its stamp of approval by the whiteness that does not mind their martyrdom. Our ancestors were terrified. Do not forget that. Allow them the humanness of fear. Forgive me for saying that my name is a burden. Every version of it. How can I offer you the variations – Shimen Suleyman, Chimene Şehitoğlu – without explaining that there are not four words alone that make my title, but thousands? We are simply the martyrs who are too afraid to die.

I think of my tattoos and the process they have taken over the years. My second draws the words 'Bismillah ir Rahman ir Raheem', the prayer my grandmother often used to part ways. The third is the Ottoman tuğra, or signature, of Suleyman the Magnificent. The fourth, high up on my shoulder, is the Turkish flag my father had bled into his arm with a desire that it may either kill him or save him.

I once stood on the veranda of my grandmother's house – the smell of burning olive leaves, the tall grass, the pine trees – and wished the street were called something different. From the veranda there was no wind in the telephone wire. It stretched motionless from the street name and far up the road.

YELLOW

VERA CHOK

I am yellow. I'm a small, yellow-skinned female and one hundred per cent ethnically Chinese. The longer I find myself in this country and the more aware I am of institutional bias, the more I feel the tensions between my Chinese ethnicity, my ex-colony Malaysian homeland, my British citizenship, and my 'American Dream' aspirational immigrant outlook.

> *I've heard that there's a kind of bird without legs that can only fly and fly, and sleep in the wind when it is tired. The bird only lands once in its life … that's when it dies.*
> – from *Days of Being Wild*, a film by Wong Kar-Wai

In recent years, I've been hearing the term 'East Asian' rather frequently and I've felt uneasy. In the process of writing this piece, I'm realising that while I am technically East Asian in terms of ethnicity and descent, I'm not East Asian in the way some people might want me to be.

Hold up. 'East Asian'? What is that, really?

Wikipedia lists China, Hong Kong, Japan, Korea, Taiwan and Mongolia as East Asia. Mongolia was a surprise to me. When I was writing this piece, no one I asked, bar one, mentioned Mongolia. Wikipedia also threw up Vietnam, which though not in the correct location, is included in the 'East Asian cultural sphere' meaning that it is 'influenced by Chinese culture'. Hmm. So are parts of Siberia or Manchurian Russia East Asian due to their cultural relations? In business, 'Asia Pacific' and 'ASEAN'[7] are other groupings of countries in that general geographical area. Who gets to label what? When I was growing up in Malaysia, I called myself Asian – I came from the continent of Asia, didn't I?

They are the real asians. The orientals are not really asian. They're just chinese.
– from 'Why do British people think Indians are Asian?', Yahoo Answers

China scares me. I don't speak any Chinese dialects, am unfamiliar with Chinese customs, and only use chopsticks under duress. My family, located in Malaysia, is part of the vast and widespread Chinese diaspora. I worry that if I ever visit China I would be shamed because of my obvious foreignness. In England, I have sometimes been asked to talk publicly about the sociopolitical landscape of China. As a British-born Chinese woman I know said, 'China is like Mozambique or Canada – a distant country but one where I happen to look like the locals.' I worry as much as the next white person about

7   ASEAN is the Association of South East Asian Nations, established in 1967 in Bangkok by the five original member countries: Indonesia, Malaysia, The Philippines, Singapore, and Thailand, joined by Brunei (1984), Vietnam (1995), Laos and Myanmar (1997), and Cambodia (1999).

'Asia Pacific' is a loose term that usually refers to East Asia, South Asia, South East Asia, Australasia and the Pacific Island nations, but may also include countries on the coast of the Eastern Pacific Ocean.

any possible threat to Western civilisation as I know it. In an interview for *Kin Podcast*, Episode 3 ('Oh Shit! I'm Not White') Dr Anna Sulan Masing and I talk about how, until we are reminded and put in our place, there are moments when we forget that we aren't white, male, or tall – things we grew up regarding as normal and desirable. In England, I am reminded often: I am yellow. Chinese.

It is Malaysia that I dream of, a land of coconut trees and equatorial heat, with its history of Malay kingdoms and a colonial legacy of Portuguese, Dutch, then British rule. My nostalgia is for the mountains, seas, and smells of this South East Asian country. My mouth is hungry for the shapes and sounds of Malaysia. Yet when I'm in Chinatown, attracted to anything that reminds me of Asia and gawping at the Chineseness of the space, or when 'East Asianness' and 'Chineseness' is ascribed to me, I find myself wondering if I would feel more at home if I surrendered to this neater role.

Being Malaysian Chinese does not make for neat explanations. Malaysia is ethnically diverse, with a population of Malay, Chinese, Indian, and indigenous groups. It is a rapidly changing, young country, having gained independence from British rule in 1957. As a child I was fuzzily aware of racial hierarchies. Simplistically, historical events led to the Chinese dominating trade, Malays farming and ruling, and everyone looking down on the Indian labourers and the indigenous population. Sweetly, propaganda in schools and on our screens held Malaysia up as a stable, harmonious, multicultural country. My closest friends weren't Chinese but when I got closer to the age when positive discrimination (that might help you get into colleges, win scholarships, obtain jobs, buy houses, etc.) might have counted against me, a family member quietly told me to re-examine my position in society. But even though

I was beginning to experience the reality of interracial jostling, being a minority in Malaysia I felt nothing like I do now.

I looked to England as an extension of my home. My parents had been British-educated and my principal was an Irish nun. I read Enid Blyton and dreamed of midnight feasts. I hung out at the British Council – a boyish Chinese girl so sun-browned people thought she was Malay, looked after so thoroughly by a Sri Lankan babysitter she smelled of curry – mouthing along to Shakespeare on VHS cassettes. But as Malaysia grew less British I believed that in order to be the fullest, happiest, most free version of myself, I had to get to English soil.

In 1914, British subjects on the ship the *Komagata Maru* were not allowed to disembark in British Columbia because they were not white British subjects. Skin colour versus citizenship. It's not black and white. When I arrived in England I felt the freedom of going about unseen and unheard, landed, as I had, in the largeness of London. But when I wanted to be heard, people look puzzled despite English being my first language. They still do, despite my not having a Malaysian accent. A yellow foreign body gets in the way.

> *Human speech is like a cracked cauldron on which we bang out tunes that make bears dance, when what we want is to move the stars to pity.*
> – from *Madame Bovary*, Gustav Flaubert

In his much-studied text *Orientalism*, Edward W. Said talks about Asia or 'The East' as being located in our 'imaginative landscape'. Said says that it is a place set apart 'geographically, morally, culturally' and that it is our distance from it that fuels our desire to know it. In the UK, 'East Asian' is replacing the word 'oriental' as the politically correct way to refer to people from the countries in that region. For many, 'oriental' keeps us mired in a romantic space, distant in both time and geography, and filled with exotic sensations. Ask a person on the street where or what 'the Orient' is and you're likely to receive a fuzzy answer. You might find an 'oriental' supermarket selling products from Turkey or another stocking Vietnamese sauces. Say 'East Asia' and what we might immediately picture is yellow people and lots of them. China, for example, has a population of close to 1.4 billion. That is 24 times as many people as in the UK. Our next gut reaction might be a flash of uneasiness. Do we associate them with cruelty, in war or against their own – think hara-kiri and unwanted baby girls, dictators and sneaky nuclear weaponry? Do we conjure up pictures of terrible smog and an unblinking disregard for the environment? Do we recall George Orwell's novel *1984*, where Eastasia, a fictitious superstate, upholds a political ideology called 'Death Worship' or the 'Obliteration of the Self'? Any of these associations, valid or invalid, might zip through our brains.

When we talk about race, the words 'black' and 'white' are familiar. 'Brown' too has come into play. I use the word 'yellow', offensive as many find it, because this is how I believe I'm seen. I use it because while we can't often tell what someone's race is, we do see colour. I use yellow because I'm not black, nor white, nor brown, and I feel I need a little flag to fly – and goodness me, what's this the band's playing? Passers-by catcall in Chinese or Japanese or use that well-known Vietnamese call-girl cry, 'Me love you long time!' referencing Kubrick's modern classic *Full Metal Jacket*. Sometimes, it's shouted in a Thai accent because we all know about the sexy ladies in

Thailand, right? Who really knows the difference between Thai and Vietnamese accents anyway, right?

Oh! This talk about sex might have you hankering to dissect 'yellow fever' and the fetishisation of the exotic female body, but hold your horses. Notice first that Thailand and Vietnam aren't East Asian countries. Technically, they're South East Asian countries alongside Indonesia, Singapore, Malaysia, etc. Uh-oh. There seem to be yellow people who don't even come from East Asia. For my money, Thailand and Vietnam – we are familiar with their cuisine, right? – are countries with yellow-looking folk. I could include Laos, Cambodia, the Philippines, and Myanmar. How do we feel about including Nepal, Bhutan, or Kazakhstan? Hawaiians and Pacific Islanders are yellowish. There's also rather a lot of tribes indigenous to other countries who look yellow e.g. the Inuit of the Arctic or some Iban subsets on the island of Borneo. Anyone notice this before? Does it matter? I reckon it's OK, right? We don't spend much time thinking about the nitty-gritty of these distant countries or the specifics of their faraway people because they don't reach our daily lives. But. What happens when they're not so far away?

The label 'East Asian' has been helpful to inch us past the 'oriental' tag. It feels like a fresh new way to talk about the yellow folk in the UK today. But the earliest recorded Chinese settlement dates to the early nineteenth century. Yellow folk have made up a large part of the UK demographic and have done so for some time. Wikipedia gives an approximate figure[8] of over 1 million British-born East Asians in the UK compared

---

8 'Approximate' because strangely, it doesn't take into account first generation immigrants. Data is fuzzy also because East Asians have historically only had the option of ticking 'Other' in ethnicity monitoring exercises.

to 1.9 million black British (3%), and 3 million South Asians (7%). East Asians are the third largest ethnic grouping in the UK but are we only now *seeing* yellow people on British soil due to recent shifts in global economics? Yellow folk. So pale and silent.

Peter Andre's hit, *Mysterious Girl*, is in the air...

Why did an old white English man in a Nottingham pub shuffle up to me and shout, 'Chinese!' to the room? Why did a young black man in Brixton murmur Chinese words to me on the street? Are these examples of racial abuse, misguided sexual advances, an assertion of male power over female, or a combination of all of the above?

In 2013, 2.4 million heterosexual interactions on the Facebook dating app 'Are You Interested?' were analysed and showed that 'all men except Asians[9] preferred Asian women'.[10] ALL. The fetishisation of the Asian female body is highly problematic. Sexual submissiveness, sexual voracity, and voicelessness is a particularly tricky and damning combination. When I googled 'Asian babes in films' (sorry!), IMDb – the key database for film and television – threw up a list called, 'Asian women White men romance movies'. The Asian women in these films worked very hard to keep their white boyfriend, mostly to no avail, and many of them

---

9   Note that this is the American usage of the word Asian, which includes East Asians, South East Asian and those from the Indian subcontinent. It is a particularity of the UK to use the word to refer to just the Indian subcontinent. For a discussion on sexual fetishisation, the American definition of the word Asian seems more useful.

10 Please note that my examples here are from a heteronormative perspective but the experiences of Asian LGBTQ+ and the intersection of sexuality, gender and race would certainly shed more light on how we classify and interact with people.

died as a consequence. Googling the less provocative phrase, 'Asian women in films' still gave me the list 'Asian American stereotypes in Hollywood movies'. In instances where I've seen Asian women in traditional,[11] hard-core pornographic films produced by Western and Japanese companies, they are the opposite of silent. They are screaming either due to extreme pleasure or extreme pain via violence. Violation scenarios are common.

Everyday Feminism's piece, '5 Ways "Asian Women Fetishes" Put Asian Women in Danger' is a basic, but on-the-nose, list. According to the piece up to 61 per cent of Asian women in America experience physical and or sexual violence from a partner in their lifetime, and over 30,000 Asian women are trafficked into the States per year.[12] I'll hazard a guess here: the fault lies not in the women but in the attitude towards us. A South East Asian woman I know said that the feeling of being objectified seems core to being an Asian woman.

Powerlessness is a particularly heavy weight to fling off. In order to be attractive to men of any colour, we are expected to be small and pliable. I know there is an alternative stereotype – the cold, automaton, dominatrix, *femme fatale* Asian woman – but we don't seem to be mail-ordering as many of them lot. There was a point in the past when I stopped dressing 'prettily' because when I was out with ANY white man, no matter his age or looks, I was

11 'Traditional' as opposed to feminist, queer or ethically made porn.
12 Yes, most data available on yellow women is American. Recall how basic information on the number of East Asians in the UK is difficult to find. Perhaps this says something about how the UK's third largest ethnic minority group is (dis)regarded.

talked over and looked down on. It was assumed that I was his escort or mail-order bride. A friend of mine meeting her white boyfriend for dinner was asked to leave a restaurant because they thought she was soliciting. I am sex positive and advocate sexual freedom of expression with consent, but I am cautious around any violent male desire to conquer/colonise a passive Asian body, especially if that male is white.

Look up American performance-maker Kristina Wong. Her grotesque but smart comedic work both disrupts the objectification of the Asian female and experiments with sexually objectifying the stereotypically emasculated Asian male. Asian American Eddie Huang's memoir, *Fresh Off the Boat*, has been transformed into a family friendly US TV series, but the rather more serious book addresses the sexlessness of the Asian male head-on: *We're allowed to play ONE role, the eunuch who can count. You seen* Romeo Must Die! *Jet Li gets NO PUSSY!* It's no overstatement to say that Aziz Ansari's TV series *Master of None* is a game-changer. How many times in media have you seen an Asian male have a sexual life? *MoN* opens with Ansari's character in the throes of sex. His sexual relationships are depicted as 'normally' as a white male's, and he has an Asian friend, played by Kelvin Yu, who is held up as a hottie in the series. This is television history, and I hope that it is this kind of TV that takes over our hearts and minds. If you happen to spot an Asian in UK media today, they are more than likely to be reinforcing racial stereotypes. Sex and power are central to the way we understand the world and both male and female Asians are very low down on the power scale.

Despite shyness and society's strong message on what makes a nice English (ha ha) girl, I feel compelled to discuss sex and the way in which we construct and perform sexually attractive selves given our constraints. Not doing so is an extremely isolating experience for me. My feelings of humiliation – unwarranted, I know, but hard to shake – from being hypersexualised and generalised about on a daily basis because of my skin colour and gender, seem abated in the not unpainful act of exposing my shame. My body as a site of violence.

Can this Little China Girl (RIP Bowie) ever step out, speak out and tell you, baby, just to shut your mouth?

> *[The oriental woman] never spoke of herself… never represented her emotions, presence or history* – Said, *Orientalism.*

Remember the old white man in the pub and the young black bloke on the street who publicly projected Chineseness onto me? How did they know that I'm ethnically Chinese? Oho. Now I don't know about you, but when my prompt is 'East Asian' not only do I think 'yellow', I think 'Chinese'. Perhaps it's the sheer number of Chinese folk – 50 million – who live outside China. There are Chinese takeaways in most towns in the UK. Chinese people make up roughly half of the total East Asian population in the UK, so yes, a yellow person on the street is most likely ethnically Chinese. Well done to the Chinese-spotting blokes! But in race monitoring exercises, yellow people – Chinese or not – have, historically, been thrown into a pot called 'Other' and data on life in the UK is sparse, and we're so silent we don't shout about the racist abuse we encounter, right?

> *Hey, look, it's Jackie Chan!*
> *Oi, chink! What are you staring at? Ching chong, ching chong!*

– a selection of insults commonly shouted at yellow people

I did not know that Chinese people are more likely than any other minority ethnic group to be subject to racial harassment and property damage ('The Fourth National Survey of Ethnic Minorities'). We don't see this on our screens. Violence against yellow folk doesn't spring to mind when people mention hate crime. I think of African Americans being shot in the street over nothing. I remember documentary footage of a Muslim woman being knocked out on the street. Chinese folk across the UK are abused, not only frequently but repeatedly – Chinese takeaway workers are sitting ducks. Owners and their families are often the only yellow family in town. A BBC *Newsbeat* (January 2015) article discussed the under-reporting of these hate crimes: it's because we're spread out across the country, and because hate crime dispensed little and often is rather difficult to prove or stop. I wonder if it's because the sexiest, most quotable statistics I could find easily on the internet[13] sound dated, dull or inconsequential unless you step back and consider what the evidence seems to indicate as a whole but can't prove quantitatively, i.e. that proportionally, Chinese people experience higher levels of fear and violence than any other minority group in the UK. Violence is only as visible as we are. Who knew that after WWII, some 2,000 Chinese seamen in Liverpool who had helped in the war effort were deported 'home' without warning? This violation was so swift and hidden that for decades their British wives and families

13 Sue Adamson et al., *Hidden from public view? Racism against the UK Chinese population*, Min Quan report, (The Monitoring Group, 2009).

thought that they had simply been left. There are a few articles online now, but only if you know what you're looking for.

What with the whitewashing of history and the darkness surrounding slavery and oppression, I don't feel as if I own, or am allowed to own, 'real suffering' because of the colour of my skin. Instead, I bear a different kind of badge, one I'm supposed to be pleased about: 'model minority'. Is yellow too pale a colour to shout about?

Yellow. What unites a Chinese, Vietnamese, Japanese, Korean, Thai, Taiw... *anyone* yellow in the UK? It's not our wildly disparate cultures nor our real or imagined homelands. It's hidden histories, made-up sex lives, violence invisible to others. In forms, the plurality of our immigrant narratives is boxed up as 'Other' but we are here. I see you.

KENDO NAGASAKI AND ME

DANIEL YORK LOH

Being a memory play, it is dimly lighted, it is sentimental,
it is not realistic.
In memory everything seems to happen to music. That
explains the fiddle in the wings.
(Tennessee Williams, *The Glass Menagerie*)

So begins Tom Wingfield, the narrator character in Tennessee
Williams's *The Glass Menagerie*.

On any given night when *The Glass Menagerie* is performed,
though, Tom Wingfield transports the audience back to 1930s
USA, where a 'huge middle class of America was matriculating
in a school for the blind' – whereas, ladies and gentlemen, I
give you 1970s Great Britain: a place that many believe was a
land of joyous liberty before the totalitarian oppression of The
Political Correctness Brigade committed the heinous Stalinist
crime of actually making it a bit difficult to take the piss out of
ethnic minorities, gay or disabled people, and only ever regard
women as either battleaxes or sex objects.

Like Tom Wingfield's memories of the 1930s, everything
about the seventies in my mind seems to happen to music. No
'fiddle in the wings' though. Instead it's a soundtrack of Gary
Glitter and Rolf Harris introduced by Jimmy Savile and Stuart

Hall to an almost constant chatter of sexist smut and racial jibes dressed in dodgy Y-Front underpants. A world where younger readers will have to imagine no Sky TV or BT Sport and where all football matches kicked off in unison at three o'clock on Saturday afternoons and the only live match you ever saw on TV was the FA Cup Final once a year.

A world where a lonely half-Chinese schoolboy in the West Country found a curious 'hero' in the inveterately cheating shape of what appeared to be a villainous Japanese wrestler called Kendo Nagasaki.

Because Kendo Nagasaki was a fellow 'oriental' (the acceptable term of the time) and far from being a dull passive silent one, Kendo Nagasaki was a badass.

In the seventies we watched *World of Sport* on a Saturday afternoon. *World of Sport* was what was known, I believe, as a 'sporting omnibus' programme. It began around midday on a Saturday, showed what mainly seemed to be fairly obscure sports such as skiing and bowls (no disrespect intended), and went all the way through to teatime when we would eagerly catch the football scores on the hilariously primitive 'vidi-printer' before turning over for *Basil Brush* and *Doctor Who*. *World of Sport* was introduced by a plummily spoken smoothie called Dickie Davies, who had the cheesiest seventies 'tache you can possibly imagine, compensated for by an endless and seemingly genuine enthusiasm for this cornucopia of sports that no one on the planet seemed much interested in.

What we really watched *World of Sport* for, though, was the wrestling. Usually on in a two-hour block and showing a succession of fights, the wrestling was *de rigeur* Saturday afternoon viewing in our house.

Nowadays it seems to be common belief that professional

wrestling is staged pantomime and not a competitive sport at all. I for one will make no attempt to either confirm or debunk this, although whenever I've seen the supposedly 'genuine' Olympic wrestling it seems to consist entirely of two men in leotards grappling tediously on a mat while being awarded points for undetectable (to the layperson's eye) displays of 'skill', lacking any of the blood, thunder and, yes, theatre of the pro wrestling I grew up watching.

Certainly I don't know of any professional wrestler who has, fessed up in public to the sport being fake. It's entirely possible they sign some form of 'secrecy contract' (like the Magic Circle perhaps) but when I have seen interviews in the press or on TV with professional wrestlers they fiercely deny there is anything 'staged' about their craft at all. I've even seen a couple of interviews where wrestlers have offered to put their press interrogators in head or arm locks to ascertain for themselves whether the sport is faked. If any professional wrestler is reading this, then please rest assured I am completely willing to take your word that it is a genuine competitive sport with no need for physical demonstrations as proof.

At the age I was at the time, it made not a jot of difference whatsoever whether it was 'real' or not and I was thrilled, every Saturday, to the exploits of the great characters of professional wrestling with ludicrous monikers such as Giant Haystacks (he was indeed giant), Big Daddy (whose sole but popular tactic was to butt his opponents with his sizeable belly), The Dynamite Kid (he was supposed to be quick … I think) and, er, Mick McManus.

Whether it was actually panto or not there were certainly heroes and villains with much booing and hissing as well as some hilarious slapstick anarchy, the two-fighter-per-team 'tag' matches in particular usually descending into riotous chaos with fighting continuing into the auditorium as the crowd bayed and roared. It was thrilling, hysterically funny, full-blooded entertainment, and made dismal provincial winter afternoons that much more bearable.

Before Kendo Nagasaki there was another 'oriental': a Japanese wrestler who appeared briefly. He was chubby with a bum fluff moustache and didn't appear to win any fights at all. He was mercilessly baited by the crowd despite appearing only to resort to the traditional wrestling villain's stock-in-trade 'dirty tactics' when it was painfully obvious he was getting thoroughly beaten. I have no memory whatsoever of his name but he was referred to by the commentator (who also seemed to despise and ridicule him) simply as 'The Japanese', as in 'oh, The Japanese is cheating now', etc.

But he was nothing like Kendo Nagasaki.

By now, the Chinese/Japanese thing was getting thoroughly confusing. I'd finished at one school full of white kids calling me a chink and transferred to another school full of white kids calling me a chink and singing songs about 'Chinese and Japanese' having 'dirty knees' (it rhymes, geddit?).

Sometimes I got angry with the singing chanting white kids and tried to hit them or throw things at them. As a result of this, as well as singing chanting white kids calling me a chink or a Jap and hurling allegations at me about the cleanliness of my knees, my world suddenly seemed to fill up with red-faced white adults shouting loudly at me that I needed to learn not to lose my temper when white kids were calling me a chink or a Jap.

I grew up surrounded by white people. At that school, there was me and my brother, plus two black kids who were also brothers. Their names were Godfrey and Geoffrey and the four of us seemed to cop racial abuse off the entire school all day every day.

Of course, the Golden Rule that all 'minority ethnic' people learn when we're growing up in Britain is that we're simply not supposed to get angry about any of this. To do so is to invite all kinds of accusations about having a chip on both shoulders and so forth. Occasionally one can join in with the rest of the majority populace and vent one's spleen about politics or inflation or the bus being late, but we soon learn we're supposed to be 'reasonable' about racism.

Even now, the 'victory' we 'politically correct killjoys' have 'won' has come at a price, in that we're rarely allowed to point out the indignities of having one's race/gender/orientation/ disability used as the butt of jokes without being implored to 'get a sense of humour, for God's sake'.

I can remember just a couple of years ago being invited on to a Radio 4 programme to discuss the broadcaster Jeremy Clarkson's use of the racist slur 'slope' when referring to a Burmese man on a sloping bridge (geddit?); I was assailed, in a preliminary pre-programme interview (it's a serious business you know), by a BBC journalist in the pressured tones one imagines an impatient farmer using to herd a particularly recalcitrant bovine animal into a field, repeatedly asking 'So, Daniel, are you *outraged* by this? Are you *outraged*?'

Confused by this and suddenly feeling unsure of my #AngryEthnic credentials I took a pause during which I could hear said Beeb journo breathing impatiently down the phone. I was shopping in Hammersmith Primark at the time (I'm ashamed to say) and took the call on my mobile phone, so you can only guess how surreal this 'outrage assessment' felt. Eventually I responded 'I just think Jeremy's a dick, basically'. Evidently disappointed by my insufficiently humourless chippiness, they relegated me to the closing 45 seconds of the discussion, to which I contributed after decamping to my favourite Hammersmith Indian restaurant (Shilpa in King Street if you're interested), where I attempted to sound articulate and measured whilst surrounded by chapattis and chutney that were admittedly far more enticing than the prospect of being outraged by the rather tired antics of a millionaire who hangs out with the Prime Minister, likes to drive fast cars, and who uses the n-word despite allegedly trying everything in his power to avoid doing so. The seventies though was the veritable heyday of political incorrectness and it was where I spent a somewhat traumatic childhood. I also had one of those haircuts that Chinese kids the world over appeared to have at the time that seem to have resulted from placing a bowl over the child's head and cutting the shape round it. Life was difficult.

From the ages of five till around 10 my 'anger' became a major issue. After being shouted at by white adults for losing my temper over being called a chink or a Jap, I would then be sat down by other white adults who would try to get to the bottom of why I was so 'aggressive' when I was called a chink or a Jap. I saw white child psychologists who actually gave me tablets – presumably to enhance the serotonin in the brain that prevents one from taking offence or feeling humiliated by gangs of white kids calling one racist names loudly and repeatedly.

At this point I was being called 'Chinese' and 'Japanese' so much I was beginning to think that 'Chinese' and 'Japanese' was literally all the same thing. I learned later of course that they are two very different and separate cultures and that the two countries have even fought wars against each other. Sometimes I wonder about a world where a solitary white kid is abused in the playground by a gang of 'ethnic minority' kids shouting 'English, German, giving us a sermon' (well, the principle's the same).

'Chinese' was what I was though, as informed by my nonplussed parents. Actually, let's qualify that: *half*-Chinese. Outside my own family I barely met any other Chinese people. The term 'East Asian' doesn't appear to have been invented at that juncture in history and the collective umbrella term for us arguably-yellow-arguably-dull-brown/olive-people-with-funny-shaped-eyes was 'oriental' – a ludicrous colonial expression, which literally means the 'furthest point east'. The mysterious 'orient' began life in the Ottoman Empire, i.e. Turkey. As civilised white men murdered, pillaged and plundered their way further across the globe, 'orientals' were found in the 'Middle' East and as the intrepid colonials went further still, 'oriental' came to sum up everyone and everything east of India. 'Oriental' has connotations of bamboo and flutes and red sunsets. It should only really be used to describe carpets, as the word has an inherent exoticism that I'm not sure a boy growing up in Wiltshire can ever fully embody. In the US 'Asian Americans' have rejected the term 'oriental'. Here, the Chinese (at least) have positively embraced it, because we appear to be a pragmatic species and aren't known as the 'model minority' for nothing. So at this confusing point of second generation immigrant experience, I accepted that I was an 'oriental' and found a 'role model' in another 'oriental': Kendo Nagasaki.

There appeared to be very few 'orientals' on TV in the seventies and the ones that were haunted me to such an extent I almost found myself wishing they weren't there. Along with 'chink' and 'China' I would be taunted with cries of 'Bruce' (Lee, naturally, though in the Land Before Home Entertainment one rarely actually *saw* Bruce), 'Kung Fu' (a TV series starring David Carradine as the supposedly mixed-race Eurasian martial arts expert with legendarily rubbish slow-motion fight sequences), 'Grasshopper' (there was a blind, bald Chinese guru in said *Kung Fu* series who would appear in flashback and advise Carradine in a ludicrously exaggerated cod-Chinese accent which many white people at the time loved to imitate), 'Hawaii Five-O' (being set in Hawaii and being an American rather than British show, it actually had a reasonably inoffensive Asian side-kick character), 'Hong Kong Phooey' (a cartoon series about a Kung Fu kicking dog in a silk dressing gown), 'Fu Manchu' (Sax Rohmer's legendarily racist cartoon Chinese villain further immortalised in a series of films starring Christopher Lee, one of which seemed to be on literally every Sunday afternoon) and 'Cato' (a character in the Peter Sellers Inspector Clouseau films who appeared for 10 minutes in every movie and got the living shit literally kicked out of him and who many white men of a certain generation seem to adore beyond all reasonable ken).

Given how few 'orientals' there were on TV at the time it was also astounding how many of them were portrayed by white men. I can vividly recall wondering whether Chinese men just didn't do acting or whether white men just loved dressing up and looking silly. Even my favourite TV programme in the world, *Doctor Who*, got in on the 'yellowface' act.

Yellowface is a form of theatrical makeup used by performers to represent an East Asian person (Wikipedia).

1970s *Doctor Who* was a very different beast to the one that adorns our screens now. There was no soppy soapy romance, no hopelessly po-faced self-aggrandisement, no superficially flashy CGI and no bombastic manipulative music. It was just cardboard sets, men in rubber suits, rattling good scripts (er … usually) and a maverick outsider travelling in time and space (what could be more attractive to a boy who was bullied at school?).

However, in one crucial area, New *Doctor Who* trumps Original *Doctor Who* hands down. The modern version positively teems with diversity of all kinds. 'Old Who', I'm afraid to say, was populated almost entirely by white people with some very occasional but fleeting ethnic stereotypes bunged in. For a remit with the whole of time and space as a palette, this is a bit crap frankly.

Somewhere in the mid-1970s, the luridly titled *Doctor Who* story, 'The Talons of Weng-Chiang' graced six consecutive Saturday evenings. A handsomely mounted Victorian Sax Rohmer homage that did, however, manage to feature, in the very same story, arguably one of the worst giant rats ever seen on TV, as well as one of the very worst examples of yellowface as a gang of silent, sinister and inscrutable (it's amazing how easily and often those words flow together) goons (the only appropriate description) appeared, led by an English actor called John Bennett sporting ridiculous false eyelids that looked like you could sit on them, skin made up yellower than a lump of cheese and speaking in a hopelessly mishmashed Chinese/Japanese hybrid accent that would have had Henry Higgins completely stumped. Not nearly so much though as the fact that the BBC still carries a website page somewhere that heaps lavish praise on Mr Bennett's staggeringly silly turn, opining that, unless they knew, a viewer might be hard-pressed to tell that the English thesp wasn't in fact Chinese. Not unless they were under the impression that Chinese people had eyelids made from recycled skateboards and talked like Yoda in *Star Wars* when he's been on the ketamine, I think.

There appeared to be no 'oriental' comedians to take the piss back and, unlike black people, we 'orientals' didn't even have any 'oriental' pop stars. There was a Japanese bloke who played bass in the video for Rod Stewart's 'Do Ya Think I'm

Sexy?' which, being Number One for what seemed like forever at the time, did at least mean that this one almost-Chinese cool-looking dude was on *Top of the Pops* every week.

And that was it.

And then along came Kendo Nagasaki.

Kendo was a proper badass. In wrestling parlance, a 'heel' as the sport's 'antagonists' are traditionally known (the term has possible biblical origins apparently). He won all his fights, dispatching his hapless opponents with consummate ease though a combination of breathtakingly agile flourishes, athletic kicks and gloriously Machiavellian skulduggery. Kendo (in my memory play) wore florid silky martial arts gear, all dragons and flames and bamboo-style lettering. He was sleek and quick, cunning and sly, made elaborate entrances to the ring where he acrobatically warmed up, revelling in the booing and baying of the crowd whom he arrogantly baited (and did so again after his inevitable victories) in what seemed, to a racially abused schoolboy, the ultimate act of ethnic defiance.

In short, Kendo Nagasaki was an out-and-out dirty villainous cheat that the crowd, viewers, commentator and other competitors loathed beyond all seeming limit – except that this fiendish 'oriental' won bout after bout with his despicable and blatant dirty tactics, appearing to positively revel in the fact that no matter how much everyone involved seemed to will it, he simply would not be beaten.

Now, 'kendo' is a form of Japanese martial art descended from ancient swordsmanship and 'Nagasaki' is of course the Japanese city famed for ever as the one that was controversially flattened by 'Fat Man', the second US atomic bomb at the tail end of World War II. So the name, as well as being completely nonsensical, was arguably offensive. But this was the 1970s, remember, when we watched publicly subsidised paedophiles on TV.

So Kendo Nagasaki was a dubiously named gangsta badman. Kendo also wore, as part of his rather florid orientalist costume, a mask. A mask with (naturally) epicanthic eye slits, that covered his entire face and made him appear even more of a villain. There was a strange wrestling rule about masked wrestlers: they could only have said mask removed when they were defeated in the ring.

But that was never happening to Kendo Nagasaki. He was quicker than everyone else, could do 'proper' kung fu (unlike that David Carradine slow-mo bollocks), and was adept at getting in cheeky little punches when the ref wasn't looking, as well as carrying on fighting when his opponent was on the deck and even laying out the ref when occasion demanded.

And I found myself silently willing on this masked man of the East as the only strong assertive role-model on TV who I could somehow relate to, albeit tenuously, despite the fact that everyone else in the entire country (the ones who watched wrestling anyway) appeared to despise Kendo Nagasaki.

And then, after what seemed like years, the fateful day arrived.

Kendo was defeated (by Mick McManus or some other bland wrestling good guy). And it was no simple KO. A wrestling 'great' like Kendo Nagasaki required the whole 'two pinfalls' – a pinfall being a move where a wrestler holds his opponent so both shoulders are on the canvas for three or five seconds (I forget which) – to finally end what was a simply glorious unbeaten reign. But this day Kendo was outsmarted, out-thought and outfought, though not out-cheated, Kendo managing to the last to go down with some defiant underhandedness.

But go down he did as he was pinned to the canvas one last time, the ref counted off and the crowd howled in jubilant primal triumph.

And then came the moment when the victor got to unmask the notorious Kendo Nagasaki as the audience bayed with glee …

Kendo knelt …

A hand tugged at his mask. I steeled myself, comforted by the fact that soon we would see Kendo's proud Asiatic features gloriously unbowed.

The hand tugged further, pulling Kendo's mask up and up and …

Off it came …

To reveal …

A white man.

!!!!????!!!!????!!!!

Another bloody white man.

White with blue eyes and blonde hair.

A cherubic-looking blond white man.

And a half-Chinese boy turned off his TV in stunned silence.

NOTE: A mere glance at the likes of Wikipedia and YouTube appears to reveal that I've probably got Kendo mixed up with another masked East Asian-themed wrestler imaginatively called 'Kung Fu' who wore rather more florid outfits than Kendo's which appear disappointingly prosaic when viewed now. There's also a clip of Kendo being unmasked by Big Daddy mid-bout and him being a balding white man with brown, not blond, hair.

It's all very confusing, but like *The Glass Menagerie* this is a 'memory' play.

An ethnic 'memory' play.

With no fiddle in the wings.

WINDOW OF OPPORTUNITY

HIMESH PATEL

When I was four years old, I tried to jump out of my bedroom window.

No, I wasn't ending it all before academia drowned my youthful optimism in a sea of social awkwardness and HB pencils. I was trying to be a Teenage Mutant Ninja Turtle.

I was obsessed with the cartoon, watching the same video over and over again at Jackie the babysitter's house. Seeing how much I loved the show, she let me keep the tape and Mum used it to keep me immobile as she worked around the house.

One afternoon, she was working in the kitchen and called for me. I didn't respond. She went to the living room to investigate, where the video was still playing but I was nowhere to be found. She called for me again. Nothing. She headed upstairs to find me, crouching on my windowsill, ready to jump.

I know how this may seem, but even at the age of four, I had enough of a grasp on physics to know that jumping down to the ground from that height wouldn't end well. I'd thought it through. You see, underneath my bedroom window was the porch roof, which was flat and [hopefully] sturdy enough to hold my weight.

The script was written.

We were running up. The director was ready to call 'action'.

And … a hand grabbed my collar from behind and yanked me back inside.

The video soon disappeared and my bedroom window was locked.

In December 2012, I was invited by the Runnymede Trust to take part in a panel discussion on race in UK film and broadcast media, at London's South Bank University. I was five years into my time at *EastEnders* and the organisers believed that young budding actors would be interested to hear my opinion on the matter. As the evening progressed, I began to feel more and more out of my depth. The other members of the panel (including one Riz Ahmed) were articulate and informed. I found myself without a point to make. I felt like I was out of the loop. In the years since that evening, the subject has become unavoidable, and rightly so. Lenny Henry's BAFTA Television Lecture in 2014 and Danny Lee Wynter's Act For Change Project are spearheading a movement that's aiming to redress the balance. I began to wonder how I had managed not to notice such a huge schism in my industry even though it directly affected me.

I think it has something to do with where I grew up. Rural Cambridgeshire, for all its tranquillity, isn't the most multicultural of places. The story of how I ended up there begins long before I was born.

In the 1960s, a lot of Indians who had settled in Kenya began moving to the UK, some taking advantage of British passports, others fleeing from increasingly severe immigration laws. My grandfather (or Dada, as I call him) lived in Nairobi, working for a company called Lamson Paragon. He was on the factory floor, making business stationery. By 1968, his two eldest sons and his eldest daughter had married and moved to the UK, leaving him in Kenya with my grandmother, their youngest daughter, and my dad. He asked Lamson Paragon for a transfer to Britain and the powers-that-be said yes.

So in 1970, my dad, aged 16, found himself in the sleepy Cambridgeshire town of St Neots, home to the factory Dada had been transferred to. It transpires that my family were the unwitting pioneers of multiculturalism in St Neots – as far as Dad can recall, they were the only South Asian family in their immediate area, perhaps even the whole town. I assumed that Dad and his family must have felt ostracised. I was wrong: Dad can't recall ever feeling that way. Whereas the segregated immigrant communities in the big cities were bearing the brunt of xenophobia, no one in St Neots seemed to have any problem with my family joining their community. This positive experience my dad had as a young adult, accepted into British society with open arms, would echo down the years and shape my own experience decades later.

During the harsh British winters, my grandparents escaped back to India. It was during one of these trips, in 1976, that my dada noticed a young girl sat on his bus. He saw her talking to a friend, laughing and smiling. He kept seeing her almost every day and wondered who she was, which family she came from. He made some enquiries and eventually found out. Fortunately, they had some family in common, so Dada sent a marriage proposal to this mutual relative, who passed it on to the girl. Or as I like to call her … Mum.

It took a while for my parents to meet though.

At the time she received the proposal, my mum was studying in India and Dad was studying in the UK. For this reason, the first time around they both said no. Then, in November 1978, my mum's family moved to the UK and my dada, so sure this girl was the perfect partner for his son, reopened the lines of communication.

As luck would have it, there was a mutual family wedding taking place and the families conspired to have my parents meet during the nuptials. The first day, the plan failed miserably. No one told Mum or Dad that they had to look out for each other and Dad, being the appointed wedding photographer, was far too preoccupied with lining up the perfect shots for the happiest day of the couple's life. So on the second day, the families attempted it again, this time informing the concerned parties to keep an eye out for each other. Alas, neither of them actually bothered to do so and attempt number two also failed.

Frustrated, Dada decided to take everyone and go over to Mum's house in London.

They arrived, introductions were made … and then the woman who would be my mum and the man who would be my dad were shoved into a room to talk. They ended up talking for 45 minutes, a pretty long time by most standards.

By January 1979, they were engaged. I asked them both what made them say yes to each other.

'I don't know,' Dad said.

'No, seriously,' I replied.

'Whatever expectations I had were fulfilled. I found someone I could get on with. Something clicked.'

'Mum?'

'I met with quite a few guys before your dad,' she explained. 'In hindsight, I've always had a strong personality and I never did what was expected of me. But your dad was different in so many ways.'

It's true, Mum did go against the grain of what was expected of a girl of her generation. Her father afforded her a good education, a rarity for girls in India at the time and this, coupled with her sheer determination, has had a profound effect on the course of my life.

Dad agreed to get married on the condition that it wouldn't be until he finished his studies, of which he still had a year remaining. Still, they were married in the eyes of the law on April 19th, 1979, and the Hindu ceremony took place a year later, on April 27th, 1980, after which Mum moved into the family home in St Neots. Dad's studies led to a job as a dental technician and Mum eventually found work at an insurance brokers. Their life together had begun.

The next decade brought a lot of changes. In 1983, my sister was born. Then, in 1985, Dad's brother-in-law told him about a shop that had come up for sale in a village called Sawtry, 16 miles up the A1. Being a shop owner himself, he advised that buying the shop would be the best thing my parents could do. After much deliberation, they decided to go for it.

I wondered whether they did it to take control of their lives, become masters of their own fate. Mum, however, says they simply took an opportunity that was afforded to them and did the best they could. Although they had my sister to look after at this point, they weren't thinking of an ideal future in which they'd be rich business owners with children who wanted for nothing. They were simply putting one foot in front of the other, learning as they went. All that was certain was that the more hard work they put in, the better the reward would be.

In 1986, they moved from the family home to the flat above the shop. Dad continued to work nine to five at the dental technician's, taking over the shop in the evening so Mum could look after my sister and do the housework. This work ethic is what forms the foundation of my life and it's knowing how hard my parents work that continues to humble me. Mum often tells me what happened when they first turned a profit of £1,000. They'd never physically seen so much cash in their lives and it was theirs to spend, but they weren't entirely sure what to do with it. So they wrapped it in a plastic bag.

'Perhaps we should hide it in the oven?' Mum suggested.

'Yeah, but if we forget it's in there we might burn it,' Dad replied.

They ended up hiding it in the drawer underneath the cooker.

In 1989, Dad gave up working as a dental technician to join Mum in working full-time at the shop. Business flourished – their hard work was paying off.

1990 was a year of contrasting emotions for my parents. In August, my dada passed away. Two months later, I was born. By now, they'd moved to a house in Sawtry. I spent the first nine years of my life there. It was a fairly lonely existence. None of my school friends lived nearby and I didn't know anyone in the area. The time spent alone here was what fired my imagination – making up for the lack of a world outside, I built imaginary worlds in my head. I wasn't just playing football in the driveway, I was playing a match at Wembley. After watching *Toy Story*, I used my old baby monitor to see if my toys were coming to life (sadly they didn't, but toys are clever like that). When I did finally make friends down the road, it turned out to be the beginning of my career as an actor – I managed to convince them that I was an American kid called Michael. This continued for some time. One of the kids was actually American and even he fell for it. I have no idea why I did it and shortly after I began this performance art piece, we moved house. I don't think they ever found out.

We moved to another village nearby, where Mum and Dad

had bought a house with a shop downstairs. The village was a tight-knit community of around 350 people (a stark contrast to 5,000 people in Sawtry) and soon enough everyone was a friend or a familiar face. The shop had been shut for over two years so my parents garnered a lot of affection simply for reopening it. Regular customers became family friends, I attended church services and played in village cricket matches. The annual village panto was a huge boost for my confidence as an actor.

For Mum and Dad, it was the closest they'd felt to home since they left India – they both originally came from tiny villages in Gujarat. Despite moving to a country 4,000 miles away, they found themselves calling a tiny village home once again. I, on the other hand, was still finding my definition of home. At the time, it meant countryside, a small community and … not many ethnic minorities.

Yet Indian culture remained a huge part of my childhood. Behind closed doors Mum only spoke to me in Gujarati so I'd learn the language. Bollywood was my introduction to cinema and the soundtrack of my childhood. Hinduism was also at the core of our household, but this is one of the aspects of my identity that left me conflicted. I was brought up and identify as a Hindu and there's no doubt that some of my earliest memories are linked to this – the smell of incense sticks and the learning of prayers that we recited at the shrine in the living room. Still, I don't know a lot about Hinduism and the philosophical intricacies of what is known to be the oldest surviving religion. Surprisingly, my mum feels the same way.

Growing up in India, she recalls faith as being a very personal thing. Each home, whilst observing the basic tenets of the religion, would favour a certain deity. She can only recall community worship at her village mandir during annual festivals, such as Navratri, Holi or Diwali. Her experience of Hinduism was of a very lenient, polytheistic religion that meant different things to different people. Having said that, I'm aware of a lot of traditions that began to clash with my liberal perceptions as I grew up – the separation of male and female seating at some weddings, funerals and festivals; the expectation of a girl to be married by a certain age (which carries across several religions) – this sort of thing made me begin to question the validity of my faith.

The ethnic demographic of my village was echoed by most of the schools I attended and especially the school where I eventually settled to do my GCSEs and A levels. I was one of two Indian guys in the entire school and the overall student population wasn't particularly diverse. Due to this being my general experience, I never saw it as an issue and I guess it wasn't – it was a pretty honest representation of the local population.

As a teenager, I struggled to fit in, but not for lack of trying. Like everyone else at that age, I followed closely what my peers were watching and listening to. So I was drawn towards bands like Arctic Monkeys, Muse and Kasabian, watched *Doctor Who*, *Harry Potter* and *Lord of the Rings*, whilst studying Shakespeare and Bertolt Brecht. Meanwhile, at home, I was still listening to Bollywood music and watching Bollywood films. My sister, who was having a cultural epiphany of her own at university, introduced me to the music of Nitin Sawhney and Niraj Chag. Yet, because no one else knew anything about these things, it was never of any interest to them.

I remember telling someone at school about *Rang De Basanti*, a Hindi film I'd seen that had a big effect on me. I wanted to lend him the DVD, but he didn't seem particularly interested. A similar attempt to introduce someone to Nitin Sawhney's music was briefly humoured and then passed by.

Looking back, this dismissal of my Indian cultural reference points must have caused me to start burying that side of my identity – if it wasn't relevant to my social growth, what use was it? Talking about any of it just drew blank looks and an awkward end to the conversation. It gradually became a very personal part of my life, rarely shared or spoken of with anyone else. Until now.

I've always been something of an outsider and at this point it's a bit of a chicken and egg situation – I'm not sure if I'm just naturally this way, or if being ostracised at an early age made me so. Either way, my teenage years at school kind of enforced the feeling. Although I made some friends, I never found a group that I got into trouble and came of age with. I kept my head down and did my work. I only really came alive in drama lessons – acting was the only thing I was confident doing. It didn't matter who I was in real life, because on the stage I could be anyone and I seemed to be good at it. Even when everyone else had seen *Bugsy Malone* and I hadn't, it didn't stop me being a part of the play. The difference in cultural background didn't seem to hold any sway here. This was what first drew me to acting – here, my propensity for imitation and jumping out of windows was actively encouraged. I could be anything that I wanted to be.

The summer before starting A levels, my life changed when I got the role on *EastEnders*. A whole world opened up to me, not just as an actor but as a person – I made lifelong friends and finally felt accepted into a family outside my own. I was riding high on the fact that I was getting to do what I loved for a living. I was working with actors I had admired for years and I was part of a show that was sewn into the fabric of British society – it was an absurd privilege for a kid from a tiny village in Cambridgeshire.

I stayed in my village for five years after starting on *EastEnders*. Keeping my family and my home near me during this time helped keep my feet on the ground – until I moved to London I still did the paper round for my parents. Outside of the job, very little changed in my life. I moved to London in 2012 and it seems strangely appropriate that it was then that I had my first brush with the issue of race on screen. London's awoken me to just how incredible multiculturalism can be and how dishonestly we're representing that in television and on film. At the same time, I began to analyse the part I've played in on-screen diversity.

Although the Masood family on *EastEnders* were specifically Pakistani Muslims, I think they were widely regarded as a kind of generic representation of a South Asian family. There were intricacies regarding their faith and how it impacted on their lives but I, as a Gujarati Hindu, could always relate to the stories my character and the Masood family were part of, and I know that there are people from various South Asian backgrounds who felt represented by the family. What I loved most about playing Tamwar was that his unique qualities had nothing to do with his ethnicity or religion – he was just like anyone else and perhaps that had a part to play in my forgetting that I was representing a huge section of our society.

Recently, I was reminded of how impactful our media can be. The Monday after the Paris attacks, a scene that we'd shot two months earlier was broadcast. In it, my character reads a Surah from the Qur'an to his girlfriend and explains to her what being a Muslim means to him. 'Be kind to people … and love them.'

In the wake of the weekend's events, it seemed to strike a chord with a lot of viewers.

This is why I became an actor. It started because I wanted

to pretend to be a mutated bipedal turtle. It became a way of escaping from the drudgery of everyday life and now I've come to see it as a responsibility. Storytelling is the most powerful way to promote our understanding of the world in which we live and the vessel to tell these stories is our media. Britain is filled with people from all corners of the earth, each with a wealth of stories to tell; sometimes, race, culture ethnicity are a key part of the narrative, sometimes not.

In discovering so much about how my family arrived here in the UK, I discovered how rich their story is with the culture and traditions of their homeland, but at its core it's a universal story about love and life. My heritage, while inherently linked to my ethnicity, only makes up a part of the role I play in society – day-to-day I'm just another face in the multicultural population of twenty-first-century Britain. If we share the gifts that people have carried across continents and acknowledge them as part of the fabric of our society, from the national curriculum to the mainstream media, we could be on the cusp of a paradigm shift in our understanding of the world.

I must have been about six when I had my first sleepover. My friend Adam had come over and we stayed up till the early hours talking about god knows what. When we finally grew tired, I looked out of my bedroom window and found myself transfixed.

Through the same bedroom window that had been locked to me, I saw my first sunrise.

It was beautiful.

IS NISH KUMAR A CONFUSED MUSLIM?

NISH KUMAR

On September 18th, 2012, I was sitting in my house. This is a common occurrence. 'Sitting in my house' is one of the things I'm best known for, amongst my group of friends, along with 'Bob Dylan trivia' and 'being asleep'. That month was a period of relaxation for me. In August I had performed a run at the Edinburgh festival of my debut stand-up show *Who is Nish Kumar?* A show that one critic had described as 'a comedy show'. The writing and subsequent execution of it had left me in a state of physical, emotional and financial exhaustion, so I had given myself a couple of weeks off in September before I began looking for a new office job so I could continue to support my dream/delusion of being a full-time comedian. My aim that month was to sit around and play a football management computer game. This may well be the least athletic endeavour of all time. It's worse than computer games where you pretend to be a footballer; at least those involve the simulation of exertion. This game requires you to do the admin for imaginary footballers. Still, everyone needs a hobby and that was mine.

Anyway, that morning I was about to return to the fictitious

dugout as Manchester United manager Phileas Q Superfly
(they let you choose your own name) when I opened my laptop
and decided to quickly check in on Facebook. My friend, the
comedian Jack Barry, had written on my wall. I clicked on
it excitedly as Jack is always good for a laugh, whether it's
onstage, in conversation or inside the internet. He had written
the following:

'Don't know if I'm the first one to show you this but this
just popped up on a meme website I was on. Apparently you're
an angry Muslim in the US.'

I was, as you can imagine, utterly baffled. Below the text of
his message was a link to a meme website called Quickmeme.
com. The link led me to a picture of my own face. This was a
surprise. If you're not expecting to see your own face, it's always
a surprise. I have no idea how twins get anything done around
each other. The picture was a publicity shot that we ended up
using as the poster for my aforementioned Edinburgh show,
and above it was the title 'CONFUSED MUSLIM'. Around
the picture, in a white font with a black outline, was text that
read:

'Angry that Christians insulted my prophet, cannot insult
Jesus as he is a prophet too.'

At this point my confusion had escalated from bafflement
to mild panic. I had not been informed that this was going to
happen. I had no idea what any of this meant. I really didn't
know what a 'meme' was. It's a point of pride to me that I stay
resolutely oblivious of much of contemporary culture. I try
to pretend this is because I'm too cerebral to be concerning
myself with all this nonsense, but in reality it's probably
a manifestation of my own intellectual insecurity. As is my
tendency to overuse polysyllabic words.

My flatmate quickly explained to me that people on the

internet share pictures with each other and they all change the caption to variations on a single theme. So he showed me one of 'surprised man' and there were loads of different captions speculating as to why this man was surprised.

But here's the thing – I am not a Muslim. My parents are Indian by birth, and as for their religious classification, my father would identify as a Hindu while my mother prays to 'all the gods, because that way I'm covered every which way'. I try to inform her that I'm not sure you can trick God, but she's convinced she's found a loophole. I wasn't offended that anyone would think I was a Muslim. There's no reason to be. In all honesty, I was offended that they hadn't recognised me as NISH KUMAR 'comedic genius and star of stage and screen' (citation needed).

Also I was pretty used to it. There's a huge Muslim population in India, as you all probably know, so people assuming that an Indian is a Muslim isn't the strangest thing in the world, despite the fact that the majority of Indians are Hindu. However, it's more likely for me. My family is from Kerala, a state in the south of India, which has a long history of immigration, dating back to the sixteenth century when Vasco Da Gama led a Portuguese delegation there. This immigration appears to have crash-landed on my face. I have a face that people seem comprehensively unable to place. I'm regularly confused for being pretty much every ethnicity other than my own (Indian).

Most strangers assume I'm from the Middle East, which isn't a problem, aside from when those people work for US customs or are themselves from the Middle East. A few times a year, in London, someone will approach me and start speaking to me in Arabic because they think they've found the reassuring familiarity of someone they share a language and culture with, in what is otherwise a strange and foreign land. I then have to dash those dreams. I used to say, 'I don't speak Arabic' but now I say 'I'm Indian', only because I don't want them to think that I am Arabian and haven't bothered to learn the language. I don't mind people thinking I'm an Arab, I just don't want them thinking I'm a lazy one.

So it wasn't a surprise, necessarily, that people would think I was a Muslim; it happened fairly regularly and I had no problem with it.

But this was a different kettle of shit.

I had no idea what this was supposed to mean. Was this a knowing joke from one Muslim to another? After all, it takes some rudimentary knowledge of the tenets of the religion to know that Jesus is a prophet in Islam. That's the kind of knowledge you don't often associate with racists, a group not known for their attention to detail. Or was this just Islamophobia with my face plastered all over it. What if people thought that I was behind this?

There were three possible alternatives and none of them were good.

1. It was a person being Islamophobic. I was therefore being racially abused and not even correctly. The only thing worse than racism is inaccurate racism. It was hurtful to me and to people who are actually Muslims.
2. It was a knowing joke made between some Muslims, of which I was now, unjustifiably, part.
3. People would think that I was involved and it was somehow part of an attempt to reinvent myself as some kind of non-white racist comedian, like a non-ironic Borat.

You might think that I was overthinking things. I would inform you that, overthinking is inevitable as a comedian. It's an occupational hazard, like being punched in the face if you're a boxer, or being roundly despised if you're a member of Coldplay. In reality, no one cared, and hardly anyone even saw the meme. That didn't stop The Good Guy (me) from boarding the Neuroses Train to Crazytown.

Here was my central concern – the great thing about joking around with your friends is that you understand each other's intent. If you make fun of your friend, there is a pre-existing understanding of your shared values and assumptions about the world. It's what comedians try really hard to do onstage. We try to establish our personalities and our beliefs so that the audience trusts us enough that when we do make a joke about a contentious subject, there's a reason for it, and it's not just crass or an expression of prejudice.

But on the internet jokes appear untethered, and out of context.

Context is all-important in comedy. Journalists and audience members will often ask you to tell them your favourite joke, but very often it's all about who tells it. It's the singer not the song. The material of a stand-up comedian is intrinsically bound up in that person's onstage identity. Nowhere else is this problem better summarised that in 'Diversity Day', an episode of the American remake of *The Office*. In the show, the hapless boss Michael Scott (played by Steve Carell) is hauled in front of a racial diversity seminar for performing Chris Rock's seminal 'N**** versus Black People' routine in the office. Scott is entirely oblivious to why a white American repeating that routine verbatim would be a problem in any circumstance, much less in an environment where he is the manager. In his frustration he says:

'How come Chris Rock can do a routine and everybody finds it hilarious and groundbreaking and then I go and do the exact same routine, same comedic timing, and people file a complaint to corporate? Is it because I'm white and Chris is black?'

This scene summarises the significance of context and intent in a much better way than the thousands of tedious blog posts and think pieces on the same subject, including the one you are currently reading.

Incidentally, it's become very fashionable to say that the US *Office* 'only really gets going in series two', which is absolute rubbish. The first episode is not great, as it's a direct remake of the UK original, but the rest of the series – including this episode – is excellent. I'm aware it's strange to stop in the middle of an essay, in what is otherwise a credible and excellent book, to talk about a sitcom that ended in 2013 but I just think it's a point that's really worth making. Anyway – the message here is context is key and Steve Carell is great.

So I was now the Confused Muslim. I wanted to contact someone, but there was no one to contact. Quickmeme was just the host website, there was no way of tracing who did it originally. The anonymity of the internet is a real problem. It facilitates the culture of 'trolling' – it's easy to say anything to someone when you don't sign your name to it. That's why 'KINGOF69ING' can spout whatever hateful nonsense he wants without fear of reprisal. In my case, it meant that someone could steal my face, and I couldn't do anything about it. I felt like Nicholas Cage in *Face/Off* before he steals John Travolta's face. Or maybe it's the other way round. I can't remember – whichever one the good one was.

In any case, the picture was a publicity photo and so was supposed to be put into the public domain. This wasn't what we had intended if I'm honest. They say all publicity is good publicity, but I'm not sure the term 'all' covers 'publicity that doesn't have your name on it and somehow could make you look like either the victim or perpetrator of a low-level hate crime'. If they did, then I salute the inventor of that phrase for the specificity of their foresight.

Without any way to trace the creator, it fell to me to establish how they had got my picture. No one had sought permission so, how had this happened? I googled the phrase 'Confused Muslim', hit the images tab and then saw a picture of my face. Then I worked backwards by clicking on the picture. It was a link to a review of my Edinburgh show. It quoted a line from my show where I described myself as 'one of the few people that's regularly confused with being both a Muslim and a Jew'. That meant that the Google algorithm, or whatever the technical term is, had picked on two words from that sentence when you searched for 'Confused Muslim'. Incidentally the other pictures on the search were Omid Djalili and Jesus Christ. What incredible company to keep. I've always seen myself as the mid-point between those two (this is obviously a joke, I don't want to start getting angry emails from ardent fans of Omid Djalili). This also means that if some other idiot decides to balance things out by doing a 'Confused Jew' meme, it'll probably be my fucking face again.

I posted the meme on my Facebook wall and my Twitter page, to friends and sympathisers of my comedy (I can't quite bring myself round to the idea that I have 'fans', I prefer to think of them as people who tolerate, rather than actively enjoy, my humour).

I had expected people to react with incredulity and outrage on my behalf. However, my expectations were quickly confounded. Instead of being passive, the internet – or at least my miniscule section of it – went to work defacing the entire meme. People started posting things like 'This is a comedian called Nish Kumar' and 'Is the Confused Muslim meme, isn't a Muslim'. A couple of my friends used it to settle some scores: 'Nish Kumar owes me a fiver'. Sadly as these are all anonymous I have no way of knowing who that fiver belongs to so will never return it. It may have something to do with those texts my friend Ed keeps sending me saying 'you owe me money'. I guess we'll never know, and in any case, I've already spent that fiver on sweets.

I often think about the person who created the meme. I imagine that they're pretty frustrated. The great thing about doing memes about cats is that cats don't tend to have the internet and ruin the meme by having their friends write things like 'Mr Whiskers did not sanction the use of this photo'. And if they do we've all got much bigger problems than my face being stolen.

There were no reprisals, or at least none of the kind that my family were worried about. When I told my mother she speculated that I'd be banned from America. I had to inform her that the CIA were probably not spending their time trawling through Quickmeme looking for suspects, otherwise Guantanamo Bay would be full of cats and that guy who sang 'Chocolate Rain'. On the plus side, if they were, it certainly would have livened up the second series of *Homeland*.

My dad was worried that it would offend religious extremists. I had to inform him that they were too busy being offended by absolutely everything in the world to worry about me. The only people I'd really been worried about offending were ordinary Muslims, who have nothing to do with terrorism and spend their time having to deal with reprisals for the actions of lunatics that have nothing to do with them. My friend, the comedian Tez Ilyas, has reassured me that they discussed it at the last big Muslim meeting, and I'm fine. However, I suspect Tez to be lying about the existence of these meetings as he always smiles as he mentions them. Then when I ask him about why he's smiling, he claims he's 'remembering a joke that he heard at the meeting and I wouldn't get it because I wasn't there', which seems pretty plausible.

The meme itself served as the inspiration for my 2013 Edinburgh show *Nish Kumar is a Comedian*, a show which most critics agreed was 'another comedy show by Nish Kumar'. Within the comedy community, it is generally agreed that the second show is the hardest one to write, a phenomenon musicians refer to as 'second album syndrome' and further evidence that all comedians just secretly wish we were as cool as musicians. The consensus was that I was given a pretty substantial hand by the meme, with one of my friends claiming 'the internet is writing your show for you' – an opinion with which I found it hard to disagree. Ironically, more people probably found out about the meme through me talking about it in my show than if I had just kept my big mouth shut. I had managed to spin a minor internet-based incident into a moderately successful comedy show, like some kind of poundshop Dave Gorman.

If you visit the website, you'll see that the meme still exists, as a monument to the strange, brief period when I was the 'confused Muslim'. That seems like as good a place as any to leave things – what with that being the name of the meme and all. It gives a nice sense of circularity and strikes a definitive tone. To be honest the rest of this all seems a bit unnecessary. I'm sure they'll edit it out of the finished book, in any case.

FORMING BLACKNESS THROUGH A SCREEN

RENI EDDO-LODGE

I have just finished writing a book about whiteness. This was a book about whiteness as a political force, how it settles like a blanket on our comprehension, how it seeps, and strangles, and silences. I wrote about whiteness from the perspective of an outsider, who – despite my university-educated, well-spoken relative privilege – has always been locked out of whiteness's exclusivity clause. Dissecting political whiteness is paramount to understanding how racism operates in Britain. So often positioned as invisible, neutral, and benign, whiteness taints every interaction we'll ever engage in.

But now I am at a loss. And although I am not a fan of binaries, spending so much time staring into the face of whiteness has forced me to ponder my blackness.

My blackness as a whole, defined not in opposition to a dominant majority, nor constructed as an undesirable 'other' by racialised forces intent on denigrating it. To ponder *my* blackness. Not the blackness that is tacked on to the phrase BAME [black, Asian and minority ethnic] for flimsy equality and diversity purposes by public sector organisations beholden to the Race Relations Act. No. Blackness defined by black folks. The celebration of melanin. For as long as I could comprehend the world, I only knew I was black because I was sure I wasn't white.

Now I want to talk about blackness, our representations of it, how we understand ourselves through the eyes of someone else. How, when I was growing up, the positive black-led and black-owned representations of blackness weren't to be found in the British Isles. Instead, they were being imported from the United States. With globalisation, this is par for the course for all aspects of our pop culture. Yet when it comes to blackness, American-centric media contributed to an erasure here.

It was a kind of displacement that went hand-in-hand with Britain's collective forgetting of black contributions to British history. The black history I learned in school was about the United States. I learned in school that on December 1st 1955, Rosa Parks was arrested for refusing to give up her seat at the front of the bus, setting off a chain of events that resulted in a bus boycott in Montgomery, Alabama. But I didn't learn that less than a decade later, a similar bus boycott took place in Bristol,[14] roughly 106 miles west from the stuffy south London classroom I was learning these facts in. British black history, positioned across the Atlantic, was as real to me as *The Simpsons*, and that was a tragedy.

I had an incredibly strong sense of heritage. Being a third generation Nigerian immigrant is not something your extended family will let you forget. I knew where I came from, but I struggled to see where I was presently at. I needed anchoring,

14 The Bristol bus boycott, led by youth worker Paul Stephenson, saw a city-wide boycott of the bus service in response to an informal colour bar that stopped black people being employed on the buses.

but the legacy of blackness I kept seeing was characterised as thoroughly American.

As a nineties child, I came of age before social media had really taken off, before normal girls were DIY-ing their own media in their bedrooms, creating blogs and YouTube channels, and reassuring their peers that black is beautiful.

I relied on television. My life was pretty sheltered. I ricocheted from the small council flat that I shared with my mum, to my school around the corner, and occasionally to a childminder. I was the only black child in a class of 30 in suburban south London. I have memories of my little white girl classmates trying to convince me that because my skin was black, my tongue was black too. I have memories of an art teacher encouraging my class to draw our 'beautiful blue eyes' whenever we got the crayons and sugar paper out. Everything around me was so starkly white that I began to believe that I would turn white sooner or later. I was quietly being written out of the narrative of humanity in my immediate surroundings.

I needed to find a blackness that was vaguely relevant to a tall, skinny, London-born-and-raised Nigerian girl, and that wasn't to be found in after school and Saturday morning television. When you're young, you translate yourself through representations of people who look like you. And when those characters look like you, but were of a different continent, and a different culture, it invited a kind of cognitive dissonance.

The first black family I saw on television was on *The Fresh Prince of Bel-Air*. For many late-eighties and early-nineties babies, the Banks were the archetypal black family, that all black people should be aiming to be. They were affluent and upper-middle-class, well-dressed, and incredibly well-educated. They even came complete with Geoffrey, the (black)

British butler. It was a complete transgression against the reality of the majority of black families' lives in America at the time, let alone black families in the UK. Even today, 20 years after these episodes first aired, white households in the States hold on average 16 times more wealth than black households. Despite the continued growth of the black middle class in the US, at the time, the Banks family were a total fantasy. And that was OK, because light-hearted entertainment is supposed to help us escape from the drudge of reality.

The Fresh Prince was as much about class as it was about race. The whole point of the show was examining the social *faux pas* that came about when lower-class Will went to live with his upper-class family. From west Philadelphia, to Bel-Air in Los Angeles. It was class that provided the most laughs, from the clashes between Will's relatives and his friend Jazz, to the withering looks of Geoffrey the butler.

As well as *The Fresh Prince*, I was peripherally aware of the Huxtable family on *The Cosby Show*, although it was a little bit before my time. As far as I can tell, the set-up was essentially the same. The Huxtables, based in Brooklyn rather than Los Angeles, were another wealthy black family breaking stereotypes. Like *The Fresh Prince,* the show had its affable, loveable patriarch, traditional family values, and more morals of the story at the end of an episode than you could shake a book of Aesop's Fables at.

But, whilst casting blackness in a positive light, the black American characters I watched were not allowed to be complex. Everyone was good deep down. If they misbehaved, it was never out of ill will, and any intra-family disagreements would be cleared up before the end of the episode. Perhaps this black-led programming was responding to programming that had gone before it that represented black people as a monolith

– lazy, uneducated and stupid. These were simplistic, narrow, and binary narratives that didn't afford us any humanity. It was predictable (and understandable), then, that the black-led response did just the opposite.

I watched black nuclear families – successful, moral along conservative Christian lines, educated and wealthy families – who deeply loved one another despite the light trials and tribulations they might endure throughout the span of a 23-minute episode. And I got it. After centuries of racist depictions of blackness, from blacked-up actors in theatre to blackface minstrels, black programme makers wanted to put their best foot forward, and not let the side down. They probably thought that in order to encourage successful black families, they had to show them in the first place. Almost 200 of *The Cosby Show*'s episodes were written by Bill Cosby himself, whilst the legendary TV and music producer Quincy Jones was at the helm of *The Fresh Prince*.

But this defensive, albeit understandable, response was just as binary and just as simplistic as the overtly racist depictions of blackness before it. It would take another couple of decades of fighting regressive stereotypes until black characters could be afforded the same kind of complexity, humanity and sometimes downright mundanity that depictions of white male characters had enjoyed for centuries.

And of course, the lionisation of the small 'c' conservative, wealthy and successful black family in these television programmes was nothing more than naked respectability politics. This was the logical conclusion of these faux positive representations of blackness, and it couldn't have been more obvious when the now disgraced, but then widely celebrated, black patriarch Bill Cosby delivered his 'Pound Cake' speech to an NAACP [National Association for the Advancement of Coloured People] event in 2004. This was the speech that launched his career as a conservative cultural commentator, and considering that *The Cosby Show* was initially based on Cosby's stand-up sketches, it wasn't surprising that respectability was a consistent theme in his work.

'Ladies and gentlemen,' said Cosby to his audience. 'These people set, they opened the doors, they gave us the right, and today, ladies and gentlemen, in our cities and public schools we have fifty per cent drop out. In our own neighbourhood, we have men in prison. No longer is a person embarrassed because they're pregnant without a husband. (Clapping.) No longer is a boy considered an embarrassment if he tries to run away from being the father of the unmarried child. (Clapping.)

'If you knock that girl up, you're going to have to run away because it's going to be too embarrassing for your family. In the old days, a girl getting pregnant had to go down South, and then her mother would go down to get her. But the mother had the baby. I said the mother had the baby. The girl didn't have a baby. The mother had the baby in two weeks. (Laughter.) We are not parenting. Ladies and gentlemen, listen to these people, they are showing you what's wrong. People putting their clothes on backwards – isn't that a sign of something going on wrong? (Laughter.)'

Ever the conservative traditionalist, Cosby blamed black people for everything, spouting rhetoric more commonly found behind closed doors at posh dinner parties. 'Those people are not Africans,' he said. 'They don't know a damned thing about Africa. With names like Shaniqua, Shaligua, Mohammed and all that crap and all of them are in jail.

'Now look, I'm telling you. It's not what they're doing to us. It's what we're not doing. Fifty per cent drop out. Look, we're raising our own ingrown immigrants. These people are fighting hard to be ignorant. There's no English being spoken, and they're walking and they're angry.'

Cosby's pound cake speech revealed the class hatred of respectability politics.

Respectability politics is the dogged belief that if black people just shape up, dress better and act right, racists would suddenly have a dramatic change of heart, and stop their racist ways. Respectability politics puts all of its faith in racist gatekeepers (telling us that we must change to appeal to their inherent, good-natured humanity), and puts none if its faith in black people living under the weight of poverty and discrimination, scrabbling, trying to make a life anyway they can. Poverty is narrow and limiting. People work within the confines of it. That they have to do that is not the problem. Poverty itself is the problem.

So, how could a lanky kid from London go about asserting black Britishness after a childhood full of seeing blackness through a conservative American cultural lens? I searched for a bit of authenticity amidst the onslaught for many years, eventually cutting off all my hair and hoping for the best, letting it grow back in tight curls, and spending time getting used to them. These were the bits of me that I had tried to erase, in pursuit of looking like the pretty, light-skinned American black women on the TV. I am loath to write about a monolithic blackness, because I know it doesn't really exist in that way. So I settled on exploring my own. To be an immigrant, good or bad, is about straddling two homes, whilst knowing you don't really belong to either. It is about both consuming versions of blackness, digging around in history until you get confirmation that you were there, whilst creating your own for the present and the future. It is up to you to make your own version of blackness in any way you can – trying on all the different versions, altering them until they fit.

BEYOND 'GOOD' IMMIGRANTS

WEI MING KAM

Years ago, my mum would sometimes call me and my siblings to the kitchen excitedly.

'Why, what's going on?' I'd ask.

'Look!' She would point at the TV, and someone Chinese would be on it.

'Oh my god,' my baby sister would groan. 'Why are you always so excited? So they're Chinese – so what?'

We rolled our eyes at each other, and trooped back to our books and Gameboys, perennially embarrassed and uncomprehending, leaving her to watch whoever the fellow East Asian was, like they were a celebrity.

A decade later, my mother's excitement seems more like surprise. I've noticed our long, gaping absence from the cultural landscape and come to recognise the mix of shock and curiosity at seeing a face like mine onscreen, a rare acknowledgement of our existence in the UK. *Look*, my mum was saying. *We're here.*

It often doesn't feel like it.

The Chinese in the UK have been called the 'hidden' or 'invisible' community,[15] given that we are perceived as

---

15 'Chinese diaspora: Britain', *BBC News*. http://news.bbc.co.uk/1/hi/world/asia-pacific/4304845.stm

ostensibly successful, assimilated into British society and self-reliant. In America, we're called 'the model minority'. We do education, food, medicine, finance, and all sorts of other things well, according to popular belief in the West.

As a journalist, Katy Lee's career choice doesn't follow the conventional well-worn stereotypes.

'My dad did want me to work really hard at school,' she says, grinning at me over Skype from her flat in Paris. 'He did want me to make lots of money when I grow up ...' We both start to giggle at the inevitability of parental anxiety. 'He's disappointed that I'm a journalist making not very much money, instead of a banker or whatever.'

Katy has worked for the international news agency Agence France-Presse for five years, moving from London to Hong Kong and then back to Europe. Her educational CV reads like this: high-achieving grammar school; Cambridge; City University for Broadcast Journalism. Half-Vietnamese, half-English, she caveats our conversation by saying that her experience has been tempered by being half-Asian. Despite that warning, her observations all feel very familiar.

'Even as a kid, before the *Tiger Mom* book was a thing,' she says. 'I was vaguely aware that as an Asian kid, I was expected to work hard at school, and that came as much from general society as it did from my dad.'

Ah, Amy Chua's *Battle Hymn of the Tiger Mother*. The hard-working, naturally-clever, silent East Asian is a pervasive stereotype, but the horrified furore around Chua's parenting memoir shows that beneath the Western awe at Chinese educational attainment is a profoundly uncomfortable fear of a seemingly alien culture. Headlines such as the BBC's 'are strict

Chinese mothers the best?'[16] jostled with claims that such parenting leads to a lack of creativity, and people predicted that Chua's children would become friendless robots.

Katy is unimpressed by this.

'It fitted very nicely into a narrative that already exists, that they already had a vague idea about,' she sighs. 'You know, [the idea that these] parents will do anything for their kids to get good grades, they're really cruel, this is exotic, so strange, it's so different from how we behave.'

We both observe that pushy parenting isn't limited to East Asian people, and she says, 'I think a lot of white parents do this, and this is what pisses me off about it.'

Integrate well. Move upwards in society. Be praised – until people worry that you're doing too well, and then they remember that you're foreign. This is perhaps best illustrated by an educational study published by Routledge in 2005, where various teachers attributed success to inherently 'Chinese' qualities while simultaneously hinting that these qualities were 'enclosed', 'denying children individuality' and in opposition to Western cultural ideas.[17]

Political relations play a part in this too. When I bring up China's economic rise, Katy nods.

'I think Britain is going through an identity crisis at the moment. Reactions to things like *Tiger Mother* are like "Who are these people, are they going to take over?"'

It's a shrewd assessment of the contradictory views that the UK has of Chinese people, and one that Jiaqi Hou agrees with.

16 'Are strict Chinese mothers the best?' *BBC News*. http://www.bbc.co.uk/news/magazine-12249215

17 Louise Archer and Becky Francis, *Understanding Minority Ethnic Achievement in Schools: Race, gender, class and 'success'*, (Routledge, 2006), 44.

'Labels can be easily removed. It's not controlled by the minority community itself, and it's related to the international political environment,' he says, when I ask him about the model minority stereotype. 'Anything can change, labels just show how vulnerable the communities are, because today they can be a model minority, but tomorrow they might not be.'

Jiaqi is the project manager of The British Chinese Project, a non-profit organisation that aims to engage the Chinese community in the political process and strengthen its social standing. When I meet him, the BC Project's advisor Cohan Chew and their media director, Jun Kit Man, they take me into a meeting room and sit across the table. It's very businesslike, and I get the feeling that Jiaqi has been asked many of the questions I put to him before.

For such an allegedly successful minority, the level of Chinese political engagement is among the lowest in Britain. The Electoral Commission found in 2006 that 30 per cent of British Chinese people weren't on the electoral register.

'The reasons are very, very complicated, it's not simply [as people] say, that Chinese people are shy, reserved, that they haven't got used to speaking out and being vocal,' Jiaqi says, with a hint of weariness. 'We have a lot of Chinese candidates, but unfortunately, most of them won't be selected to safe seats. So that dramatically reduces the chance of them winning. If we are looking at those Chinese who have never registered [to vote], or have never voted, language barrier is always the first reason.'

He goes on to talk about the large number of people working long hours in catering, who don't have the time for politics, and the ugly history of Chinese exclusion from other forms of employment.

A pause, then very firmly: 'These are all related reasons, it should not be thought of as simply culture. I strongly disagree with anyone who has that opinion.'

The lack of interest in wider civic participation that the low voter registration suggests, is compounded by a pervading distrust of police. In 2013 the BC Project published a report on the Chinese community's relations with the police, and 43.8 per cent of those who did not report a crime selected 'do not think the perpetrator will be caught' or 'do not see any point in reporting', as reasons for their inaction and apathy.[18] Statements from the respondents included feeling that the police reacted too slowly after reporting the crime, and, worryingly, 'many felt that the police failed in their responsibility to make them feel safe and were instead "intimidating".'[19] None of this sounds like a completely happy community.

When I ask Jiaqi if he feels their concerns are being taken seriously, he tells me, frustrated, 'A friend of mine got robbed in her apartment and all of our friends, we called the police, but they said, "We don't have police patrolling that area, we can't do anything".' He continues, 'So basically after an hour the police finally went there, but only because we had more than 50 people calling for the same issue.'

Not much seems to have changed since Min Quan's eye-opening report on racism against the Chinese in 2009. A part of The Monitoring Group, Min Quan's study was prompted by the 2005 murder of Mi Gao Huang Chen outside his takeaway in Wigan in an attack by more than 20 white youths. The reaction of the investigating officer in the case was a classic example of systemic racism. '[He] denied the murder

---

18 All-Party Parliamentary Group on the Chinese in Britain, *Chinese Community and Policing Report 2013*, (British China Project), 16.

19 *Chinese Community and Policing Report 2013.*

was racially motivated and dismissed [Mi Gao's partner] Ms Jia's accusations of police incompetence as "sheer nonsense".[20]

Despite repeated warnings about racial harassment, the officer also described the murder as 'unforeseeable'.[21] Min Quan's study notes that, 'Eileen [Jia] remained isolated. In fact, her ethnic origin seemed to work against her. As a Chinese person she was stereotyped as being self-reliant; and not in need of the kind of support offered to other families of murder victims.'[22] She left the UK shortly after the trial.

The case is an extreme example of police indifference towards racial abuse suffered by Chinese people, but the report makes it clear that it is far from isolated, saying that 'there are perhaps even higher levels of racial violence or harassment than those experienced by any other minority group.'[23]

Unsurprisingly, it's not just outright abuse that is an issue for the British Chinese. A paper on inequality for the Joseph Rowntree Foundation in 2011 found that 'inequality levels are also extremely high. Despite the high median levels of resources, poverty rates are above average for both adults and children.'[24] But the illusion that the community as a whole is prospering is, for some East Asians, something to be embraced.

20 'Girlfriend blames police as "racist" killers jailed', *The Guardian*. http://www.theguardian.com/uk/2005/dec/17/ukcrime.race

21 'Takeaway murder teenagers named', *BBC News*. http://news.bbc.co.uk/1/hi/england/manchester/4424766.stm

22 Sue Adamson et al., *Hidden from public view? Racism against the UK Chinese population*, Min Quan report, (The Monitoring Group, 2009).

23 Sue Adamson et al., *Hidden from public view?*

24 Lucinda Platt, 'Inequality within Ethnic Groups', *JRF Programme: Poverty and Ethnicity*, (Joseph Rowntree Foundation, 2011), 14.

This attitude was epitomised by a piece by Clarissa Tan in 2014 in the *Spectator* [25] in which she proclaimed confidently that, 'Britain has many challenges … racism isn't one of them.'

She goes on to say, 'The danger with crying racism at every turn is that it conceals real problems … an Ofsted inspector recently raised the issue of working-class white schoolchildren being overlooked and without representation versus ethnic groups …'

Nothing, of course, about the fact that despite being among the highest achievers in our schools, Chinese male graduates in 2004/5 could expect to earn 25 per cent less than white male graduates. [26]

That particular ceiling is only one of many she ignores. 'I have been welcomed and accepted in this country, and – uncool as this may sound – I feel grateful for this,' she says, towards the end of the article. It seems like a very low bar for gratitude.

'Thinking about the model minority thing,' I say, 'there will probably be some people I talk to who think, "Oh it's a good thing!"'

Viki abandons her sushi completely.

'No it's not! People who think that think, "It's positive racism", which is the most ridiculous phrase I've ever heard in my life.'

Viki Cheung works in publishing. We're sitting in a Japanese restaurant in Chinatown on a Sunday, attempting to

---

25 'Britain has major problems – racism isn't one of them', *The Spectator*. http://www.spectator.co.uk/2014/02/how-racist-is-britain/

26 Yaojun Li, Fiona Devine, Anthony Heath, 'Equality Group Inequalities in Education, Earnings and Employment', Equality and Human Rights Commission, (2008), Executive summary, iii.

chat in between the endless plates being brought to our table.

'You're treating all East Asians as a homogenous mass,' she continues. 'We're all individual people, why is this such a struggle to see that?'

I mention the absurd dichotomy that the phrase 'model minority' indirectly suggests. She nods. 'Yes. In the same mouthful as saying, "East Asians are the model minority because they're quiet and hardworking", [you imply] black people are apparently loud and lazy.'

I ask Viki if she feels she has to push back against stereotypes. She considers this for a second, and replies, 'I am far more outspoken at work than I ever thought I would be, on work issues. I'm aware that if I'm not it's contributing to the "quiet, sensible [stereotype]".' I nod, understanding. There are very few East Asian people in publishing. 'And I'm going to have to be even more me to combat that, especially because I'm a woman. I would rather be thought of as opinionated.'

Even as I think about how much hard work that sounds, she says, 'It was an active choice I made. It's a choice I made a long time ago, but I amped it up since coming to work in publishing, which is a very white industry.' She shrugs. 'I'm a very outspoken person anyway, it's not a facade in any way, it's just a more me version of me, out of necessity because I don't want ...'

Viki stops for a few seconds. 'It's a really heavy lot of things that I have to think about to not be stereotyped. And I have no idea if my efforts are even working.'

Sensible, quiet, shy ... some things just follow us around. The idea of not complaining being an admirable trait, is something that struck Katy Lee during our Skype chat.

'I do think it's interesting that this idea of being a model minority is tied up with essentially being quiet,' she says. 'Just sitting back, not complaining about stuff, and getting on with making money. Being quiet is considered a really good quality.'

Especially when it comes to the rights of others to make racist jokes at someone else's expense.

The week before we chatted, it was announced that Janette Tough, a white actor, had been cast as a Japanese designer in *Ab Fab: The Movie*. Amidst the fury that the decision unleashed, newspapers published opinion pieces (by writers who weren't East Asian) on the row. Helen Lewis in the *Guardian* wondered why drag wasn't considered as bad as yellowface. The *Telegraph* managed to comprehend that blackface is 'fundamentally racist', and yet decided that Ab Fab's yellowface was merely mocking a nation. 'No country is immune to satire – and nor should it be,' they concluded.

Be quiet. Stop complaining. Let us have our fun. Don't be so sensitive. You're normally quiet, aren't you?

Katy sighs with disappointment.

'The yellowface thing is a really good example. I think I was listening to some comedians the other day [they were talking about] what accent it's acceptable to do and saying, "Well, like obviously you can't do a Jamaican one, but like I think Chinese is pretty OK," and well no, it isn't!'

'People expect me to be a good worker. Professional etc., I think this is because of the stereotype that we are smart and nerdy and thus seen to be a hard worker.'

I stare at the email and grin. I found Rebecca Yip's blog through her YouTube channel a few weeks ago. Both are called *Asianchemnerd*. Her family is from Hong Kong, and she moved back there from the UK to do her chemistry PhD a year ago. After reading about her reasons for doing so ('I had some awful times with racist people [in] secondary school'), I emailed her asking for a chat.

'Born in UK but ethnically Chinese, everyone looked at me to be an outsider,' she wrote back. She doesn't, unsurprisingly, escape systemic prejudice in academia either. 'Generally, professors tend to be white men. I feel that we do have to prove ourselves more than a white man.'

She mentions a racist incident in the UK involving her boyfriend, who is Indian. 'I want to bring up my family in a place that is safe, and they feel welcome and they can feel like they can reach their full potential, without holding back because of their race.'

In the UK, she says, there will always be something holding them back.

As I watch her Chinese New Year video, I wonder: how many other people like her leave this country to find better things?

'I do feel that there're better work opportunities elsewhere. What I want to do personally, I want to work in Britain. I'm British and I want to work here.' Paul Courtenay Hyu, otherwise known as 'Chinese Elvis', is giving me the lowdown on life as a jobbing Chinese actor in the Curzon Soho café.

I mention the steady stream of British black actors honing their potential in America, and he nods.

'Well it's happening to a very small extent with the East Asians. Elaine Tan is over there and she's working her arse off.' He adds in a satisfied tone, 'And she is the main person in our episode of *Doctor Who*. So there are two Chinese in it, and she's got a Geordie accent, and pretty good too, I have to say. And I do my Yorkshire accent.'

He mentions Singapore and Hong Kong as other places that British Chinese seek work in.

'They're more like the kung fu guys, the ones who can do stunts. A lot of Singaporeans go back to Singapore because it's just better [than the UK]. Anybody who has a right to work there seems to go back quite often ...' He reels off a list of other actors who work in Singapore. 'Adrian Pang hasn't been back for about fifteen years and I don't blame him, because he's just staying busy, whereas here we're scrabbling for shit.'

He mentions very casually that he went to drama school with an actor from *The Hobbit*. I gape at him for a second, and he grimaces at the memory of seeing his old classmate in the trailer.

'The majority of us British actors – apart from Ben Wong, literally apart from him – we haven't had the opportunities that all our white peers have had,' he says. 'So whilst we might in the 80s have had the equivalent talent and potential, they've had a chance to develop it, and we're just sat there stagnating going ...' He grabs a Curzon café menu and puts on what white people call a Chinese accent, then mimes being a waiter. 'Ohhhh we talk like 'dis, a Chinese menu for one?' I wince, and he slaps the menu down on the coffee table. 'That's what we've done, so we aren't as technically on top of it as we should be. That's an unforeseen consequence of not getting the same opportunities.' Paul picks up the menu again, exasperated. 'You have to be better than you should be in order just to keep up. Women say that, don't they, you have to be better just to stay par. I think that's what we suffer from as well.

'We pay our taxes, we deserve something, it's only fair. We pay our fucking BBC licence, we deserve to see somebody on *EastEnders*! Surely after 30 years of East-fucking-Enders we must have had a Chinese family on it ... at least once ... for six months?'

* * *

He's not the only person thinking this. Everyone I spoke to for this essay voiced annoyance or puzzlement at the lack of East Asians in British media who weren't stereotypes. From illegal immigrants in *Casualty* to Triad members in *Sherlock*, hardly anyone writing for the British screen (or book) seems capable of imagining British East Asians as British. If we're not villains à la Fu Manchu, we're delicate women who need saving, usually by white men (Gemma Chan in *Sherlock*), or comedy material.

Even Katie Leung of Harry Potter fame, arguably the most famous British Chinese actor we have, recently expressed frustration at how limiting her roles are. 'More and more when I see a script that requires a Chinese accent of any kind, I flinch a little bit,' she said, in an interview with the *Herald on Sunday*.

News coverage, rare though it is, is hardly better, going between the extremes of criminality or some comment on the model minority story, usually to do with education.

We're not seen as human, because we never get to be complex individuals. Our defining characteristic is generally our foreignness. Even news reports about education carry an undertone of fear of a culturally alien other and of being usurped, both here and internationally. Being a model minority is code for being on perpetual probation. Hostility towards the 'yellow peril' is never far from the surface.

It's easy to cling to a position of privilege when it acts as protection from the ever-present danger of being seen as outsiders, but playing to the myth of the 'good immigrant' does not lead to real equality, or even acceptance. Breaking out of the 'model minority' box and looking beyond that status towards humanity and freedom is the long game.

'YOU CAN'T SAY THAT! STORIES HAVE TO BE ABOUT WHITE PEOPLE'

DARREN CHETTY

A few years ago, I taught a Year 2 class in east London. I had built up a good bank of multicultural picture books and resources and shared these with the class whenever seemed appropriate. When it came time for the class to write their own stories, I suggested that they used the name of someone in their family for their protagonist. I wanted them to draw on their own backgrounds, but was worried about 'making an issue of race'. When it came to sharing their stories, I noticed only one boy had acted upon my suggestion, naming his main character after his uncle. He had recently arrived from Nigeria and was eager to read his story to the class. However, when he read out the protagonist's name another boy, who was born in Britain and identified as Congolese, interrupted him. 'You can't say that!' he said. 'Stories have to be about white people.'

Let me back up for a second.

I've spent almost two decades teaching children aged between four and 11, in English primary schools that serve multiracial, multicultural, multifaith communities. Over that time, I have come to notice that whenever children are asked to write a story in school, children of colour[27] will write a story featuring characters with 'traditional' English names who speak English as a first language. This has been the case across the schools I have taught in with barely an exception. Yet, I don't recall it ever being discussed by teachers in these schools or on any of the courses on writing that I attended over the years.

My own attempts to open up conversations about what I have noticed have had some success but have also been met with angry responses from a loud minority of teachers. In one case, I recall being asked, 'Why are you making an issue of race when children are colour-blind?'

The question contains an assumption, namely that children are 'colour-blind'. I think this might stem from a belief that children do not attach any significance to racialised identities, particularly in twenty-first-century multi-ethnic urban classrooms, because we inhabit a post-racial world. If children were writing stories where the race[28] of characters was varied and random, there might be some merit in claiming that children are colour-blind. However, even the strongest advocates of racial colour-blindness do not argue that all people are white ... and English. They argue that race no longer matters. If that's true, why are young children of colour and young white children writing exclusively about white characters?

I'm confident the boy who said that stories had to be about

27 I use here 'children of colour' and 'people of colour' to refer to those who are racialised as 'other than white'. Originating in the USA, this term is used increasingly in the UK. Alternative terms include 'Black Asian and Minority Ethnic' (BAME), racially minoritised and 'Global Majority'.

28 I view race as socially constructed and agree with Gary Younge that it is 'a nonsense' that nevertheless affects our lives and thus should be talked about.

white people was being sincere and indeed, in the ensuing class discussion there was a fair bit of uncertainty about who could and couldn't be in stories. I was surprised and confused by this. Why did my students without fail write stories about children from very different backgrounds to themselves? And why were these characters always white? Why hadn't my efforts to offer a culturally diverse reading diet made clear to them that stories could be about absolutely anyone?

At the time, I don't think I realised what I was up against.

If you are a teacher, try this with your class. Ask them to write down their favourite 25 children's book characters. Then ask them to count how many of those characters are white (and look for other patterns too, such as gender and disability). If you're not a teacher, ask any child you know. Or maybe ask the staff in a bookshop to show you the picture-books with a black boy, or a mixed-race girl or a Muslim child as the protagonist. I tried this once and received a lot of help in searching from a clearly panicked shopkeeper – but very few books.

Booksellers like Letterbox Library provide a service valued by many parents and teachers in going the extra mile to locate books featuring people traditionally under-represented in children's literature. Of course, booksellers can only sell books that get published. And the stories I hear from people in publishing and from authors leads me to wonder if some UK publishers share the same confusion I observed in that Year 2 class. Namely, an uncertainty about the place of stories featuring people of colour and the place of people of colour in stories.

A South Asian author told me that she was advised to change her name for a book cover in order to broaden its appeal, and another writer was advised that unless they were writing an 'issue' book, their book-cover protagonist should not be black, as this would result in fewer copies being purchased. Whether or not such advice is based on evidence – do white book buyers *really* shy away from buying books because they feature black characters? – it seems that this concern with race and commercial viability certainly troubles this idea of 'colour-blindness' or 'post-raciality' in the UK.

Not only that, it means that, as a teacher, I have fewer books at my disposal to demonstrate to BAME children that stories can be about people like them.

Chimamanda Ngozi Adichie recalls that the stories she wrote as a seven-year-old in Nigeria were based on the kinds of stories she read, featuring characters who were 'white and blue-eyed, they played in the snow, they ate apples'. According to Adichie, this wasn't just about experimentation or an active imagination, 'because all I had read were books in which characters were foreign, I had become convinced that books by their very nature had to have foreigners in them and had to be about things with which I could not personally identify.'[29] We learn so many things from reading stories, including the conventions of stories such as good versus evil, confronting our fears and that danger often lurks in the woods. The problem is that, when one of these conventions is that children in stories are white, English and middle-class, than you may come to learn that your own life does not qualify as subject material. Adichie describes this as 'The Danger of a Single Story' – a danger that extends to stories which, whilst appearing to be 'diverse', rely on stereotypes and thus limit the imagination.

Children's literature professor Rudine Sims Bishop offers

---

29 'The danger of a single story', Chimanda Ngozi Adichie TED talk. https://www.ted.com/talks/chimamanda_adichie_the_danger_of_a_single_story/transcript?language=en

a useful metaphor for helping us think about what is at stake here. Whilst acknowledging that 'good literature reaches across cultural and ethnic borders to touch us all as human',[30] she argues that books can act as both mirrors and windows for children. 'Windows' offer us a chance to look closely at a view of the world we may not have previously seen. Those windows might take us out to escapist fantasy or provide a view of lives we have not previously seen. These are notions familiar and vital to writers, teachers and those of us who care about stories. But Sims Bishop adds that books might also mirror our lives in some aspects and that children from the dominant culture tend to have books as mirrors whilst children who have been historically 'ignored – or worse ridiculed' do not, and that this communicates important messages about the extent to which 'they are valued in the social context in which they are growing up'. Recognising that a window can be a barrier, Sims Bishop later added the idea of the sliding glass door as 'a way to suggest that a book can offer … a lived experience for a reader'.[31]

It was a concern over the lack of stories that allow all children to see themselves in the fiction they read – books as mirrors – that motivated Verna Wilkins to establish Tamarind Books, first as an author and then also as a publisher. Wilkins recalls her son coming home with a self-portrait in which he had painted his face 'bright pink'. She recalls the conversation:

'Is this you?' I asked feebly.
'Yes,' came the confident reply.
'Are you that colour?'
'No. The teacher gave out flesh colour to everyone!'

---

30 Rudine Sims Bishop, 'Reflections on the Development of African American Children's Literature', *Journal of Children's Literature*, 38:2, (Fall 2012).

31 Ibid.

'*Oh. Fine. I have a lovely brown crayon and we can fix that right now.*'

'*No!*' *he said. 'It has to be that colour. It's for a book!*'[32]

My classroom story is remarkably similar to Wilkins's story of this conversation but took place over 20 years later. I certainly don't want to diminish the huge impact that Tamarind has had on children's publishing but I'm confident Wilkins would agree with me that there's a need for more like her in children's publishing, as campaigns like #WeNeedDiverseBooks are arguing. Wilkins made the decision to focus on books with everyday representations of black children rather than what she terms book about 'issues'. Wilkins has good reasons for doing this but it does mean that stories like hers with her son, and mine with my class, which invite us to explore ideas around childhood, racism and the arts would probably not be published by Tamarind, however well-written.

I've written elsewhere about how the books that often are recommended as dealing in some way with racism do so through metaphor and animal allegories.[33] There may well be benefits to this – not least the avoidance of further portrayals of children of colour as victims – but this also means its hard to find portrayals of children of colour thriving in a world where racism exists. A much-discussed example is J.K. Rowling's 'Harry Potter' series. The books are seen by many as arguing for inclusivity and tolerance, tackling challenging themes such as racial purity and oppression. These themes are explored through fantasy figures such as wizards, giants and elves. At

32 Verna Wilkins, 'The Right To Be Seen', Patrick Hardy Lecture, October 29th, 2008.

33 Darren Chetty, 'The Elephant in the Room: Picturebooks, Philosophy for Children and Racism', *Childhood and Philosophy* , Vol. 10 No 9, (2014).

the same time, amongst the teachers and pupils at Hogwarts, there are very few people of colour and no clear explanation of why that might be. So a story that has so much to say about racism on an allegorical level at the same time depicts people of colour as marginal without exploring their marginalisation.

Malorie Blackman has shown that compelling stories that do not shy away from racism can be written for children with her 'Noughts and Crosses' series, whilst also demonstrating that there are so many stories beyond racism to be told about children of colour. In 2014, in her role as the presiding Children's Laureate, Blackman spoke out about how diversifying the characters in children's literature would benefit all readers. In a piece for Sky News, which itself became a news story after she was misquoted in the original title, Blackman is quoted as saying,

'You want to escape into fiction as well and read about other people, other cultures, other lives, other planets and so on. But I think there is a very significant message that goes out when you cannot see yourself at all in the books you are reading. I think it is saying "well, you may be here, but do you really belong?"'[34]

Clearly, not everyone agreed. However, despite receiving racist abuse online Blackman vowed not to be silenced, and mainstream newspapers ran stories about children's literature, diversity and marginalisation.[35]

I don't think such marginalisation is limited to children's books. As well as books, the children I taught were learning about stories from film and television. One popular show

---

34 'Call for more ethnic diversity in kids' books', *Sky News.* http://news.sky.com/story/1323753/call-for-more-ethnic-diversity-in-kids-books

35 'Malorie Blackman facest racist abuse after call to diversify children's books'. *The Guardian.* http://www.theguardian.com/books/2014/aug/26/malorie-blackman-racist-abuse-diversity-childrens-books

amongst pupils I've taught over the years is set in the very area of England where we live. When it was launched in 1985, *EastEnders* was lauded for its inner-city realism and diversity.

Creator/producer Julia Smith declared that 'We don't make life, we reflect it.' She also said, 'We decided to go for a realistic, fairly outspoken type of drama which could encompass stories about homosexuality, rape, unemployment, racial prejudice, etc., in a believable context. Above all, we wanted realism.'[36]

In 2009, the BBC compiled a list of the 100 *EastEnders'* characters with the most 'doof doof'[37] cliffhangers – an indication, albeit an imprecise one, of who has the main storyline. As the BBC website says, 'Impact after all is the bedrock of the perfect cliffhanger.'[38]

According to the 2011 Census, inner east London boroughs have populations that are somewhere between 45–71 per cent BAME. So, how many of the top 50 most impactful characters in this programme, set in the East End of London and aiming for realism, were BAME?

None.

Many of the children I was teaching watched *EastEnders*. Given the chance they'd talk about current storylines. Perhaps, as well as learning about dramatic plotting they were learning that people who looked like them and their parents were 'supporting cast' not 'lead roles'. Perhaps this again comes

---

36 Christine Geraghty, *Women and Soap Opera: A Study of Prime Time Soaps*, (Cambridge, Polity Press, 1991).

37 Doof Doof refers to the drums that kick in as the theme tune plays at the end of the show.

38 'Who has the most doof doofs?', *BBC*. http://www.bbc.co.uk/programmes/articles/1wZjwgr7519fmWF6m10wgz1/who-has-the-most-doof-doofs

down to questions of audience … for whom are these stories produced? What do the creators assume, rightly or wrongly, about their audience?

In her essay *Playing in the Dark*, Toni Morrison argues that 'the readers of virtually all of American fiction have been positioned as white'.[39] Karen Sands O'Connor, a professor specialising in Black British children's literature, says of West Indian writers who came to Britain, 'In order to be writers, they had to tell their own stories; in order to be published authors, they had to do it in a way acceptable to their mostly white British audience.'[40]

So who is the reader for children's writing in a classroom? I think that's probably a complicated question – but in a very literal sense it is the teacher. Teachers read their students' writing and teach them about the kind of things they hope or expect to see whilst reading.

After reflecting on my experience with my Year 2 class, the following year – whilst teaching Year 5 – I was emboldened to experiment. What would happen if for just one lesson I insisted they write about a character from a similar ethnic, religious and linguistic background as themselves – just as I sometimes insist they try to include a fronted adverbial, a moral dilemma or a tricolon?

First we discussed ourselves in terms of, amongst other things, language, family migration, physical appearance including skin and hair, religion, hobbies and clothes. Then I asked the children to write a character who was similar

---

39   Toni Morrison, *Playing in the Dark: Whiteness and the Literary Imagination*, (Harvard University Press, 1992), xiv.

40   Karen Sands-O'Connor, *Soon Come Home To This Island: West Indians in British Children's Literature*, (2007), 140.

in some but not necessarily all of these categories. As I modelled this process for them, I realised that previously I too often defaulted to 'traditional' English names and white characters when writing in class. Now, I tried to draw on my own experience, creating composite characters from family members and applying some of the writing techniques we'd noted in our class reading.

Then they wrote. Clearly, many of them enjoyed the lesson and many produced their best piece of writing. Here are a couple of examples:

Bang! As I stormed to head teacher Mrs Paula's office my head filled with fear. Fear of exclusion!

Mrs Paula was a short, slim, young white woman with red ruddy cheeks. She was a stern woman who hated disobedience and inappropriateness. As I stroked my black hair, my smooth lips crumpled and my creamy brown face turned red with worry.

Michael

Maryam Patel was a twelve-year-old girl, whose parents were Indian, but she was born in Britain. She was a fairly religious person. However, Maryam thought one does not have to wear a headscarf to be religious. She loved her red straight hair. Her hair was as red as blood. She had decided to dye her hair as she hated her dark brown hair. She loved football and the club she supported was Liverpool. One day I will play for the Liverpool women, she thought.

Nabila

I want to avoid making huge claims here. However, I do sense a greater emotional engagement with the story from the children and the beginnings of an authorial voice in both Michael's dramatic first-person opening and Nabila's character description. Nabila is not writing the 'single story' stereotype of Muslim girls. She is writing something far more interesting. There is genuine characterisation in the paragraph not just a short list of features, which I often encounter. More than that, there is some insight in this nine-year-old's writing – and I think that is precisely because she is using her own life as inspiration for her creativity whilst drawing on her reading of fiction. Her descriptive paragraph comes after a lesson looking closely at descriptions by a range of children's authors, which is where the idea of including the protagonist's thought or principle as well as a simple physical description emerged. As her teacher, I tried to get her to focus on a range of structures for describing a character and then give her clear encouragement to draw on her own experiences and those of the people she knew well.

I am not claiming any expertise here, rather sharing a story from my teaching. In many ways I have only scratched the surface and I've tried to include other voices in this essay for those who want to go deeper. I developed my practice from one of just offering a more diverse range of stories in the classroom to modelling writing that drew on my own background so as to signal to my students that they may do the same. I made time to have discussions with students that developed our language for describing skin colour and hair texture and recognised the diversity in the classroom and the lack of diversity in the stories we were writing. I shared examples of how writers explore character's thoughts and feelings so that stories become specific, memorable and something that resonate with us as human beings. I'm not suggesting teachers should always do this but rather that they try it and then review the results; perhaps along with the children they teach.

When I initially wrote about this issue, many people commented saying either that I'd articulated something they'd felt but not said, or that I'd made them see something they'd previously not noticed. A few people were clearly annoyed by it or just dismissive. But many began telling their own stories, often tales of frustration with classroom environments and children's literature – as former children, as parents, as teachers. Perhaps in the telling of these tales, of being the antagonist battling against omission and absence, we can become protagonists, writing ourselves into a richer, multilayered narrative – beyond a single story.

Speaking to Nabila, she told me she had never written about an Indian heritage and/or Muslim character before. Nobody had ever told her she shouldn't. But at the same time, nobody had ever explicitly given her permission. Subsequently, she wrote two further full stories about 'Maryam Patel'. The third instalment described Maryam's trip to India.

Trust me, it was a good read.

An earlier version of this chapter appeared on Media Diversified.[41]

---

41 'You can't do that! Stories have to be about White people', Media Diversified. https://mediadiversified.org/2013/12/07/you-cant-do-that-stories-have-to-be-about-white-people/

ON GOING HOME

KIERAN YATES

I'm looking out of the window midway through the eight-hour journey back to my homeland and thinking of the countless diasporic tales of going home I've read over the years. I consider how the sea has inspired a thousand clichés, about never feeling quite whole, of experiencing an identity cut into neat, disembodied pieces. Staring out it suddenly becomes so clear why we contribute our experiences to a canon saturated with tales of diaspora drama. From Rushdie's 'imaginary homeland' to Naipaul's 'sugar cane and sugar cane', to each reference of a billowing sari in the wind, it's ironic how fraught literature has been with Kipling-esque throwback exoticism. But for any writer, the poetry of crossing oceans to rediscover our home is irresistible, and perhaps for many of those writers who were rarely given opportunities to champion their homes it was too tempting to draw from the multicoloured utopian visions of lush green jungles and air scented with milk and honey. As a fragmented world allows for more nuance now it's obvious that in reality, it's the details of these experiences, not the grand clichés that really reveal the most about ourselves and our journeys.

It's been eight years since I've returned to Punjab. Last time, I was a student, which enabled me to swerve questions about marriage and career, but now I'm officially an adult everything will be up for scrutiny. I'm making mental notes about how best to sidestep the lines of questioning in the courtrooms of family living rooms and kitchens, as we pass over Turkey. I see the mountains below and think about when my granddad made this journey over 40 years ago in the opposite direction, on a Boeing 747 to London Heathrow.

The Britain that accepted him, the place I call home, is now experiencing a period of rejection. The last year has seen a depressing attack on many immigrant communities, as the aggressive rhetoric of adhering to 'British values' has catapulted itself into political and social policy. Cameron specifically targets Muslim women for their poor language skills, the tabloid media demonises refugees on a daily basis, and the rhetoric encouraging us to prove our allegiance to the country's best interests, makes the place I call home feel less safe for people who, largely, look like me.

As the tannoy announces in both Hindi and English that we can unfasten our seatbelts, I consider how the demonising of language is a depressingly familiar narrative – these new plans (that actually pop up every few years) proposing the enforcement of English lessons, as a way of promoting integration under the guise of celebrating British values.

In reality, proposals like this create even more forensic side-eyes that you notice when you're speaking your mother tongue on the train to Kings Cross, or forget yourself in a quiet café and finding yourself speaking Punjabi too loudly on the phone to your cousin.

I know that language can be painful, and so too do a generation of immigrants who have arrived here through different pathways. For them, language is the great battle to fight, and for many it's a war you always feel like you're losing. Even when you get the language, unless you shed your accent, you're continually reminded of your difference. For Indians, our accent has almost become a universal in-joke. The Apu-*thank-you-come-again* novelty, the ingrained Western truth that 'everything sounds funny with an Indian accent!' is an imprint of cultural worth. French accents are sexy, intelligent; Americans (in rap, anyway) cool and culturally appropriated; Indians are comedic – a fact that made the 'One Pound Fish' guy a brief chart hit thanks to tongue-in-cheek purchases from middle England. Whenever I think of his 'novelty act' that 'the nation' loved, I'm amazed that even as recently as 2012, that colonial spirit of finding humour in difference lived on in the hearty laughs of people using my granddad's accent to be entertained. His Indian/British accent was a map of where he'd been and what he'd seen. He travelled from our village in Bahowal to Delhi, to Southall, to Calgary. His voice mirrored those journeys, a living imprint of his memories, and revealed the things he didn't about himself.

Language acquisition is of course a result of age, prior education, resources, and access, rather than a simple time-plus-effort equation. A fact that the current dangerous political rhetoric erases with its snappily presented policy; it's difficult to argue with. Who can protest against the idea of more resources for immigrants? The only problem with this is that those who speak the language of their homeland first, before the language of the coloniser, are made to wade in thick, asphyxiating shame. That they should fall victim to the threateningly punitive 'learn-or-get-out' deal that political rhetoric is ramping up, is obvious. For anyone who has actually seen someone learn a language, it's safe to say that the school of 'well you live here, just learn the language!' thought isn't quite as easy as that. And remember, even when you get it, people will still take the piss.

Next to me is my one-year-old cousin. He is flicking the tray compartment up and down repeatedly, fascinated. My mind is immediately back to my nanaji, who had never travelled on a plane before his journey to London, and I think of how he must have been fascinated by this tray and the cup holders and the plastic cutlery and the window shutters, and how he must have craned to see these same views below.

After a nine-hour drive I'm in the pinde, in my home village of Bahowal. This is where my family comes from, where generations of us have lived, worked and died. My cousins are staring at my sari in adoration. I'm embarrassed at how unnecessarily extravagant it is. My grandma is enjoying the attention I'm getting, but my cheeks are red and I'm terrified of my relatives thinking that I revel in this uncomfortable showboating.

We spend three weeks in this village, disconnected from the internet, showers, unable to walk around unchaperoned. I struggle with the details. I'm scared of the high-speed scooters my cousins whizz around on, which are victims to the untarmacked roads. My reticence to just fearlessly hop on one with my sari on makes me look like some kind of nanny-state soldier trying to enforce Draconian traffic safety and I'm heckled until I finally just shut up and submit. The buckets of water I collect from the well are the exact height of my knees and every time I walk with them, I knock them over, spilling water everywhere, to the entertainment of the neighbourhood children who come to watch me every morning. Even my long, perfectly pointed acrylic nails give away my cushy life, devoid of manual labour, and every time flour gets stuck in them when I'm in the kitchen, making chapattis, I can hear my grandma tutting next to me. My attempts to realign myself with a traditional Punjabi identity fall flat and I'm getting it wrong over and over.

My Punjabi identity back home is a fairly typical second generation one. It's Hoshiarpur football T-shirts as streetwear in London, Bhangra and grime playing out of your cousin's BMW, sending pictures of you in Air Max 90s and a sari to a WhatsApp group. Being a British Asian in 2016 is about being in on the joke when in comes to reclaiming parts of our identity you're supposed to feel ashamed about.

I wear sari tops in the rave, blast Bhangra in the car, make friends with corner-shop owners and teach co-workers about Vaisakhi, delicately explaining to them why saying 'Salaam Alaikum' to a Sikh is a misstep. I grew up revelling in being a typical Southall girl, finding familiarity in the shaved eyebrows of my older male cousins, before moving to a white community where people didn't get me and I noticed just how different I was. Being dragged out of my comfort zone enabled me to discover a new kind of British identity and eventually my family got used to my weirdness, that I wanted to be a writer, that I had white and black friends, that I wanted to stay in reading *Harry Potter* instead of going to the Mega Mela on the common.

At home, the coding is pitched right and I've learned how to navigate my identity in white spaces, in family spaces, in my own. But here, in this village, my specific adoption of Punjab through my own lens is scrutinised by my family and found lacking. They don't understand my jokes, my observations, my London-twanged Punjabi.

This becomes particularly apparent at times, like when my masi catches me on the roof of our house where I've escaped with my sister (it's the only place you can get any privacy and I'm so bored of the local gossip and eternal tea-making below). I'm making a video of a faux toothpaste advert, spinning around as I bite into some sugar cane and flash my pearly whites into the camera (my grandmother swears by sugar cane as the answer to pristine white teeth). I'm winking into the camera and making 'ColCane' taglines in an Indian accent, and my masi berates me for acting like a child. She doesn't understand me, what I find funny, why I'm so weird and different. She constantly compares me to my cousin, who looks like a Kardashian, works as a teacher and has just had an arranged marriage to some heartthrob doctor son. They are cooing over pictures of her while I'm spoken about in tones of puzzlement and sympathy. I overhear my uncle's wife noting that she heard me listening to 'black music' in the bathroom (Fetty Wap) and that I was probably 'messaging a boy' (untrue, no data) and that I always wake up too late (true, but jet lag?).

Going back to the pinde flags up all the things I can't do properly – my rotis aren't round enough, my hands aren't steady enough to apply mendhi, my teeth are too weak to pull sugar cane. While my job as a journalist requires me to artfully draw out other people's voices, I'm unable to give myself one that doesn't present me as pretty inadequate. I am what my favourite cousin calls a 'proper paki' when I'm at home, owing to my love of 'freshie' interior details, Zee TV and old-fashioned songs – but here I'm a fraud, 'a proper coconut' (as my other cousin calls me), too modern to gain favour with the simple tasks, and too strange to be adored by my masis. Despite this, I love every minute of my inadequacy, and it's the intimacy of the unsaid – that they describe me as beautiful when I'm not there, that they worry when I'm out of sight – that allows me to grow roots.

Our next stop is in Delhi.

My 15-year-old cousin in Delhi who reminds me of a desi Paris Hilton illustrates that there is a different code here. Her opening question on seeing me is, 'What's your favourite cosmetic product?', spoken in a city-dwelling modern Delhi drawl that I recognise from Bollywood, aping Karisma Kapoor.

It signals that being humble about what you have isn't the state of play here.

As I arrive, she sees me in my thick, unfashionable suit of heavy embroidered gold thread and as she stands in designer pyjamas, I can see she's visibly disappointed.

'Why are you wearing that?' she asks me.

The answer is that I endured the hellish car trip in said suit to look respectful – my tracksuit is in the boot – and it now seems that I've been scratching my neck on this heavy chuni for the last 10 hours for nothing. When we arrive, my other younger cousin, who is almost 10, runs out to greet me excitedly – somehow, it's been relayed through family Chinese whispers that I'm a fashion journalist and she's expecting a Chanel-clad, high-fashion, vogue catwalk model. What she sees is my matted hair and shapeless, outdated (as her sister has just let me know) suit and she's confused. I'm wearing my nani's sandals and I can see her looking at my dusty, unmanicured feet.

Her mum, my ex-model masi, looks at my eyebrows. I had them threaded before I left, by my Topshop regular, but by now they're unruly and grown out, and I haven't trusted anyone to do them here through fear of getting them too thin (like my last trip). It's unfathomable to my masi why I have bad eyebrows and the trio stare, amazed at my terrible make-up. In a post-desi YouTuber world it's incomprehensible to my cool teen cousins that I would arrive un-contoured and un-highlighted.

I try to explain that 'I'm sorry I look very tired, it was a long journey', and they're nodding but in a way that suggests that they would probably look immaculate had they done the same and that I'm too lazy to care how I look.

All in all, I don't think I'm quite what they were expecting.

Over the weekend my cousin takes me through her selfie wall, which has over 100 colour print-outs of pouting selfies she has taken. We bond over our love of Zayn Malik, she's disappointed at my lack of knowledge about Shruti Arjun Anand, a make-up YouTuber, after I told her I was 'into make-up' (I am, but not on a par with her forensic knowledge, bordering on maniacal) and her mum berates me for feeling uncomfortable asking their servant to make me food.

My unironic love of Bollywood classics and Honey Singh are judged quickly and expertly by my aunty in Delhi, a middle-class ex-model who cites Indian 'cinema' as an interest and has five Fair'n'Lovely products in her bathroom. At one point I spread a thick layer of the lightening cream on my face for Snapchat declaring my fairness and she's staring at me, wondering what's funny. I know the rules but I don't quite impress, and before I know it, it ceases to matter because we're en route to Delhi airport, on our way back home.

The taxi driver as we were driving to the airport opened the doors and on hearing me speak boomed, 'Ah! You're from London?!'

The accusation hung in the air and after a second I had to begrudgingly acknowledge that I was. Opening your mouth reveals more than you might like about who you are and where you come from. We've created routing responses for the monotonous, bordering-on-parodic regularity with which we are asked where we're 'from', and in India you are forced to admit, that it's London.

His son was from here and while my mum was on the phone and we darted across the city, we spoke about Modi and Britain and Zayn Malik and Kajol and Adidas tracksuits and his love of Fruit Pastilles and my inability to make round rotis.

I realised that this was where I understood myself, in snatched conversations, in connections, in the beauty of the throwaway details that it's my job to discover. It's why I was a born journalist, asking questions about the world and myself while always feeling just outside it. I will always be fascinated by seemingly inconsequential details and while my difference makes me strange back home in Britain – where people like me are made to feel like outsiders – in India, reminding myself that I have a stake in two worlds is what makes me able to love and respect them and absorb the details that simultaneously empower and disempower me. Knowing when to speak and knowing when to silently observe is a code that thousands of immigrants before me have learned to manoeuvre to their own end. For me, it will always be on the page where I find my voice most comfortably. I celebrate those who are more articulate than me, standing proud, and proclaiming their additional identities.

Walking onto the plane, as the hum of Anglo-Indian accents on each seat shuffles through the air alongside the many bags, I prepare to stow away my own language now I'm returning to my home in London, an adult again.

Returning home isn't so much reinforcing the crippling clean-cut duality of my identity, like writers have historically professed to feel, it's about how just how anomalous I am in both worlds. The plurality of my strangeness – of being split, of being Indian, too fresh, too Western, too bizarre, too independent, isn't as welcome as I hoped.

I see coming back to my village as significant, thanks to my privilege of being able to leave. But also because I can simultaneously cherry-pick my favourite aspects of my culture for anecdotes back home and social media, and keep the private, painful reflective ones for myself. This is what so many second-and-third generation immigrants experience visiting their homeland. We fine-tune the ability to find the nuances funny, deflecting the crushing weight of displacement and diaspora drama that becomes part of our everyday.

As we board, and I take my last look around the airport adverts of cosmetic creams selling 'lighter, brighter' skin, I think of every time I've made a joke about Fair'n'Lovely cream that has fallen flat because white colleagues have looked so horrified.

I learned quickly that there are certain jokes the white community can't ever really find funny because the punchline means wading through gasps of horror or sympathy, or worse, lengthy explanations whenever you make a quip about skin lightening, arranged marriage or hate crimes. Learning the comedic levels of rooms is part of the immigrant experience, and even going home reinforces how learned and Western mine is. I know when to keep quiet; keeping quiet is all part of the displacement and I think of how keeping your head down is a crucial physicality of the immigrant experience. When people bemoan this generation constantly craning their heads downwards on their phones, I can't help but think of all those heads looking down, avoiding trouble, not wanting to draw attention to themselves or their differences. Of my granddad and his friends keeping their eyes fixed on the floor – perhaps people just didn't notice it back then.

I feel the shudder of the plane's wheels hit the ground and I'm jolted, physically, back into action. My phone is accepting three weeks of WhatsApp messages and now the announcement is made in English first. The Bollywood film I'm watching is cut short and I'm looking out on to the gangway and the rain hits the tarmac and I wait in my seat, indulging in this no man's land of the plane before I'm forced to leave. The wind hits my face and I understand how people define these moments as poetic examples of duality – cold from hot, grey from colour. But for me, there is no neat duality, no cleanly sliced elements of my identity that are in opposition. There is no hollow insecurity about rootlessness because those additional details and stories I've learned are additions to our identity, not losses. Being aware of inadequacies or seeing your own strangeness through different eyes, gives us a wholeness that allows us to see the world with humour, nuance, and complexity. The notion of fragments is not what defines me – the gift my grandfather gave me was that his life as a good immigrant allowed me, generations later, to recognise the power and strength of that experience. We've never really been split, never been cut in half, we've just been silent about how we've been empowered because we haven't always felt it, have been too busy being good immigrants, not making a fuss, and quieting down when people felt uncomfortable. Rewriting the narrative of retracing our journeys has, for me, derailed those ideas of losing our internal battles of identity and cemented a simple fact – we've never had anything to lose, only everything to gain.

FLAGS

COCO KHAN

Letters, they were the key. As long as you could find a letter stating the address of the flat you'd found yourself in, you could call a taxi and sneak off without waking him, indeed without anyone ever knowing you'd been there.

That was a trick I learned with Felix – Felix with the peroxide hair so blonde it could (in the right light) appear to be a continuation of his porcelain skin. Blue-eyed Felix in the patent Dr. Martens and the MA1 jacket. I remember him distinctly: six-feet tall, ravenous roll-up smoker, aloof in demeanour but animated quickly by discussions about sculpture, which he was studying. I met him a few times, at various art shows – mutual friends, cursory chit-chat, nothing special.

When Felix and I eventually had sex, it was based on very little conversation. I like to imagine that it was my raw, potent animal power that did it – that the shirt with stains from breakfast made his heart skip a beat; that he watched me from across the room hovering around the canapé table and his loins stirred; that he once saw me pull up my ill-fitting jeans while balancing not just one, but two plastic cups of warm white wine and thought *now that is a woman of true brilliance.* But I suspect the free bar at the after-show party had something to do with it.

We had sex in the dark because the light bulb burst as soon as we switched it on. He offered to fix it but I said it didn't matter. After, Felix slept soundly but I tossed and turned. As dawn broke, light began to filter into the room, and for the first time I came to see, to learn, something personal about him.

He had flags, lots of flags. Union Jack flags everywhere, all over the room. Reality had jolted and the world was vibrating from the impact. Suddenly, the room felt blindingly bright, and claustrophobically small. One flag was tacked to the door, another took the form of a desktop mug crammed full of pens. Hung up on the rails was a button-down Union Jack shirt that felt like it had been pulled from a costume cupboard and, to my alarm and bewilderment, the very bed we lay on – a red, white and blue striped spread.

Between the shock, confusion and increasing alcohol withdrawal, my body began to turn. Only a shrill ringing filled my ears now, while piercing shards of glass made themselves present inside my head. *Who? Who? Who?* I kept asking myself, *Who is this person? Why wouldn't he mention them, didn't he know how they'd make me feel? Was that supposed to be a part of it? Is this a game, a fantasy, some imperial-themed kink that I didn't know about?*

The flags, the boots, the jacket – a terrifying thought began to dawn on me. *A skinhead. He's a skinhead, a stealth skinhead with hair. I thought he was an art student, that it was fashion not fascism …*

I pulled the covers off my body, quietly and slowly, and after putting on my dress, I gathered up my belongings and left.

By the time I hit 16, I felt I had gleaned everything about relationships I possibly could have from my immediate surroundings. E12 was a working-class neighbourhood, mixed racially but with more South Asians than most, and despite being part of London, it had a distinctly small-town feel – comforting and suffocating in equal measures.

From the adults in my community, I learned that sex was something to steer clear of unless it was within marriage (or you knew how to keep it a secret). From the kids at school – mostly other brown kids like myself – I learned that sex was something to steer clear of, unless you were a boy (or you knew how to keep it a secret). From Bollywood, I learned that men with handlebar moustaches are evil, that men in white linen flares are good, and that women were damned if they do, and damned if they don't, whatever the situation. In the background of all of this were the independent women of Destiny's Child and the guiltless hedonism of *Sex and the City*, which we weren't supposed to watch, but knew how to keep it secret.

Back then, I lacked confidence but felt at least that I was wise to the world. I was certain that, unlike many of my teenage friends who found themselves in difficult situations, I had a view of the bigger picture even though I'd had no practice. I understood men were allowed to be reckless and hurtful, but it was women who'd get the blame. It was always women who were made to hide. Strange how something so banal and everyday had become so powerful.

There was my best friend, Praveena, who, when she was 17, fell for an older man. He was 32 at the time, but she was young and naïve, not suspecting that this love could have been somewhat predatory. Praveena and the Predator had made a sex tape, which, in retrospect, should have been handed in to the police. Somehow this tape made its way into her brother's possession – and then her father's – and Praveena was told she would never be allowed out of the house unsupervised again until she was married.

For a long while, I would cover for Praveena and say she was studying at my house, when in fact we were out at some under-18's club night. Over the years, my own overprotective mother began to loosen up, and understood that I was a sensible girl who didn't need constant monitoring – not least because I kicked up quite the fuss if I was. Soon, she began to cover for us too, answering the house phone and speaking to Praveena's mum in Urdu – *yes the girls are studying hard, very hard indeed.*

I learned a lot from my mum. She came to the UK in an arranged marriage that was unhappy for many years. She divorced her husband, struggling to raise two children singlehandedly, and when she eventually found love, bore another child: me. My father didn't work out, and he had the privilege of returning to his old wife, scar free. I only found out many years later quite how burdensome it had been for my mother – people, sometimes even close relatives, made her feel ashamed for falling in love, and, I suppose, unwittingly, for bringing me into this world.

Although she never publicly approved of Praveena, or later, me, I know she had a quiet sympathy – a sympathy for women who dared to take a chance.

'I've decided to give it a go, this whole sex thing, I want to have a pop.'

'Right. Okay.'

I was talking to Stacey, my study buddy from Sixth-form College. Stacey was 18, and as fiery as her wavy red hair. She drove a distinctive purple Nissan Micra, which clashed marvellously with her appearance. She was always nipping around in that thing, getting speeding fines, making blowjob gestures at any rubberneckers at traffic nights. Stacey ended up dropping out of college when she fell pregnant. She and her entire family moved out of the neighbourhood before the baby was born – rumour had it, her boyfriend's father had paid them to leave, to hide them away somewhere.

'So where should I start?'

'You don't have to start, it just happens doesn't it? You just have to let it.'

For Stacey, maybe that was true. I wasn't – and never have been – the girl who walked into a room and made heads turn. I was always that little bit too short, too fat, too dark. Besides, I didn't want sex to be something that just happened to me, like a tragedy.

'Anyway, don't you want it to be special?'

'If I'm waiting for someone who is actually hot and awesome to just rock up and say they want me, I'm going to be waiting a while. Look, I don't want to go to uni next month as a virgin – I'll have my own place – I don't want it hanging over me; get it over with so I can have some fun. Mate, I'm a safe-sex evangelist, I know what I'm doing. Honestly I'm not going to make the same mistakes as everyone else but I don't see why I should miss out, life's too short.'

'Well, what about Sandeep? He's cute, you said you liked him. You can borrow my car if you want, just make sure you don't bring it back gross.'

'Is it bad to say that I really hope I'm good? You know, in bed. I really hope I'm a natural. I mean, how am I supposed to know what to do?'

'You don't have to know. They know. You just follow their lead'

'How do they know?'

'They just do, don't they? Dirty mags, I guess. And they talk, they're always talking about shagging. Listen, you'll be fine. Practice makes perfect.'

* * *

When I came back to London after university, I was cockier than ever. I'd learned a lot in those four years away. I'd learned how to flirt, how to party exceptionally hard, how to orgasm, and how to tell any man who was selfish, pressuring, or downright unwelcome to fuck off without a second thought.

I'd read a lot of books, fantastic books from heroic women who ventured into the darkest corners of humanity and returned with messages of equality and hope; working toward a day when sex would no longer be about power, about stealing something from someone else, but instead about shared joy. I wanted to have that joy in my life, on terms that suited me, and felt it was possible. I enjoyed my independence and my close female friendships; I wasn't scared to grow attached to the right man and some chance dalliances did develop into more formal relationships. As for the rejections, well they were all part of growing as a person.

I had life in the bag. I'd laugh thinking about the younger me, curled up like a pretzel in a Nissan Micra, so threatened by the hard cock in my hand, whispering soothing nothings at it as though it were a wild animal that could attack me at any moment. And the laughs kept coming, for years. The nocturnal life – bars, clubs, parties – were already silly enough without the unexpected thrill of meeting someone. I took great pride in regaling my friends with female-focused bedroom tales, stories that had no doubt been around for millennia but never seen the light of day. How else were we going to make sex equally ours if we didn't talk freely about it?

So I'm on top of this guy like a cowgirl champion. My belly's there, it's hanging out, and I'm like, swish-my-hair I don't care. But then, I'm not even joking, I start to get vertigo, like actual Alfred-Hitchcock-James-Stewart spinning around like a Spirograph

vertigo. Do you think too much wine can induce vertigo? Cowgirl,
down! Dismount!

Then, one day, it was talking freely that changed everything.

'So am I your first?'

'Was I that bad?!' I said laughing.

'No no, I mean, white boy. Am I your first white boy?' he
grinned widely.

'Afraid not. I've had all the races, and before you ask, yes
they were all better than you.'

He smiled genuinely. 'You're my first. I've only ever been
with white girls so I'm glad I have.'

I hadn't thought a great deal about the colour of my skin, or
theirs, but now I couldn't get it off my mind.

Is that why they want me?

I asked myself that question every day for weeks and months
after that, and not just about the white boys, but the black
boys, and even Asians like me. At first, I ignored it. What was
the big deal? How different was it really to any of the quick
judgement calls we make on who we fancy? But I felt uneasy,
and I couldn't shake the feeling. I wondered if he went back to
his friends and told the 'I shagged an Asian girl' story over the
'I had a great time last night' story.

I felt defeated.

I decided I had to take control of the situation. I tried for
a while to wear it like a badge of honour, imagining myself
as some kind of sexual crusader, breaking down stereotypes
with the power of banging. I took it seriously, like it was the
Olympics and my nation's hopes rested on my shoulders. I
took time to learn new sexy moves, and pulled many muscles
attempting some impossible tantric pose that no modern
human being could possibly do. On dates I would tolerate the
vaguely insulting stereotypical questions, patiently answering,

'No, I have never been promised to a man I've never met. Actually I can barely cook at all.'

Perhaps worse were the apologisers. The ones that were like, 'I just want to check, is this okay with you?' before watching an episode of *Homeland*.

Eventually, I couldn't take any of it anymore.

The first time I was called a paki, I was at primary school. I must have been around seven years old – eight maybe – and I was in the lunch hall queuing for school dinner. Somehow, an argument had broken out between me and another girl in my class, Amy. We were arguing about something completely meaningless (as children will do) when it came out. I'm not sure if she even knew what she was saying; she looked surprised as the words passed her lips – 'you are a paki'.

It was like time had stood still. Even at that age, I knew this was a step too far; up shot my hand, *Miss! Miss!* I called a dinner lady over. Now, this dinner lady was more a dinner nan; a grey-haired, older woman, who must have been hard of hearing because, when I told her that Amy had called me a paki, she replied in complete earnestness, in her thick East End accent, and said: *she called you a packet? A packet of what, love?*

After that, I didn't hear the word again until I found it spray-painted on the side of our house: 'Pakis go home, NF'. I always found it mildly amusing that they signed their name. Why? As though we wouldn't know who it was? Just in case we mistook it for the racially themed high jinks we brown people were always up to.

Days later, my older brother and some of his friends frogmarched a scrawny, trembling white teenage boy to our house. He was the culprit and he was here to apologise.

'It was a dare,' he said. 'I didn't mean it, I'm sorry.'

'Let him go,' said Mum. 'Can't you see he's crying? He's just a child.'

He couldn't have been more than 13, he had those awkward teen proportions where the hands and feet are huge, but the rest of the body hasn't caught up.

He was a skinhead but he wasn't scary. Indeed, there was something strikingly clown-like about him – huge cherry-red Dr Martens, strangely high-waisted trousers, braces, shirt buttoned up to the top. As he scooted off he turned back to me before he'd disappeared around the corner and, raising his arm, did a Nazi salute. Then, he was gone.

I didn't expect to see Felix ever again, but he was hard to miss. He was tall, and his hair was unmistakable. He didn't seem pleased to see me, but he did remember who I was, which was something. Maybe I *was* the only non-Aryan he lured back to his flag dungeon after all.

We exchanged courtesies, talked sculpture, he rolled up two cigarettes, put one behind his ear and held the other out to me, saying, 'I can't remember if you smoke or not.'

Outside, we sat on the curb and smoked. He joked that I could have left a note and I explained truthfully that his whole flag get-up was nothing short of terrifying.

'As if you wouldn't have just fucking stayed, and actually asked me about it.' He paused, catching the expression on my face. 'I do understand. I know the flag's a bit, you know, sensitive, and maybe I should have said something. I'm sorry if I intimidated you. No, I definitely should have said something but hey, I was drunk and distracted by the hot girl in my room.' He leaned over and bumped his shoulder against mine. 'You know there wasn't a moment when I was hanging those flags and I thought, Well I wonder what would happen if there was an Asian person in this room? To be honest I didn't think there was going to be any girls in that room at all.'

'So you're not extremely right-wing with a Kryptonite for weird but-notably-babe-ish Asian girls that is secretly tearing you up inside?'

'Ha, no. My dad was a punk in the 70s – and not a racist one – so we always had flags in our house. I brought them to the flat because they remind me of home, that's all.'

A queue was beginning to form at the door now. The bar was getting busier, the music sounding louder and louder each time the door swung open.

'I guess I should apologise too maybe. I'm sorry I didn't give you the chance to explain. I had this really weird experience a few months before we hooked up where this dude basically told me he was happy that I was Asian and it really freaked me out –'

'Yeesh'

'– I don't know, did he want me to be grateful or something, that he chose me? Did it make him feel better about himself that he was a cool, right-on guy? You know, I just want to have some fun, while I'm young and I don't have a mortgage or kids or whatever, but there's always something, some bullshit thing, that turns whatever could just be really cool, into something horrible. And you know, I do want to keep meeting people and having fun, whether it's a one-off thing or something more, I'm open to what life wants to give me. But that comment, it's just ruining it for me. I'm always thinking, does this person actually want me or am I a brown-shaped thing that will do? It's a real mood-killer to say the least. I wish I could just find a way to know for sure'

'Can I make a suggestion?'

'Is your suggestion getting a taxi and going back to your punk palace, because if it is, I'm up for it?'

'Ah see, I don't think my girlfriend will like that very much. But, I was going to say, why don't you try *talking* to the guys, getting to know them for real—'

'I've tried that and it's even worse, so many stupid, shitty questions—'

'Well then, don't keep talking to them if they're douchebags. If you want to engage 'cos they're nice but a bit daft then cool but if you don't want to, then don't. It's not your job to try and correct everything. We should go inside, the bouncer is getting angry.'

'No, I think I'm going to go home. Would you be really offended if I said I hope I never see you again?'

'Why?'

'Because you're great and I feel annoyed at myself for disappearing.'

His eyes smiled. 'Okay, well tell you what, I'll disappear now, and we're even. Just make sure you remember what I said.'

'Sounds good.'

I gathered up my handbag and put on my coat slowly, watching him as he put out his cigarette. He shook my hand, formally like at the end of a job interview, and with a perfunctory 'yes, sir' nod clicked his heels together theatrically. He walked through the entrance and turning back just before the door closed behind him gave me a wink. Then, he was gone.

CUTTING THROUGH (ON BLACK BARBERSHOPS AND MASCULINITY)

INUA ELLAMS

*If Africa was a bar, what would your country be drinking/
doing?*
– @SiyandaWrites

Last year, Botswanan writer Siyanda Moutsiwa tweeted a
'classic writing prompt' designed for workshops on character
interaction. 50,000 tweets later, #IfAfricaWasABar was
trending. The answers came in thick, fast, vicious, tragic,
insightful, insulting and illuminating. It shed an unashamed
light on African geopolitics, on what Africans thought of other
Africans, what they thought about Europeans and finally, on a
project I had started two years before.

*#IfAfricaWasABar Europeans would spike all the drinks
then sell antidotes to everyone at a later date.*
– @ChetoManji

When I became an immigrant and left Nigeria aged 12, my
father and I began cutting each other's hair. We lived in Dublin,
where whenever I followed my white Irish friends to get their

haircuts, I'd see panic cross the faces of their barbers who had little or no experience of cutting African hair. I learned not to ask. I'd sit, watching the business conducted in almost absolute silence. Everything changed when we moved to Peckham in London and I came across the familiar bastions of masculinity that are African and Caribbean barbershops. Late into the night, light would pour out of glass-fronted shops stuffed full of Afro/Caribbean men holding court and I dived back into that world. I discovered conversation of the broadest nature, from football to parenting, Creole languages to nutrition and I started writing 'Barbershop Chronicles' – a play about what African men inside them talked about. A month into it and I wanted to go bigger, to see if conversation on the continent mirrored conversation here, to see what indigenous Africans thought about us in the diaspora, and what Africans thought of other Africans. I left England and travelled to South Africa, Zimbabwe, Kenya, Uganda, Nigeria and Ghana and #IfAfricaWasABar brought my findings into sharp focus.

South Africa

In 2013, two days after Nelson Mandela died, I arrived in Johannesburg. Africa's most respected statesman, mythic and legendary figure, most esteemed father, had passed and the country was in shock. The men I spoke with talked of nothing else. Their emotions ranged from loss at his death, to disgust at his portrayal, to frustration that he died without seeing his 'rainbow nation', to suspicion at backroom deals he might have made for peace. They believed South Africa was still gripped by apartheid and mentioned a study released the previous year, which found that 40 per cent of white South Africans didn't think apartheid was wrong. Millie, a writer and art director I met, explained that the demons of the regime were never exorcised. After it was abolished, the generations of men who had been emasculated, called 'boy' under the regime, who came forward with stories of kidnapped, maimed or murdered family members, were told to forgive and forget. The Truth and Reconciliation Commission was set up in such a way that all the perpetrators had to do was come forward and apologise. Not many came forward, and of those who did, not many apologised.

'They never got to get mad and no one was held accountable,' Millie said. 'This is why crime is so violent in South Africa, why we are the rape capital of the world.'

Millie believed deep-seated mental health issues have only calcified and festered and this frustration is taken out on women.

Andile, a travelling IT Consultant, talked about how alcoholism was rife in the 'coloured' community he came from. His ancestors worked vineyards for white South Africans and were not paid in money or food, but in barrels of wine, which left a thirst for alcohol in his blood. Every single member of his family suffered and complete abstinence was his only cure.

I met Shoni who took me to Yeoville, the most multi-ethnic neighbourhood in sub-Saharan Africa. Walking, we heard a mixture of tongues: languages from Cameroon, Ghana, Zimbabwe, Tanzania, Nigeria, Malawi, Jamaica, Trinidad and Zambia spliced with South African ones: Zulu, Afrikaans and Xhosa. The following year, a spate of xenophobic killings would grip the nation. Marching mobs, protesting immigration, would kill seven black immigrants from other African countries, echoing 2008's outbreak where 67 were killed. At the time, I knew nothing of the events of 2008 and couldn't have predicted the future, but I left South Africa with the impression that it was a melting pot of ideas: deeply African in traditional ways, yet so deeply marked by inherited British elitism that it looked down on other African nations – even as it sought to unify its 12 tribes under one identity.

> *#IfAfricaWasABar South Africa would be drinking all kinds of alcohol and begging them to get along in its stomach.*
> – @SiyandaWrites

Zimbabwe

I was meant to travel to Harare, but hadn't been granted a visa. I resolved to interview Zimbabwean barbers and clients in Jo'burg. They were everywhere: when sanctions were placed on Zimbabwe because of President Mugabe's violent land reform programmes, three million Zimbabweans fled to South Africa. Dwain, a musician, explained that this, and Zimbabwean conservatism, were the reasons why he left – there wasn't a market for the music he wished to make. Now, everything had changed.

After I explained the project, he guessed I wasn't granted a visa because of my job.

'Uncle Bob … (the affectionate name for Robert Mugabe),' he told me, 'doesn't trust writers from the West. They always lying, exaggerating about him.'

He added that I'd have had problems finding barbers and clients anyway because dreadlocks are BIG in Zimbabwe: men are growing, not cutting locks. In 1980, after bloody battles defeating imperialism and British Rule, Bob Marley sang at their Independence Day celebration. That sowed a legacy and culture of Rastafarianism, which Dwain said, 'is all about spirituality, consciousness and self-pride. This is why we respect Uncle Bob now … he stands for consciousness and self-pride.'

I thought back to Mandela's burial, which had been aired live on South African television. Of the politicians, heads of state, presidents, vice presidents, royalty and dignitaries in attendance, Mugabe got the loudest, longest, most rapturous applause.

'This is because South Africans recognised he succeeded where Mandela failed: getting land back.' Dwain believed that Zimbabweans were natural farmers. In the neighbourhood in which he was born, most grew their own food with their bare hands. 'This is why losing land to colonisers was a big deal, why winning it back meant so much.'

Dwain introduced himself as one of the 'born frees' who grew up in a free Zimbabwe. He had turned from hip-hop to Chimurenga music. Chimurenga is the Shona word for 'struggle' harking back to the battles and liberation of the seven tribes of his country. As he spoke, the pride of surviving those times shook like a knife in his voice, sharpening his words.

#IfAfricaWasABar Zimbabwe would be telling stories about how it fought the bouncers to get inside.
– @TheGaryCahill

Kenya

I landed in a half-empty Nairobi, three days before Christmas. Though English and Swahili are the official languages of Kenya, Sheng, which I'm not versed in, is the language of gossip. It was difficult to find barbers and clients I could speak with, but after two days I found Ian.

Ian asked, 'Who discovered Mount Kenya?'. I said I didn't know. 'Kenyan textbooks will tell you that a German missionary, Johann Krapf, discovered Mount Kenya. How is that possible when my ancestors had been grazing cattle there for centuries? There are 42 tribes in Kenya, you think not a single one of us looked up and thought *That's a very big hill, let's go check it out.* We need to reform our entire educational system and teach an Afrocentric syllabus.'

The conversation turned to two new government laws. One he called the 'Madonna Law', after the pop star famously adopted a Malawian orphan, introduced tougher regulations for foreigners wishing to adopt Kenyan orphans. Allegations of child-trafficking were rife. The second was regarding business, demanding that 30 per cent of government contracts be awarded to women, young and disabled people.

'Already, she, I mean women, are running around Nairobi with big ideas and contracts, but she doesn't have the capacity to do the job,' he said.

He feared that domestic Kenyan life would suffer, society would crumble and men would loose their standing in their own families. He felt Kenya was not prepared for this change. As he spoke, I got the fleeting sense that the 'she' he mentioned was none other than his own wife. We talked for four solid hours after the shop had shut, and he seemed reluctant to return home.

Two days later, I journeyed to a barbershop in the 'Calif' neighbourhood, where evidence of new businesses were everywhere.

In celebration of Barak Obama's Kenyan roots, there were buildings named 'Barak Bakery', 'Obama's Corner', 'Obama's Barber' and 'Yes We Can Limited'. Conversations were wild … everything from Kenyan witchcraft versus Nigerian witchcraft, to love-potions, adequate punishment for rapists, 'acceptable' bestiality, cross-border travel, and the strength of the Kenyan shilling against the Ugandan shilling. There was also pride in Kenya's ability to attract Chinese investments, who, the barbers commented, were becoming the forty-third tribe of Kenya.

If the South Africans were searching for their identity and Zimbabweans proud of liberating theirs, the Kenyans were celebrating new wealth, enterprise and global recognition.

> *#IfAfricaWasABar Kenya would be the loud 'new money' drunk, telling everyone about his cousin Barack who done made it in the States.*
> – @ShikoNguru

Uganda

I travelled to Uganda next. Compared to South Africans, Kenyans were a chilled-out folk. Compared to Ugandans, Kenyans were absolute firecrackers. Ugandans seemed to stride with a deep and lengthy leisure through all aspects of life, such that at the airport, I felt like I was merely queuing at a supermarket.

In the first few days, the taxi driver from the airport and Patricia of the British Council painted a picture of the linguistic landscape in Uganda. The driver said that whereas 100 per cent of Kenyans speak Swahili, only 30 per cent of Ugandans did. He spoke proudly, as though it elevated them above the Kenyans. Patricia added that during the Liberation War between Uganda and Tanzania, Idi Amin distrusted government officials who'd been educated in England and spoke English better than he did. He deposed a lot of them,

gave their jobs to those he trusted and insisted duties of office
be executed in Swahili. Those years were brutal and after the
war Swahili became synonymous with military dictatorship, so,
the people rebelled and chose English as their official language
but spoke mostly in their tribal tongues.

My contact was Dre, a soft-spoken, loose-limbed starving
artist who had an interest in etymology. He explained that of
the 56 tribes in the country, the Buganda (hence the country's
name) are the largest.

He told me, 'Baganda' is the plural for 'Muganda', which is
what you call a lone Bugandan, and 'Luganda' is their language.

Easy.

I tracked down a shop with a magnificently welcoming
barber called Simon. Where the South Africans searched for
their identity, Zimbabweans proud of liberating theirs, Kenyans
were celebrating wealth, the Ugandans overwhelmingly spoke
of romance and its complications.

Simon was flabbergasted when he discovered that as a
Nigerian, I didn't have two girlfriends and almost kicked me
out of his shop when I admitted I didn't have a single one.

He had two, suspected that not only did they know of each
other, they were fine with it. Jackson, a handsome 22-year-old
model chimed in, detailing his girlfriends, but the most in-
depth conversation was with Mark, who explained that neither
did he believe in nor 'love' his wife. He believed in 'Godly' love
– love for orphans, animals, the disabled etc., but romantic or
'Human' love deposed objective thinking, which he believed
was foolish and dangerous to marriages.

Weeks before, the government had passed a law giving
the death penalty to homosexuals and weeks later, the death
penalty clause would be substituted with life imprisonment.
At the time, when I raised the topic, the clientele echoed the

sentiment that it wasn't the Ugandan way, that it threatened the dowry system, which was still part of society.

Mark, who did not 'love' but deeply respected and cherished his wife, had paid sixty cows for her. The men explained that marriages were the only opportunities fathers had to gain back some of costs of raising a child; husbands paid for daughters. If men married each other or women married each other, there'd be no one paying for anyone and wouldn't everything fall apart?

#IfAfricaWasABar Uganda is the guy getting really angry that two girls are kissing across the room.
– @ImranGarda

Nigeria

Because I was travelling to my own homeland, I did no preparation whatsoever. I expected to naturally synchronise with its barbershop culture, for it to embrace its prodigal son. As soon as the plane touched down in Lagos, I noticed two things. One, West African heat must be some brand of hellfire – unrelenting and merciless compared to the East's – and, two, the people.

Nigerians are crazy – a different breed of African man. Never before has the East–West divide been so apparent to me. The sheer breakneck speed of Lagos life and the feeling that everything is happening simultaneously ... isn't a feeling. It is real. There are 371 tribes in the country, 500 languages spoken, which makes sense of why so much doesn't quite work in Lagos.

I stayed on Victoria Island among the rich elite. During the first three days, my internal compass evaporated under the heat and the poor directions I was given. When I finally found barbershops and collapsed into the chairs exhausted, I discovered the barbers refused to talk unless I paid them, and rich clients thinking themselves too good to converse, remained resolutely silent.

Wole, the lone contact I had in the theatre industry, took me to the spots he knew but they were either staffed by non-English speakers or barbers who, without payment dismissed the project. On one of the dejected rides back to the hotel, I asked why 'This House Is Not For Sale' was spray-painted on so many properties. Wole explained that Nigerian conmen had perfected a way of breaking into and selling properties when their owners holidayed. The writing on the wall was the only sure way of safeguarding homes.

'419 …' he added – the moniker for Nigerian con men – '… refers to section 419 of the Nigerian Criminal Code which deals with obtaining property by false pretences.'

On my last day, I poured my woes into the open ears of Wallace, the driver who taxied me to the airport. He patiently listened, feigned annoyance that I hadn't called him and without missing a beat, did his best to portray barbershop culture on the mainland where he and the working class lived. It was a whole other world. Men come specifically to talk, food hawkers come by to feed clients, and because of the constant lack of electricity, boys in the hood come to charge their phones. In the darkness of Nigerian nights, they're the only places with electricity, they glow, literally, like beacons of the community where 'men come to be men,' Wallace told me.

As the plane took off, I remembered something Wole said. 'There are phrases you see when arriving in major cities, "Welcome to LA" a billboard will say, "Welcome to London" another, but ours reads "This is Lagos".' It is a statement. Its subtext is "Enter at your own peril", "Sink or Swim", or as Wallace put it: 'Hustle or die'.

I can't fault that mentality, it is relentless and enterprising.

#IfAfricaWasABar Nigeria would own it.
– @MduThaParty

Ghana

On landing in Accra, I noticed the country felt like the older, calmer, wiser brother to hot-headed Nigeria, as though it had harmonised its 70 tribes where we had failed desperately. Because there is a healthy rivalry between the two countries, as a Nigerian, it pains me to say this.

The first two days were spent with Aunty Mary, a friend's mother, who embraced me as her own, and the rest of the week I stayed with a mentor and his family, so perhaps the cumulative effect of their domestic lives slowed me down. I was no longer a travelling bachelor. I was a surrogate son in one house, a new uncle in the other. Whatever it was, something had changed. I found barbershops easily and the best one within walking distance of the house. The conversations were not of business, politics, infidelity or crime, but of family, language and fatherhood. A client recounted a childhood memory involving his father. Another, the beauty of the Ga language. An experienced father gave advice on raising daughters to a new father. A linguist talked on similarities of pidgin languages.

'It takes a whole village to raise 'is child' is one of the many sayings indicative of the nature of African communities. It points to the deeply socialist structures many were built on before colonisation and capitalism changed them. Of all the cities I'd visited, this philosophy seemed most alive in Accra, such that it had inhabited Christianity and localised it. Aunt Mary was in the church business. On the first day, Ebo, who worked for her, asked if I'd accompany him on his morning errands. It involved visiting a church Aunt Mary was building. I jumped in the taxi and minutes later, we stood before an unpainted concrete structure the size of a small sports stadium. Inside lay high-tech sound systems, pulpits and podiums for preachers, a broad stage with a cascading blue curtain, magnificent natural light through slits cut in the roof and large windows for cross-ventilation. It sat four thousand people comfortably. A primary school was attached to one side of the church, architectural plans for a secondary school had just been completed, and behind lay a small but rapidly expanding shop. Ebo explained about the financial ecosystem built into the church, those it employs, the lives it supports, how vital it'd become to the neighbourhood, how, some Sundays, so many attend that they set up a canopy and cinema screen to relay the service to those standing outside.

#IfAfricaWasABar Ghana would be that guy who gets drunk and starts – for some reason – talking about how much God loves us all.
– @SiyandaWrites

England

One night in Battersea a young actor entered the barbershop and admitted he doubted he'd get the role he'd just auditioned for. We asked what the role was.

He said, 'Black man.'

'Anything else?' I asked.

'Strong black man,' he said and continued that he doubted he fitted the director's concept of 'black' masculinity.

I asked what his concept was, he said he didn't have one. I claimed this was his problem, until he asked if anyone really had a definite grasp on what 'black' was, or 'masculinity', for that matter. We failed to answer him then, and I fail still, but travelling had given me a broader sense of the issue.

The term 'Black' was employed by African Americans as both a political and socially conscious alternative to 'negro' (or the much darker *nigger*). It was as an act of defiance, self-identification, and as a way to distance themselves from the 'African' label, which had abundantly negative connotations at the time. Nowadays, the label is used for darker-skinned people of sub-Saharan descent everywhere: in the Americas, Asia, Europe and on the Africa continent itself. In Europe where whiteness is the default, blackness stands in contrast and any race is 'other'. On the African continent, not only is blackness NOT the default, given North Africans who are generally lighter-skinned, but blackness isn't the default in all sub-Saharan countries; countries like South Africa, Angola, Namibia or Zambia have large British, French or German communities. In the countries I visited that have a greater percentage of 'black' nationals, the concerns, motivations and emotions of the men I met differed, not just from country to country, but within countries, along tribal and socio-economic lines – differences so sharp and clear they had become stereotypes. Dividing them along tribal lines, those six countries alone break down to 558 different types of 'black' men. 'Black' men from all 54 African countries live in England, so even a conservative estimate would put a least 1,000 different types of them in the country.

England is also home to 'black' men from the various

Caribbean Islands, from North and South America, as well as 'black' men born in England, who have never touched African soil … men of different tribes, temperaments, natures, political and socio-economic backgrounds and beliefs. Despite these obvious nuances, phrases like 'black-on-black crime' or 'black community' are used to suggest a monolith and when there are disagreements within said monolith, it is portrayed as dysfunctional, rebellious, animalistic and mutinous. The African continent is so vast the land can hold Portugal, Spain, Belgium, France, Germany, Switzerland, Italy, Eastern Europe, India, United States, China, Japan and the United Kingdom at the same damn time. As we know the earliest human, 'Lucy', was found in Ethiopia, it's safe to say inhabitants of these countries and all of humanity came from sub-Saharan Africa, that sub-Saharan Africans are genetically coded with all of humanity's assemblage, that they contain all hues, variations and cultures: eye shape, pupil colour, hair texture, hip thickness, bone density, finger width, tongue and skin tone. To put it mildly then, it is insulting, reductive, counter-productive, lazy, disingenuous and deeply, deeply, deeply, problematic to attach a single label – one of Western invention as a shield against racism, one as porous a description of skin pigmentation, as 'black' – to a group of people so vastly varied and numerous. Whenever we beg for nuances, for our differences to be articulated, for more diversity and accuracy in how our communities are described, in the characters written for 'black' actors on stage, on television, or in film, our voices are either silenced or ignored.

#IfAfricaWasABar there would be a load of groupies hanging around outside claiming they know what's going on inside better than the bar staff.
– @fil

WEARING WHERE YOU'RE AT: IMMIGRATION AND UK FASHION

SABRINA MAHFOUZ

I thought you'd be, you know, darker ... You don't look at all how I imagined ... Well, I have to say, I thought you'd look more, ha ha, I suppose, foreign ... You look a bit, English though ... It's quite a relief you're, well, you know ...

These comments were spoken by different people of different backgrounds at different times of my life, but put together they could easily be one continuous musing by a confused person on what it means to have a name that indicates non-whiteness, but a skin tone that indicates a happy harmony with the politically and economically dominant racial group of the previous few centuries. There is so much to delve into from this that it would require another essay with a different focus. What I'd like to particularly point out from it for the purposes of this piece are two things. Firstly, that the way whiteness is defined seems to differ person to person, country to country. Many people from North Africa and the Middle East regard themselves as white, whilst stating that there are also black people of that nationality. In Egypt, for example, those who have a darker skin tone and more of a sub-Saharan African physiognomy may be called 'Black Egyptians' by other Egyptians who, if pressed, would self-classify as 'White Egyptians' – even though they themselves would most certainly be regarded as a non-white ethnic minority in a white majority country such as the UK or USA. It is interesting to note that the classifying seems to be done by those with lighter pigmentation. This is a direct colonial legacy of course, encouraging racial divides and appealing to those with a lighter skin tone to self-classify as white in order to create feelings of superiority and aspirations of assimilation into the politically dominant race, which they are not recognised as being once outside of their locality. The first existing documentation on racial classification was François Bernier's, written in 1684. Bernier divides all of humankind into four racial groups – calling those who live in Europe, North Africa, South Asia as well as the Native Americans to be of the same race, whilst sub-Saharan Africans were another, as were the Lapp race (indigenous people from Lapland area). The Central, South and South East Asians were the final category.[42] This 'typological model' influenced later anthropologists such as Johann Friedrich Blumenbach who created explicitly racist theories, which in turn influenced the eugenics movement and the persistence of the slave trade. Although these theories, and Bernier's simplistic classification system, are thankfully now wholly discredited, we can see from the self-classifications of Egyptians, as mentioned above, that this original theory still permeates the consciousness of people. There are those who would narrow these outdated categories even further. I have had conversations with educated people

---

42 Siep Stuurman, 'François Bernier and the Invention of Racial Classification', *History Workshop Journal*, Issue 50 (Autumn 2000), 1–21.

of all ethnicities in the UK who truly believe that if someone is not black, then they are white and vice versa. This narrow and negating dual classification tool has been promulgated so that people are unwittingly encouraged to choose 'sides' and discouraged from regarding race as something unfixed and far more complex than many seem ready to admit. I see this as a huge societal issue that can only be dismantled by constant discussion, hence my inclusion of it here, even though it could be argued to sit slightly outside of the remit I have set myself. However, as this is an essay that talks of race throughout, I'd ask the reader to bear in mind the above and to note that despite the imperfection of all classification systems, I will be using the classification of whiteness throughout which relates mainly to Northern and Central European ancestry.

The second aspect of the above I'd like to pluck apart is my own discomfort at feeling as if I don't meet people's expectations of what somebody from 'somewhere else' should look like. This reclassification of my identity by others has often made me feel guilty that I have this background, and even more so that I am connected to and highly interested in it. It is part of our endemic racism that we immediately attribute the experience of otherness to somebody who fulfils what otherness is supposed to aesthetically be. Whilst I appreciate that any negative experiences of otherness are exacerbated if you *do* occupy that aesthetic, it is part of the problem if we do not accept, or expect, diverse heritage experiences from those who don't conform to our inherited and constructed ideas of what 'diversity' looks like.

I am a bit white. I'm part-Danish and part-English via Wales. I'm also as much part-Amerindian and Madeiran Guyanese. But the largest part of my heritage is Egyptian, which is where the Arabic Muslim surname comes from and why some of the (openly pleased) people quoted at the start of this piece thought I would look 'more foreign'.

I have seen these surprised smiles enough to know I am not in a position to complain about my ability to assimilate into the cold embrace of dominance due to my pale skin tone; but on a micro level, I think that whenever anyone questions your identity, you have the right to get a bit pissed off and on a macro level, what this questioning represents is problematic, as I've already talked about. What I've found interesting and worrying in varying degrees is the extent to which my ethnic identities can be validated, dismissed, or even prove offensive to others in the UK, just from me wearing a particular piece of clothing, arguably a luxury others who look 'less white' don't ever get.

I'll share a couple of examples. My Egyptian great-grandmother and my Guyanese great-grandmother both wore headwear in styles reflective of the country and time they were in. My Egyptian great-grandmother wore a thin, silky turban of sorts, with a costume jewel in the middle, fashionable but conservative in the days when not many middle-class women in Egypt covered their heads. She was a practicing Muslim, but in those days this did not mean what it often does today in terms of Egyptian women's attire. She chose it partly because her husband was an active Islamic scholar and both of them felt more comfortable if she covered her head in public, as they were often attending places of worship and religious importance. The other factor was that despite Egypt being credited with the emergence of the turban thousands of years ago, it had unexpectedly become globally fashionable in the 1950s, so she was doubly happy. My Guyanese great-grandmother wore colourful cotton scarves tied up around the front of her head in little knots, a style that those with African heritage had popularised in the country, many of whom she had grown up with in the city orphanage as a mixed-up, light-eyed child, nobody would take in.

Waiting at the bus stop in South London one day, I was wearing a black turban similar to the style my Egyptian great-grandmother wore. I hardly knew her, but I have always been more comfortable with my head covered, albeit not in a traditionally religion-specific style. When living in Cairo for a few years of my life at various times and whilst exploring aspects of my faith, I have worn hijab, but in London I have always worn a wide variety of head coverings. On this particular turban-wearing day, a white English man came up to me just before I stepped onto the bus, pointed at my head-covering and shouted, '*All Muslims should die*', before scurrying away to dissolve in the acid of his hatred (hopefully). I am well aware that this is light conversation compared to what Muslim women wearing hijab or niqab have to face every day in this country. But it astounded me, as it always does, that somebody could be driven to such vociferousness by a piece of cloth and the 'difference' this might represent.

Another day, once again in south London, but this time *on* a bus (all of this is making me think I should probably just save up for a car), I was wearing a headscarf similar to the ones my Guyanese great-grandmother used to wear. Two girls who appeared to be of mixed heritage behind me were loudly complaining about '*white people wearing black people's headscarves like a trend*' and stared at me pointedly when their stop came along and they left the bus. I understand appropriation is a very real, very sinister thing. Cultures who are left devastated by Western power and policies – in some cases almost entirely annihilated by them (such as the Aboriginal and Native American peoples) – are constantly used as sources to 'inspire' fashion trends and art of all kinds.[43] At the same time, in the case of this scenario, I feel strongly that headscarves are not owned by one culture and, even if they were, what the comment made by the young women highlights again is this problematic assumption of an individual's heritage based purely on an aesthetic they appear to fulfil. Maybe I should have said all of this to them through the open window. But I didn't because I was busy playing a game on my phone and let's be honest, confrontation on London transport is always better as a 'shoulda woulda coulda'.

Except for the one time on a night bus to Lewisham around 12 years ago, when I heard two drunk, young, white men abuse two much younger black men at the back of the top deck. There were quite a few passengers, but they all stared ahead. I got up and told them to leave it out. I was wearing a faux snakeskin pink biker jacket from Morgan (don't, I know). Both of the young men left the boys at the back and came swaggering towards me. As one of them started taking his belt off to presumably threaten to hit me with or take down his jeans more efficiently, the other one provided the commentary.

'*You think you're fucking J. Lo, don't you?*', he said, pointing at my jacket.

The upside of this distraction caused by my dubious fashion choice was that the other boys ran off the bus unbothered.

Meanwhile, I was trying to simultaneously figure out why my wanting to be J. Lo in a snakeskin jacket (which I didn't, I really only ever listened to UK Garage) made him so angry he was ready to unleash a belt buckle into my face. I was saved

---

43 See Kristin Knox's *Culture to Catwalk* (London, Bloomsbury, 2011), for numerous contemporary examples of fashion appropriation.

by a tannoy announcement that the driver was recording what was going on and the two racists rushed down the stairs, out of the doors and on their merry way. That story, though loosely related, was a slight detour on what is basically a wondering on my part as to both fashion's impact on the identity of immigrants and the children of immigrants in the UK and the impact of immigration on current British fashions.

I asked the two direct immigrants in my family – my granddad (from Guyana) and my dad (from Egypt) – to tell me what they could recall about their experience with British fashion when entering the country as an outsider.

My granddad arrived in Hartlepool in the 1950s on a merchant navy ship that had set sail from Guyana, shown the young Pedro the metropolis of New York and the arbitrary aggression of the open ocean. It was due to carry on around the globe, but my granddad hired a moped and decided he liked the sights he saw around the north of England.

There were the ladies, in their stilettos, nipped-in waists and flouncy skirts. He had Ray-Bans, Hawaiian shirts and could freestyle on the bongo drums. This made him an instant celebrity in the foggy streets of the North-East. There were just enough Caribbean immigrants in the area for him to have allies and understanding, but not too much competition when it came to novelty.

Flip-flops were the items he remembers as having the biggest shock factor. Now one of the most-worn items of footwear in the warmer months, in the 1950s British people were as likely to be seen in them as they were to move to Germany. My grandma, from the North-east of England with Welsh heritage, could never fully get over his apparent disregard for the looks people gave him if they went to the pub and he had his toes out. He says he did it *for* the looks, his toes were freezing and anyway, he preferred winkle-pickers, a British fad he discovered after a few nights out in Newcastle.

My dad arrived in Britain in the 1980s, having already married my mum in Cairo. He was subjected to months of interrogation and mockery of his marriage to a British woman before he was granted temporary citizenship. He wanted to fit in. But not with the fuddy-duddy pen pushers who made up the majority in the south London suburb where he lived, oh no. He wanted to fit in with the fashion crowd, with the young ones living it up in one of the coolest cities in the world. He might have been married, but he was in his early twenties and his love of the disco life was made of strong stuff (it still is).

It's likely he funded the entire leather jacket industry at the time and he was certainly a fan of the plain white T-shirt. He stocked up on Levi's and loafers; he left the socks in the drawer. One thing he couldn't get on board with though, was the clean-cut coiffed hair look. He had the moustache and slight beard of Cairo movie stars and he removed them for nobody, not even the Home Office.

A country wears where it is at. Most people can visit a place and, after seeing a few dozen passers-by, make a judgement based on the fashions being worn about a number of cultural, social and political aspects of that place, whether they're conscious of doing this or not. They may be wrong – that's the tricky thing with judgements after all, they're no science. For example, standing at Old Street Underground station entrance on a Thursday at 8.30am and the first groups of people that pass by have smart suits on, but they wear backpacks and more casual shoes than brogues and stilettos. They have scarves on. I can make a judgement based on those simple observations that this area is business-orientated but slightly more casual and youthful in approach than Westminster or Mayfair and it's cold outside. These judgements may be partly right, but stand in the same spot at 9pm and the people I observe are wearing party clothes, many of them outside of the mainstream, metallic trousers and neon glasses, multiple piercings and bubble coats. This could lead me to think the area is one full of bars, clubs and somewhere more alternative than, say, the West End. Again, this would be partly true, though not the whole story. Most of us like to imagine our individuality is reflected in our style and reveals nothing about the system we are inextricably linked to, but of course it does.

So is what the UK's wearing today related in any way to immigration?

Yes.

Even in the most mundane high street stores you'll see colours, fabrics and styles that have been taken from every part of the globe. The ones that are popular here are often ones that originate from the very places that have a large diaspora in the UK.

Indian embroidery, East African beaded jewellery, Caribbean colour palettes, North African styles such as the kaftan, West African prints – the list continues. In no way does this mean the people from these diasporas are the ones buying (or making) these things, but it does indicate how these groups have heavily influenced what is perceived as 'British style' today. A quick Google image search shows plenty of the above included in the visual definition of 'British style', alongside a multitude of well-tailored jackets, tartan patterns and twinsets.

Of course, nothing can be called 'British' without including the huge array of cultural influences that make Britain what it is, but sometimes that is not what it feels like. The rhetoric around the term 'British' insidiously attempts to equate it with a pre-multicultural England (whenever that was, seeing as North Africans were guarding Hadrian's Wall nearly 2,000 years ago, but whatever) that owes its celebrated arts, style and 'values' to nothing and nobody except the ancient British families and their rambling estates that get rolled out for every period drama.

Despite this grievance with the whitewashing of British history, I readily admit it's not only elsewhere that has inspired British fashion. It also works the other way around. Many immigrants came to the UK, were inspired by the fashions they found here and integrated these into their existing wardrobe – resulting in London in particular being world-renowned for some of the most exciting and eccentric clothing combinations.

However, by not widely acknowledging the influence immigrant groups and individuals have had on UK fashion, we allow the story of colonial superiority in all realms to perpetuate.

I see fashion as the cultural crystal ball, an immediacy reflecting what will later be seen in other art forms, once the artists have had time to filter the nuance and the nausea into a cohesive piece of work.

Fashion-makers (and in this I include designers, printmakers, sewers, pattern-cutters, and others I don't have the expertise to credit) are driven by a practical need, as well as a creative and financial one; to create things that people can wear. They don't always have time to filter or to muse on the profundity of a moment – they take the moment and sew it onto fabric and we see it walking down the street and don't think twice about it, unless to admire or object to it.

After saying all of this – what, specifically, is the majority of Britain wearing in 2016?

I couldn't find any research that had been done into individual items of clothing purchased in Britain, outside of broad categories such as 'shoes' or 'leather goods'. There was no literature on how immigration, outside of very specific groups, had influenced British fashion and it is easy to see why. The impact of immigration to the UK on contemporary UK clothing is impossible to accurately document. Therefore what follows are simply some of my musings, triggered by my fruitless searching for studies on the subject.

Amazon, despite its dubious morality regarding workers' rights, thankfully came up trumps with a current list of the top 20 bestselling clothing items on the UK site. Not all UK residents use Amazon, or even the internet. I have no illusion that this is the definitive source of purchasing information for the country. However, I do think it reflects at least a part of our national fashion footprint and so I have chosen to expand on some of the items shown there, evaluating how their emergence into a top 20 list could *possibly* be linked with immigration to the UK.

Number nine on the list is a 'Ladies Chiffon Wrap Scarf'. It has flowers printed on it and comes in a multitude of colours.

Chiffon as a fabric was invented in early-twentieth-century India. It can be made from silk, cotton or polyester fibres, but nowadays is most widely available as polyester. This particular wrap scarf is reminiscent of traditional Indian scarves that have been worn for thousands of years, with a European-influenced flower design printed on them.

Indians have been present in the UK for hundreds of years – as have people from many areas of the world – albeit in small numbers to begin with. Global trade has been happening since people were able to travel and this resulted in traders and workers living temporarily or permanently in countries outside of their birthplace. India was under various forms of British colonial rule from 1612, so this migration of traders and workers would have been even greater. There is evidence of Indian seamen being buried in London during the 1600s and one probable theory is that the East India Company employed Indian seamen for their voyages back to Britain and their home.[44] The first large migration to the UK by Indian women, who brought with them versions of the fantastic chiffon scarves that today sell so prolifically in the mainstream, seems to have been from Kenya in 1968, when 100,000 Indians arrived in Britain following Kenyan independence from Britain – mostly as families invited here and promised passports and citizenship. The scarves worn by these women were already reflected in the popular Western fashions of the time – the loose-flowing hippy garments and Indian-influenced designs. Much fashion of that era disappeared along with the feelings of peace and love, but the chiffon scarf evidently remains a strong staple. This is likely to be due to its versatility, durability, resistance to wrinkling and its ability to be stored in very small spaces. All of these traits became even more important by the advent of mass access to international travel. The 'twice migrants' of Indian origin knew this well, having travelled the globe with their belongings more times than most. Who knows if they would have had any idea that the scarves that covered them, warmed them and cooled them would become one of the most worn fashion items in Britain less than 50 years later.

---

44 Rozina Visram, *Asians in Britain – 400 Years of History*, (London, Pluto Press, 2002).

Worryingly, number two in the most popular clothing bought on Amazon.co.uk is the 'FeelinGirl Latex 9 Steel Boned Waist Training Corset Cincher for Women'. Considering the Rational Dress Movement (1881) was a significant player in feminist activism and eventual suffrage for women, campaigning as they did to free women from clothing that 'impeded physical movement or deformed the figure',[45] it is depressing to see this elaborately named item of clothing maintain such a prominent position on the sales list, at a time when many women and men say there's no need for feminism and/or feel a discomfort at describing themselves as a feminist. This discomfort must pale in comparison to the aches imposed by wearing the chart-topping 'Steel Boned Waist Cincher'. French migration to Britain brought along the early obsessions with corset-wearing, although its current popularity may be more directly linked to TOWIE or Kim K. It's generally accepted that the garment first became popular in Italy and was introduced to France by Catherine de Médici in the sixteenth century.[46] It was also during the 1500s that the largest numbers of French migrated to Britain to put down permanent roots, as the Protestant Huguenots fled religious persecution in their homeland. It is from this point onward that corsets become common in Britain and throughout Europe, something which doesn't change (although the style of the corset does) until the 1920s, as women had been asked to stop buying corsets in order to save steel for the war from 1917.[47] They continued to exist as items of fashion worn in Britain for

45 *The Rational Dress Society Gazette*, (1889).

46 Elizabeth Ewing, *Dress and Undress: A History of Women's Underwear*, (London, Batsford,1978).

47 'Mary Phelps Jacob', Phelps Family History in America. http://phelpsfamilyhistory.com/bios/mary_phelps_jacob.asp

stage costumes and in sex shops as 'erotic wear'. Perhaps their mainstream popularity resumed in the 1990s with the onset of pseudo-female empowerment branding, such as the mass commercialisation of 'raunchy lingerie' by companies like Ann Summers.

Prior to writing this, I would have imagined that the French presence in Britain had resulted in far more stylish items of popular fashion than the 'cincher', but there you go.

Now, the moment we've all been waiting for – the number one selling item of clothing on the UK site of Amazon … The white T-Shirt. It's been there for 1,887 days. What is it about white T-shirts? I own two, but I just wear them under furry vintage jumpers to stop the scratchiness sending me barmy. I borrow my partner's sometimes for bed. They have long been worn by all sexes, yet there still seems to be something quietly masculine about them. Perhaps this is attributable to their origins. Worn as all-in-one undergarments in early nineteenth-century America, these 'union suits' were hailed as emancipatory fashion for women, allowing them to wear more comfortable and 'masculine' clothing in an effort to rid themselves of the restrictions placed on them by society and manifested for all to see in the fashions of the time. These then became two-piece undergarments worn by both sexes and in the late nineteenth century buttonless versions were issued as standard US Navy undershirts. Around the same time, these easy to slip on garments became popular globally amongst miners and stevedores (a waterfront manual labourer involved in loading and unloading ships). They were convenient for hot environments and comfortable to work in underneath layers in cold environments. This global popularity may have been initiated by the US Navy presence from the 1820s in all

African countries where the British Navy was stationed.[48] I am purely speculating, but it is possible that the dockworkers in these countries used the white T-shirt more than the British Navy did, as all of the British Armed Forces have their own strict uniform codes. Considering that in the early twentieth century, Britain began urgently recruiting people from its vast colonies to work on British ships and dockyards[49] and large numbers of Somali, Sudanese and Yemeni dockworkers took up the offer of employment, perhaps they were the ones who brought the white T-shirt to British docks long before Hollywood did – influencing fashion (and Amazon sales) in a way they would surely be unable to predict, or benefit from. Whatever the truth about its introduction to Britain is, this enduring popularity of the plain white tee is surely down to more than just practicality? I would make some guesses that it speaks to individualism's irony and capitalism's sustenance by allowing the wearer (and the 'viewer') to project any of their multiple identities onto the blank face of the top. It allows the wearer to appear theoretically classless and unclassifiable.

As my dad showed with his very own collection of bright white T-shirts, this rare opportunity for equality is often more valuable to an immigrant than others could ever imagine.

48 Christopher Lloyd, *The Navy and the Slave Trade: The Suppression of the African Slave Trade in the Nineteenth Century*, (Hove, Psychology Press,1968).

49 David Killingray, *Africans in Britain*, (Hove, Psychology Press, 1994).

AIRPORTS AND AUDITIONS

RIZ AHMED

To begin with, auditions taught me to get through airports. In the end, it was the other way around.

I'm an actor. Since I was a teenager I've had to play different characters, negotiating the cultural expectations of a Pakistani family, Brit-Asian rudeboy culture, and a scholarship to private school. The fluidity of my own personal identity on any given day was further compounded by the changing labels assigned to Asians in general.

As children in the 80s, when my brother and I were stopped near our home by a skinhead and a knife was put to his throat, we were black. A decade later the knife to my throat was held by another 'paki', a label we wore with swagger in the Brit-Asian subculture and gang culture of the 90s. The next time I found myself as helplessly cornered, it was in a windowless room at Luton airport. My arm was in a painful wrist-lock and my collars pinned to the wall by British intelligence officers. It was 'post 9/11', and I was now labelled a Muslim.

As a minority, no sooner do you learn to polish and cherish one chip on your shoulder, it's taken off you and swapped out for another. The jewellery of your struggles is forever on loan, like the Koh-i-Noor. You are intermittently handed this

Necklace of labels to hang around your neck, neither of your choosing nor making, both constricting and decorative.

Part of the reason I became an actor was the promise that I might be able to help stretch these Necklaces, and that the teenage version of myself might breathe a little easier as a result. If the films I re-enacted as a kid could humanise mutants and aliens, maybe there was hope for us.

But portrayals of ethnic minorities worked in stages, I realised, so I'd have to strap in for a long ride.

Stage One is the two-dimensional stereotype – the minicab driver/terrorist/cornershop owner. It tightens the Necklace.

Stage Two is the subversive portrayal, taking place on 'ethnic' terrain but aiming to challenge stereotypes. It loosens the Necklace.

And Stage Three is the Promised Land, where you play a character whose story is not intrinsically linked to his race. In the Promised Land, I'm not a terror suspect, nor a victim of forced marriage. In the Promised Land, my name might even be Dave. In the Promised Land, there is no Necklace.

I started acting professionally during the post 9/11 boom for Stage One stereotypes, but I avoided them at the behest of my 18-year-old self. Luckily there was also a tiny speck of Stage Two stuff taking shape, subverting those stereotypes, and I managed to get in on the act.

My first film was in this mode, Michael Winterbottom's *The Road to Guantanamo*. It told the story of a group of friends from Birmingham who were illegally detained and tortured there. When it won a prestigious award at the Berlin Film Festival, we were euphoric. For those who saw it, the inmates went from orange jumpsuits to human beings.

But airport security hadn't got the memo. Returning to the glamour of Luton Airport after our festival win, ironically-named 'British intelligence officers' frog-marched me to an unmarked room where they insulted, threatened, then attacked me.

'What kinda film you making? Did you become an actor to further the Muslim struggle?' an officer screamed, twisting my arm to the point of snapping.

The question is disturbing not only because it endangers artistic expression, but because it suggests our security services don't quite grasp the nature of the terror threat we all face. A presentation outlining Al-Qaeda's penchant for 'theatrical' attacks may have been taken a little literally. Their suspicion of thespians may also explain why those Guantanamo Bay prisoners are so goddamn photogenic.

It turned out that what those Special Branch officers did was illegal. I was asked by activist lawyers if I wanted to sue, but instead I wrote an account of the incident and sent it to a few journalists. A story about the illegal detention of the actors from a film about illegal detention turned out to be too good to ignore. I was glad to shed some light on this depressing state of affairs.

I went on to write a song inspired by the incident, called 'Post 9/11 Blues', full of sage advice like: 'We're all suspects so watch your back, I farted and got arrested for a chemical attack.' The song got the attention of Chris Morris, who cast me in *Four Lions*.

In the end, having my arm nearly torn off by people whose salary I pay led to me exploring loads of Stage Two work – loosening the Necklace. It felt good, but what about Stage Three, the Promised Land?

It turned out there was no clear pathway for an actor of colour in the UK to go to Stage Three – to play 'just a bloke'. Producers all said they wanted to work with me, but they had nothing I could feasibly act in. The stories that needed to be told in the multicultural mid-2000s were about the all-white mid-1700s, it seemed. I heard rumours that the Promised Land was not in Britain at all, but in Hollywood.

The reason for this is simple. America uses its stories to export a myth of itself, just like the UK. The reality of Britain is vibrant multi-culturalism, but the myth we export is an all-white world of Lords and Ladies. Conversely, American society is pretty segregated, but the myth they export is of a racial melting-pot solving crimes and fighting aliens side by side.

So America is where I was headed. But it would not be an easy journey.

You see, the pitfalls of the audition room and the airport interrogation room are the same. They are places where the threat of rejection is real. They're also places where you're reduced to your marketability or threat-level, where the length of your facial hair can be a deal breaker, where you are seen, and hence see yourself, in reductive labels – never as 'just a bloke called Dave'. The post 9/11 Necklace tightens around your neck.

I had so far managed to avoid this in the audition room, but now I faced the same threat at US airports. It didn't help that *The Road to Guantanamo* had left my passport stamped with an Axis of Evil world tour – shooting in Pakistan, Afghanistan, and Iran within six months. I spent the flight sweating in defiance of air-conditioning, wondering what would await me.

When I landed, the officer assessing me shared my skin colour. I wondered whether this was a good sign or if he was one of the legendarily patriotic Cuban borders officers I had heard about, determined to assess how star-spangled I was with a thumb up the anus.

He looked at my passport, then at me, frowned and drew a big 'P' over my immigration card. I immediately thought it stood for Paki.

'Protocol!'

I was led down a long corridor without explanation before turning in to a side room that felt instantly familiar.

Apart from a Chinese family and a South American pilot battling the indignity with his spotless uniform, the holding pen was filled with 20 slight variations of my own face, now all staring at me. Kinda like a Bollywood remake of *Being John Malkovich*. It's a reminder that you are a type, whose face says things before your mouth opens. You are a signifier before you are a person. You are back at Stage One.

The holding room also had that familiar audition room fear. Everyone is nervous, but the prospect of solidarity is undercut by competition. You're all fighting to graduate out of this reductive purgatory and into some recognition of your unique personhood. In one way or another you are all saying, 'I'm not like the rest of them.'

The fresh-faced desk officer was no older than 23. By the time I was called up to audition for him, my spiel to explain the passport stamps was ready. I'd show a letter from the film's producer, I'd say 'award-winning film', and I'd flash a shiny new DVD. But the kid questioning me seemed more nervous than I was. He'd clearly been to the same 'beware bloodthirsty actors' seminar as the intelligence officers at Luton.

'Step back from the counter!'

I was pinballed up the chain for a proper interrogation with a dangerously fat man and his moustache. I sat and waited, rehearsing my lines. When the interrogation came, it was more of a car crash than my *Slumdog Millionaire* audition.

'Oh yeah? Afghanistan? What kinda movie were you making there?'

The question shot through me with a shudder. It reminded me of the questions I faced at Luton airport, but also of the question I ask myself all the time. Was I adding to the catalogue of Stage One, Two, or Three? Was it a film my 18-year-old self wanted? Would it make the Necklace looser or tighter?

I thought about the right way to answer him. *The Road to Guantanamo* was a documentary-drama, but maybe saying I was in a documentary about Guantanamo Bay wouldn't be wise. Drama should do.

I said, 'Erm, it's an award-winning drama called *The Road to Guantanamo*.'

There was a long silence. He raised an eyebrow. I offered up the DVD; it had a photo of me handcuffed in an orange jumpsuit on its cover. I immediately regretted it. Longer silence. Second eyebrow went up. He leaned in.

'Do you know anyone who wants to do harm to the United States?'

I shook my head and made Hugh Grant noises, venturing a 'gosh!' in there somewhere. He absorbed my performance before holding up a book from my luggage. It was Mohsin Hamid's novel *The Reluctant Fundamentalist*.[50]

'What's this book?'

I explained, but he wasn't really listening. He deployed a state-of-the-art intelligence protocol by Googling me, which returned a news clipping about the Luton Airport incident. Fuck. My heart sank. This was it. No Hollywood for me. I was

---

50 Though I didn't know it at the time, I would go on to act in the film adaptation of *The Reluctant Fundamentalist* – I'm sure in part because its title doubled as a description of my casting perils up until that point.

never gonna be Brad Pitt. I wasn't even gonna be Apu from the fucking *Simpsons*. What was I thinking?

When after an agonising three hours I was waved through, I couldn't believe it. I felt relieved, grateful, lucky – and then suddenly incensed.

On the way out past my look-alikes, I gave a loud 'As-Salaam aliekum'.

No one leapt to return the greeting. Perhaps they lacked the safety net of a convincing 'gosh!'.

I joined a friend in Manhattan for dinner, apologising for being three hours late, and zoned out while they discussed astrology. Someone at the dinner turned to me.

'You're such a terrorist,' she said.

I blinked. What the fuck? My face screwed itself into the expression I wish I'd pulled instead of mewling apologetically at the border officers.

'What the fuck is that supposed to mean?'

My friend put her arm on mine and squeezed.

'Riz, she asked if you're a Sagittarius.'

I swallowed. Baffled faces pinned me with concern.

'Right. Sorry. Yeah. Yes, I am,' I said.

A similar version of the same thing happened again soon after. And again. And again. And again. I grew belligerent.

One officer asked if I had had any military training. My school had a cadet-force programme that I was swiftly ejected from, but I just answered 'yes' without expanding. I was asked if I had travelled to Iran, Iraq, or Afghanistan recently.

'All except Iraq, but if it helps I've also been to Pakistan and Saudi Arabia,' I smiled.

Childish perhaps, but the situation itself is infantilising. Feigning obliviousness to an officer's suspicion and refusing to pander to it was my only defence.

But the farce rolled on.

Twice when applying for a US Work Visa I was subjected to a Section 221G – a lengthy background check against a global database of terrorists – which almost lost me the jobs. I saw the email correspondence between the state department and my attorney:

'Hey Bill, looking at your client Mr Ahmed – pretty British-sounding name, huh? Saw his "Post 9/11 Blues" song, what's with the "I heart Osama" routine?'

Fair enough, you might think. Search him. Look at his racial profile and his passport stamps and his dangerously hilarious rap lyrics. But since I had been let into the US and deemed safe just the previous month, another rigmarole this month was obviously fruitless. The possibility of radicalising me in under thirty days is laughable if you know how entrenched I am in a Satanic Internet Porn addiction (and the CIA and NSA surely do).

In the end, I was always let in, so these airport auditions were technically a success. But they involved the experience of being typecast, and when that happens enough, you internalise the role written for you by others. Now, like an over-eager method actor, I was struggling to break character.

I tried not to ingest all the signs telling me I was a suspect. I tried not to buy into the story world of this 'protocol' or its Stage One stereotype of who I was. But when you have always moulded your identity to your environment and had your Necklace picked out by others, it's not easy. I couldn't see myself as 'just a bloke'. I failed at every single audition I went up for.

Rehearsing a scene beds a role into you. But sometimes if you over-rehearse it without unearthing any new meaning in it, you can suddenly forget your lines. You realise that you are on a stage, not in the real world. The scene's emotional power and your immersion in it disappears.

And so it dawned on me that these searches were a fictional role-play taking place in a bubble, rather than an assessment of my worth.

This was the way to see it.

And it turns out this is also the way to see auditions.

The protocol lost its chokehold on me, and I started getting roles again.

One big job secured me a proper US visa, and soon I was getting waved through without the protocol. I began inching towards the Promised Land.

Now, both at auditions and airports, I find myself on the right side of the same velvet rope with which I was once clotheslined. But this isn't a success story. I see most of my fellow Malkoviches still arched back, spines bent to snapping as they try to limbo under that rope. So although these days it's likely that no one resembles me in the waiting room for an acting audition, the same is also true of everyone being waved through with me at US immigration. In both spaces, my exception proves the rule.

Don't get me wrong: although my US airport experience is smoother, I still get stopped before boarding a plane at Heathrow every time I fly to America. But now I find it hilarious rather than bruising. Easy for me to laugh with my work visa and strategically deployed 'gosh!', perhaps. But it's also easy for me to laugh, because the more I travel, the more ridiculous the procedures become.

Heathrow airport draws its staff from the nearby Asian suburbs of Hounslow and Southall. My 'random selection' flying to LA was so reliable that as I started travelling more, I went through a six-month stretch of being searched by the same middle-aged Sikh guy. I instinctively started calling him Uncle, as is the custom for Asian elders. He started calling me 'beta', or son, as he went through my luggage apologetically. It was heart-warming, but veered dangerously close to incest every time he had to frisk my crotch.

'How are you, son?'

'I'm er, ooh, er, good, Uncle.'

As I've travelled more I've also done more film work, increasing the chances of being recognised by the young Asian staff at Heathrow. I have had my films quoted back at me by someone rifling through my underpants, and been asked for selfies by someone swabbing me for explosives.

The last kid who searched me, a young Muslim boy with an immaculate line-beard and goatee, was particularly apologetic.

'Sorry, bro. If it makes you feel any better, they search me before I fly too.'

We laughed, not because he was joking, but because he was deadly serious. It was the perfect encapsulation of the minority's shifting and divided self, forced to internalise the limitations imposed on us just to get by, on the wrong side of the velvet rope even when (maybe *especially* when) you're on the right side of it. We cracked jokes and bumped fists.

As I left, he called after me with a question.

'Bro, what kinda film you doing next?'

I looked at the ID badge hanging from a string around his neck. I told him I hoped it would be one he liked.

PERPETUATING CASTEISM

SARAH SAHIM

Most people are aware of the discriminatory Indian caste system, but many do not realise that this form of intra-racial segregation has extended beyond South Asia and into the United Kingdom through the diaspora. While the British were not directly responsible for the caste system's creation, their own system of classism and the violence of racism imposed on Indians during colonisation reinforced it.

Caste is an ancient and complex social stratification system, with Dalits (Marathi for 'oppressed') at the very bottom and Brahmins – the spiritual and scholarly class – at the top. Such is the status of Dalits in Indian society that they are excluded from the *varna* (an ancient Hindu form of classifying civilisation) entirely.

Those around today are still paying for – or, for those who are privileged, reaping the benefits of – the results of past generations' mistakes with regards to casteism. Caste continues to affect our lives despite it being supposedly eradicated. There is a colonial 'hangover' of sorts and it isn't just limited to the borders of India. It pervades other countries and the Indian diaspora. It takes place in Britain itself: the colonial source. Yet, the question remains: why do Indians who have migrated to Britain (as well as other Western countries, such as the

United States) and their children continue this discriminatory practice?

'Caste' itself was a British construction, showing up on Indian census forms in 1871.[51] This helped create a hierarchy of castes that worked to give Brahmins more privilege and societal advantages through their misunderstanding of the complex *varna*. This is not to say that the system on its own – prior to British arrival – was without fault. And notwithstanding discrimination based on caste being illegal in India, casteism has permeated factions of Indian society both domestically and internationally. The caste system has supposedly been eradicated from India,[52] and was not necessarily part of the original structural inequality in other countries in the Indian diaspora. However, casteism is just as vehement today, and those who refuse to acknowledge its existence are in abundance.

The relationship between castes is also complex. As a young light-skinned woman with a Gujarati Brahmin mother and Afghan Pashtun father, I have access to a wealth of privilege: something I have taken for granted. My family never concerned themselves with casteism and neither did I: we didn't discriminate or abide by its rules. However, this 'caste-blind' attitude is extremely harmful and you cannot and must not turn a blind eye to injustices that your people are responsible for. I have the freedom to be wilfully ignorant, but others, especially Dalits, cannot afford to do so.

The recent suicide of Rohith Vemula, a Dalit, on

---

51 'Caste not class is the main British problem, Lords', *The Huffington Post*. http://www.huffingtonpost.co.uk/jasdev-singh-rai/caste-not-class-is-the-ma_b_2989148.html

52 'Why India is still fighting over caste system', *CNN*. http://www.cnn.com/2015/08/28/asia/india-gujarat-caste-protests/

January 17th 2016, reified the horrific realities of caste-based discrimination, especially amongst younger Indians. Vemula was a 25-year-old PhD student at the University of Hyderabad. Just two weeks away from turning 26, Vemula hanged himself after being expelled from his accommodation because the university refused to carry on paying him a grant of 25,000 rupees per month, an apparently clear case of caste-based discrimination by an academic institution.

In his suicide note he wrote, 'I always was rushing. Desperate to start a life. All the while, some people, for them, life itself is curse. My birth is my fatal accident.'

His death subsequently sparked protest and a much-needed discussion about the state of casteism in India.

One of the ways the conversation has evolved is through New York-based journalist Yashica Dutt's *Documents of Dalit Discrimination* blog on Tumblr.[53] The page is intended for Dalits and witnesses of Dalit discrimination to share their stories; a 'safe space for conversation that goes beyond "reservation" and "merit" and voices that echo the hurt so many of us suffer silently'.[54]

As well as charting the history of discrimination, she also seeks to record the toll that the caste system continues to exact on it lower caste victims. The page documents instances of casteism denial – which in itself is casteist – instances of slurs being used against Dalits, job discrimination, assuming

---

53 Documents of Dalit Discrimination (blog). http://dalitdiscrimination.tumblr. com/

54 'Coming out as a Dalit in Rohith's memory: New York journalist's project to document discrimination', *The News Minute*. http://www.thenewsminute. com/article/coming-out-dalit-rohith%E2%80%99s-memory-new-york-journalist%E2%80%99s-project-document-discrimination-38083

that someone of a lower caste was employed due to positive discrimination, unprovoked physical abuse, and how many Dalits have to attempt to pass as Brahmin in order to circumvent all of these experiences. 'Passing' is not only a precarious decision, but the fact that it is possible at all, just goes to prove that delineations between caste are meaningless and harmful. Dutt even used the blog to recount an abhorrently violent incident that happened to her own mother: '[Her neighbour] had … hit her with two different mid-sized boulders from a distance of less than two feet. One he brutally bruised her face with, using its sharp end. The other, he used to strike her forehead.' These were stones that her mother had used to block sewage coming from his drain. Unfortunately the neighbour did not stop there as he 'kick[ed] her twice in the shin and [struck her], using the boulders'. She immediately contacted the police but the neighbour denied attacking her. The police were of no use and she told Dutt this was because 'everyone knows our caste'. This encapsulates the myopia through which perpetuators of the caste system perceive their world and just how tangible its effects are, but is only one of hundreds of thousands of stories about the mistreatment of Dalits.

The South Asian non-binary and trans 'performance art duo' DarkMatter tweeted on May 30th, 2014, 'Hinduism is a huge and complex and contradictory religion but it has been repurposed by upper caste for nationalism #NoHindutva', which was just one of a series of tweets about casteism.[55] It's evident that the issue of casteism and exploring methods to undo the poisonous nature of this obsolete and divisive

55 Twitter user @DarkMatterPoets. https://twitter.com/DarkMatterPoets/ status/472505155817316353

structure is one that younger people prioritise. While conversations about casteism by white people and non-South Asian people of colour can easily career into racist, xenophobic, or culturally insensitive sentiment, that does not mean that the conversation should not be held at all. It should be led by people who bear the brunt of casteism: lower castes, depressed classes, Dalits.

After the supposed end of the caste system in India, a system akin to positive discrimination emerged there, a so-called 'quota system'. This was developed to help disadvantaged castes succeed without regard to their social status. The system created groups of 'Other Backward Classes', 'Scheduled Castes', and 'Scheduled Tribes'. Though it was intended to counter years of oppression of lower castes,[56] systems such as this one are not always successful. Despite attempting to mitigate institutional oppression, putting people in a workplace where they might be assumed to be there only because of this, brings about its own issues. Quite a few instances of everyday casteism mentioned on Dutt's blog discuss problems with the quota system. Some of them expressed worry about accepting scholarships because they had been pretending to be Brahmin.[57]

In Dutt's *Huffington Post* article 'Today, I'm Coming Out As Dalit', she articulates the struggle of passing. 'I was born in a Dalit family in Ajmer, Rajasthan. And I grew up learning to hide it. My convent school education, a non-Dalit-sounding last name, and a skin colour that was "dusky but still not dirty", eased

56 'Why India is still fighting over caste system', *CNN*. http://www.cnn.com/2015/08/28/asia/india-gujarat-caste-protests/
57 Documents of Dalit Discrimination (blog). http://dalitdiscrimination.tumblr.com/post/137820923502/i-never-came-out-of-my-shell-became-introverted

my passing as a non-Dalit,'[58] Dutt writes. She also mentions that early in her career as a journalist she wrote about things associated with upper castes that she thought would help her continue to pass as non-Dalit, such as 'fashion and lifestyle'.[59]

One thing that Vemula's suicide did for Dalits such as Dutt was remind them that their pain was rooted in oppression: not in shame or the notion that they are 'dirty'. This victim-blaming mentality echoes the negatives of colonialism too. Removing the actual source of the blame serves to place it on those who are experiencing the most pain in society; the most marginalised. Vemula's suicide is still a tragedy, but with young trailblazers and activists like Dutt, there is a chance that he might be one of the last. What Dutt, *Documents of Dalit Discrimination*, and other Dalits who are seeking self-empowerment and community empowerment are doing is similar to what Dr Ambedkar argued for.[60] He stressed that he wished for Dalits to gain 'self-pride, self-improvement, and self-confidence so as to have an equal share in society'.[61]

The census imposed on India by the British Empire in 1871 served to solidify the institutionalisation of caste for years to come, many remnants of which have survived into the

---

58 'Today, I'm coming out as Dalit', *The Huffington Post*. http://www.huffingtonpost. in/yashica-dutt-/why-im-coming-out-as-dali_b_9035094.html

59 'Coming out as a Dalit in Rohith's memory', *The News Minute*. http://www.thenewsminute.com/article/coming-out-dalit-rohith %E2%80%99s-memory-new-york-journalist%E2%80%99s-project-document-discrimination-38083

60 India's first minister of law and justice and prominent campaigner against the caste system.

61 N.S. Gehlot, 'Dr Ambedkar, Mahatma Gandhi, and Dalit Movement', *The Indian Journal of Political Science*, Vol.54, No.3/4 (July–Dec 1991), 382–387.

modern era. The way the caste system manifests itself today is the combined product of both the British and privileged Indians. Another article that followed Vemula's suicide makes this clear: 'The discussion surrounding the suicide on the other hand is evidence of the colonial hangover our society suffers from; of our incapability to elucidate societal divisions without resorting to the concept of caste, which was born out of a combined effort on the part of the British and the Brahmins to maintain governing status in the country'.[62] The first census in 1871 counted and classified Indian people based on caste, which contributed to the institutionalisation of the caste system under British colonial rule.

This step to maintain British and Brahmin Indian power demonstrates the British involvement in modern casteism, and they must be held accountable. The British also used other means of classifying Indians[63] as they had with many other colonised populations, including skin colour/shade, head measurements, body measurements, and other objectifying means, designed to help determine physical traits and their supposed relation to caste. This embodied archaic distinctions anthropologists used to separate 'Negroids', 'Mongoloids', 'Iranids', and other offensive racial classifications. Western colonialism stunted many societies' ability to advance by enforcing regressive views on race, gender, and sexuality. Though some may try to argue that colonialism was, on balance, a good

---

62 'Our obsession with caste is really a colonial hangover', *The Indian Express*. http://indianexpress.com/article/blogs/rohith-vemula-dalit-suicide-hyderabad-our-obsession-with-caste-is-really-a-colonial-hangover/

63 'Caste not class is the main British problem, Lords', *The Huffington Post*. http://www.huffingtonpost.co.uk/jasdev-singh-rai/caste-not-class-is-the-ma_b_2989148.html

thing (a sentiment that derives from the British believing they abolished 'uncivilised' cultural practices), the fact of the matter is that the British ruled with an ardent cruelty that stemmed from their inflated sense of racial superiority,[64] and they passed this attitude on to Brahmins (not to mention that the notion of the British 'civilising' other cultures is inherently racist).

While Gandhi was regarded as a bastion of peaceful protest who fought against the evil British Empire, his methods left many unsatisfied, including Dr Ambedkar. Granted, Gandhi's efforts ameliorated the anti-colonialism movement but that does not automatically render him unaccountable for his casteism. Gandhi opposed Dr Ambedkar's demand for separate electorates for the Dalits, dating back to 1931 at the Second Round Table Conference in London.[65] Dalits then protested against Gandhi's stance on this situation upon his return to Mumbai. And when the lower and depressed classes were given separate electorates, Gandhi went on a petulant hunger strike in protest until Dr Ambedkar relented. Dr Ambedkar was concerned that without their own electorate, the Dalits would remain 'at the mercy of the Hindus' and, with hindsight, it looks as though his fears were justified. Gandhi, on the other hand, believed that 'untouchability' would soon be a thing of the past.[66] The reframing and manipulation of history has been in Gandhi's favour. A hunger strike is seen to be a valiant form of political defiance and this further romanticises perceptions of Gandhi. This sentiment is not shared by the lower castes,

---

64 'Wake up, Britain. Should the empire really be a source of pride?', *The Guardian*. http://www.theguardian.com/commentisfree/2016/jan/23/britain-empire-pride-poll

65 N.S. Gehlot, 'Dr Ambedkar, Mahatma Gandhi, and Dalit Movement'.

66 N.S. Gehlot, 'Dr Ambedkar, Mahatma Gandhi, and Dalit Movement'.

however, as their lack of political power remains unaltered.

Despite the part the British played in helping to reinforce this caste discrimination, the racism practised by white British people extends to all, not just those of a lower caste. Racial discrimination does not distinguish between Dalits and Brahmins; to racists, all Indians are the same. Even when the politics of respectability encourage variation in the way Indians of different castes or socio-economic status are treated in Britain, the end result is still racial discrimination.

Racism in society often works through a divide and conquer strategy, more often than not it is also intertwined with classism as well as other forms of oppression. Structural racism can divide a community that would be stronger together, by keeping individual groups entrenched in their own class – in this case, caste discrimination. This form of racism combined with the inflated white British sense of self-importance means that from the outside it appears that they dismiss casteism without holding themselves accountable. In some ways, one could argue that lingering caste discrimination in the UK is fortified by British classism – a capitalist structure that seeks to segregate people without any chance of social mobility is very reminiscent of the Indian caste system.

British Indians are the largest minority community in Britain[67] and while most young British Indians may not pay much mind to the caste system, they are no doubt still on the receiving end of its negative effects as it manifests in many ways. Although children are independent and formulate their own opinions, watching their elders partake in the caste system

---

67 'British Indians seek legal protection from caste system', *CBC World.* http://www.cbc.ca/news/world/british-indians-seek-legal-protection-from-caste-system-1.2224275

can leave a lasting impression and encourage them to become directly complicit in casteism. Their privilege as upper-caste Indians gives them an arbitrarily higher status over other Indian children who might have to resort to hiding their caste, even in a country where the Indian caste system is not a familiar concept. Those who are conscious of, and engage in, the boundaries that casteism presents, perpetuate discriminatory and odious practices such as forbidding inter-caste marriage so as not to 'spoil' a bloodline. But the divide extends beyond marital relationships as higher castes make efforts to exclude lower castes from partaking in events and functions that are intended to bring communities together for dancing and celebrations. This is particularly rife in the North Indian community as many British Gujaratis host and attend garbas (a form of traditional Gujarati dance with sticks), which are segregated by caste and most are exclusively attended by the higher castes.

Whether an Indian from a higher caste admits it or not, they are always indirectly complicit in perpetuating the caste system, because their existence means that they're more advantaged than Dalits by default. Young children have been known to taunt other children from lower castes with casteist slurs[68] and British-born Hindu Indians are still at risk of being shunned for their caste, no matter what generation.[69] They experience caste discrimination at work, '… in public services, music, social media as well as at religious and community

---

68 'No escape from caste prejudice even in UK', *The Times of India*. http://timesofindia.indiatimes.com/nri/No-escape-from-caste-prejudice-even-in-UK/articleshow/18998712.cms

69 'British Indians seek legal protection from caste system', *CBC World*. http://www.cbc.ca/news/world/british-indians-seek-legal-protection-from-caste-system-1.2224275

spaces',[70] and when casteist slurs like 'Jat'[71] are being used in lieu of 'dirty' it evokes a cause for concern.

In 2013, British Indians protested to the British government about casteism, demanding government protection. While these protests were successful, with the British government eventually agreeing to explicitly prohibit caste discrimination within the 2010 Equalities Act, changing the law does not simply end discrimination right there and then. When systems of oppression are so deeply ingrained in the Indian – and human – psyche, it's impossible for people to do a complete *volte face* with regards to their bigotry, even if it is illegal. All British Indians are still subject to white supremacy[72], despite Britain's claims that race is less important in this than class. Additionally, it's hard to ignore that Britain was the perpetrator of modern casteism and thus the hierarchical social order in India. Usually those claims that racism is no longer an issue are paired with assertions that the United States is the sole culprit of institutional racism. While it is true that the United States has a huge history of and problem with racism, that does not erase the history of racism and white supremacy in Britain. It was Britain who formed the second point on the transatlantic slave trade triangle (the path African slaves would travel in order to reach America) and most recently, the death of Sarah Reed – a London black woman who died in 2012 after a brutal beating while in police custody – bears

---

70 'Long range of prejudice', *Outlook Magazine*. http://www.outlookindia.com/article/long-range-of-prejudice/293121

71 The Jat people are an Indo-Aryan people based in Northern India and Pakistan, most of whom still live in farming communities.

72 The notion of 'white supremacy' in this instance is to be taken as a global concept rather than in the context of America's relationship with black and Native American citizens.

many similarities to the fate of Sandra Bland, who died under mysterious circumstances in a Texas prison cell in 2015.

In order for anti-racism to become a reality – at least in the context of Indians – it's important for Indians higher than Dalit on the *varna* to be fully aware of the arbitrary privileges bestowed upon them and those who possess major social and financial power to make the environment safer for Dalits. This is not something that can happen overnight. Acknowledging the pain that Dalits experience is the first step. The conversation of caste cannot start and end with Vemula's suicide. The work of today's existing generations fighting against caste discrimination cannot go unnoticed either. Yashica Dutt's *Documents of Dalit Discrimination* and the work of other activists like DarkMatter is vital in moving forward into a future that betters the lives of the lower castes and in turn enhances the lives of all castes.

The British must be held accountable for their reinforcing of the caste system and their continuing indirect support of discriminatory practices. It's clear that the caste system, taken to the extreme it has been, is not an inherently Indian convention. If the British are partially responsible for classifying Indians during colonialism, why is there a need to continue this practice – why not abolish caste discrimination and work as a better-formed community, embracing the diversity of the castes, to challenge British authority? Indulging casteism is not going to earn upper castes the privilege that white Brits have by design. It is clear that the continuation of caste is not beneficial for anyone in the Indian community and especially within white institutions. Looking down on lower castes or classes and using them to navigate your way to the top does not guarantee you will achieve a white person's status in this white supremacist world. Uniting against white oppressors can only be achieved by eradicating these quasi-sectarian oppressions.

SHADE

SALENA GODDEN

Shade: Comparative darkness and coolness caused by shelter from direct sunlight.

The darker part of a picture.

A position of relative inferiority or obscurity.

To publicly criticise or express contempt for someone, to act in a casual or disrespectful manner towards someone, throwing shade, acting kinda shady.

Sometimes I think I am about the same shade as Beyoncé. But it is hard to tell because it depends how much light they give her. Some days I think I'm about the same shade as Rihanna but that's also difficult to say as she switches shade too. Your shade is not skin deep. Your shade is not just about your heart and soul; your religion and spirituality, your elders and your history, your connection to a country, to geography and to a time and place. Your shade is an industry, your shade is a token, shade is a passport, shade is a cage and shade is a status.

You tick: Other.

I am in Bangkok. The billboards on the streets and sides of buses are dominated by adverts for a skin-lightening product called 'Snail White'. Glossy pictures of westernised Thai

girls with cheerleader smiles and faces of palest ivory. In the
markets and restaurants I observe Thai residents with bleached
skin and powder-white faces; in the streets some wear gloves
protecting their brown hands and thick white tights to conceal
brown legs in 40-degree heat. I never noticed this so much
before. I think I missed a memo, but the internet informs me
that skin bleaching has been trending for years – from India
to Africa, the Caribbean, all over the world, skin bleaching
is big business and the shade of your skin is your freedom or
your prison. The colour of the outside of you dictates existence
and acceptance. Your shade is the symbol of your wealth, your
beauty, your worth and your success.

Here we are then, this is Britain, where white people dye
themselves as brown as tea stains. The desire to tan continues
to thrive, people toasting themselves to sunbed death. The
first sign of a UK heatwave and our beaches and parks are
awash with salmon pink bodies and barbecued lobster faces.
Celebrities on the covers of gossip magazines are crab orange;
reality television stars are streaky antique teak.

Wherever you live, wherever you are from, it seems it is
all about shade. Universally we are divided and whatever
shade you are born it is not right or good enough. We are in
a giant brainwash, we are being organised by colour and tone,
the natural shade of your skin must be improved, altered and
filtered. Your skin is a living organ. Your skin is the casing
for your sausage-meat soul. And the armour for your muscles,
bones and flesh. Skin is the protective layer of the interior of
you with the exterior world, but it is always wrong. You are
too white or too black. Too light is bad? Too dark is bad? I get
confused. I am in the middle here. Hang on a minute, what
shade am I to you?

My mother is the same shade as Oprah or Maya. Some

summers I have seen my big brother almost as brown as Idris but closer to Obama in the winter. Bob Marley was mixed, Jamaican and Celtic, same as me, his shade looks pale in some photos, sometimes much darker. You see, it all depends on the filter and the time of year, it all depends on the light, it all depends on the shade. It depends on what point people are trying to make, to advertise things, to sell you things, to make money. That is the point, to get the shade right, to make shade the issue. To give shade, to put someone in the shade, to put someone in their place, to let someone know they are less, more or less, because of their shade. Advertising companies, big corporations, banks and politicians need to maintain this, to control the division of people through racism and shade, throwing shade of difference and indifference, good immigrant and bad immigrant, refugee and benefit scrounger. This keeps us in our place, humans bickering, focusing on their differences, distracted, and at each other's throats, competing and separating –

Divide and rule.

I now imagine a giant separating people like he is recycling glass at the bottle bank: brown skin glass there, yellow skin glass here, white skin glass over there. But most people aren't simply one or the other, either black or white. What about me? Where are you putting the two-tone people?

I wish the giant would pick the glass people up and hold us all up to the light. Then he'd see that together and united as a people we are a beautiful picture, a multicoloured mosaic, a glorious stained-glass window. But the giant just scratches his head and continues flinging people in separate buckets. Referencing his colour chart guide for shades of human – Paddy Field Brown is Poverty. Greasy Chip White is Skint.

Black Panther Beret Black is Super Bowl Uproar. Shot Teenager is Chalk On Bloody Concrete. Crack White is Baby Momma's Bitch. Geisha is Pink Cherry Blossom. Ping Pong is Ladyboy White. LA Orange is Porn Slut. Tangerine Queen is Essex Teak. Cardboard Grey is Benefit Scrounger. Rat Tail Beige is Food Bank. Cheerleader Pink is Under-Age Pop Tart. Fox Hunt is Tory. War Crime is Blood Diamond Red. Arab Oil is Gold Dust. Drowned Brown is Refugee. Immigrant Brown is Better Media Coverage. The giant shrugs. He throws some people in the *other* bucket and some in the sea to die. His supervisor reminds him it is vital to tell the difference between Immigrant Brown and Refugee Brown. Let's be diligent about that. Let's make sure we pay attention.

News just in …

What is the shade?

Boko Harem Black. Entire village. Over 80 people burnt to death in their homes.

No. Not newsworthy. Not important.

Bring Back Our Girls.

No. Not Today.

Black Lives Matter.

No. Not Today.

Say Her Name.

Not newsworthy.

Terrorist bomb, blood on European soil.

Headline. Front page.

The indifference is clear. The difference is as clear as oil and gold. We must know the divide. Know your shade. Whose shade are you on? Whose side are you on? None of us can ever un-see the violent images of immigrant children washed up on beaches and plastered over the front page of newspapers. Or the ashy broken babies trapped beneath rubble and bomb debris. How safe are the children? How safe is it for immigrant children in transit? All over the world, wherever they end up, whatever the shade of their skin, refugee brown or immigrant brown, who is protecting the kids from the predators, traffickers, from rape and murder?

Do you mind me asking you a question: where do you come from?

You tick: Other.

I pull up a chair and wait to be processed. I wait here while you print off your labels, and consider me for your boxes marked black as in black-black or black as in brown-black, or brown as in half-black or brown as in half-caste. But hang on a minute. Surely if I am from two colours, two races, I am two shades, and therefore not half-caste, not half anything, but whole, I am double-caste. But half sounds shadier. Half is best because half means less. You lose. You are half a person. We don't want you getting all empowered, now do we.

Half-caste.

Half-breed.

Mulatto.

Ah, now there's a shady word we don't hear too often, but a word used liberally throughout my teenage years. And most recently a word revived in the US press in a piece about Halle Berry, a shitty article that debated what we should call her mixed children. How rude and how old money is the word mulatto? That word is pure shade with its connotations and meanings. The word mulatto comes from the Spanish and Portuguese – it is derived from *mula*, meaning mule, the hybrid offspring of a horse and a donkey. But I am not a mule and I am not made from two species.

My parents are Jamaican and Irish-English. My passport is British and I have lived in England all my life. My fire and spirit is pure Maroon rebel. They didn't teach us about the significance of the Maroons at school, but growing up Jamaican it was always *Black History Month* back home. My grandparents wanted me to know where we all came from, how the Maroons rebelled to rise and fight against slavery. Through storytelling in the kitchen my grandparents gave me history lessons, a map and a time machine.

Welcome aboard my Good Ship. Let us sail to the colourful island of mixed identity. You are free to use your own rules and savvy because they haven't invented a filter for our shade yet. You are a pirate and you're itinerant. You eat from the cooking pot of mixed culture and bathe in the cool shade of being mixed-race. You disembark and hesitate, your pen hovers over your boarding pass.

You tick: Other.

'I don't think of you as black, not really black-black …'

Not black enough. But not white enough either. You are in the playground and you keep your mouth shut as your classmates argue. 'She's not black, she's brown, but she's not black-black, not like really black …' Your plaits are too frizzy and messed up for the Strawberry Shortcake girls, you are too loud and bright and boisterous for them. Maybe they are too girly and pink for you, anyway. They smell of Parma violets and baby powder. You smell of cocoa butter. You stay in the shade they provide, you find your own light inside, you find strength and you are taught that you are outside.

You tick: Other.

There's a rising fashion for golden-brown skin and curly hair. Mothers at the school gates coo and nudge each other.

'She's so lucky, she has a sun tan all year around, mine comes out of a bottle!' They laugh as someone's mum pats your head, her hand bounces a bit.

'I wish I had your curly hair, can I touch it?'

You tick: Other.

After school, spotty white teenagers in Tacchini tracksuits writhe and jolt, body-popping and breakdancing, competing at caterpillars and windmills on a piece of lino in the street to hip-hop on their ghetto blaster – they call it a Ghetto Blaster. Breakdance has exploded and suddenly everyone wants to be a rapper, everyone wants to be *other*. These same white boys who might have teased you and called you *golliwog* a year or two ago, now suddenly call you 'sister' in a fake Yardie accent.

You tick: Other.

You go to live in the city. You and your friends have been studying drama and you go for castings, auditions for extra work and modelling jobs. Most of the time you are turned away for being too exotic. Casting agents look at you with a puzzled expression and shrug and say:

'We don't book your look … we don't really specialise in exotic girls.'

Someone suggests you join an agency for *exotic people* and scribbles down an address. You are penniless and desperate for work so you go. When you get there, there are film stills of aliens, photographs of dwarfs on the walls. Ah, penny drops! Of course, brown people belong in the circus, with the aliens and the dwarves, not in beauty campaigns, but with the elephant man, with the outsiders and the other others. You give them your CV and hope to get offered extra work, non-speaking parts the prostitute, drug dealer or dead girl. You get a part as an extra in a prison riot scene, it pays the rent that month.

You tick: Other.

My mother is a black immigrant. She was born in Port Antonio, Jamaica. She lived in the Robinson family home on Colonels Ridge, Bulls Head Mountain. There are more shades of green there, and more shades of sky, than anywhere else in the world, it is so beautiful. My mother's tropical childhood days were idyllic. She was barefoot and carefree, picking mango fresh from the tree and swimming in clear, warm turquoise oceans. My mother had no idea what England was, or who King George was. She knew nothing of the war, there was no shortage of sugar, cocoa or coffee. Jamaica was the centre of the world. Her father was in the RAF and posted to Dover and so just before my mother's seventh birthday, December 1951, my grandmother and my mother left that warm paradise and stepped onto a banana boat to set sail for England to join my grandfather.

The passage took several weeks. My mum vaguely remembers the ocean crossing, my grandmother making friends with the other passengers. Most of all she remembers how they switched boats off the coast of Ireland and she was terrified as she was winched across from the shipping boat onto a passenger ship, as though she were just like a box of bananas. My mother had been born in the colourful paint box of Barrington Watson and suddenly she found herself in the coal grey industrial frame of a Lowry. England was one long bitter winter's day; my seven-year-old mother shivered at the docks in a short-sleeved cotton dress. Her feet, so used to being bare, were now shoved into these hard shoes she hated. And the flags were all at half mast, King George had just died, February, 1952.

She remembers all of this as a traumatic time.

Back in Jamaica they had told her how wonderful England was, that the streets were paved with gold. But she recalls arriving to find an atmosphere of lost hope, of people's dreams being dashed, a collective depression and disappointment. Newcomers to England found it hard and cold, cold with animosity, cold in the shade cast on them.

She has an early memory of a white child, just opposite, across the street, pointing at her:

'Mummy, Mummy, look at the blackie.'

The mother yanks her child's hand,

'Now, now, dear, don't stare.'

At her new English school, my mum remembers the teachers, how they always put the immigrant children to work together in groups. The brown faces, teeth chattering, shivering on the field, stuck in pairs for sports. Keeping the outsiders outside, keeping the others, other. The newcomers were united as outsiders and lived in a community. One of my grandmother's first friends when she arrived in England was a neighbour, a Polish woman who showed her some practical things, like the way to the shops and how to keep the house warm and keep out the draughts. That Polish immigrant neighbour knitted my mum her first wool cardigan, a kindness my mother remembers even now.

Meanwhile my father was white, his mother was an Irish immigrant. We don't know much about this side of my story because he was adopted and his birth mother disappeared without trace. My paternal grandmother was an Irish 15-year-old scullery maid, working below stairs in a big house. When she fell pregnant with my dad, the case went to Juvenile Court, she said she'd been *taken advantage of* by the lord of the manor, the big boss of the house had got her in the family way. It is all very *Downton Abbey* in my mind, but not much of a happy ending, this 15-year-old girl disappeared as the ink dried on the adoption papers and we now know nothing of my Irish roots. And the fact remains that my paternal grandfather must have been a wealthy and reprehensible brute as he kept his name well out of it and off the record. It was his word against hers in the 1940s, that of a poor 15-year-old Irish immigrant maid against a white man of means and wealth, she didn't stand a chance did she? And nor do immigrant teenagers in this century. Wherever they end up, wash up, whatever the shade, refugee or immigrant, torn away from their parents and homes, I repeat my question: who is protecting the kids from traffickers, from rape and murder?

My parents fell in love and married in the swinging 1960s. They were part of a circle of open-minded, cosmopolitan groovers, musicians and bohemians. My father was a brilliant jazz musician and my mother was a go-go dancer. That was how they met, my father down in the pit, looking up at the legs.

Every time I tell people my father was a jazz musician they picture him as a black man and my mother as the white, funny, isn't it?

But away from their mix of bohemian jazz friends and swinging sixties hippy circle, the prejudice showed its ugly self, primarily as an ignorant curiosity about their sexual relationship. People sniggered and said the most filthy things, the racist connotation being that my mum was untameable and wild from the jungle. Men would nudge each other dirtily and make crass jokes that my father was a lucky man, the common joke going along the lines of:

'… I bet he has his work cut out in the bedroom.'

The fetishisation of the sexuality of black people comes from centuries of dirty dark shade. It starts with sleazy old jokes that black men have huge cocks, or that black women are hyper-sexual, and it festers to become something toxic and sinister. This continues now, mostly unquestioned, with the sexual objectification of women, rounded fat bottoms and full lips all across the media industry. But once the canned laughter dies down or the fashion shoot is done and dusted, and you stop and take a cold hard look at the root history of these jokes and stereotypes, it all comes from a shade so bleak and so ignorant, that it has a sub-human subtext to it – brown people for sale in a human pet shop window.

When my mother had her babies she remembers that the immigrants, the black and Asian mothers, were all put together at one end of one ward. She recalls some nurses were unkind, a bit snotty, making sure they knew they were in the shade, that they were being cast aside, treated differently and were somehow inferior. And afterwards, in the street, as a new mum were proudly pushing her pram, people would stop to look, peering in, curious to see her offspring. Staring down at me, a chubby pale blonde bundle in the pram.

'Are you sure that's your baby?' they'd ask rudely, without a flicker of thought for the hurt that comment might cause.

James Robertson, my great-great-great grandfather, is known in my family as the Colonel. By the time he died he was in fact a General, General James Robertson. A Scottish man, who we recently discovered is buried at Edinburgh University. The Robertson mausoleum is in Greyfriars Cemetery. His oil painting hangs in the National Army Museum, it is a portrait of a white man in a white wig, red jacket, medals and epaulettes. I believe that he was rewarded for his excellence in capturing

Maroons with hunting dogs. I feel uncomfortable when I see his portrait, and visiting his grave I can visualise it all–

Gnarling dogs snapping in the moonlight, Maroon warriors waiting in ambush, camouflaged in the rain forest undergrowth, a human fox hunt, the masts of distant ships, hidden treasure, piracy and subterfuge. We weren't taught about the Maroons at school. They were renown for inventive guerrilla warfare and fierce courage, living by the Maroon mantra that called for them to fear no death:

'To never bow head or knee, to hear only their own voice, to stand in the shadow of none and to be masters of their own destiny.'

Robertson was given land in Jamaica, and this whole area of Clarendon is still called Colonel's Ridge to this day. Robertson married a Maroon - she was in fact a Zulu princess - and through miseducation and misdirection his name changed from Robertson to Robinson, he didn't correct anyone's spelling because he faired better in Jamaica. He abandoned his wife and children in Scotland for a life living as a wealthy plantation owner in the blue mountains of Jamaica.

So now what shade are we? I am a child of immigrants, the first being this Scots man, Robertson or Robinson, an immigrant from Scotland to Jamaica. We are all connected. We live in the shade and shadow of secrets and lies, this shared dirty history of colonialism, rape, land theft and slavery. Slavery was abolished, at a cost, with promises of land and wealth and freedom. Jamaica may have gained independence from Britain in 1962 but today we still chase those broken promises and fight for truth, justice and reparations.

Now, these are just a handful of the things that I hardly ever talk about, these are memories that give me uneasy feelings of doubt and things that remind me that to some I am nothing but a shade. And these are also the moments that inspire me to keep writing and to keep fighting to speak and to be heard and to be read. This shade I wear, this outer skin, this isn't a lovely natural perm or a lucky all-year tan, this is my past, present and future, this shade is my identity. As a kid I was the curly-haired, brown girl with bright green eyes. I was an alien and I stood out in the school group photographs, you can spot us right away, me and my brother; the two grinning brown faces in a sea of white. But you pass any playground now and there are millions of us. I occasionally work in schools, teaching poetry workshops and giving talks, and I'm delighted to walk into a classroom to see a sea of countless colours and mixes, beautiful mixed-up, double-dipped, curly-tops. Most of us are mixed something or other, the world is majorly populated with minorities.

We tick: Other.

There is a dream, a grand idealism, that mixed-race people are the hope for change, the peacekeepers, we are the people with an *other* understanding, with an invested interest in everyone being treated equally as we have a foot and a loyalty in many camps, with all shades. We are like love bombs planted in the minefield of black and white. It is as if our parents intended to make us, with courage, and on purpose, as vessels of empathy, bridges for the cultural divide and diplomats for diversity and equality.

As you grow older, as a mixed-race person, you become a chameleon, you are born with natural camouflage. When you travel everyone assumes you are some version of Latino or Spanish. In the first minutes of meeting you, people have to figure out what shade you are and this is your superpower, it buys you valuable time. People will show their hand and ask,

'Where do you come from?'

And if you reply, 'I just jumped on the tube at Tottenham Court Road,' they'll tut and shake their head.

'No,' they say, 'where do you come from, as in …'

Pause '… *come from*, come from?'

You earn time to chameleon, to camouflage, to make your shade darker or lighter. To morph into what is required or expected. Whatever it takes to survive, whatever it takes to be heard, whatever it takes to get the job. Whatever armour you must wear that day. It's all positive discrimination. Right? No. Wrong. Very. Wrong.

You hesitate, your pen hovers over your boarding pass.

You tick: Other.

Being other, another shade, hasn't ever been a free pass: at the time of writing this I have been reading articles about the aggressive backlash aimed at actress Zoe Saldana for not being *black enough* to play Nina Simone in a new biopic of Simone's later years. As far as Saldana is concerned she is black enough, and woman enough and good enough. When confronted like this, are they asking her to pass up the opportunity to play Nina? Should she know her shade and therefore her place? Decent lead parts for strong female actors are so few and far between, I am keen to see how she plays it. In spite of the shade thrown her way, I suspect Saldana will have worked ten times harder to prove she is good enough, a skilled actor, to portray the legend that is Nina.

For me, being another shade has not been a guarantee of being published by a BAME publisher, to be included in black literary magazines, or that my work will be supported by the black press or BAME media. I haven't relied on tokenism or any positive discrimination. I have, however, always felt that I have to work ten times as hard and that my voice is mine, but that it is different. I keep my head down, I keep on keeping on and I show up to work to write every day. I like to believe that I am booked for festivals and events and published for my merit and talent, and not for the tokenism of my shade or even my gender. I have hope and feel strongly that diversity and equality is improving in the UK, it's a long and slow simmer, but I have seen improvement since I started out in 1994. I perform regularly, and share the stage with a comparatively even mix of boys and girls, black, mixed and white. But we still have such a long way to go; the headline acts are still mostly white and male. I continue to survive and thrive due to my own tenacity and the generous support of others, people who identify as being other: the warriors and outcasts, rebels and renegades, the revolutionaries, the circus, the outsiders and underdogs, the working-class heroes, the punks and the poets and the LGBTQ+ community too. We have learned to belong in the un-belonging. Spirited and colourful souls, of all shades.

We tick: Other.

Some people seem to think that BAME writers, *coloured folk*, are all in some clique, saluting our saviour Zadie Smith sipping coconut water and sharing jerk chicken sauce recipes. That is not true. And neither is it true that BAME writers write with BAME readerships in mind. It also isn't true that all our books solely contain stories for each other, about each other, and about our roots, like travel diaries, tales that will only interest other homesick BAME people. I call bullshit on all of that. The shade of your skin is not the whole content of you and your work. The shade of your skin should not be the measure of your worth. The shade of your skin is not your only audience nor should it be a limitation.

The universal job of being a writer is to write, to write with empathy, to be brave and honest, to find joy conveying a journey and in sharing your passion. Your ink is replenished by your life experiences, by taking off the mask and using your limitless imagination, by stepping out of the shade and into the light. As a woman may write in the voice of a man, I don't see why a writer cannot imagine the voice of another shade and culture, that is what imagination is all about. Whatever shade you are, as a writer, you have just one task each day, one battle, and that is you against the blank page. Every writer should have just that in mind, nothing else matters, just that one fight is more than enough to contend with, each and every morning.

You and your pen against the empty page.

Britain is an island surrounded by salt seawater and inhabited by people of every shade. On a whole I do not think of people as flocks of sheep but more as shoals of fish, swimming to find food and heat and migrating to survive. We could protect each other better if we swam together in unison, we could protect each other from great white sharks dominating everything. We could, but we are like fish, as fickle as fish.

I finish writing this piece at Arvon. I'm working at the writing residency, The Hurst in rural Shropshire. This week I'm tutoring an all-BAME and all-female group of writers, poets and playwrights. I just discovered that this is the first time that Arvon have programmed an all-BAME and all-women course since Arvon began in 1968. I feel honoured to be chosen to be here this week. I observe the women sharing stories, the challenges of being women writers, the struggles to be funded and to publish work. I am stunned by the openness of the dialogue, moreover the shocking lack of confidence which comes from having to lower your expectations, shrinking your dream because of a stream of constant rejection and the lack of opportunities here in the UK, especially if you are a BAME woman and aged over 30. Above all, this week is evidence to me of things improving, new platforms being provided and good people helping to change things. Things are slowly getting better, I can see an improvement since the 1990s, but it is just taking way too long.

All I can do is keep on keeping on, keep sailing my Good Ship.

Human colour is the colour I'm truly interested in, the colour of your humanity. May the size of your heart and the depth of your soul be your currency. Welcome aboard my Good Ship. Let us sail to the colourful island of mixed identity. You can eat from the cooking pot of mixed culture and bathe in the cool shade of being mixed-race. There is no need for a passport. There are no borders. We are all citizens of the world. Whatever shade you are, bring your light, bring your colour, bring your music and your books, your stories and your histories, and climb aboard. United as a people we are a million majestic colours, together we are a glorious stained-glass window. We are building a cathedral of otherness, brick by brick and book by book. Raise your glass of rum, let's toast to the minorities who are the majority. There is no stopping time, nor the blurring of lines or the blending of shades. With a spirit of hope I leave you now. I drink to our sameness and to our unique differences. This is the twenty-first century and we share this, we live here, in the future. It is a beautiful morning, it is first light on the time of being other, so get out from that shade and feel the warmth of being outside.

You tick: Other.

THE WIFE OF A TERRORIST

MISS L

Doctor.

Lawyer.

Farmer.

Librarian.

A villain with a good heart.

Hairdresser.

One by one, accepting smiles spread around the room as our fates were tantalisingly dished out. The person next to me is bequeathed 'Nurse'. She's happy. She tells me later that she'd been fearing 'Student'. We are all pleased for her.

It's my turn next. I'm in a drama studio, sitting in a circle with the 33 other people that I've spent the last three years with. Three years spent desperately clinging to the hope that we will leave this place and won't spend the rest of our days working in a call centre instead of setting the BBC alight with our acting majesty.

Today is an infamous day in drama school folklore. This is the day that we are all going to discover how to best market ourselves. After three years of trying to make ourselves as versatile as possible, we are now going to be told how the world would be seeing us. Our training is almost at an end. Just a few weeks to go until we're kicked out into the world, desperately waving our *Complete Works of Shakespeare* like it's a ticket for the *Titanic*. Sat before us is the head of the acting school, a woman who has been getting to know us for three years and is now telling us what it's worth.

She turns to me and there's a pause. Wow, I think. A dramatic pause. Clearly this is going to be good. My versatility over the last three years must mean my tutor can't possibly pick just one role for me. I can practically hear every film studio sweeping their doorsteps in preparation for my arrival. She takes a deep breath and I suddenly realise what she's going to say.

'Terrorist.'

People laugh. I even think I laugh. I'd honestly been expecting 'pharmacist'.

'Actually, no,' she says, changing her mind. Well of course, she'd realised what a narrow-minded thing that was to say. That's okay, we've all been there, we've all put our recycling in the regular rubbish without thinking of our great, great, great-grandchildren and the awful world we're creating for them.

She looks at me again and says, 'The wife of a terrorist'.

Now I'm definitely laughing. Three years of getting up at 7am, three years of movement classes that made my feet bleed, three years of singing that made me cry at my atrocious voice, three years of phonetics that made me want to rip my own soul out, three years of time, money, effort, hope, love, hate, hangovers and it was all to play the wife of a terrorist, the most silent, unseen role you can possibly think of.

I wish I'd had the courage to shout back. I wish I'd found my voice before she moved on to tell me that the man sat next to me would be best suited to play a politician. I'm reeling harder than the time Dad was doing Ramadan so it meant we had to wait until the evening for our Christmas dinner ... I know, our household was nothing if not multicultural.

Until now, acting was being everything that I wasn't. I, the brown girl at school with a funny name, had played everything. I'd been a villager from Oz, I'd been Jack Frost, I'd even played Gordie from *Stand By Me* when, aged 10, my friend and I inexplicably decided to turn it into a full-length play for our class. Yes, I, a 10-year-old girl with frizzy hair and a better moustache than all the boys in my class, had pretended, in 1993 in front of our Year Five class and painfully patient teacher Mr East, to have a leech on my penis. It's this kind of tolerance of my foolish endeavours that almost definitely lead me to believe I could prance about for a living. When you've spent most of your life wanting to make a living out of pretending to be someone else, suddenly being told you can only play one role because of how you look is quite the rap across the jazz hands. One of the first steps to becoming an actor, after the realisation that people will always ask if you've been in anything they might've seen, is telling yourself it's okay to want to be other people. It's not that you don't want to be you, it's that you also enjoy not being you, and that's fine. You took the Halloween fancy dress invite, and instead of just buying a cheap wig like most people, you decided to make a career out of it.

The whole point of acting is versatility. Of course, there are some actors who make a glorious living out of playing the same role for ever more, but the reason why we become actors is because we never know which role will come in next. Look at Meryl Streep, you need to set aside a whole day if you want to spend some time with her CV. I kept telling myself there would be other roles on offer to me. If Renée Zellweger could play Bridget Jones then I was allowed to dream of being more than sad set dressing. I'd played Jack Frost, goddammit. Really though, that wasn't the problem on that warm spring afternoon in April. The problem was that I'd finally been told how the industry would see me, and it was only on my walk home that I had the withering realisation that I was being judged by both my skin colour and my gender.

The first question I had to deal with was why I was being seen as the wife of a terrorist. I'm going to go out on a pretty strong limb here and say that, despite the fact I once drunkenly broke a locker, this wasn't due to any particularly disruptive tendencies I'd shown at drama school. In fact, I was so keen to not disrupt things that I even rather foolishly once came in for a dance showing with chronic food poisoning. I often wonder how many people in the world have attempted a grand *jeté* to Kanye West and contemplated which orifice is going to give way first. So no, that can't be it. Therefore, I'm going to have to make a pretty bold assumption, much like she did, that my terrorist casting is down to the colour of my skin and my slightly unpronounceable name. Apparently, because of this, I was much less likely to be a doctor and far more likely to be something that has sadly become synonymous with the Middle East.

Now don't get me wrong, I was under no illusions that I was going to be the next Lizzie Bennet. I'd already come to terms with the fact that I was probably never going to appear in a Sunday teatime adaptation. Those quaint period dramas were never going to be for me, girls with my complexion don't get to wear a corset as their father worries about the upper field drainage. I mean, it's supposedly fine to cast white actors in ethnic minority roles (Angelina Jolie, Emma Stone, Mickey Rooney, I could go on …) but the other way round? There's more chance of seeing Benedict Cumberbatch in the dole queue. This would be fine if ringlets and riding crops didn't reign supreme on our TV screens, but you currently can't look at a screen without seeing a white person worrying about a dowry. It's no wonder ethnic actors are heading to America instead, somewhere they have a chance of not being elbowed out by corsets and fancy hats.

As a kid who grew up being mildly obsessed with *Brief Encounter*, the realisation that I'd never get to be in any of these of course made me sad, but I consoled myself with the fact that this was the twenty-first century. This was the era of diversity and I, a woman once called 'funny-coloured' by one of her drama school peers when wondering how she'd be best described, should surely thrive. I hate to go on about it but, come on, I'D PLAYED JACK FROST. The sallow-skinned girl with a big nose had played the whitest male character the world has ever seen. So why was I being pigeonholed before I'd even begun?

I should be used to assumptions being made about me since it has been happening pretty much my whole life. From kids at school incorrectly calling me 'paki' to teachers constantly presuming that I and the other Middle Eastern girl at school must be sisters, despite us having different surnames. And then there is, of course, this conversation:

'So where are you from?'

'Oxford.'

'No, where are you really from?'

'It's a little village in the sticks. You really won't have heard of it.'

'No, like where are you originally from?'

'Do you want my address?'

'No, what's your heritage?'

Your heritage, like you're an antique vase or a listed building. The other lesson I quickly learned was that being unwhite also seems to mean that people make assumptions about what you can do. I remember once going to an audition for another familiar scenario, 'Middle Eastern woman in a relationship with a white man and they have to fight everyone's prejudices'. The audition was so far away that I nearly had to pack my stuff up in 100ml bottles, and I got there to find it was being held in the director's attic. Already this didn't bode well. We did the scene and he frowned at me. 'Can you do the scene in Hindi for me?'

'Nope.'

'I think it would be a good idea.'

'But I can't speak Hindi.'

'Why not?'

'Because I'm not from India.'

He grabs my printed out CV. 'Well, what do you speak?'

'English.'

'And you don't speak any other languages? You should be ashamed of yourself.'

Should I? Would they be saying this to a white actor who hadn't bothered to learn German? At no point had I claimed to speak Hindi, and nor should I, but people can presume I can, just because I look a little bit like I might come from somewhere near there. It's also been presumed I can speak the following (deep breath) Italian, Spanish, Portuguese, Hebrew, Farsi, Arabic, Urdu and Turkish.

The wife of a terrorist.

Suddenly being released into the world as a newly trained actor is tough enough but I also had to contend with being both Middle Eastern and a woman. This is something I've battled against since day one and is the reason why I set up my *Casting Call Woe* blog. Born out of frustration and horror, it's a look at the very worst casting calls I've seen on my desperate hunt for work. From female roles described as 'her cleavage is her best feature' to actors being asked to do an 'immigrant accent', it's a terrifying insight into the stereotypes still being maintained despite it supposedly being the twenty-first century.

I'd love to say that once I stepped out into the big, bad world I actually got to play a whole host of interesting roles. I mean I did, sort of. Over the last 10 years I played an eight-year-old boy, a nine-year-old girl and even a stag, but a good 75 per cent of the roles I went up for very much fell under the heading of Middle Eastern Women. If I wasn't auditioning for the wife of a terrorist (yes, she was right), then I was up for the role she hadn't warned me of, that of a woman in an arranged marriage. It was nice that there were some surprises still in store for me but, really, a BAFTA nomination would've been nicer.

In fact, it was the arranged marriage situation that I found myself in most. Pretty much every role I went for was either being set up for an arranged marriage or was suffering terribly during one. One particular role I went up for was of a woman desperate to escape her marriage. I turned up to the audition to find a note tacked to the door saying the room was no longer available and instead to go and wait outside the McDonald's. Odd, but whatever. I wandered around to find that the audition was actually being held inside the McDonald's. Great. Because there's nothing that aids getting into the character of someone who's just set themselves on fire than seeing someone tucking into their cheeseburger. I checked a few months later and saw that the very white director had decided to cast herself instead. I consoled myself that night with a KFC.

When I complain about the lack of female representation in film and TV, I can guarantee someone will helpfully shout some suggestions in my face. Granted, these suggestions will probably be from a few years ago (yes, *Girls*, *Bridesmaids*, *Mean Girls* … funny how they all have something female in the title …) but they tend to shy away when I bemoan the lack of Middle Eastern females. They might flounder for a bit and then quietly – just in case they're wrong and they can then claim I misheard it, like someone pretending not to hear a question in the pub quiz because they know they really should know the answer – they'll mutter, 'Princess Jasmine?' 200,000 years of humans and all we get is a Disney princess to represent us. To be fair to them, Middle Eastern women are few and far between when it comes to the roles we see on our screens and stages. There's a reason why you can't think of any famous wives of terrorists, because who would remember a woman in a hijab who features in the corner of one shot? Once you've exhausted P-Jaz and Cleopatra, you're already starting to run out of ideas. More recent additions include Ms Marvel, *Persepolis* and *A Girl Walks Home Alone at Night*; there's progress, but it's slow and can just as easily take a step backwards rather than forwards.

Much of this came from the fact that I was graduating during the Noughties, a time when our perception of the Middle East was particularly primed to be one based around fear and misunderstanding. Maybe if I'd been graduating a bit earlier then I might've been able to play the wife of a taxi driver or a kebab shop owner, maybe the wife of a rug maker if I was really lucky.

There are such connotations linked with being Middle Eastern that you generally can't play a role unless it has something to do with your race. Sure, I can play a doctor or a lawyer or a street cleaner, but only if I'm being forced into an arranged marriage in the background or providing a cover-up for my terrorist husband. If there's some really daring casting then I might get to play a character that defies my father's wishes, if that happens then maybe I get to wear a nice dress and not wear a hijab. But very rarely do I get to play a role that isn't defined by the preconceptions made about the colour of my skin.

What really gets me is that all the roles are so helpless, and this is something that's often true of a lot of female roles. Every role I go up for that is specifically Middle Eastern is a woman that is basically having her life controlled, and her story is that she's either suffering through it or trying to escape it. In fact, I'm reading a casting call for such a role right now, 'a rebellious Pakistani Muslim girl who lives with her traditional father and brother. She decides to run away with her boyfriend.' Now, don't get me wrong, these are stories that should be told but we're mistaken to think that Middle Eastern women are limited to being in unhappy relationships. Also, not only are they hugely limiting for Middle Eastern actresses but they're massively insulting to Middle Eastern men.

Looking back over all the Middle Eastern Wife roles I've been up for, not one of them has been in a happy marriage. She's either there because she's been forced to or she's dealing with a terrorist husband through gritted teeth. And of all the Middle Eastern Non-Wife roles I've been for, not one of them has had a father or brother who isn't trying to get them to marry someone. How boringly limiting is that? There are no roles for Middle Eastern girls to aspire to, no roles to show the world that we're capable of more than being a prop in a hijab.

All this is what lead me to, shamefully, deciding to change my name when I first graduated. I've never been ashamed of how I look or the fact that cold callers take a deep breath before attempting the concoction of letters that I call my name, but I couldn't cope with the fact that I was pigeonholing myself before I'd even started. I'd spent so long having assumptions made about me and now, suddenly, I was being handed this little ticket that might allow my acting abilities a second thought. Of course, it was a hideous idea. The name never really scanned properly. I'd suddenly made myself that random person from school on Facebook who gets married and changes their name. Every time they pop up on your feed, you totally forget who they are and only vaguely remember when you squint at their terrible picture. I lived with that feeling as my name for two years until, thankfully, a director I was working with was the first person to be honest with me and sat me down to tell me I'd made a huge mistake. That afternoon, I changed it back and, since then, I've embraced everything that being a part-Iraqi, part-Iranian, part-British actress is.

Yes, I will play the role of a wife or wife-to-be. Yes, I know that I sometimes get work purely because I'm a good diversity box-ticker. Yes, I'll never be cast in *Pride and Prejudice*. But none of that really matters because I get to represent a bunch of incredible women who are so vastly unrepresented. And that's what acting is. It's about telling people's stories as honestly and faithfully as we possibly can. It's being entrusted with a person and showing them to the world. It's not just about us as actors being represented, it's about the people we represent and making sure their tales are told.

Excitingly, as I write this, I've just been asked to audition for the lead in a short film. It's the role of a high-powered Syrian lawyer. She's also married to a controlling husband. Roll on Princess bloody Jasmine.

WHAT WE TALK ABOUT WHEN WE TALK ABOUT TOKENISM

BIM ADEWUNMI

The comments section is different for every story on the internet. For stories about diversity – whether that be across gender, disability, sexual orientation or race – though, there are a few that crop up with a regularity that would be reassuring if it weren't so depressingly samey.

A quick perusal across the breadth of the internet throws up the one that gets me the most heated: the 'but do you want tokenism?' defence. I mean, practically every gathering of internet-opinions has its version of this question; well-meaning people asking – with baffled internet-expressions – if what we as people of colour want is 'tokenism' in popular (and not-so-popular) culture. This is how 'reasonable' people – the people who work alongside you, and manage to have nuanced conversations about so many things in daily life – respond to a call to have more than one type of person in the cultural representations of human life that we absorb every day. I feel sure I have seen every variant of this comment and I am compelled to ask: why is it that the only options ever offered are 'tokenism' (this internet-person's objective, overwhelming concern) or total, yawning absence? How is it, that in 2016, there are only these two stark choices? To paraphrase Eddie Izzard's classic sketch: why do we have to be so 'cake or death' about this?

Sometimes, there are addenda, gracious add-ons, like: 'I'm happy to see people of colour as characters in this TV show *if* the plot calls for it' or 'why put a black dude in the cast "just because"?' (Again, there are many variations of these.) It is important to understand precisely what is being said there: the story that everyone can relate to, the character that we as an audience are supposed to be able to project ourselves onto with the most ease, the 'universal', is white. The default is *always* white. There are no vacancies in that spot – ever – for people of colour. No Nigerian-British everyman. No unexceptional Bangladeshi-British Joe Bloggs/Jaleel Begum. Characters of colour only make it into the mix specifically 'when the role calls for it'.

Let that sink in for a moment.

Whiteness – or, you know, white people – exists as the basic template. And that template covers all human experience, by the way: the ability to be special or ordinary, handsome or ugly, tall or short, interesting or dull as ditchwater. On the other hand, *our* presence in popular culture (as well as in non-stereotypical 'issue' roles) must always be justified. Our place at the table has to be *earned*. We must somehow show we are worthy of inclusion in representations of the culture that we live and breathe in. Does that black woman deserve to be on that show? Give the exact reason that Chinese-British man is in this scene. Explain the series of decisions that led us to having this mixed-race boy in this film. Please show your working for maximum marks.

We live in an age where fandom is less on the fringes: regular people make their own homemade costumes and go to comic conventions now, not just the geeks of yore. So we know the patter of the showrunner who is getting some audience heat – they were 'hesitant' to include POC POVs in their shows because they were 'worried' about issues of 'authenticity'. For about five seconds after hearing these responses, I nod and understand. That quickly passes, though; what I want to do is call up their offices to set up a meeting to discuss *exactly* what they imagine people of colour (usually in the city, town or village the writer is her/himself from) do so damn differently. *Then* I want to offer my services (for a substantial fee, obviously – I'm no martyr) to help them 'bridge the gap'. Here's what black people do: we breathe air, we drink water and we fart noxious gases, just like other people. Our hopes and dreams are similar, and alongside the various hardships we may suffer because of the way we look or where we come from, we largely do the same things – and that includes all the frivolous things too. Things like eating cupcakes, or wanting the chance to write a self-involved collection of essays (let's not even get started on the publishing industry), having sex with unsuitable boys and being monstrously self-obsessed. There, I'm a consultant. NOW, WHERE'S MY CHEQUE?

As an enthusiastic fan of popular culture – and a human being in possession of the full complement of human desires and emotions, narcissism high among them – I like to see myself in the surrounding culture. I want to see a girl with natural hair, or a weave, or relaxed hair and I want to see her doing everything: I want her to go to the movies, I want her to find a cure for a rare disease, I want her to work as a shop girl, I want her to save the world when the apocalypse comes, I want her to fall in love, I want her to fight aliens, and I want her to laugh a lot. As things stand, she simply doesn't exist. This sad state of affairs means I thrilled quietly when I saw Storm in the X-Men movies (even though she has a frankly insulting and vague 'African' accent in the first one – WHO ACTUALLY SPEAKS LIKE THAT, HALLE?), and I squealed and called my sister when I saw Nicole Beharie in the trailer for Steve McQueen's *Shame*. It means I got excited when I read in a 2012 report from the Directors Guild of America that Shonda Rhimes used 67 per cent female or minority ethnic directors in the making of her show *Scandal*.[73]

I'm a big telly fan. It's one of my favourite things in the world – I can quote most of *Friends* (my favourite sitcom of all time, despite its monochrome core cast and myriad flaws) from memory, just give me the prompt – but I am not involved directly in making telly. I don't wish to downplay the importance and necessity of having a diverse writers' room system – clearly there are too few people of colour in these rooms, and that's before we even get into the class issue. But it seems obvious to me, a naïve layman with beautiful dreams, that there are three steps to writing a good character of colour:

1. Write a stonkingly good, well-rounded character
2. Make the 'effort' to cast a person of colour
3. That's it!

I've seen real life applications of this groundbreaking technique in *The Good Wife*, *Master of None*, *Chewing Gum*, and *Community*, among others. But maybe I'm wrong. Maybe there are huge hurdles to clear in order to make television that looks like the world, hurdles that the layman just can't see or comprehend. If you're reading this and do make entertainment television, please correct me if I've somehow misunderstood the complexities.

---

73 'DGA says diversity among TV directors stalled: report', Deadline Hollywood. http://deadline.com/2012/09/directors-guild-diversity-study-tv-directors-veep-dallas-344300/

It appears clear to me that there is a gap in what people mean when they say things like 'we're all one race – the human race' and how they actually see the world. The thing that means a person cannot imagine seeing a Asian man as a superhero (you know, that set of fictional beings with special powers) is pretty much the same thing that makes a person cringe away from feeling empathy for a fictional dying black girl (Rue, played by Amandla Stenberg in *The Hunger Games*). It leaks into the everyday, too – if you cannot bring yourself to imagine us as real, rounded individuals with feelings equal to your own on screen, how does that affect your ability to do so when you encounter us on the street, at your workplace, in your bed, in your life?

It doesn't have to be this way. Consider these words from Mindy Kaling back in September 2012:

When you are the only Indian-American female lead in a television show, you seem to be making sweeping statements about that person simply because you are that person and the only one, whereas, for instance, Steve Carell – he's not making sweeping generalisations about white American men on his show because there's so many different white American men on different shows. So I get worried by doing this character that people think that I'm saying that about all those people. And I just have the weight of that on my shoulders, which is something that I do envy other performers for not having.

This is just the everyday shit of being a pop culture fan living in black skin. And it's so tiring.

DEATH IS A MANY-HEADED MONSTER

VINAY PATEL

My father's father, my dada, is staring at me, trying to wrap his head around what I've just told him.

'Crocodiles?'

I nod.

'Yes, Dada.'

By the staircase in my house there is a framed photo of a woman that I've passed every day of my six years. I've always known, looking at that photo, that this woman died when I was very little, littler than I am now. I've always known that this woman is my mother, a mother being someone a bit like my grandma, my Ba, but younger and with better English. I know that when someone dies, it means they're not around anymore. I even know how it can happen.

'Too many angry white shells,' is how Dad, sitting on the edge of my bed late one night, explained lupus to me. Despite mishearing 'cells' as 'shells' and imagining my insides as a tiny beach, I'm already more *au fait* with death than your average kid.

But the possibilities of what death might be like for the person dying have only recently snuck up on me and they are more horrifying than any movie monster. At bedtime, before I switch off the light, I picture death. I see myself floating in a void for a finite but excruciatingly long amount of time before being allowed into heaven. Like fifty thousand years. Long enough for you to lose all sense of self, all points of reference. Maybe Mum, trembling and alone, is a few years into that long haul. Then the idea of time vanishes and I grapple with the darkest thought to enter my young mind so far: when you die, you are dead for ever. No feeling. No thinking. Just nothing. Forever. I started to leave the light on. However, the stillness of a lit room in an otherwise dark street had its own sense of a timeless void so I would throw myself into different worlds in order to escape. I would read – *Star Wars* novels, a copy of *Great Expectations* someone had bought me without irony, *Improving Your Golf Swing,* whatever I could find – until a drowsy adult would stumble past (I come from a family of light sleepers) and check in. I'd pretend to have dropped off mid-sentence, they would turn the light off and I would hope I had tired myself out enough not to think.

Thankfully, this exhausting state of affairs could now come to an end since, on my way to confront my bed, I've poked my head in to watch a BBC nature documentary someone's left running on the living room telly and I've heard something wonderful, something that's going to change my life for ever and I've run upstairs to tell my dada. I repeat myself to him to dispel the confusion on his face:

'Yeah, crocodiles! They said on the TV that crocodiles reincarnate and if crocodiles can reincarnate, I can too.'

The idea of death being final might have been new to me but this reincarnation lark was not. Nobody had explicitly talked to me about it yet, but it featured very strongly in the children's storybooks I'd been given depicting the two central

Hindu myths, the *Mahabharata* and the *Ramayana*. These were epics about Gods-incarnate and 10-headed demons and arrows that could destroy seas. They were tales where at the start a woman could be spurned by a suitor and kill herself from the shame, only to turn up near the end, born into the body of a young warrior prince, ready to revenge herself on her former lover. What a twist! However, twists are devices for stories and whilst I thought they were awesome stories, it was clear to me that there was no connection between those mythic worlds and my reality.

That had all changed now. Already at the age of six there was a deep part of me that recognised David Attenborough's calm voice as one that spoke with a weight of knowledge. I could trust what this man from the documentary told me about the world because this wasn't a story, this was *science*.

It takes Dada a while, but he eventually figures out that this is yet another mishearing on my part and what Mr Attenborough actually said was 'crocodiles reproduce', not 'crocodiles reincarnate'. My dada is a proud, self-taught businessman who likes to pamper his grandkids, using the gains from a lifetime of hard work to create a cushion from the harshness of the world that he never had. So to crush the hopes of a child and then round it off with a much-needed chat about the birds and bees must've been quite tricky. But he bloody well managed it.

My thoughts about The End spread from bedtime to every spare moment. Showers are particularly bad. They start off well enough; I enjoy being naked, our boiler is the absolute business and our showerhead provides several options to keep things fresh. And then, as the ballast of everyday cares drop away, my mind inevitably drifts to the moment of my death and I consider how one minute I'll exist and the next I won't, that the line was that fine, that it was absolutely, definitely going to happen to me one day. One day I won't touch or smell or see or even care that I couldn't and …

Screaming.

Eventually, always, I ended up screaming in terror for a good minute or so until the small worries of life crept back in.

'You might be dead one day, buddy,' they'd say. 'But you've still got us to deal with.' I was never more grateful for Monday morning homework hand-in than in those moments.

My poor concerned Ba asked me every time what was wrong, and I always sulked the question off. How could she empathise or understand? She was full of the comforting conviction of faith, so much so that she dedicated half of every morning to the shrine in her bedroom – bringing a flame from downstairs in a tiny golden cup and placing it before her equally tiny idols of the Gods, of which there a multitude. I only recognised the bronze Hanuman that I had picked up myself from a ramshackle market stall in Ahmedabad. I was told that I could choose the God I wanted to be the one who would look after me and I went for Hanuman, the mercurial monkey king from my *Ramayana* story book. He spends his time wrestling, arguing with mountains and burning down cities with his tail for japes. That's the guy I want watching my back. When I pointed him out, the merchant nodded, applied some badly-painted plastic eyes to the metal, and handed him over. I found it really funny to see this boss-eyed monkey man sitting on my ba's immaculate shrine but it was clear to me from this practised routine, during which you *must not* disturb her, that it all meant a lot to her. Any solutions to my screaming were going to come from this faith, this dedication and I didn't trust them.

None of this anxiety was helped by the family events I was now trusted to come to. Typical of immigrants from poor countries, my extended family was huge on both sides, which meant an endless stream of weddings and funerals, at which I knew no one and cared very little. The weddings were traditionally Indian: flowers, saris, bad dancing, carefully portioned food served into specially made plastic trays with dividers that helpfully kept your khichdi and puri dry and separate from the dhey. The funerals, on the other hand, had a stronger English infusion. Black suits, churches and solemnity. The weddings were boring but at least you could run around and have fun with the other kids. No such luck at the funerals. All there was to do was absorb the sadness and hope that if you fell over, someone might take you home early.

I eventually tamed my existential dread by doing what I continue to do with all deadlines to this day: I pushed it back. I can't remember what triggered it but one day I just told myself 'It's OK, I'll find religion when I'm twenty-one', and with that I was satisfied that All Would Be Well One Day. It was a Pascalian pragmatism that held for a couple of years until, ever so gradually, the obvious issue reared its head.

Exactly **which** religion would I be finding?

Being raised in a Hindu family but going to an explicitly Christian school (where I played Joseph in the nativity play, yet somehow lost out on Mowgli in *The Jungle Book* to a ginger kid called Charlie) in a nominally Christian country meant a strong dissonance not just in tolerance of spices and film lengths but also in end-of-life theories. With Hinduism there wasn't even an Abrahamic link like there was between Judaism, Islam and Christianity that would allow you to do a reasoned 'well, when you think about it, it's all from the same place, the same people, what do the differences really matter?' number on it.

People I loved, people I trusted, people I thought were cool, all backed wildly different beliefs about what happened after death and how to live the life that came before it. My grandmothers had a fervent Hindu faith, but adding together everyone else around me it was clear there were so many others available to offer a contradiction: my Sikh friends with their little swords and turbans; the proud owners of the Punjabi kebab house I'd visit with my dad on Commercial Street with Islamic art on their walls; my Chinese teacher at primary school who taught me all about which numbers were lucky and which weren't in her culture; even a Jehovah's Witness who turned up at our door once and made a good go of explaining how she was one of the chosen few. There seemed to be as many ways to live as there were to be dead. They couldn't all be right, even if I wanted them to be, which led me to what felt like the only logical conclusion: they're all wrong. Dread had morphed into pragmatism, which now gave way to a wary, sometimes sneering atheism shared by my sister and dad – the cynical school run trio – that carried me through secondary education and informed my choice of friends.

It wasn't until university and my encounters with the Christian Union there that I found anything matching my grandmothers for intensity of belief. These weren't the half-hearted C of E types I knew from home, or traditional old ladies for whom religion went a long way to standing in for the education denied to them. These CU types were confident, smart and *nice* – so bloody nice. It's hard to be snarky about people who hand out free cheese toasties with a smile and no expectations. I became good friends with a few of them and started to see how their faith helped guide their lives. It gave them patience, hope, a mission, all things I was desperately lacking in. I was still cynical about religion but I could see the appeal; when compared to a first-year student body loaded with horny drunks, it was hard not to think that the world would actually be better off with more people like them – community-minded and doing regular Good Deeds – than people like me.

To show my appreciation, I made posters about how their hall rep was 'a really fucking great guy!', which wasn't appreciated. Eventually I started going to their meet-up groups, along with my Belgian Goth flatmate, Michael. He was there to give them a hard time, I was there to listen.

As it happens, God did finally find me during second year, two years before my self-imposed deadline, but it wasn't the Christian Union that got me in the end, despite their best efforts. I was lucky enough to have all four grandparents around for my childhood; however, the counterweight of that luck was knowing you were going to see them all die one day and you wondered which would go first. It wasn't the one I was expecting. It turned out to be one of my grandmothers, my mother's mother, my biji ba (a name, along with biji dada, that I think of with much affection, but which basically means 'other grandma' and 'other grandad' – useful in distinguishing between them but somewhat suggestive of a bit of a hierarchy). She was both the youngest and the most devout. One of the last things she said from her hospital bed was, 'I'm coming back as a bird.'

Hearing this, I wanted to reply, 'That's stupid, you're here, be here, don't be talking about being somewhere else, something else.'

I didn't, of course. I couldn't crush her like my grandfather had done to me. She wasn't six like I was but sixty-six which, to my mind, was still far too young for this to happen. She was the first person that I really knew to go and I found that first death is the evil mirror universe version of first love – life-changing, raw, an experience that will superficially come again but will never be felt in the same way.

My childhood was spent between the homes of both sides of my family, and if the photo of Mum in my dad's house was a subtle memento mori, the funeral home opposite my mum's parents' estate was an altogether more overt one, somewhere they were probably going to end up if the place stayed in business long enough, and so it proved. They had Biji Ba in the back room of that funeral home (isn't it strange they're called homes?), her concrete-grey, stern face – an expression she'd never worn in life – contrasted with the bright sari she'd been draped in. The colour amongst the grey felt a fitting tribute to her time in this country. Before I left, I decided I really, really needed to knock on her forehead. Was she in there? In the void? A bird? There was, of course, no reply.

The funeral and the events around it I went into with a detached clarity. Living within two religious traditions had robbed me of any belief in the holy or spiritual but it allowed me a greater appreciation for why those traditions are important. They hold us when we need it. Traditions are just nonsense that binds, and whilst the nonsense might take on a different hue, the binding is universal.

My grief lingered and, in the time it was with me, it felt possible to believe that maybe, just maybe, my grandma *was* a bird. I tortured my sceptical brain around the science of it – we're all just atoms to be rearranged, right? – and it felt that there must be something to this world that I was missing. I wanted to believe that the sacrifices my family had made to create a life for me, that took them so far from their home, would be validated somehow by a merciful god. It had to be. Had to. So I asked my newly widowed biji dada for a copy of the *Bhagavad Gita*, which he gladly provided. In doing so, he told me of his own journey from non-belief to belief over his years moving through the last outposts of Empire and ending up in his ex-council house in Battersea. Is it harder to have faith when you're in another land, I wondered? Or, in a search for meaning and purity in a place that can often resent you, does your faith harden in reaction?

For my part, I started to push against my evangelical friends who I had previously got on so well with. What did *they* think had happened to Biji Ba? To my mum? What did they think would happen to me, this heathen in their midst?

During a night I'm not particularly proud of, I pushed one of them so hard that she confessed that, yes, they thought my mum and grandma were in hell and that I was going to end up there too ... but she prayed that I wouldn't. I was being a prick. She was my friend. She was in tears. She clearly found it agony to say it. But she did say it, and I told her to go fuck herself. It was ugly, and proved an uglier time still for Exeter evangelicals in general as their group found themselves in disputes with other Christian societies as well as the secularism of the uni itself. An increasingly rancorous chain of events that culminated in them attempting to sue the student union[74].

Meanwhile, I dived into the *Bhagavad Gita* and was thrilled to find more poetic, adult versions of the storybooks I had as a kid. I spoke to priests. Read forums. Did I know Hinduism isn't a religion but more a pagan-style collection of beliefs? No, I did not. Did I realise you could worship Jesus and still be a Hindu? No way. This was great. It all tied up! Hinduism was older than everything else, it was flexible, if there was one that

---

74 'Christian group to take university to court', *The Guardian*. http://www. theguardian.com/education/2007/jul/27/highereducation.uk2

was going to be *right* across the millennia it had to be this one – the faith I needed had been staring me in the face ever since birth. I was brown Luke Skywalker. I was a Hindu, like my mother before me. Of course. Of course! Peace and purpose were around the corner.

This religious ecstasy lasted, all in all, about a couple of months before withering away.

Nowadays, having for the most part accepted I'm just a chimp with airs, with no mighty sky chimp looking out for me, I think less about what happens to the souls of me and my loved ones after and more about what will be done with our actual bodies, which we at least have some control over.

At the time of writing this essay, I still have three grandparents left. Fingers crossed this figure doesn't shift too significantly before publication, but it will one day and how they choose to be mourned says as much about their journey as their actions in life. Three generations of my family have been born on three different continents: most of my grandparents in India, both parents in Kenya, me in England along with my sister and cousins. Asia. Africa. Europe. Every continent we've been through has left a mark on us. I'm half-amused, half-annoyed that the little Gujarati I speak is infused with Swahili words and dialect, a coded language fully available only to those who have made that particular journey. Broadly useless to me, but in itself a wonderful reminder of how far they've come in every sense. We are happy to change and adapt even something so fundamentally important to us as language in order to start sinking into our new homes. In death, though, so far they've all returned to the 'motherland' and had their ashes spread over the Ganges. There's a religious element to that of course but, in choosing this way to be laid to rest, it suggests to me that this diaspora, these brave wanderers, always yearned for home no matter how successful they were at integrating abroad.

What about me then? After all, I'm racking up the days myself and when I dwell on the numbers they warp into curious, morbid trivia. This year, for example, I turn thirty and so soon my mum – that picture on the wall – will become, in a way, the youngest member of our family. If my sister and I live until we're eighty, it will have been a whole hundred years from my family arriving in the UK to someone born here dying here. And, I imagine, we'll also wind up getting our ashes spread here or somewhere nearby. We aren't religious. There's no spiritual connection to some 'homeland' for us. Will that be the final moment of integration? When we've not just been born, lived and died in this country, but are interred somewhere in its soil as well? When there's, to rephrase an old poem, some corner of an English field that is forever foreign.

For my part, I hope in death I create another branch to my family's story. If I die where I am now, I don't believe I'll reincarnate, I don't think I'm going to heaven or hell or the void, but at least I will already be home.

THE UNGRATEFUL COUNTRY

MUSA OKWONGA

So here's my experience of growing up in Britain; it was always a case of making sure that I was grateful. Maybe that wasn't such a bad attitude to have; after all, my parents were brought to the UK as refugees, fleeing the hyper-violent regime of Idi Amin, and so there was no question that they had been given a second chance at life. At the time of their departure, Amin was busily wiping out anyone who might represent a future threat to his rule, and my parents – then attendees of two of the best schools in Uganda – were firmly within his target demographic. And so they came to West Drayton, and a few years later I turned up: the eldest son of two doctors, with an eagerness to please their adopted country.

I didn't notice that eagerness until I was 11, when I was given a bursary to attend Sunningdale, a boys' prep school. Until that point, I hadn't given much thought to my skin colour, since everywhere I'd studied before had been racially diverse: now, though, I was one of two black pupils out of 130. What's more, my new peers and their families weren't like the white people I had met before, whose lives were reassuringly everyday, and who generally only owned the one home. My new classmates seemed to have the most glamorous of existences. Many of them lived abroad. Their holidays were spent skiing and shooting. One had a butler. The richest ones were always the most shabbily dressed: if a boy had holes in his sweater, he was more likely than not to be descended from some emperor.

Following the overthrow of Idi Amin in 1981, my father returned to Uganda to help build what he believed would be a better country. He became the military physician for Major General Oyite-Ojok, the commander who defeated Amin, and he died with him. On December 3rd, 1983, their helicopter crashed – or, most likely, was shot down – in a moment that was seen as the turning-point in the struggle for control of the country. My mother, widowed, was left to raise four young children alone; and with her attention divided between us and endless shifts as a local GP, I learned that the last thing she needed was additional problems from me. No: what she needed was for me to be smart, dutiful and responsible. So I turned up at Sunningdale School, black and from a miraculously solvent single-parent home, amongst the sons of white millionaires.

I became an unofficial ambassador for black people. There were so few of us in the boarding-school world that I felt driven every week to prove that we could be just as good as our white counterparts. Returning home for my holidays, I saw the implications of a world where people were judged by their skin alone. My cousins and I were starting to be stop-searched by police, on one occasion merely for waiting by a bus stop. 'Loitering' became a code word for 'being dark-skinned in broad daylight'. And here I was, at school with boys whose parents had the potential to change things for people who looked like me; with boys who, one day, might be running the country themselves. I approached my studies with a furious sense of mission: believing that, if I made a good impression here, I could help to erode some of our society's firmest prejudices.

Maybe, in attending Sunningdale, I felt as much of an immigrant as my parents had in their schooldays. My mother had gone to Gayaza High School, in Kampala. As one of its few pupils from the northern part of the country, she had been mocked by her classmates, who said that members of her tribe were rumoured to have monkey tails. Perhaps, like my parents landing in the UK, I was in an alien landscape, grateful for the opportunity I had been given. It didn't help that, never having been taught Latin, Greek, French or Tudor history, I was immediately bottom of almost every single class. I only remain thankful for being good at English, which allowed me to reassure those around me that I wasn't academically useless, and for being decent at football, which among most boys that age was a pretty immediate path to social acceptance.

After two years at Sunningdale, I found myself at Eton College. This, I told myself quietly, was The Big Time. I had watched a documentary about it on Channel 4, *Class of 91*, and was captivated. Here, I thought, was a place an outsider had to go to prove himself. Some of the world's greatest leaders had been here, and now their sons were presumably going there too. If I was to achieve anything in life, I had to acquit myself against them, and excel. As Frank Sinatra once sang of New York, if I could make it there, I could make it anywhere.

I took to my studies with such a spectacular seriousness that, for a couple of years, I carried my work around school in a briefcase. That must have looked excessively formal, even by the standards of a school where we wore wedding clothes to class. Desperate to make the best of an education that so few people, let alone black ones, would ever experience, I got involved in every school activity I could. If there was an arts magazine anywhere in sight, I wanted to edit it; if there was a school society I liked the look of, I wanted to run it. I enjoyed my work, but I didn't much enjoy my social life. Whenever I went back home, I discovered that I was considered too posh to hang out with most of the locals there; and during the school holidays I rarely saw my classmates, since most of them seemed to have prohibitively expensive tastes. Moreover, there had been the warning that an Old Etonian, one of my mother's patients, had asked her to pass on to me when I was just about to start my first term there. 'Tell him he will never be one of them,' he said. I scoffed at that advice then, but with each passing term I was less and less sure.

I remained grateful to the UK. Then the murder of Stephen Lawrence in 1993, horrifying in itself, exposed a police force so addled with discrimination and alleged corruption that it could not even complete what, at first, seemed to be a reasonably routine investigation. Lawrence's death annihilated the lies we told ourselves – that if we were just good little black boys and girls, that if we just stayed away from the bad crowds, no harm would come to us. Lawrence was a budding architect who spent most of his final hours playing video games with his best friend; it didn't get anymore innocuous than that. Yet that didn't stop him from encountering a gang of white youths who found his mere presence so offensive that they spontaneously set upon him and stabbed him to death.

In the five years between Lawrence's murder and the end of my time at boarding-school, I was grateful for the sanctuary of Eton. West Drayton, for that period, endured a surge of racism apparently at odds with the normal torpor of this suburb. The British National Party, oblivious to the fact that black people lived in our particular cul-de-sac, posted campaign fliers through our door. Studying at the local library, I found National Front logos carved into one of the desks. Heading towards the train station, I found stickers bearing considerate advice for foreigners. 'West London pakis beware,' they read. 'Combat 18 in the area.'

And there, next to Yiewsley Methodist Church and along a wall 30 metres across by 10 metres high, you could find graffitied every form of white power insignia you could imagine. The one I remember best was a burgundy Ku Klux Klan logo, lovingly stencilled inside a star: it looked like the kind of thing a sponsor might emblazon across a football shirt. Once, a man waited for my sister and me to emerge from the local opticians, and then, seeing that we had crossed the street to avoid him, opened his leather jacket to reveal a patchwork of swastikas of various different shades and sizes. Multiracial racism, if you will.

Eton taught me some vital things about people and their judgments. One was that I could not change some of my peers' perceptions of black people merely by being as hardworking and as agreeable as possible; I became the exception that proved their rule. I realised this when having a pub meal with a friend. Out of nowhere, he launched into an astonishing rant against migrants, and, when I pointed out that my parents and I were no different from those he was denigrating, he told me that 'I don't see you as a migrant, Musa. I see you as a friend'.

Even the calling-card of being an Etonian was not enough to shield me from prejudice in the upper-class world. I will never forget the time when, just after my A levels, I went to stay at a friend's flat in West London. His stepfather had not been at home when I had dropped off my bag earlier that afternoon. When I returned that evening, though, the stepfather took one look at me and asked me to leave, not even allowing me to enter the house. It was a quarter-to-midnight as my friend shamefacedly handed me my bag on his doorstep, and stepped back into his home.

I only really started being myself when I was 22, a year after I left university. During my three years at Oxford, where there were fewer than 100 black students of African or Caribbean descent out of a total 15,000, I still felt I had ambassadorial responsibility. I was used to being part of an ethnic minority by now.

I started being myself at 22, because that's when I had my first drop of alcohol. I don't mean to say that drink liberated me, in some profoundly spiritual way: I simply mean that I felt comfortable enough to get drunk. Because, until my friend passed me that first fateful shot of tequila, I had tried my very best to keep control. As ridiculous as it might seem, I believed that since my white peers had grown up seeing so many negative stereotypes of black people their entire lives, I had a duty to counteract as many of them as possible. That meant never getting drunk, never getting that Afro I had long wanted, never taking the joint when it was offered. And, in truth, I was a little scared about what my intoxication might reveal. I was afraid that, beneath my straight-laced veneer of the Good Immigrant, there seethed a boorish, brutal womaniser. And, of course, no such monster emerged. I was merely a slightly louder, slightly merrier version of my sober self. And I saw then, after several years, that I had absorbed many of the racial stereotypes that I had feared others would see in me. Raised without a father, lacking many black male role models – most of whom were probably quietly struggling away just like me – I was left only with media portrayals of what black men were, and most of those were overwhelmingly negative. What's more, 22 was also the age when I realised that I was attracted to men as well as women: an experience that was traumatic at the time, but for which I am now thankful. It was so life-altering an event that it forced me no longer to see myself as some sort of diplomat for my people, but instead to live for myself. London was a place where identity did not matter nearly so much as it had until that point in my life. Surrounded by Turks, Kiwis, Poles, Nigerians and many more, there was no need to worry further about who I was, but simply to get on with the business of being.

I thought I would never again see anti-immigration feeling as strong as I did in my teens, and so when UKIP's votes started to rise rapidly I was taken by surprise. By the 2015 general election, they found themselves walking away with 6,346 votes, over a quarter of those claimed by the winner of the seat for Uxbridge and South Ruislip, one Boris Johnson. In hindsight, though, UKIP's progress makes total sense. A sprinkling of foreign-looking people here and there was all very well, but the arrival of many of us at once bewildered locals who were not accustomed to such swift cultural change. That was to say nothing of white working-class people who found themselves undercut by labourers from the EU and beyond, who were prepared to work for far less. To some of them, it must have felt like looting.

And here's the problem. There's only so much you can do to convince your fellow citizens that a multiracial society is A Good Thing, especially when they perceive that it's hitting them too hard in their pockets. It's remarkable how so many of the country's economic problems were blamed, not on the misfiring calculations of the financial sector, but instead on the ills of mass immigration. The momentum was probably building from around 2005, when Michael Howard's Conservative Party put out a billboard campaign I saw each day on my way into work. 'Are you thinking what we're thinking?' it said. And just in case you weren't sure, it gave you the punchline: 'It's not racist to impose limits on immigration'. That second sentence always made me pause. It wasn't inherently racist to impose limits on admission – after all, if a nightclub is full, it's not racist to say that no-one else can come in. What is racist is when you begin denying admission to people purely on the basis of their race and culture – which, incidentally, is something that has been happening in London nightclubs for years.

There's nothing new about a country wanting to cherry-pick the best of all the foreigners who want to come over. Some might even argue that there's nothing wrong with it. But as I got older, I began to notice more and more that the very moment immigrants were seen as contributing anything less than wholesomely to the national effort, they were viewed with contempt. It was as if, even though we had been born here, we were still seen as guests, our social acceptance only conditional upon our very best behaviour. I began to have less tolerance for this infantilising outlook, particularly when I looked at how much of the capital's, and indeed the country's, lowest-paid work was being done by immigrants with very little complaint. If there was anyone ungrateful about their presence in the country, it wasn't them, it was Britain.

And this, I think, is what I hoped to see the media coverage of the immigration discourse – a recognition of what people like my parents brought to the country, both economically and culturally. But that nuance was often absent, and took a *Daily Mail*-esque tone.

I remember, during the 2012 Olympic Games, the *Mail*, having taken offence at a scene from the opening ceremony, which featured a happily married mixed-race couple, wrote the next day that '[the ceremony] was supposed to be a representation of modern life in England but it is likely to be a challenge for the organisers to find an educated white middle-aged mother and black father living together with a happy family in such a set-up'.[75] And to my surprise, because I am normally a fairly temperate soul, I lost it.

I think I lost it because the *Mail*, presumably read with approval by millions, had finally exploded the lie that had been comforting so many of us for so long – that even if you lived a decent, law-abiding life, there were countless communities in this country that might never accept you, merely because of how you looked. The thought that a black man somewhere in the UK might somehow have infiltrated the affections of a white woman apparently filled the *Mail* with disgust. Perhaps this story affected me so much because the *Mail* said what I feared so many white middle- and upper-class parents silently believed: that someone like me would never be good enough.

By now I was in my mid-thirties, and travelling abroad with work. During these short trips, I would occasionally check back in with the British press, and the anti-immigrant anger in its pages struck me time and again. These days, though, I was increasingly greeting that fury not with fury but exhaustion. I was tired, as one of the few black journalists writing with reasonable frequency for some of the country's main publications, of being summoned by the media to defend the basic dignity of black people; of being called upon every single time a public figure said something flagrantly bigoted, or, as they or many of their softly cackling fans might put it, 'provocative'. It felt more like bear-baiting than how the news ought to work. I was better than this: black people were better than this. Since my schooldays I hoped that the quality of

75 The *Daily Mail* pulled the article after all the backlash, but thanks to the wonders of the internet, you can find it here: http://www.freezepage. com/1343493744VDGIBPHPUW

my writing might one day speak for itself; now, though, I was becoming The Race Commentator. It was all that some news editors would come to me for. For a period of several months, I turned down every single media invitation to debate or write about race, even as they increased in frequency. *Let others discuss it among themselves*, I thought. *Let others sit and reflect on just how low the discourse has fallen.*

Here's the truth of the matter. I find racism boring – really dull. I wish it didn't exist, and have spent most of my life trying to help to counteract many of its worst effects in society. Contrary to the belief of some of the digital pitchforkers who jab away at the bottom of each of my blogs, I genuinely wish that I never had to write about it again. Unfortunately, however, that is a luxury that I do not have. Because even though we're well into the second decade of the twenty-first century, young black people are still being shot on sight in the USA because they are regarded as inherently criminal due to their skin colour; black people are dying unexplained at police hands; black people are having disproportionate trouble renting apartments in the world's most cosmopolitan cities or even getting job interviews because of the foreign-looking names on their CVs.

I had just grown tired of all of this. More pertinently, on a personal level, I had grown tired of spending my time fighting those battles in the country of my birth. Naïvely wishful as it seems, I had thought that there would by now have been a better public understanding of why so many immigrants seek to come to the United Kingdom. I had thought that there would be a greater level of awareness about the British Empire and its historical role in shaping the world as we see it today. But I was wrong, and to that extent I had to admit some form of defeat.

I decided to leave the United Kingdom. The decision was heartbreaking. I never thought it was something I could do. I had long since realised that if there was greatness in Britain, then it lay in its everyday citizens, and not in its institutions. Britain was not great because of its papers and politicians who relentlessly denigrated us, it was great in spite of them. Britain was great because of the spontaneous community spirit you saw as soon as a small town was flooded, because of the volunteers who turned out in their tens of thousands to act as stewards for the Olympic Games. But that wasn't a spirit that I felt my country was doing nearly enough to nurture.

I quietly shuffled off to Germany. It wasn't lost on me that the very advice that racists in the UK had long spat at foreigners – 'if you don't like it, then go ahead and leave' – was that which I took. I suppose; in that sense, they won. I had my new home of Berlin to look forward to – one which, though not without racial issues of its own, had shown a great willingness to embrace newcomers from all quarters. A year or so after my arrival, this city of misfits greeted thousands of Syrians, fleeing war in their homeland. A cluster of supremely grateful immigrants, they were looking, just as my parents had done, to make a new life, to form part of a greater and hopefully more glorious whole: and, in their welcome, I saw confirmation that a town this generous was the perfect place to start again.

ACKNOWLEDGEMENTS

Thanks so much to:

The Secret Cabal.

Nikesh: Thank you to everyone at Unbound, especially Rachael and John, for supporting and championing this project; all the contributors, Katie, Niven Govinden, Julia Kingsford and Charlie Campbell, Sarah Shaffi, Melissa Cox, Candice Carty-Williams, Harpreet Purewal, Elaine Wong, everyone at *Watershed/Rife Magazine*, Sam Asumadu and Henna Butt from Media Diversified (especially for publishing an earlier version of Darren Chetty's essay), Sunny Singh, James Smythe and Will Wiles, Nerm and Sangna Chauhan, Anita Rani, Josh Idehen, Nimer Rashed, Sam Binnie, Sharan Dhaliwal, Josie Long and Neil Griffiths and everyone at Arts Emergency.

Extra special thanks to Chimene Suleyman, Rosie Knight, Inua Ellams and Musa Okwonga for level heads and emotional support.

Vera: Thank you to Haruka Abe, Julie Cheung-Inhin, Shera Chok, Kathryn Golding, Catriona James, Jennifer Lim, Diana Ly, Anna Sulan Masing, Rani Moorthy, and Caroline Teo for talking to me as I mulled over the intersection between East Asianness and gender. Thank you Daniel York for being a champion, and James for the support. Love to GS, CAG, SLF, JT, LS and TWH..

Inua: Thanks to Siyanda Moutsiwa.

Ming: Thanks to Katy Lee, Jackie Tang and Viki Cheung, Katy's friend Vera, Jiaqi Hou, Jun Kit Man and Cohan Chew from The BC Project, Paul Courtenay-Hyu, Nina Crisp, Kim Liu Leach, Rebecca Yip, Professor Yaojun Li, Louie Stowell, Jeremy Curtis, Katherine Webber, Kevin Tsang, Alice Sutherland-Hawes, Manisha Matharu, Kwaku Osei-Afrifa, Joelyn Rolston-Esdelle, and Jasnam Channe. Final thanks to my family and to Liz Wawrykow.

Kieran: Thanks to Bally Yates.

Riz: Thank you to Bilal Qureshi, Farrah Jarral and Anya Raza.

Daniel: Thank you to Jennifer Lim and Elaine Wong.

Sarah: Thank you to Haleem, Rabia, Ishwarlal, Tarla, Hanif, Meena, Amina, Samie, and Roxanne for standing by my side and believing in me. I'd also like to thank my friends and masala chai for keeping me going.

Musa: For my parents, the two immigrants who gave me everything they had.

Bim: For Ade, who is the reason I am a writer.

Darren: Thanks to Samantha Asumadu and Media Diversified. Thanks to Judith Suissa, Sam Berkson and Bréanainn Lambkin for helpful comments on my writing. Thanks to Steve Cockett, Geoff Fox and Steve Williams for encouraging me to share my stories. Thanks to the primary school children who have shared their stories with me. Special thanks to Rageshri Chetty, for her love, support and inspiration.

Miss L: Thanks to T, my mum, dad and nan.

Chimene: Always, Mum and Dad. And the Turkish Cypriot community who have more strength than they are ever recognised for.

Nish: Amy Annette, Jack Barry, Tez Ilyas, Sara Pascoe and whoever made the 'Confused Muslim' meme.

Himesh: Thank you to the friends I've made since the beginning of my career for feeding my soul and showing me a world beyond my front door – I'd still be naïve and clueless without you. Thank you to my sister for setting the stage, to my dad for his silent wisdom, to my mum for putting love above all else and to all three of them for opening the window and giving me the faith to leap through.

Coco: Thank you to Beena for making me, and Stephen for rating me (enough to get me writing).

Salena: Thanks and love to my Mum, to my elders and cousins, and my mixed up immigrant family. Thanks to my Dickie. Thank you to Nikesh and all the crowd funding Unbound comrades for making this extraordinary book happen.

Vinay: Thanks for my grandparents for putting my hardships into context and loving me before I was even born.

Varaidzo: For my siblings.

Thank you to immigrants, the children of immigrants, relatives of immigrants, friends of immigrants, employers of immigrants, and anyone who made a journey from there to here and opened the world up in the process. This is for you.

SUPPORTERS

Unbound is a new kind of publishing house. Our books are funded directly by readers. This was a very popular idea during the late eighteenth and early nineteenth centuries. Now we have revived it for the internet age. It allows authors to write the books they really want to write and readers to support the writing they would most like to see published.

The names listed below are of readers who have pledged their support and made this book happen. If you'd like to join them, visit: www.unbound.co.uk.

With special thanks to
Harriet Tyce, Super Friend of *The Good Immigrant*.

@BooksandJohn
Tom Abba
Lauren Ace
Claire Adam
Gemma Addy
Morenike Adebayo
Crud Man Adz
Kate Agar
Ore Agbaje-Williams
Afua Agyeman-Mensah
Ailah Ahmed
Mediah Ahmed
Jon Aitken

Furquan Akhtar
Karen Al-Jeboury
Aria Alagha
Carolina Albuerne
Georgie Aldridge
Emma Alexander
Max Alexander
Firdos Ali
Becca Allen
David Alsmeyer
Amy Alward
Tanuja Amarasuriya
Annissa Amrani

J. Ander
Stuart Anderson
Josephine Andrews
Christina Angeloudes
Susan Angoy
Catherine Annabel
Mark Appleton
Clare Archibald
Marian Armour
Jesse Armstrong
Stuart Armstrong
Jason Arthur
Will Ashon
A. J. Ashworth
Jenn Ashworth
Claire Askew
Cicely Aspinall
Tim Atack
Tanya Atapattu
Jacqueline Auma
Suzanne Azzopardi
Bolu Babalola
Hannah Bacon
Suki Badesha
Dinesh Kumar Badhan
Zara Bain
Ali Baker
Amanda Baker
Upekha Bandaranayake
Adam Banks
Catherine Banner
Fozia Bano
Tutku TUTS Barbaros
Kate Barker

Paul Barley
Sarah Barnard
Chris Barnes
Amanda Barokh
Nick Barreto
Georgia Barrington
Cara Barry
Stuart Bartholomew
Cath Barton
Neda Barzegar-Befroei
Avneet Basra
Jessica Bateman
Bath Novel Award
Georgina Bawden
Rachael Beale
Cole Beauchamp
Charles Beckett
Mark Beechill
Farhana Begum
Jo Bell
Carolyn Belson
Julianne Benford
Jendella Benson
Trine M Bergestuen
Claire Berliner
Gillian Best
Sanjeev Bhaskar
Nirpal Bhogal
Nikki Bi
Karn Bianco
Elizabeth Billinger
Georgie Billings
Sam Binnie
William Binns

Bugs Binny
Matthew Birnbaum
Indira Birnie
Joshua Bishop
Sophia Blackwell
Joanna Blake
Ellie and James
    Blatchley-Asfa
Hana Blumenfeld
Pascal Blunk
Rich Boakes
Amna Boheim
Steph Boland
Thomas Bonnick
Shane Boothby
Ruth Boreham
Euan Borland
Mair Bosworth
Emily Boulter
Andy Bower
Gavin Bower
Deborah Bowman
Jo Bradshaw
Serena Braida
Eishar Brar
Joti Brar
John Brassey
Carys Bray
Corrie Bray
Richard W H Bray
Bread Matters Cultural
    Foundation
Miriam Brent
Andy Brereton

Madeleine Brettingham
Laura Brewis
Sam Brhaspati
Laura Brooke
Chris Brosnahan
Jack Brougham
Ellie Broughton
Helen Brown
Kat Brown
Lauren Brown
Pendrick Brown
Nick Bryan
Josh Bryson
Gary Budden
Clare Bullock
Cheresse Burke
Ed Burness
Peter Burns
Cai Burton
Jessie Burton
Rachael Burton
Anna Burtt
Virginie Busette
Aisha Bushby
Sam Byers
Tanya Byrne
Helen Cadbury
Lucy Caldwell
Kit Caless
Eleni Calligas
Neill Cameron
Sophie Cameron
Alia, Luke & Zara
    Campbell-Crawford

Kirby Costa Campos
Rosie Canning
Anna Carey
Perdita Cargill-Thompson
Clare Carlin
Caroline Carpenter
Daniel Carpenter
Victoria Carr
Tobias Carroll
Eva Carson
Joel Casey
David Castle
Stephanie Catala
Lucy Catchpole
Nao Cathcart
Karan Chadda
Yann Chalmers
Niki Chang
Priya Changela
Zelda Chappel
Sarah Chappell
Elisabeth Charis
Ava Charles
KJ Charles
Tom Chatfield
Hinesh Chauhan
Navreet Chawla
Andy Checker
Darren Chetty
Dushy Chetty
Rageshri Chetty
Viki Cheung
Lumiere Chieh
Alex Chisholm
Zen Cho
Vera Chok

Sarah Chong
Ekwy Chukwuji-Nnene
Matt Clacher
Nick Clark
Caro and Cat Clarke
Evelyn Clegg
Laura Clements
Roxanne Coady
Dave Coates
Richard Coatsworth
Matteo Cocco
Alex Cochran
Jacob Cockcroft
Jonathan Coe
Joe Coghlan
Oliver Colegrave
Julian Coleman
Fen Coles
David Collier
Andrew Collins
Simon Collinson
Jane Commane
Louise Conlin
Sinéad Conneely
Philip Connor
Rosie Cooke
Josephine Corcoran
Isabel Costello
Charlie Coulthard
M. Cox
Dan Coxon
Ellie Craven
John Crawford
Maria Crawford
Kate Crowther
Thom Cuell

Shannon Cullen
Fiona Cummins
James Cuningham
Rachel Cutts
Poetcurious DaGriot
Ciarán Ua Dálaigh
Wasi Daniju
Ishita DasGupta
A M Dassu
Rishi Dastidar
Sheila David
Beth Davies
Hannah Davies
Harriet Fear Davies
Maxine Davies
Sara Davies
Dan Davis
Daniel M Davis
Hayley Davis
Joshua Davis
Susie Day
Becca Day-Preston
Rachael de Moravia
Peter de Silva
Jim Dean
Will Dean
Will Dean
Elelta Demissie
Grace Denton
JF Derry
Ellie Devereux
Sandi Dheensa
Roseanna Dias
Marija Maher Diffenthal
Lanré Diko
Ben Dilley

Tom Dissonance
Isobel Dixon
Sareeta Domingo
Kirsty Doole
Louise Doughty
Nina Douglas
Corin Douieb
Tiernan Douieb
Angela Drayton
Sam Dub
Jane Duffus
Hannah Duncan
Rachael Dunlop
Edmund Dunsdon
Joe Dunthorne
Sam Eades
Kathryn Eastman
Cariad Eccleston
Jean Hannah Edelstein
Steven Edwards
Aniefiok Ekpoudom
elaine.wong elaine.wong
Lauren Elkin
Matthew Elliott
Joanna Ellis
Camilla Elworthy
Luke Emery
Mine Ertanin
Fergus Evans
Tanis Eve
Stuart Evers
Charlotte Eyre
Katherine Fabian
Megan Farr
Claire Farrow
Jumoke Fashola

Rahnuma Feist-Hassan
Emma Felber
Gillian Fenner
Abigail Fenton
Manisha Ferdinand
Rebecca Ferdinand
Hannah Ferguson
Maria Fernandes
Jamie Fewery
William Fiennes
Nathan Filer
Becky Fincham
Ailsa Fineron
Natalya Fineron
Arlene Finnigan
David Fisher
Anna-Marie Fitzgerald
Kim Fitzpatrick
Jean Flack
Catherine Fleming
Chrissy Fleps
Catherine Fletcher
Chelsey Flood
Sarah Flynn
Christina Fontaine
Louise Forbes
Susan Ford
Charlotte Forfieh
Charles Forsdick
Lauren Fortune
Nicola Foxfield
Dan Franklin
Sarah Franklin
Sarah-Jane Franklin
Laura Fraser

Maureen Freely
Tim Freeman
Naomi Frisby
Hilary Gallo
Cathy Galvin
Dian Garrett
Duncan Gates
Vanessa Gebbie
Amro Gebreel
Emma Geen
Jonathan Gibbs
Daniele Gibney
Jo Gibson
Aly Gillani
Salena Godden
Richard Godwin
Caroline Goldsmith
Sophie Goldsworthy
Maya Goodfellow
Sophie Goodfellow
Charlotte Goodhart
Serine Goodmond
Kim Curran Goodson
Sakura Gooneratne
Sam Gordon
Chris 'Chairs' Gough
Miles Gould
Santhie Lau Goundar
Niven Govinden
Roshni Goyate
Samuel Gray
Martin Greaves
Mrinalini Greedharry
Michelle Green
Bedene Greenspan

Ami Greko
Siobhán Grennan
Chris Gribble
Helen Griffiths
John Griffiths
Guy Gunaratne
Rohan Gunatillake
Julia H
Daniel Hahn
Francesca Haig
Matt Haig
Steve Haines
Sue Haldemann
Emylia Hall
Mary Halton
Thomas Hamid
Chris Hamilton-Emery
Kirsten Han
Ellen Harber
Jessica Harby
Donna Hardcastle
Louise Hare
Jonathan Harper
Mary-Anne Harrington
Claire R E Harris
Jane Harris
Richard Harris
Shelley Harris
Kate Harrison
Ruth Harrison
A.F. Harrold
Damian Harte
Madeleine Hartley
Françoise Harvey
Ramsey Hassan

Louise Hawkins
Paula Hawkins
Molly Ker Hawn
Lucy Hay
David Hayden
Rob Haynes
Abbie Headon
Nick Hearne
Eric Heath
Rachel Heath
David Hebblethwaite
Alexandra Heminsley
Michael Henry
Emma Herdman
Johanna Herman
Marta Bausells Hernanz
Tania Hershman
Imali Hettiarachchi
Philip Hewitt
Clare Hey
Tim Higginbotham
Colin Hill
Matt Hill
Sabina Hinchliffe
Juliet Hirst
Tom Hodges
Ed Hogan
Rachel Holdsworth
J.A. Holten
Sarah Honey
Antonia Honeywell
Seth Honnor
Jennifer Hunt
David Hunter
Kirsty Hunter

Rebecca Hunter
Emteaz Hussain
Rabiah Hussain
Sairish Hussain
Vicaas Hussain
Louise Hussey
Emma Hutson
Lizzie Huxley-Jones
Ben Immanuel
Suzey Ingold
Tanya J.
Nico Jabin
Sinead Jack
Jade Jackman
Diane Jackson
Rob Jackson
Lisa Jacobs
Lorna Jaggard
Anna James
Rebecca James
Emma Jamison
Jay Jay
Anna Jean
Diana Jeater
Hamza Jeetooa
Lisa Jenkins
Elizabeth Jenner
Natalie Jester-Carter
Jan Jewkes
Tara John
Amber Yeshpaul Johnson
Catherine Johnson
Holly Johnson
Kate Johnson
Mitchell Jones

Nicholas Jones
Sammy Jones
Susan Liu Jones
Zainab Juma
Kamal Kainth
Karthik Kakarala
Savita Kalhan
Wei Ming Kam
Prithi Kanakamedala
Nikita Kanani
Hannah Kaner
Dino Karapittis
Isha Karki
Julia Karmo
Shaheen Kasmani
Sandy Kaur
Robert Kazandjian
Seamus Keaveny
Anna Kelly
Stephen Kelman
Al Kennedy
Ross Kennedy
Laura Kenwright
Rachael Kerr
Amy Key
Simon Key
Hammad Khan
Katie Khan
Mariam Khan
Mobeena Khan
Shahjehan Khan
Henna Khan-Hussain
Saida Khanom
Alison Kidd
Dan Kieran

Peter King
Julia Kingsford
Daniel Kitson
Hannah Knowles
Joseph Knowles
Ian Korner
Maris Kreizman
Jessica Krstičević
Joanna Kurlbaum
Pierre L'Allier
Mit Lahiri
Zoe Lambert
Breanainn Lambkin
Stefanie Lamprinidi
Line Langebek
Sara Langham
Patrick Langley
Jo Lansdowne
Becky Lavender
Patrice Lawrence
Tom Leach
Diane Leedham
Helen Legg
Elizabeth Lehtola
Ilona Leighton-Goodall
Chloe Leila
Paula D Lennon
George Lester
Tala Levin
Philip Levine
Sydney Levinson
Liza Levy
Fredrik Lindroth
Rob Lingo
Colm Linnane

Dan Lipscombe
Cath Little
Olivia Little
Natasha Ying Liu
Marilyn Livingstone
Frances Lynch Llewellyn
Josie Long
Éireann Lorsung
Laurie Louise
Catherine Love
Jo Lovesdancing
Charlie Lowe
Juliet Lubega
Rachael Lucas
DeAndra Lupu
Frances Lynn
Amelia MacDonald
Karen MacKelvie
Michael MacKian
Lorna Mackinnon
Seonaid Macleod
Lucy Macnab
Jon Macqueen
Anand Madhvani
Ravi Madhvani
Anthony Madigan
Erin Maguire
Hannah Maguire
Mellini Mahadevan
Crystal Mahey-Morgan
Francesca Main
Marianthi Makra
Claire Malcolm
Gita Malhotra
Ayisha Malik

Preeya Malkan
Gautam Malkani
Jane Maltby
Halimah Manan
Philippa Manasseh
Kat Mandu
Rachel Mann
Sophie Manners
Sarah Manvel
Rebecca Marcus
Eben Marks
Ellen Marsh
Ella Marshall
Lucy Marshall
Philippa Martin
Kate Mascarenhas
Sapphire Mason-Brown
Janina Matthewson
Ada Mau
Chloe Mavrommatis
Paul May
Sarah May
Stephen May
Kevin Maynard
Jazza MC
Rachel McCormack
Chris McCrudden
Lexie McD
Heather McDaid
Eleanor McDowall
Amanda McGrath
Jon McGregor
John Patrick McHugh
Sarah McIntyre
Belinda McKeon

Anna McKerrow
Kate McNaughton
Kiera McNeice
Martin McNulty
Marie-Anne McQuay
Tessa McWatt
Elizabeth Meade
Glen Mehn
Chloe Meineck
Mina Meiß
Joe Melia
Zak Mensah
Erinna Mettler
Jess Meyer
Sophia Miah
Carly Miller
James Miller
Duncan Mills
Bridget Minamore
Priya Minhas
Saima Mir
Sam Missingham
Anupa Mistry
Malissa Mistry
Josie Mitchell
Pete Mitchell
John Mitchinson
Lucy Moffatt
Virginia Moffatt
Stefan Mohamed
Sarah Monk
Penny Montague
James Montgomery
Mimi-Beth Montgomery
Maxine Monu

Safia Moore
Simon Moreton
Lou Morgan
Charlotte Morris
Cas Morrison
Kate Morrison
Emma Morsi
Juliette Motamed
Durre Mughal
Nafisa Muhtadi
Tanya Mukherjee
Diane Mulholland
Holly Muller
Helen Murphy
Mike Murphy
Rebekah Murrell
Holly Muse
Benjamin Myers
Keshini Naidoo
Fergal Nally
Eric Nash
Stu Nathan
Carlo Navato
Kate Neilan
Graeme Neill
Rachel Nelken
Nerm Nerm
Lorraine Newman
Lydia Nicholas
David Nicholls
Gary Nicol
Jenni Nock
Poppy North
Alexandra Notay
Gosia Nowicka

Khush Nubian
Kevin O'Connor
Meghan O'Dea
Tania O'Donnell
Catherine O'Flynn
Jenny O'Gorman
Dan O'Hara
Emma O'Mahony
Sadhbh O'Sullivan
Therese O'Sullivan
Marsha Gosho Oakes
Rachel Oakes
Georgia Odd
Kam Odedra
Antonia Odunlami
Pey Pey Oh
Natalie Ohlson
Irenosen Okojie
Musa Okwonga
Aimee Oliver
Karen Onojaife
Tasha Onwuemezi
Emily Oram
Elizabeth Orayinka
Katharine Orton
Adam Osborne
Gabrielle Osrin
Susannah Otter
Meg Otto
Marsha Oza
Samuel Palin
Anthony Thomas Palma
Amit V Pansuria
Muna Parajuli
Leonie Parish

Helen Parker
John Parker
Julia Parker
Siena Parker
Claire Parry
Nik Partridge
Damyanti Patel
Jayesh Patel
Maatin Patel
Nikesh Patel
Radha M Patel
Vibhuti Patel
Vinay Patel
Claire Patel-Campbell
Tash Payne
Richard Peabody
Poppy Peacock
Jo Pearson
Genevieve Pegg
Bianca Pellet
Penny Pepper
Tom Percival
Steve Perfect
Sarah Perry
Pamela Peter-Agbia
Bohdan Piasecki
Joe Pickering
Juliet Pickering
Magda Pieta
Candice Pires
Kevin Pocock
Fabia Pollard
Justin Pollard
Lauren Pope
David Porter

Max Porter
positiveimageproject
Nina Pottell
Jackie Potter
Anna Poulton
Lizzie Poulton
Chris Power
Smriti Prasadam-Halls
Alex Preston
Elizabeth Preston
Sharron Preston
Tina Price-Johnson
Simon Prosser
James Pulford
Harpreet Purewal
Emma Pusill
Alice Quigley
Kate Quine
Hazel Quinlan
Sanaa Qureshi
Mandy Rabin
Faisel Rahman
Zara Rahman
Matthew Railton
Kavya Rajagopalan
Polly Randall
Simran Randhawa
Tejal Rao
Nimer Rashed
Leila Rasheed
Kate Raworth
Stephanie Reynolds
Reardon
Clare Reddington
Matt Reid

Nina Renshaw
Cathy Rentzenbrink
Emma Reynolds
Francesca Riccardi
Rahul Ricky
Lorna Riley
Amber Rithalia
Lee.Robb@sky.com Robb
Charmion Roberts
Fay Roberts
Sean Roberts
Imogen Robertson
Neil Robertson
Miriam Robinson
Rachael Robinson
Katie Roden
Anna Roderick
Cynthia Rodríguez
Robyn Roscoe
Annah Ross
Rebecca Rouillard
RowanHisayoBuchanan
Emilie Joy Rowell
C.N. Rowen
Joanne Rowling
Tinni Guha Roy
Harold Rubin
Georgina Ruffhead
Reshma Ruia
Helen Rule
Katherine Rundell
Jalpa Ruparelia
Jonathan Ruppin
Bernadette Russell
Tom Ryan

William Rycroft
Helen Rye
Sid Sagar
Amrit Saggu
Sarah Sahim
SF Said
David Salariya
Melinda Salisbury
Charly Salvesen-Ford
Daisy Samuel
Ana Sánchez-Arce
Christoph Sander
Siân Sanders
Rajpreet Sandhu
Sarah Sandow
Rachel Sanger
Harvinder Sangha
Sathnam Sanghera
Luiza Sauma
Isabel Saunders
Tim Saxton
Samuel Schafer
Erich Schottstaedt
Matthew David Scott
James Scudamore
Cherokee Seebalack
Katharine Segal
Gemma Seltzer
Adeep Sethi
Sarah Shaffi
Amit Shah
Nikhil Shah
Alom Shaha
Farhana Shaikh
Wendy Shakespeare

ShamPhat Sham
Maria Shamin
Samantha Shannon
Dale Shaw
Lucy Shaw
Richard Sheehan
Alexandra Sheppard
Emily Shipp
Leo Shire
Nadia Shireen
Jai Shukla
Neena Shukla
Nikesh Shukla
Grace Ibidolapo Shutti
Amardeep Sian
Kay Sidebottom
Jess Siggers
Joanna Silber
Julia Silk
Ranbir Singh
Sid Singh
Sunny Singh
Leilah Skelton
Jon Slack
Anna Slater
Stephen Slocombe
Iesha Small
Claire Smith
Wendy Smithers
Richard Smyth
James Smythe
Mahsuda Snaith
Amy Zamarripa Solis
Leela Soma
Natasha Soobramanien

Chitra Soundar
Kitty Spence
Josh Spero
Vanessa Bellaar Spruijt
Truda Spruyt
Shefali Srivastava
Emma Stanford
Helen Stanton
Zoe Stavri
Ian Steadman
Cathryn Steele
Daneet Steffens
Katherine Stephen
Robin Stevens
Claire Stewart
Lucy Stewart
Roz Stobart
Peter Stojanovic
Katie Stone
Louie Stowell
Kay Stratton
Emma Strong
Chris Styles
Sarah Such
    and Tony White
Zerrin Suleyman
Recep Süleyman
JC Sutcliffe
Tom Sutcliffe
Alice Sutherland-Hawes
Karolina Sutton
Pete Sutton
SWight SWight
Susie Symes
Laura Taflinger

Paul Talbot
Zeba Talkhani
Preti Taneja
Abeeha Tariq
Shema Tariq
Daniel Tatarsky
Amy Taylor
C M Taylor
Jennifer Taylor
Justine Taylor
Marjorie Taylor
David Taylor-Matthews
Hannah Fort Teller
Matthew Teller
Ally Temple
James Thomas
Joanna Thomas
Caroline Thompson
Fiona Thompson
Selina Thompson
Mike Scott Thomson
Tim Thornton
Rhys Timson
Clare Titley
Charles Tocock
Alice Tomlinson
Francine Toon
Bethan Townsend
Emma Townshend
Angelique Tran Van Sang
Anthony Trevelyan
Claire Trévien
Daniel Trilling
Thomas Truong
Catt Turney

Eleanor Turney
Rik Ubhi
Nilopar Uddin
Asad Ullah
Jack Underwood
Emma Unsworth
Jo Unwin
Bahul Upadhyaya
Mayur Upadhyaya
Reshma Upadhyaya
Shaun Usher
Sabrina Uswak
Francois van Zyl
Liz Vater
Mark Vent
Sophie Verass
Rahul Verma
Iana Vidal
Kelly Vien
Eduard von Fischer
Johanna von Fischer
Erica Wagner
Julia Wainwright
Christopher Wakling
Eloise Wales
Lindsay Waller-Wilkinson
Joanna Walsh
Judi Walsh
Jemma Walton
Miranda Ward
Celeste Ward-Best
Ellie Warren
Emma Warren
Sarah Watkins
Liz Wawrykow

Katherine Webber
Matthew Welton
James Westby
Janet Weston
Emily Wheeler
Hannah Whelan
Jayne White
Simon White
Katy Whitehead
David Whitehouse
Zoe Whitfield
Alison Whittaker-Stewart
Charlotte Wicks
Kishani Widyaratna
Will Wiles
Rebecca Wilkie
Leah Wilkins
Sara Willard
Andrew Wille
Andrew Williams
Eley Williams
James Wills
Fiona Wilson
Johanna Wilson
Terri & Howard
      Windling-Gayton
Gretchen Woelfle
T.M. Wolf
Amy Wong
Joe Wong
Liza Wonga
Jess Woo
Benjamin Wood
Katherine Woodfine
Michelle Woolfenden

Marie Wright
Evie Wyld
Llinos Wynn-Jones
Jane Yates
Pete Yelding
Farrah Yusuf
Helen Zaltzman
Justin Zaman
Eva Zienau